D0708246

THE COLLECTED SHORT STORIES
OF
D. H. LAWRENCE

THE PHOENIX EDITION OF D. H. LAWRENCE

D. H. LAWRENCE

*The Collected
Short Stories*

BOOK CLUB ASSOCIATES
LONDON

This edition published 1974 by
Book Club Associates
By arrangement with Wm. Heinemann Ltd.

Printed in Great Britain by
Richard Clay (The Chaucer Press), Ltd.,
Bungay, Suffolk

CONTENTS

A MODERN LOVER

I

THE road was heavy with mud. It was labour to move along it. The old, wide way, forsaken and grown over with grass, used not to be so bad. The farm traffic from Coney Grey must have cut it up. The young man crossed carefully again to the strip of grass on the other side.

It was a dreary, out-of-doors track, saved only by low fragments of fence and occasional bushes from the desolation of the large spaces of arable and of grassland on either side, where only the unopposed wind and the great clouds mattered, where even the little grasses bent to one another indifferent of any traveller. The abandoned road used to seem clean and firm. Cyril Mersham stopped to look round and to bring back old winters to the scene, over the ribbed red land and the purple wood. The surface of the field seemed suddenly to lift and break. Something had startled the peewits, and the fallow flickered over with pink gleams of birds white-breasting the sunset. Then the plovers turned, and were gone in the dusk behind.

Darkness was issuing out of the earth, and clinging to the trunks of the elms which rose like weird statues, lessening down the wayside. Mersham laboured forwards, the earth sucking and smacking at his feet. In front the Coney Grey farm was piled in shadow on the road. He came near to it, and saw the turnips heaped in a fabulous heap up the side of the barn, a buttress that rose almost to the eaves, and stretched out towards the cart-ruts in the road. Also, the pale breasts of the turnips got the sunset, and they were innumerable orange glimmers piled in the dusk. The two labourers who were pulping at the foot of the mound stood shadow-like to watch as he passed, breathing the sharp scent of turnips.

It was all very wonderful and glamorous here, in the old places that had seemed so ordinary. Three-quarters of the scarlet sun was settling among the branches of the elm in front, right ahead where he would come soon. But when he arrived at the brow where the hill swooped downwards, where the broad road ended suddenly, the sun had vanished from the space before him, and the evening star was white where the night urged up against the retreating, rose-coloured billow of day. Mersham passed through the stile and sat upon the remnant of the thorn tree on the brink of the valley. All the wide space before him was full of a mist of rose, nearly to his feet. The large ponds were hidden, the farms, the fields, the far-off coal-mine, under the rosy outpouring of twilight. Between him and the spaces of Leicestershire and the hills of Derbyshire, between him and all the South Country which he had fled, was the splendid rose-red strand of sunset, and the white star keeping guard.

Here, on the lee-shore of day, was the only purple showing of the woods and the great hedge below him; and the roof of the farm below him, with a film of smoke rising up. Unreal, like a dream which wastes a sleep with unrest, was the South and its hurrying to and fro. Here, on the farther shore of the sunset, with the flushed tide at his feet, and the large star flashing with strange laughter, did he himself naked walk with lifted arms into the quiet flood of life.

What was it he wanted, sought in the slowly-lapsing tide of days? Two years he had been in the large city in the south. There always his soul had moved among the faces that swayed on the thousand currents in that node of tides, hovering and wheeling and flying low over the faces of the multitude like a sea-gull over the waters, stopping now and again, and taking a fragment of life – a look, a contour, a movement – to feed upon. Of many people, his friends, he had asked that they would kindle again the smouldering embers of their experience; he had blown the low fires gently with his breath, and had leaned his face towards their glow, and had breathed in the words that rose like fumes from the revived embers, till he was sick with the strong drug of sufferings and ecstasies and sensations, and the dreams that ensued. But most folk had choked out the fires of their fiercer experience with rubble of sentimentality and stupid fear, and rarely could he feel the hot destruction of Life fighting out its way.

Surely, surely somebody could give him enough of the philtre of life to stop the craving which tortured him hither and thither, enough to satisfy for a while, to intoxicate him till he could laugh the crystalline laughter of the star, and bathe in the retreating flood of twilight like a naked boy in the surf, clasping the waves and beating them and answering their wild clawings with laughter sometimes, and sometimes gasps of pain.

He rose and stretched himself. The mist was lying in the valley like a flock of folded sheep; Orion had strode into the sky, and the Twins were playing towards the West. He shivered, stumbled down the path, and crossed the orchard, passing among the dark trees as if among people he knew.

II

He came into the yard. It was exceedingly, painfully muddy. He felt a disgust of his own feet, which were cold, and numbed, and heavy.

The window of the house was uncurtained, and shone like a yellow moon, with only a large leaf or two of ivy, and a cord of honeysuckle hanging across it. There seemed a throng of figures moving about the fire. Another light gleamed mysteriously among the out-buildings. He heard a voice in the cow-shed, and the impatient movement of a cow, and the rhythm of milk in the bucket.

He hesitated in the darkness of the porch; then he entered without knocking. A girl was opposite him, coming out of the dairy doorway with a loaf of bread. She started, and they stood a moment looking at each other across the room. They advanced to each other; he took her hand, plunged overhead, as it were, for a moment in her great brown eyes. Then he let her go, and looked aside, saying some words of greeting. He had not kissed her; he realised that when he heard her voice:

'When did you come?'

She was bent over the table, cutting bread-and-butter. What was it in her bowed, submissive pose, in the dark, small head with its black hair twining and hiding her face, that made him wince and shrink and close over his soul that had been open like a foolhardy flower to the night? Perhaps it was her very submission, which trammelled him, throwing the responsibility of her wholly on him, making him shrink from the burden of her.

Her brothers were home from the pit. They were two well-built lads of twenty and twenty-one. The coal-dust over their faces was like a mask, making them inscrutable, hiding any glow of greeting, making them strangers. He could only see their eyes wake with a sudden smile, which sank almost immediately, and they turned aside. The mother was kneeling at a big brown stew-jar in front of the open oven. She did not rise, but gave him her hand, saying: 'Cyril! How are you?' Her large dark eyes wavered and left him. She continued with the spoon in the jar.

His disappointment rose as water suddenly heaves up the side of a

3

ship. A sense of dreariness revived, a feeling, too, of the cold wet mud that he had struggled through.

These were the people who, a few months before, would look up in one fine broad glow of welcome whenever he entered the door, even if he came daily. Three years before, their lives would draw together into one flame, and whole evenings long would flare with magnificent mirth, and with play. They had known each other's lightest and deepest feelings. Now, when he came back to them after a long absence, they withdrew, turned aside. He sat down on the sofa under the window, deeply chagrined. His heart closed tight like a fir-cone, which had been open and full of naked seeds when he came to them.

They asked him questions of the South. They were starved for news, they said, in that God-forsaken hole.

'It is such a treat to hear a bit of news from outside,' said the mother.

News! He smiled, and talked, plucking for them the leaves from off his tree: leaves of easy speech. He smiled, rather bitterly, as he slowly reeled off his news, almost mechanically. Yet he knew – and that was the irony of it – that they did not want his 'records'; they wanted the timorous buds of his hopes, and the unknown fruits of his experience, full of the taste of tears and what sunshine of gladness had gone to their ripening. But they asked for his 'news', and, because of some subtle perversity, he gave them what they begged, not what they wanted, not what he desired most sincerely to give them.

Gradually he exhausted his store of talk, that he had thought was limitless. Muriel moved about all the time, laying the table and listening, only looking now and again across the barren garden of his talk into his windows. But he hardened his heart and turned his head from her. The boys had stripped to their waists, and had knelt on the hearth-rug and washed themselves in a large tin bowl, the mother sponging and drying their backs. Now they stood wiping themselves, the firelight bright and rosy on their fine torsos, their heavy arms swelling and sinking with life. They seemed to cherish the firelight on their bodies. Benjamin, the younger, leaned his breast to the warmth, and threw back his head, showing his teeth in a voluptuous little smile. Mersham watched them, as he had watched the peewits and the sunset.

Then they sat down to their dinners, and the room was dim with the steam of food. Presently the father and the eldest brother were in from the cow-sheds, and all assembled at table. The conversation went haltingly; a little badinage on Mersham's part, a few questions on politics from the father. Then there grew an acute, fine feeling of discord.

4

Mersham, particularly sensitive, reacted. He became extremely attentive to the others at table, and to his own manner of eating. He used English that was exquisitely accurate, pronounced with the Southern accent, very different from the heavily-sounded speech of the home folk. His nicety contrasted the more with their rough, country habit. They became shy and awkward, fumbling for something to say. The boys ate their dinners hastily, shovelling up the mass as a man shovels gravel. The eldest son clambered roughly with a great hand at the plate of bread-and-butter. Mersham tried to shut his eyes. He kept up all the time a brilliant tea-talk that they failed to appreciate in that atmosphere. It was evident to him; without forming the idea, he felt how irrevocably he was removing them from him, though he had loved them. The irony of the situation appealed to him, and added brightness and subtlety to his wit. Muriel, who had studied him so thoroughly, confusedly understood. She hung her head over her plate, and ate little. Now and again she would look up at him, toying all the time with her knife – though it was a family for ugly hands – and would address him some barren question. He always answered the question, but he invariably disregarded her look of earnestness, lapped in his unbreakable armour of light irony. He acknowledged, however, her power in the flicker of irritation that accompanied his reply. She quickly hid her face again.

They did not linger at tea, as in the old days. The men rose, with an 'Ah well!' and went about their farm-work. One of the lads lay sprawling for sleep on the sofa; the other lighted a cigarette and sat with his arms on his knees, blinking into the fire. Neither of them ever wore a coat in the house, and their shirt-sleeves and their thick bare necks irritated the stranger still further by accentuating his strangeness. The men came tramping in and out to the boiler. The kitchen was full of bustle, of the carrying of steaming water, and of draughts. It seemed like a place out of doors. Mersham shrank up in his corner, and pretended to read the *Daily News*. He was ignored, like an owl sitting in the stalls of cattle.

'Go in the parlour, Cyril. Why don't you? It's comfortable there.'

Muriel turned to him with this reproach, this remonstrance, almost chiding him. She was keenly aware of his discomfort, and of his painful discord with his surroundings. He rose without a word and obeyed her.

The parlour was a long, low room with red colourings. A bunch of mistletoe hung from the beam, and thickly-berried holly was over the pictures – over the little gilt-blazed water-colours that he hated so much because he had done them in his 'teens, and nothing is so hateful as the self one has left. He dropped in the tapestried chair called the Countess, and thought of the changes which this room had seen in him. There, by that hearth, they had threshed the harvest of their youth's experience, gradually burning the chaff of sentimentality and false romance that covered the real grain of life. How infinitely far away, now, seemed *Jane Eyre* and George Eliot. These had marked the beginning. He smiled as he traced the graph onwards, plotting the points with Carlyle and Ruskin, Schopenhauer and Darwin and Huxley, Omar Khayyam, the Russians, Ibsen and Balzac; then Guy de Maupassant and *Madame Bovary*. They had parted in the midst of *Madame Bovary*. Since then had come only Nietzsche and William James. They had not done so badly, he thought, during those years which now he was apt to despise a little, because of their dreadful strenuousness, and because of their later deadly, unrelieved seriousness. He wanted her to come in and talk about the old times. He crossed to the other side of the fire and lay in the big horse-hair chair, which pricked the back of his head. He looked about, and stuffed behind him the limp green cushions that were always sweating down.

It was a week after Christmas. He guessed they had kept up the holly and mistletoe for him. The two photographs of himself still occupied the post of honour on the mantelpiece; but between them was a stranger. He wondered who the fellow could be; good-looking he seemed to be; but a bit of a clown beside the radiant, subtle photos of himself. He smiled broadly at his own arrogance. Then he remembered that Muriel and her people were leaving the farm come Lady-day. Immediately, in valediction, he began to call up the old days, when they had romped and played so boisterously, dances, and wild charades, and all mad games. He was just telling himself that those were the days, the days of unconscious, ecstatic fun, and he was smiling at himself over his information, when she entered.

She came in, hesitating. Seeing him sprawling in his old abandonment, she closed the door softly. For a moment or two she sat, her elbows on her knees, her chin in her hands, sucking her little finger, and withdrawing it from her lips with a little pop, looking all the while in the fire. She was waiting for him, knowing all the time he would not begin. She was trying to feel him, as it were. She wanted to assure herself of him after so many months. She dared not look at him directly. Like all brooding, constitutionally earnest souls, she gave herself away unwisely, and was defenceless when she found herself pushed back, rejected so often with contempt.

'Why didn't you tell me you were coming?' she asked at last.

'I wanted to have exactly one of the old tea-times, and evenings.'

'Ay!' she answered with hopeless bitterness. She was a dreadful pessimist. People had handled her so brutally, and had cheaply thrown away her most sacred intimacies.

He laughed, and looked at her kindly.

'Ah, well, if I'd thought about it I should have known this was what to expect. It's my own fault.'

'Nay,' she answered, still bitterly; 'it's not your fault. It's ours. You bring us to a certain point, and when you go away, we lose it all again, and receive you like creatures who have never known you.'

'Never mind,' he said easily. 'If it is so, it is! How are you?'

She turned and looked full at him. She was very handsome; heavily moulded, coloured richly. He looked back smiling into her big, brown, serious eyes.

'Oh, I'm very well,' she answered, with puzzled irony. 'How are you?'

'Me? You tell me. What do you think of me?'

'What do I think?' She laughed a little nervous laugh and shook her head. 'I don't know. Why – you look well – and very much of a gentleman.'

'Ah – and you are sorry?'

'No – No, I am not! No! Only you're different, you see.'

'Ah, the pity! I shall never be as nice as I was at twenty-one, shall I?' He glanced at his photo on the mantelpiece, and smiled, gently chaffing her.

'Well – you're different – it isn't that you're not so nice, but different. I always think you're like that, really.'

She too glanced at the photo, which had been called the portrait of an intellectual prig, but which was really that of a sensitive, alert, exquisite boy. The subject of the portrait lay smiling at her. Then it turned voluptuously, like a cat spread out in the chair.

'And this is the last of it all —!'

She looked up at him, startled and pitiful.

'Of this phase, I mean,' he continued, indicating with his eyes the room, the surroundings. 'Of Crossleigh Bank, I mean, and this part of our lives.'

'Ay!' she said, bowing her head, and putting into the exclamation all her depth of sadness and regret. He laughed.

'Aren't you glad?' he asked.

She looked up, startled, a little shocked.

'Good-bye's a fine word,' he explained. 'It means you're going to have a change, and a change is what you, of all people, want.'

Her expression altered as she listened.

'It's true,' she said. 'I do.'

'So you ought to say to yourself, "What a treat! I'm going to say good-bye directly to the most painful phase of my life." You make up your mind it shall be the most painful, by refusing to be hurt so much in the future. There you are! "Men at most times are masters of their fates," etcetera.'

She pondered his method of reasoning, and turned to him with a little laughter that was full of pleading and yearning.

'Well,' he said, lying, amiably smiling, 'isn't that so? – and aren't you glad?'

'Yes!' she nodded. 'I am – very glad.'

He twinkled playfully at her, and asked, in a soft voice :

'Then what do you want?'

'Yes,' she replied, a little breathlessly. 'What do I?' She looked at him with a rash challenge that pricked him.

'Nay,' he said, evading her, 'do you even ask me that?'

She veiled her eyes, and said, meekly in excuse :

'It's a long time since I asked you anything, isn't it?'

'Ay! I never thought of it. Whom have you asked in the interim?'

'Whom have I asked?' – she arched her brows and laughed a mono-syllable of scorn.

'No one, of course!' he said, smiling. 'The world asks questions of you, you ask questions of me, and I go to some oracle in the dark, don't I?'

She laughed with him.

'No!' he said, suddenly serious. 'Supposing you must answer me a big question – something I can never find out by myself?'

He lay out indolently in the chair and began smiling again. She turned to look with intensity at him, her hair's fine foliage all loose

8

round her face, her dark eyes haunted with doubt, her finger at her lips. A slight perplexity flickered over his eyes.

'At any rate,' he said, 'you have something to give me.'

She continued to look at him with dark, absorbing eyes. He probed her with his regard. Then he seemed to withdraw, and his pupils dilated with thought.

'You see,' he said, 'life's no good but to live – and you can't live your life by yourself. You must have a flint and a steel, both, to make the spark fly. Supposing you be my flint, my white flint, to spurt out red fire for me?'

'But how do you mean?' she asked breathlessly.

'You see,' he continued, thinking aloud as usual: 'thought – that's not life. It's like washing and combing and carding and weaving the fleece that the year of life has produced. Now I think – we've carded and woven to the end of our bundle – nearly. We've got to begin again – you and me – living together, see? Not speculating and poetising together – see?'

She did not cease to gaze absorbedly at him.

'Yes?' she whispered, urging him on.

'You see – I'll come back to you – to you —' He waited for her.

'But,' she said huskily, 'I don't understand.'

He looked at her with aggressive frankness, putting aside all her confusions.

'Fibber!' he said gently.

'But —' she turned in her chair from him – 'but not clearly.'

He frowned slightly:

'Nay, you should be able by now to use the algebra of speech. Must I count up on your fingers for you what I mean, unit by unit, in bald arithmetic?'

'No – no!' she cried, justifying herself; 'but how can I understand – the change in you? You used to say – you couldn't. – Quite opposite.'

He lifted his head as if taking in her meaning.

'Ah, yes, I have changed. I forget. I suppose I must have changed in myself. I'm older – I'm twenty-six. I used to shrink from the thought of having to kiss you, didn't I?' He smiled very brightly, and added, in a soft voice: 'Well – I don't, now.'

She flushed darkly and hid her face from him.

'Not,' he continued, with slow, brutal candour – 'not that I know any more than I did then – what love is – as you know it – but – I think you're beautiful – and we know each other so well – as we know nobody else, don't we? And so we ...'

His voice died away, and they sat in a tense silence, listening to the noise outside, for the dog was barking loudly. They heard a voice speaking and quieting him. Cyril Mersham listened. He heard the clatter of the barn door latch, and a slurring ring of a bicycle-bell brushing the wall.

'Who is it?' he asked, unsuspecting.

She looked at him, and confessed with her eyes, guiltily, beseeching. He understood immediately.

'Good Lord! – Him?' He looked at the photo on the mantelpiece. She nodded with her usual despair, her finger between her lips again. Mersham took some moments to adjust himself to the new situation.

'Well! – so *he's* in my place! Why didn't you tell me?'

'How could I? – he's not. Besides – you never would have a place.' She hid her face.

'No,' he drawled, thinking deeply. 'I wouldn't. It's my fault altogether.' Then he smiled, and said whimsically: 'But I thought you kept an old pair of my gloves in the chair beside you.'

'So I did, so I did!' she justified herself again with extreme bitterness, 'till you asked me for them. You told me to – to take another man – and I did as you told me – as usual.'

'Did I tell you? – did I tell you? I suppose I must. I suppose I am a fool. And do you like him?'

She laughed aloud, with scorn and bitterness.

'He's very good – and he's very fond of me.'

'Naturally!' said Mersham, smiling and becoming ironical. 'And how firmly is he fixed?'

IV

She was mortified, and would not answer him. The question for him now was how much did this intruder count. He looked, and saw she wore no ring – but perhaps she had taken it off for his coming. He began diligently to calculate what attitude he might take. He had looked for many women to wake his love, but he had been always disappointed. So he had kept himself virtuous, and waited. Now he would wait no longer. No woman and he could ever understand each

10

other so well as he and Muriel whom he had fiercely educated into womanhood along with his own struggling towards a manhood of independent outlook. They had breathed the same air of thought, they had been beaten with the same storms of doubt and disillusionment, they had expanded together in days of pure poetry. They had grown so; spiritually, or rather psychically, as he preferred to say, they were married; and now he found himself thinking of the way she moved about the house.

The outer door had opened and a man had entered the kitchen, greeting the family cordially, and without any formality. He had the throaty, penetrating voice of a tenor singer, and it came distinctly over the vibrating rumble of the men's talking. He spoke good, easy English. The boys asked him about the 'iron-men' and the electric haulage, and he answered them with rough technicalities, so Mersham concluded he was a working electrician in the mine. They continued to talk casually for some time, though there was a false note of secondary interest in it all. Then Benjamin came forward and broke the check, saying, with a dash of braggart taunting:

'Muriel's in th' parlour, Tom, if you want her.'

'Oh, is she? I saw a light in; I thought she might be.' He affected indifference, as if he were kept thus at every visit. Then he added, with a touch of impatience, and of the proprietor's interest: 'What is she doing?'

'She's talking. Cyril Mersham's come from London.'

'What! – is *he* here?'

Mersham sat listening, smiling. Muriel saw his eyelids lift. She had run up her flag of challenge taut, but continually she slackened towards him with tenderness. Now her flag flew out bravely. She rose, and went to the door.

'Hello!' she said, greeting the stranger with a little song of welcome in one word, such as girls use when they become aware of the presence of their sweetheart.

'You've got a visitor, I hear,' he answered.

'Yes. Come along, come in!'

She spoke softly, with much gentle caressing.

He was a handsome man, well set-up, rather shorter than Mersham. The latter rose indolently, and held out his hand, smiling curiously into the beautiful, generous blue eyes of the other.

'Cyril – Mr. Vickers.'

Tom Vickers crushed Mersham's hand, and answered his steady,

11

smiling regard with a warm expansion of feeling, then bent his head, slightly confused.

'Sit here, will you?' said Mersham, languidly indicating the armchair.

'No, no, thanks, I won't. I shall do here, thanks.' Tom Vickers took a chair and placed it in front of the fire. He was confusedly charmed with Mersham's natural frankness and courtesy.

'If I'm not intruding,' he added, as he sat down.

'No, of course not!' said Muriel, in her wonderfully soft, fond tones – the indulgent tone of a woman who will sacrifice anything to love.

'Couldn't!' added Mersham lazily. 'We're always a public meeting, Muriel and I. Aren't we, Miel? We're discussing affinities, that ancient topic. You'll do for an audience. We agree so beastly well, we two. We always did. It's her fault. Does she treat you so badly?'

The other was rather bewildered. Out of it all he dimly gathered that he was suggested as the present lover of Muriel, while Mersham referred to himself as the one discarded. So he smiled, reassured.

'How – badly?' he asked.

'Agreeing with you on every point?'

'No, I can't say she does that,' said Vickers, smiling, and looking with little warm glances at her.

'Why, we never disagree, you know!' she remonstrated, in the same deep indulgent tone.

'I see,' Mersham said languidly, and yet keeping his wits keenly to the point. '*You* agree with everything *she* says. Lord, how interesting!'

Muriel arched her eyelids with a fine flare of intelligence across at him, and laughed.

'Something like that,' answered the other man, also indulgently, as became a healthy male towards one who lay limply in a chair and said clever nothings in a lazy drawl. Mersham noted the fine limbs, the solid, large thighs, and the thick wrists. He was classifying his rival among the men of handsome, healthy animalism, and good intelligence, who are children in simplicity, who can add two and two, but never xy and yx. His contours, his movements, his repose were, strictly, lovable. 'But,' said Mersham to himself, 'if I were blind, or sorrowful, or very tired, I should not want him. He is one of the men, as George Moore says, whom his wife would hate after a few years for the very way he walked across the floor. I can imagine him with a family of children, a fine father. But unless he had a domestic wife —'

12

Muriel had begun to make talk to him.

'Did you cycle?' she asked, in that irritating private tone so common to lovers, a tone that makes a third person an impertinence.

'Yes – I was rather late,' he replied, in the same caressing manner. The sense did not matter, the caress was everything.

'Didn't you find it very muddy?'

'Well, I did – but not any worse than yesterday.'

Mersham sprawled his length in the chair, his eyelids almost shut, his fine white hands hanging over the arms of the chair like dead-white stoats from a bough. He was wondering how long Muriel would endure to indulge her sweetheart thus. Soon she began to talk second-hand to Mersham. They were speaking of Tom's landlady.

'You don't care for her, do you?' she asked, laughing insinuatingly, since the shadow of his dislike for other women heightened the radiance of his affection for her.

'Well, I can't say that I love her.'

'How is it you always fall out with your landladies after six months? You must be a wretch to live with.'

'Nay, I don't know that I am. But they're all alike; they're jam and cakes at first, but after a bit they're dry bread.'

He spoke with solemnity, as if he uttered a universal truth. Mersham's eyelids flickered now and again. Muriel turned to him:

'Mr. Vickers doesn't like lodgings,' she said.

Mersham understood that Vickers therefore wanted to marry her; he also understood that as the pretendant tired of his landladies, so his wife and he would probably weary one another. He looked this intelligence at Muriel, and drawled:

'Doesn't he? Lodgings are ideal. A good lodger can always boss the show, and have his own way. It's the time of his life.'

'I don't think!' laughed Vickers.

'It's true,' drawled Mersham torpidly, giving his words the effect of droll irony. 'You're evidently not a good lodger. You only need to sympathise with a landlady – against her husband generally – and she'll move heaven and earth for you.'

'Ah!' laughed Muriel, glancing at Mersham. 'Tom doesn't believe in sympathising with women – especially married women.'

'I don't!' said Tom emphatically, '– it's dangerous.'

'You leave it to the husband,' said Mersham.

'I do that! I don't want 'em coming to me with their troubles. I should never know the end.'

13

'Wise of you. Poor woman! So you'll broach your barrel of sympathy for your wife, eh, and for nobody else?'

'That's it. Isn't that right?'

'Oh, quite. Your wife will be a privileged person. Sort of home-brewed beer to drink *ad infinitum*? Quite all right, that!'

'There's nothing better,' said Tom, laughing.

'Except a change,' said Mersham. 'Now, I'm like a cup of tea to a woman.'

Muriel laughed aloud at this preposterous cynicism, and knitted her brows to bid him cease playing ball with bombs.

'A fresh cup each time. Women never weary of tea. Muriel, I can see you having a rich time. Sort of long after-supper drowse with a good husband.'

'Very delightful!' said Muriel sarcastically.

'If she's got a good husband, what more can she want?' asked Tom, keeping the tone of banter, but really serious and somewhat resentful.

'A lodger – to make things interesting.'

'Why,' said Muriel, intervening, 'do women like you so?'

Mersham looked up at her, quietly, smiling into her eyes. She was really perplexed. She wanted to know what he put in the pan to make the balance go down so heavily on his side. He had, as usual, to answer her seriously and truthfully, so he said: 'Because I can make them believe that black is green or purple – which it is, in reality.' Then, smiling broadly as she wakened again with admiration for him, he added: 'But you're trying to make me conceited, Miel – to stain my virgin modesty.'

Muriel glanced up at him with softness and understanding, and laughed low. Tom gave a guffaw at the notion of Mersham's virgin modesty. Muriel's brow wrinkled with irritation, and she turned from her sweetheart to look in the fire.

v

Mersham, all unconsciously, had now developed the situation to the climax he desired. He was sure that Vickers would not count seriously in Muriel's movement towards himself. So he turned away, uninterested.

The talk drifted for some time, after which he suddenly bethought himself:

'I say, Mr. Vickers, will you sing for us? You do sing, don't you?'

14

'Well – nothing to speak of,' replied the other modestly, wondering at Mersham's sudden change of interest. He looked at Muriel.

'Very well,' she answered him, indulging him now like a child. 'But —' she turned to Mersham – 'but do you, really?'

'Yes, of course. Play some of the old songs. Do you play any better?' She began 'Honour and Arms'.

'No, not that!' cried Mersham. 'Something quiet – "*Sois triste et sois belle*".' He smiled gently at her, suggestively. 'Try "*Du bist wie eine Blume*," or "*Pur dicesti*".'

Vickers sang well, though without much imagination. But the songs they sang were the old songs that Mersham had taught Muriel years before, and she played with one of his memories in her heart. At the end of the first song, she turned and found him looking at her, and they met again in the poetry of the past.

'Daffodils,' he said softly, his eyes full of memories.

She dilated, quivered with emotion, in response. They had sat on the rim of the hill, where the wild daffodils stood up to the sky, and there he had taught her, singing line by line: '*Du bist wie eine Blume*.' He had no voice, but a very accurate ear.

The evening wore on to ten o'clock. The lads came through the room on their way to bed. The house was asleep save the father, who sat alone in the kitchen, reading *The Octopus*. They went in to supper.

Mersham had roused himself and was talking well. Muriel stimulated him, always, and turned him to talk of art and philosophy – abstract things that she loved, of which only he had ever spoken to her, of which only he could speak, she believed, with such beauty. He used quaint turns of speech, contradicted himself waywardly, then said something sad and whimsical, all in a wistful, irresponsible manner so that even the men leaned indulgent and deferential to him.

'Life,' he said, and he was always urging this on Muriel in one form or another, 'life is beautiful, so long as it is consuming you. When it is rushing through you, destroying you, life is glorious. It is best to roar away, like a fire with a great draught, white-hot to the last bit. It's when you burn a slow fire and save fuel that life's not worth having.'

'You believe in a short life and a merry,' said the father.

'Needn't be either short or merry. Grief is part of the fire of life – and suffering – they're the root of the flame of joy, as they say. No! With life, we're like the man who was so anxious to provide for his old age that he died at thirty from inanition.'

'That's what we're not likely to do,' laughed Tom.

'Oh, I don't know. You live most intensely in human contact – and that's what we shrink from, poor timid creatures, from giving our souls to somebody to touch; for they, bungling fools, will generally paw it with dirty hands.'

Muriel looked at him with dark eyes of grateful understanding. She herself had been much pawed, brutally, by her brothers. But, then, she had been foolish in offering herself.

'And,' concluded Mersham, 'you are washed with the whitest fire of life – when you take a woman you love – and understand.'

Perhaps Mersham did not know what he was doing. Yet his whole talk lifted Muriel as in a net, like a sea-maiden out of the waters, and placed her in his arms, to breathe his thin, rare atmosphere. She looked at him, and was certain of his pure earnestness, and believed implicitly he could not do wrong.

Vickers believed otherwise. He would have expressed his opinion, whatever it might be, in an: 'Oh, ay, he's got plenty to say, and he'll keep on saying it – but, hang it all . . . !'

For Vickers was an old-fashioned, inarticulate lover; such as has been found the brief joy and the unending disappointment of a woman's life. At last he found he must go, as Mersham would not precede him. Muriel did not kiss him good-bye, nor did she offer to go out with him to his bicycle. He was angry at this, but more angry with the girl than with the man. He felt that she was fooling about, 'showing off' before the stranger. Mersham was a stranger to him, and so, in his idea, to Muriel. Both young men went out of the house together, and down the rough brick track to the barn. Mersham made whimsical little jokes: 'I wish my feet weren't so fastidious. They dither when they go in a soft spot like a girl who's touched a toad. Hark at that poor old wretch – she sounds as if she'd got whooping-cough.'

'A cow is not coughing when she makes that row,' said Vickers.

'Pretending, is she? – to get some Owbridge's? Don't blame her. I guess she's got chilblains, at any rate. Do cows have chilblains, poor devils?'

Vickers laughed and felt he must take this man into his protection. 'Mind,' he said, as they entered the barn, which was very dark. 'Mind your forehead against this beam.' He put one hand on the beam, and stretched out the other to feel for Mersham. 'Thanks,' said the latter gratefully. He knew the position of the beam to an inch, however dark the barn, but he allowed Vickers to guide him past it. He rather enjoyed being taken into Tom's protection.

Vickers carefully struck a match, bowing over the ruddy core of light and illuminating himself like some beautiful lantern in the midst of the high darkness of the barn. For some moments he bent over his bicycle-lamp, trimming and adjusting the wick, and his face, gathering all the light on its ruddy beauty, seemed luminous and wonderful. Mersham could see the down on his cheeks above the razor-line, and the full lips in shadow beneath the moustache, and the brush of the eyebrows between the light.

'After all,' said Mersham, 'he's very beautiful; she's a fool to give him up.'

Tom shut the lamp with a snap, and carefully crushed the match under his foot. Then he took the pump from the bicycle, and crouched on his heels in the dimness, inflating the tyre. The swift, unerring, untiring stroke of the pump, the light balance and the fine elastic adjustment of the man's body to his movements pleased Mersham.

'She could have,' he was saying to himself, 'some glorious hours with this man – yet she'd rather have me, because I can make her sad and set her wondering.'

But to the man he was saying:

'You know, love isn't the twin-soul business. With you, for instance, women are like apples on a tree. You can have one that you can reach. Those that look best are overhead, but it's no good bothering with them. So you stretch up, perhaps you pull down a bough and just get your fingers round a good one. Then it swings back and you feel wild and you say your heart's broken. But there are plenty of apples as good for you no higher than your chest.'

Vickers smiled, and thought there was something in it – generally; but for himself, it was nothing.

They went out of the barn to the yard gate. He watched the young man swing over his saddle and vanish, calling 'Good-night.'

'*Sic transit*,' he murmured – meaning Tom Vickers, and beautiful lustihood that is unconscious like a blossom.

Mersham went slowly in the house. Muriel was clearing away the supper things, and laying the table again for the men's breakfasts. But she was waiting for him as clearly as if she had stood watching in the doorway. She looked up at him, and instinctively he lifted his face towards her as if to kiss her. They smiled, and she went on with her work.

The father rose, stretching his burly form, and yawning. Mersham put on his overcoat.

'You will come a little way with me?' he said. She answered him with her eyes. The father stood, large and silent, on the hearth-rug. His sleepy, mazed disapproval had no more effect than a little breeze which might blow against them. She smiled brightly at her lover, like a child, as she pinned on her hat.

It was very dark outside in the starlight. He groaned heavily, and swore with extravagance as he went ankle-deep in mud.

'See, you should follow me. Come here,' she commanded, delighted to have him in charge.

'Give me your hand,' he said, and they went hand-in-hand over the rough places. The fields were open, and the night went up to the magnificent stars. The wood was very dark, and wet; they leaned forward and stepped stealthily, and gripped each other's hands fast with a delightful sense of adventure. When they stood and looked up a moment, they did not know how the stars were scattered among the tree-tops till he found the three jewels of Orion right in front.

There was a strangeness everywhere, as if all things had ventured out alive to play in the night, as they do in fairy-tales; the trees, the many stars, the dark spaces, and the mysterious waters below uniting in some magnificent game.

They emerged from the wood on to the bare hillside. She came down from the wood-fence into his arms, and he kissed her, and they laughed low together. Then they went on across the wild meadows where there was no path.

'Why don't you like him?' he asked playfully.

'Need you ask?' she said simply.

'Yes. Because he's heaps nicer than I am.'

She laughed a full laugh of amusement.

'He is! Look! He's like summer, brown and full of warmth. Think how splendid and fierce he'd be —'

'Why do you talk about him?' she said.

'Because I want you to know what you're losing – and you won't till you see him in my terms. He is very desirable – I should choose him in preference to me – for myself.'

'Should you?' she laughed. 'But,' she added with soft certainty, 'you don't understand.'

'No – I don't. I suppose it's love; your sort, which is beyond me. I shall never be blindly in love, shall I?'

'I begin to think you never will,' she answered, not very sadly. 'You won't be blindly anything.'

'The voice of love!' he laughed; and then: 'No, if you pull your flowers to pieces, and find how they pollinate, and where are the ovaries, you don't go in blind ecstasies over to them. But they mean more to you; they are intimate, like friends of your heart, not like wonderful, dazing fairies.'

'Ay!' she assented, musing over it with the gladness of understanding him. 'And then?'

Softly, almost without words, she urged him to the point.

'Well,' he said, 'you think I'm a wonderful, magical person, don't you? – and I'm not – I'm not as good, in the long run, as your Tom, who thinks you are a wonderful, magical person.'

She laughed and clung to him as they walked. He continued, very carefully and gently: 'Now, I don't imagine for a moment that you are princessy or angelic or wonderful. You often make me thundering mad because you're an ass...'

She laughed low with shame and humiliation.

'Nevertheless – I come from the south to you – because – well, with you I can be just as I feel, conceited or idiotic, without being afraid to be myself...' He broke off suddenly. 'I don't think I've tried to make myself out to you – any bigger or better than I am?' he asked her wistfully.

'No,' she answered, in beautiful, deep assurance. 'No! That's where it is. You have always been so honest. You are more honest than anybody ever —' She did not finish, being deeply moved. He was silent for some time, then he continued, as if he must see the question to the end with her:

'But, you know – I do like you not to wear corsets. I like to see you move inside your dress.'

She laughed, half shame, half pleasure.

'I wondered if you'd notice,' she said.

'I did – directly.' There was a space of silence, after which he resumed: 'You see – we would marry tomorrow – but I can't keep myself. I am in debt —'

She came close to him, and took his arm.

'– And what's the good of letting the years go, and the beauty of one's youth —?'

'No,' she admitted, very slowly and softly, shaking her head.

'So – well! – you understand, don't you? And if you're willing – you'll come to me, won't you? – just naturally, as you used to come and go to church with me? – and it won't be – it won't be me coaxing you – reluctant? Will it?'

They had halted in front of a stile which they would have to climb. She turned to him in silence, and put up her face to him. He took her in his arms, and kissed her, and felt the night mist with which his moustache was drenched, and he bent his head and rubbed his face on her shoulder, and then pressed his lips on her neck. For a while they stood in silence, clasped together. Then he heard her voice, muffled in his shoulder, saying:

'But – but, you know – it's much harder for the woman – it means something so different for a woman.'

'One can be wise,' he answered, slowly and gently. 'One need not blunder into calamities.'

She was silent for a time. Then she spoke again.

'Yes, but – if it should be – you see – I couldn't bear it.'

He let her go, and they drew apart, and the embrace no longer choked them from speaking. He recognised the woman defensive, playing the coward against her own inclinations, and even against her knowledge.

'If – if!' he exclaimed sharply, so that she shrank with a little fear. 'There need be no ifs – need there?'

'I don't know,' she replied, reproachfully, very quietly.

'If I say so —' he said, angry with her mistrust. Then he climbed the stile, and she followed.

'But you *do* know,' he exclaimed. 'I have given you books —'

'Yes, but —'

'But what?' He was getting really angry.

'It's so different for a woman – you don't know.'

He did not answer this. They stumbled together over the mole-hills, under the oak trees.

'And look – how we should have to be – creeping together in the dark —'

This stung him; at once, it was as if the glamour went out of life. It was as if she had tipped over the fine vessel that held the wine of his desire, and had emptied him of all his vitality. He had played a difficult, deeply-moving part all night, and now the lights suddenly switched out, and there was left only weariness. He was silent, tired, very tired, bodily and spiritually. They walked across the wide, dark meadow with sunken heads. Suddenly she caught his arm.

'Don't be cold with me!' she cried.

He bent and kissed in acknowledgment the lips she offered him for love.

20

'No,' he said drearily; 'no, it is not coldness – only – I have lost hold – for to-night.' He spoke with difficulty. It was hard to find a word to say. They stood together, apart, under the old thorn tree for some minutes, neither speaking. Then he climbed the fence, and stood on the highway above the meadow.

At parting also he had not kissed her. He stood a moment and looked at her. The water in a little brook under the hedge was running, chuckling with extraordinary loudness: away on Nethermere they heard the sad, haunting cry of the wild-fowl from the North. The stars still twinkled intensely. He was too spent to think of anything to say; she was too overcome with grief and fear and a little resentment. He looked down at the pale blotch of her face upturned from the low meadow beyond the fence. The thorn boughs tangled above her, drooping behind her like the roof of a hut. Beyond was the great width of the darkness. He felt unable to gather his energy to say anything vital.

'Good-bye,' he said. 'I'm going back – on Saturday. But – you'll write to me. Good-bye.'

He turned to go. He saw her white uplifted face vanish, and her dark form bend under the boughs of the tree, and go out into the great darkness. She did not say good-bye.

THE OLD ADAM

THE maid who opened the door was just developing into a handsome womanhood. Therefore she seemed to have the insolent pride of one newly come to an inheritance. She would be a splendid woman to look at, having just enough of Jewish blood to enrich her comeliness into beauty. At nineteen her fine grey eyes looked challenge, and her warm complexion, her black hair looped up slack, enforced the sensuous folding of her mouth.

She wore no cap nor apron, but a well-looking sleeved overall such as even very ladies don.

The man she opened to was tall and thin, but graceful in his energy. He wore white flannels, carried a tennis-racket. With a light bow to the maid he stepped beside her on the threshold. He was one of those who attract by their movement, whose movement is watched unconsciously, as we watch the flight of a sea-bird waving its wing leisurely. Instead of entering the house, the young man stood beside the maid-servant and looked back into the blackish evening. When in repose, he had the diffident, ironic bearing so remarkable in the educated youth of to-day, the very reverse of that traditional aggressiveness of youth.

'It is going to thunder, Kate,' he said.

'Yes, I think it is,' she replied, on an even footing.

The young man stood a moment looking at the trees across the road, and on the oppressive twilight.

'Look,' he said, 'there's not a trace of colour in the atmosphere, though it's sunset; all a dark, lustrous grey; and those oaks kindle green like a low fire – see!'

'Yes,' said Kate, rather awkwardly.

'A troublesome sort of evening; must be, because it's your last with us.'

'Yes,' said the girl, flushing and hardening.

There was another pause; then:

'Sorry you're going?' he asked, with a faint tang of irony.

'In some ways,' she replied, rather haughtily.

He laughed, as if he understood what was not said, then, with an 'Ah well!' he passed along the hall.

22

The maid stood for a few moments clenching her young fists, clenching her very breast in revolt. Then she closed the door.

Edward Severn went into the dining-room. It was eight o'clock, very dark for a June evening; on the dusk-blue walls only the gilt frames of the pictures glinted pale. The clock occupied the room with its delicate ticking.

The door opened into a tiny conservatory that was lined with a grape-vine. Severn could hear, from the garden beyond, the high prattling of a child. He went to the glass door.

Running down the grass by the flower-border was a little girl of three, dressed in white. She was very bonny, very quick and intent in her movements; she reminded him of a fieldmouse which plays alone in the corn, for sheer joy. Severn lounged in the doorway, watching her. Suddenly she perceived him. She started, flashed into greeting, gave a little gay jump, and stood quite still again, as if pleading.

'Mr. Severn,' she cried, in wonderfully coaxing tones: 'Come and see this.'

'What?' he asked.

'Com' and see it,' she pleaded.

He laughed, knowing she only wanted to coax him into the garden; and he went.

'Look,' she said, spreading out her plump little arm.

'What?' he asked.

The baby was not going to admit that she had tricked him thither for her amusement.

'All gone up to buds,' she said, pointing to the closed marigolds. Then 'See!' she shrieked, flinging herself at his legs, grasping the flan-nel of his trousers, and tugging at him wildly. She was a wild little Mænad. She flew shrieking like a revelling bird down the garden, glanc-ing back to see if he were coming. He had not the heart to desist, but went swiftly after her. In the obscure garden, the two white figures darted through the flowering plants, the baby, with her full silk skirts, scudding like a ruffled bird, the man, lithe and fleet, snatching her up and smothering his face in hers. And all the time her piercing voice re-echoed from his low calls of warning and of triumph as he hunted her. Often she was really frightened of him; then she clung fast round his neck, and he laughed and mocked her in a low, stirring voice, whilst she protested.

The garden was large for a London suburb. It was shut in by a high dark embankment, that rose above a row of black poplar trees. And over the spires of the trees, high up, slid by the golden-lighted trains, with the soft movement of caterpillars and a hoarse, subtle noise.

Mrs. Thomas stood in the dark doorway watching the night, the trains, the flash and run of the two white figures.

'And now we must go in,' she heard Severn say.

'No,' cried the baby, wild and defiant as a bacchanal. She clung to him like a wild-cat.

'Yes,' he said. 'Where's your mother?'

'Give me a swing,' demanded the child.

He caught her up. She strangled him hard with her young arms.

'I said, where's your mother?' he persisted, half smothered.

'She's op'tairs,' shouted the child. 'Give me a swing.'

'I don't think she is,' said Severn.

'She is. Give me a swing, a swi-i-ing!'

He bent forward, so that she hung from his neck like a great pendant. Then he swung her, laughing low to himself while she shrieked with fear. As she slipped he caught her to his breast.

'Mary!' called Mrs. Thomas, in that low, songful tone of a woman when her heart is roused and happy.

'Mary!' she called, long and sweet.

'Oh, no!' cried the child quickly.

But Severn bore her off. Laughing, he bowed his head and offered to the mother the baby who clung round his neck.

'Come along here,' said Mrs. Thomas roguishly, clasping the baby's waist with her hands.

'Oh, no,' cried the child, tucking her head into the young man's neck.

'But it's bed-time,' said the mother. She laughed as she drew at the child to pull her loose from Severn. The baby clung tighter, and laughed, feeling no determination in her mother's grip. Severn bent his head to loosen the child's hold, bowed, and swung the heavy baby on his neck. The child clung to him, bubbling with laughter; the mother drew at her baby, laughing low, while the man swung gracefully, giving little jerks of laughter.

'Let Mr. Severn undress me,' said the child, hugging close to the young man, who had come to lodge with her parents when she was scarce a month old.

'You're in high favour to-night,' said the mother to Severn. He laughed, and all three stood a moment watching the trains pass and re-

24

pass in the sky beyond the garden-end. Then they went indoors, and Severn undressed the child.

She was a beautiful girl, a bacchanal with her wild, dull-gold hair tossing about like a loose chaplet, her hazel eyes shining daringly, her small, spaced teeth glistening in little passions of laughter within her red, small mouth. The young man loved her. She was such a little bright wave of wilfulness, so abandoned to her impulses, so white and smooth as she lay at rest, so startling as she flashed her naked limbs about. But she was growing too old for a young man to undress.

She sat on his knee in her high-waisted night-gown, eating her piece of bread-and-butter with savage little bites of resentment: she did not want to go to bed. But Severn made her repeat a Pater Noster. She lisped over the Latin, and Mrs. Thomas, listening, flushed with pleasure; although she was a Protestant, and although she deplored the unbelief of Severn, who had been a Catholic.

The mother took the baby to carry her to bed. Mrs. Thomas was thirty-four years old, full-bosomed and ripe. She had dark hair that twined lightly round her low, white brow. She had a clear complexion, and beautiful brows, and dark-blue eyes. The lower part of her face was heavy.

'Kiss me,' said Severn to the child.

He raised his face as he sat in the rocking-chair. The mother stood beside, looking down at him, and holding the laughing rogue of a baby against her breast. The man's face was uptilted, his heavy brows set back from the laughing tenderness of his eyes, which looked dark, because the pupil was dilated. He pursed up his handsome mouth, his thick close-cut moustache roused.

He was a man who gave tenderness, but who did not ask for it. All his own troubles he kept, laughingly, to himself. But his eyes were very sad when quiet, and he was too quick to understand sorrow, not to know it.

Mrs. Thomas watched his fine mouth lifted for kissing. She leaned forward, lowering the baby, and suddenly, by a quick change in his eyes, she knew he was aware of her heavy woman's breasts approaching down to him. The wild rogue of a baby bent her face to his, and then, instead of kissing him, suddenly licked his cheek with her wet, soft tongue. He started back in aversion, and his eyes and his teeth flashed with a dangerous laugh.

'No, no,' he laughed, in low strangled tones. 'No dog-lick, my dear, oh no!'

25

The baby chuckled with glee, gave one wicked jerk of laughter, that came out like a bubble escaping.

He put up his mouth again, and again his face was horizontal below the face of the young mother. She looked down on him as if by a kind of fascination.

'Kiss me, then,' he said with thick throat.

The mother lowered the baby. She felt scarcely sure of her balance. Again the child, when near to his face, darted out her tongue to lick him. He swiftly averted his face, laughing in his throat.

Mrs. Thomas turned her face aside; she would see no more.

'Come then,' she said to the child. 'If you won't kiss Mr. Severn nicely —'

The child laughed over the mother's shoulder like a squirrel crouched there. She was carried to bed.

It was still not quite dark; the clouds had opened slightly. The young man flung himself into an arm-chair, with a volume of French verse. He read one lyric, then he lay still.

'What, all in the dark!' exclaimed Mrs. Thomas, coming in. 'And reading by *this* light.' She rebuked him with timid affectionateness. Then, glancing at his white-flannelled limbs sprawled out in the gloom, she went to the door. There she turned her back to him, looking out.

'Don't these flags smell strongly in the evening?' she said at length.

He replied with a few lines of the French he had been reading.

She did not understand. There was a peculiar silence.

'A peculiar, brutal, carnal scent, iris,' he drawled at length. 'Isn't it?'

She laughed shortly, saying: 'Eh, I don't know about that.'

'It is,' he asserted calmly.

He rose from his chair, went to stand beside her at the door.

There was a great sheaf of yellow iris near the window. Farther off, in the last twilight, a gang of enormous poppies balanced and flapped their gold-scarlet, which even the darkness could not quite put out.

'We ought to be feeling very sad,' she said after a while.

'Why?' he asked.

'Well – isn't it Kate's last night?' she said, slightly mocking.

'She's a tartar, Kate,' he said.

'Oh, she's too rude, she is really! The way she criticises the things you do, and her insolence —'

'The things *I* do?' he asked.

26

'Oh no; you can't do anything wrong. It's the things *I* do.' Mrs. Thomas sounded very much incensed.

'Poor Kate, she'll have to lower her key,' said Severn.

'Indeed she will, and a good thing too.'

There was silence again.

'It's lightning,' he said at last.

'Where?' she asked, with a suddenness that surprised him. She turned, met his eyes for a second. He sank his head, abashed.

'Over there in the north-east,' he said, keeping his face from her. She watched his hand rather than the sky.

'Oh,' she said uninterestedly.

'The storm will wheel round, you'll see,' he said.

'I hope it wheels the other way, then.'

'Well, it won't. You don't like lightning, do you? You'd even have to take refuge with Kate if I weren't here.'

She laughed quietly at his irony.

'No,' she said, quite bitterly. 'Mr. Thomas is never in when he's wanted.'

'Well, as he won't be urgently required, we'll acquit him, eh?'

At that moment a white flash fell across the blackness. They looked at each other, laughing. The thunder came broken and hesitatingly.

'I think we'll shut the door,' said Mrs. Thomas, in normal, sufficiently distant tones. A strong woman, she locked and bolted the stiff fastenings easily. Severn pressed on the light. Mrs. Thomas noticed the untidiness of the room. She rang, and presently Kate appeared.

'Will you clear baby's things away?' she said, in the contemptuous tone of a hostile woman. Without answering, and in her superb, unhastening way, Kate began to gather up the small garments. Both women were aware of the observant, white figure of the man standing on the hearth. Severn balanced with a fine, easy poise, and smiled to himself, exulting a little to see the two women in this state of hostility. Kate moved about with bowed defiant head. Severn watched her curiously; he could not understand her. And she was leaving to-morrow. When she had gone out of the room, he remained still standing, thinking. Something in his lithe, vigorous balance, so alert, and white, and independent, caused Mrs. Thomas to glance at him from her sewing.

'I will let the blinds down,' he said, becoming aware that he was attracting attention.

'Thank you,' she replied conventionally.

He let the lattice blinds down, then flung himself into his chair.

Mrs. Thomas sat at the table, near him, sewing. She was a good-looking woman, well made. She sat under the one light that was turned on. The lamp-shade was of red silk lined with yellow. She sat in the warm-gold light. There was established between the two a peculiar silence, like suspense, almost painful to cach of thcm, yct which neither would break. Severn listened to the snap of her needle, looked from the movement of her hand to the window, where the lightning beat and fluttered through the lattice. The thunder was as yet far off.

'Look,' he said, 'at the lightning.'

Mrs. Thomas started at the sound of his voice, and some of the colour went from her face. She turned to the window.

There, between the cracks of the venetian blinds, came the white flare of lightning, then the dark. Several storms were in the sky. Scarcely had one sudden glare fluttered and palpitated out, than another covered the window with white. It dropped, and another flew up, beat like a moth for a moment, then vanished. Thunder met and overlapped; two battles were fought together in the sky.

Mrs. Thomas went very pale. She tried not to look at the window, yet, when she felt the lightning blench the lamplight, she watched, and each time a flash leaped on the window, she shuddered. Severn, all unconsciously, was smiling with roused eyes.

'You don't like it?' he said, at last, gently.

'Not much,' she answered, and he laughed.

'Yet all the storms are a fair way off,' he said. 'Not one near enough to touch us.'

'No, but,' she replied, at last laying her hands in her lap, and turning to him, 'it makes me feel worked up. You don't know how it makes me feel, as if I couldn't contain myself.'

She made a helpless gesture with her hand. He was watching her closely. She seemed to him pathetically helpless and bewildered; she was eight years older than he. He smiled in a strange, alert fashion, like a man who feels in jeopardy. She bent over her work, stitching nervously. There was a silence in which neither of them could breathe freely.

Presently a bigger flash than usual whitened through the yellow lamplight. Both glanced at the window, then at each other. For a moment it was a look of greeting; then his eyes dilated to a smile, wide with recklessness. He felt her waver, lose her composure, become incoherent. Seeing the faint helplessness of coming tears, he felt his heart thud to a crisis. She had her face at her sewing.

Severn sank in his chair, half suffocated by the beating of his heart. Yet, time after time, as the flashes came, they looked at each other, till in the end they both were panting, and afraid, not of the lightning but of themselves and of each other.

He was so much moved that he became conscious of his perturbation. 'What the deuce is up?' he asked himself, wondering. At twenty-seven, he was quite chaste. Being highly civilised, he prized women for their intuition, and because of the delicacy with which he could transfer to them his thoughts and feelings, without cumbrous argument. From this to a state of passion he could only proceed by fine gradations, and such a procedure he had never begun. Now he was startled, astonished, perturbed, yet still scarcely conscious of his whereabouts. There was a pain in his chest that made him pant, and an involuntary tension in his arms, as if he must press someone to his breast. But the idea that this someone was Mrs. Thomas would have shocked him too much had he formed it. His passion had run on subconsciously, till now it had come to such a pitch it must drag his conscious soul into allegiance. This, however, would probably never happen; he would not yield allegiance, and blind emotion, in this direction, could not carry him alone.

Towards eleven o'clock Mr. Thomas came in.

'I wonder you come home at all,' Severn heard Mrs. Thomas say as her husband stepped indoors.

'I left the office at half-past ten,' the voice of Thomas replied, disagreeably.

'Oh, don't try to tell me that old tale,' the woman answered contemptuously.

'I didn't try anything at all, Gertie,' he replied with sarcasm. 'Your question was answered.'

Severn imagined him bowing with affected, magisterial dignity, and he smiled. Mr. Thomas was something in the law.

Mrs. Thomas left her husband in the hall, came and sat down again at table, where she and Severn had just finished supper, both of them reading the while.

Thomas came in, flushed very red. He was of middle stature, a thickly-built man of forty, good-looking. But he had grown round-shouldered with thrusting forward his chin in order to look the aggressive, strong-jawed man. He *had* a good jaw; but his mouth was small and nervously pinched. His brown eyes were of the emotional, affectionate sort, lacking pride or any austerity.

He did not speak to Severn nor Severn to him. Although as a rule the

29

two men were very friendly, there came these times when, for no reason whatever, they were sullenly hostile. Thomas sat down heavily, and reached his bottle of beer. His hands were thick, and in their movement rudimentary. Severn watched the thick fingers grasp the drinking-glass as if it were a treacherous enemy.

'Have you *had* supper, Gertie?' he asked, in tones that sounded like an insult. He could not bear that these two should sit reading as if he did not exist.

'Yes,' she replied, looking up at him in impatient surprise. 'It's late enough.' Then she buried herself again in her book.

Severn ducked low and grinned. Thomas swallowed a mouthful of beer.

'I wish you could answer my questions, Gertie, without superfluous *de*-tail,' he said nastily, thrusting out his chin at her as if cross-examining.

'Oh,' she said indifferently, not looking up. 'Wasn't my answer right, then?'

'Quite – I thank you,' he answered, bowing with great sarcasm. It was utterly lost on his wife.

'Hm-hm!' she murmured in abstraction, continuing to read.

Silence resumed. Severn was grinning to himself, chuckling.

'I *had* a compliment paid me to-night, Gertie,' said Thomas, quite amicably, after a while. He still ignored Severn.

'Hm-hm!' murmured his wife. This was a well-known beginning. Thomas valiantly struggled on with his courtship of his wife, swallowing his spleen.

'Councillor Jarndyce, in full committee—Are you listening, Gertie?'

'Yes,' she replied, looking up for a moment.

'You know Councillor Jarndyce's style,' Thomas continued, in the tone of a man determined to be patient and affable: '– the courteous Old English Gentleman —'

'Hm-hm!' replied Mrs. Thomas.

'He was speaking in reply to . . .' Thomas gave innumerable wearisome details, which no one heeded.

'Then he bowed to me, then to the Chairman – "I am compelled to say, Mr. Chairman, that we have *one* cause for congratulation; we are inestimably fortunate in *one* member of our staff; there is one point of which we can always be sure – the point of *law*; and it is an important point, Mr. Chairman."

'He bowed to the Chairman, he bowed to me. And you should have heard the applause all round that Council Chamber – that great, horse-shoe table, you don't know how impressive it is. And every face turned to me, and all round the board: "Hear – Hear!" You don't know what respect I command in *business*, Mrs. Thomas.'

'Then let it suffice you,' said Mrs. Thomas, calmly indifferent.

Mr. Thomas bit his bread-and-butter.

'The fat-head's had two drops of Scotch, so he's drawing on his imagination,' thought Severn chuckling deeply.

'I thought you said there was no meeting to-night,' Mrs. Thomas suddenly and innocently remarked after a while.

'There was a meeting, *in camera*,' replied her husband, drawing himself up with official dignity. His excessive and wounded dignity convulsed Severn; the lie disgusted Mrs. Thomas in spite of herself.

Presently Thomas, always courting his wife and insultingly overlooking Severn, raised a point of politics, passed a lordly opinion very offensive to the young man. Severn had risen, stretched himself, and laid down his book. He was leaning on the mantelpiece in an indifferent manner, as if he scarcely noticed the two talkers. But hearing Thomas pronounce like a boor upon the Woman's Bill, he roused himself, and coolly contradicted his landlord. Mrs. Thomas shot a look of joy at the white-clad young man who lounged so scornfully on the hearth. Thomas cracked his knuckles one after another, and lowered his brown eyes, which were full of hate. After a sufficient pause, for his timidity was stronger than his impulse, he replied with a phrase that sounded final. Severn flipped the sense out of it with a few words. In the argument Severn, more cultured and far more nimble-witted than his antagonist, who hauled up his answers with a lawyer's show of invincibility, but who had not any fineness of perception, merely spiked his opponent's pieces and smiled at him. Also the young man enjoyed himself by looking down scornfully, straight into the brown eyes of his senior all the time, so that Thomas writhed.

Mrs. Thomas, meantime, took her husband's side against women, without reserve. Severn was angry; he was scornfully angry with her. Mrs. Thomas glanced at him from time to time, a little ecstasy lighting her fine blue eyes. The irony of her part was delicious to her. If she had sided with Severn, that young man would have pitied the forlorn man, and been gentle with him.

The battle of words had got quieter and more intense. Mrs. Thomas made no move to check it. At last Severn was aware he and Thomas were both getting overheated. Thomas had doubled and dodged painfully, like a half-frenzied rabbit that will not realise it is trapped. Finally his efforts had moved even his opponent to pity. Mrs. Thomas was not pitiful. She scorned her husband's dexterity of argument, when his intellectual dishonesty was so evident to her. Severn uttered his last phrases, and would say no more. Then Thomas cracked his knuckles one after the other, turned aside, consumed with morbid humiliation, and there was silence.

'I will go to bed,' said Severn. He would have spoken some conciliatory words to his landlord; he lingered with that purpose; but he could not bring his throat to utter his purpose.

'Oh, before you go, do you mind, Mr. Severn, helping Mr. Thomas down with Kate's box? You may be gone before he's up in the morning, and the cab comes at ten. Do you mind?'

'Why should I?' replied Severn.

'Are you ready, Joe?' she asked her husband.

Thomas rose with the air of a man who represses himself and is determined to be patient.

'Where is it?' he asked.

'On the top landing. I'll tell Kate, and then we shan't frighten her. She has gone to bed.'

Mrs. Thomas was quite mistress of the situation; both men were humble before her. She led the way, with a candle, to the third floor. There on the little landing, outside the closed door, stood a large tin trunk. The three were silent because of the baby.

'Poor Kate,' Severn thought. 'It's a shame to kick her out into the world, and all for nothing.' He felt an impulse of hate towards womankind.

'Shall I go first, Mr. Severn?' asked Thomas.

It was surprising how friendly the two men were, as soon as they had something to do together, or when Mrs. Thomas was absent. Then they were comrades, Thomas, the elder, the thick-set, playing the protector's part, though always deferential to the younger, whimsical man.

'I had better go first,' said Thomas kindly. 'And if you put this round the handle, it won't cut your fingers.'

He offered the young man a little flexible book from his pocket. Severn had such small, fine hands that Thomas pitied them.

Severn raised one end of the trunk. Leaning back, and flashing a smile to Mrs. Thomas, who stood with the candle, he whispered: 'Kate's got a lot more impediments than I have.'

'I know it's heavy,' laughed Mrs. Thomas.

Thomas, waiting at the brink of the stairs, saw the young man tilting his bare throat towards the smiling woman, and whispering words which pleased her.

'At your pleasure, sir,' he said in his most grating and official tones.

'Sorry,' Severn flung out scornfully.

The elder man retreated very cautiously, stiffly lowering himself down one stair, looking anxiously behind.

'Are you holding the light for *me*, Gertie?' he snapped sarcastically, when he had managed one stair. She lifted the candle with a swoop. He was in a bustle and a funk. Severn, always indifferent, smiled slightly, and lowered the box with negligent ease of movement. As a matter of fact, three-quarters of the heavy weight pressed on Thomas. Mrs. Thomas watched the two figures from above.

'If I slip now,' thought Severn, as he noticed the anxious, red face of his landlord, 'I should squash him like a shrimp,' and he laughed to himself.

'Don't come yet,' he called softly to Mrs. Thomas, whom he heard following. 'If you slip, your husband's bottom-most under the smash. "Beware the fearful avalanche!"'

He laughed, and Mrs. Thomas gave a little chuckle. Thomas, very red and flustered, glanced irritably back at them, but said nothing.

Near the bottom of the staircase there was a twist in the stairs. Severn was feeling particularly reckless. When he came to the turn, he chuckled to himself, feeling his house-slippers unsafe on the narrowed, triangular stairs. He loved a risk above all things, and a subconscious instinct made the risk doubly sweet when his rival was under the box. Though Severn would not knowingly have hurt a hair of his landlord's head.

When Thomas was beginning to sweat with relief, being only one step from the landing, Severn did slip, quite accidentally. The great box crashed as if in pain, Severn glissaded down the stairs. Thomas was flung backwards across the landing, and his head went thud against the banister post. Severn, seeing no great harm done, was struggling to his feet, laughing and saying: 'I'm awfully sorry —' when Thomas got up. The elder man was infuriated like a bull. He saw the laughing face of Severn and he went mad. His brown eyes flared.

'You —, you did it on purpose!' he shouted, and straightway he fetched the young man two heavy blows, upon the jaw and ear. Thomas, a footballer and a boxer in his youth, had been brought up among the roughs of Swansea; Severn in a religious college in France.

The young man had never been struck in the face before. He instantly went white and mad with rage. Thomas stood on guard, fists up. But on the small, lumbered landing there was no room for fight. Moreover, Severn had no instinct of fisticuffs. With open, stiff fingers, the young man sprang on his adversary. In spite of the blow he received, but did not feel, he flung himself again forward, and then, catching Thomas's collar, brought him down with a crash. Instantly his exquisite hands were dug in the other's thick throat, the linen collar having been torn open. Thomas fought madly, with blind, brute strength. But the other lay wrapped on him like a white steel, his rare intelligence concentrated, not scattered; concentrated on strangling Thomas swiftly. He pressed forward, forcing his landlord's head over the edge of the next flight of stairs. Thomas, stout and full-blooded, lost every trace of self-possession; he struggled like an animal at slaughter. The blood came out of his nose over his face; he made horrid choking sounds as he struggled.

Suddenly Severn felt his face turned between two hands. With a shock of real agony, he met the eyes of Kate. She bent forward, she captured his eyes.

'What do you think you're doing?' she cried in frenzy of indignation. She learned over him in her night-dress, her two black plaits hanging perpendicular. He hid his face, and took his hands away. As he kneeled to rise, he glanced up the stairs. Mrs. Thomas stood against the banisters, motionless in a trance of horror and remorse. He saw the remorse plainly. Severn turned away his face, and was wild with shame. He saw his landlord kneeling, his hands at his throat, choking, rattling, and gasping. The young man's heart filled with remorse and grief. He put his arms round the heavy man, and raised him, saying tenderly:

'Let me help you up.'

He had got Thomas up against the wall, when the choked man began to slide down again in collapse, gasping all the time pitifully.

'No, stand up; you're best standing up,' commanded Severn sharply, rearing his landlord up again. Thomas managed to obey, stupidly. His nose still bled, he still held his throat and gasped with a crowing sound. But his breathing was getting deeper.

'Water, Kate – and sponge – cold,' said Severn.

Kate was back in an instant. The young man bathed his landlord's face and temples and throat. The bleeding ceased directly, the stout man's breathing became a series of irregular, jerky gasps, like a child that has been sobbing hard. At last he took a long breath, and his breast

34

settled into regular stroke, with little fluttering interruptions. Still holding his hand to his throat, he looked up with dazed, piteous brown eyes, mutely wretched and appealing. He moved his tongue as if to try it, put back his head a little, and moved the muscles of his throat. Then he replaced his hands on the place that ached.

Severn was grief-stricken. He would willingly, at that moment, have given his right hand for the man he had hurt.

Mrs. Thomas, meanwhile, stood on the stairs, watching: for a long time she dared not move, knowing she would sink down. She watched. One of the crises of her life was passing. Full of remorse, she passed over into the bitter land of repentance. She must no longer allow herself to hope for anything for herself. The rest of her life must be spent in self-abnegation: she must seek for no sympathy, must ask for no grace in love, no grace and harmony in living. Henceforward, as far as her own desires went, she was dead. She took a fierce joy in the anguish of it.

'Do you feel better?' Severn asked of the sick man. Thomas looked at the questioner with tragic brown eyes, in which was no anger, only mute self-pity. He did not answer, but looked like a wounded animal, very pitiable. Mrs. Thomas quickly repressed an impulse of impatient scorn, replacing it with a numb, abstract sense of duty, lofty and cold.

'Come,' said Severn, full of pity, and gentle as a woman. 'Let me help you to bed.'

Thomas, leaning heavily on the young man, whose white garments were dabbed with blood and water, stumbled forlornly into his room. There Severn unlaced his boots and got off the remnant of his collar. At this point Mrs. Thomas came in. She had taken her part; she was weeping also.

'Thank you, Mr. Severn,' she said coldly. Severn, dismissed, slunk out of the room. She went up to her husband, took his pathetic head upon her bosom, and pressed it there. As Severn went downstairs, he heard the few sobs of the husband, among the quick sniffing of the wife's tears. And he saw Kate, who had stood on the stairs to see all went well, climb up to her room with cold, calm face.

He locked up the house, put everything in order. Then he heated some water to bathe his face, which was swelling painfully. Having finished his fomentations, he sat thinking bitterly, with a good deal of shame.

As he sat, Mrs. Thomas came down for something. Her bearing was cold and hostile. She glanced round to see all was safe. Then:

'You will put out the light when you go to bed, Mr. Severn,' she said, more formally than a landlady at the seaside would speak. He was insulted: any ordinary being would turn off the light on retiring. Moreover, almost every night it was he who locked up the house, and came last to bed.

'I will, Mrs. Thomas,' he answered. He bowed, his eyes flickering with irony, because he knew his face was swollen.

She returned again after having reached the landing.

'Perhaps you wouldn't mind helping *me* down with the box,' she said, quietly and coldly. He did not reply, as he would have done an hour before, that he certainly should not help her, because it was a man's job, and she must not do it. Now, he rose, bowed, and went upstairs with her. Taking the greater part of the weight, he came quickly downstairs with the load.

'Thank you; it's very good of you. Good-night,' said Mrs. Thomas, and she retired.

In the morning Severn rose late. His face was considerably swollen. He went in his dressing-gown across to Thomas's room. The other man lay in bed, looking much the same as ever, but mournful in aspect, though pleased within himself at being coddled.

'How are you this morning?' Severn asked.

Thomas smiled, looked almost with tenderness up at his friend.

'Oh, I'm all right, thanks,' he replied.

He looked at the other's swollen and bruised cheek, then again, affectionately, into Severn's eyes.

'I'm sorry' – with a glance of indication – 'for that,' he said simply. Severn smiled with his eyes, in his own winsome manner.

'I didn't know we were such essential brutes,' he said. 'I thought I was so civilised . . .'

Again he smiled, with a wry, stiff mouth. Thomas gave a deprecating little grunt of a laugh.

'Oh, I don't know,' he said. 'It shows a man's got some fight in him.'

He looked up in the other's face appealingly. Severn smiled, with a touch of bitterness. The two men grasped hands.

To the end of their acquaintance, Severn and Thomas were close friends, with a gentleness in their bearing, one towards the other. On the other hand, Mrs. Thomas was only polite and formal with Severn, treating him as if he were a stranger.

Kate, her fate disposed of by her 'betters', passed out of their three lives.

36

HER TURN

SHE was his second wife, and so there was between them that truce which is never held between a man and his first woman.

He was one for the women, and as such, an exception among the colliers. In spite of their prudery, the neighbour women liked him; he was big, naïve, and very courteous with them; he was so, even to his second wife.

Being a large man of considerable strength and perfect health, he earned good money in the pit. His natural courtesy saved him from enemies, while his fresh interest in life made his presence always agreeable. So he went his own way, had always plenty of friends, always a good job down pit.

He gave his wife thirty-five shillings a week. He had two grown-up sons at home, and they paid twelve shillings each. There was only one child by the second marriage, so Radford considered his wife did well.

Eighteen months ago, Bryan and Wentworth's men were out on strike for eleven weeks. During that time, Mrs. Radford could neither cajole nor entreat nor nag the ten shillings strike-pay from her husband. So that when the second strike came on, she was prepared for action.

Radford was going, quite inconspicuously, to the publican's wife at the 'Golden Horn'. She is a large, easy-going lady of forty, and her husband is sixty-three, moreover crippled with rheumatism. She sits in the little bar-parlour of the wayside public-house, knitting for dear life, and sipping a very moderate glass of Scotch. When a decent man arrives at the three-foot width of bar, she rises, serves him, surveys him over, and, if she likes his looks, says:

'Won't you step inside, sir?'

If he steps inside, he will find not more than one or two men present. The room is warm, quite small. The landlady knits. She gives a few polite words to the stranger, then resumes her conversation with the man who interests her most. She is straight, highly-coloured, with indifferent brown eyes.

'What was that you asked me, Mr. Radford?'

'What is the difference between a donkey's tail and a rainbow?' asked Radford, who had a consuming passion for conundrums.

'All the difference in the world,' replied the landlady.

'Yes, but what special difference?'

'I s'll have to give it up again. You'll think me a donkey's head, I'm afraid.'

'Not likely. But just you consider now, wheer . . .'

The conundrum was still under weigh, when a girl entered. She was swarthy, a fine animal. After she had gone out:

'Do you know who that is?' asked the landlady.

'I can't say as I do,' replied Radford.

'She's Frederick Pinnock's daughter, from Stony Ford. She's courting our Willy.'

'And a fine lass, too.'

'Yes, fine enough, as far as that goes. What sort of a wife'll she make him, think you?'

'You just let me consider a bit,' said the man. He took out a pocketbook and a pencil. The landlady continued to talk to the other guests.

Radford was a big fellow, black-haired, with a brown moustache, and darkish blue eyes. His voice, naturally deep, was pitched in his throat, and had a peculiar, tenor quality, rather husky, and disturbing. He modulated it a good deal as he spoke, as men do who talk much with women. Always, there was a certain indolence in his carriage.

'Our mester's lazy,' his wife said. 'There's many a bit of a jab wants doin', but get him to do it if you can.'

But she knew he was merely indifferent to the little jobs, and not lazy.

He sat writing for about ten minutes, at the end of which time, he read:

'I see a fine girl full of life.

I see her just ready for wedlock,

But there's jealousy between her eyebrows

And jealousy on her mouth.

I see trouble ahead.

Willy is delicate.

She would do him no good.

She would never see when he wasn't well,

She would only see what she wanted —'

So, in phrases, he got down his thoughts. He had to fumble for expression, and therefore anything serious he wanted to say he wrote in 'poetry', as he called it.

Presently, the landlady rose, saying:

'Well, I s'll have to be looking after our mester. I s'll be in again before we close.'

Radford sat quite comfortably on. In a while, he too bade the company good-night.

When he got home, at a quarter-past eleven, his sons were in bed, and his wife sat awaiting him. She was a woman of medium height, fat and sleek, a dumpling. Her black hair was parted smooth, her narrow-opened eyes were sly and satirical, she had a peculiar twang in her rather sleering voice.

'Our missis is a puss-puss,' he said easily, of her. Her extraordinarily smooth, sleek face was remarkable. She was very healthy.

He never came in drunk. Having taken off his coat and his cap, he sat down to supper in his shirt-sleeves. Do as he might, she was fascinated by him. He had a strong neck, with the crisp hair growing low. Let her be angry as she would yet she had a passion for that neck of his, particularly when she saw the great vein rib under the skin.

'I think, missis,' he said, 'I'd rather ha'e a smite o' cheese than this meat.'

'Well, can't you get it yourself?'

'Yi, surely I can,' he said, and went out to the pantry.

'I think, if yer comin' in at this time of night, you can wait on yourself,' she justified herself.

She moved uneasily in her chair. There were several jam-tarts alongside the cheese on the dish he brought.

'Yi, Missis, them tan-tafflins'll go down very nicely,' he said.

'Oh, will they! Then you'd better help to pay for them,' she said, amiably, but determined.

'Now what art after?'

'What am I after? Why, can't you think?' she said sarcastically.

'I'm not for thinkin', missis.'

'No, I know you're not. But wheer's my money? You've been paid the Union to-day. Wheer do I come in?'

'Tha's got money, an' tha mun use it.'

'Thank yer. An' 'aven't you none, as well?'

'I hadna, not till we was paid, not a ha'p'ny.'

'Then you ought to be ashamed of yourself to say so.'

' 'Appen so.'

'We'll go shares wi' th' Union money,' she said. 'That's nothing but what's right.'

'We shonna. Tha's got plenty o' money as tha can use.'

39

'Oh, all right,' she said. 'I will do.'

She went to bed. It made her feel sharp that she could not get at him.

The next day, she was just as usual. But at eleven o'clock she took her purse and went up town. Trade was very slack. Men stood about in gangs, men were playing marbles everywhere in the streets. It was a sunny morning. Mrs. Radford went into the furnisher-and-upholsterer's shop.

'There's a few things,' she said to Mr. Allcock, 'as I'm wantin' for the house, and I might as well get them now, while the men's at home, and can shift me the furniture.'

She put her fat purse on to the counter with a click. The man should know she was not wanting 'strap'. She bought linoleum for the kitchen, a new wringer, a breakfast-service, a spring mattress, and various other things, keeping a mere thirty shillings, which she tied in a corner of her handkerchief. In her purse was some loose silver.

Her husband was gardening in a desultory fashion when she got back home. The daffodils were out. The colts in the field at the end of the garden were tossing their velvety brown necks.

'Sithee here, missis,' called Radford, from the shed which stood half-way down the path. Two doves in a cage were cooing.

'What have you got?' asked the woman, as she approached. He held out to her in his big, earthy hand a tortoise. The reptile was very, very slowly issuing its head again to the warmth.

'He's wakkened up betimes,' said Radford.

'He's like th' men, wakened up for a holiday,' said the wife. Radford scratched the little beast's scaly head.

'We pleased to see him out,' he said.

They had just finished dinner, when a man knocked at the door.

'From Allcock's!' he said.

The plump woman took up the clothes-basket containing the crockery she had bought.

'Whativer hast got theer?' asked her husband.

'We've been wantin' some breakfast-cups for ages, so I went up town an' got 'em this mornin',' she replied.

He watched her taking out the crockery.

'Hm!' he said. 'Tha's been on th' spend, seemly.'

Again there was a thud at the door. The man had put down a roll of linoleum. Mr. Radford went to look at it.

'They come rolling in!' he exclaimed.

'Who's grumbled more than you about the raggy oilcloth of this kitchen?' said the insidious, cat-like voice of the wife.

'It's all right, it's all right,' said Radford.

The carter came up the entry with another roll, which he deposited with a grunt at the door.

'An' how much do you reckon this lot is?' he asked.

'Oh, they're all paid for, don't worry,' replied the wife.

'Shall yer gi'e me a hand, mester?' asked the carter.

Radford followed him down the entry, in his easy, slouching way. His wife went after. His waistcoat was hanging loose over his shirt. She watched his easy movement of well-being as she followed him, and she laughed to herself.

The carter took hold of one end of the wire mattress, dragged it forth.

'Well, this is a corker!' said Radford, as he received the burden.

'Now the mangle!' said the carter.

'What dost reckon tha's been up to, missis?' asked the husband.

'I said to myself last wash-day, if I had to turn that mangle again, tha'd ha'e ter wash the clothes thyself.'

Radford followed the carter down the entry again. In the street, women were standing watching, and dozens of men were lounging round the cart. One officiously helped with the wringer.

'Gi'e him thrippence,' said Mrs. Radford.

'Gi'e him thysen,' replied her husband.

'I've no change under half a crown.'

Radford tipped the carter, and returned indoors. He surveyed the array of crockery, linoleum, mattress, mangle, and other goods crowding the house and the yard.

'Well, this is a winder!' he repeated.

'We stood in need of 'em enough,' she replied.

'I hope tha's got plenty more from wheer they came from,' he replied dangerously.

'That's just what I haven't.' She opened her purse. 'Two half-crowns, that's every copper I've got i' th' world.'

He stood very still as he looked.

'It's right,' she said.

There was a certain smug sense of satisfaction about her. A wave of anger came over him, blinding him. But he waited and waited. Suddenly his arm leapt up, the fist clenched, and his eyes blazed at her. She shrank away, pale and frightened. But he dropped his fist to his side, turned, and went out, muttering. He went down to the shed that stood in the middle of the garden. There he picked up the tortoise, and stood with bent head, rubbing its horny head.

She stood hesitating, watching him. Her heart was heavy, and yet there was a curious, cat-like look of satisfaction round her eyes. Then she went indoors and gazed at her new cups, admiringly.

The next week he handed her his half-sovereign without a word.

'You'll want some for yourself,' she said, and she gave him a shilling. He accepted it.

STRIKE-PAY

STRIKE-MONEY is paid in the Primitive Methodist Chapel. The crier was round quite early on Wednesday morning to say that paying would begin at ten o'clock.

The Primitive Methodist Chapel is a big barn of a place, built, designed, and paid for by the colliers themselves. But it threatened to fall down from its first form, so that a professional architect had to be hired at last to pull the place together.

It stands in the Square. Forty years ago, when Bryan and Wentworth opened their pits, they put up the 'squares' of miners' dwellings. They are two great quadrangles of houses, enclosing a barren stretch of ground, littered with broken pots and rubbish, which forms a square, a great, sloping, lumpy playground for the children, a drying-ground for many women's washing.

Wednesday is still wash-day with some women. As the men clustered round the Chapel, they heard the thud-thud-thud of many pouches, women pounding away at the wash-tub with a wooden pestle. In the Square the white clothes were waving in the wind from a maze of clothes-lines, and here and there women were pegging out, calling to the miners, or to the children who dodged under the flapping sheets.

Ben Townsend, the Union agent, has a bad way of paying. He takes the men in order of his round, and calls them by name. A big, oratorical man with a grey beard, he sat at the table in the Primitive school-room, calling name after name. The room was crowded with colliers, and a great group pushed up outside. There was much confusion. Ben dodged from the Scargill Street list to the Queen Street. For this Queen Street men were not prepared. They were not to the fore.

'Joseph Grooby – Joseph Grooby! Now, Joe, where are you?'

'Hold on a bit, Sorry!' cried Joe from outside. 'I'm shovin' up.'

There was a great noise from the men.

'I'm takin' Queen Street. All you Queen Street men should be ready. Here you are, Joe,' said the Union agent loudly.

'Five children!' said Joe, counting the money suspiciously.

'That's right, I think,' came the mouthing voice. 'Fifteen shillings, is it not?'

'A bob a kid,' said the collier.

'Thomas Sedgwick—How are you, Tom? Missis better?'

'Ay, 'er's shapin' nicely. Tha'rt hard at work to-day, Ben.' This was sarcasm on the idleness of a man who had given up the pit to become a Union agent.

'Yes. I rose at four to fetch the money.'

'Dunna hurt thysen,' was the retort, and the men laughed.

'No – John Merfin!'

But the colliers, tired with waiting, excited by the strike spirit, began to rag. Merfin was young and dandiacal. He was choir-master at the Wesleyan Chapel.

'Does your collar cut, John?' asked a sarcastic voice out of the crowd.

'Hymn Number Nine.

> "Diddle-diddle dumpling, my son John
> Went to bed with his best suit on," '

came the solemn announcement.

Mr. Merfin, his white cuffs down to his knuckles, picked up his half-sovereign, and walked away loftily.

'Sam Coutts!' cried the paymaster.

'Now, lad, reckon it up,' shouted the voice of the crowd, delighted.

Mr. Coutts was a straight-backed ne'er-do-well. He looked at his twelve shillings sheepishly.

'Another two-bob – he had twins a-Monday night – get thy money, Sam, tha's earned it – tha's addled it, Sam; dunna go be-out it. Let him ha' the two bob for 'is twins, mister,' came the clamour from the men around.

Sam Coutts stood grinning awkwardly.

'You should ha' given us notice, Sam,' said the paymaster suavely. 'We can make it all right for you next week—'

'Nay, nay, nay,' shouted a voice. 'Pay on delivery – the goods is there right enough.'

'Get thy money, Sam, tha's addled it,' became the universal cry, and the Union agent had to hand over another florin, to prevent a disturbance. Sam Coutts grinned with satisfaction.

'Good shot, Sam,' the men exclaimed.

'Ephraim Wharmby,' shouted the pay-man.

A lad came forward.

'Gi' him sixpence for what's on t'road,' said a sly voice.

'Nay, nay,' replied Ben Townsend; 'pay on delivery.'

There was a roar of laughter. The miners were in high spirits.

In the town they stood about in gangs, talking and laughing. Many sat on their heels in the market-place. In and out of the public-houses they went, and on every bar the half-sovereigns clicked.

'Comin' ter Nottingham wi' us, Ephraim?' said Sam Coutts to the slender, pale young fellow of about twenty-two.

'I'm non walkin' that far of a gleamy day like this.'

'He has na got the strength,' said somebody, and a laugh went up.

'How's that?' asked another pertinent voice.

'He's a married man, mind yer,' said Chris Smitheringale, 'an' it ta'es a bit o' keepin' up.'

The youth was teased in this manner for some time.

'Come on ter Nottingham wi's; tha'll be safe for a bit,' said Coutts.

A gang set off, although it was only eleven o'clock. It was a nine-mile walk. The road was crowded with colliers travelling on foot to see the match between Notts and Aston Villa. In Ephraim's gang were Sam Coutts, with his fine shoulders and his extra florin, Chris Smitheringale, fat and smiling, and John Wharmby, a remarkable man, tall, erect as a soldier, black-haired and proud; he could play any musical instrument, he declared.

'I can play owt from a comb up'ards. If there's music to be got outer a thing, I back I'll get it. No matter what shape or form of instrument you set before me, it doesn't signify if I nivir clapped eyes on it before, I's warrant I'll have a tune out of it in five minutes.'

He beguiled the first two miles so. It was true, he had caused a sensation by introducing the mandoline into the townlet, filling the hearts of his fellow-colliers with pride as he sat on the platform in evening dress, a fine soldierly man, bowing his black head, and scratching the mewing mandoline with hands that had only to grasp the 'instrument' to crush it entirely.

Chris stood a can round at the 'White Bull' at Gilt Brook. John Wharmby took his turn at Kimberley top.

'We wunna drink again,' they decided, 'till we're at Cinder Hill. We'll non stop i' Nuttall.'

They swung along the high-road under the budding trees. In Nuttall churchyard the crocuses blazed with yellow at the brim of the balanced, black yews. White and purple crocuses clipt up over the graves, as if the churchyard were bursting out in tiny tongues of flame.

'Sithee,' said Ephraim, who was an ostler down pit, 'sithee, here comes the Colonel. Sithee at his 'osses how they pick their toes up, the beauties!'

The Colonel drove past the men, who took no notice of him.

'Hast heard, Sorry,' said Sam, 'as they're com'n out i' Germany, by the thousand, an' begun riotin'?'

'An' comin' out i' France simbitar,' cried Chris.

The men all gave a chuckle.

'Sorry,' shouted John Wharmby, much elated, 'we oughtna ter go back under a twenty per cent rise.'

'We should get it,' said Chris.

'An' easy! They can do nowt bi-out us, we'n on'y ter stop out long enough.'

'I'm willin',' said Sam, and there was a laugh. The colliers looked at one another. A thrill went through them as if an electric current passed.

'We'n on'y ter stick out, an' we s'll see who's gaffer.'

'Us!' cried Sam. 'Why, what can they do again' us, if we come out all over th' world?'

'Nowt!' said John Wharmby. 'Th' mesters is bobbin' about like corks on a cassivoy a'ready.' There was a large natural reservoir, like a lake, near Bestwood, and this supplied the simile.

Again there passed through the men that wave of elation, quickening their pulses. They chuckled in their throats. Beyond all consciousness was this sense of battle and triumph in the hearts of the working-men at this juncture.

It was suddenly suggested at Nuttall that they should go over the fields to Bulwell, and into Nottingham that way. They went single file across the fallow, past the wood, and over the railway, where now no trains were running. Two fields away was a troop of pit ponies. Of all colours, but chiefly of red or brown, they clustered thick in the field, scarcely moving, and the two lines of trodden earth patches showed where fodder was placed down the field.

'Theer's the pit 'osses,' said Sam. 'Let's run 'em.'

'It's like a circus turned out. See them skewbawd 'uns – seven skewbawd,' said Ephraim.

The ponies were inert, unused to freedom. Occasionally one walked round. But there they stood, two thick lines of ruddy brown and piebald and white, across the trampled field. It was a beautiful day, mild, pale blue, a 'growing day', as the men said, when there was the silence of swelling sap everywhere.

'Let's ha'e a ride,' said Ephraim.

46

The younger men went up to the horses.

'Come on – co-oop, Taffy – co-oop, Ginger.'

The horses tossed away. But having got over the excitement of being above-ground, the animals were feeling dazed and rather dreary. They missed the warmth and the life of the pit. They looked as if life were a blank to them.

Ephraim and Sam caught a couple of steeds, on whose backs they went careering round, driving the rest of the sluggish herd from end to end of the field. The horses were good specimens, on the whole, and in fine condition. But they were out of their element.

Performing too clever a feat, Ephraim went rolling from his mount. He was soon up again, chasing his horse. Again he was thrown. Then the men proceeded on their way.

They were drawing near to miserable Bulwell, when Ephraim, remembering his turn was coming to stand drinks, felt in his pocket for his beloved half-sovereign, his strike-pay. It was not there. Through all his pockets he went, his heart sinking like lead.

'Sam,' he said, 'I believe I'n lost that ha'ef a sovereign.'

'Tha's got it somewheer about thee,' said Chris.

They made him take off his coat and waistcoat. Chris examined the coat, Sam the waistcoat, whilst Ephraim searched his trousers.

'Well,' said Chris, 'I'n foraged this coat, an' it's non theer.'

'An' I'll back my life as th' on'y bit a metal on this wa'scoat is the buttons,' said Sam.

'An' it's non in my breeches,' said Ephraim. He took off his boots and his stockings. The half-sovereign was not there. He had not another coin in his possession.

'Well,' said Chris, 'we mun go back an' look for it.'

Back they went, four serious-hearted colliers, and searched the field, but in vain.

'Well,' said Chris, 'we s'll ha'e ter share wi' thee, that's a'.'

'I'm willin',' said John Wharmby.

'An' me,' said Sam.

'Two bob each,' said Chris.

Ephraim, who was in the depths of despair, shamefully accepted their six shillings.

In Bulwell they called in a small public-house, which had one long room with a brick floor, scrubbed benches and scrubbed tables. The central space was open. The place was full of colliers, who were drinking. There was a great deal of drinking during the strike, but not a vast amount drunk. Two men were playing skittles, and the rest were betting. The seconds sat on either side the skittle-board, holding caps of money, sixpences and coppers, the wagers of the 'backers'.

Sam, Chris, and John Wharmby immediately put money on the man who had their favour. In the end Sam declared himself willing to play against the victor. He was the Bestwood champion. Chris and John Wharmby backed him heavily, and even Ephraim the Unhappy ventured sixpence.

In the end, Sam had won half a crown, with which he promptly stood drinks and bread and cheese for his comrades. At half-past one they set off again.

It was a good match between Notts and Villa – no goals at half-time, two-none for Notts at the finish. The colliers were hugely delighted, especially as Flint, the forward for Notts, who was an Underwood man well known to the four comrades, did some handsome work, putting the two goals through.

Ephraim determined to go home as soon as the match was over. He knew John Wharmby would be playing the piano at the 'Punch Bowl', and Sam, who had a good tenor voice, singing, while Chris cut in with witticisms, until evening. So he bade them farewell, as he must get home. They, finding him somewhat of a damper on their spirits, let him go.

He was the sadder for having witnessed an accident near the football-ground. A navvy, working at some drainage, carting an iron tip-tub of mud and emptying it, had got with his horse on to the deep deposit of ooze which was crusted over. The crust had broken, the man had gone under the horse, and it was some time before the people had realised he had vanished. When they found his feet sticking out, and hauled him forth, he was dead, stifled dead in the mud. The horse was at length hauled out, after having its neck nearly pulled from the socket.

Ephraim went home vaguely impressed with a sense of death, and loss, and strife. Death was loss greater than his own, the strike was a battle greater than that he would presently have to fight.

He arrived home at seven o'clock, just when it had fallen dark. He lived in Queen Street with his young wife, to whom he had been married two months, and with his mother-in-law, a widow of sixty-four. Maud was the last child remaining unmarried, the last of eleven.

Ephraim went up the entry. The light was burning in the kitchen. His mother-in-law was a big, erect woman, with wrinkled, loose face, and cold blue eyes. His wife was also large, with very vigorous fair hair, frizzy like unravelled rope. She had a quiet way of stepping, a certain cat-like stealth, in spite of her large build. She was five months pregnant.

'Might we ask wheer you've been to?' inquired Mrs. Marriott, very erect, very dangerous. She was only polite when she was very angry.

'I'n bin ter th' match.'

'Oh, indeed!' said the mother-in-law. 'And why couldn't we be told as you thought of jaunting off?'

'I didna know mysen,' he answered, sticking to his broad Derbyshire.

'I suppose it popped into your mind, an' so you darted off,' said the mother-in-law dangerously.

'I didna. It wor Chris Smitheringale who exed me.'

'An' did you take much invitin'?'

'I didna want ter goo.'

'But wasn't there enough man beside your jacket to say no?'

He did not answer. Down at the bottom he hated her. But he was, to use his own words, all messed up with having lost his strike-pay and with knowing the man was dead. So he was more helpless before his mother-in-law, whom he feared. His wife neither looked at him nor spoke, but kept her head bowed. He knew she was with her mother.

'Our Maud's been waitin' for some money, to get a few things,' said the mother-in-law.

In silence, he put five-and-sixpence on the table.

'Take that up, Maud,' said the mother.

Maud did so.

'You'll want it for us board, shan't you?' she asked, furtively, of her mother.

'Might I ask if there's nothing you want to buy yourself, first?'

'No, there's nothink I want,' answered the daughter.

Mrs. Marriott took the silver and counted it.

'And do you,' said the mother-in-law, towering upon the shrinking son, but speaking slowly and statelily, 'do you think I'm going to keep you and your wife for five and sixpence a week?'

'It's a' I've got,' he answered sulkily.

'You've had a good jaunt, my sirs, if it's cost four and sixpence. You've started your game early, haven't you?'

He did not answer.

'It's a nice thing! Here's our Maud an' me been sitting since eleven o'clock this morning! Dinner waiting and cleared away, tea waiting and washed up; then in he comes crawling with five and sixpence. Five and sixpence for a man an' wife's board for a week, if you please!'

Still he did not say anything.

'You must think something of yourself, Ephraim Wharmby!' said his mother-in-law. 'You must think something of yourself. You suppose, do you, *I'm* going to keep you an' your wife, while you make a holiday, off on the nines to Nottingham, drink an' women.'

'I've neither had drink nor women, as you know right well,' he said.

'I'm glad we know summat about you. For you're that close, anybody'd think we was foreigners to you. You're a pretty little jockey, aren't you? Oh, it's a gala time for you, the strike is. That's all men strike for, indeed. They enjoy themselves, they do that. Ripping and racing and drinking, from morn till night, my sirs!'

'Is there on'y tea for me?' he asked, in a temper.

'Hark at him! Hark-ye! Should I ask you whose house you think you're in? Kindly order me about, do. Oh, it makes him big, the strike does. See him land home after being out on the spree for hours, and give his orders, my sirs! Oh, strike sets the men up, it does. Nothing have they to do but guzzle and gallivant to Nottingham. Their wives'll keep them, oh yes. So long as they get something to eat at home, what more do they want! What more *should* they want, prithee? Nothing! Let the women and children starve and scrape, but fill the man's belly, and let him have his fling. My sirs, indeed, I think so! Let tradesmen go – what do they matter! Let rent go. Let children get what they can catch. Only the man will see *he's* all right. But not here, though!'

'Are you goin' ter gi'e me ony bloody tea?'

His mother-in-law started up.

'If tha dares ter swear at me, I'll lay thee flat.'

'Are yer – goin' ter – gi'e me – any blasted, rotten, còssed, blòody tèa?' he bawled, in a fury, accenting every other word deliberately.

'Maud!' said the mother-in-law, cold and stately, 'If you gi'e him any tea after that, you're a trollops.' Whereupon she sailed out to her other daughters.

Maud quietly got the tea ready.

'Shall y'ave your dinner warmed up?' she asked.

'Ay.'

She attended to him. Not that she was really meek. But – he was *her* man, not her mother's.

50

THE WITCH *A LA MODE*

WHEN Bernard Coutts alighted at East Croydon he knew he was tempting Providence.

'I may just as well,' he said to himself, 'stay the night here, where I am used to the place, as go to London. I can't get to Connie's forlorn spot to-night, and I'm tired to death, so why shouldn't I do what is easiest?'

He gave his luggage to a porter.

Again, as he faced the approaching tram-car: 'I don't see why I shouldn't go down to Purley. I shall just be in time for tea.'

Each of these concessions to his desires he made against his conscience. But beneath his sense of shame his spirit exulted.

It was an evening of March. In the dark hollow below Crown Hill the buildings accumulated, bearing the black bulk of the church tower up into the rolling and smoking sunset.

'I know it so well,' he thought. 'And love it,' he confessed secretly in his heart.

The car ran on familiarly. The young man listened for the swish, watched for the striking of the blue splash overhead, at the bracket. The sudden fervour of the spark, splashed out of the mere wire, pleased him.

'Where does it come from?' he asked himself, and a spark struck bright again. He smiled a little, roused.

The day was dying out. One by one the arc lamps fluttered or leaped alight, the strand of copper overhead glistened against the dark sky that now was deepening to the colour of monkshood. The tram-car dipped as it ran, seeming to exult. As it came clear of the houses, the young man, looking west, saw the evening star advance, a bright thing approaching from a long way off, as if it had been bathing in the surf of the daylight, and now was walking shorewards to the night. He greeted the naked star with a bow of the head, his heart surging as the car leaped.

'It seems to be greeting me across the sky – the star,' he said, amused by his own vanity.

Above the colouring of the afterglow the blade of the new moon hung sharp and keen. Something recoiled in him.

'It is like a knife to be used at a sacrifice,' he said to himself. Then, secretly: 'I wonder for whom?'

He refused to answer this question, but he had the sense of Constance, his betrothed, waiting for him in the Vicarage in the north. He closed his eyes.

Soon the car was running full-tilt from the shadow to the fume of yellow light at the terminus, where shop on shop and lamp beyond lamp heaped golden fire on the floor of the blue night. The car, like an eager dog, ran in home, sniffing with pleasure the fume of lights.

Coutts flung away uphill. He had forgotten he was tired. From the distance he could distinguish the house, by the broad white cloth of alyssum flowers that hung down the garden walls. He ran up the steep path to the door, smelling the hyacinths in the dark, watching for the pale fluttering of daffodils and the steadier show of white crocuses on the grassy banks.

Mrs. Braithwaite herself opened the door to him.

'There!' she exclaimed. 'I expected you. I had your card saying you would cross from Dieppe to-day. You wouldn't make up your mind to come here, not till the last minute, would you? No – that's what I expected. You know where to put your things; I don't think we've altered anything in the last year.'

Mrs. Braithwaite chattered on, laughing all the time. She was a young widow, whose husband had been dead two years. Of medium height, sanguine in complexion and temper, there was a rich oily glisten in her skin and in her black hair, suggesting the flesh of a nut. She was dressed for the evening in a long gown of soft, mole-coloured satin.

'Of course, I'm delighted you've come,' she said at last, lapsing into conventional politeness, and then, seeing his eyes, she began to laugh at her attempt at formality.

She let Coutts into a small, very warm room that had a dark, foreign sheen, owing to the black of the curtains and hangings covered thick with glistening Indian embroidery, and to the sleekness of some Indian ware. A rosy old gentleman, with exquisite white hair and side-whiskers, got up shakily and stretched out his hand. His cordial expression of welcome was rendered strange by a puzzled, wondering look of old age, and by a certain stiffness of his countenance, which now would only render a few expressions. He wrung the newcomer's hand heartily, his manner contrasting pathetically with his bowed and trembling form.

'Oh, why – why, yes, it's Mr. Coutts! H'm – ay. Well, and how are you – h'm? Sit down, sit down.' The old man rose again, bowing,

52

waving the young man into a chair. 'Ay! well, and how are you? ...
What? Have some tea – come on, come along; here's the tray. Laura,
ring for fresh tea for Mr. Coutts. But I will do it.' He suddenly remembered his old gallantry, forgot his age and uncertainty. Fumbling, he
rose to go to the bell-pull.

'It's done, Pater – the tea will be in a minute,' said his daughter in
high, distinct tones. Mr. Cleveland sank with relief into his chair.

'You know, I'm beginning to be troubled with rheumatism,' he explained in confidential tones. Mrs. Braithwaite glanced at the young
man and smiled. The old gentleman babbled and chattered. He had no
knowledge of his guest beyond the fact of his presence; Coutts might
have been any other young man, for all his host was aware.

'You didn't tell us you were going away. Why didn't you?' asked
Laura, in her distinct tones, between laughing and reproach. Coutts
looked at her ironically, so that she fidgeted with some crumbs on the
cloth.

'I don't know,' he said. 'Why do we do things?'

'I'm sure I don't know. Why do we? Because we want to, I suppose,'
and she ended again with a little run of laughter. Things were so amusing, and she was so healthy.

'Why *do* we do things, Pater?' she suddenly asked in a loud voice,
glancing with a little chuckle of laughter at Coutts.

'Ay – why do we do things? What things?' said the old man, beginning to laugh with his daughter.

'Why, any of the things that we do.'

'Eh? Oh!' The old man was illuminated, and delighted. 'Well, now,
that's a difficult question. I remember, when I was a little younger, we
used to discuss Free Will – got very hot about it ...' He laughed, and
Laura laughed, then said, in a high voice:

'Oh! Free Will! We shall really think you're *passé*, if you revive
that, Pater.'

Mr. Cleveland looked puzzled for a moment. Then, as if answering a
conundrum, he repeated:

'Why do we do things? Now, why *do* we do things?'

'I suppose,' he said, in all good faith, 'it's because we can't help it –
eh? What?'

Laura laughed. Coutts showed his teeth in a smile.

'That's what I think, Pater,' she said loudly.

'And are you still engaged to your Constance?' she asked of Coutts,
with a touch of mockery this time. Coutts nodded.

'And how is she?' asked the widow.

'I believe she is very well – unless my delay has upset her,' said Coutts, his tongue between his teeth. It hurt him to give pain to his fiancée, and yet he did it wilfully.

'Do you know, she always reminds me of a Bunbury – I call her your Miss Bunbury,' Laura laughed.

Coutts did not answer.

'We missed you *so* much when you first went away,' Laura began, re-establishing the proprieties.

'Thank you,' he said. She began to laugh wickedly.

'On Friday evenings,' she said, adding quickly: 'Oh, and this is Friday evening, and Winifred is coming just as she used to – how long ago? – ten months?'

'Ten months,' Coutts corroborated.

'Did you quarrel with Winifred?' she asked suddenly.

'Winifred never quarrels,' he answered.

'I don't believe she does. Then why *did* you go away? You are such a puzzle to me, you know – and I shall never rest till I have had it out of you. Do you mind?'

'I like it,' he said, quietly, flashing a laugh at her.

She laughed, then settled herself in a dignified, serious way.

'No, I can't make you out at all – nor can I Winifred. You *are* a pair! But it's you who are the real wonder. When are you going to be married?'

'I don't know—When I am sufficiently well off.'

'I *asked* Winifred to come to-night,' Laura confessed. The eyes of the man and woman met.

'Why is she so ironic to me? – does she really like me?' Coutts asked of himself. But Laura looked too bonny and jolly to be fretted by love.

'And Winifred won't tell me a word,' she said.

'There is nothing to tell,' he replied.

Laura looked at him closely for a few moments. Then she rose and left the room.

Presently there arrived a German lady with whom Coutts was slightly acquainted. At about half-past seven came Winifred Varley. Courts heard the courtly old gentleman welcoming her in the hall, heard her low voice in answer. When she entered, and saw him, he knew it was a shock to her, though she hid it as well as she could. He suffered too. After hesitating for a second in the doorway, she came forward, shook hands without speaking, only looking at him with rather frightened blue eyes. She was of medium height, sturdy in build. Her face was white and impassive, without the least trace of a smile. She was a blonde of twenty-eight, dressed in a white gown just short enough not to touch the ground. Her throat was solid and strong, her arms heavy and white and beautiful, her blue eyes heavy with unacknowledged passion. When she had turned away from Coutts, she flushed vividly. He could see the pink in her arms and throat, and he flushed in answer.

'That blush would hurt her,' he said to himself, wincing.

'I did not expect to see you,' she said, with a reedy timbre of voice, as if her throat were half-closed. It made his nerves tingle.

'No – nor I you. At least...' He ended indefinitely.

'You have come down from Yorkshire?' she asked. Apparently she was cold and self-possessed. Yorkshire meant the Rectory where his fiancée lived; he felt the sting of sarcasm.

'No,' he answered. 'I am on my way there.'

There was a moment's pause. Unable to resolve the situation, she turned abruptly to her hostess.

'Shall we play, then?'

They adjourned to the drawing-room. It was a large room upholstered in dull yellow. The chimney-piece took Coutts' attention. He knew it perfectly well, but this evening it had a new, lustrous fascination. Over the mellow marble of the mantel rose an immense mirror, very translucent and deep, like deep grey water. Before this mirror, shining white as moons on a soft grey sky, was a pair of statues in alabaster, two feet high. Both were nude figures. They glistened under the side lamps, rose clean and distinct from their pedestals. The Venus leaned slightly forward, as if anticipating someone's coming. Her attitude of suspense made the young man stiffen. He could see the clean suavity of her shoulders and waist reflected white on the deep mirror. She shone, catching, as she leaned forward, the glow of the lamp on her lustrous marble loins.

Laura played Brahms; the delicate, winsome German lady played Chopin; Winifred played on her violin a Grieg sonata, to Laura's accompaniment. After having sung twice, Coutts listened to the music. Unable to criticise, he listened till he was intoxicated. Winifred, as she played, swayed slightly. He watched the strong forward thrust of her neck, the powerful and angry striking of her arm. He could see the outline of her figure; she wore no corsets; and he found her of resolute independent build. Again he glanced at the Venus bending in suspense. Winifred was blonde with a solid whiteness, an isolated woman.

All the evening, little was said, save by Laura. Miss Syfurt exclaimed continually: 'Oh, that is fine! You play gra-and, Miss Varley, don't you know. If I could play the violin – ah! the violin!'

It was not later than ten o'clock when Winifred and Miss Syfurt rose to go, the former to Croydon, the latter to Ewell.

'We can go by car together to West Croydon,' said the German lady, gleefully, as if she were a child. She was a frail, excitable little woman of forty, naïve and innocent. She gazed with bright brown eyes of admiration on Coutts.

'Yes, I am glad,' he answered.

He took up Winifred's violin, and the three proceeded downhill to the tram-terminus. There a car was on the point of departure. They hurried forward. Miss Syfurt mounted the step. Coutts waited for Winifred. The conductor called:

'Come along, please, if you're going.'

'No,' said Winifred. 'I prefer to walk this stage.'

'We can walk from West Croydon,' said Coutts.

The conductor rang the bell.

'Aren't you coming?' cried the frail, excitable little lady, from the footboard. 'Aren't you coming? – Oh!'

'I walk from West Croydon every day; I prefer to walk here, in the quiet,' said Winifred.

'Aw! aren't you coming with me?' cried the little lady, quite frightened. She stepped back, in supplication, towards the footboard. The conductor impatiently buzzed the bell. The car started forward, Miss Syfurt staggered, was caught by the conductor.

'Aw!' she cried, holding her hand out to the two who stood on the road, and breaking almost into tears of disappointment. As the tram darted forward she clutched at her hat. In a moment she was out of sight.

Coutts stood wounded to the quick by this pain given to the frail, child-like lady.

'We may as well,' said Winifred, 'walk over the hill to "The Swan".' Her note had that intense reedy quality which always set the man on edge; it was the note of her anger, or, more often, of her tortured sense of discord. The two turned away, to climb the hill again. He carried the violin; for a long time neither spoke.

'Ah, how I hate her, how I hate her!' he repeated in his heart. He

56

winced repeatedly at the thought of Miss Syfurt's little cry of supplication. He was in a position where he was not himself, and he hated her for putting him there, forgetting that it was he who had come, like a moth to the candle. For half a mile he walked on, his head carried stiffly, his face set, his heart twisted with painful emotion. And all the time, as she plodded, head down, beside him, his blood beat with hate of her, drawn to her, repelled by her.

At last, on the high-up, naked down, they came upon those meaningless pavements that run through the grass, waiting for the houses to line them. The two were thrust up into the night above the little flowering of the lamps in the valley. In front was the daze of light from London, rising midway to the zenith, just fainter than the stars. Across the valley, on the blackness of the opposite hill, little groups of lights like gnats seemed to be floating in the darkness. Orion was heeled over the West. Below, in a cleft in the night, the long, low garland of arc lamps strung down the Brighton Road, where now and then the golden tram-cars flew along the track, passing each other with a faint, angry sound.

'It is a year last Monday since we came over here,' said Winifred, as they stopped to look about them.

'I remember – but I didn't know it was then,' he said. There was a touch of hardness in his voice. 'I don't remember our dates.'

After a wait, she said in a very low, passionate tones:

'It *is* a beautiful night.'

'The moon has set, and the evening star,' he answered; 'both were out as I came down.'

She glanced swiftly at him to see if this speech was a bit of symbolism. He was looking across the valley with a set face. Very slightly, by an inch or two, she nestled towards him.

'Yes,' she said, half-stubborn, half-pleading. 'But the night is a very fine one, for all that.'

'Yes,' he replied, unwillingly.

Thus, after months of separation, they dove-tailed into the same love and hate.

'You are staying down here?' she asked at length, in a forced voice. She never intruded a hair's-breadth on the most trifling privacy; in which she was Laura's antithesis; so that this question was almost an impertinence for her. He felt her shrink.

'Till the morning – then Yorkshire,' he said cruelly.

He hated it that she could not bear outspokenness.

At that moment a train across the valley threaded the opposite darkness with its gold thread. The valley re-echoed with vague threat. The two watched the express, like a gold-and-black snake, curve and dive seawards into the night. He turned, saw her full, fine face tilted up to him. It showed pale, distinct, and firm, very near to him. He shut his eyes and shivered.

'I hate trains,' he said, impulsively.

'Why?' she asked, with a curious, tender little smile that caressed, as it were, his emotion towards her.

'I don't know; they pitch one about here and there . . .'

'I thought,' she said, with faint irony, 'that you preferred change.'

'I do like life. But now I should like to be nailed to something, if it were only a cross.'

She laughed sharply, and said, with keen sarcasm:

'Is it so difficult, then, to let yourself be nailed to a cross? I thought the difficulty lay in getting free.'

He ignored her sarcasm on his engagement.

'There is nothing now that matters,' he said, adding quickly, to forestall her: 'Of course I'm wild when dinner's late, and so on; but . . . apart from those things . . . nothing seems to matter.'

She was silent.

'One goes on – remains in office, so to speak; and life's all right – only, it doesn't seem to matter.'

'This does sound like complaining of trouble because you've got none,' she laughed.

'Trouble . . .' he repeated. 'No, I don't suppose I've got any. Vexation, which most folk call trouble; but something I really grieve about in my soul – no, nothing. I wish I had.'

She laughed again sharply; but he perceived in her laughter a little keen despair.

'I find a lucky pebble. I think, now I'll throw it over my left shoulder, and wish. So I spit over my little finger, and throw the white pebble behind me, and then, when I want to wish, I'm done. I say to myself: "Wish," and myself says back: "I don't want anything." I say again: "Wish, you fool," but I'm as dumb of wishes as a newt. And then, because it rather frightens me, I say in a hurry: "A million of money." Do *you* know what to wish for when you see the new moon?'

She laughed quickly.

'I think so,' she said. 'But my wish varies.'

'I wish mine did,' he said, whimsically lugubrious.

She took his hand in a little impulse of love.

They walked hand in hand on the ridge of the down, bunches of lights shining below, the big radiance of London advancing like a wonder in front.

'You know ...' he began, then stopped.

'I don't ...' she ironically urged.

'Do you want to?' he laughed.

'Yes; one is never at peace with oneself till one understands.'

'Understands what?' he asked brutally. He knew she meant that she wanted to understand the situation he and she were in.

'How to resolve the discord,' she said, balking the issue. He would have liked her to say: 'What you want of me.'

'Your foggy weather of symbolism, as usual,' he said.

'The fog is not of symbols,' she replied, in her metallic voice of displeasure. 'It may be symbols are candles in a fog.'

'I prefer my fog without candles. I'm the fog, eh? Then I'll blow out your candle, and you'll see me better. Your candles of speech, symbols and so forth, only lead you more wrong. I'm going to wander blind, and go by instinct, like a moth that flies and settles on the wooden box his mate is shut up in.'

'Isn't it an *ignis fatuus* you are flying after, at that rate?' she said.

'Maybe, for if I breathe outwards, in the positive movement towards you, you move off. If I draw in a vacant sigh of soulfulness, you flow nearly to my lips.'

'This is a very interesting symbol,' she said, with sharp sarcasm.

He hated her, truly. She hated him. Yet they held hands fast as they walked.

'We are just the same as we were a year ago,' he laughed. But he hated her, for all his laughter.

When, at the 'Swan and Sugar-Loaf', they mounted the car, she climbed to the top, in spite of the sharp night. They nestled side by side, shoulders caressing, and all the time that they ran under the round lamps neither spoke.

At the gate of a small house in a dark tree-lined street, both waited a moment. From her garden leaned an almond tree whose buds, early this year, glistened in the light of the street lamp, with theatrical effect. He broke off a twig.

'I always remember this tree,' he said; 'how I used to feel sorry for it when it was full out, and so lively, at midnight in the lamplight. I thought it must be tired.'

59

'Will you come in?' she asked tenderly.

'I did get a room in town,' he answered, following her.

She opened the door with her latch-key, showing him, as usual, into the drawing-room. Everything was just the same; cold in colouring, warm in appointment; ivory-coloured walls, blond, polished floor, with thick ivory-coloured rugs; three deep arm-chairs in pale amber, with large cushions; a big black piano, a violin-stand beside it; and the room very warm with a clear red fire, the brass shining hot. Coutts, according to his habit, lit the piano-candles and lowered the blinds.

'I say,' he said; 'this is a variation from your line!'

He pointed to a bowl of magnificent scarlet anemones that stood on the piano.

'Why?' she asked, pausing in arranging her hair at the small mirror.

'On the *piano*!' he admonished.

'Only while the table was in use,' she smiled, glancing at the litter of papers that covered her table.

'And then – *red* flowers!' he said.

'Oh, I thought they were such a fine piece of colour,' she replied.

'I would have wagered you would buy freesias,' he said.

'Why?' she smiled. He pleased her thus.

'Well – for their cream and gold and restrained, bruised purple, and their scent. I can't believe you bought scentless flowers!'

'What!' She went forward, bent over the flowers.

'I had not noticed,' she said, smiling curiously, 'that they were scentless.'

She touched the velvet black centres.

'Would you have bought them had you noticed?' he asked.

She thought for a moment, curiously.

'I don't know ... probably I should not.'

'You would never buy scentless flowers,' he averred. 'Any more than you'd love a man because he was handsome.'

'I did not know,' she smiled. She was pleased.

The housekeeper entered with a lamp, which she set on a stand.

'You will illuminate me?' he said to Winifred. It was her habit to talk to him by candle-light.

'I have thought about you – now I will look at you,' she said quietly, smiling.

'I see—To confirm your conclusions?' he asked.

Her eyes lifted quickly in acknowledgment of his guess.

'That is so,' she replied.

'Then,' he said, 'I'll wash my hands.'

He ran upstairs. The sense of freedom, of intimacy, was very fascinating. As he washed, the little everyday action of twining his hands in the lather set him suddenly considering his other love. At her house he was always polite and formal; gentlemanly, in short. With Connie he felt the old, manly superiority; he was the knight, strong and tender, she was the beautiful maiden with a touch of God on her brow. He kissed her, he softened and selected his speech for her, he forbore from being the greater part of himself. She was his betrothed, his wife, his queen, whom he loved to idealise, and for whom he carefully modified himself. She should rule him later on – that part of him which was hers. But he loved her, too, with a pitying, tender love. He thought of her tears upon her pillow in the northern Rectory, and he bit his lip, held his breath under the strain of the situation. Vaguely he knew she would bore him. And Winifred fascinated him. He and she really played with fire. In her house, he was roused and keen. But she was not, and never could be, frank. So he was not frank, even to himself. Saying nothing, betraying nothing, immediately they were together they began the same game. Each shuddered, each defenceless and exposed, hated the other by turns. Yet they came together again. Coutts felt a vague fear of Winifred. She was intense and unnatural – and he became unnatural and intense, beside her.

When he came downstairs she was fingering the piano from the score of 'Walküre'.

'First wash in England,' he announced, looking at his hands. She laughed swiftly. Impatient herself of the slightest soil, his indifference to temporary grubbiness amused her.

He was a tall, bony man, with small hands and feet. His features were rough and rather ugly, but his smile was taking. She was always fascinated by the changes in him. His eyes, particularly, seemed quite different at times; sometimes hard, insolent, blue; sometimes dark, full of warmth and tenderness; sometimes flaring like an animal's.

He sank wearily into a chair.

'My chair,' he said, as if to himself.

She bowed her head. Of compact physique, uncorseted, her figure bowed richly to the piano. He watched the shallow concave between her shoulders, marvelling at its rich solidity. She let one arm fall loose, he looked at the shadows in the dimples of her elbow. Slowly smiling a look of brooding affection, of acknowledgment upon him for a forgetful moment, she said:

'And what have you done lately?'

'Simply nothing,' he replied quietly. 'For all that these months have been so full of variety, I think they will sink out of my life; they will evaporate and leave no result; I shall forget them.'

Her blue eyes were dark and heavy upon him, watching. She did not answer. He smiled faintly at her.

'And you?' he said, at length.

'With me it is different,' she said quietly.

'You sit with your crystal,' he laughed.

'While you tilt...' She hung on her ending.

He laughed, sighed, and they were quiet awhile.

'I've got such a skinful of heavy visions, they come sweating through my dreams,' he said.

'Whom have you read?' She smiled.

'Meredith. Very healthy,' he laughed.

She laughed quickly at being caught.

'Now, have you found out all you want?' he asked.

'Oh, no,' she cried with full throat.

'Well, finish, at any rate. I'm not diseased. How are you?'

'But ... but...' she stumbled on doggedly. 'What *do* you intend to do?'

He hardened the line of his mouth and eyes, only to retort with immediate lightness:

'Just go on.'

This was their battlefield: she could not understand how he could marry: it seemed almost monstrous to her; she fought against his marriage. She looked up at him, witch-like, from under bent brows. Her eyes were dark blue and heavy. He shivered, shrank with pain. She was so cruel to that other, common, everyday part of him.

'I wonder you dare go on like it,' she said.

'Why dare?' he replied. 'What's the odds?'

'I don't know,' she answered, in deep, bitter displeasure.

'And I don't care,' he said.

'But...' she continued, slowly, gravely pressing the point: 'You know what you intend to do.'

'Marry – settle – be a good husband, good father, partner in the business; get fat, be an amiable gentleman – Q.E.F.'

'Very good,' she said, deep and final.

'Thank you.'

'I did not congratulate you,' she said.

'Ah!' His voice tailed off into sadness and self-mistrust. Meanwhile she watched him heavily. He did not mind being scrutinised: it flattered him.

'Yes, it is, or may be, very good,' she began; 'but *why* all this? – *why*?'

'And why not? And why? – Because I want to.'

He could not leave it thus flippantly.

'You know, Winifred, we should only drive each other into insanity, you and I: become abnormal.'

'Well,' she said, 'and even so, why the other?'

'My marriage? – I don't know. Instinct.'

'One has so many instincts,' she laughed bitterly.

That was a new idea to him.

She raised her arms, stretched them above her head, in a weary gesture. They were fine, strong arms. They reminded Coutts of Euripides' 'Bacchae': white, round arms, long arms. The lifting of her arms lifted her breasts. She dropped suddenly as if inert, lolling her arms against the cushions.

'I really don't see why you should be,' she said drearily, though always with a touch of a sneer, 'why we should always – be fighting.'

'Oh, yes, you do,' he replied. It was a deadlock which he could not sustain.

'Besides,' he laughed, 'it's your fault.'

'Am I *so* bad' she sneered.

'Worse,' he said.

'But' – she moved irritably – 'is this to the point?'

'What point?' he answered; then, smiling: 'You know you only like a wild-goose chase.'

'I do,' she answered plaintively. 'I miss you very much. You snatch things from the Kobolds for me.'

'Exactly,' he said in a biting tone. 'Exactly! That's what you want me for. I am to be your crystal, your "genius". My length of blood and bone you don't care a rap for. Ah, yes, you like me for a crystal-glass, to see things in: to hold up to the light. I'm a blessed Lady-of-Shalott looking-glass for you.'

'You talk to *me*,' she said, dashing his fervour, 'of my fog of symbols!'

'Ah, well, if so, 'tis your own asking.'

'I did not know it.' She looked at him coldly. She was angry.

'No,' he said.

Again, they hated each other.

'The old ancients,' he laughed, 'gave the gods the suet and intestines: at least, I believe so. They ate the rest. You shouldn't be a goddess.'

'I wonder, among your rectory acquaintances, you haven't learned better manners,' she answered in cold contempt. He closed his eyes, lying back in his chair, his legs sprawled towards her.

'I suppose we're civilised savages,' he said sadly. All was silent.

At last, opening his eyes again, he said: 'I shall have to be going directly, Winifred; it is past eleven...' Then the appeal in his voice changed to laughter. 'Though I know I shall be winding through all the *Addios* in "Traviata" before you can set me travelling.' He smiled gently at her, then closed his eyes once more, conscious of deep, but vague, suffering. She lay in her chair, her face averted, rosily, towards the fire. Without glancing at her he was aware of the white approach of her throat towards her breast. He seemed to perceive her with another, unknown sense that acted all over his body. She lay perfectly still and warm in the fire-glow. He was dimly aware that he suffered.

'Yes,' she said at length; 'if we were linked together we should only destroy each other.'

He started, hearing her admit, for the first time, this point of which he was so sure.

'You should never *marry* anyone,' he said.

'And you,' she asked in irony, 'must offer your head to harness and be bridled and driven?'

'There's the makings of quite a good, respectable trotter in me,' he laughed. 'Don't you see it's what I *want* to be?'

'I'm not sure,' she laughed in return.

'I think so.'

They were silent for a time. The white lamp burned steadily as moonlight, the red fire like sunset; there was no stir or flicker.

'And what of you?' he asked.

She crooned a faint, tired laugh.

'If you are jetsam, as you say you are,' she answered, 'I am flotsam. I shall lie stranded.'

'Nay,' he pleaded. 'When were you wrecked?'

She laughed quickly, with a sound like a tinkle of tears.

'Oh, dear Winifred!' he cried despairingly.

She lifted her arms towards him, hiding her face between them, looking up through the white closure with dark, uncanny eyes, like an

64

invocation. His breast lifted towards her uptilted arms. He shuddered, shut his eyes, held himself rigid. He heard her drop her arms heavily.

'I must go,' he said in a dull voice.

The rapidly-chasing quivers that ran in tremors down the front of his body and limbs made him stretch himself, stretch hard.

'Yes,' she assented gravely; 'you must go.'

He turned to her. Again looking up darkly, from under her lowered brows, she lifted her hands like small white orchids towards him. Without knowing, he gripped her wrists with a grasp that circled his blood-red nails with white rims.

'Good-bye,' he said, looking down at her. She made a small, moaning noise in her throat, lifting her face so that it came open and near to him like a suddenly-risen flower, borne on a strong white stalk. She seemed to extend, to fill the world, to become atmosphere and all. He did not know what he was doing. He was bending forward, his mouth on hers, her arms round his neck, and his own hands, still fastened on to her wrists, almost bursting the blood under his nails with the intensity of their grip. They remained for a few moments thus, rigid. Then, weary of the strain, she relaxed. She turned her face, offered him her throat, white, hard, and rich, below the ear. Stooping still lower, so that he quivered in every fibre at the strain, he laid his mouth to the kiss. In the intense silence, he heard the deep, dull pulsing of her blood, and a minute click of a spark within the lamp.

Then he drew her from the chair up to him. She came, arms always round his neck, till at last she lay along his breast as he stood, feet planted wide, clasping her tight, his mouth on her neck. She turned suddenly to meet his full, red mouth in a kiss. He felt his moustache prick back into his lips. It was the first kiss she had genuinely given. Dazed, he was conscious of the throb of one great pulse, as if his whole body were a heart that contracted in throbs. He felt, with an intolerable ache, as if he, the heart, were setting the pulse in her, in the very night, so that everything beat from the throb of his overstrained, bursting body.

The hurt became so great it brought him out of the reeling stage to distinct consciousness. She clipped her lips, drew them away, leaving him her throat. Already she had had enough. He opened his eyes as he bent with his mouth on her neck, and was startled; there stood the objects of the room, stark; there, close below his eyes, were the half-sunk lashes of the woman, swooning on her unnatural ebb of passion. He saw her thus, knew that she wanted no more of him than that kiss.

65

And the heavy form of this woman hung upon him. His whole body ached like a swollen vein, with heavy intensity, while his heart grew dead with misery and despair. This woman gave him anguish and a cutting-short like death; to the other woman he was false. As he shivered with suffering, he opened his eyes again, and caught sight of the pure ivory of the lamp. His heart flashed with rage.

A sudden involuntary blow of his foot, and he sent the lamp-stand spinning. The lamp leaped off, fell with a smash on the fair, polished floor. Instantly a bluish hedge of flame quivered, leaped up before them. She had lightened her hold round his neck, and buried her face against his throat. The flame veered at her, blue, with a yellow tongue that licked her dress and her arm. Convulsive, she clutched him, almost strangled him, though she made no sound.

He gathered her up and bore her heavily out of the room. Slipping from her clasp, he brought his arms down her form, crushing the starting blaze of her dress. His face was singed. Staring at her, he could scarcely see her.

'I am not hurt,' she cried. 'But you?'

The housekeeper was coming; the flames were sinking and waving up in the drawing-room. He broke away from Winifred, threw one of the great woollen rugs on to the flame, then stood a moment looking at the darkness.

Winifred caught at him as he passed her.

'No, no,' he answered, as he fumbled for the latch. 'I'm not hurt. Clumsy fool I am – clumsy fool!'

In another instant he was gone, running with burning-red hands held out blindly, down the street.

NEW EVE AND OLD ADAM

I

'AFTER all,' she said, with a little laugh, 'I can't see it was so wonderful of you to hurry home to me, if you are so cross when you do come.'

'You would rather I stayed away?' he asked.

'I wouldn't mind.'

'You would rather I had stayed a day or two in Paris – or a night or two.'

She burst into a jeering 'pouf!' of laughter.

'You!' she cried. 'You and Parisian Nights' Entertainment! What a fool you would look.'

'Still,' he said, 'I could try.'

'You *would*!' she mocked. 'You would go dribbling up to a woman. "Please take me – my wife is so unkind to me!"'

He drank his tea in silence. They had been married a year. They had married quickly, for love. And during the last three months there had gone on almost continuously that battle between them which so many married people fight, without knowing why. Now it had begun again. He felt the physical sickness rising in him. Somewhere down in his belly the big, feverish pulse began to beat, where was the inflamed place caused by the conflict between them.

She was a beautiful woman of about thirty, fair, luxuriant, with proud shoulders and a face borne up by a fierce, native vitality. Her green eyes had a curiously puzzled contraction just now. She sat leaning on the table against the tea-tray, absorbed. It was as if she battled with herself in him. Her green dress reflected in the silver, against the red of the firelight. Leaning abstractedly forward, she pulled some primroses from the bowl, and threaded them at intervals in the plait which bound round her head in the peasant fashion. So, with her little starred fillet of flowers, there was something of the Gretchen about her. But her eyes retained the curious half-smile.

Suddenly her face lowered gloomily. She sank her beautiful arms, laying them on the table. Then she sat almost sullenly, as if she would not give in. He was looking away out of the window. With a quick movement she glanced down at her hands. She took off her wedding-ring, reached to the bowl for a long flower-stalk, and shook the ring glittering round and round upon it, regarding the spinning gold, and spinning it as if she would spurn it. Yet there was something about her of a fretful, naughty child as she did so.

The man sat by the fire, tired, but tense. His body seemed so utterly still because of the tension in which it was held. His limbs, thin and vigorous, lay braced like a listening thing, always vivid for action, yet held perfectly still. His face was set and expressionless. The wife was all the time, in spite of herself, conscious of him, as if the cheek that was turned towards him had a sense which perceived him. They were both rendered elemental, like impersonal forces, by the battle and the suffering.

She rose and went to the window. Their flat was the fourth, the top storey of a large house. Above the high-ridged, handsome red roof opposite was an assembly of telegraph wires, a square, squat frame-work, towards which hosts of wires sped from four directions, arriving in darkly-stretched lines out of the white sky. High up, at a great height, a seagull sailed. There was a noise of traffic from the town beyond.

Then, from behind the ridge of the house-roof opposite a man climbed up into the tower of wires, belted himself amid the netted sky, and began to work, absorbedly. Another man, half-hidden by the roof-ridge, stretched up to him with a wire. The man in the sky reached down to receive it. The other, having delivered, sank out of sight. The solitary man worked absorbedly. Then he seemed drawn away from his task. He looked round almost furtively, from his lonely height, the space pressing on him. His eyes met those of the beautiful woman who stood in her afternoon-gown, with flowers in her hair, at the window.

'I like you,' she said, in her normal voice.

Her husband, in the room with her, looked round slowly and asked: 'Whom do you like?'

Receiving no answer, he resumed his tense stillness.

She remained watching at the window, above the small, quiet street of large houses. The man, suspended there in the sky, looked across at her and she at him. The city was far below. Her eyes and his met across the lofty space. Then, crouching together again into his forgetfulness, he hid himself in his work. He would not look again. Presently he climbed down, and the tower of wires was empty against the sky.

The woman glanced at the little park at the end of the clear, grey

68

street. The diminished, dark-blue form of a soldier was seen passing between the green stretches of grass, his spurs giving the faintest glitter to his walk.

Then she turned hesitating from the window, as if drawn by her husband. He was sitting still motionless, and detached from her, hard; held absolutely away from her by his will. She wavered, then went and crouched on the hearth-rug at his feet, laying her head on his knee.

'Don't be horrid with me!' she pleaded, in a caressing, languid, impersonal voice. He shut his teeth hard, and his lips parted slightly with pain.

'You know you love me,' she continued, in the same heavy, sing-song way. He breathed hard, but kept still.

'Don't you?' she said, slowly, and she put her arms round his waist, under his coat, drawing him to her. It was as if flames of fire were running under his skin.

'I have never denied it,' he said woodenly.

'Yes,' she pleaded, in the same heavy, toneless voice. 'Yes. You are always trying to deny it.' She was rubbing her cheek against his knee, softly. Then she gave a little laugh, and shook her head. 'But it's no good.' She looked up at him. There was a curious light in his eyes, of subtle victory. 'It's no good, my love, is it?'

His heart ran hot. He knew it was no good trying to deny he loved her. But he saw her eyes, and his will remained set and hard. She looked away into the fire.

'You hate it that you have to love me,' she said, in a pensive voice through which the triumph flickered faintly. 'You hate it that you love me – and it is petty and mean of you. You hate it that you had to hurry back to me from Paris.'

Her voice had become again quite impersonal, as if she were talking to herself.

'At any rate,' he said, 'it is your triumph.'

She gave a sudden, bitter-contemptuous laugh.

'Ha!' she said. 'What is triumph to me, you fool! You can have your triumph. I should be only too glad to give it you.'

'And I to take it.'

'Then take it,' she cried, in hostility. 'I offer it you often enough.'

'But you never mean to part with it.'

'It is a lie. It is you, you, who are too paltry to take a woman. How often do I fling myself at you —'

'Then don't – don't.'

69

'Ha! – and if I don't – I get nothing out of you. Self! self! that is all you are.'

His face remained set and expressionless. She looked up at him. Suddenly she drew him to her again, and hid her face against him.

'Don't kick me off, Pietro, when I come to you,' she pleaded.

'You *don't* come to me,' he answered stubbornly.

She lifted her head a few inches away from him and seemed to listen, or to think.

'What do I do, then?' she asked, for the first time quietly.

'You treat me as if I were a piece of cake, for you to eat when you wanted.'

She rose from him with a mocking cry of scorn, that yet had something hollow in its sound.

'Treat you like a piece of cake, do I!' she cried. 'I, who have done all I have for you!'

There was a knock, and the maid entered with a telegram. He tore it open.

'No answer,' he said, and the maid softly closed the door.

'I suppose it is for you,' he said, bitingly, rising and handing her the slip of paper. She read it, laughed, then read it again, aloud:

' "Meet me Marble Arch 7.30 – theatre – Richard." Who is Richard?' she asked, looking at her husband rather interested. He shook his head.

'Nobody of mine,' he said. 'Who is he?'

'I haven't the faintest notion,' she said, flippantly.

'But,' and his eyes went bullying, 'you *must* know.'

She suddenly became quiet, and jeering, took up his challenge.

'Why must I know?' she asked.

'Because it isn't for me, therefore it must be for you.'

'And couldn't it be for anybody else?' she sneered.

' "Moest, 14 Merrilies Street," ' he read, decisively.

For a second she was puzzled into earnestness.

'Pah, you fool,' she said, turning aside. 'Think of your own friends,' and she flung the telegram away.

'It is not for me,' he said, stiffly and finally.

'Then it is for the man in the moon – I should think *his* name is Moest,' she added, with a pouf of laughter against him.

'Do you mean to say you know nothing about it?' he asked.

'Do you mean to say,' she mocked, mouthing the words, and sneering; 'Yes, I do mean to say, poor little man.'

70

He suddenly went hard with disgust.

'Then I simply don't believe you,' he said coldly.

'Oh – don't you believe me!' she jeered, mocking the touch of sententiousness in his voice. 'What a calamity. The poor man doesn't believe!'

'It couldn't possibly be any acquaintance of mine,' he said slowly.

'Then hold your tongue!' she cried harshly. 'I've heard enough of it.'

He was silent, and soon she went out of the room. In a few minutes he heard her in the drawing-room, improvising furiously. It was a sound that maddened him: something yearning, yearning, striving, and something perverse, that counteracted the yearning. Her music was always working up towards a certain culmination, but never reaching it, falling away in a jangle. How he hated it. He lit a cigarette, and went across to the sideboard for a whisky and soda. Then she began to sing. She had a good voice, but she could not keep time. As a rule it made his heart warm with tenderness for her, hearing her ramble through the songs in her own fashion, making Brahms sound so different by altering his time. But to-day he hated her for it. Why the devil couldn't she submit to the natural laws of the stuff!

In about fifteen minutes she entered, laughing. She laughed as she closed the door, and as she came to him where he sat.

'Oh,' she said, 'you silly thing, you silly thing! Aren't you a stupid clown?'

She crouched between his knees and put her arms round him. She was smiling into his face, her green eyes looking into his, were bright and wide. But somewhere in them, as he looked back, was a little twist that could not come loose to him, a little cast, that was like an aversion from him, a strain of hate for him. The hot waves of blood flushed over his body, and his heart seemed to dissolve under her caresses. But at last, after many months, he knew her well enough. He knew that curious little strain in her eyes, which was waiting for him to submit to her, and then would spurn him again. He resisted her while ever it was there.

'Why don't you let yourself love me?' she asked, pleading, but a touch of mockery in her voice. His jaw set hard.

'Is it because you are afraid?'

He heard the slight sneer.

'Of what?' he asked.

'Afraid to trust yourself?'

There was silence. It made him furious that she could sit there caressing him and yet sneer at him.

'What *have* I done with myself?' he asked.

'Carefully saved yourself from giving all to me, for fear you might lose something.'

'Why should I lose anything?' he asked.

And they were both silent. She rose at last and went away from him to get a cigarette. The silver box flashed red with firelight in her hands. She struck a match, bungled, threw the stick aside, lit another.

'What did you come running back for?' she asked, insolently, talking with half-shut lips because of the cigarette. 'I told you I wanted peace. I've had none for a year. And for the last three months you've done nothing but try to destroy me.'

'You have not gone frail on it,' he answered sarcastically.

'Nevertheless,' she said, 'I am ill inside me. I am sick of you – sick. You make an eternal demand, and you give nothing back. You leave one empty.' She puffed the cigarette in feminine fashion, then suddenly she struck her forehead with a wild gesture. 'I have a ghastly, empty feeling in my head,' she said. 'I feel I simply *must* have rest – I must.'

The rage went through his veins like flame.

'From your labours?' he asked, sarcastically, suppressing himself.

'From you – from *you*?' she cried, thrusting forward her head at him. 'You, who use a woman's soul up, with your rotten life. I suppose it is partly your health, and you can't help it,' she added, more mildly. 'But I simply can't stick it – I simply can't, and that is all.'

She shook her cigarette carelessly in the direction of the fire. The ash fell on the beautiful Asiatic rug. She glanced at it, but did not trouble. He sat, hard with rage.

'May I ask how I use you up, as you say?' he asked.

She was silent a moment, trying to get her feeling into words. Then she shook her hand at him passionately, and took the cigarette from her mouth.

'By – by following me about – by not leaving me *alone*. You give me no peace – *I* don't know what you do, but it is something ghastly.'

Again the hard stroke of rage went down his mind.

'It is very vague,' he said.

'I know,' she cried. 'I can't put it into words – but there it is. You – you don't love. I pour myself out to you, and then – there's nothing there – you simply aren't there.'

72

He was silent for some time. His jaw set hard with fury and hate.

'We have come to the incomprehensible,' he said. 'And now, what about Richard?'

It had grown nearly dark in the room. She sat silent for a moment. Then she took the cigarette from her mouth and looked at it.

'I'm going to meet him,' her voice, mocking, answered out of the twilight.

His head went molten, and he could scarcely breathe.

'Who is he?' he asked, though he did not believe the affair to be anything at all, even if there were a Richard.

'I'll introduce him to you when I know him a little better,' she said.

He waited.

'But who is he?'

'I tell you, I'll introduce him to you later.'

There was a pause.

'Shall I come with you?'

'It would be like you,' she answered, with a sneer.

The maid came in, softly, to draw the curtains and turn on the light. The husband and wife sat silent.

'I suppose,' he said, when the door was closed again, 'you are wanting a Richard for a rest?'

She took his sarcasm simply as a statement.

'I am,' she said. 'A simple, warm man who would love me without all these reservation and difficulties. That is just what I do want.'

'Well, you have your own independence,' he said.

'Ha,' she laughed. 'You needn't tell me that. It would take more than you to rob me of my independence.'

'I meant your own income,' he answered quietly, while his heart was plunging with bitterness and rage.

'Well,' she said, 'I will go and dress.'

He remained without moving, in his chair. The pain of this was almost too much. For some moments the great, inflamed pulse struck through his body. It died gradually down, and he went dull. He had not wanted to separate from her at this point of their union; they would probably, if they parted in such a crisis, never come together again. But if she insisted, well then, it would have to be. He would go away for a month. He could easily make business in Italy. And when he came back, they could patch up some sort of domestic arrangement, as most other folk had to do.

73

He felt full and heavy inside, and without the energy for anything. The thought of having to pack and take a train to Milan appalled him; it would mean such an effort of will. But it would have to be done, and so he must do it. It was no use his waiting at home. He might stay in town a night, at his brother-in-law's, and go away the next day. It were better to give her a little time to come to herself. She was really impulsive. And he did not really want to go away from her.

He was still sitting thinking, when she came downstairs. She was in costume and furs and toque. There was a radiant, half-wistful, half-perverse look about her. She was a beautiful woman, her bright, fair face set among the black furs.

'Will you give me some money?' she said. 'There isn't any.'

He took two sovereigns, which she put in her little black purse. She would go without a word of reconciliation. It made his heart set hard again.

'You would like me to go away for a moment?' he said, calmly.

'Yes,' she answered, stubbornly.

'All right, then, I will. I must stop in town for to-morrow, but I will sleep at Edmund's.'

'You could do that, couldn't you?' she said, accepting his suggestion, a little bit hesitating.

'If you want me to.'

'I'm so *tired*!' she lamented.

But there was exasperation and hate in the last word, too.

'Very well,' he answered.

She finished buttoning her glove.

'You'll go, then?' she said suddenly, brightly, turning to depart. 'Good-bye.'

He hated her for the flippant insult of her leave-taking.

'I shall be at Edmund's to-morrow,' he said.

'You will write to me from Italy, won't you?'

He would not answer the unnecessary question.

'Have you taken the dead primroses out of your hair?' he asked.

'I haven't,' she said.

And she unpinned her hat.

'Richard *would* think me cracked,' she said, picking out the crumpled, creamy fragments. She strewed the withered flowers carelessly on the table, set her hat straight.

'Do you *want* me to go?' he asked, again, rather yearning.

She knitted her brows. It irked her to resist the appeal. Yet she had

74

in her breast a hard, repellent feeling for him. She had loved him, too. She had loved him dearly. And – he had not seemed to realise her. So that now she *did* want to be free of him for a while. Yet the love, the passion she had had for him clung about her. But she did want, first and primarily, to be free of him again.

'Yes,' she said, half pleading.

'Very well,' he answered.

She came across to him, and put her arms round his neck. Her hatpin caught his head, but he moved, and she did not notice.

'You don't mind very much, do you, my love?' she said caressingly.

'I mind all the world, and all I am,' he said.

She rose from him, fretted, miserable, and yet determined.

'I *must* have some rest,' she repeated.

He knew that cry. She had had it, on occasions, for two months now. He had cursed her, and refused either to go away or to let her go. Now he knew it was no use.

'All right,' he said. 'Go and get it from Richard.'

'Yes.' She hesitated. 'Good-bye,' she called, and was gone.

He heard her cab whirr away. He had no idea whither she was gone – but probably to Madge, her friend.

He went upstairs to pack. Their bedroom made him suffer. She used to say, at first, that she would give up anything rather than her sleeping with him. And still they were always together. A kind of blind helplessness drove them to one another, even when, after he had taken her, they only felt more apart than ever. It had seemed to her that he had been mechanical and barren with her. She felt a horrible feeling of aversion from him, inside her, even while physically she still desired him. His body had always a kind of fascination for her. But had hers for him? He seemed, often, just to have served her, or to have obeyed some impersonal instinct for which she was the only outlet, in his loving her. So at last she rose against him, to cast him off. He seemed to follow her so, to draw her life into his. It made her feel she would go mad. For he seemed to do it just blindly, without having any notion of her herself. It was as if she were sucked out of herself by some non-human force. As for him, he seemed only like an instrument for his work, his business, not like a person at all. Sometimes she thought he was a big fountain-pen which was always sucking at her blood for ink.

He could not understand anything of this. He loved her – he could not bear to be away from her. He tried to realise her and to give her what she wanted. But he could not understand. He could not understand her accusations against him. Physically, he knew, she loved him, or had loved him, and was satisfied by him. He also knew that she would have loved another man nearly as well. And for the rest, he was only himself. He could not understand what she said about his using her and giving her nothing in return. Perhaps he did not think of her, as a separate person from himself, sufficiently. But then he did not see, he could not see that she had any real personal life, separate from himself. He tried to think of her in every possible way, and to give her what she wanted. But it was no good; she was never at peace. And lately there had been growing a breach between them. They had never come together without his realising it, afterwards. Now he must submit, and go away.

And her quilted dressing-gown – it was a little bit torn, like most of her things – and her pearl-backed mirror, with one of the pieces of pearl missing – all her untidy, flimsy, lovable things hurt him as he went about the bedroom, and made his heart go hard with hate, in the midst of his love.

II

Instead of going to his brother-in-law's, he went to an hotel for the night. It was not till he stood in the lift, with the attendant at his side, that he began to realise that he was only a mile or so away from his own home, and yet farther away than any miles could make him. It was about nine o'clock. He hated his bedroom. It was comfortable, and not ostentatious; its only fault was the neutrality necessary to an hotel apartment. He looked round. There was one semi-erotic Florentine picture of a lady with cat's eyes, over the bed. It was not bad. The only other ornament on the walls was the notice of hours and prices of meals and rooms. The couch sat correctly before the correct little table, on which the writing-sachet and ink-stand stood mechanically. Down below, the quiet street was half illuminated, the people passed sparsely, like stunted shadows. And of all times of the night, it was a quarter-past nine. He thought he would go to bed. Then he looked at the white-and-glazed doors which shut him off from the bath. He would bath, to pass the time away. In the bath-closet everything was so comfortable and white and warm – too warm; the level, unvarying heat of the atmosphere, from which there was no escape anywhere, seemed so hideously hotel-like; this central-heating forced a unity into the great building, making it more than ever like an enormous box with incubating cells. He loathed it. But at any rate the bath-closet was human, white and business-like and luxurious.

He was trying, with the voluptuous warm water, and the exciting thrill of the shower-bath, to bring back the life into his dazed body. Since she had begun to hate him, he had gradually lost that physical pride and pleasure in his own physique which the first months of married life had given him. His body had gone meaningless to him again, almost as if it were not there. It had wakened up, there had been the physical glow and satisfaction about his movements of a creature which rejoices in itself; a glow which comes on a man who loves and is loved passionately and successfully. Now this was going again. All the life was accumulating in his mental consciousness, and his body felt like a piece of waste. He was not aware of this. It was instinct which made him want to bathe. But that, too, was a failure. He went under the shower-spray with his mind occupied by business, or some care of affairs, taking the tingling water almost without knowing it, stepping out mechanically, as a man going through a barren routine. He was dry again, and looking out of the window, without having experienced anything during the last hour.

Then he remembered that she did not know his address. He scribbled a note and rang to have it posted.

As soon as he had turned out the light, and there was nothing left for his mental consciousness to flourish amongst, it dropped, and it was dark inside him as without. It was his blood, and the elemental male in it, that now rose from him; unknown instincts suffocated him, and he could not bear it, that he was shut in this great, warm building. He wanted to be outside, with space springing from him. But, again, the reasonable being in him knew it was ridiculous, and he remained staring at the dark, having the horrible sensation of a roof low down over him; whilst that dark, unknown being, which lived below all his consciousness in the eternal gloom of his blood, heaved and raged blindly against him.

It was not his thoughts that represented him. They spun like straws or the iridescence of oil on a dark stream. He thought of her, sketchily, spending an evening of light amusement with the symbolical Richard. That did not mean much to him. He did not really speculate about Richard. He had the dark, powerful sense of her, how she wanted to get away from him and from the deep, underneath intimacy which had gradually come between them, back to the easy, everyday life where one knows nothing of the underneath, so that it takes its way apart from the consciousness. She did not want to have the deeper part of herself in direct contact with or under the influence of any other intrinsic being. She wanted, in the deepest sense, to be free of him. She could not bear the close, basic intimacy into which she had been drawn. She wanted her life for herself. It was true, her strongest desire had been previously to know the contact through the whole of her being, down to the very bottom. Now it troubled her. She wanted to disengage his roots. Above, in the open, she would live. But she must live perfectly free of herself, and not, at her source, be connected with anybody. She was using this symbolical Richard as a spade to dig him away from her. And he felt like a thing whose roots are all straining on their hold, and whose elemental life, that blind source, surges backwards and forwards darkly, in a chaos, like something which is threatened with spilling out of its own vessel.

This tremendous swaying of the most elemental part of him continued through the hours, accomplishing his being, whilst superficially he thought of the journey, of the Italian he would speak, how he had left his coat in the train, and the rascally official interpreter had tried to give him twenty lire for a sovereign – how the man in the hat-shop in the Strand had given him the wrong change – of the new shape in hats, and the new felt – and so on. Underneath it all, like the sea under a pleasure pier, his elemental, physical soul was heaving in great waves through his blood and his tissue, the sob, the silent lift, the slightly-washing fall away again. So his blood, out of whose darkness everything rose, being moved to its depth by her revulsion, heaved and swung towards its own rest, surging blindly to its own re-settling.

Without knowing it, he suffered that night almost more than he had ever suffered during his life. But it was all below his consciousness. It was his life itself at storm, not his mind and his will engaged at all.

In the morning he got up, thin and quiet, without much movement anywhere, only with some of the clearing afterstorm. His body felt like a clean, empty shell. His mind was limpidly clear. He went through the business of the toilet with a certain accuracy, and at breakfast, in the restaurant, there was about him that air of neutral correctness which makes men seem so unreal.

At lunch, there was a telegram for him. It was like her to telegraph. 'Come to tea, my dear love.'

As he read it, there was a great heave of resistance in him. But then he faltered. With his consciousness, he remembered how impulsive and eager she was when she dashed off her telegram, and he relaxed. It went without saying that he would go.

III

When he stood in the lift going up to his own flat, he was almost blind with the hurt of it all. They had loved each other so much in his first home. The parlour-maid opened to him, and he smiled at her affectionately. In the golden-brown and cream-coloured hall – Paula would have nothing heavy or sombre about her – a bush of rose-coloured azaleas shone, and a little tub of lilies twinkled naïvely.

She did not come out to meet him.

'Tea is in the drawing-room,' the maid said, and he went in while she was hanging up his coat. It was a big room, with a sense of space, and a spread of whity carpet almost the colour of unpolished marble – and grey and pink border; of pink roses on big white cushions, pretty Dresden china, and deep chintz-covered chairs and sofas which looked as if they were used freely. It was a room where one could roll in soft, fresh-comfort, a room which had not much breakable in it, and which seemed, in the dusky spring evening, fuller of light than the streets outside.

Paula rose, looking queenly and rather radiant, as she held out her hand. A young man whom Peter scarcely noticed rose on the other side of the hearth.

'I expected you an hour ago,' she said, looking into her husband's eyes. But though she looked at him, she did not see him. And he sank his head.

'This is another Moest,' she said, presenting the stranger. 'He knows Richard, too.'

The young man, a German of about thirty, with a clean-shaven æsthetic face, long black hair brushed back a little wearily or bewildered from his brow, and inclined to fall in an odd loose strand again, so that he nervously put it back with his fine hand, looked at Moest and bowed. He had a finely-cut face, but his dark-blue eyes were strained, as if he did not quite know where he was. He sat down again, and his pleasant figure took a self-conscious attitude, of a man whose business it was to say things that should be listened to. He was not conceited or affected – naturally sensitive and rather naïve; but he could only move in an atmosphere of literature and literary ideas; yet he seemed to know there was something else, vaguely, and he felt rather at a loss. He waited for the conversation to move his way, as, inert, an insect waits for the sun to set it flying.

'Another Moest,' Paula was pronouncing emphatically. 'Actually another Moest, of whom we have never heard, and under the same roof with us.'

The stranger laughed, his lips moving nervously over his teeth.

'You are in this house?' Peter asked, surprised.

The young man shifted in his chair, dropped his head, looked up again.

'Yes,' he said, meeting Moest's eyes as if he were somewhat dazzled. 'I am staying with the Lauriers, on the second floor.'

He spoke English slowly, with a quaint, musical quality in his voice, and a certain rhythmic enunciation.

'I see; and the telegram was for you?' said the host.

'Yes,' replied the stranger, with a nervous little laugh.

'My husband,' broke in Paula, evidently repeating to the German what she had said before, for Peter's benefit this time, 'was quite convinced I had an *affaire*' – she pronounced it in the French fashion – 'with this terrible Richard.'

The German gave his little laugh, and moved, painfully self-conscious, in his chair.

'Yes,' he said, glancing at Moest.

'Did you spend a night of virtuous indignation?' Paula laughed to her husband, 'imagining my perfidy?'

'I did not,' said her husband. 'Were you at Madge's?'

'No,' she said. Then, turning to her guest: 'Who is Richard, Mr. Moest?'

'Richard,' began the German, word by word, 'is my cousin.' He glanced quickly at Paula, to see if he were understood. She rustled her skirts, and arranged herself comfortably, lying, or almost squatting, on the sofa by the fire. 'He lives in Hampstead.'

'And what is he like?' she asked, with eager interest.

The German gave his little laugh. Then he moved his fingers across his brow, in his dazed fashion. Then he looked, with his beautiful blue eyes, at his beautiful hostess.

'I —' He laughed again nervously. 'He is a man whose parts – are not very much – very well known to me. You see,' he broke forth, and it was evident he was now conversing to an imaginary audience – 'I cannot easily express myself in English. I – I never have talked it. I shall

80

speak, because I know nothing of modern England, a kind of Renaissance English.'

'How lovely!' cried Paula. 'But if you would rather, speak German. We shall understand sufficiently.'

'I would rather hear some Renaissance English,' said Moest.

Paula was quite happy with the new stranger. She listened to descriptions of Richard, shifting animatedly on her sofa. She wore a new dress, of a rich red-tile colour, glossy and long and soft, and she had threaded daisies, like buttons, in the braided plait of her hair. Her husband hated her for these familiarities. But she was beautiful too, and warm-hearted. Only, through all her warmth and kindliness, lay, he said, at the bottom, an almost feline selfishness, a coldness.

She was playing to the stranger – nay, she was not playing, she was really occupied by him. The young man was the favourite disciple of the most famous present-day German poet and *Meister*. He himself was occupied in translating Shakespeare. Having been always a poetic disciple, he had never come into touch with life save through literature, and for him, since he was a rather fine-hearted young man, with a human need to live, this was a tragedy. Paula was not long in discovering what ailed him, and she was eager to come to his rescue.

It pleased her, nevertheless, to have her husband sitting by, watching her. She forgot to give tea to anyone. Moest and the German both helped themselves, and the former attended also to his wife's cup. He sat rather in the background, listening, and waiting. She had made a fool of him with her talk to this stranger of 'Richard'; lightly and flippantly she had made a fool of him. He minded, but was used to it. Now she had absorbed herself in this dazed, starved, literature-bewildered young German, who was, moreover, really lovable, evidently a gentleman. And she was seeing in him her mission – 'just as', said Moest bitterly to himself, 'she saw her mission in me, a year ago. She is no woman. She's got a big heart for everybody, but it must be like a common-room; she's got no private, sacred heart, except perhaps for herself, where there's no room for a man in it.'

At length the stranger rose to go, promising to come again.

'Isn't he adorable?' cried Paula, as her husband returned to the drawing-room. 'I think he is simply adorable.'

'Yes!' said Moest.

'He called this morning to ask about the telegram. But, poor devil, isn't it a shame what they've done to him?'

'What who have done to him?' her husband asked coldly, jealous.

'Those literary creatures. They take a young fellow like that, and stick him up among the literary gods, like a mantelpiece ornament, and there he has to sit, being a minor ornament, while all his youth is gone. It is criminal.'

'He should get off the mantelpiece, then,' said Moest.

But inside him his heart was black with rage against her. What had she, after all, to do with this young man, when he himself was being smashed up by her? He loathed her pity and her kindliness, which was like a charitable institution. There was no core to the woman. She was full of generosity and bigness and kindness, but there was no heart in her, no security, no place for one single man. He began to understand now sirens and sphinxes and the other Greek fabulous female things. They had not been created by fancy, but out of bitter necessity of the man's human heart to express itself.

'Ha!' she laughed, half contemptuous. 'Did *you* get off your miserable, starved isolation by yourself? – you didn't. You had to be fetched down, and I had to do it.'

'Out of your usual charity,' he said.

'But you can sneer at another man's difficulties,' she said.

'Your name ought to be Panacea, not Paula,' he replied.

He felt furious and dead against her. He could even look at her without the tenderness coming. And he was glad. He hated her. She seemed unaware. Very well; let her be so.

'Oh, but he makes me so miserable, to see him!' she cried. 'Self-conscious, can't get into contact with anybody, living a false literary life like a man who takes poetry as a drug. – One *ought* to help him.'

She was really earnest and distressed.

'Out of the frying-pan into the fire,' he said.

'I'd rather be in the fire any day, than in a frying-pan,' she said, abstractedly, with a little shudder. She never troubled to see the meaning of her husband's sarcasms.

They remained silent. The maid came in for the tray, and to ask him if he would be in to dinner. He waited for his wife to answer. She sat with her chin in her hands, brooding over the young German, and did not hear. The rage flashed up in his heart. He would have liked to smash her out of this false absorption.

'No,' he said to the maid. 'I think not. Are you at home for dinner, Paula?'

'Yes,' she said.

And he knew by her tone, easy and abstracted, that she intended him to stay, too. But she did not trouble to say anything.

At last, after some time, she asked:

'What did you do?'

'Nothing – went to bed early,' he replied.

'Did you sleep well?'

'Yes, thank you.'

And he recognised the ludicrous civilities of married people, and he wanted to go. She was silent for a time. Then she asked, and her voice had gone still and grave:

'Why don't you ask me what I did?'

'Because I don't care – you just went to somebody's for dinner.'

'Why don't you care what I do? Isn't it your place to care?'

'About the things you do to spite me? – no!'

'Ha!' she mocked. 'I did nothing to spite you. I was in deadly earnest.'

'Even with your Richard?'

'Yes,' she cried. 'There *might* have been a Richard. What did you care!'

'In that case you'd have been a liar and worse, so why should I care about you then?'

'You *don't* care about me,' she said, sullenly.

'You say what you please,' he answered.

She was silent for some time.

'And did you do absolutely nothing last night?' she asked.

'I had a bath and went to bed.'

Then she pondered.

'No,' she said, 'you don't care for me.'

He did not trouble to answer. Softly, a little china clock rang six.

'I shall go to Italy in the morning,' he said.

'Yes.'

'And,' he said, slowly, forcing the words out, 'I shall stay at the Aquila Nera at Milan – you know my address.'

'Yes,' she answered.

'I shall be away about a month. Meanwhile you can rest.'

'Yes,' she said, in her throat, with a little contempt of him and his stiffness. He, in spite of himself, was breathing heavily. He knew that this parting was the real separation of their souls, marked the point beyond which they could go no farther, but accepted the marriage as a comparative failure. And he had built all his life on his marriage. She accused him of not loving her. He gripped the arms of his chair. Was there something in it? Did he only want the attributes which went along with her, the peace of heart which a man has in living to one woman, even if the love between them be not complete; the singleness and unity in his life that made it easy; the fixed establishment of himself as a married man with a home; the feeling that he belonged somewhere, that one woman existed – not was paid but *existed* – really to take care of him; was it these things he wanted, and not her? But he wanted her for these purposes – her, and nobody else. But was that not enough for her? Perhaps he wronged her – it was possible. What she said against him was in earnest. And what she said in earnest he had to believe, in the long run, since it was the utterance of her being. He felt miserable and tired.

When he looked at her, across the gathering twilight of the room, she was staring into the fire and biting her finger-nail, restlessly, restlessly, without knowing. And all his limbs went suddenly weak, as he realised that she suffered too, that something was gnawing at her. Something in the look of her, the crouching, dogged, wondering look made him faint with tenderness for her.

'Don't bite your finger-nails,' he said quietly, and, obediently, she took her hand from her mouth. His heart was beating quickly. He could feel the atmosphere of the room changing. It had stood aloof, the room, like something placed round him, like a great box. Now everything got softer, as if it partook of the atmosphere, of which he partook himself, and they were all one.

His mind reverted to her accusations, and his heart beat like a caged thing against what he could not understand. She said he did not love her. But he knew that in his way, he did. In his way – but was his way wrong? His way was himself, he thought, struggling. Was there something wrong, something missing in his nature, that he could not love? He struggled, as if he were in a mesh, and could not get out. He did not want to believe that he was deficient in his nature. Wherein was he deficient? It was nothing physical. She said he would not come out of himself, that he was no good to her, because he could not get outside himself. What did she mean? Not outside himself! It seemed like some acrobatic feat, some slippery, contortionist trick. No, he could not understand. His heart flashed hot with resentment. She did nothing but find fault with him. What did she care about him, really, when she could taunt him with not being able to take a light woman when he was in Paris? Though his heart, forced to do her justice, knew that for this she loved him, really.

But it was too complicated and difficult, and already, as they sat thinking, it had gone wrong between them and things felt twisted, horribly twisted, so that he could not breathe. He must go. He could dine at the hotel and go to the theatre.

'Well,' he said casually, 'I must go. I think I shall go and see "The Black Sheep".'

She did not answer. Then she turned and looked at him with a queer, half-bewildered, half-perverse smile that seemed conscious of pain. Her eyes, shining rather dilated and triumphant, and yet with something heavily yearning behind them, looked at him. He could not understand, and, between her appeal and her defiant triumph, he felt as if his chest was crushed so that he could not breathe.

'My love,' she said, in a little singing, abstract fashion, her lips somehow sipping towards him, her eyes shining dilated; and yet he felt as if he were not in it, himself.

His heart was a flame that prevented his breathing. He gripped the chair like a man who is going to be put under torture.

'What?' he said, staring back at her.

'Oh, my love!' she said softly, with a little, intense laugh on her face, that made him pant. And she slipped from her sofa and came across to him quickly, and put her hand hesitating on his hair. The blood struck like flame across his consciousness, and the hurt was keen like joy, like the releasing of something that hurts as the pressure is relaxed and the movement comes, before the peace. Afraid, his fingers touched her hand, and she sank swiftly between his knees, and put her face on his breast. He held her head hard against his chest, and again and again the flame went down his blood, as he felt her round, small, nut of a head between his hands pressing into his chest where the hurt had been bruised in so deep. His wrists quivered as he pressed her head to him, as he felt the deadness going out of him; the real life released, flowing into his body again. How hard he had shut it off, against her, when she hated him. He was breathing heavily with relief, blindly pressing her head against him. He believed in her again.

She looked up, laughing, childish, inviting him with her lips. He bent to kiss her, and as his eyes closed, he saw hers were shut. The feeling of restoration was almost unbearable.

'Do you love me?' she whispered, in a little ecstasy.

He did not answer, except with the quick tightening of his arms, clutching her a little closer against him. And he loved the silkiness of her hair, and its natural scent. And it hurt him that the daisies she had threaded in should begin to wither. He resented their hurting her by their dying.

He had not understood. But the trouble had gone off. He was quiet, and he watched her from out of his sensitive stillness, a little bit dimly, unable to recover. She was loving to him, protective, and bright, laughing like a glad child too.

'We must tell Maud I shall be in to dinner,' he said.

That was like him – always aware of the practical side of the case, and the appearances. She laughed a little bit ironically. Why should she have to take her arm from round him, just to tell Maud he would be in to dinner?

'I'll go,' she said.

He drew the curtains and turned on the light in the big lamp that stood in a corner. The room was dim, and palely warm. He loved it dearly.

His wife, when she came back, as soon as she had closed the door, lifted her arms to him in a little ecstasy, coming to him. They clasped each other closer, body to body. And the intensity of his feeling was so fierce, he felt himself going dim, fusing into something soft and plastic between her hands. And this connection with her was bigger than life or death. And at the bottom of his heart was a sob.

She was gay and winsome at the dinner. Like lovers, they were just deliciously waiting for the night to come up. But there remained in him always the slightly broken feeling which the night before had left.

'And you won't go to Italy,' she said, as if it were an understood thing.

She gave him the best things to eat, and was solicitous for his welfare – which was not usual with her. It gave him deep, shy pleasure. He remembered a verse she was often quoting as one she loved. He did not know it for himself:

> 'On my breasts I warm thy foot-soles;
> Wine I pour, and dress thy meats;
> Humbly, when my lord disposes,
> Lie with him on perfumed sheets.'

She said it to him sometimes, looking up at him from the pillow. But it never seemed real to him. She might, in her sudden passion, put his feet between her breasts. But he never felt like a lord, never more pained and insignificant than at those times. As a little girl, she must have subjected herself before her dolls. And he was something like her lordliest plaything. He liked that too. If only . . .

Then, seeing some frightened little way of looking at him which she had, the pure pain came back. He loved her, and it would never be peace between them; she would never belong to him, as a wife. She would take him and reject him, like a mistress. And perhaps for that reason he would love her all the more; it might be so.

But then, he forgot. Whatever was or was not, now she loved him. And whatever came after, this evening he was the lord. What matter if he were deposed to-morrow, and she hated him!

Her eyes, wide and candid, were staring at him a little bit wondering, a little bit forlorn. She knew he had not quite come back. He held her close to him.

'My love,' she murmured consolingly. 'My love.'

And she put her fingers through his hair, arranging it in little, loose curves, playing with it and forgetting everything else. He loved that dearly, to feel the light lift and touch – touch of her finger-tips making his hair, as she said, like an Apollo's. She lifted his face to see how he looked, and, with a little laugh of love, kissed him. And he loved to be made much of by her. But he had the dim, hurting sense that she would not love him to-morrow, that it was only her great need to love that exalted him to-night. He *knew* he was no king; he did not feel a king, even when she was crowning and kissing him.

'Do you love me?' she asked, playfully whispering.

He held her fast and kissed her, while the blood hurt in his heart-chambers.

'You know,' he answered, with a struggle.

Later, when he lay holding her with a passion intense like pain, the words blurted from him:

'Flesh of my flesh. Paula! – Will you —?'

'Yes, my love,' she answered consolingly.

He bit his mouth with pain. For him it was almost an agony of appeal.

'But, Paula – I mean it – flesh of my flesh – a wife?'

She tightened her arms round him without answering. And he knew, and she knew, that she put him off like that.

87

IV

Two months later, she was writing to him in Italy: 'Your idea of your woman is that she is an expansion, no, a *rib* of yourself, without any existence of her own. That I am a being by myself is more than you can grasp. I wish I could absolutely submerge myself in a man – and *so I do*. I *always* loved you . . .

'You will say "I was patient." Do you call that patient, hanging on for your needs, as you have done? The innermost life you have *always* had of me, and you held yourself aloof because you were afraid.

'The unpardonable thing was you told me you loved me. – Your *feelings* have hated me these three months, which did not prevent you from taking my love and every breath from me. – Underneath you undermined me, in some subtle, corrupt way that I did not see because I believed you, when you told me you loved me . . .

'The insult of the way you took me these last three months I shall never forgive you. I honestly *did* give myself, and always in vain and rebuffed. The strain of it all has driven me quite mad.

'You say I am a tragédienne, but I don't do any of your perverse undermining tricks. You are always luring one into the open like a clever enemy, but you keep safely under cover all the time.

'This practically means, for me, that life is over, my belief in life – I hope it will recover, but it never could do so with you . . .'

To which he answered: 'If I kept under cover it is funny, for there isn't any cover now. – And you can hope, pretty easily, for your own recovery apart from me. For my side, without you, I am done . . . But you lie to yourself. You *wouldn't* love *me*, and you won't be able to love anybody else – except yourself.'

THE PRUSSIAN OFFICER

I

THEY had marched more than thirty kilometres since dawn, along the white, hot road where occasional thickets of trees threw a moment of shade, then out into the glare again. On either hand, the valley, wide and shallow, glittered with heat; dark-green patches of rye, pale young corn, fallow and meadow and black pine woods spread in a dull, hot diagram under a glistening sky. But right in front the mountains ranged across, pale blue and very still, snow gleaming gently out of the deep atmosphere. And towards the mountains, on and on, the regiment marched between the rye-fields and the meadows, between the scraggy fruit trees set regularly on either side the high road. The burnished, dark-green rye threw off a suffocating heat, the mountains drew gradually nearer and more distinct. While the feet of the soldiers grew hotter, sweat ran through their hair under their helmets, and their knapsacks could burn no more in contact with their shoulders, but seemed instead to give off a cold, prickly sensation.

He walked on and on in silence, staring at the mountains ahead, that rose sheer out of the land, and stood fold behind fold, half earth, half heaven, the heaven, the barrier with slits of soft snow, in the pale, bluish peaks.

He could now walk almost without pain. At the start, he had determined not to limp. It had made him sick to take the first steps, and during the first mile or so, he had compressed his breath, and the cold drops of sweat had stood on his forehead. But he had walked it off. What were they after all but bruises! He had looked at them, as he was getting up: deep bruises on the backs of his thighs. And since he had made his first step in the morning, he had been conscious of them, till now he had a tight, hot place in his chest, with suppressing the pain, and holding himself in. There seemed no air when he breathed. But he walked almost lightly.

The Captain's hand had trembled at taking his coffee at dawn: his orderly saw it again. And he saw the fine figure of the Captain wheeling on horseback at the farmhouse ahead, a handsome figure in pale-blue uniform with facings of scarlet, and the metal gleaming on the black helmet and the sword-scabbard, and dark streaks of sweat coming on the silky bay horse. The orderly felt he was connected with that figure moving so suddenly on horseback: he followed it like a shadow, mute and inevitable and damned by it. And the officer was always aware of the tramp of the company behind, the march of his orderly among the men.

The Captain was a tall man of about forty, grey at the temples. He had a handsome, finely-knit figure, and was one of the best horsemen in the West. His orderly, having to rub him down, admired the amazing riding-muscles of his loins.

For the rest, the orderly scarcely noticed the officer any more than he noticed himself. It was rarely he saw his master's face: he did not look at it. The Captain had reddish-brown, stiff hair, that he wore short upon his skull. His moustache was also cut short and bristly over a full, brutal mouth. His face was rather rugged, the cheeks thin. Perhaps the man was the more handsome for the deep lines in his face, the irritable tension of his brow, which gave him the look of a man who fights with life. His fair eyebrows stood bushy over light-blue eyes that were always flashing with cold fire.

He was a Prussian aristocrat, haughty and overbearing. But his mother had been a Polish countess. Having made too many gambling debts when he was young, he had ruined his prospects in the Army, and remained an infantry captain. He had never married: his position did not allow of it, and no woman had ever moved him to it. His time he spent riding – occasionally he rode one of his own horses at the races – and at the officers' club. Now and then he took himself a mistress. But after such an event, he returned to duty with his brow still more tense, his eyes still more hostile and irritable. With the men, however, he was merely impersonal, though a devil when roused; so that, on the whole, they feared him, but had no great aversion from him. They accepted him as the inevitable.

To his orderly he was at first cold and just and indifferent: he did not fuss over trifles. So that his servant knew practically nothing about him, except just what orders he would give, and how he wanted them obeyed. That was quite simple. Then the change gradually came.

The orderly was a youth of about twenty-two, of medium height, and well built. He had strong, heavy limbs, was swarthy, with a soft, black, young moustache. There was something altogether warm and young about him. He had firmly marked eyebrows over dark, expressionless eyes, that seemed never to have thought, only to have received life direct through his senses, and acted straight from instinct.

Gradually the officer had become aware of his servant's young vigorous, unconscious presence about him. He could not get away from the sense of the youth's person, while he was in attendance. It was like a warm flame upon the older man's tense, rigid body, that had become almost unliving, fixed. There was something so free and self-contained about him, and something in the young fellow's movement, that made the officer aware of him. And this irritated the Prussian. He did not choose to be touched into life by his servant. He might easily have changed his man, but he did not. He now very rarely looked direct at his orderly, but kept his face averted, as if to avoid seeing him. And yet as the young soldier moved unthinking about the apartment, the elder watched him, and would notice the movement of his strong young shoulders under the blue cloth, the bend of his neck. And it irritated him. To see the soldier's young, brown, shapely peasant's hand grasp the loaf or the wine-bottle sent a flash of hate or of anger through the elder man's blood. It was not that the youth was clumsy: it was rather the blind, instinctive sureness of movement of an unhampered young animal that irritated the officer to such a degree.

Once, when a bottle of wine had gone over, and the red gushed out on to the tablecloth, the officer had started up with an oath, and his eyes, bluey like fire, had held those of the confused youth for a moment. It was a shock for the young soldier. He felt something sink deeper, deeper into his soul, where nothing had ever gone before. It left him rather blank and wondering. Some of his natural completeness in himself was gone, a little uneasiness took its place. And from that time an undiscovered feeling had held between the two men.

Henceforward the orderly was afraid of really meeting his master. His subconsciousness remembered those steely blue eyes and the harsh brows, and did not intend to meet them again. So he always stared past his master, and avoided him. Also, in a little anxiety, he waited for the three months to have gone, when his time would be up. He began to feel a constraint in the Captain's presence, and the soldier even more than the officer wanted to be left alone, in his neutrality as servant.

He had served the Captain for more than a year, and knew his duty. This he performed easily, as if it were natural to him. The officer and his commands he took for granted, as he took the sun and the rain, and he served as a matter of course. It did not implicate him personally.

But now if he were going to be forced into a personal interchange with his master he would be like a wild thing caught, he felt he must get away.

But the influence of the young soldier's being had penetrated through the officer's stiffened discipline, and perturbed the man in him. He, however, was a gentleman, with long, fine hands and cultivated movements, and was not going to allow such a thing as the stirring of his innate self. He was a man of passionate temper, who had always kept himself suppressed. Occasionally there had been a duel, an outburst before the soldiers. He knew himself to be always on the point of breaking out. But he kept himself hard to the idea of the Service. Whereas the young soldier seemed to live out his warm, full nature, to give it off in his very movements, which had a certain zest, such as wild animals have in free movement. And this irritated the officer more and more.

In spite of himself, the Captain could not regain his neutrality of feeling towards his orderly. Nor could he leave the man alone. In spite of himself, he watched him, gave him sharp orders, tried to take up as much of his time as possible. Sometimes he flew into a rage with the young soldier, and bullied him. Then the orderly shut himself off, as it were out of earshot, and waited, with sullen, flushed face, for the end of the noise. The words never pierced to his intelligence, he made himself, protectively, impervious to the feelings of his master.

He had a scar on his left thumb, a deep seam going across the knuckle. The officer had long suffered from it, and wanted to do something to it. Still it was there, ugly and brutal on the young, brown hand. At last the Captain's reserve gave way. One day, as the orderly was smoothing out the tablecloth, the officer pinned down his thumb with a pencil, asking:

'How did you come by that?'

The young man winced and drew back at attention.

'A wood axe, Herr Hauptmann,' he answered.

The officer waited for further explanation. None came. The orderly went about his duties. The elder man was sullenly angry. His servant avoided him. And the next day he had to use all his will-power to avoid seeing the scarred thumb. He wanted to get hold of it and — A hot flame ran in his blood.

He knew his servant would soon be free, and would be glad. As yet, the soldier had held himself off from the elder man. The Captain grew madly irritable. He could not rest when the soldier was away, and when he was present, he glared at him with tormented eyes. He hated those fine, black brows over the unmeaning, dark eyes, he was infuriated by the free movement of the handsome limbs, which no military discipline could make stiff. And he became harsh and cruelly bullying, using contempt and satire. The young soldier only grew more mute and expressionless.

'What cattle were you bred by, that you can't keep straight eyes? Look me in the eyes when I speak to you.'

And the soldier turned his dark eyes to the other's face, but there was no sight in them: he stared with the slightest possible cast, holding back his sight, perceiving the blue of his master's eyes, but receiving no look from them. And the elder man went pale, and his reddish eyebrows twitched. He gave his order, barrenly.

Once he flung a heavy military glove into the young soldier's face. Then he had the satisfaction of seeing the black eyes flare up into his own, like a blaze when straw is thrown on a fire. And he had laughed with a little tremor and a sneer.

But there were only two months more. The youth instinctively tried to keep himself intact: he tried to serve the officer as if the latter were an abstract authority and not a man. All his instinct was to avoid personal contact, even definite hate. But in spite of himself the hate grew, responsive to the officer's passion. However, he put it in the background. When he had left the Army he could dare acknowledge it. By nature he was active, and had many friends. He thought what amazing good fellows they were. But, without knowing it, he was alone. Now this solitariness was intensified. It would carry him through his term. But the officer seemed to be going irritably insane, and the youth was deeply frightened.

The soldier had a sweetheart, a girl from the mountains, independent and primitive. The two walked together, rather silently. He went with her, not to talk, but to have his arm round her, and for the physical contact. This eased him, made it easier for him to ignore the Captain; for he could rest with her head fast against his chest. And she, in some unspoken fashion, was there for him. They loved each other.

The Captain perceived it, and was mad with irritation. He kept the young man engaged all the evenings long, and took pleasure in the dark look that came on his face. Occasionally, the eyes of the two men met, those of the younger sullen and dark, doggedly unalterable, those of the elder sneering with restless contempt.

The officer tried hard not to admit the passion that had got hold of him. He would not know that his feeling for his orderly was anything but that of a man incensed by his stupid, perverse servant. So, keeping quite justified and conventional in his consciousness, he let the other thing run on. His nerves, however, were suffering. At last he slung the end of a belt in his servant's face. When he saw the youth start back, the pain-tears in his eyes and the blood on his mouth, he had felt at once a thrill of deep pleasure and of shame.

But this, he acknowledged to himself, was a thing he had never done before. The fellow was too exasperating. His own nerves must be going to pieces. He went away for some days with a woman.

It was a mockery of pleasure. He simply did not want the woman. But he stayed on for his time. At the end of it, he came back in an agony of irritation, torment, and misery. He rode all the evening, then came straight in to supper. His orderly was out. The officer sat with his long, fine hands lying on the table, perfectly still, and all his blood seemed to be corroding.

At last his servant entered. He watched the strong, easy young figure, the fine eyebrows, the thick black hair. In a week's time the youth had got back his old well-being. The hands of the officer twitched and seemed to be full of mad flame. The young man stood at attention, unmoving, shut off.

The meal went in silence. But the orderly seemed eager. He made a clatter with the dishes.

'Are you in a hurry?' asked the officer, watching the intent, warm face of his servant. The other did not reply.

'Will you answer my question?' said the Captain.

'Yes, sir,' replied the orderly, standing with his pile of deep Army plates. The Captain waited, looked at him, then asked again:

'Are you in a hurry?'

'Yes, sir,' came the answer, that sent a flash through the listener.

'For what?'

'I was going out, sir.'

'I want you this evening.'

There was a moment's hesitation. The officer had a curious stiffness of countenance.

'Yes, sir,' replied the servant, in his throat.

'I want you to-morrow evening also – in fact you may consider your evenings occupied, unless I give you leave.'

The mouth with the young moustache set close.

'Yes, sir,' answered the orderly, loosening his lips for a moment.

He again turned to the door.

94

'And why have you a piece of pencil in your ear?'

The orderly hesitated, then continued on his way without answering. He set the plates in a pile outside the door, took the stump of pencil from his ear, and put it in his pocket. He had been copying a verse for his sweetheart's birthday card. He returned to finish clearing the table. The officer's eyes were dancing, he had a little, eager smile.

'Why have you a piece of pencil in your ear?' he asked.

The orderly took his hands full of dishes. His master was standing near the great green stove, a little smile on his face, his chin thrust forward. When the young soldier saw him his heart suddenly ran hot. He felt blind. Instead of answering, he turned dazedly to the door. As he was crouching to set down the dishes, he was pitched forward by a kick from behind. The pots went in a stream down the stairs, he clung to the pillar of the banisters. And as he was rising he was kicked heavily again and again, so that he clung sickly to the post for some moments. His master had gone swiftly into the room and closed the door. The maid-servant downstairs looked up the staircase and made a mocking face at the crockery disaster.

The officer's heart was plunging. He poured himself a glass of wine, part of which he spilled on the floor, and gulped the remainder, leaning against the cool, green stove. He heard his man collecting the dishes from the stairs. Pale, as if intoxicated, he waited. The servant entered again. The Captain's heart gave a pang, as of pleasure, seeing the young fellow bewildered and uncertain on his feet with pain.

'Schöner!' he said.

The soldier was a little slower in coming to attention.

'Yes, sir!'

The youth stood before him, with pathetic young moustache, and fine eyebrows very distinct on his forehead of dark marble.

'I asked you a question.'

'Yes, sir.'

The officer's tone bit like acid.

'Why had you a pencil in your ear?'

Again the servant's heart ran hot, and he could not breathe. With dark, strained eyes, he looked at the officer, as if fascinated. And he stood there sturdily planted, unconscious. The withering smile came into the Captain's eyes, and he lifted his foot.

'I forgot it – sir,' panted the soldier, his dark eyes fixed on the other man's dancing blue ones.

'What was it doing there?'

He saw the young man's breast heaving as he made an effort for words.

'I had been writing.'

'Writing what?'

Again the soldier looked him up and down. The officer could hear him panting. The smile came into the blue eyes. The soldier worked his dry throat, but could not speak. Suddenly the smile lit like a flame on the officer's face, and a kick came heavily against the orderly's thigh. The youth moved sideways. His face went dead, with two black, staring eyes.

'Well?' said the officer.

The orderly's mouth had gone dry, and his tongue rubbed in it as on dry brown-paper. He worked his throat. The officer raised his foot. The servant went stiff.

'Some poetry, sir,' came the crackling, unrecognisable sound of his voice.

'Poetry, what poetry?' asked the Captain, with a sickly smile.

Again there was the working in the throat. The Captain's heart had suddenly gone down heavily, and he stood sick and tired.

'For my girl, sir,' he heard the dry, inhuman sound.

'Oh!' he said, turning away. 'Clear the table.'

'Click!' went the soldier's throat; then again, 'click!' and then the half-articulate:

'Yes, sir.'

The young soldier was gone, looking old, and walking heavily.

The officer, left alone, held himself rigid, to prevent himself from thinking. His instinct warned him that he must not think. Deep inside him was the intense gratification of his passion, still working powerfully. Then there was a counteraction, a horrible breaking down of something inside him, a whole agony of reaction. He stood there for an hour motionless, a chaos of sensations, but rigid with a will to keep blank his consciousness, to prevent his mind grasping. And he held himself so until the worst of the stress had passed, when he began to drink, drank himself to an intoxication, till he slept obliterated. When he woke in the morning he was shaken to the base of his nature. But he had fought off the realisation of what he had done. He had prevented his mind from taking it in, had suppressed it along with his instincts, and the conscious man had nothing to do with it. He felt only as after a bout of intoxication, weak, but the affair itself all dim and not to be recovered. Of the drunkenness of his passion he successfully refused remembrance. And when his orderly appeared with coffee, the officer assumed the same self he had had the morning before. He refused the event of the past night – denied it had ever been – and was successful in his denial. He had not done any such thing – not he himself. Whatever there might be lay at the door of a stupid insubordinate servant.

The orderly had gone about in a stupor all the evening. He drank some beer because he was parched, but not much, the alcohol made his feeling come back, and he could not bear it. He was dulled, as if nine-tenths of the ordinary man in him were inert. He crawled about disfigured. Still, when he thought of the kicks, he went sick, and when he thought of the threat of more kicking, in the room afterwards, his heart went hot and faint, and he panted, remembering the one that had come. He had been forced to say: 'For my girl.' He was much too done even to want to cry. His mouth hung slightly open, like an idiot's. He felt vacant, and wasted. So, he wandered at his work, painfully, and very slowly and clumsily, fumbling blindly with the brushes, and finding it difficult, when he sat down, to summon the energy to move again. His limbs, his jaw, were slack and nerveless. But he was very tired. He got to bed at last, and slept inert, relaxed, in a sleep that was rather stupor than slumber, a dead night of stupefaction shot through with gleams of anguish.

In the morning were the manoeuvres. But he woke even before the bugle sounded. The painful ache in his chest, the dryness of his throat, the awful steady feeling of misery made his eyes come awake and dreary at once. He knew, without thinking, what had happened. And he knew that the day had come again, when he must go on with his round. The last bit of darkness was being pushed out of the room. He would have to move his inert body and go on. He was so young, and had known so little trouble, that he was bewildered. He only wished it would stay night, so that he could lie still, covered up by the darkness. And yet nothing would prevent the day from coming, nothing would save him from having to get up and saddle the Captain's horse, and make the Captain's coffee. It was there, inevitable. And then, he thought, it was impossible. Yet they would not leave him free. He must go and take the coffee to the Captain. He was too stunned to understand it. He only knew it was inevitable – inevitable, however long he lay inert.

At last, after heaving at himself, for he seemed to be a mass of inertia, he got up. But he had to force every one of his movements from behind, with his will. He felt lost, and dazed, and helpless. Then he clutched hold of the bed, the pain was so keen. And looking at his thighs he saw the darker bruises on his swarthy flesh, and he knew that if he pressed one of his fingers on one of the bruises, he should faint. But he did not want to faint – he did not want anybody to know. No one should ever know. It was between him and the Captain. There were only the two people in the world now – himself and the Captain.

Slowly, economically, he got dressed and forced himself to walk. Everything was obscure, except just what he had his hands on. But he managed to get through his work. The very pain revived his dull senses. The worst remained yet. He took the tray and went up to the Captain's room. The officer, pale and heavy, sat at the table. The orderly, as he saluted, felt himself put out of existence. He stood still for a moment submitting to his own nullification – then he gathered himself, seemed to regain himself, and then the Captain began to grow vague, unreal, and the younger soldier's heart beat up. He clung to this situation – that the Captain did not exist – so that he himself might live. But when he saw his officer's hand tremble as he took the coffee, he felt everything falling shattered. And he went away, feeling as if he himself were coming to pieces, disintegrated. And when the Captain was there on horseback, giving orders, while he himself stood, with rifle and knapsack, sick with pain, he felt as if he must shut his eyes – as if he must shut his eyes on everything. It was only the long agony of marching with a parched throat that filled him with one single, sleep-heavy intention: to save himself.

II

He was getting used even to his parched throat. That the snowy peaks were radiant among the sky, that the whity-green glacier-river twisted through its pale shoals, in the valley below, seemed almost supernatural. But he was going mad with fever and thirst. He plodded on uncomplaining. He did not want to speak, not to anybody. There were two gulls, like flakes of water and snow, over the river. The scent of green rye soaked in sunshine came like a sickness. And the march continued, monotonously, almost like a bad sleep.

At the next farmhouse, which stood low and broad near the high road, tubs of water had been put out. The soldiers clustered round to drink. They took off their helmets, and the steam mounted from their wet hair. The Captain sat on horseback, watching. He needed to see his orderly. His helmet threw a dark shadow over his light, fierce eyes, but his moustache and mouth and chin were distinct in the sunshine. The orderly must move under the presence of the figure of the horseman. It was not that he was afraid, or cowed. It was as if he was disembowelled, made empty, like an empty shell. He felt himself as nothing, a shadow creeping under the sunshine. And, thirsty as he was, he could scarcely drink, feeling the Captain near him. He would not take off his helmet to wipe his wet hair. He wanted to stay in shadow, not to be forced into consciousness. Starting, he saw the light heel of the officer prick the belly of the horse; the Captain cantered away, and he himself could relapse into vacancy.

Nothing, however, could give him back his living place in the hot, bright morning. He felt like a gap among it all. Whereas the Captain was prouder, overriding. A hot flash went through the young servant's body. The Captain was firmer and prouder with life, he himself was empty as a shadow. Again the flash went through him, dazing him out. But his heart ran a little firmer.

The company turned up the hill, to make a loop for the return. Below, from among the trees, the farm-bell clanged. He saw the labourers, mowing bare-foot at the thick grass, leave off their work and go downhill, their scythes hanging over their shoulders, like long, bright claws curving down behind them. They seemed like dream-people, as if they had no relation to himself. He felt as in a blackish dream: as if all the other things were there and had form, but he himself was only a consciousness, a gap that could think and perceive.

The soldiers were tramping silently up the glaring hill-side. Gradually his head began to revolve, slowly, rhythmically. Sometimes it was dark before his eyes, as if he saw this world through a smoked glass, frail shadows and unreal. It gave him a pain in his head to walk.

The air was too scented, it gave no breath. All the lush green-stuff seemed to be issuing its sap, till the air was deathly, sickly with the smell of greenness. There was the perfume of clover, like pure honey and bees. Then there grew a faint acrid tang – they were near the beeches; and then a queer clattering noise, and a suffocating, hideous smell; they were passing a flock of sheep, a shepherd in a black smock, holding his crook. Why should the sheep huddle together under this fierce sun? He felt that the shepherd would not see him, though he could see the shepherd.

At last there was the halt. They stacked rifles in a conical stack, put down their kit in a scattered circle around it, and dispersed a little, sitting on a small knoll high on the hill-side. The chatter began. The soldiers were steaming with heat, but were lively. He sat still, seeing the blue mountains rising upon the land, twenty kilometres away. There was a blue fold in the ranges, then out of that, at the foot, the broad, pale bed of the river, stretches of whity-green water between pinkish-grey shoals among the dark pine woods. There it was, spread out a long way off. And it seemed to come downhill, the river. There was a raft being steered, a mile away. It was a strange country. Nearer, a red-roofed, broad farm with white base and square dots of windows crouched beside the wall of beech foliage on the wood's edge. There were long strips of rye and clover and pale green corn. And just at his feet, below the knoll, was a darkish bog, where globe flowers stood breathless still on their slim stalks. And some of the pale gold bubbles were burst, and a broken fragment hung in the air. He thought he was going to sleep.

Suddenly something moved into this coloured mirage before his eyes. The Captain, a small, light-blue and scarlet figure, was trotting evenly between the strips of corn, along the level brow of the hill. And the man making flag-signals was coming on. Proud and sure moved the horse-man's figure, the quick, bright thing, in which was concentrated all the light of this morning, which for the rest lay fragile, shining shadow. Submissive, apathetic, the young soldier sat and stared. But as the horse slowed to a walk, coming up the last steep path, the great flash flared over the body and soul of the orderly. He sat waiting. The back of his head felt as if it were weighted with a heavy piece of fire. He did not want to eat. His hands trembled slightly as he moved them. Mean-while the officer on horseback was approaching slowly and proudly. The tension grew in the orderly's soul. Then again, seeing the Captain ease himself on the saddle, the flash blazed through him.

The Captain looked at the patch of light blue and scarlet, and dark head, scattered closely on the hill-side. It pleased him. The command pleased him. And he was feeling proud. His orderly was among them in common subjection. The officer rose a little on his stirrups to look. The young soldier sat with averted, dumb face. The Captain relaxed on his seat. His slim-legged, beautiful horse, brown as a beech nut, walked proudly uphill. The Captain passed into the zone of the company's atmosphere: a hot smell of men, of sweat, of leather. He knew it very well. After a word with the lieutenant, he went a few paces higher, and sat there, a dominant figure, his sweat-marked horse swishing its tail, while he looked down on his men, on his orderly, a nonentity among the crowd.

The young soldier's heart was like fire in his chest, and he breathed with difficulty. The officer, looking downhill, saw three of the young soldiers, two pails of water between them, staggering across a sunny green field. A table had been set up under a tree, and there the slim lieutenant stood, importantly busy. Then the Captain summoned himself to an act of courage. He called his orderly.

The flame leapt into the young soldier's throat as he heard the command, and he rose blindly, stifled. He saluted, standing below the officer. He did not look up. But there was the flicker in the Captain's voice.

'Go to the inn and fetch me ...' the officer gave his commands. 'Quick!' he added.

At the last word, the heart of the servant leapt with a flash, and he felt the strength come over his body. But he turned in mechanical obedience, and set off at a heavy run downhill, looking almost like a bear, his trousers bagging over his military boots. And the officer watched this blind, plunging run all the way.

But it was only the outside of the orderly's body that was obeying so humbly and mechanically. Inside had gradually accumulated a core into which all the energy of that young life was compact and concentrated. He executed his commission, and plodded quickly back uphill. There was a pain in his head as he walked that made him twist his features unknowingly. But hard there in the centre of his chest was himself, himself, firm, and not to be plucked to pieces.

The Captain had gone up into the wood. The orderly plodded through the hot, powerfully smelling zone of the company's atmosphere. He had a curious mass of energy inside him now. The Captain was less real than himself. He approached the green entrance to the wood. There, in the half-shade, he saw the horse standing, the sunshine and the flickering shadow of leaves dancing over his brown body. There was a clearing where timber had lately been felled. Here, in the gold-green shade beside the brilliant cup of sunshine, stood two figures, blue and pink, the bits of pink showing out plainly. The Captain was talking to his lieutenant.

The orderly stood on the edge of the bright clearing, where great trunks of trees, stripped and glistening, lay stretched like naked, brown-skinned bodies. Chips of wood littered the trampled floor, like splashed light, and the bases of the felled trees stood here and there, with their raw, level tops. Beyond was the brilliant, sunlit green of a beech.

'Then I will ride forward,' the orderly heard his Captain say. The lieutenant saluted and strode away. He himself went forward. A hot flash passed through his belly, as he tramped towards his officer.

The Captain watched the rather heavy figure of the young soldier stumble forward, and his veins, too, ran hot. This was to be man to man between them. He yielded before the solid, stumbling figure with bent head. The orderly stooped and put the food on a level-sawn tree-base. The Captain watched the glistening, sun-inflamed, naked hands. He wanted to speak to the young soldier, but could not. The servant propped a bottle against his thigh, pressed open the cork, and poured out the beer into the mug. He kept his head bent. The Captain accepted the mug.

'Hot!' he said, as if amiably.

The flame sprang out of the orderly's heart, nearly suffocating him. 'Yes, sir,' he replied, between shut teeth.

And he heard the sound of the Captain's drinking, and he clenched his fists, such a strong torment came into his wrists. Then came the faint clang of the closing of the pot-lid. He looked up. The Captain was watching him. He glanced swiftly away. Then he saw the officer stoop and take a piece of bread from the tree-base. Again the flash of flame went through the young soldier, seeing the stiff body stoop beneath him, and his hands jerked. He looked away. He could feel the officer was nervous. The bread fell as it was being broken. The officer ate the other piece. The two men stood tense and still, the master laboriously chewing his bread, the servant staring with averted face, his fist clenched.

Then the young soldier started. The officer had pressed open the lid of the mug again. The orderly watched the lip of the mug, and the white hand that clenched the handle, as if he were fascinated. It was raised. The youth followed it with his eyes. And then he saw the thin, strong throat of the elder man moving up and down as he drank, the strong jaw working. And the instinct which had been jerking at the young man's wrists suddenly jerked free. He jumped, feeling as if it were rent in two by a strong flame.

The spur of the officer caught in a tree root, he went down backwards with a crash, the middle of his back thudding sickeningly against a sharp-edged tree-base, the pot flying away. And in a second the orderly, with serious, earnest young face, and underlip between his teeth, had got his knee in the officer's chest and was pressing the chin backward over the farther edge of the tree-stump, pressing, with all his heart behind in a passion of relief, the tension of his wrists exquisite with relief. And with the base of his palms he shoved at the chin, with all his might. And it was pleasant, too, to have that chin that hard jaw already slightly rough with beard, in his hands. He did not relax one hair's breadth, but, all the force of all his blood exulting in his thrust, he shoved back the head of the other man, till there was a little 'cluck' and a crunching sensation. Then he felt as if his head went to vapour. Heavy convulsions shook the body of the officer, frightening and horrifying the young soldier. Yet it pleased him, too, to repress them. It pleased him to keep his hands pressing back the chin, to feel the chest of the other man yield in expiration to the weight of his strong, young knees, to feel the hard twitchings of the prostrate body jerking his own whole frame, which was pressed down on it.

But it went still. He could look into the nostrils of the other man, the eyes he could scarcely see. How curiously the mouth was pushed out, exaggerating the full lips, and the moustache bristling up from them. Then, with a start, he noticed the nostrils gradually filled with blood. The red brimmed, hesitated, ran over, and went in a thin trickle down the face to the eyes.

It shocked and distressed him. Slowly, he got up. The body twitched and sprawled there, inert. He stood and looked at it in silence. It was a pity *it* was broken. It represented more than the thing which had kicked and bullied him. He was afraid to look at the eyes. They were hideous now, only the whites showing, and the blood running to them. The face of the orderly was drawn with horror at the sight. Well, it was so. In his heart he was satisfied. He had hated the face of the Captain. It was extinguished now. There was a heavy relief in the orderly's soul. That was as it should be. But he could not bear to see the long, military body lying broken over the tree-base, the fine fingers crisped. He wanted to hide it away.

Quickly, busily, he gathered it up and pushed it under the felled tree trunks, which rested their beautiful, smooth length either end on the logs. The face was horrible with blood. He covered it with the helmet. Then he pushed the limbs straight and decent, and brushed the dead leaves off the fine cloth of the uniform. So, it lay quite still in the shadow under there. A little strip of sunshine ran along the breast, from a chink between the logs. The orderly sat by it for a few moments. Here his own life also ended.

Then, through his daze, he heard the lieutenant, in a loud voice, explaining to the men outside the wood, that they were to suppose the bridge on the river below was held by the enemy. Now they were to march to the attack in such and such a manner. The lieutenant had no gift of expression. The orderly, listening from habit, got muddled. And when the lieutenant began it all again he ceased to hear.

He knew he must go. He stood up. It surprised him that the leaves were glittering in the sun, and the chips of wood reflecting white from the ground. For him a change had come over the world. But for the rest it had not – all seemed the same. Only he had left it. And he could not go back. It was his duty to return with the beer-pot and the bottle. He could not. He had left all that. The lieutenant was still hoarsely explaining. He must go, or they would overtake him. And he could not bear contact with anyone now.

He drew his fingers over his eyes, trying to find out where he was. Then he turned away. He saw the horse standing in the path. He went up to it and mounted. It hurt him to sit in the saddle. The pain of keeping his seat occupied him as they cantered through the wood. He would not have minded anything, but he could not get away from the sense of being divided from the others. The path led out of the trees. On the edge of the wood he pulled up and stood watching. There in the spacious sunshine of the valley soldiers were moving in a little swarm. Every now and then, a man harrowing on a strip of fallow shouted to his oxen, at the turn. The village and the white-towered church was small in the sunshine. And he no longer belonged to it – he sat there, beyond, like a man outside in the dark. He had gone out from everyday life into the unknown and he could not, he even did not want to go back.

Turning from the sun-blazing valley, he rode deep into the wood. Tree trunks, like people standing grey and still, took no notice as he went. A doe, herself a moving bit of sunshine and shadow, went running through the flecked shade. There were bright green rents in the foliage. Then it was all pine wood, dark and cool. And he was sick with pain, and had an intolerable great pulse in his head, and he was sick. He had never been ill in his life. He felt lost, quite dazed with all this.

Trying to get down from the horse, he fell, astonished at the pain and his lack of balance. The horse shifted uneasily. He jerked its bridle and sent it cantering jerkily away. It was his last connection with the rest of things.

But he only wanted to lie down and not be disturbed. Stumbling through the trees, he came on a quiet place where beeches and pine trees grew on a slope. Immediately he had lain down and closed his eyes, his consciousness went racing on without him. A big pulse of sickness beat in him as if it throbbed through the whole earth. He was burning with dry heat. But he was too busy, too tearingly active in the incoherent race of delirium to observe.

III

He came to with a start. His mouth was dry and hard, his heart beat heavily, but he had not the energy to get up. His heart beat heavily. Where was he? – the barracks – at home? There was something knocking. And, making an effort, he looked round – trees, and litter of greenery, and reddish, bright, still pieces of sunshine on the floor. He did not believe he was himself, he did not believe what he saw. Something was knocking. He made a struggle towards consciousness, but relapsed. Then he struggled again. And gradually his surroundings fell into relationship with himself. He knew, and a great pang of fear went through his heart. Somebody was knocking. He could see the heavy, black rags of a fir tree overhead. Then everything went black. Yet he did not believe he had closed his eyes. He had not. Out of the blackness sight slowly emerged again. And someone was knocking. Quickly, he saw the blood-disfigured face of his Captain, which he hated. And he held himself still with horror. Yet, deep inside him, he knew that it was so, the Captain should be dead. But the physical delirium got hold of him. Someone was knocking. He lay perfectly still, as if dead, with fear. And he went unconscious.

When he opened his eyes again he started, seeing something creeping swiftly up a tree trunk. It was a little bird. And the bird was whistling overhead. Tap-tap-tap – it was the small, quick bird rapping the tree trunk with its beak, as if its head were a little round hammer. He watched it curiously. It shifted sharply, in its creeping fashion. Then, like a mouse, it slid down the bare trunk. Its swift creeping sent a flash of revulsion through him. He raised his head. It felt a great weight. Then, the little bird ran out of the shadow across a still patch of sunshine, its little head bobbing swiftly, its white legs twinkling brightly for a moment. How neat it was in its build, so compact, with piece of white on its wings. There were several of them. They were so pretty – but they crept like swift, erratic mice, running here and there among the beech-mast.

He lay down again exhausted, and his consciousness lapsed. He had a horror of the little creeping birds. All his blood seemed to be darting and creeping in his head. And yet he could not move.

He came to with a further ache of exhaustion. There was the pain in his head, and the horrible sickness, and his inability to move. He had never been ill in his life. He did not know where he was or what he was. Probably he had got sunstroke. Or what else? – he had silenced the Captain for ever – some time ago – oh, a long time ago. There had been blood on his face, and his eyes had turned upwards. It was all right, somehow. It was peace. But now he had got beyond himself. He had never been here before. Was it life, or not life? He was by himself. They were in a big, bright place, those others, and he was outside. The town, all the country, a big bright place of light: and he was outside, here, in the darkened open beyond, where each thing existed alone. But they would all have to come out there sometime, those others. Little, and left behind him, they all were. There had been father and mother and sweetheart. What did they all matter? This was the open land.

He sat up. Something scuffled. It was a little brown squirrel running in lovely undulating bounds over the floor, its red tail completing the undulation of its body – and then, as it sat up, furling and unfurling. He watched it, pleased. It ran on again, friskily, enjoying itself. It flew wildly at another squirrel, and they were chasing each other, and making little scolding, chattering noises. The soldier wanted to speak to them. But only a hoarse sound came out of his throat. The squirrels burst away – they flew up the trees. And then he saw the one peeping round at him, half-way up a tree trunk. A start of fear went through him, though in so far as he was conscious, he was amused. It still stayed, its little keen face staring at him half-way up the tree trunk, its little ears pricked up, its clawey little hands clinging to the bark, its white breast reared. He started from it in panic.

Struggling to his feet, he lurched away. He went on walking, walking, looking for something – for a drink. His brain felt hot and inflamed for want of water. He stumbled on. Then he did not know anything. He went unconscious as he walked. Yet he stumbled on, his mouth open.

When, to his dumb wonder, he opened his eyes on the world again, he no longer tried to remember what it was. There was thick, golden light behind golden-green glitterings, and tall, grey-purple shafts, and darknesses farther off, surrounding him, growing deeper. He was conscious of a sense of arrival. He was amid the reality, on the real, dark bottom. But there was the thirst burning in his brain. He felt lighter, not so heavy. He supposed it was newness. The air was muttering with

106

thunder. He thought he was walking wonderfully swiftly and was coming straight to relief – or was it to water?

Suddenly he stood still with fear. There was a tremendous flare of gold, immense – just a few dark trunks like bars between him and it. All the young level wheat was burnished gold glaring on its silky green. A woman, full-skirted, a black cloth on her head for head-dress, was passing like a block of shadow through the glistening, green corn, into the full glare. There was a farm, too, pale blue in shadow, and the timber black. And there was a church spire, nearly fused away in the gold. The woman moved on, away from him. He had no language with which to speak to her. She was the bright, solid unreality. She would make a noise of words that would confuse him, and her eyes would look at him without seeing him. She was crossing there to the other side. He stood against a tree.

When at last he turned, looking down the long, bare grove whose flat bed was already filling dark, he saw the mountains in a wonder-light, not far away, and radiant. Behind the soft, grey ridge of the nearest range the farther mountains stood golden and pale grey, the snow all radiant like pure, soft gold. So still, gleaming in the sky, fashioned pure out of the ore of the sky, they shone in their silence. He stood and looked at them, his face illuminated. And like the golden, lustrous gleaming of the snow he felt his own thirst bright in him. He stood and gazed, leaning against a tree. And then everything slid away into space.

During the night the lightning fluttered perpetually, making the whole sky white. He must have walked again. The world hung livid round him for moments, fields a level sheen of grey-green light, trees in dark bulk, and the range of clouds black across a white sky. Then the darkness fell like a shutter, and the night was whole. A faint flutter of a half-revealed world, that could not quite leap out of the darkness! – Then there again stood a sweep of pallor for the land, dark shapes looming, a range of clouds hanging overhead. The world was a ghostly shadow, thrown for a moment upon the pure darkness, which returned ever whole and complete.

And the mere delirium of sickness and fever went on inside him – his brain opening and shutting like the night – then sometimes convulsions of terror from something with great eyes that stared round a tree – then the long agony of the march, and the sun decomposing his blood – then the pang of hate for the Captain, followed by a pang of tenderness and ease. But everything was distorted, born of an ache and resolving into an ache.

107

In the morning he came definitely awake. Then his brain flamed with the sole horror or thirstiness! The sun was on his face, the dew was steaming from his wet clothes. Like one possessed, he got up. There, straight in front of him, blue and cool and tender, the mountains ranged across the pale edge of the morning sky. He wanted them – he wanted them alone – he wanted to leave himself and be identified with them. They did not move, they were still and soft, with white, gentle markings of snow. He stood still, mad with suffering, his hands crisping and clutching. Then he was twisting in a paroxysm on the grass.

He lay still, in a kind of dream of anguish. His thirst seemed to have separated itself from him, and to stand apart, a single demand. Then the pain he felt was another single self. Then there was the clog of his body, another separate thing. He was divided among all kinds of separate things. There was some strange, agonised connection between them, but they were drawing farther apart. Then they would all split. The sun, drilling down on him, was drilling through the bond. Then they would all fall, fall through the everlasting lapse of space. Then again, his consciousness reasserted itself. He roused on to his elbow and stared at the gleaming mountains. There they ranked, all still and wonderful between earth and heaven. He stared till his eyes went black, and the mountains, as they stood in their beauty, so clean and cool, seemed to have it, that which was lost in him.

IV

When the soldiers found him, three hours later, he was lying with his face over his arm, his black hair giving off heat under the sun. But he was still alive. Seeing the open, black mouth the young soldiers dropped him in horror.

He died in the hospital at night, without having seen again.

The doctors saw the bruises on his legs, behind, and were silent.

The bodies of the two men lay together, side by side, in the mortuary, the one white and slender, but laid rigidly at rest, the other looking as if every moment it must rouse into life again, so young and unused, from a slumber.

THE THORN IN THE FLESH

I

A WIND was running, so that occasionally the poplars whitened as if a flame flew up them. The sky was broken and blue among moving clouds. Patches of sunshine lay on the level fields, and shadows on the rye and the vineyards. In the distance, very blue, the cathedral bristled against the sky, and the houses of the city of Metz clustered vaguely below, like a hill.

Among the fields by the lime trees stood the barracks, upon bare, dry ground, a collection of round-roofed huts of corrugated iron, where the soldiers' nasturtiums climbed brilliantly. There was a tract of vegetable garden at the side, with the soldiers' yellowish lettuces in rows, and at the back the big, hard drilling-yard surrounded by a wire fence.

At this time in the afternoon, the huts were deserted, all the beds pushed up, the soldiers were lounging about under the lime trees waiting for the call to drill. Bachmann sat on a bench in the shade that smelled sickly with blossom. Pale green, wrecked lime flowers were scattered on the ground. He was writing his weekly post card to his mother. He was a fair, long, limber youth, good-looking. He sat very still indeed, trying to write his post card. His blue uniform, sagging on him as he sat bent over the card, disfigured his youthful shape. His sunburnt hand waited motionless for the words to come. 'Dear mother' – was all he had written. Then he scribbled mechanically: 'Many thanks for your letter with what you sent. Everything is all right with me. We are just off to drill on the fortifications —' Here he broke off and sat suspended, oblivious of everything, held in some definite suspense. He looked again at the card. But he could write no more. Out of the knot of his consciousness no word would come. He signed himself, and looked up, as a man looks to see if anyone has noticed him in his privacy.

There was a self-conscious strain in his blue eyes, and a pallor about his mouth, where the young, fair moustache glistened. He was almost girlish in his good looks and his grace. But he had something of military consciousness, as if he believed in the discipline for himself, and found

109

satisfaction in delivering himself to his duty. There was also a trace of youthful swagger and dare-devilry about his mouth and his limber body, but this was in suppression now.

He put the post card in the pocket of his tunic, and went to join a group of his comrades who were lounging in the shade, laughing and talking grossly. Today he was out of it. He only stood near to them for the warmth of the association. In his own consciousness something held him down.

Presently they were summoned to ranks. The sergeant came out to take command. He was a strongly built, rather heavy man of forty. His head was thrust forward, sunk a little between his powerful shoulders, and the strong jaw was pushed out aggressively. But the eyes were smouldering, the face hung slack and sodden with drink.

He gave his orders in brutal, barking shouts, and the little company moved forward, out of the wire-fenced yard to the open road, marching rhythmically, raising the dust. Bachmann, one of the inner file of four deep, marched in the airless ranks, half suffocated with heat and dust and enclosure. Through the moving of his comrades' bodies, he culd see the small vines dusty by the roadside, the poppies among the tares fluttering and blown to pieces, the distant spaces of sky and fields all free with air and sunshine. But he was bound in a very dark enclosure of anxiety within himself.

He marched with his usual ease, being healthy and well adjusted. But his body went on by itself. His spirit was clenched apart. And ever the few soldiers drew nearer and nearer the town, ever the consciousness of the youth became more gripped and separate, his body worked by a kind of mechanical intelligence, a mere presence of mind.

They diverged from the high road and passed in single file down a path among trees. All was silent and green and mysterious, with shadow of foliage and long, green, undisturbed grass. Then they came out in the sunshine on a moat of water, which wound silently between the long, flowery grass, at the foot of the earthworks, that rose in front in terraces walled smooth on the face, but all soft with long grass at the top. Marguerite daisies and lady's-slipper glimmered white and gold in the lush grass, preserved here in the intense peace of the fortifications. Thickets of trees stood round about. Occasionally a puff of mysterious wind made the flowers and the long grass that crested the earthworks above bow and shake as with signals of oncoming alarm.

The group of soldiers stood at the end of the moat, in their light blue and scarlet uniforms, very bright. The sergeant was giving them in-

110

structions, and his shout came sharp and alarming in the intense, untouched stillness of the place. They listened, finding it difficult to make the effort of understanding.

Then it was over, and the men were moving to make preparations. On the other side of the moat the ramparts rose smooth and clear in the sun, sloping slightly back. Along the summit grass grew and tall daisies stood ledged high, like magic, against the dark green of the tree-tops behind. The noise of the town, the running of tram-cars, was heard distinctly, but it seemed not to penetrate this still place.

The water of the moat was motionless. In silence the practice began. One of the soldiers took a scaling-ladder, and passing along the narrow ledge at the foot of the earthworks, with the water of the moat just behind him, tried to get a fixture on the slightly sloping wall-face. There he stood, small and isolated, at the foot of the wall, trying to get his ladder settled. At last it held, and the clumsy, groping figure in the baggy blue uniform began to clamber up. The rest of the soldiers stood and watched. Occasionally the sergeant barked a command. Slowly the clumsy blue figure clambered higher up the wall-face. Bachmann stood with his bowels turned to water. The figure of the climbing soldier scrambled out on to the terrace up above, and moved, blue and distinct, among the bright green grass. The officer shouted from below. The soldier tramped along, fixed the ladder in another spot, and carefully lowered himself on to the rungs. Bachmann watched the blind foot groping in space for the ladder, and he felt the world fall away beneath him. The figure of the soldier clung cringing against the face of the wall, cleaving, groping downwards like some unsure insect working its way lower and lower, fearing every movement. At last, sweating and with a strained face, the figure had landed safely and turned to the group of soldiers. But still it had a stiffness and a blank mechanical look, was something less than human.

Bachmann stood there heavy and condemned, waiting for his own turn and betrayal. Some of the men went up easily enough, and without fear. That only showed it could be done lightly, and made Bachmann's case more bitter. If only he could do it lightly, like that.

His turn came. He knew intuitively that nobody knew his condition. The officer just saw him as a mechanical thing. He tried to keep it up, to carry it through on the face of things. His inside gripped tight, as yet under control, he took the ladder and went along under the wall. He placed his ladder with quick success, and wild, quivering hope possessed him. Then blindly he began to climb. But the ladder was not

111

very firm; and at every hitch a great, sick melting feeling took hold of him. He clung on fast. If only he could keep that grip on himself, he would get through. He knew this, in agony. What he could not understand was the blind gush of white-hot fear, that came with great force whenever the ladder swerved, and which almost melted his belly and all his joints, and left him powerless. If once it melted all his joints and his belly, he was done. He clung desperately to himself. He knew the fear, he knew what it did when it came, he knew he had only to keep a firm hold. He knew all this. Yet, when the ladder swerved and his foot missed, there was the great blast of fear blowing on his heart and bowels, and he was melting weaker and weaker, in a horror of fear and lack of control, melting to fall.

Yet he groped slowly higher and higher, always staring upwards with desperate face, and always conscious of the space below. But all of him, body and soul, was growing hot to fusion point. He would have to let go for very relief's sake. Suddenly his heart began to lurch. It gave a great, sickly swoop, rose, and again plunged in a swoop of horror. He lay against the wall inert as if dead, inert, at peace, save for one deep core of anxiety, which knew that it was *not* all over, that he was still high in space against the wall. But the chief effort of will was gone.

There came into his consciousness a small, foreign sensation. He woke up a little. What was it? Then slowly it penetrated him. His water had run down his leg. He lay there, clinging, still with shame, half conscious of the echo of the sergeant's voice thundering from below. He waited, in depth of shame beginning to recover himself. He had been shamed so deeply. Then he could go on, for his fear for himself was conquered. His shame was known and published. He must go on.

Slowly he began to grope for the rung above, when a great shock shook through him. His wrists were grasped from above, he was being hauled out of himself up, up to the safe ground. Like a sack he was dragged over the edge of the earthworks by large hands, and landed there on his knees, grovelling in the grass to recover command of himself, to rise up on his feet.

Shame, blind shame and ignominy overthrew his spirit and left it writhing. He stood there shrunk over himself, trying to obliterate himself.

Then the presence of the officer who had hauled him up made itself felt upon him. He heard the panting of the elder man, and then the voice came down on his veins like a fierce whip. He shrank in tension of shame.

'Put up your head – eyes front,' shouted the enraged sergeant, and mechanically the soldier obeyed the command, forced to look into the eyes of the sergeant. The brutal, hanging face of the officer violated the youth. He hardened himself with all his might from seeing it. The tearing noise of the sergeant's voice continued to lacerate his body.

Suddenly he set back his head, rigid, and his heart leapt to burst. The face had suddenly thrust itself close, all distorted and showing the teeth, the eyes smouldering into him. The breath of the barking words was on his nose and mouth. He stepped aside in revulsion. With a scream the face was upon him again. He raised his arm, involuntarily, in self-defence. A shock of horror went through him, as he felt his forearm hit the face of the officer a brutal blow. The latter staggered, swerved back, and with a curious cry, reeled backwards over the ramparts, his hands clutching the air. There was a second of silence, then a crash to water.

Bachmann, rigid, looked out of his inner silence upon the scene. Soldiers were running.

'You'd better clear,' said one young, excited voice to him. And with immediate instinctive decision he started to walk away from the spot. He went down the tree-hidden path to the high road where the trams ran to and from the town. In his heart was a sense of vindication, of escape. He was leaving it all, the military world, the shame. He was walking away from it.

Officers on horseback rode sauntering down the street, soldiers passed along the pavement. Coming to the bridge, Bachmann crossed over to the town that heaped before him, rising from the flat, picturesque French houses down below at the water's edge, up a jumble of roofs and chasms of streets, to the lovely dark cathedral with its myriad pinnacles making points at the sky.

He felt for the moment quite at peace, relieved from a great strain. So he turned along by the river to the public gardens. Beautiful were the heaped, purple lilac trees upon the green grass, and wonderful the walls of the horse-chestnut trees, lighted like an altar with white flowers on every ledge. Officers went by, elegant and all coloured, women and girls sauntered in the chequered shade. Beautiful it was, he walked in a vision, free.

But where was he going? He began to come out of his trance of delight and liberty. Deep within him he felt the steady burning of shame in the flesh. As yet he could not bear to think of it. But there it was, submerged beneath his attention, the raw, steady-burning shame.

It behoved him to be intelligent. As yet he dared not remember what he had done. He only knew the need to get away, away from everything he had been in contact with.

But now? A great pang of fear went through him. He could not bear his shamed flesh to be put again between the hands of authority. Already the hands had been laid upon him, brutally upon his nakedness, ripping open his shame and making him maimed, crippled in his own control.

Fear became an anguish. Almost blindly he was turning in the direction of the barracks. He could not take the responsibility of himself. He must give himself up to someone. Then his heart, obstinate in hope, became obsessed with the idea of his sweetheart. He would make himself her responsibility.

Blenching as he took courage, he mounted the small, quick-hurrying tram that ran out of the town in the direction of the barracks. He sat motionless and composed, static.

He got out at the terminus and went down the road. A wind was still running. He could hear the faint whisper of the rye, and the stronger swish as a sudden gust was upon it. No one was about. Feeling detached and impersonal, he went down a field-path between the low vines. Many little vine trees rose up in spires, holding out tender pink shoots, waving their tendrils. He saw them distinctly, and wondered over them. In a field a little way off, men and women were taking up the hay. The bullock-wagon stood by on the path, the men in their blue shirts, the women with white cloths over their heads carried hay in their arms to the cart, all brilliant and distinct upon the shorn, glowing green acres. He felt himself looking out of darkness on to the glamorous brilliant beauty of the world around him, outside him.

The Baron's house, where Emilie was maid-servant, stood square and mellow among trees and garden and fields. It was an old French grange. The barracks was quite near. Bachmann walked, drawn by a single purpose, towards the courtyard. He entered the spacious, shadowy, sun-swept place. The dog, seeing a soldier, only jumped and whined for greeting. The pump stood peacefully in a corner, under a lime tree, in the shade.

The kitchen door was open. He hesitated, then walked in, speaking shyly and smiling involuntarily. The two women started, but with pleasure. Emilie was preparing the tray for afternoon coffee. She stood beyond the table, drawn up, startled, and challenging, and glad. She had the proud, timid eyes of some wild animal, some proud animal. Her black hair was closely banded, her grey eyes watched steadily. She wore a peasant dress of blue cotton sprigged with little red roses, that buttoned tight over her strong maiden breasts.

At the table sat another young woman, the nursery governness, who was picking cherries from a huge heap, and dropping them into a bowl. She was young, pretty, freckled.

'Good day!' she said pleasantly. 'The unexpected.'

Emilie did not speak. The flush came in her dark cheek. She stood stood watching, between fear and a desire to escape, and on the other hand joy that kept her in his presence.

'Yes,' he said, bashful and strained, while the eyes of the two women were upon him. 'I've got myself in a mess this time.'

'What?' asked the nursery governess, dropping her hands in her lap. Emilie stood rigid.

Bachmann could not raise his head. He looked sideways at the glistening, ruddy cherries. He could not recover the normal world.

'I knocked Sergeant Huber over the fortifications down into the moat,' he said. 'It was accident – but —'

And he grasped at the cherries, and began to eat them, unknowing, hearing only Emilie's little exclamation.

'You knocked him over the fortifications!' echoed Fräulein Hesse in horror. 'How?'

Spitting the cherry-stones into his hand, mechanically, absorbedly, he told them.

'Ach!' exclaimed Emilie sharply.

'And how did you get here?' asked Fräulein Hesse.

'I ran off,' he said.

There was a dead silence. He stood, putting himself at the mercy of the women. There came a hissing from the stove, and a stronger smell of coffee. Emilie turned swiftly away. He saw her flat, straight back and her strong loins, as she bent over the stove.

'But what are you going to do?' said Fräulein Hesse, aghast.

115

'I don't know,' he said, grasping at more cherries. He had come to an end.

'You'd better go to the barracks,' she said. 'We'll get the Herr Baron to come and see about it.'

Emilie was swiftly and quietly preparing the tray. She picked it up, and stood with the glittering china and silver before her, impassive, waiting for his reply. Bachmann remained with his head dropped, pale and obstinate. He could not bear to go back.

'I'm going to try to get into France,' he said.

'Yes, but they'll catch you,' said Fräulein Hesse.

Emilie watched with steady, watchful grey eyes.

'I can have a try, if I could hide till to-night,' he said.

Both women knew what he wanted. And they all knew it was no good. Emilie picked up the tray, and went out. Bachmann stood with his head dropped. Within himself he felt the dross of shame and incapacity.

'You'd never get away,' said the governess.

'I can try,' he said.

To-day he could not put himself between the hands of the military. Let them do as they liked with him to-morrow, if he escaped to-day.

They were silent. He ate cherries. The colour flushed bright into the cheeks of the young governess.

Emilie returned to prepare another tray.

'He could hide in your room,' the governess said to her.

The girl drew herself away. She could not bear the intrusion.

'That is all I can think of that is safe from the children,' said Fräulein Hesse.

Emilie gave no answer. Bachmann stood waiting for the two women. Emilie did not want the close contact with him.

'You could sleep with me,' Fräulein Hesse said to her.

Emilie lifted her eyes and looked at the young man, direct, clear, reserving herself.

'Do you want that?' she asked, her strong virginity proof against him.

'Yes – yes —' he said uncertainly, destroyed by shame.

She put back her head.

'Yes,' she murmured to herself.

Quickly she filled the tray, and went out.

'But you can't walk over the frontier in a night,' said Fräulein Hesse.

'I can cycle,' he said.

Emilie returned, a restraint, a neutrality in her bearing.

'I'll see if it's all right,' said the governess.

In a moment or two Bachmann was following Emilie through the square hall, where hung large maps on the walls. He noticed a child's blue coat with brass buttons on the peg, and it reminded him of Emilie walking holding the hand of the youngest child, whilst he watched, sitting under the lime tree. Already this was a long way off. That was a sort of freedom he had lost, changed for a new, immediate anxiety.

They went quickly, fearfully up the stairs and down a long corridor. Emilie opened her door, and he entered, ashamed, into her room.

'I must go down,' she murmured, and she departed, closing the door softly.

It was a small, bare, neat room. There was a little dish for holy water, a picture of the Sacred Heart, a crucifix, and a *prie-Dieu*. The small bed lay white and untouched, the wash-hand bowl of red earth stood on a bare table, there was a little mirror and a small chest of drawers. That was all.

Feeling safe, in sanctuary, he went to the window, looking over the courtyard at the shimmering, afternoon country. He was going to leave this land, this life. Already he was in the unknown.

He drew away into the room. The curious simplicity and severity of the little Roman Catholic bedroom was foreign but restoring to him. He looked at the crucifix. It was a long, lean, peasant Christ carved by a peasant in the Black Forest. For the first time in his life Bachmann saw the figure as a human thing. It represented a man hanging there in helpless torture. He stared at it, closely, as if for new knowledge.

Within his own flesh burned and smouldered the restless shame. He could not gather himself together. There was a gap in his soul. The shame within him seemed to displace his strength and his manhood.

He sat down on his chair. The shame, the roused feeling of exposure acted on his brain, made him heavy, unutterably heavy.

Mechanically, his wits all gone, he took off his boots, his belt, his tunic, put them aside, and lay down, heavy, and fell into a kind of drugged sleep.

Emilie came in a little while, and looked at him. But he was sunk in sleep. She saw him lying there inert, and terribly still, and she was afraid. His shirt was unfastened at the throat. She saw his pure white flesh, very clean and beautiful. And he slept inert. His legs, in the blue uniform trousers, his feet in the coarse stockings, lay foreign on her bed. She went away.

III

She was uneasy, perturbed, to her last fibre. She wanted to remain clear, with no touch on her. A wild instinct made her shrink away from any hands which might be laid on her.

She was a foundling, probably of some gipsy race, brought up in a Roman Catholic Rescue Home. A naïve, paganly religious being, she was attached to the Baroness, with whom she had served for seven years, since she was fourteen.

She came into contact with no one, unless it were with Ida Hesse, the governess. Ida was a calculating, good-natured, not very straightforward flirt. She was the daughter of a poor country doctor. Having gradually come into connection with Emilie, more an alliance than an attachment, she put no distinction of grade between the two of them. They worked together, sang together, walked together, and went together to the rooms of Franz Brand, Ida's sweetheart. There the three talked and laughed together, or the women listened to Franz, who was a forester, playing on his violin.

In all this alliance there was no personal intimacy between the young women. Emilie was naturally secluded in herself, of a reserved, native race. Ida used her as a kind of weight to balance her own flighty movement, but the quick, shifty governess, occupied always in her dealings with admirers, did all she could to move the violent nature of Emilie towards some connection with men.

But the dark girl, primitive yet sensitive to a high degree, was fiercely virgin. Her blood flamed with rage when the common soldiers made the long, sucking, kissing noise behind her as she passed. She hated them for their almost jeering offers. She was well protected by the Baroness.

And her contempt of the common men in general was ineffable. But she loved the Baroness, and she revered the Baron, and she was at her ease when she was doing something for the service of a gentleman. Her whole nature was at peace in the service of real masters or mistresses. For her, a gentleman had some mystic quality that left her free and proud in service. The common soldiers were brutes, merely nothing. Her desire was to serve.

She held herself aloof. When, on Sunday afternoon, she had looked through the windows of the Reichshalle in passing, and had seen the soldiers dancing with the common girls, a cold revulsion and anger had possessed her. She could not bear to see the soldiers taking off their belts and pulling open their tunics, dancing with their shirts showing through the open, sagging tunic, their movements gross, their faces transfigured and sweaty, their coarse hands holding their coarse girls under the arm-pits, drawing the female up to their breasts. She hated to see them clutched breast to breast, the legs of the men moving grossly in the dance.

At evening, when she had been in the garden, and heard on the other side of the hedge the sexual, inarticulate cries of the girls in the embraces of the soldiers, her anger had been too much for her, and she had cried, loud and cold:

'What are you doing there, in the hedge?'

She would have had them whipped.

But Bachmann was not quite a common soldier. Fräulein Hesse had found out about him, and had drawn him and Emilie together. For he was a handsome, blond youth, erect and walking with a kind of pride, unconscious yet clear. Moreover, he came of a rich farming stock, rich for many generations. His father was dead, his mother controlled the moneys for the time being. But if Bachmann wanted a hundred pounds at any moment, he could have them. By trade he, with one of his brothers, was a wagon-builder. The family had the farming, smithy, and wagon-building of their village. They worked because that was the form of life they knew. If they had chosen, they could have lived independent upon their means.

In this way, he was a gentleman in sensibility, though his intellect was not developed. He could afford to pay freely for things. He had, moveover, his native, fine breeding. Emilie wavered uncertainly before him. So he became her sweetheart, and she hungered after him. But she was virgin, and shy, and needed to be in subjection, because she was primitive and had no grasp on civilised forms of living, nor on civilised purposes.

IV

At six o'clock came the inquiry of the soldiers: Had anything been seen of Bachmann? Fräulein Hesse answered, pleased to be playing a rôle:

'No, I've not seen him since Sunday – have you, Emilie?'

'No, I haven't seen him,' said Emilie, and her awkwardness was

119

construed as bashfulness. Ida Hesse, stimulated, asked questions, and played her part.

'But it hasn't killed Sergeant Huber?' she cried in consternation.

'No. He fell into the water. But it gave him a bad shock, and smashed his foot on the side of the moat. He's in hospital. It's a bad look-out for Bachmann.'

Emilie, implicated and captive, stood looking on. She was no longer free, working with all this regulated system which she could not understand and which was almost god-like to her. She was put out of her place. Bachmann was in her room, she was no longer the faithful in service serving with religious surety.

Her situation was intolerable to her. All evening long the burden was upon her, she could not live. The children must be fed and put to sleep. The Baron and Baroness were going out, she must give them light refreshment. The man-servant was coming in to supper after returning with the carriage. And all the while she had the insupportable feeling of being out of the order, self-responsible, bewildered. The control of her life should come from those above her, and she should move within that control. But now she was out of it, uncontrolled and troubled. More than that, the man, the lover, Bachmann, who was he, what was he? He alone of all men contained for her the unknown quality which terrified her beyond her service. Oh, she had wanted him as a distant sweetheart, not close, like this, casting her out of her world.

When the Baron and Baroness had departed, and the young man-servant had gone out to enjoy himself, she went upstairs to Bachmann. He had wakened up, and sat dimly in the room. Out in the open he heard the soldiers, his comrades, singing the sentimental songs of the nightfall, the drone of the concertina rising in accompaniment.

> *'Wenn ich zu mei ... nem Kinde geh' ...*
> *In seinem Au ... g die Mutter seh' ....'*

But he himself was removed from it now. Only the sentimental cry of young, unsatisfied desire in the soldiers' singing penetrated his blood and stirred him subtly. He let his head hang; he had become gradually roused: and he waited in concentration, in another world.

The moment she entered the room where the man sat alone, waiting intensely, the thrill passed through her, she died in terror, and after the death, a great flame gushed up, obliterating her. He sat in trousers and shirt on the side of the bed. He looked up as she came in, and she

120

shrank from his face. She could not bear it. Yet she entered near to him.

'Do you want anything to eat?' she said.

'Yes,' he answered, and she stood in the twilight of the room with him, he could only hear his heart beat heavily. He saw her apron just level with his face. She stood silent, a little distance off, as if she would be there for ever. He suffered.

As if in a spell she waited, standing motionless and looming there, he sat rather crouching on the side of the bed. A second will in him was powerful and dominating. She drew gradually nearer to him, coming up slowly, as if unconscious. His heart beat up swfitly. He was going to move.

As she came quite close, almost invisibly he lifted his arms and put them round her waist, drawing her with his will and desire. He buried his face into her apron, into the terrible softness of her belly. And he was a flame of passion intense about her. He had forgotten. Shame and memory were gone in a whole, furious flame of passion.

She was quite helpless. Her hands leapt, fluttered, and closed over his head, pressing it deeper into her belly, vibrating as she did so. And his arms tightened on her, his hands spread over her loins, warm as flame on her loveliness. In was intense anguish of bliss for her, and she lost consciousness.

When she recovered, she lay translated in the peace of satisfaction.

It was what she had had no inkling of, never known could be. She was strong with eternal gratitude. And he was there with her. Instinctively with an instinct of reverence and gratitude, her arms tightened in a little embrace upon him who held her thoroughly embraced.

And he was restored and completed, close to her. That little, twitching, momentary clasp of acknowledgment that she gave him in her satisfaction, roused his pride unconquerable. They loved each other, and all was whole. She loved him, he had taken her, she was given to him. It was right. He was given to her, and they were one, complete.

Warm, with a glow in their hearts and faces, they rose again, modest, but transfigured with happiness.

'I will get you something to eat,' she said, and in joy and security of service again, she left him, making a curious little homage of departure. He sat on the side of the bed, escaped, liberated, wondering, and happy.

V

Soon she came again with the tray, followed by Fräulein Hesse. The two women watched him eat, watching the pride and wonder of his being, as he sat there blond and naïve again. Emilie felt rich and complete. Ida was a lesser thing than herself.

'And what are you going to do?' asked Fräulein Hesse, jealous.

'I must get away,' he said.

But words had no meaning for him. What did it matter? He had the inner satisfaction and liberty.

'But you'll want a bicycle,' said Ida Hesse.

'Yes,' he said.

Emilie sat silent, removed and yet with him, connected with him in passion. She looked from this talk of bicycles and escape.

They discussed plans. But in two of them was the one will, that Bachmann should stay with Emilie. Ida Hesse was an outsider.

It was arranged, however, that Ida's lover should put out his bicycle, leave it at the hut where he sometimes watched. Bachmann should fetch it in the night, and ride into France. The hearts of all three beat hot in suspense, driven to thought. They sat in a fire of agitation.

Then Bachmann would get away to America, and Emilie would come and join him. They would be in a fine land then. The tale burned up again.

Emilie and Ida had to go round to Franz Brand's lodging. They departed with slight leave-taking. Bachmann sat in the dark, hearing the bugle for retreat sound out of the night. Then he remembered his post card to his mother. He slipped out after Emilie, gave it her to post. His manner was careless and victorious, hers shining and trustful. He slipped back to shelter.

There he sat on the side of the bed, thinking. Again he went over the events of the afternoon, remembering his own anguish of apprehension because he had known he could not climb the wall without fainting with fear. Still, a flush of shame came alight in him at the memory. But he said to himself: 'What does it matter? – I can't help it, well then I can't. If I go up a height, I get absolutely weak, and can't help myself.' Again memory came over him, and a gush of shame, like fire. But he sat and endured it. It had to be endured, admitted, and accepted. 'I'm not a coward, for all that,' he continued. 'I'm not afraid of danger. If I'm made that way, that heights melt me and make me let go my water' – it was torture for him to pluck at this truth – 'if I'm made like that, I shall have to abide by it, that's all. It isn't all of me.' He thought of Emilie, and was satisfied. 'What I am, I am; and let it be enough,' he thought.

Having accepted his own defect, he sat thinking, waiting for Emilie, to tell her. She came at length, saying that Franz could not arrange about his bicycle this night. It was broken. Bachmann would have to stay over another day.

They were both happy. Emilie, confused before Ida, who was excited and prurient, came again to the young man. She was stiff and dignified with an agony of unusedness. But he took her between his hands, and uncovered her, and enjoyed almost like madness her helpless, virgin body that suffered so strongly, and that took its joy so deeply. While the moisture of torment and modesty was still in her eyes, she clasped him closer, and closer, to the victory and the deep satisfaction of both of them. And they slept together, he in repose still satisfied and peaceful, and she lying close in her static reality.

VI

In the morning, when the bugle sounded from the barracks they rose and looked out of the window. She loved his body that was proud and blond and able to take command. And he loved her body that was soft and eternal. They looked at the faint grey vapour of summer steaming off from the greenness and ripeness of the fields. There was no town anywhere, their look ended in the haze of the summer morning. Their bodies rested together, their minds tranquil. Then a little anxiety stirred in both of them from the sound of the bugle. She was called back to her old position, to realise the world of authority she did not understand but had wanted to serve. But this call died away again from her. She had all.

She went downstairs to her work, curiously changed. She was in a new world of her own, that she had never even imagined, and which was the land of promise for all that. In this she moved and had her being. And she extended it to her duties. She was curiously happy and absorbed. She had not to strive out of herself to do her work. The doing came from within her without call or command. It was a delicious outflow, like sunshine, the activity that flowed from her and put her tasks to rights.

Bachmann sat busily thinking. He would have to get all his plans ready. He must write to his mother, and she must send him money to Paris. He would go to Paris, and from thence, quickly, to America. It had to be done. He must make all preparations. The dangerous part was the getting into France. He thrilled in anticipation. During the day he would need a time-table of the trains going to Paris – he would need to think. It gave him delicious pleasure, using all his wits. It seemed such an adventure.

This one day, and he would escape then into freedom. What an agony of need he had for absolute, imperious freedom. He had won to his own being, in himself and Emilie, he had drawn the stigma from his shame, he was beginning to be himself. And now he wanted madly to be free to go on. A home, his work, and absolute freedom to move and to be, in her, with her, this was his passionate desire. He thought in a kind of ecstasy, living an hour of painful intensity.

Suddenly he heard voices, and a tramping of feet. His heart gave a great leap, then went still. He was taken. He had known all along. A complete silence filled his body and soul, a silence like death, a suspension of life and sound. He stood motionless in the bedroom, in perfect suspension.

Emilie was busy passing swiftly about the kitchen preparing the children's breakfasts when she heard the tramp of feet and the voice of the Baron. The latter had come in from the garden, and was wearing an old green linen suit. He was a man of middle stature, quick, finely made, and of whimsical charm. His right hand had been shot in the Franco-Prussian war, and now, as always when he was much agitated, he shook it down at his side, as if it hurt. He was talking rapidly to a young, stiff ober-leutnant. Two private soldiers stood bearishly in the doorway.

Emilie, shocked out of herself, stood pale and erect, recoiling.

'Yes, if you think so, we can look,' the Baron was hastily and irascibly saying.

'Emilie,' he said, turning to the girl, 'did you put a post card to the mother of this Bachmann in the box last evening?'

Emilie stood erect and did not answer.

'Yes?' said the Baron sharply.

'Yes, Herr Baron,' replied Emilie, neutral.

The Baron's wounded hand shook rapidly in exasperation. The lieutenant drew himself up still more stiffly. He was right.

'And do you know anything of the fellow?' asked the Baron looking at her with his blazing, greyish-golden eyes. The girl looked back at him steadily, dumb, but her whole soul naked before him. For two seconds he looked at her in silence. Then in silence, ashamed and furious, he turned away.

'Go up!' he said, with his fierce, peremptory command, to the young officer.

The lieutenant gave his order, in military cold confidence, to the soldiers. They all tramped across the hall. Emilie stood motionless, her life suspended.

The Baron marched swiftly upstairs and down the corridor, the lieutenant and the common soldiers followed. The Baron flung open the door of Emilie's room, and looked at Bachmann, who stood watching, standing in shirt and trousers beside the bed, fronting the door. He was perfectly still. His eyes met the furious, blazing look of the Baron. The latter shook his wounded hand, and then went still. He looked into the eyes of the soldier, steadily. He saw the same naked soul exposed, as if he looked really into the *man*. And the man was helpless, the more helpless for his singular nakedness.

'Ha!' he exclaimed impatiently, turning to the approaching lieutenant.

The latter appeared in the doorway. Quickly his eyes travelled over the bare-footed youth. He recognised him as his object. He gave the brief command to dress.

Bachmann turned round for his clothes. He was very still, silent in himself. He was in an abstract, motionless world. That the two gentlemen and the two soldiers stood watching him, he scarcely realised. They could not see him.

Soon he was ready. He stood at attention. But only the shell of his body was at attention. A curious silence, a blankness, like something eternal, possessed him. He remained true to himself.

The lieutenant gave the order to march. The little procession went down the stairs with careful, respectful tread, and passed through the hall to the kitchen. There Emilie stood with her face uplifted, motionless and expressionless. Bachmann did not look at her. They knew each other. They were themselves. Then the little file of men passed out into the courtyard.

The Baron stood in the doorway watching the four figures in uniform pass through the chequered shadows under the lime trees. Bachmann was walking neutralised, as if he were not there. The lieutenant went brittle and long, the two soldiers lumbered beside. They passed out into the sunny morning, growing smaller, going towards the barracks.

The Baron turned into the kitchen. Emilie was cutting bread.

'So he stayed the night here?' he said.

The girl looked at him, scarcely seeing. She was too much herself. The Baron saw the dark, naked soul of her body in her unseeing eyes.

'What were you going to do?' he asked.

'He was going to America,' she replied, in a still voice.

'Pah! You should have sent him straight back,' fired the Baron.

Emilie stood at his bidding, untouched.

'He's done for now,' he said.

But he could not bear the dark, deep nakedness of her eyes, that scarcely changed under this suffering.

'Nothing but a fool,' he repeated, going away in agitation, and preparing himself for what he could do.

DAUGHTERS OF THE VICAR

I

MR. LINDLEY was first vicar of Aldecross. The cottages of this tiny hamlet had nestled in peace since their beginning, and the country folk had crossed the lanes and farm-land, two or three miles, to the parish church at Greymeed, on the bright Sunday mornings.

But when the pits were sunk, blank rows of dwellings started up beside the high roads, and a new population, skimmed from the floating scum of workmen, was filled in, the cottages and the country people almost obliterated.

To suit the convenience of these new collier-inhabitants, a church must be built at Aldecross. There was not too much money. And so the little building crouched like a humped stone-and-mortar mouse, with two little turrets at the west corners for ears, in the fields near the cottages and the apple trees, as far as possible from the dwellings down the high road. It had an uncertain, timid look about it. And so they planted big-leaved ivy, to hide its shrinking newness. So that now the little church stands buried in its greenery, stranded and sleeping among the fields, while the brick houses elbow nearer and nearer, threatening to crush it down. It is already obsolete.

The Reverend Ernest Lindley, aged twenty-seven, and newly married, came from his curacy in Suffolk to take charge of his church. He was just an ordinary young man, who had been to Cambridge and taken orders. His wife was a self-assured young woman, daughter of a Cambridgeshire rector. Her father had spent the whole of his thousand a year, so that Mrs. Lindley had nothing of her own. Thus the young married people came to Aldecross to live on a stipend of about a hundred and twenty pounds, and to keep up a superior position.

They were not very well received by the new, raw, disaffected population of colliers. Being accustomed to farm labourers, Mr. Lindley had considered himself as belonging indisputably to the upper or ordering classes. He had to be humble to the county families, but still, he was of their kind, whilst the common people were something different. He had no doubts of himself.

127

He found, however, that the collier population refused to accept this arrangement. They had no use for him in their lives, and they told him so, callously. The women merely said: 'they were throng,' or else: 'Oh, it's no good you coming here, we're Chapel.' The men were quite good-humoured so long as he did not touch them too nigh, they were cheerfully contemptuous of him, with a preconceived contempt he was powerless against.

At last, passing from indignation to silent resentment, even, if he dared have acknowledged it, to conscious hatred of the majority of his flock, and unconscious hatred of himself, he confined his activities to a narrow round of cottages, and he had to submit. He had no particular character, having always depended on his position in society to give him position among men. Now he was so poor, he had no social standing even among the common vulgar tradespeople of the district, and he had not the nature nor the wish to make his society agreeable to them, nor the strength to impose himself where he would have liked to be recognised. He dragged on, pale and miserable and neutral.

At first his wife raged with mortification. She took on airs and used a high hand. But her income was too small, the wrestling with tradesmen's bills was too pitiful, she only met with general, callous ridicule when she tried to be impressive.

Wounded to the quick of her pride. she found herself isolated in an indifferent, callous population. She raged indoors and out. But soon she learned that she must pay too heavily for her outdoor rages, and then she only raged within the walls of the rectory. There her feeling was so strong that she frightened herself. She saw herself hating her husband, and she knew that, unless she were careful, she would smash her form of life and bring catastrophe upon him and upon herself. So in very fear she went quiet. She hid, bitter and beaten by fear, behind the only shelter she had in the world, her gloomy, poor parsonage.

Children were born one every year; almost mechanically, she continued to perform her maternal duty, which was forced upon her. Gradually, broken by the suppressing of her violent anger and misery and disgust, she became an invalid and took to her couch.

The children grew up healthy, but unwarmed and rather rigid. Their father and mother educated them at home, made them very proud and very genteel, put them definitely and cruelly in the upper classes, apart from the vulgar around them. So they lived quite isolated. They were good-looking, and had that curiously clean, semi-transparent look of the genteel, isolated and poor.

Gradually Mr. and Mrs. Lindley lost all hold on life, and spent their hours, weeks, and years merely haggling to make ends meet, and bitterly repressing and pruning their children into gentility, urging them to ambition, weighting them with duty. On Sunday morning the whole family, except the mother, went down the lane to church, the long-legged girls in skimpy frocks, the boys in black coats and long, grey, unfitting trousers. They passed by their father's parishioners with mute clear faces, childish mouths closed in pride that was like a doom to them, and childish eyes already unseeing. Miss Mary, the eldest, was the leader. She was a long, slim thing with a fine profile and a proud, pure look of submission to a high fate. Miss Louisa, the second, was short and plump and obstinate-looking. She had more enemies than ideals. She looked after the lesser children, Miss Mary after the elder. The collier children watched the pale, distinguished procession of the vicar's family pass mutely by, and they were impressed by the air of gentility and distance, they made mock of the trousers of the small sons, they felt inferior in themselves, and hate stirred their hearts.

In her time, Miss Mary received as governess a few little daughters of tradesmen; Miss Louisa managed the house and went among her father's church-goers, giving lessons on the piano to the colliers' daughters at thirteen shillings for twenty-six lessons.

II

One winter morning, when his daughter Mary was about twenty years old, Mr. Lindley, a thin, unobtrusive figure in his black overcoat and his wideawake, went down into Aldecross with a packet of white papers under his arm. He was delivering the parish almanacs.

A rather pale, neutral man of middle age, he waited while the train thumped over the level-crossing, going up to the pit which rattled busily just along the line. A wooden-legged man hobbled to open the gate, Mr. Lindley passed on. Just at his left hand, below the road and the railway, was the red roof of a cottage, showing through the bare twigs of apple trees. Mr. Lindley passed round the low wall, and descended the worn steps that led from the highway down to the cottage which crouched darkly and quietly away below the rumble of passing trains and the clank of coal-carts, in a quiet little underworld of its own. Snowdrops with tight-shut buds were hanging very still under the bare currant bushes.

The clergyman was just going to knock when he heard a clinking noise, and turning saw through the open door of a black shed just behind him an elderly woman in a black lace cap stooping among reddish big cans, pouring a very bright liquid into a tundish. There was a smell of paraffin. The woman put down her can, took the tundish and laid it on a shelf, then rose with a tin bottle. Her eyes met those of the clergyman.

'Oh, is it you, Mr. Lin'ley!' she said, in a complaining tone. 'Go in.'

The minister entered the house. In the hot kitchen sat a big, elderly man with a great grey beard, taking snuff. He grunted in a deep, muttering voice, telling the minister to sit down, and then took no more notice of him, but stared vacantly into the fire. Mr. Lindley waited.

The woman came in, the ribbons of her black lace cap, or bonnet, hanging on her shawl. She was of medium stature, everything about her was tidy. She went up a step out of the kitchen, carrying the paraffin-tin. Feet were heard entering the room up the step. It was a little haberdashery shop, with parcels on the shelves of the walls, a big, old-fashioned sewing-machine with tailor's work lying round it, in the open space. The woman went behind the counter, gave the child who had entered the paraffin-bottle, and took from her a jug.

'My mother says shall yer put it down,' said the child, and she was gone. The woman wrote in a book, then came into the kitchen with her jug. The husband, a very large man, rose and brought more coal to the already hot fire. He moved slowly and sluggishly. Already he was going dead; being a tailor, his large form had become an encumbrance to him. In his youth he had been a great dancer and boxer. Now he was taciturn, and inert. The minister had nothing to say, so he sought for his phrases. But John Durant took no notice, existing silent and dull.

Mrs. Durant spread the cloth. Her husband poured himself beer into a mug, and began to smoke and drink.

'Shall you have some?' he growled through his beard at the clergyman, looking slowly from the man to the jug, capable of this one idea.

'No, thank you,' replied Mr. Lindley, though he would have liked some beer. He must set the example in a drinking parish.

'We need a drop to keep us going,' said Mrs. Durant.

She had rather a complaining manner. The clergyman sat on uncomfortably while she laid the table for the half-past ten lunch. Her husband drew up to eat. She remained in her little round arm-chair by the fire.

She was a woman who would have liked to be easy in her life, but to whose lot had fallen a rough and turbulent family, and a slothful husband who did not care what became of himself or anybody. So, her rather good-looking square face was peevish, she had that air of having been compelled all her life to serve unwillingly, and to control where she did not want to control. There was about her, too, that masterful aplomb of a woman who has brought up and ruled her sons: but even them she had ruled unwillingly. She had enjoyed managing her little haberdashery shop, riding in the carrier's cart to Nottingham, going through the big warehouses to buy her goods. But the fret of managing her sons she did not like. Only she loved her youngest boy, because he was her last, and she saw herself free.

This was one of the houses the clergyman visited occasionally. Mrs. Durant, as part of her regulation, had brought up all her sons in the Church. Not that she had any religion. Only, it was what she was used to. Mr. Durant was without religion. He read the fervently evangelical *Life of John Wesley* with a curious pleasure, getting from it a satisfaction as from the warmth of the fire, or a glass of brandy. But he cared no more about John Wesley, in fact, than about John Milton, of whom he had never heard.

Mrs. Durant took her chair to the table.

'I don't feel like eating,' she sighed.

'Why – aren't you well?' asked the clergyman, patronising.

'It isn't that,' she sighed. She sat with shut, straight mouth. 'I don't know what's going to become of us.'

But the clergyman had ground himself down so long that he could not easily sympathise.

'Have you any trouble?' he asked.

'Ay, have I any trouble!' cried the elderly woman. 'I shall end my days in the workhouse.'

The minister waited unmoved. What could she know of poverty in her little house of plenty!

'I hope not,' he said.

'And the one lad as I wanted to keep by me —' she lamented.

The minister listened without sympathy, quite neutral.

'And the lad as would have been a support to my old age! What is going to become of us?' she said.

The clergyman, justly, did not believe in the cry of poverty, but wondered what had become of the son.

'Has anything happened to Alfred?' he asked.

'We've got word he's gone for a Queen's sailor,' she said sharply.

'He has joined the Navy!' exclaimed Mr. Lindley. 'I think he could scarcely have done better – to serve his Queen and country on the sea . . .'

'He is wanted to serve *me*,' she cried. 'And I wanted my lad at home.'

Alfred was her baby, her last, whom she had allowed herself the luxury of spoiling.

'You will miss him,' said Mr. Lindley, 'that is certain. But this is no regrettable step for him to have taken – on the contrary.'

'That's easy for you to say, Mr. Lindley,' she replied tartly. 'Do you think I want my lad climbing ropes at another man's bidding, like a monkey —'

'There is no *dishonour*, surely, in serving in the Navy?'

'Dishonour this dishonour that,' cried the angry old woman. 'He goes and makes a slave of himself, and he'll rue it.'

Her angry, scornful impatience nettled the clergyman, and silenced him for some moments.

'I do not see,' he retorted at last, white at the gills and inadequate, 'that the Queen's service is any more to be called slavery than working in a mine.'

'At home he was at home, and his own master. *I* know he'll find a difference.'

'It may be the making of him,' said the clergyman. 'It will take him away from bad companionship and drink.'

Some of the Durants' sons were notorious drinkers, and Alfred was not quite steady.

'And why indeed shouldn't he have his glass?' cried the mother. 'He picks no man's pocket to pay for it!'

Ther clergyman stiffened at what he thought was an allusion to his own profession, and his unpaid bills.

'With all due consideration, I am glad to hear he has joined the Navy,' he said.

'Me with my old age coming on, and his father working very little! I'd thank you to be glad about something else besides that, Mr. Lindley.'

The woman began to cry. Her husband, quite impassive, finished his lunch of meat-pie, and drank some beer. Then he turned to the fire, as if there were no one in the room but himself.

'I shall respect all men who serve God and their country on the sea, Mrs. Durant,' said the clergyman stubbornly.

'That is very well, when they're not your sons who are doing the dirty work. It makes a difference,' she replied tartly.

'I should be proud if one of my sons were to enter the Navy.'

'Ay – well – we're not all of us made alike —'

The minister rose. He put down a large folded paper.

'I've brought the almanac,' he said.

Mrs. Durant unfolded it.

'I do like a bit of colour in things,' she said, petulantly.

The clergyman did not reply.

'There's that envelope for the organist's fund —' said the old woman, and rising, she took the thing from the mantelpiece, went into the shop, and returned sealing it up.

'Which is all I can afford,' she said.

Mr. Lindley took his departure, in his pocket the envelope containing Mrs. Durant's offering for Miss Louisa's services. He went from door to door delivering the almanacs, in dull routine. Jaded with the monotony of the business, and with the repeated effort of greeting half-known people, he felt barren and rather irritable. At last he returned home.

In the dining-room was a small fire. Mrs. Lindley, growing very stout, lay on her couch. The vicar carved the cold mutton: Miss Louisa, short and plump and rather flushed, came in from the kitchen; Miss Mary, dark, with a beautiful white brow and grey eyes, served the vegetables; the children chattered a little, but not exuberantly. The very air seemed starved.

'I went to the Durants,' said the vicar, as he served out small portions of mutton; 'it appears Alfred has run away to join the Navy.'

'Do him good,' came the rough voice of the invalid.

Miss Louisa, attending to the youngest child, looked up in protest.

'Why has he done that?' asked Mary's low, musical voice.

'He wanted some excitement, I suppose,' said the vicar. 'Shall we say grace?'

The children were arranged, all bent their heads, grace was pronounced, at the last word every face was being raised to go on with the interesting subject.

'He's just done the right thing, for once,' came the rather deep voice of the mother; 'save him from becoming a drunken sot, like the rest of them.'

'They're not *all* drunken, mama,' said Miss Louisa, stubbornly.

'It's no fault of their upbringing if they're not. Walter Durant is a standing disgrace.'

133

'As I told Mrs. Durant,' said the vicar, eating hungrily, 'it is the best thing he could have done. It will take him away from temptation during the most dangerous years of his life – how old is he – nineteen?'

'Twenty,' said Miss Louisa.

'Twenty!' repeated the vicar. 'It will give him wholesome discipline and set before him some sort of standard of duty and honour – nothing could have been better for him. But —'

'We shall miss him from the choir,' said Miss Louisa, as if taking opposite sides to her parents.

'That is as it may be,' said the vicar. 'I prefer to know he is safe in the Navy than running the risk of getting into bad ways here.'

'Was he getting into bad ways?' asked the stubborn Miss Louisa.

'You know, Louisa, he wasn't quite what he used to be,' said Miss Mary gently and steadily. Miss Louisa shut her rather heavy jaw sulkily. She wanted to deny it, but she knew it was true.

For her he had been a laughing, warm lad, with something kindly and something rich about him. He had made her feel warm. It seemed the days would be colder since he had gone.

'Quite the best thing he could do,' said the mother with emphasis.

'I think so,' said the vicar. 'But his mother was almost abusive because I suggested it.'

He spoke in an injured tone.

'What does she care for her children's welfare?' said the invalid. 'Their wages is all her concern.'

'I suppose she wanted him at home with her,' said Miss Louisa.

'Yes, she did – at the expense of his learning to be a drunkard like the rest of them,' retorted her mother.

'George Durant doesn't drink,' defended her daughter.

'Because he got burned so badly when he was nineteen – in the pit – and that frightened him. The Navy is a better remedy than that, at least.'

'Certainly,' said the vicar. 'Certainly.'

And to this Miss Louisa agreed. Yet she could not but feel angry that he had gone away for so many years. She herself was only nineteen.

III

It happened when Miss Mary was twenty-three years old that Mr. Lindley was very ill. The family was exceedingly poor at the time, such a lot of money was needed, so little was forthcoming. Neither Miss Mary nor Miss Louisa had suitors. What chance had they? They met no eligible young men in Aldecross. And what they earned was a mere drop in a void. The girls' hearts were chilled and hardened with fear of this perpetual, cold penury, this narrow struggle, this horrible nothingness of their lives.

A clergyman had to be found for the church work. It so happened the son of an old friend of Mr. Lindley's was waiting three months before taking up his duties. He would come and officiate, for nothing. The young clergyman was keenly expected. He was not more than twenty-seven, a Master of Arts of Oxford, had written his thesis on Roman Law. He came of an old Cambridgeshire family, had some private means, was going to take a church in Northamptonshire with a good stipend, and was not married. Mrs. Lindley incurred new debts, and scarcely regretted her husband's illness.

But when Mr. Massy came there was a shock of disappointment in the house. They had expected a young man with a pipe and a deep voice, but with better manners than Sidney, the eldest of the Lindleys. There arrived instead a small, *chétif* man, scarcely larger than a boy of twelve, spectacled, timid in the extreme, without a word to utter at first; yet with a certain inhuman self-sureness.

'What a little abortion!' was Mrs. Lindley's exclamation to herself on first seeing him, in his buttoned-up clerical coat. And for the first time for many days she was profoundly thankful to God that all her children were decent specimens.

He had not normal powers of perception. They soon saw that he lacked the full range of human feelings, but had rather a strong philosophical mind, from which he lived. His body was almost unthinkable, in intellect he was something definite. The conversation at once took a balanced, abstract tone when he participated. There was no spontaneous exclamation, no violent assertion or expression of personal conviction, but all cold, reasonable assertion. This was very hard on Mrs. Lindley. The little man would look at her, after one of her pronouncements, and then give, in his thin voice, his own calculated version, so that she felt as if she were tumbling into thin air through a hole in the flimsy floor on which their conversation stood. It was she who felt a fool. Soon she was reduced to a hardy silence.

Still, at the back of her mind, she remembered that he was an unattached gentleman, who would shortly have an income altogether of six or seven hundred a year. What did the man matter, if there were pecun-

135

iary ease! The man was a trifle thrown in. After twenty-two years her sentimentality was ground away, and only the millstone of poverty mattered to her. So she supported the little man as a representative of a decent income.

His most irritating habit was that of a sneering little giggle, all on his own, which came when he perceived or related some illogical absurdity on the part of another person. It was the only form of humour he had. Stupidity in thinking seemed to him exquisitely funny. But any novel was unintelligibly meaningless and dull, and to an Irish sort of humour he listened curiously, examining it like mathematics, or else simply not hearing. In normal human relationship he was not there. Quite unable to take part in simple everyday talk, he padded, silently round the house, or sat in the dining-room looking nervously from side to side, always apart in a cold, rarefied little world of his own. Sometimes he made an ironic remark, that did not seem humanly relevant, or he gave his little laugh, like a sneer. He had to defend himself and his own insufficiency. And he answered questions grudgingly, with a yes or no, because he did not see their import and was nervous. It seemed to Miss Louisa he scarcely distinguished one person from another, but that he liked to be near to her, or to Miss Mary, for some sort of contact which stimulated him unknown.

Apart from all this, he was the most admirable workman. He was unremittingly shy, but perfect in his sense of duty: as far as he could conceive Christianity, he was a perfect Christian. Nothing that he realised he could do for anyone did he leave undone, although he was so incapable of coming into contact with another being that he could not proffer help. Now he attended assiduously to the sick man, investigated all the affairs of the parish or the church which Mr. Lindley had in control, straightened out accounts, made lists of the sick and needy, padded round with help and to see what he could do. He heard of Mrs Lindley's anxiety about her sons, and began to investigate means of sending them to Cambridge. His kindness almost frightened Miss Mary. She honoured it so, and yet she shrank from it. For, in it all Mr. Massy seemed to have no sense of any person, any human being whom he was helping: he only realised a kind of mathematical working out, solving of given situations, a calculated well-doing. And it was as if he had accepted the Christian tenets as axioms. His religion consisted in what his scrupulous, abstract mind approved of.

Seeing his acts, Miss Mary must respect and honour him. In consequence she must serve him. To this she had to force herself, shuddering

136

and yet desirous, but he did not perceive it. She accompanied him on his visiting in the parish, and whilst she was cold with admiration for him, often she was touched with pity for the little padding figure with bent shoulders, buttoned up to the chin in his overcoat. She was a handsome, calm girl, tall, with a beautiful repose. Her clothes were poor, and she wore a black silk scarf, having no furs. But she was a lady. As the people saw her walking down Aldecross beside Mr. Massy they said:

'My word, Miss Mary's got a catch. Did you ever see such a sickly little shrimp!'

She knew they were talking so, and it made her heart grow hot against them, and she drew herself as it were protectively towards the little man beside her. At any rate, she could see and give honour to his genuine goodness.

He could not walk fast, or far.

'You have not been well?' she asked, in her dignified way.

'I have an internal trouble.'

He was not aware of her slight shudder. There was silence, whilst she bowed to recover her composure, to resume her gentle manner towards him.

He was fond of Miss Mary. She had made it a rule of hospitality that he should always be escorted by herself or by her sister on his visits in the parish, which were not many. But some mornings she was engaged. Then Miss Louisa took her place. It was no good Miss Louisa's trying to adopt to Mr. Massy an attitude of queenly service. She was unable to regard him save with aversion. When she saw him from behind, thin and bent-shouldered, looking like a sickly lad of thirteen, she disliked him exceedingly, and felt a desire to put him out of existence. And yet a deeper justice in Mary made Louisa humble before her sister.

They were going to see Mr. Durant, who was paralysed and not expected to live. Miss Louisa was crudely ashamed at being admitted to the cottage in company with the little clergyman.

Mrs. Durant was, however, much quieter in the face of her real trouble.

'How is Mr. Durant?' asked Louisa.

'He is no different – and we don't expect him to be,' was the reply. The little clergyman stood looking on.

They went upstairs. The three stood for some time looking at the bed, at the grey head of the old man on the pillow, the grey beard over the sheet. Miss Louisa was shocked and afraid.

'It is so dreadful,' she said, with a shudder.

'It is how I always thought it would be,' replied Mrs. Durant.

Then Miss Louisa was afraid of her. The two women were uneasy, waiting for Mr. Massy to say something. He stood, small and bent, too nervous to speak.

'Has he any understanding?' he asked at length.

'Maybe,' said Mrs. Durant. 'Can you hear, John?' she asked loudly. The dull blue eye of the inert man looked at her feebly.

'Yes, he understands,' said Mrs. Durant to Mr. Massy. Except for the dull look in his eyes, the sick man lay as if dead. The three stood in silence. Miss Louisa was obstinate but heavy-hearted under the load of unlivingness. It was Mr. Massy who kept her there in discipline. His non-human will dominated them all.

Then they heard a sound below, a man's footsteps, and a man's voice called subduedly:

'Are you upstairs, mother?'

Mrs. Durant started and moved to the door. But already a quick, firm step was running up the stairs.

'I'm a bit early, mother,' a troubled voice said, and on the landing they saw the form of the sailor. His mother came and clung to him. She was suddenly aware that she needed something to hold on to. He put his arms round her, and bent over her, kissing her.

'He's not gone, mother?' he asked anxiously, struggling to control his voice.

Miss Louisa looked away from the mother and son who stood together in the gloom on the landing. She could not bear it that she and Mr. Massy should be there. The latter stood nervously, as if ill at ease before the emotion that was running. He was a witness nervous, unwilling, but dispassionate. To Miss Louisa's hot heart it seemed all, all wrong that they should be there.

Mrs. Durant entered the bedroom, her face wet.

'There's Miss Louisa and the vicar,' she said, out of voice and quavering.

Her son, red-faced and slender, drew himself up to salute. But Miss Louisa held out her hand. Then she saw his hazel eyes recognise her for a moment, and his small white teeth showed in a glimpse of the greeting she used to love. She was covered with confusion. He went round to the bed; his boots clicked on the plaster roof, he bowed with dignity.

'How are you, dad?' he said, laying his hand on the sheet, faltering.

138

But the old man stared fixedly and unseeing. The son stood perfectly still for a few minutes, then slowly recoiled. Miss Louisa saw the fine outline of his breast, under the sailor's blue blouse, as his chest began to heave.

'He doesn't know me,' he said, turning to his mother. He gradually went white.

'No, my boy!' cried the mother, pitiful, lifting her face. And suddenly she put her face against his shoulder, he was stooping down to her, holding her against him, and she cried aloud for a moment or two. Miss Louisa saw his sides heaving, and heard the sharp hiss of his breath. She turned away, tears streaming down her face. The father lay inert upon the white bed, Mr. Massy looked queer and obliterated, so little now that the sailor with his sun-burned skin was in the room. He stood waiting. Miss Louisa wanted to die, she wanted to have done. She dared not turn round again to look.

'Shall I offer a prayer?' came the frail voice of the clergyman, and all kneeled down.

Miss Louisa was frightened of the inert man upon the bed. Then she felt a flash of fear of Mr. Massy, hearing his thin, detached voice. And then, calmed, she looked up. On the far side of the bed were the head of the mother and son, the one in the black lace cap, with the small white nape of the neck beneath, the other, with brown, sun-scorched hair too close and wiry to allow of a parting, and neck tanned firm, bowed as if unwillingly. The great grey beard of the old man did not move, the prayer continued. Mr. Massy prayed with a pure lucidity that they all might conform to the higher Will. He was like something that dominated the bowed heads, something dispassionate that governed them inexorably. Miss Louisa was afraid of him. And she was bound, during the course of the prayer, to have a little reverence for him. It was like a foretaste of inexorable, cold death, a taste of pure justice.

That evening she talked to Mary of the visit. Her heart, her veins were possessed by the thought of Alfred Durant as he held his mother in his arms; then the break in his voice, as she remembered it again and again, was like a flame through her; and she wanted to see his face more distinctly in her mind, ruddy with the sun, and his golden-brown eyes, kind and careless, strained now with a natural fear, the fine nose tanned hard by the sun, the mouth that could not help smiling at her. And it went through her with pride, to think of his figure, a fine jet of life.

'He is a handsome lad,' said she to Miss Mary, as if he had not been a year older than herself. Underneath was the deeper dread, almost hatred, of the inhuman being of Mr. Massy. She felt she must protect herself and Alfred from him.

'When I felt Mr. Massy there,' she said, 'I almost hated him. What right had he to be there!'

'Surely he has all right,' said Miss Mary after a pause. 'He is *really* a Christian.'

'He seems to me nearly an imbecile,' said Miss Louisa.

Miss Mary, quiet and beautiful, was silent for a moment:

'Oh, no,' she said. 'Not *imbecile*—'

'Well then – he reminds me of a six months' child – or a five months' child – as if he didn't have time to get developed enough before he was born.'

'Yes,' said Miss Mary, slowly. 'There is something lacking. But there is something wonderful in him: and he is really *good*—'

'Yes,' said Miss Louisa, 'it doesn't seem right that he should be. What right has *that* to be called goodness!'

'But it *is* goodness,' persisted Mary. Then she added, with a laugh: 'And come, you wouldn't deny that as well.'

There was a doggedness in her voice. She went about very quietly. In her soul, she knew what was going to happen. She knew that Mr. Massy was stronger than she, and that she must submit to what he was. Her physical self was prouder, stronger than he, her physical self disliked and despised him. But she was in the grip of his moral, mental being. And she felt the days allotted out to her. And her family watched.

IV

A few days after, old Mr. Durant died. Miss Louisa saw Alfred once more, but he was stiff before her now, treating her not like a person, but as if she were some sort of will in command and he a separate, distinct will waiting in front of her. She had never felt such utter steel-plate separation from anyone. It puzzled her and frightened her. What had become of him? And she hated the military discipline – she was antagonistic to it. Now he was not himself. He was the will which obeys set over against the will which commands. She hesitated over accepting this. He had put himself out of her range. He had ranked himself inferior, subordinate to her. And that was how he could get away from her, that was how he would avoid all connection with her: by fronting her impersonally from the opposite camp, by taking up the abstract position of an inferior.

She went brooding steadily and sullenly over this, brooding and brooding. Her fierce, obstinate heart could not give way. It clung to its own rights. Sometimes she dismissed him. Why should he, her inferior, trouble her?

Then she relapsed to him, and almost hated him. It was his way of getting out of it. She felt the cowardice of it, his calmly placing her in a superior class, and placing himself inaccessibly apart, in an inferior, as if she, the sentient woman who was fond of him, did not count. But she was not going to submit. Dogged in her heart she held on to him.

v

In six months' time Miss Mary had married Mr. Massy. There had been no love-making, nobody had made any remark. But everybody was tense and callous with expectation. When one day Mr. Massy asked for Mary's hand, Mr. Lindley started and trembled from the thin, abstract voice of the little man. Mr. Massy was very nervous, but so curiously absolute.

'I shall be very glad,' said the vicar, 'but of course the decision lies with Mary herself.' And his still feeble hand shook as he moved a Bible on his desk.

The small man, keeping fixedly to his idea, padded out of the room to find Miss Mary. He sat a long time by her, while she made some conversation, before he had readiness to speak. She was afraid of what was coming, and sat stiff in apprehension. She felt as if her body would rise and fling him aside. But her spirit quivered and waited. Almost in expectation she waited, almost wanting him. And then she knew he would speak.

'I have already asked Mr. Lindley,' said the clergyman, while suddenly she looked with aversion at his little knees, 'if he would consent to my proposal.' He was aware of his own disadvantage, but his will was set.

She went cold as she sat, and impervious, almost as if she had become stone. He waited a moment nervously. He would not persuade her. He himself never even heard persuasion, but pursued his own course. He looked at her, sure of himself, unsure of her, and said:

'Will you become my wife, Mary?'

141

Still her heart was hard and cold. She sat proudly.

'I should like to speak to mama first,' she said.

'Very well,' replied Mr. Massy. And in a moment he padded away.

Mary went to her mother. She was cold and reserved.

'Mr. Massy has asked me to marry him, mama,' she said. Mrs. Lindley went on staring at her book. She was cramped in her feeling.

'Well, and what did you say?'

They were both keeping calm and cold.

'I said I would speak to you before answering him.'

This was equivalent to a question. Mrs. Lindley did not want to reply to it. She shifted her heavy form irritably on the couch. Miss Mary sat calm and straight, with closed mouth.

'Your father thinks it would not be a bad match,' said the mother, as if casually.

Nothing more was said. Everybody remained cold and shut-off. Miss Mary did not speak to Miss Louisa, the Reverend Ernest Lindley kept out of sight.

At evening Miss Mary accepted Mr. Massy.

'Yes, I will marry you,' she said, with even a little movement of tenderness towards him. He was embarrassed, but satisfied. She could see him making some movement towards her, could feel the male in him, something cold and triumphant, asserting itself. She sat rigid, and waited.

When Miss Louisa knew, she was silent with bitter anger against everybody, even against Mary. She felt her faith wounded. Did the real things to her not matter after all? She wanted to get away. She thought of Mr. Massy. He had some curious power, some unanswerable right. He was a will that they could not controvert. Suddenly a flush started in her. If he had come to her she would have flipped him out of the room. He was never going to touch *her*. And she was glad. She was glad that her blood would rise and exterminate the little man, if he came too near to her, no matter how her judgment was paralysed by him, no matter how he moved in abstract goodness. She thought she was perverse to be glad, but glad she was. 'I would just flip him out of the room,' she said, and she derived great satisfaction from the open statement. Nevertheless, perhaps she ought still to feel that Mary, on her plane, was a higher being than herself. But then Mary was Mary, and she was Louisa, and that also was inalterable.

Mary, in marrying him, tried to become a pure reason such as he was, without feeling or impulse. She shut herself up, she shut herself rigid against the agonies of shame and the terror of violation which came at first. She *would* not feel, and she *would* not feel. She was a pure will acquiescing to him. She elected a certain kind of fate. She would be good and purely just, she would live in a higher freedom than she had ever known, she would be free of mundane care, she was a pure will towards right. She had sold herself, but she had a new freedom. She had got rid of her body. She had sold a lower thing, her body, for a higher thing, her freedom from material things. She considered that she paid for all she got from her husband. So, in kind of independence, she moved proud and free. She had paid with her body: that was henceforward out of consideration. She was glad to be rid of it. She had bought her position in the world – that henceforth was taken for granted. There remained only the direction of her activity towards charity and high-minded living.

She could scarcely bear other people to be present with her and her husband. Her private life was her shame. But then, she could keep it hidden. She lived almost isolated in the rectory of the tiny village miles from the railway. She suffered as if it were an insult to her own flesh, seeing the repulsion which some people felt for her husband, or the special manner they had of treating him, as if he were a 'case'. But most people were uneasy before him, which restored her pride.

If she had let herself, she would have hated him, hated his padding round the house, his thin voice devoid of human understanding, his bent little shoulders and rather incomplete face that reminded her of an abortion. But rigorously she kept her position. She took care of him and was just to him. There was also a deep, craven fear of him, something slave-like.

There was not much fault to be found with his behaviour. He was scrupulously just and kind according to his lights. But the male in him was cold and self-complete, and utterly domineering. Weak, insufficient little thing as he was, she had not expected this of him. It was something in the bargain she had not understood. It made her hold her head, to keep still. She knew, vaguely, that she was murdering herself. After all, her body was not quite so easy to get rid of. And this manner of disposing of it – ah, sometimes she felt she must rise and bring about death, lift her hand for utter denial of everything, by a general destruction.

He was almost unaware of the conditions about him. He did not fuss in the domestic way, she did as she liked in the house. Indeed, she was a great deal free of him. He would sit obliterated for hours. He was kind, and almost anxiously considerate. But when he considered he was right, his will was just blindly male, like a cold machine. And on most points he was logically right, or he had with him the right of the creed they both accepted. It was so. There was nothing for her to go against.

Then she found herself with child, and felt for the first time horror, afraid before God and man. This also she had to go through – it was the right. When the child arrived, it was a bonny, healthy lad. Her heart hurt in her body, as she took the baby between her hands. The flesh that was trampled and silent in her must speak again in the boy. After all, she had to live – it was not so simple after all. Nothing was finished completely. She looked and looked at the baby, and almost hated it, and suffered an anguish of love for it. She hated it because it made her live again in the flesh, when she *could* not live in the flesh, she could not. She wanted to trample her flesh down, down, extinct, to live in the mind. And now there was this child. It was too cruel, too racking. For she must love the child. Her purpose was broken in two again. She had to become amorphous, purposeless, without real being. As a mother, she was a fragmentary, ignoble thing.

Mr. Massy, blind to everything else in the way of human feeling, became obsessed by the idea of his child. When it arrived, suddenly it filled the whole world of feeling for him. It was his obsession, his terror was for its safety and well-being. It was something new, as if he himself had been born a naked infant, conscious of his own exposure, and full of apprehension. He who had never been aware of anyone else, all his life, now was aware of nothing but the child. Not that he ever played with it, or kissed it, or tended it. He did nothing for it. But it dominated him, it filled, and at the same time emptied his mind. The world was all baby for him.

This his wife must also bear, his question: 'What is the reason that he cries?' – his reminder, at the first sound: 'Mary, that is the child,' – his restlessness if the feeding-time were five minutes past. She had bargained for this – now she must stand by her bargain.

VI

Miss Louisa, at home in the dingy vicarage, had suffered a great deal over her sister's wedding. Having once began to cry out against it, during the engagement, she had been silenced by Mary's quiet: 'I don't agree with you about him, Louisa, I *want* to marry him.' Then Miss

Louisa had been angry deep in her heart, and therefore silent. This dangerous state started the change in her. Her own revulsion made her recoil from the hitherto undoubted Mary.

'I'd beg the streets barefoot first,' said Miss Louisa, thinking of Mr. Massy.

But evidently Mary could perform a different heroism. So she, Louisa the practical, suddenly felt that Mary, her ideal, was questionable after all. How could she be pure – one cannot be dirty in act and spiritual in being. Louisa distrusted Mary's high spirituality. It was no longer genuine for her. And if Mary were spiritual and misguided, why did not her father protect her? Because of the money. He disliked the whole affair, but he backed away, because of the money. And the mother frankly did not care: her daughters could do as they liked. Her mother's pronouncement:

'Whatever happens to *him*, Mary is safe for life,' – so evidently and shallowly a calculation, incensed Louisa.

'I'd rather be safe in the workhouse,' she cried.

'Your father will see to that,' replied her mother brutally. This speech, in its directness, so injured Miss Louisa that she hated her mother deep, deep in her heart, and almost hated herself. It was a long time resolving itself out, this hate. But it worked and worked, and at last the young woman said:

'They are wrong – they are all wrong. They have ground out their souls for what isn't worth anything, and there isn't a grain of love in them anywhere. And I *will* have love. They want us to deny it. They've never found it, so they want to say it doesn't exist. But I *will* have it. I *will* love – it is my birthright. I will love the man I marry – that is all I care about.'

So Miss Louisa stood isolated from everybody. She and Mary had parted over Mr. Massy. In Louisa's eyes, Mary was degraded, married to Mr. Massy. She could not bear to think of her lofty, spiritual sister degraded in the body like this. Mary was wrong, wrong, wrong: she was not superior, she was flawed, incomplete. The two sisters stood apart. They still loved each other, they would love each other as long as they lived. But they had parted ways. A new solitariness came over the obstinate Louisa, and her heavy jaw set stubbornly. She was going on her own way. But which way? She was quite alone, with a blank world before her. How could she be said to have any way? Yet she had her fixed will to love, to have the man she loved.

VII

When her boy was three years old, Mary had another baby, a girl. The three years had gone by monotonously. They might have been an eternity, they might have been brief as a sleep. She did not know. Only, there was always a weight on top of her, something that pressed down her life. The only thing that had happened was that Mr. Massy had had an operation. He was always exceedingly fragile. His wife had soon learned to attend to him mechanically, as part of her duty.

But this third year, after the baby girl had been born, Mary felt oppressed and depressed. Christmas drew near: the gloomy, unleavened Christmas of the rectory, where all the days were of the same dark fabric. And Mary was afraid. It was as if the darkness were coming upon her.

'Edward, I should like to go home for Christmas,' she said, and a certain terror filled her as she spoke.

'But you can't leave baby,' said her husband, blinking.

'We can all go.'

He thought, and started in his collective fashion.

'Why do you wish to go?' he asked.

'Because I need a change. A change would do me good, and it would be good for the milk.'

He heard the will in his wife's voice, and was at a loss. Her language was unintelligible to him. But somehow he felt that Mary was set upon it. And while she was breeding, either about to have a child, or nursing, he regarded her as a special sort of being.

'Wouldn't it hurt baby to take her by the train?' he said.

'No,' replied the mother, 'why should it?'

They went. When they were in the train it began to snow. From the window of his first-class carriage the little clergyman watched the big flakes sweep by, like a blind drawn across the country. He was obsessed by thought of the baby, and afraid of the draughts of the carriage.

'Sit right in the corner,' he said to his wife, 'and hold baby close back.'

She moved at his bidding, and stared out of the window. His eternal presence was like an iron weight on her brain. But she was going partially to escape for a few days.

'Sit on the other side, Jack,' said the father. 'It is less draughty. Come to this window.'

146

He watched the boy in anxiety. But his children were the only beings in the world who took not the slightest notice of him.

'Look, mother, look!' cried the boy. 'They fly right in my face' – he meant the snowflakes.

'Come into this corner,' repeated his father, out of another world.

'He's jumped on this one's back, mother, an' they're riding to the bottom!' cried the boy, jumping with glee.

'Tell him to come on this side,' the little man bade his wife.

'Jack, kneel on this cushion,' said the mother, putting her white hand on the place.

The boy slid over in silence to the place she indicated, waited still for a moment, then almost deliberately, stridently cried:

'Look at all those in the corner, mother, making a heap,' and he pointed to the cluster of snowflakes with finger pressed dramatically on the pane, and he turned to his mother a bit ostentatiously.

'All in a heap!' she said.

He had seen her face, and had her response, and he was somewhat assured. Vaguely uneasy, he was reassured if he could win her attention.

They arrived at the vicarage at half-past two, not having had lunch.

'How are you, Edward?' said Mr. Lindley, trying on his side to be fatherly. But he was always in a false position with his son-in-law, frustrated before him, therefore, as much as possible, he shut his eyes and ears to him. The vicar was looking thin and pale and ill-nourished. He had gone quite grey. He was, however, still haughty; but, since the growing-up of his children, it was a brittle haughtiness, that might break at any moment and leave the vicar only an impoverished, pitiable figure. Mrs. Lindley took all the notice of her daughter, and of the children. She ignored her son-in-law. Miss Louisa was clucking and laughing and rejoicing over the baby. Mr. Massy stood aside, a bent, persistent little figure.

'Oh a pretty! – a little pretty! oh a cold little pretty come in a railway train!' Miss Louisa was cooing to the infant, crouching on the hearth-rug, opening the white woollen wraps and exposing the child to the fireglow.

'Mary,' said the little clergyman, 'I think it would be better to give baby a warm bath; she may take cold.'

'I think it is not necessary,' said the mother, coming and closing her hand judiciously over the rosy feet and hands of the mite. 'She is not chilly.'

'Not a bit,' cried Miss Louisa. 'She's not caught cold.'

'I'll go and bring her flannels,' said Mr. Massy, with one idea.

'I can bath her in the kitchen then,' said Mary, in an altered, cold tone.

'You can't, the girl is scrubbing there,' said Miss Louisa. 'Besides, she doesn't want a bath at this time of day.'

'She'd better have one,' said Mary, quietly, out of submission. Miss Louisa's gorge rose, and she was silent. When the little man padded down with the flannels on his arm, Mrs. Lindley asked:

'Hadn't *you* better take a hot bath, Edward?'

But the sarcasm was lost on the little clergyman. He was absorbed in the preparations round the baby.

The room was dull and threadbare, and the snow outside seemed fairy-like by comparison, so white on the lawn and tufted on the bushes. Indoors the heavy pictures hung obscurely on the walls, everything was dingy with gloom.

Except in the fireglow, where they had laid the bath on the hearth. Mrs. Massy, her black hair always smoothly coiled and queenly, kneeled by the bath, wearing a rubber apron, and holding the kicking child. Her husband stood holding the towels and the flannels to warm. Louisa, too cross to share in the joy of the baby's bath, was laying the table. The boy was hanging on the door-knob, wrestling with it to get out. His father looked round.

'Come away from the door, Jack,' he said ineffectually. Jack tugged harder at the knob as if he did not hear. Mr. Massy blinked at him.

'He must come away from the door, Mary,' he said. 'There will be a draught if it is opened.'

'Jack, come away from the door, dear,' said the mother, dexterously turning the shiny wet baby on to her towelled knee, then glancing round: 'Go and tell Auntie Louisa about the train.'

Louisa, also afraid to open the door, was watching the scene on the hearth. Mr. Massy stood holding the baby's flannel, as if assisting at some ceremonial. If everybody had not been subduedly angry, it would have been ridiculous.

'I want to see out of the window,' Jack said. His father turned hastily.

'Do *you* mind lifting him on to a chair, Louisa,' said Mary hastily. The father was too delicate.

When the baby was flannelled, Mr. Massy went upstairs and returned with four pillows, which he set in the fender to warm. Then he stood watching the mother feed her child, obsessed by the idea of his infant.

Louisa went on with her preparations for the meal. She could not have told why she was so sullenly angry. Mrs. Lindley, as usual, lay silently watching.

Mary carried her child upstairs, followed by her husband with the pillows. After a while he came down again.

'What is Mary doing? Why doesn't she come down to eat?' asked Mrs. Lindley.

'She is staying with baby. The room is rather cold. I will ask the girl to put in a fire.' He was going absorbedly to the door.

'But Mary has had nothing to eat. It is *she* who will catch cold,' said the mother, exasperated.

Mr. Massy seemed as if he did not hear. Yet he looked at his mother-in-law, and answered:

'I will take her something.'

He went out. Mrs. Lindley shifted on her couch with anger. Miss Louisa glowered. But no one said anything, because of the money that came to the vicarage from Mr. Massy.

Louisa went upstairs. Her sister was sitting by the bed, reading a scrap of paper.

'Won't you come down and eat?' the younger asked.

'In a moment or two,' Mary replied, in a quiet, reserved voice, that forbade anyone to approach her.

It was this that made Miss Louisa most furious. She went downstairs, and announced to her mother:

'I am going out. I may not be home to tea.'

VIII

No one remarked on her exit. She put on her fur hat, that the village people knew so well, and the old Norfolk jacket. Louisa was short and plump and plain. She had her mother's heavy jaw, her father's proud brow, and her own grey, brooding eyes that were very beautiful when she smiled. It was true, as the people said, that she looked sulky. Her chief attraction was her glistening, heavy, deep-blonde hair, which shone and gleamed with a richness that was not entirely foreign to her.

'Where am I going?' she said to herself, when she got outside in the

149

snow. She did not hesitate, however, but by mechanical walking found herself descending the hill towards Old Aldecross. In the valley that was black with trees, the colliery breathed in stertorous pants, sending out high conical columns of steam that remained upright, whiter than the snow on the hills, yet shadowy, in the dead air. Louisa would not acknowledge to herself whither she was making her way, till she came to the railway crossing. Then the bunches of snow in the twigs of the apple tree that leaned towards the fence told her she must go and see Mrs. Durant. The tree was in Mrs. Durant's garden.

Alfred was now at home again, living with his mother in the cottage below the road. From the highway hedge, by the railway crossing, the snowy garden sheered down steeply, like the side of a hole, then dropped straight in a wall. In this depth the house was snug, its chimney just level with the road. Miss Louisa descended the stone stairs, and stood below in the little back-yard, in the dimness and the semi-secrecy. A big tree leaned overhead, above the paraffin-hut. Louisa felt secure from all the world down there. She knocked at the open door, then looked round. The tongue of garden narrowing in from the quarry bed was white with snow: she thought of the thick fringes of snowdrops it would show beneath the currant bushes in a month's time. The ragged fringe of pinks hanging over the garden brim behind her was whitened now with snowflakes, that in summer held white blossom to Louisa's face. It was pleasant, she thought, to gather flowers that stooped to one's face from above.

She knocked again. Peeping in, she saw the scarlet glow of the kitchen, red firelight falling on the brick floor and on the bright chintz cushions. It was alive and bright as a peep-show. She crossed the scullery, where still an almanac hung. There was no one about. 'Mrs. Durant,' called Louisa softly, 'Mrs. Durant.'

She went up the brick step into the front room, that still had its little shop counter and its bundles of goods, and she called from the stair-foot. Then she knew Mrs. Durant was out.

She went into the yard, to follow the old woman's footsteps up the garden path.

She emerged from the bushes and raspberry canes. There was the whole quarry bed, a wide garden white and dimmed, brindled with dark bushes, lying half submerged. On the left, overhead, the little colliery train rumbled by. Right away at the back was a mass of trees.

Louisa followed the open path, looking from right to left, and then she gave a cry of concern. The old woman was sitting rocking slightly among the ragged snowy cabbages. Louisa ran to her, found her whimpering with little, involuntary cries.

'Whatever have you done?' cried Louisa, kneeling in the snow.

'I've – I've – I was pulling a brussels-sprout stalk – and – oh-h! – something tore inside me. I've had a pain,' the old woman wept from shock and suffering, gasping between her whimpers, – 'I've had a pain there – a long time – and now – oh – oh!' She panted, pressed her hand on her side, leaned as if she would faint, looking yellow against the snow. Louisa supported her.

'Do you think you could walk now?' she asked.

'Yes,' gasped the old woman.

Louisa helped her to her feet.

'Get the cabbage – I want it for Alfred's dinner,' panted Mrs. Durant. Louisa picked up the stalk of brussels-sprouts, and with difficulty got the old woman indoors. She gave her brandy, laid her on the couch, saying:

'I'm going to send for a doctor – wait just a minute.'

The young woman ran up the steps to the public-house a few yards away. The landlady was astonished to see Miss Louisa.

'Will you send for a doctor at once to Mrs. Durant,' she said with some of her father in her commanding tone.

'Is something the matter?' fluttered the landlady in concern.

Louisa, glancing out up the road, saw the grocer's cart driving to Eastwood. She ran and stopped the man, and told him.

Mrs. Durant lay on the sofa, her face turned away, when the young woman came back.

'Let me put you to bed,' Louisa said. Mrs. Durant did not resist.

Louisa knew the ways of the working people. In the bottom drawer of the dresser she found dusters and flannels. With the old pit-flannel she snatched out the oven shelves, wrapped them up, and put them in the bed. From the son's bed she took a blanket, and, running down, set it before the fire. Having undressed the little old woman, Louisa carried her upstairs.

'You'll drop me, you'll drop me!' cried Mrs. Durant.

Louisa did not answer, but bore her burden quickly. She could not light a fire, because there was no fire-place in the bedroom. And the floor was plaster. So she fetched the lamp, and stood it lighted in one corner.

'It will air the room,' she said.

'Yes,' moaned the old woman.

Louisa ran with more hot flannels, replacing those from the oven shelves. Then she made a bran-bag and laid it on the woman's side. There was a big lump on the side of the abdomen.

'I've felt it coming a long time,' moaned the old lady, when the pain was easier, 'but I've not said anything; I didn't want to upset our Alfred.'

Louisa did not see why 'our Alfred' should be spared.

'What time is it?' came the plaintive voice.

'A quarter to four.'

'Oh!' wailed the old lady, 'he'll be here in half an hour, and no dinner ready for him.'

'Let me do it?' said Louisa, gently.

'There's that cabbage – and you'll find the meat in the pantry – and there's an apple-pie you can hot up. But *don't you* do it —!'

'Who will, then?' asked Louisa.

'I don't know,' moaned the sick woman, unable to consider.

Louisa did it. The doctor came and gave serious examination. He looked very grave.

'What is it, doctor?' asked the old lady, looking up at him with old, pathetic eyes in which already hope was dead.

'I think you've torn the skin in which a tumour hangs,' he replied.

'Ay!' she murmured, and she turned away.

'You see, she may die any minute – and it *may* be swaled away,' said the old doctor to Louisa.

The young woman went upstairs again.

'He says the lump may be swaled away, and you may get quite well again,' she said.

'Ay!' murmured the old lady. It did not deceive her. Presently she asked:

'Is there a good fire?'

'I think so,' answered Louisa.

'He'll want a good fire,' the mother said. Louisa attended to it.

Since the death of Durant, the widow had come to church occasionally, and Louisa had been friendly to her. In the girl's heart the purpose was fixed. No man had affected her as Alfred Durant had done, and to that she kept. In her heart, she adhered to him. A natural sympathy existed between her and his rather hard, materialistic mother.

Alfred was the most lovable of the old woman's sons. He had grown up like the rest, however, headstrong and blind to everything but his own will. Like the other boys, he had insisted on going into the pit as

152

soon as he left school, because that was the only way speedily to become a man, level with all the other men. This was a great chagrin to his mother, who would have liked to have this last of her sons a gentleman.

But still he remained constant to her. His feeling for her was deep and unexpressed. He noticed when she was tired, or when she had a new night-cap. And he bought little things for her occasionally. She was not wise enough to see how much he lived by her.

At the bottom he did not satisfy her, he did not seem manly enough. He liked to read books occasionally, and better still he liked to play the piccolo. It amused her to see his head nod over the instrument as he made an effort to get the right note. It made her fond of him, with tenderness, almost pity, but not with respect. She wanted a man to be fixed, going his own way without knowledge of women. Whereas she knew Alfred depended on her. He sang in the choir because he liked singing. In the summer he worked in the garden, attended to the fowls and pigs. He kept pigeons. He played on Saturday in the cricket or football team. But to her he did not seem the man, the independent man her other boys had been. He was her baby – and whilst she loved him for it, she was a little bit contemptuous of him.

There grew up a little hostility between them. Then he began to drink, as the others had done; but not in their blind, oblivious way. He was a little self-conscious over it. She saw this, and she pitied it in him. She loved him most, but she was not satisfied with him because he was not free of her. He could not quite go his own way.

Then at twenty he ran away and served his time in the Navy. This had made a man of him. He had hated it bitterly, the service, the subordination. For years he fought with himself under the military discipline, for his own self-respect, struggling through blind anger and shame and a cramping sense of inferiority. Out of humiliation and self-hatred he rose into a sort of inner freedom. And his love for his mother, whom he idealised, remained the fact of hope and of belief.

He came home again, nearly thirty years old, but naïve and inexperienced as a boy, only with a silence about him that was new: a sort of dumb humility before life, a fear of living. He was almost quite chaste. A strong sensitiveness had kept him from women. Sexual talk was all very well among men, but somehow it had no application to living women. There were two things for him, the *idea* of women, with which he sometimes debauched himself, and real women, before whom he felt a deep uneasiness, and a need to draw away. He shrank and

153

defended himself from the approach of any woman. And then he felt ashamed. In his innermost soul he felt he was not a man, he was less than the normal man. In Genoa he went with an under-officer to a drinking-house where the cheaper sort of girl came in to look for lovers. He sat there with his glass, the girls looked at him, but they never came to him. He knew that if they did come he could only pay for food and drink for them, because he felt a pity for them, and was anxious lest they lacked good necessities. He could not have gone with one of them; he knew it, and was ashamed, looking with curious envy at the swaggering, easy-passionate Italian whose body went to a woman by instinctive impersonal attraction. They were men, he was not a man. He sat feeling short, feeling like a leper. And he went away imagining sexual scenes between himself and a woman, walking wrapt in this indulgence. But when the ready woman presented herself, the very fact that she was a palpable woman made it impossible for him to touch her. And this incapacity was like a core of rottenness in him.

So several times he went, drunk, with his companions, to the licensed prostitute-houses abroad. But the sordid insignificance of the experience appalled him. It had not been anything really: it meant nothing. He felt as if he were, not physically, but spiritually impotent: not actually impotent, but intriniscally so.

He came home with this secret, never changing burden of his unknown, unbestowed self torturing him. His Navy training left him in perfect physical condition. He was sensible of, and proud of his body. He bathed and used dumb-bells, and kept himself fit. He played cricket and football. He read books and began to hold fixed ideas which he got from the Fabians. He played his piccolo and was considered an expert. But at the bottom of his soul was always this canker of shame and incompleteness: he was miserable beneath all his healthy cheerfulness, he was uneasy and felt despicable among all his confidence and superiority of ideas. He would have changed with any mere brute, just to be free of himself, to be free of this shame of self-consciousness. He saw some collier lurching straight forward without misgiving, pursuing his own satisfactions, and he envied him. Anything, he would have given for this spontaneity and this blind stupidity which went to its own satisfaction direct.

IX

He was not unhappy in the pit. He was admired by the men, and well enough liked. It was only he himself who felt the difference between himself and the others. He seemed to hide his own stigma. But he was never sure that the others did not really despise him for a ninny, as being less a man than they were. Only he pretended to be more manly, and was surprised by the ease with which they were deceived. And, being naturally cheerful, he was happy at work. He was sure of himself there. Naked to the waist, hot and grimy with labour, they squatted on their heels for a few minutes and talked, seeing each other dimly by the light of the safety lamps, while the black coal rose jutting round them, and the props of wood stood like little pillars in the low, black, very dark temple. Then the pony came and the gang-lad with a message from Number 7, or with a bottle of water from the horse-trough or some news of the world above. The day passed pleasantly enough. There was an ease, a go-as-you-please about the day underground, a delightful camaraderie of men shut off alone from the rest of the world, in a dangerous place, and a variety of labour, holing, loading, timbering, and a glamour of mystery and adventure in the atmosphere, that made the pit not unattractive to him when he had again got over his anguish of desire for the open air and the sea.

This day there was much to do and Durant was not in humour to talk. He went on working in silence through the afternoon.

'Loose-all!' came, and they tramped to the bottom. The whitewashed underground office shone brightly. Men were putting out their lamps. They sat in dozens round the bottom of the shaft, down which black, heavy drops of water fell continuously into the sump. The electric lights shone away down the main underground road.

'Is it raining?' asked Durant.

'Snowing,' said an old man, and the younger was pleased. He liked to go up when it was snowing.

'It'll just come right for Christmas?' said the old man.

'Ay,' replied Durant.

'A green Christmas, a fat churchyard,' said the other sententiously.

Durant laughed, showing his small, rather pointed teeth.

The cage came down, a dozen men lined on. Durant noticed tufts of snow on the perforated, arched roof of the chain, and he was pleased.

He wondered how it liked its excursion underground. But already it was getting soppy with black water.

He liked things about him. There was a little smile on his face. But underlying it was the curious consciousness he felt in himself.

The upper world came almost with a flash, because of the glimmer of snow. Hurrying along the bank, giving up his lamp at the office, he smiled to feel the open about him again, all glimmering round him with snow. The hills on either hand were pale blue in the dusk, and the hedges looked savage and dark. The snow was trampled between the railway lines. But far ahead, beyond the black figures of miners moving home, it became smooth again, spreading right up to the dark wall of the coppice.

To the west there was a pinkness, and a big star hovered half revealed. Below, the lights of the pit came out crisp and yellow among the darkness of the buildings, and the lights of Old Aldecross twinkled in rows down the bluish twilight.

Durant walked glad with life among the miners, who were all talking animatedly because of the snow. He liked their company, he liked the white dusky world. It gave him a little thrill to stop at the garden gate and see the light of home down below, shining on the silent blue snow.

X

By the big gate of the railway, in the fence, was a little gate, that he kept locked. As he unfastened it, he watched the kitchen light that shone on to the bushes and the snow outside. It was a candle burning till night set in, he thought to himself. He slid down the steep path to the level below. He liked making the first marks in the smooth snow. Then he came through the bushes to the house. The two women heard his heavy boots ring outside on the scraper, and his voice as he opened the door:

'How much worth of oil do you reckon to save by that candle, mother?' He liked a good light from the lamp.

He had just put down his bottle and snap-bag and was hanging his coat behind the scullery door, when Miss Louisa came upon him. He was startled, but he smiled.

His eyes began to laugh – then his face went suddenly straight, and he was afraid.

'Your mother's had an accident,' she said.

156

'How?' he exclaimed.

'In the garden,' she answered. He hesitated with his coat in his hands. Then he hung it up and turned to the kitchen.

'Is she in bed?' he asked.

'Yes,' said Miss Louisa, who found it hard to deceive him. He was silent. He went into the kitchen, sat down heavily in his father's old chair, and began to pull off his boots. His head was small, rather finely shapen. His brown hair, close and crisp, would look jolly whatever happened. He wore heavy, moleskin trousers that gave off the stale, exhausted scent of the pit. Having put on his slippers, he carried his boots into the scullery.

'What is it?' he asked, afraid.

'Something internal,' she replied.

He went upstairs. His mother kept herself calm for his coming. Louisa felt his tread shake the plaster floor of the bedroom above.

'What have you done?' he asked.

'It's nothing, my lad,' said the old woman, rather hard. 'It's nothing. You needn't fret, my boy, it's nothing more the matter with me than I had yesterday, or last week. The doctor said I'd done nothing serious.'

'What were you doing?' asked her son.

'I was pulling up a cabbage, and I suppose I pulled too hard; for, oh – there was such a pain—'

Her son looked at her quickly. She hardened herself.

'But who doesn't have a sudden pain sometimes, my boy? We all do.'

'And what's it done?'

'I don't know,' she said, 'but I don't suppose it's anything.'

The big lamp in the corner was screened with dark green screen, so that he could scarcely see her face. He was strung tight with apprehension and many emotions. Then his brow knitted.

'What did you go pulling your inside out at cabbages for,' he asked, 'and the ground frozen? You'd go on dragging and dragging, if you killed yourself.'

'Somebody's got to get them,' she said.

'You needn't do yourself harm.'

But they had reached futility.

Miss Louisa could hear plainly downstairs. Her heart sank. It seemed so hopeless between them.

'Are you sure it's nothing much, mother?' he asked, appealing, after a little silence.

'Ay, it's nothing,' said the old woman, rather bitter.

'I don't want you to – to – to be badly – you know.'

'Go an' get your dinner,' she said. She knew she was going to die: moreover, the pain was torture just then. 'They're only cosseting me up a bit because I'm an old woman. Miss Louisa's *very* good – and she'll have got your dinner ready, so you'd better go and eat it.'

He felt stupid and ashamed. His mother put him off. He had to turn away. The pain burned in his bowels. He went downstairs. The mother was glad he was gone, so that she could moan with pain.

He had resumed the old habit of eating before he washed himself. Miss Louisa served his dinner. It was strange and exciting to her. She was strung up tense, trying to understand him and his mother. She watched him as he sat. He was turned away from his food, looking in the fire. Her soul watched him, trying to see what he was. His black face and arms were uncouth, he was foreign. His face was masked black with coal-dust. She could not see him, she could not know him. The brown eyebrows, the steady eyes, the coarse, small moustache above the closed mouth – these were the only familiar indications. What was he, as he sat there in his pit-dirt? She could not see him, and it hurt her.

She ran upstairs, presently coming down with flannels and the bran-bag, to heat them, because the pain was on again.

He was half-way through his dinner. He put down the fork, suddenly nauseated.

'They will soothe the wrench,' she said. He watched, useless and left out.

'Is she bad?' he asked.

'I think she is,' she answered.

It was useless for him to stir or comment. Louisa was busy. She went upstairs. The poor old woman was in a white, cold sweat of pain. Louisa's face was sullen with suffering as she went about to relieve her. Then she sat and waited. The pain passed gradually, the old woman sank into a state of coma. Louisa still sat silent by the bed. She heard the sound of water downstairs. Then came the voice of the old mother, faint but unrelaxing:

'Alfred's washing himself – he'll want his back washing —'

Louisa listened anxiously, wondering what the sick woman wanted.

'He can't bear if his back isn't washed —' the old woman persisted, in a cruel attention to his needs. Louisa rose and wiped the sweat from the yellowish brow.

'I will go down,' she said soothingly.

'If you would,' murmured the sick woman.

Louisa waited a moment. Mrs. Durant closed her eyes, having discharged her duty. The young woman went downstairs. Herself, or the man, what did they matter? Only the suffering woman must be considered.

Alfred was kneeling on the hearth-rug, stripped to the waist, washing himself in a large panchion of earthenware. He did so every evening, when he had eaten his dinner; his brothers had done so before him. But Miss Louisa was strange in the house.

He was mechanically rubbing the white lather on his head, with a repeated, unconscious movement, his hand every now and then passing over his neck. Louisa watched. She had to brace herself to this also. He bent his head into the water, washed it free of soap, and pressed the water out of his eyes.

'Your mother said you would want your back washing,' she said.

Curious how it hurt her to take part in their fixed routine of life! Louisa felt the almost repulsive intimacy being forced upon her. It was all so common, so like herding. She lost her own distinctness.

He ducked his face round, looking up at her in what was a very comical way. She had to harden herself.

'How funny he looks with his face upside down,' she thought. After all, there was a difference between her and the common people. The water in which his arms were plunged was quite black, the soap-froth was darkish. She could scarcely conceive him as human. Mechanically, under the influence of habit, he groped in the black water, fished out soap and flannel, and handed them backward to Louisa. Then he remained rigid and submissive, his two arms thrust straight in the panchion, supporting the weight of his shoulders. His skin was beautifully white and unblemished, of an opaque, solid whiteness. Gradually Louisa saw it: this also was what he was. It fascinated her. Her feelings of separateness passed away: she ceased to draw back from contact with him and his mother. There was this living centre. Her heart ran hot. She had reached some goal in this beautiful, clear, male body. She loved him in a white, impersonal heat. But the sun-burnt, reddish neck and ears: they were more personal, more curious. A tenderness rose in her, she loved even his queer ears. A person – an intimate being he was to her. She put down the towel and went upstairs again, troubled in her heart. She had only seen one human being in her life – and that was Mary. All the rest were strangers. Now her soul was going to open, she was going to see another. She felt strange and pregnant.

'He'll be more comfortable,' murmured the sick woman abstractedly, as Louisa entered the room. The latter did not answer. Her own heart was heavy with its own responsibility. Mrs. Durant lay silent awhile, then she murmured plaintively:

'You mustn't mind, Miss Louisa.'

'Why should I?' replied Louisa, deeply moved.

'It's what we're used to,' said the old woman.

And Louisa felt herself excluded again from their life. She sat in pain, with the tears of disappointment distilling in her heart. Was that all?

Alfred came upstairs. He was clean, and in his shirt-sleeves. He looked a workman now. Louisa felt that she and he were foreigners, moving in different lives. It dulled her again. Oh, if she could only find some fixed relations, something sure and abiding.

'How do you feel?' he said to his mother.

'It's a bit better,' she replied wearily, impersonally. This strange putting herself aside, this abstracting herself and answering him only what she thought good for him to hear, made the relations between mother and son poignant and cramping to Miss Louisa. It made the man so ineffectual, so nothing. Louisa groped as if she had lost him. The mother was real and positive – he was not very actual. It puzzled and chilled the young woman.

'I'd better fetch Mrs. Harrison?' he said, waiting for his mother to decide.

'I suppose we shall have to take somebody,' she replied.

Miss Louisa stood by, afraid to interfere in their business. They did not include her in their lives, they felt she had nothing to do with them, except as a help from outside. She was quite external to them. She felt hurt and powerless against this unconscious difference. But something patient and unyielding in her made her say:

'I will stay and do the nursing: you can't be left.'

The other two were shy, and at a loss for an answer.

'We s'll manage to get somebody,' said the old woman wearily. She did not care very much what happened, now.

'I will stay until to-morrow, in any case,' said Louisa. 'Then we can see.'

'I'm sure you've no right to trouble yourself,' moaned the old woman. But she must leave herself in my hands.

Miss Louisa felt glad that she was admitted, even in an official capacity. She wanted to share their lives. At home they would need her, now Mary had come. But they must manage without her.

'I must write a note to the vicarage,' she said.

Alfred Durant looked at her inquiringly, for her service. He had always that intelligent readiness to serve, since he had been in the Navy. But there was a simple independence in his willingness, which she loved. She felt nevertheless it was hard to get at him. He was so deferential, quick to take the slightest suggestion of an order from her, implicitly, that she could not get at the man in him.

He looked at her very keenly. She noticed his eyes were golden brown, with a very small pupil, the kind of eyes that can see a long way off. He stood alert, at military attention. His face was still rather weather-reddened.

'Do you want pen and paper?' he asked, with deferential suggestion to a superior, which was more difficult for her than reserve.

'Yes, please,' she said.

He turned and went downstairs. He seemed to her so self-contained, so utterly sure in his movement. How was she to approach him? For he would take not one step towards her. He would only put himself entirely and impersonally at her service, glad to serve her, but keeping himself quite removed from her. She could see he felt real joy in doing anything for her, but any recognition would confuse him and hurt him. Strange it was to her, to have a man going about the house in his shirt-sleeves, his waistcoat unbuttoned, his throat bare, waiting on her. He moved well, as if he had plenty of life to spare. She was attracted by his completeness. And yet, when all was ready, and there was nothing more for him to do, she quivered, meeting his questioning look.

As she sat writing, he placed another candle near her. The rather dense light fell in two places on the overfoldings of her hair till it glistened heavy and bright, like a dense golden plumage folded up. Then the nape of her neck was very white, with fine down and pointed wisps of gold. He watched it as if it were a vision, losing himself. She was all that was beyond him, of revelation and exquisiteness. All that was ideal and beyond him, she was that – and he was lost to himself in looking at her. She had no connection with him. He did not approach her. She was there like a wonderful distance. But it was a treat, having her in the house. Even with this anguish for his mother tightening about him, he was sensible of the wonder of living this evening. The candles glistened on her hair, and seemed to fascinate him. He felt a little awe of her, and a sense of uplifting, that he and she and his mother should be together for a time, in the strange, unknown atmosphere. And, when he got out of the house, he was afraid. He saw the stars above ringing

161

with fine brightness, the snow beneath just visible, and a new night was gathering round him. He was afraid almost with obliteration. What was this new night ringing about him, and what was he? He could not recognise himself nor any of his surroundings. He was afraid to think of his mother. And yet his chest was conscious of her, and of what was happening to her. He could not escape from her, she carried him with her into an unformed, unknown chaos.

XI

He went up the road in an agony, not knowing what it was all about, but feeling as if a red-hot iron were gripped round his chest. Without thinking, he shook two or three tears on to the snow. Yet in his mind he did not believe his mother would die. He was in the grip of some greater consciousness. As he sat in the hall of the vicarage, waiting whilst Mary put things for Louisa into a bag, he wondered why he had been so upset. He felt abashed and humbled by the big house, he felt again as if he were one of the rank and file. When Miss Mary spoke to him, he almost saluted.

'An honest man,' thought Mary. And the patronage was applied as salve to her own sickness. She had station, so she could patronise: it was almost all that was left to her. But she could not have lived without having a certain position. She could never have trusted herself outside a definite place, nor respected herself except as a woman of superior class.

As Alfred came to the latch-gate, he felt the grief at his heart again, and saw the new heavens. He stood a moment looking northward to the Plough climbing up the night, and at the far glimmer of snow in distant fields. Then his grief came on like physical pain. He held tight to the gate, biting his mouth, whispering 'Mother!' It was a fierce, cutting, physical pain of grief, that came on in bouts, as his mother's pain came on in bouts, and was so acute he could scarcely keep erect. He did not know where it came from, the pain, nor why. It had nothing to do with his thoughts. Almost it had nothing to do with him. Only it gripped him and he must submit. The whole tide of his soul, gathering in its unknown towards this expansion into death, carried him with it help-lessly, all the fritter of his thought and consciousness caught up as nothing, the heave passing on towards its breaking, taking him farther than he had ever been. When the young man had regained himself, he

162

went indoors, and there he was almost gay. It seemed to excite him. He felt in high spirits: he made whimsical fun of things. He sat on one side of his mother's bed. Louisa on the other, and a certain gaiety seized them all. But the night and the dread was coming on.

Alfred kissed his mother and went to bed. When he was half undressed the knowledge of his mother came upon him, and the suffering seized him in its grip like two hands, in agony. He lay on the bed screwed up tight. It lasted so long, and exhausted him so much, that he fell asleep, without having the energy to get up and finish undressing. He awoke after midnight to find himself stone cold. He undressed and got into bed, and was soon asleep again.

At a quarter to six he woke, and instantly remembered. Having pulled on his trousers and lighted a candle, he went into his mother's room. He put his hand before the candle flame so that no light fell on the bed.

'Mother!' he whispered.

'Yes,' was the reply.

There was a hesitation.

'Should I go to work?'

He waited, his heart was beating heavily.

'I think I'd go, my lad.'

His heart went down in a kind of despair.

'You want me to?'

He let his hand down from the candle flame. The light fell on the bed. There he saw Louisa lying looking up at him. Her eyes were upon him. She quickly shut her eyes and half buried her face in the pillow, her back turned to him. He saw the rough hair like bright vapour about her round head, and the two plaits flung coiled among the bedclothes. It gave him a shock. He stood almost himself, determined. Louisa cowered down. He looked, and met his mother's eyes. Then he gave way again, and ceased to be sure, ceased to be himself.

'Yes, go to work, my boy,' said the mother.

'All right,' replied he, kissing her. His heart was down at despair, and bitter. He went away.

'Alfred!' cried his mother faintly.

He came back with beating heart.

'What, mother?'

'You'll always do what's right, Alfred?' the mother asked, beside herself in terror now he was leaving her. He was too terrified and bewildered to know what she meant.

163

'Yes,' he said.

She turned her cheek to him. He kissed her, then went away in bitter despair. He went to work.

XII

By midday his mother was dead. The word met him at the pit-mouth. As he had known, inwardly, it was not a shock to him, and yet he trembled. He went home quite calmly, feeling only heavy in his breathing.

Miss Louisa was still at the house. She had seen to everything possible. Very succinctly, she informed him of what he needed to know. But there was one point of anxiety for her.

'You *did* half expect it – it's not come as a blow to you!' she asked, looking up at him. Her eyes were dark and calm and searching. She too felt lost. He was so dark and inchoate.

'I suppose – yes,' he said stupidly. He looked aside, unable to endure her eyes on him.

'I could not bear to think you might not have guessed,' she said.

He did not answer.

He felt it a great strain to have her near him at this time. He wanted to be alone. As soon as the relatives began to arrive, Louisa departed and came no more. While everything was arranging, and a crowd was in the house, whilst he had business to settle, he went well enough, with only those uncontrollable paroxysms of grief. For the rest, he was superficial. By himself, he endured the fierce, almost insane bursts of grief which passed again and left him calm, almost clear, just wonder-ing. He had not known before that everything could break down, that he himself could break down, and all be a great chaos, very vast and wonderful. It seemed as if life in him had burst its bounds, and he was lost in a great, bewildering flood, immense and unpeopled. He himself was broken and spilled out amid it all. He could only breathe panting in silence. Then the anguish came on again.

When all the people had gone from the Quarry Cottage, leaving the young man alone with an elderly housekeeper, then the long trial began. The snow had thawed and frozen, a fresh fall had whitened the grey, this then began to thaw. The world was a place of loose grey slosh. Alfred had nothing to do in the evenings. He was a man whose life had been filled up with small activities. Without knowing it, he had been centralised, polarised in his mother. It was she who had kept him. Even now, when the old housekeeper had left him, he might still have gone on in his old way. But the force and balance of his life was lacking. He sat pretending to read, all the time holding his fists clenched, and holding himself in, enduring he did not know what. He walked the black and sodden miles of field-paths, till he was tired out: but all this was only running away from whence he must return. At work he was all right. If it had been summer he might have escaped by working in the garden till bedtime. But now, there was no escape, no relief, no help. He, perhaps, was made for action rather than for understanding; for doing than for being. He was shocked out of his activities, like a swimmer who forgets to swim.

For a week, he had the force to endure this suffocation and struggle, then he began to get exhausted, and knew it must come out. The instinct of self-preservation became strongest. But there was the question: Where was he to go? The public-house really meant nothing to him, it was no good going there. He began to think of emigration. In another country he would be all right. He wrote to the emigration offices.

On the Sunday after the funeral, when all the Durant people had attended church, Alfred had seen Miss Louisa, impassive and reserved, sitting with Miss Mary, who was proud and very distant, and with the other Lindleys, who were people removed. Alfred saw them as people remote. He did not think about it. They had nothing to do with his life. After service Louisa had come to him and shaken hands.

'My sister would like you to come to supper one evening, if you would be so good.'

He looked at Miss Mary, who bowed. Out of kindness, Mary had proposed this to Louisa, disapproving of her even as she did so. But she did not examine herself closely.

'Yes,' said Durant awkwardly, 'I'll come if you want me.' But he vaguely felt that it was misplaced.

'You'll come to-morrow evening, then, about half-past six.'

He went. Miss Louisa was very kind to him. There could be no music, because of the babies. He sat with his fists clenched on his thighs, very quiet and unmoved, lapsing, among all those people, into a kind of muse or daze. There was nothing between him and them. They knew it as well as he. But he remained very steady in himself, and the evening passed slowly. Mrs. Lindley called him 'young man'.

'Will you sit here, young man?'

He sat there. One name was as good as another. What had they to do with him?

Mr. Lindley kept a special tone for him, kind, indulgent, but patronising. Durant took it all without criticism or offence, just submitting. But he did not want to eat – that troubled him, to have to eat in their presence. He knew he was out of place. But it was his duty to stay yet awhile. He answered precisely, in monosyllables.

When he left he winced with confusion. He was glad it was finished. He got away as quickly as possible. And he wanted still more intensely to go right away, to Canada.

Miss Louisa suffered in her soul, indignant with all of them, with him too, but quite unable to say why she was indignant.

XIII

Two evenings after, Louisa tapped at the door of the Quarry Cottage, at half-past six. He had finished dinner, the woman had washed up and gone away, but still he sat in his pit-dirt. He was going later to the New Inn. He had begun to go there because he must go somewhere. The mere contact with other men was necessary to him, the noise, the warmth, the forgetful flight of the hours. But still he did not move. He sat alone in the empty house till it began to grow on him like something unnatural.

He was in his pit-dirt when he opened the door.

'I have been wanting to call – I thought I would,' she said, and she went to the sofa. He wondered why she wouldn't use his mother's round arm-chair. Yet something stirred in him, like anger, when the housekeeper placed herself in it.

'I ought to have been washed by now,' he said, glancing at the clock, which was adorned with butterflies and cherries, and the name of 'T. Brooks, Mansfield'. He laid his black hands along his mottled dirty arms. Louisa looked at him. There was the reserve, and the simple neutrality towards her, which she dreaded in him. It made it impossible for her to approach him.

'I am afraid,' she said, 'that I wasn't kind in asking you to supper.'

'I'm not used to it,' he said, smiling with his mouth, showing the interspaced white teeth. His eyes, however, were steady and unseeing.

'It's not *that*,' she said hastily. Her repose was exquisite and her dark

166

grey eyes rich with understanding. He felt afraid of her as she sat there, as he began to grow conscious of her.

'How do you get on alone?' she asked.

He glanced away to the fire.

'Oh —' he answered, shifting uneasily, not finishing his answer.

Her face settled heavily.

'How close it is in this room. You have such immense fires. I will take off my coat,' she said.

He watched her take off her hat and coat. She wore a cream cashmere blouse embroidered with gold silks. It seemed to him a very fine garment, fitting her throat and wrists close. It gave him a feeling of pleasure and cleanness and relief from himself.

'What were you thinking about, that you didn't get washed?' she asked, half intimately. He laughed, turning aside his head. The whites of his eyes showed very distinct his black face.

'Oh,' he said, 'I couldn't tell you.'

There was a pause.

'Are you going to keep this house on?' she asked.

He stirred in his chair, under the question.

'I hardly know,' he said. 'I'm very likely going to Canada.'

Her spirit became very quiet and attentive.

'What for?' she asked.

Again he shifted restlessly on his seat.

'Well,' – he said slowly – 'to try the life.'

'But which life?'

'There's various things – farming or lumbering or mining. I don't mind much what it is.'

'And is that what you want?'

He did not think in these terms, so he could not answer.

'I don't know,' he said, 'till I've tried.'

She saw him drawing away from her for ever.

'Aren't you sorry to leave this house and garden?' she asked.

'I don't know,' he answered reluctantly. 'I suppose our Fred would come in – that's what he's wanting.'

'You don't want to settle down?' she asked.

He was leaning forward on the arms of his chair. He turned to her. Her face was pale and set. It looked heavy and impassive, her hair shone richer as she grew white. She was to him something steady and immovable and eternal presented to him. His heart was hot in an anguish of suspense. Sharp twitches of fear and pain were in his limbs. He turned his whole body away from her. The silence was unendurable. He could not bear her to sit there any more. It made his heart get hot and stifled in his breast.

'Were you going out to-night?' she asked.

'Only to the New Inn,' he said.

Again there was silence.

She reached for her hat. Nothing else was suggested to her. She *had* to go. He sat waiting for her to be gone, for relief. And she knew that if she went out of that house as she was, she went out a failure. Yet she continued to pin on her hat; in a moment she would have to go. Something was carrying her.

Then suddenly a sharp pang, like lightning, seared her from head to foot, and she was beyond herself.

'Do you want me to go?' she asked, controlled, yet speaking out of a fiery anguish, as if the words were spoken from her without her intervention.

He went white under his dirt.

'Why?' he asked, turning to her in fear, compelled.

'Do you want me to go?' she repeated.

'Why?' he asked again.

'Because I wanted to stay with you,' she said, suffocated, with her lungs full of fire.

His face worked, he hung forward a little, suspended, staring straight into her eyes, in torment, in an agony of chaos, unable to collect himself. And as if turned to stone, she looked back into his eyes. The souls were exposed bare for a few moments. It was agony. They could not bear it. He dropped his head, whilst his body jerked with little sharp twitchings.

She turned away for her coat. Her soul had gone dead in her. Her hands trembled, but she could not feel any more. She drew on her coat. There was a cruel suspense in the room. The moment had come for her to go. He lifted his head. His eyes were like agate, expressionless, save for the black points of torture. They held her, she had no will, no life any more. She felt broken.

'Don't you want me?' she said helplessly.

A spasm of torture crossed his eyes, which held her fixed.

'I – I —' he began, but he could not speak. Something drew him from his chair to her. She stood motionless, spellbound, like a creature given up as prey. He put his hand tentatively, uncertainly, on her arm. The expression of his face was strange and inhuman. She stood utterly

168

motionless. Then clumsily he put his arms round her, and took her, cruelly, blindly, straining her till she nearly lost consciousness, till he himself had almost fallen.

Then, gradually, as he held her gripped, and his brain reeled round, and he felt himself falling, falling from himself, and whilst she, yielded up, swooned to a kind of death of herself, a moment of utter darkness came over him, and they began to wake up again as if from a long sleep. He was himself.

After a while his arms slackened, she loosened herself a little, and put her arms round him, as he held her. So they held each other close, and hid each against the other for assurance, helpless in speech. And it was ever her hands that trembled more closely upon him, drawing him nearer into her, with love.

And at last she drew back her face and looked up at him, her eyes wet, and shining with light. His heart, which saw, was silent with fear. He was with her. She saw his face all sombre and inscrutable, and he seemed eternal to her. And all the echo of pain came back into the rarity of bliss, and all her tears came up.

'I love you,' she said, her lips drawn to sobbing. He put down his head against her, unable to hear her, unable to bear the sudden coming of the peace and passion that almost broke his heart. They stood together in silence whilst the thing moved away a little.

At last she wanted to see him. She looked up. His eyes were strange and glowing, with a tiny black pupil. Strange, they were, and powerful over her. And his mouth came to hers, and slowly her eyelids closed, as his mouth sought hers closer and closer, and took possession of her.

They were silent for a long time, too much mixed up with passion and grief and death to do anything but hold each other in pain and kiss with long, hurting kisses wherein fear was transfused into desire. At last she disengaged herself. He felt as if his heart were hurt, but glad, and he scarcely dared look at her.

'I'm glad,' she said also.

He held her hands in passionate gratitude and desire. He had not yet the presence of mind to say anything. He was dazed with relief.

'I ought to go,' she said.

He looked at her. He could not grasp the thought of her going, he knew he could never be separated from her any more. Yet he dared not assert himself. He held her hands tight.

'Your face is black,' she said.

He laughed.

'Yours is a bit smudged,' he said.

They were afraid of each other, afraid to talk. He could only keep her near to him. After a while she wanted to wash her face. He brought her some warm water, standing by and watching her. There was something he wanted to say, that he dared not. He watched her wiping her face, and making tidy her hair.

'They'll see your blouse is dirty,' he said.

She looked at her sleeves and laughed for joy.

He was sharp with pride.

'What shall you do?' he asked.

'How?' she said.

He was awkward at a reply.

'About me,' he said.

'What do you want me to do?' she laughed.

He put his hand out slowly to her. What did it matter!

'But make yourself clean,' she said.

XIV

As they went up the hill, the night seemed dense with the unknown. They kept close together, feeling as if the darkness were alive and full of knowledge, all around them. In silence they walked up the hill. At first the street lamps went their way. Several people passed them. He was more shy than she, and would have let her go had she loosened in the least. But she held firm.

Then they came into the true darkness, between the fields. They did not want to speak, feeling closer together in silence. So they arrived at the vicarage gate. They stood under the naked horse-chestnut tree.

'I wish you didn't have to go,' he said.

She laughed a quick little laugh.

'Come to-morrow,' she said, in a low tone, 'and ask father.'

She felt his hand close on hers.

She gave the same sorrowful little laugh of sympathy. Then she kissed him, sending him home.

At home, the old grief came on in another paroxysm, obliterating Louisa, obliterating even his mother for whom the stress was raging like a burst of fever in a wound. But something was sound in his heart.

XV

The next evening he dressed to go to the vicarage, feeling it was to be done, not imagining what it would be like. He would not take this seriously. He was sure of Louisa, and this marriage was like fate to him. It filled him also with a blessed feeling of fatality. He was not responsible, neither had her people anything really to do with it.

They ushered him into the little study, which was fireless. By and by the vicar came in. His voice was cold and hostile as he said:

'What can I do for you, young man?'

He knew already, without asking.

Durant looked up at him, again like a sailor before a superior. He had the subordinate manner. Yet his spirit was clear.

'I wanted, Mr. Lindley —' he began respectfully, then all the colour suddenly left his face. It seemed now a violation to say what he had to say. What was he doing there? But he stood on, because it had to be done. He held firmly to his own independence and self-respect. He must not be indecisive. He must put himself aside: the matter was bigger than just his personal self. He must not feel. This was his highest duty.

'You wanted —' said the vicar.

Durant's mouth was dry, but he answered with steadiness:

'Miss Louisa – Louisa – promised to marry me —'

'You asked Miss Louisa if she would marry you – yes —' corrected the vicar. Durant reflected he had not asked her this:

'If she would marry me, sir. I hope you – don't mind.'

He smiled. He was a good-looking man, and the vicar could not help seeing it.

'And my daughter was willing to marry you?' said Mr. Lindley.

'Yes,' said Durant seriously. It was pain to him, nevertheless. He felt the natural hostility between himself and the elder man.

'Will you come this way?' said the vicar. He led into the dining-room, where were Mary, Louisa, and Mrs. Lindley. Mr. Massy sat in a corner with a lamp.

'This young man has come on your account, Louisa?' said Mr. Lindley.

'Yes,' said Louisa, her eyes on Durant, who stood erect, in discipline. He dared not look at her, but he was aware of her.

'You don't want to marry a collier, you little fool,' cried Mrs. Lindley harshly. She lay obese and helpless upon the couch, swathed in a loose dove-grey gown.

'Oh, hush, Mother,' cried Mary, with quiet intensity and pride.

'What means have you to support a wife?' demanded the vicar's wife roughly.

'I!' Durant replied, starting. 'I think I can earn enough.'

'Well, and how much?' came the rough voice.

'Seven and six a day,' replied the young man.

'And will it get to be any more?'

'I hope so.'

'And are you going to live in that poky little house?'

'I think so,' said Durant, 'if it's all right.'

He took small offence, only was upset, because they would not think him good enough. He knew that, in their sense, he was not.

'Then she's a fool, I tell you, if she marries you,' cried the mother roughly, casting her decision.

'After all, mama, it is Louisa's affair,' said Mary distinctly, 'and we must remember —'

'As she makes her bed, she must lie – but she'll repent it,' interrupted Mrs. Lindley.

'And after all,' said Mr. Lindley, 'Louisa cannot quite hold herself free to act entirely without consideration for her family.'

'What do you want, Papa?' asked Louisa sharply.

'I mean that if you marry this man, it will make my position very difficult for me, particularly if you stay in this parish. If you were moving quite away, it would be simpler. But living here in a collier's cottage, under my nose, as it were – it would be almost unseemly. I have my position to maintain, and a position which may not be taken lightly.'

'Come over here, young man,' cried the mother, in her rough voice, 'and let us look at you.'

Durant, flushing, went over and stood – not quite at attention, so that he did not know what to do with his hands. Miss Louisa was angry to see him standing there, obedient and acquiescent. He ought to show himself a man.

'Can't you take her away and live out of sight?' said the mother. 'You'd both of you be better off.'

'Yes, we can go away,' he said.

'Do you want to?' asked Miss Mary clearly.

172

He faced round. Mary looked very stately and impressive. He flushed.

'I do if it's going to be a trouble to anybody,' he said.

'For yourself, you would rather stay?' said Mary.

'It's my home,' he said, 'and that's the house I was born in.'

'Then' – Mary turned clearly to her parents, 'I really don't see how you can make the conditions, papa. He has his own rights, and if Louisa wants to marry him —'

'Louisa, Louisa!' cried the father impatiently. 'I cannot understand why Louisa should not behave in the normal way. I cannot see why she should only think of herself, and leave her family out of count. The thing is enough in itself, and she ought to try to ameliorate it as much as possible. And if —'

'But I love the man, papa,' said Louisa.

'And I hope you love your parents, and I hope you want to spare them as much of the – the loss of prestige as possible.'

'We *can* go away to live,' said Louisa, her face breaking to tears. At last she was really hurt.

'Oh yes, easily,' Durant replied hastily, pale, distressed.

There was dead silence in the room.

'I think it would really be better,' murmured the vicar, mollified.

'Very likely it would,' said the rough-voiced invalid.

'Though I think we ought to apologise for asking such a thing,' said Mary haughtily.

'No,' said Durant. 'It will be best all round.' He was glad there was no more bother.

'And shall we put up the banns here or go to the registrar?' he asked clearly, like a challenge.

'We will go to the registrar,' replied Louisa decidedly.

Again there was a dead silence in the room.

'Well, if you will have your own way, you must go your own way,' said the mother emphatically.

All the time Mr. Massy had sat obscure and unnoticed in a corner of the room. At this juncture he got up, saying:

'There is baby, Mary.'

Mary rose and went out of the room, stately; her little husband padded after her. Durant watched the fragile, small man go, wondering.

'And where,' asked the vicar, almost genial, 'do you think you will go when you are married?'

Durant started.

'I was thinking of emigrating,' he said.

'To Canada? Or where?'

'I think to Canada.'

'Yes, that would be very good.'

Again there was a pause.

'We shan't see much of you then, as a son-in-law,' said the mother, roughly but amicably.

'Not much,' he said.

Then he took his leave. Louisa went with him to the gate. She stood before him in distress.

'You won't mind them, will you?' she said humbly.

'I don't mind them, if they don't mind me!' he said. Then he stooped and kissed her.

'Let us be married soon,' she murmured, in tears.

'All right,' he said. 'I'll go to-morrow to Barford.'

A FRAGMENT OF STAINED GLASS

BEAUVALE is, or was, the largest parish in England. It is thinly populated, only just netting the stragglers from shoals of houses in three large mining villages. For the rest, it holds a great tract of woodland, fragment of old Sherwood, a few hills of pasture and arable land, three collieries, and, finally, the ruins of a Cistercian abbey. These ruins lie in a still rich meadow at the foot of the last fall of woodland, through whose oaks shines a blue of hyacinths, like water, in Maytime. Of the abbey, there remains only the east wall of the chancel standing, a wild thick mass of ivy weighting one shoulder, while pigeons perch in the tracery of the lofty window. This is the window in question.

The vicar of Beauvale is a bachelor of forty-two years. Quite early in life some illness caused a slight paralysis of his right side, so that he drags a little, and so that the right corner of his mouth is twisted up into his cheek with a constant grimace, unhidden by a heavy moustache. There is something pathetic about this twist on the vicar's countenance: his eyes are so shrewd and sad. It would be hard to get near to Mr. Colbran. Indeed, now, his soul has some of the twist to his face, so that, when he is not ironical, he is satiric. Yet a man of more complete tolerance and generosity scarcely exists. Let the boors mock him, he merely smiles on the other side, and there is no malice in his eyes, only a quiet expression of waiting till they have finished. His people do not like him, yet none could bring forth an accusation against him, save that 'You never can tell when he's having you.'

I dined the other evening with the vicar in his study. The room scandalises the neighbourhood because of the statuary which adorns it: a Laocoön and other classic copies, with bronze and silver Italian Renaissance works. For the rest, it is all dark and tawny.

Mr, Colbran is an archaeologist. He does not take himself seriously, however, in his hobby, so that nobody knows the worth of his opinions on the subject.

'Here you are,' he said to me after dinner, 'I've found another paragraph for my great work.'

'What's that?' I asked.

'Haven't I told you I was compiling a Bible of the English people –

the Bible of their hearts – their exclamations in presence of the unknown? I've found a fragment at home, a jump at God from Beauvale.'

'Where?' I asked, startled.

The vicar closed his eyes whilst looking at me.

'Only on parchment,' he said.

Then, slowly, he reached for a yellow book, and read, translating as he went:

'Then, while we chanted, came a crackling at the window, at the great east window, where hung our Lord on the Cross. It was a malicious coveitous Devil wrathed by us, rended the lovely image of the glasse. We saw the iron clutches of the fiend pick the window, and a face flaming red like fire in a basket did glower down on us. Our hearts melted away, our legs broke, we thought to die. The breath of the wretch filled the chapel.

'But our dear Saint, etc., etc., came hastening down heaven to defend us. The fiend began to groan and bray – he was daunted and beat off.

'When the sun up-rose, and it was morning, some went out in dread upon the thin snow. There the figure of our Saint was broken and thrown down, whilst in the window was a wicked hole as from the Holy Wounds the Blessed Blood was run out at the touch of the Fiend, and on the snow was the Blood, sparkling like gold. Some gathered it up for the joy of this House....'

'Interesting,' I said. 'Where's it from?'

'Beauvale records – fifteenth century.'

'Beauvale Abbey,' I said; 'they were only very few, the monks. What frightened them, I wonder.'

'I wonder,' he repeated.

'Somebody climbed up,' I supposed, 'and attempted to get in.'

'What?' he exclaimed, smiling.

'Well, what do you think?'

'Pretty much the same,' he replied. 'I glossed it out for my book.'

'Your great work? Tell me.'

He put a shade over the lamp so that the room was almost in darkness.

'Am I more than a voice?' he asked.

'I can see your hand,' I replied. He moved entirely from the circle of light. Then his voice began, sing-song, sardonic:

'I was a serf at Rollestoun's, Newthorp Manor, master of the stables, I was. One day a horse bit me as I was grooming him. He was an old enemy of mine. I fetched him a blow across the nose. Then, when he

176

got a chance, he lashed out at me and caught me a gash over the mouth. I snatched at a hatchet and cut his head. He yelled, fiend as he was, and strained for me with all his teeth bare. I brought him down.

'For killing him they flogged me till they thought I was dead. I was sturdy, because we horse-serfs got plenty to eat. I was sturdy, but they flogged me till I did not move. The next night I set fire to the stables, and the stables set fire to the house. I watched and saw the red flame rise and look out of the window, I saw the folk running, each for himself, master no more than one of a frightened party. It was freezing, but the heat made me sweat. I saw them all turn again to watch, all rimmed with red. They cried, all of them, when the roof went in, when the sparks splashed up at rebound. They cried then like dogs at the bagpipes howling. Master cursed me, till I laughed as I lay under a bush quite near.

'As the fire went down I got frightened. I ran for the woods with fire blazing in my eyes and crackling in my ears. For hours I was all fire. Then I went to sleep under the bracken. When I woke it was evening. I had no mantle, was frozen stiff. I was afraid to move, lest all the sores of my back should be broken like thin ice. I lay still until I could bear my hunger no longer. I moved then to get used to the pain of movement, when I began to hunt for food. There was nothing to be found but hips.

'After wandering about till I was faint I dropped again in the bracken. The boughs above me creaked with frost. I started and looked round. The branches were like hair among the starlight. My heart stood still. Again there was a creak, creak, and suddenly a whoop, that whistled in fading. I fell down in the bracken like dead wood. Yet, by the peculiar whistling sound at the end, I knew it was only the ice bending or tightening in the frost. I was in the woods above the lake, only two miles from the Manor. And yet, when the lake whooped hollowly again, I clutched the frozen soil, every one of my muscles as stiff as the stiff earth. So all the night long I dare not move my face, but pressed it flat down, and taut I lay as if pegged down and braced.

'When morning came still I did not move, I lay still in a dream. By afternoon my ache was such it enlivened me. I cried, rocking my breath in the ache of moving. Then again I became fierce. I beat my hands on the rough bark to hurt them, so that I should not ache so much. In such a rage I was I swung my limbs to torture till I fell sick with pain. Yet I fought the hurt, fought it and fought by twisting and flinging myself, until it was overcome. Then the evening began to draw on. All day the sun had not loosened the frost. I felt the sky chill again towards afternoon. Then I knew the night was coming, and, remembering the great space I had just come through, horrible so that it seemed to have made me another man, I fled across the wood.

'But in my running I came upon the oak where hanged five bodies. There they must hang, bar-stiff, night after night. It was a terror worse than any. Turning, blundering through the forest, I came out where the trees thinned, where only hawthorns, ragged and shaggy, went down to the lake's edge.

'The sky across was red, the ice on the water glistened as if it were warm. A few wild geese sat out like stones on the sheet of ice. I thought of Martha. She was the daughter of the miller at the upper end of the lake. Her hair was red like beech leaves in a wind. When I had gone often to the mill with the horses she had brought me food.

' "I thought," said I to her, " 'twas a squirrel sat on your shoulder. 'Tis your hair fallen loose."

' "They call me the fox," she said.

' "Would I were your dog," said I. She would bring me bacon and good bread, when I called at the mill with the horses. The thought of cakes of bread and of bacon made me reel as if drunk. I had torn at the rabbit-holes, I had chewed wood all day. In such a dimness was my head that I felt neither the soreness of my wounds nor the cuts of thorns on my knees, but stumbled towards the mill, almost past fear of man and death, panting with fear of the darkness that crept behind me from trunk to trunk.

'Coming to the gap in the wood, below which lay the pond, I heard no sound. Always I knew the place filled with the buzz of water, but now it was silent. In fear of this stillness I ran forward, forgetting myself, forgetting the frost. The wood seemed to pursue me. I fell, just in time, down by a shed wherein were housed the few wintry pigs. The miller came riding in on his horse, and the barking of dogs was for him. I heard him curse the day, curse his servant, curse me, whom he had been out to hunt, in his rage of wasted labour, curse all. As I lay I heard inside the shed a sucking. Then I knew that the sow was there, and that the most of her sucking pigs would be already killed for to-morrow's Christmas. The miller, from forethought to have young at that time, made profit by his sucking pigs that were sold for the mid-winter feast.

'When in a moment all was silent in the dusk, I broke the bar and came into the shed. The sow grunted, but did not come forth to discover me. By and by I crept in towards her warmth. She had but three young left, which now angered her, she being too full of milk. Every now and again she slashed at them and they squealed. Busy as she was with them, I in the darkness advanced towards her. I trembled so that scarce dared I trust myself near her, for long dared not put my naked face towards her. Shuddering with hunger and fear, I at last fed of her, guarding my face with my arm. Her own full young tumbled squealing against me, but she, feeling her ease, lay grunting. At last, I, too, lay drunk, swooning.

'I was roused by the shouting of the miller. He, angered by his daughter who wept, abused her, driving her from the house to feed the swine. She came, bowing under a yoke, to the door of the shed. Finding the pin broken she stood afraid, then, as the sow grunted, she came cautiously in. I took her with my arm, my hand over her mouth. As she struggled against my breast my heart began to beat loudly. At last she knew it was I. I clasped her. She hung in my arms, turning away her face, so that I kissed her throat. The tears blinded my eyes, I know not why, unless it were the hurt of my mouth, wounded by the horse, was keen.

' "They will kill you," she whispered.

' "No," I answered.

'And she wept softly. She took my head in her arms and kissed me, wetting me with her tears, brushing me with her keen hair, warming me through.

' "I will not go away from here," I said. "Bring me a knife, and I will defend myself."

' "No," she wept. "Ah, no!"

'When she went I lay down, pressing my chest where she had rested on the earth, lest being alone were worse emptiness than hunger.

'Later she came again. I saw her bend in the doorway, a lanthorn hanging in front. As she peered under the redness of her falling hair, I was afraid of her. But she came with food. We sat together in the dull light. Sometimes still I shivered and my throat would not swallow.

' "If," said I, "I eat all this you have brought me, I shall sleep till somebody finds me."

'Then she took away the rest of the meat.

' "Why," said I, "should I not eat?" She looked at me in tears of fear.

' "What?" I said, but still she had no answer. I kissed her, and the hurt of my wounded mouth angered me.

179

' "Now there is my blood," said I, "on your mouth." Wiping her smooth hand over her lips, she looked thereat, then at me.

' "Leave me," I said, "I am tired." She rose to leave me.

' "But bring a knife," I said. Then she held the lanthorn near my face, looking as at a picture.

' "You look to me," she said, "like a stirk that is roped for the axe. Your eyes are dark, but they are wide open."

' "Then I will sleep," said I, "but will not wake too late."

' "Do not stay here," she said.

' "I will not sleep in the wood," I answered, and it was my heart that spoke, "for I am afraid. I had better be afraid of the voice of man and dogs, than the sounds in the woods. Bring me a knife, and in the morning I will go. Alone will I not go now."

' "The searchers will take you," she said.

' "Bring me a knife," I answered.

' "Ah, go," she wept.

' "Not now – I will not —"

'With that she lifted the lanthorn, lit up her own face and mine. Her blue eyes dried of tears. Then I took her to myself, knowing she was mine.

' "I will come again," she said.

'She went, and I folded my arms, lay down and slept.

'When I woke, she was rocking me wildly to rouse me.

' "I dreamed," said I, "that a great heap, as if it were a hill, lay on me and above me."

'She put a cloak over me, gave me a hunting-knife and a wallet of food, and other things I did not note. Then under her own cloak she hid the lanthorn.

' "Let us go," she said, and blindly I followed her.

'When I came out into the cold someone touched my face and my hair.

' "Ha!" I cried, "who now —" Then she swiftly clung to me, hushed me.

' "Someone has touched me," I said aloud, still dazed with sleep.

' "Oh, hush!" she wept. " 'Tis snowing." The dogs within the house began to bark. She fled forward, I after her. Coming to the ford of the stream she ran swiftly over, but I broke through the ice. Then I knew where I was. Snowflakes, fine and rapid, were biting at my face. In the wood there was no wind nor snow.

' "Listen," said I to her, "listen, for I am locked up with sleep."

180

' "I hear roaring overhead," she answered. "I hear in the trees like great bats squeaking."

' "Give me your hand," said I.

'We heard many noises as we passed. Once as there uprose a whiteness before us, she cried aloud.

' "Nay," said I, "do not untie thy hand from mine," and soon we were crossing fallen snow. But ever and again she started back from fear.

' "When you draw back my arm," I said, angry, "you loosen a weal on my shoulder."

'Thereafter she ran by my side like a fawn beside its mother.

' "We will cross the valley and gain the stream," I said. "That will lead us on its ice as on a path deep into the forest. There we can join the outlaws. The wolves are driven from this part. They have followed the driven deer."

'We came directly on a large gleam that shaped itself up among flying grains of snow.

' "Ah!" she cried, and she stood amazed.

'Then I thought we had gone through the bounds into faery realm, and I was no more a man. How did I know what eyes were gleaming at me between the snow, what cunning spirits in the draughts of air? So I waited for what would happen, and I forgot her, that she was there. Only I could feel the spirits whirling and blowing about me.

'Whereupon she clung upon me, kissing me lavishly, and, were dogs or men or demons come upon us at that moment, she had let us be stricken down, nor heeded not. So we moved forward to the shadow that shone in colours upon the passing snow. We found ourselves under a door of light which shed its colours mixed with snow. This Martha had never seen, nor I, this door open for a red and brave issuing like fires. We wondered.

' "It is faery," she said, and after a while, "Could one catch such — Ah, no!"

'Through the snow shone bushes of red and blue.

' "Could one have such a little light like a red flower – only a little, like a rose-berry scarlet on one's breast! – then one were singled out as Our Lady."

'I flung off my cloak and my burden to climb up the face of the shadow. Standing on rims of stone, then in pockets of snow, I reached upward. My hand was red and blue, but I could not take the stuff. Like colour of a moth's wing it was on my hand, it flew on the increasing snow. I stood higher on the head of a frozen man, reached higher my hand. Then I felt the bright stuff cold. I could not pluck it off. Down below she cried to me to come again to her. I felt a rib that yielded, I struck at it with my knife. There came a gap in the redness. Looking through, I saw below as it were white stunted angels, with sad faces lifted in fear. Two faces they had each, and round rings of hair. I was afraid. I grasped the shining red, I pulled. Then the cold man under me sank, so I fell as if broken on to the snow.

'Soon I was risen again, and we were running downwards towards the stream. We felt ourselves eased when the smooth road of ice was beneath us. For a while it was resting, to travel thus evenly. But the wind blew round us, the snow hung upon us, we leaned us this way and that, towards the storm. I drew her along, for she came as a bird that stems lifting and swaying against the wind. By and by the snow came smaller, there was no wind in the wood. Then I felt nor labour, nor cold. Only I knew the darkness drifted by on either side, that overhead was a lane of paleness where a moon fled us before. Still, I can feel the moon fleeing from me, can feel the trees passing round me in slow dizzy reel, can feel the hurt of my shoulder and my straight arm torn with holding her. I was following the moon and the stream, for I knew where the water peeped from its burrow in the ground there were shelters of the outlaw. But she fell, without sound or sign.

'I gathered her up and climbed the bank. There all round me hissed the larchwood, dry beneath, and laced with its dry-fretted cords. For a little way I carried her into the trees. Then I laid her down till I cut flat hairy boughs. I put her in my bosom on this dry bed, so we swooned together through the night. I laced her round and covered her with myself, so she lay like a nut within its shell.

'Again, when morning came, it was pain of cold that woke me. I groaned, but my heart was warm as I saw the heap of red hair in my arms. As I looked at her, her eyes opened into mine. She smiled – from out of her smile came fear. As if in a trap she pressed back her head.

' "We have no flint," said I.

' "Yes – in the wallet, flint and steel and tinder-box," she answered.

' "God yield you blessing," I said.

'In a place a little open I kindled a fire of larch boughs. She was afraid of me, hovering near, yet never crossing a space.

' "Come," said I, "let us eat this food."

' "Your face," she said, "is smeared with blood."

'I opened out my cloak.

' "But come," said I, "you are frosted with cold."

'I took a handful of snow in my hand, wiping my face with it, which then I dried on my cloak.

' "My face is no longered painted with blood. You are no longer afraid of me. Come here then, sit by me while we eat."

'But as I cut the cold bread for her, she clasped me suddenly, kissing me. She fell before me, clasped my knees to her breast, weeping. She laid her face down to my feet, so that her hair spread like a fire before me. I wondered at the woman. "Nay," I cried. At that she lifted her face to me from below. "Nay," I cried, feeling my tears fall. With her head on my breast, my own tears rose from their source, wetting my cheek and her hair, which was wet with the rain of my eyes.

'Then I remembered and took from my bosom the coloured light of that night before. I saw it was black and rough.

' "Ah," said I, "this is magic."

' "The black stone!" she wondered.

' "It is magic," she answered.

' "Shall I throw it?" said I, lifting the stone, "shall I throw it away, for fear?"

' "It shines!" she cried, looking up, "it shines like the eye of a creature at night, the eye of a wolf in the doorway."

' " 'Tis magic," I said, "let me throw it from us." But nay, she held my arm.

' "It is red and shining," she cried.

' "It is a bloodstone," I answered. "It will hurt us, we shall die in blood."

' "But give it to me," she answered.

' "It is red of blood," I said.

' "Ah, give it to me," she called.

' "It is my blood," I said.

' "Give it," she commanded, low.

' "It is my life-stone," I said.

' "Give it me," she pleaded.

'I gave it her. She held it up, she smiled, she smiled in my face, lifting her arms to me. I took her with my mouth, her mouth, her white throat. Nor she ever shrank, but trembled with happiness.

'What woke us, when the woods were filling again with shadow, when the fire was out, when we opened our eyes and looked up as if drowned, into the light which stood bright and thick on the tree-tops, what woke us was the sound of wolves....'

'Nay,' said the vicar, suddenly rising, 'they lived happily ever after.'
'No,' I said.

THE SHADES OF SPRING

I

IT was a mile nearer through the wood. Mechanically, Syson turned up by the forge and lifted the field-gate. The blacksmith and his mate stood still, watching the trespasser. But Syson looked too much a gentleman to be accosted. They let him go on in silence across the small field to the wood.

There was not the least difference between this morning and those of the bright springs, six or eight years back. White and sandy-gold fowls still scratched round the gate, littering the earth and the field with feathers and scratched-up rubbish. Between the two thick holly bushes in the wood-hedge was the hidden gap, whose fence one climbed to get into the woods; the bars were scored just the same by the keeper's boots. He was back in the eternal.

Syson was extraordinarily glad. Like an uneasy spirit he had returned to the country of his past, and he found it waiting for him, unaltered. The hazel still spread glad little hands downwards, the bluebells here were still wan and few, among the lush grass and in shade of the bushes.

The path through the wood, on the very brow of a slope, ran winding easily for a time. All around here twiggy oaks, just issuing their gold, and floor spaces diapered with woodruff, with patches of dog-mercury and tufts of hyacinth. Two fallen trees still lay across the track. Syson jolted down a steep, rough slope, and came again upon the open land, this time looking north as through a great window in the wood. He stayed to gaze over the level fields of the hill-top, at the village which strewed the bare upland as if it had tumbled off the passing wagons of industry, and been forsaken. There was a stiff, modern, grey little church, and blocks and rows of red dwellings lying at random; at the back, the twinkling headstocks of the pit, and the looming pit-hill. All was naked and out-of-doors, not a tree! It was quite unaltered.

Syson turned, satisfied, to follow the path that sheered downhill into the wood. He was curiously elated, feeling himself back in an enduring vision. He started. A keeper was standing a few yards in front, barring the way.

'Where might you be going this road, sir?' asked the man. The tone of his question had a challenging twang. Syson looked at the fellow with an impersonal, observant gaze. It was a young man of four- or five-and-twenty, ruddy and well favoured. His dark blue eyes now stared aggressively at the intruder. His black moustache, very thick, was cropped short over a small, rather soft mouth. In every other respect the fellow was manly and good-looking. He stood just above middle height; the strong forward thrust of his chest, and the perfect ease of his erect, self-sufficient body, gave one the feeling that he was taut with animal life, like the thick jet of a fountain balanced in itself. He stood with the butt of his gun on the ground, looking uncertainly and questioningly at Syson. The dark, restless eyes of the trespasser, examining the man and penetrating into him without heeding his office, troubled the keeper and made him flush.

'Where is Naylor? Have you got his job?' Syson asked.

'You're not from the House, are you?' inquired the keeper. It could not be, since everyone was away.

'No, I'm not from the House,' the other replied. It seemed to amuse him.

'Then might I ask where you were making for?' said the keeper, nettled.

'Where I am making for?' Syson repeated. 'I am going to Willey-Water Farm.'

'This isn't the road.'

'I think so. Down this path, past the well, and out by the white gate.'

'But that's not the public road.'

'I suppose not. I used to come so often, in Naylor's time, I had forgotten. Where is he, by the way?'

'Crippled with rheumatism,' the keeper answered reluctantly.

'Is he?' Syson exclaimed in pain.

'And who might you be?' asked the keeper, with a new intonation.

'John Adderley Syson; I used to live in Cordy Lane.'

'Used to court Hilda Millership?'

Syson's eyes opened with a pained smile. He nodded. There was an awkward silence.

'And you – who are you?' asked Syson.

'Arthur Pilbeam – Naylor's my uncle,' said the other.

'You live here in Nuttall?'

'I'm lodgin' at my uncle's – at Naylor's.'

'I see!'

'Did you say you was goin' down to Willey-Water?' asked the keeper.

'Yes.'

There was a pause of some moments, before the keeper blurted: '*I'm courtin' Hilda Millership.*'

The young fellow looked at the intruder with a stubborn defiance, almost pathetic. Syson opened new eyes.

'Are you?' he said, astonished. The keeper flushed dark.

'She and me are keeping company,' he said.

'I didn't know!' said Syson. The other man waited uncomfortably.

'What, is the thing settled?' asked the intruder.

'How, settled?' retorted the other sulkily.

'Are you going to get married soon, and all that?'

The keeper stared in silence for some moments, impotent.

'I suppose so,' he said, full of resentment.

'Ah!' Syson watched closely.

'I'm married myself,' he added, after a time.

'You are?' said the other incredulously.

Syson laughed in his brilliant, unhappy way.

'This last fifteen months,' he said.

The keeper gazed at him with wide, wondering eyes, apparently thinking back, and trying to make things out.

'Why, didn't you know?' asked Syson.

'No, I didn't,' said the other sulkily.

There was silence for a moment.

'Ah well!' said Syson, 'I will go on. I suppose I may.' The keeper stood in silent opposition. The two men hesitated in the open, grassy space, set round with small sheaves of sturdy bluebells; a little open platform on the brow of the hill. Syson took a few indecisive steps forward, then stopped.

'I say, how beautiful!' he cried.

He had come in full view of the downslope. The wide path ran from his feet like a river, and it was full of bluebells, save for a green winding thread down the centre, where the keeper walked. Like a stream the path opened into azure shallows at the levels, and there were pools of bluebells, with still the green thread winding through, like a thin current of ice-water through blue lakes. And from under the twig-purple of

187

the bushes swam the shadowed blue, as if the flowers lay in flood water over the woodland.

'Ah, isn't it lovely!' Syson exclaimed; this was his past, the country he had abandoned, and it hurt him to see it so beautiful. Wood-pigeons cooed overhead, and the air was full of the brightness of birds singing.

'If you're married, what do you keep writing to her for, and sending her poetry books and things?' asked the keeper. Syson stared at him, taken aback and humiliated. Then he began to smile.

'Well,' he said, 'I did not know about you...'

Again the keeper flushed darkly.

'But if you are married —' he charged.

'I am,' answered the other cynically.

Then, looking down the blue, beautiful path, Syson felt his own humiliation. 'What right *have* I to hang on to her?' he thought, bitterly, self-contemptuous.

'She knows I'm married and all that,' he said.

'But you keep sending her books,' challenged the keeper.

Syson, silenced, looked at the other man quizzically, half pitying. Then he turned.

'Good day,' he said, and was gone. Now, everything irritated him: the two sallows, one all gold and perfume and murmur, one silver-green and bristly, reminded him that here he had taught her about pollination. What a fool he was! What god-forsaken folly it all was!

'Ah well,' he said to himself; 'the poor devil seems to have a grudge against me. I'll do my best for him.' He grinned to himself, in a very bad temper.

II

The farm was less than a hundred yards from the wood's edge. The wall of trees formed the fourth side to the open quadrangle. The house faced the wood. With tangled emotions, Syson noted the plum blossom falling on the profuse, coloured primroses, which he himself had brought here and set. How they had increased! There were thick tufts of scarlet, and pink, and pale purple primroses under the plum trees. He saw somebody glance at him through the kitchen window, heard men's voices.

The door opened suddenly: very womanly she had grown! He felt himself going pale.

'You? – Addy!' she exclaimed, and stood motionless.

'Who?' called the farmer's voice. Men's low voices answered. Those low voices, curious and almost jeering, roused the tormented spirit in the visitor. Smiling brilliantly at her, he waited.

'Myself – why not?' he said.

The flush burned very deep on her cheek and throat.

'We are just finishing dinner,' she said.

'Then I will stay outside.' He made a motion to show that he would sit on the red earthenware pipkin that stood near the door among the daffodils, and contained the drinking-water.

'Oh no, come in,' she said hurriedly. He followed her. In the doorway, he glanced swiftly over the family, and bowed. Everyone was confused. The farmer, his wife, and the four sons sat at the coarsely laid dinner-table, the men with arms bare to the elbows.

'I am sorry I come at lunch-time,' said Syson.

'Hello, Addy!' said the farmer, assuming the old form of address, but his tone cold. 'How are you?'

And he shook hands.

'Shall you have a bit?' he invited the young visitor, but taking for granted the offer would be refused. He assumed that Syson was become too refined to eat so roughly. The young man winced at the imputation.

'Have you had any dinner?' asked the daughter.

'No,' replied Syson. 'It is too early. I shall be back at half-past one.'

'You call it lunch, don't you?' asked the eldest son, almost ironical. He had once been an intimate friend of this young man.

'We'll give Addy something when we've finished,' said the mother, an invalid, deprecating.

'No – don't trouble. I don't want to give you any trouble,' said Syson.

'You could allus live on fresh air an' scenery,' laughed the youngest son, a lad of nineteen.

Syson went round the buildings, and into the orchard at the back of the house, where daffodils all along the hedgerow swung like yellow, ruffled birds on their perches. He loved the place extraordinarily, the hills ranging round, with bear-skin woods covering their giant shoulders, and small red farms like brooches clasping their garments; the blue streak of water in the valley, the bareness of the home pasture, the sound of myriad-threaded bird-singing, which went mostly unheard. To his last day, he would dream of this place, when he felt the sun on his face, or saw the small handfuls of snow between the winter twigs, or smelt the coming of spring.

Hilda was very womanly. In her presence he felt constrained. She was twenty-nine, as he was, but she seemed to him much older. He felt foolish, almost unreal beside her. She was so static. As he was fingering some shed plum blossom on a low bough, she came to the back door to shake the tablecloth. Fowls raced from the stack-yard, birds rustled from the trees. Her dark hair was gathered up in a coil like a crown on her head. She was very straight, distant in her bearing. As she folded the cloth, she looked away over the hills.

Presently Syson returned indoors. She had prepared eggs and curd cheese, stewed gooseberries and cream.

'Since you will dine to-night,' she said, 'I have only given you a light lunch.'

'It is awfully nice,' he said. 'You keep a real idyllic atmosphere – your belt of straw and ivy buds.'

Still they hurt each other.

He was uneasy before her. Her brief, sure speech, her distant bearing, were unfamiliar to him. He admired again her grey-black eyebrows, and her lashes. Their eyes met. He saw, in the beautiful grey and black of her glance, tears and a strange light, and at the back of all, calm acceptance of herself, and triumph over him.

He felt himself shrinking. With an effort he kept up the ironic manner.

She sent him into the parlour while she washed the dishes. The long low room was refurnished from the Abbey sale, with chairs upholstered in claret-coloured rep, many years old, and an oval table of polished walnut, and another piano, handsome, though still antique. In spite of the strangeness, he was pleased. Opening a high cupboard let into the thickness of the wall, he found it full of his books, his old lesson-books, and volumes of verse he had sent her, English and German. The daffodils in the white window-bottoms shone across the room, he could almost feel their rays. The old glamour caught him again. His youthful water-colours on the wall no longer made him grin; he remembered how fervently he had tried to paint for her, twelve years before.

She entered, wiping a dish, and he saw again the bright, kernel-white beauty of her arms.

'You are quite splendid here,' he said, and their eyes met.

'Do you like it?' she asked. It was the old, low, husky tone of intimacy. He felt a quick change beginning in his blood. It was the old, delicious sublimation, the thinning, almost the vaporising of himself, as if his spirit were to be liberated.

'Aye,' he nodded, smiling at her like a boy again. She bowed her head.

'This was the countess's chair,' she said in low tones. 'I found her scissors down here between the padding.'

'Did you? Where are they?'

Quickly, with a lilt in her movement, she fetched her workbasket, and together they examined the long-shanked old scissors.

'What a ballad of dead ladies!' he said, laughing, as he fitted his fingers into the round loops of the countess's scissors.

'I knew you could use them,' she said, with certainty. He looked at his fingers, and at the scissors. She meant his fingers were fine enough for the small-looped scissors.

'That is something to be said for me,' he laughed, putting the scissors aside. She turned to the window. He noticed the fine, fair down on her cheeks and her upper lip, and her soft, white neck, like the throat of a nettle flower, and her forearms, bright as newly blanched kernels. He was looking at her with new eyes, and she was a different person to him. He did not know her. But he could regard her objectively now. He did not know her. But he could regard her objectively now.

'Shall we go out awhile?' she asked.

'Yes!' he answered. But the predominant emotion, that troubled the excitement and perplexity of his heart, was fear, fear of that which he saw. There was about her the same manner, the same intonation in her voice, now as then, but she was not what he had known her to be. He knew quite well what she had been for him. And gradually he was realising that she was something quite other, and always had been.

She put no covering on her head, merely took off her apron, saying: 'We will go by the larches.' As they passed the old orchard, she called him in to show him a blue-tit's nest in one of the apple trees, and a sycock's in the hedge. He rather wondered at her surety, at a certain hardness like arrogance hidden under her humility.

'Look at the apple buds,' she said, and he then perceived myriads of little scarlet balls among the drooping boughs. Watching his face, her eyes went hard. She saw the scales were fallen from him, and at last he was going to see her as she was. It was the thing she had most dreaded in the past, and most needed, for her soul's sake. Now he was going to see her as she was. He would not love her, and he would know he never could have loved her. The old illusion gone, they were strangers, crude

191

and entire. But he would give her her due – she would have her due from him.

She was brilliant as he had not known her. She showed him nests: a jenny wren's in a low bush.

'See this jinty's!' she exclaimed.

He was surprised to hear her use the local name. She reached carefully through the thorns, and put her finger in the nest's round door.

'Five!' she said. 'Tiny little things.'

She showed him nests of robins, and chaffinches, and linnets, and buntings; of a wagtail beside the water.

'And if we go down, nearer the lake, I will show you a kingfisher's....'

'Among the young fir trees,' she said, 'there's a throstle's or a blackie's on nearly every bough, every ledge. The first day, when I had seen them all. I felt as if I mustn't go in the wood. It seemed a city of birds: and in the morning, hearing them all, I thought of the noisy early markets. I was afraid to go in my own wood.'

She was using the language they had both of them invented. Now it was all her own. He had done with it. She did not mind his silence, but was always dominant, letting him see her wood. As they came along a marshy path where forget-me-nots were opening in a rich blue drift: 'We know all the birds, but there are many flowers we can't find out,' she said. It was half an appeal to him, who had known the names of things.

She looked dreamily across to the open fields that slept in the sun.

'I have a lover as well, you know,' she said, with assurance, yet dropping again almost into the intimate tone.

This woke in him the spirit to fight her.

'I think I met him. He is good-looking – also in Arcady.'

Without answering, she turned into a dark path that led uphill, where the trees and undergrowth were very thick.

'They did well,' she said at length, 'to have various altars to various gods, in old days.'

'Ah yes!' he agreed. 'To whom is the new one?'

'There are no old ones,' she said. 'I was always looking for this.'

'And whose is it?' he asked.

'I don't know,' she said, looking full at him.

'I'm very glad, for your sake,' he said, 'that you are satisfied.'

'Aye – but the man doesn't matter so much?' she said. There was a pause.

'No!' he exclaimed, astonished, yet recognising her as her real self.

'It is one's self that matters,' she said. 'Whether one is being one's own self and serving one's own God.'

There was silence, during which he pondered. The path was almost flowerless, gloomy. At the side, his heels sank into soft clay.

III

'I,' she said, very slowly, 'I was married the same night as you.'

He looked at her.

'Not legally, of course,' she replied. 'But – actually.'

'To the keeper?' he said, not knowing what else to say.

She turned to him.

'You thought I could not?' she said. But the flush was deep in her cheek and throat, for all her assurance.

Still he would not say anything.

'You see' – she was making an effort to explain – 'I had to understand also.'

'And what does it amount to, this *understanding*?' he asked.

'A very great deal – does it not to you?' she replied. 'One is free.'

'And you are not disappointed?'

'Far from it!' Her tone was deep and sincere.

'You love him?'

'Yes, I love him.'

'Good!' he said.

This silenced her for a while.

'Here, among his things, I love him,' she said.

His conceit would not let him be silent.

'It needs this setting?' he asked.

'It does,' she cried. 'You were always making me to be not myself.'

He laughed shortly.

'But is it a matter of surroundings?' he said. He had considered her all spirit.

'I am like a plant,' she replied. 'I can only grow in my own soil.'

They came to a place where the undergrowth shrank away, leaving a bare, brown space, pillared with the brick-red and purplish trunks of pine trees. On the fringe, hung the sombre green of elder trees, with flat flowers in bud, and below were bright, unfurling pennons of fern. In the

193

midst of the bare space stood a keeper's log hut. Pheasant-coops were lying about, some occupied by a clucking hen, some empty.

Hilda walked over the brown pine-needles to the hut, took a key from among the eaves, and opened the door. It was a bare wooden place with a carpenter's bench and form, carpenter's tools, an axe, snares, traps, some skins pegged down, everything in order. Hilda closed the door. Syson examined the weird flat coats of wild animals, that were pegged down to be cured. She turned some knotch in the side wall, and disclosed a second, small apartment.

'How romantic!' said Syson.

'Yes. He is very curious – he has some of a wild animal's cunning – in a nice sense – and he is inventive, and thoughtful – but not beyond a certain point.'

She pulled back a dark green curtain. The apartment was occupied almost entirely by a large couch of heather and bracken, on which was spread an ample rabbit-skin rug. On the floor were patchwork rugs of cat-skin, and a red calf-skin, while hanging from the wall were other furs. Hilda took down one, which she put on. It was a cloak of rabbit-skin and of white fur, with a hood, apparently of the skins of stoats. She laughed at Syson from out of this barbaric mantle, saying:

'What do you think of it?'

'Ah —! I congratulate you on your man,' he replied.

'And look!' she said.

In a little jar on a shelf were some sprays, frail and white, of the first honeysuckle.

'They will scent the place at night.'

He looked round curiously.

'Where does he come short, then?' he asked. She gazed at him for a few moments. Then, turning aside:

'The stars aren't the same with him,' she said. 'You could make them flash and quiver, and the forget-me-nots come up at me like phosphorescence. You could make things *wonderful*. I have found it out – it is true. But I have them all for myself, now.'

He laughed, saying:

'After all, stars and forget-me-nots are only luxuries. You ought to make poetry.'

'Aye,' she assented. 'But I have them all now.'

Again he laughed bitterly at her.

She turned swiftly. He was leaning against the small window of the tiny, obscure room, and was watching her, who stood in the doorway, still cloaked in her mantle. His cap was removed, so she saw his face and head distinctly in the dim room. His black, straight, glossy hair was brushed clean back from his brow. His black eyes were watching her, and his face, that was clear and cream, and perfectly smooth, was flickering.

'We are very different,' she said bitterly.

Again he laughed.

'I see you disapprove of me,' he said.

'I disapprove of what you have become,' she said.

'You think we might' – he glanced at the hut – 'have been like this – you and I?'

She shook her head.

'You! No; never! You plucked a thing and looked at it till you had found out all you wanted to know about it, then you threw it away,' she said.

'Did I?' he asked. 'And could your way never have been my way? I suppose not.'

'Why should it?' she said. 'I am a separate being.'

'But surely two people sometimes go the same way,' he said.

'You took me away from myself,' she said.

He knew he had mistaken her, had taken her for something she was not. That was his fault, not hers.

'And did you always know?' he asked.

'No – you never let me know. You bullied me. I couldn't help myself. I was glad when you left me, really.'

'I know you were,' he said. But his face went paler, almost deathly luminous.

'Yet,' he said, 'it was you who sent me the way I have gone.'

'I!' she exclaimed, in pride.

'You *would* have me take the Grammar School scholarship – and you would have me foster poor little Botell's fervent attachment to me, till he couldn't live without me – and because Botell was rich and influential. You triumphed in the wine-merchant's offer to send me to Cambridge, to befriend his only child. You wanted me to rise in the world. And all the time you were sending me away from you – every new success of mine put a separation between us, and more for you than for me. You never wanted to come with me: you wanted just to send me to see what it was like. I believe you even wanted me to marry a lady. You wanted to triumph over society in me.'

'And I am responsible,' she said, with sarcasm.

'I distinguished myself to satisfy you,' he replied.

'Ah!' she cried, 'you always wanted change, change, like a child.'

'Very well! And I am a success, and I know it, and I do some good work. But – I thought you were different. What right have you to a man?'

'What do you want?' she said, looking at him with wide, fearful eyes.

He looked back at her, his eyes pointed, like weapons.

'Why, nothing,' he laughed shortly.

There was a rattling at the outer latch, and the keeper entered. The woman glanced round, but remained standing, fur-cloaked, in the inner doorway. Syson did not move.

The other man entered, saw, and turned away without speaking. The two also were silent.

Pilbeam attended to his skins.

'I must go,' said Syson.

'Yes,' she replied.

'Then I give you "To our vast and varying fortunes." ' He lifted his hand in pledge.

' "To our vast and varying fortunes," ' she answered gravely, and speaking in cold tones.

'Arthur!' she said.

The keeper pretended not to hear. Syson, watching keenly, began to smile. The woman drew herself up.

'Arthur!' she said again, with a curious upward inflection, which warned the two men that her soul was trembling on a dangerous crisis.

The keeper slowly put down his tool and came to her.

'Yes,' he said.

'I wanted to introduce you,' she said, trembling.

'I've met him a'ready,' said the keeper.

'Have you? It is Addy, Mr. Syson, whom you know about. – This is Arthur, Mr. Pilbeam,' she added, turning to Syson. The latter held out his hand to the keeper, and they shook hands in silence.

'I'm glad to have met you,' said Syson. 'We drop our correspondence, Hilda?'

'Why need we?' she asked.

The two men stood at a loss.

'Is there no need?' said Syson.

Still she was silent.

'It is as you will,' she said.

They went all three together down the gloomy path.

' "Qu'il était bleu, le ciel, et grand l'espoir," ' quoted Syson, not knowing what to say.

'What do you mean?' she said. 'Besides, *we* can't walk in *our* wild oats – we never sowed any.'

Syson looked at her. He was startled to see his young love, his nun, his Botticelli angel, so revealed. It was he who had been the fool. He and she were more separate than any two strangers could be. She only wanted to keep up a correspondence with him – and he, of course, wanted it kept up, so that he would write to her, like Dante to some Beatrice who had never existed save in the man's own brain.

At the bottom of the path she left him. He went along with the keeper, towards the open, towards the gate that closed on the wood. The two men walked almost like friends. They did not broach the subject of their thoughts.

Instead of going straight to the high-road gate, Syson went along the woods' edge, where the brook spread out in a little bog, and under the alder trees, among the reeds, great yellow stools and bosses of marigolds shone. Threads of brown water trickled by, touched with gold from the flowers. Suddenly there was a blue flash in the air, as a kingfisher passed.

Syson was extraordinarily moved. He climbed the bank to the gorse bushes, whose sparks of blossom had not yet gathered into a flame. Lying on the dry brown turf, he discovered sprigs of tiny purple milk-wort and pink spots of lousewort. What a wonderful world it was – marvellous, for ever new. He felt as if it were underground, like the fields of monotone hell, notwithstanding. Inside his breast was a pain like a wound. He remembered the poem of William Morris, where in the Chapel of Lyonesse a knight lay wounded, with the truncheon of a spear deep in his breast, lying always as dead, yet did not die, while day after day the coloured sunlight dipped from the painted window across the chancel, and passed away. He knew now it never had been true, that which was between him and her, not for a moment. The truth had stood apart all the time.

Syson turned over. The air was full of the sound of larks, as if the sunshine above were condensing and falling in a shower. Amid this bright sound, voices sounded small and distinct.

'But if he's married, an' quite willing to drop it off, what has ter against it?' said the man's voice.

'I don't want to talk about it now. I want to be alone.'

Syson looked through the bushes. Hilda was standing in the wood, near the gate. The man was in the field, loitering by the hedge, and playing with the bees as they settled on the white bramble flowers.

There was silence for a while, in which Syson imagined her will among the brightness of the larks. Suddenly the keeper exclaimed 'Ah!' and swore. He was gripping at the sleeve of his coat, near the shoulder. Then he pulled off his jacket, threw it on the ground, and absorbedly rolled up his shirtsleeves right to the shoulder.

'Ah!' he said vindictively, as he picked out the bee and flung it away. He twisted his fine, bright arm, peering awkwardly over his shoulder.

'What is it?' asked Hilda.

'A bee – crawled up my sleeve,' he answered.

'Come here to me,' she said.

The keeper went to her, like a sulky boy. She took his arm in her hands.

'Here it is – and the sting left in – poor bee!'

She picked out the sting, put her mouth to his arm, and sucked away the drop of poison. As she looked at the red mark her mouth had made, and at his arm, she said, laughing:

'That is the reddest kiss you will ever have.'

When Syson next looked up, at the sound of voices, he saw in the shadow the keeper with his mouth on the throat of his beloved, whose head was thrown back, and whose hair had fallen, so that one rough rope of dark brown hair hung across his bare arm.

'No,' the woman answered. 'I am not upset because he's gone. You won't understand....'

Syson could not distinguish what the man said. Hilda replied, clear and distinct:

'You know I love you. He has gone quite out of my life – don't trouble about him....' He kissed her, murmuring. She laughed hollowly.

'Yes,' she said, indulgent. 'We will be married, we will be married. But not just yet.' He spoke to her again. Syson heard nothing for a time. Then she said:

'You must go home now, dear – you will get no sleep.'

Again was heard the murmur of the keeper's voice, troubled by fear and passion.

'But why should we be married at once?' she said. 'What more would you have, by being married? It is most beautiful as it is.'

At last he pulled on his coat and departed. She stood at the gate, not watching him, but looking over the sunny country.

When at last she had gone, Syson also departed, going back to town.

SECOND BEST

'OH, I'm tired!' Frances exclaimed petulantly, and in the same instant she dropped down on the turf, near the hedge-bottom. Anne stood a moment surprised, then, accustomed to the vagaries of her beloved Frances, said:

'Well, and aren't you always likely to be tired, after travelling that blessed long way from Liverpool yesterday?' and she plumped down beside her sister. Anne was a wise young body of fourteen, very buxom, brimming with common sense. Frances was much older, about twenty-three, and whimsical, spasmodic. She was the beauty and the clever child of the family. She plucked the goose-grass buttons from her dress in a nervous, desperate fashion. Her beautiful profile, looped above with black hair, warm with the dusky-and-scarlet complexion of a pear, was calm as a mask, her thin brown hand plucked nervously.

'It's not the journey,' she said, objecting to Anne's obtuseness. Anne looked inquiringly at her darling. The young girl, in her self-confident, practical way, proceeded to reckon up this whimsical creature. But suddenly she found herself full in the eyes of Frances; felt two dark, hectic eyes flaring challenge at her, and she shrank away. Frances was peculiar for these great, exposed looks, which disconcerted people by their violence and their suddenness.

'What's a matter, poor old duck?' asked Anne, as she folded the slight, wilful form of her sister in her arms. Frances laughed shakily, and nestled down for comfort on the budding breasts of the strong girl.

'Oh, I'm only a bit tired,' she murmured, on the point of tears.

'Well, of course you are, what do you expect?' soothed Anne. It was a joke to Frances that Anne should play elder, almost mother to her. But then, Anne was in her unvexed teens; men were like big dogs to her: while Frances, at twenty-three, suffered a good deal.

The country was intensely morning-still. On the common everything shone beside its shadow, and the hill-side gave off heat in silence. The brown turf seemed in a low state of combustion, the leaves of the oaks were scorched brown. Among the blackish foliage in the distance shone the small red and orange of the village.

The willows in the brook-course at the foot of the common suddenly shook with a dazzling effect like diamonds. It was a puff of wind. Anne resumed her normal position. She spread her knees, and put in her lap a handful of hazel nuts, whity-green leafy things, whose one cheek was tanned between brown and pink. These she began to crack and eat. Frances, with bowed head, mused bitterly.

'Eh, you know Tom Smedley?' began the young girl, as she pulled a tight kernel out of its shell.

'I suppose so,' replied Frances sarcastically.

'Well, he gave me a wild rabbit what he'd caught, to keep with my tame one – and it's living.'

'That's a good thing,' said Frances, very detached and ironic.

'Well, it *is*! He reckoned he'd take me to Ollerton Feast, but he never did. Look here, he took a servant from the rectory; I saw him.'

'So he ought,' said Frances.

'No, he oughtn't! And I told him so. And I told him I should tell you – an' I have done.'

Click and snap went a nut between her teeth. She sorted out the kernel, and chewed complacently.

'It doesn't make much difference,' said Frances.

'Well, 'appen it doesn't; but I was mad with him all the same.'

'Why?'

'Because I was; he's no right to go with a servant.'

'He's a perfect right,' persisted Frances, very just and cold.

'No, he hasn't, when he'd said he'd take me.'

Frances burst into a laugh of amusement and relief.

'Oh no; I'd forgot that,' she said, adding, 'and what did he say when you promised to tell me?'

'He laughed and said: "She won't fret her fat over that." '

'And she won't,' sniffed Frances.

There was silence. The common, with its sere, blonde-headed thistles, its heaps of silent bramble, its brown-husked gorse in the glare of sunshine, seemed visionary. Across the brook began the immense pattern of agriculture, white chequering of barley stubble, brown squares of wheat, khaki patches of pasture, red stripes of fallow, with the woodland and the tiny village dark like ornaments, leading away to the distance, right to the hills, where the check-pattern grew smaller and smaller, till, in the blackish haze of heat, far off, only the tiny white squares of barley stubble showed distinct.

'Eh, I say, here's a rabbit-hole!' cried Anne suddenly. 'Should we watch if one comes out? You won't have to fidget, you know.'

The two girls sat perfectly still. Frances watched certain objects in her surroundings: they had a peculiar, unfriendly look about them: the weight of greenish elderberries on their purpling stalks; the twinkling of the yellowing crab-apple that clustered high up in the hedge, against the sky: the exhausted, limp leaves of the primroses lying flat in the hedge-bottom: all looked strange to her. Then her eyes caught a movement. A mole was moving silently over the warm, red soil, nosing, shuffling hither and thither, flat, and dark as a shadow, shifting about, and as suddenly brisk, and as silent, like a very ghost of *joie de vivre*. Frances started, from habit was about to call on Anne to kill the little pest. But, to-day her lethargy of unhappiness was too much for her. She watched the little brute paddling, snuffing, touching things to discover them, running in blindness, delighted to ecstasy by the sunlight and the hot, strange things that caressed its belly and its nose. She felt a keen pity for the little creature.

'Eh, our Fran, look there! It's a mole.'

Anne was on her feet, standing watching the dark, unconscious beast. Frances frowned with anxiety.

'It doesn't run off, does it?' said the young girl softly. Then she stealthily approached the creature. The mole paddled fumblingly away. In an instant Anne put her foot upon it, not too heavily. Frances could see the struggling, swimming movement of the little pink hands of the brute, the twisting and twitching of its pointed nose, as it wrestled under the sole of the boot.

'It *does* wriggle!' said the bonny girl, knitting her brows in a frown at the eerie sensation. Then she bent down to look at her trap. Frances could now see, beyond the edge of the boot-sole, the heaving of the velvet shoulders, the pitiful turning of the sightless face, the frantic rowing of the flat, pink hands.

'Kill the thing,' she said, turning away her face.

'Oh – I'm not,' laughed Anne, shrinking. 'You can, if you like.'

'I *don't* like,' said Frances, with quiet intensity.

After several dabbing attempts, Anne succeeded in picking up the little animal by the scruff of its neck. It threw back its head, flung its long blind snout from side to side, the mouth open in a peculiar oblong, with tiny pinkish teeth at the edge. The blind, frantic mouth gaped and writhed. The body, heavy and clumsy, hung scarcely moving.

'Isn't it a snappy little thing,' observed Anne, twisting to avoid the teeth.

'What are you going to do with it?' asked Frances sharply.

'It's got to be killed – look at the damage they do. I s'll take it home and let dadda or somebody kill it. I'm not going to let it go.'

She swaddled the creature clumsily in her pocket handkerchief and sat down beside her sister. There was an interval of silence, during which Anne combated the efforts of the mole.

'You've not had much to say about Jimmy this time. Did you see him often in Liverpool?' Anne asked suddenly.

'Once or twice,' replied Frances, giving no sign of how the question troubled her.

'And aren't you sweet on him any more, then?'

'I should think I'm not, seeing that he's engaged.'

'Engaged? Jimmy Barrass! Well, of all things! I never thought *he'd* get engaged.'

'Why not, he's as much right as anybody else?' snapped Frances.

Anne was fumbling with the mole.

' 'Appen so,' she said at length; 'but I never thought Jimmy would, though.'

'Why not?' snapped Frances.

'*I* don't know – this blessed mole, it'll not keep still! – who's he got engaged to?'

'How should I know?'

'I thought you'd ask him; you've known him long enough. I s'd think he thought he'd get engaged now he's a Doctor of Chemistry.'

Frances laughed in spite of herself.

'What's that got to do with it?' she asked.

'I'm sure it's got a bit. He'll want to feel *somebody* now, so he's got engaged. Hey, stop it; go in!'

But at this juncture the mole almost succeeded in wriggling clear. It wrestled and twisted frantically, waved its pointed blind head, its mouth standing open like a little shaft, its big, wrinkled hands spread out.

'Go in with you!' urged Anne, poking the little creature with her forefinger, trying to get it back into the handkerchief. Suddenly the mouth turned like a spark on her finger.

'Oh!' she cried, 'he's bit me.'

She dropped him to the floor. Dazed, the blind creature fumbled round. Frances felt like shrieking. She expected him to dart away in a flash, like a mouse, and there he remained groping; she wanted to cry to him to be gone. Anne, in a sudden decision of wrath, caught up her sister's walking-cane. With one blow the mole was dead. Frances was startled and shocked. One moment the little wretch was fussing in the heat, and the next it lay like a little bag, inert and black – not a struggle, scarce a quiver.

'It is dead!' Frances said breathlessly. Anne took her finger from her mouth, looked at the tiny pin-pricks, and said:

'Yes, he is, and I'm glad. They're vicious little nuisances, moles are.' With which her wrath vanished. She picked up the dead animal.

'Hasn't it got a beautiful skin,' she mused, stroking the fur with her forefinger, then with her cheek.

'Mind,' said Frances sharply. 'You'll have the blood on your skirt!' One ruby drop of blood hung on the small snout, ready to fall. Anne shook it off on to some harebells. Frances suddenly became calm; in that moment, grown-up.

'I suppose they have to be killed,' she said, and a certain rather dreary indifference succeeded to her grief. The twinkling crab-apples, the glitter of brilliant willows now seemed to her trifling, scarcely worth the notice. Something had died in her, so that things lost their poignancy. She was calm, indifference overlying her quiet sadness. Rising, she walked down to the brook course.

'Here, wait for me,' cried Anne, coming tumbling after.

Frances stood on the bridge, looking at the red mud trodden into pockets by the feet of cattle. There was not a drain of water left, but everything smelled green, succulent. Why did she care so little for Anne, who was so fond of her! she asked herself. Why did she care so little for anyone? She did not know, but she felt a rather stubborn pride in her isolation and indifference.

They entered a field where stooks of barley stood in rows, the straight, blonde tresses of the corn streaming on to the ground. The stubble was bleached by the intense summer, so that the expanse glared white. The next field was sweet and soft with a second crop of seeds; thin, straggling clover whose little pink knobs rested prettily in the dark green. The scent was faint and sickly. The girls came up in single file, Frances leading.

Near the gate a young man was mowing with the scythe some fodder for the afternoon feed of the cattle. As he saw the girls he left off working and waited in an aimless kind of way. Frances was dressed in white muslin, and she walked with dignity, detached and forgetful. Her lack of agitation, her simple, unheeding advance made him nervous. She had loved the far-off Jimmy for five years, having had in return his half-measures. This man only affected her slightly.

Tom was of medium stature, energetic in build. His smooth, fair-skinned face was burned red, not brown, by the sun, and this ruddiness enhanced his appearance of good humour and easiness. Being a year older than Frances, he would have courted her long ago had she been so inclined. As it was, he had gone his uneventful way amiably, chatting with many a girl, but remaining unattached, free of trouble for the most part. Only he knew he wanted a woman. He hitched his trousers just a trifle self-consciously as the girls approached. Frances was a rare, delicate kind of being, whom he realised with a queer and delicious stimulation in his veins. She gave him a slight sense of suffocation. Somehow, this morning she affected him more than usual. She was dressed in white. He, however, being matter-of-fact in his mind, did not realise. His feeling had never become conscious, purposive.

Frances knew what she was about. Tom was ready to love her as soon as she would show him. Now that she could not have Jimmy, she did not poignantly care. Still, she would have something. If she could not have the best – Jimmy, whom she knew to be something of a snob – she would have the second best, Tom. She advanced rather indifferently.

'You are back, then!' said Tom. She marked the touch of uncertainty in his voice.

'No,' she laughed, 'I'm still in Liverpool,' and the undertone of intimacy made him burn.

'This isn't you, then?' he asked.

Her heart leapt up in approval. She looked in his eyes, and for a second was with him.

'Why, what do you think?' she laughed.

He lifted his hat from his head with a distracted little gesture. She liked him, his quaint ways, his humour, his ignorance, and his slow masculinity.

'Here, look here, Tom Smedley,' broke in Anne.

'A moudiwarp! Did you find it dead?' he asked.

'No, it bit me,' said Anne.

'Oh, aye! An' that got your rag out, did it?'

'No, it didn't!' Anne scolded sharply. 'Such language!'

'Oh, what's up wi' it?'

'I can't bear you to talk broad.'

'Can't you?'

He glanced at Frances.

'It isn't nice,' Frances said. She did not care, really. The vulgar

205

speech jarred on her as a rule; Jimmy was a gentleman. But Tom's manner of speech did not matter to her.

'I like you to talk *nicely*,' she added.

'Do you,' he replied, tilting his hat, stirred.

'And generally you *do*, you know,' she smiled.

'I s'll have to have a try,' he said, rather tensely gallant.

'What?' she asked brightly.

'To talk nice to you,' he said. Frances coloured furiously, bent her head for a moment, then laughed gaily, as if she liked this clumsy hint.

'Eh now, you mind what you're saying,' cried Anne, giving the young man an admonitory pat.

'You wouldn't have to give yon mole many knocks like that,' he teased, relieved to get on safe ground, rubbing his arm.

'No, indeed, it died in one blow,' said Frances, with a flippancy that was hateful to her.

'You're not so good at knockin' 'em?' he said, turning to her.

'I don't know, if I'm cross,' she said decisively.

'No?' he replied, with alert attentiveness.

'I could,' she added, harder, 'if it was necessary.'

He was slow to feel her difference.

'And don't you consider it *is* necessary?' he asked, with misgiving.

'W – ell – is it?' she said, looking at him steadily, coldly.

'I reckon it is,' he replied, looking away, but standing stubborn.

She laughed quickly.

'But it isn't necessary for *me*,' she said, with slight contempt.

'Yes, that's quite true,' he answered.

She laughed in a shaky fashion.

'*I know it is*,' she said; and there was an awkward pause.

'Why, would you *like* me to kill moles then?' she asked tentatively, after a while.

'They do us a lot of damage,' he said, standing firm on his own ground, angered.

'Well, I'll see the next time I come across one,' she promised defiantly. Their eyes met, and she sank before him, her pride troubled. He felt uneasy and triumphant and baffled, as if fate had gripped him. She smiled as she departed.

'Well,' said Anne, as the sisters went through the wheat stubble; 'I don't know what you two's been jawing about, I'm sure.'

'Don't you?' laughed Frances significantly.

206

'No, I don't. But, at any rate, Tom Smedley's a good deal better to my thinking than Jimmy, so there – and nicer.'

'Perhaps he is,' said Frances coldly.

And the next day, after a secret, persistent hunt, she found another mole playing in the heat. She killed it, and in the evening, when Tom came to the gate to smoke his pipe after supper, she took him the dead creature.

'Here you are then!' she said.

'Did you catch it?' he replied, taking the velvet corpse into his fingers and examining it minutely. This was to hide his trepidation.

'Did you think I couldn't?' she asked, her face very near his.

'Nay, I didn't know.'

She laughed in his face, a strange little laugh that caught her breath, all agitation, and tears, and recklessness of desire. He looked frightened and upset. She put her hand to his arm.

'Shall you go out wi' me?' he asked, in a difficult, troubled tone.

She turned her face away, with a shaky laugh. The blood came up in him, strong, overmastering. He resisted it. But it drove him down, and he was carried away. Seeing the winsome, frail nape of her neck, fierce love came upon him for her, and tenderness.

'We s'll 'ave to tell your mother,' he said. And he stood, suffering, resisting his passion for her.

'Yes,' she replied, in a dead voice. But there was a thrill of pleasure in this death.

THE SHADOW IN THE ROSE GARDEN

A RATHER small young man sat by the window of a pretty seaside cottage trying to persuade himself that he was reading the newspaper. It was about half-past eight in the morning. Outside, the glory roses hung in the morning sunshine like little bowls of fire tipped up. The young man looked at the table, then at the clock, then at his own big silver watch. An expression of stiff endurance came on to his face. Then he rose and reflected on the oil-paintings that hung on the walls of the room, giving careful but hostile attention to 'The Stag at Bay'. He tried the lid of the piano, and found it locked. He caught sight of his own face in a little mirror, pulled his brown moustache, and an alert interest sprang into his eyes. He was not ill-favoured. He twisted his moustache. His figure was rather small, but alert and vigorous. As he turned from the mirror a look of self-commiseration mingled with his appreciation of his own physiognomy.

In a state of self-suppression, he went through into the garden. His jacket, however, did not look dejected. It was new, and had a smart and self-confident air, sitting upon a confident body. He contemplated the Tree of Heaven that flourished by the lawn, then sauntered on to the next plant. There was more promise in a crooked apple tree covered with brown-red fruit. Glancing round, he broke off an apple and, with his back to the house, took a clean, sharp bite. To his surprise the fruit was sweet. He took another. Then again he turned to survey the bed-room windows overlooking the garden. He started, seeing a woman's figure; but it was only his wife. She was gazing across to the sea, apparently ignorant of him.

For a moment or two he looked at her, watching her. She was a good-looking woman, who seemed older than he, rather pale, but healthy, her face yearning. Her rich auburn hair was heaped in folds on her fore-head. She looked apart from him and his world, gazing away to the sea. It irked her husband that she should continue abstracted and in ignor-ance of him; he pulled poppy fruits and threw them at the window. She started, glanced at him with a wild smile, and looked away again. Then almost immediately she left the window. He went indoors to meet her.

She had a fine carriage, very proud, and wore a dress of soft white muslin.

'I've been waiting long enough,' he said.

'For me or for breakfast?' she said lightly. 'You know we said nine o'clock. I should have thought you could have slept after the journey.'

'You know I'm always up at five, and I couldn't stop in bed after six. You might as well be in pit as in bed, on a morning like this.'

'I shouldn't have thought the pit would occur to you, here.'

She moved about examining the room, looking at the ornaments under glass covers. He, planted on the hearth-rug, watched her rather uneasily, and grudgingly indulgent. She shrugged her shoulders at the apartment.

'Come,' she said, taking his arm, 'let us go into the garden till Mrs. Coates brings the tray.'

'I hope she'll be quick,' he said, pulling his moustache. She gave a short laugh, and leaned on his arm as they went. He had lighted a pipe.

Mrs. Coates entered the room as they went down the steps. The delightful, erect old lady hastened to the window for a good view of her visitors. Her china-blue eyes were bright as she watched the young couple go down the path, he walking in an easy, confident fashion, with his wife on his arm. The landlady began talking to herself in a soft, Yorkshire accent.

'Just of a height they are. She wouldn't ha' married a man less than herself in stature, I think, though he's not her equal otherwise.' Here her granddaughter came in, setting a tray on the table. The girl went to the old woman's side.

'He's been eating the apples, Gran',' she said.

'Has he, my pet? Well, if he's happy, why not?'

Outside, the young, well-favoured man listened with impatience to the chink of the tea-cups. At last, with a sigh of relief, the couple came in to breakfast. After he had eaten for some time, he rested a moment and said:

'Do you think it's any better place than Bridlington?'

'I do,' she said, 'infinitely! Besides, I am at home here – it's not like a strange sea-side place to me.'

'How long were you here?'

'Two years.'

He ate reflectively.

'I should ha' thought you'd rather go to a fresh place,' he said at length.

She sat very silent, and then, delicately, put out a feeler.

'Why?' she said. 'Do you think I shan't enjoy myself?'

He laughed comfortably, putting the marmalade thick on his bread. 'I hope so,' he said.

She again took no notice of him.

'But don't say anything about it in the village, Frank,' she said casually. 'Don't say who I am, or that I used to live here. There's nobody I want to meet, particularly, and we should never feel free if they knew me again.'

'Why did you come, then?'

' "Why?" Can't you understand why?'

'Not if you don't want to know anybody.'

'I came to see the place, not the people.'

He did not say any more.

'Women,' she said, 'are different from men. I don't know why I wanted to come – but I did.'

She helped him to another cup of coffee, solicitously.

'Only,' she resumed, 'don't talk about me in the village.' She laughed shakily. 'I don't want my past brought up against me, you know.' And she moved the crumbs on the cloth with her finger-tip.

He looked at her as he drank his coffee; he sucked his moustache, and putting down his cup, said phlegmatically:

'I'll bet you've had a lot of past.'

She looked with a little guiltiness, that flattered him, down at the table-cloth.

'Well,' she said, caressive, 'you won't give me away, who I am, will you?'

'No,' he said, comforting, laughing, 'I won't give you away.'

He was pleased.

She remained silent. After a moment or two she lifted her head, saying:

'I've got to arrange with Mrs. Coates, and do various things. So you'd better go out by yourself this morning – and we'll be in to dinner at one.'

'But you can't be arranging with Mrs. Coates all morning,' he said.

'Oh, well – then I've some letters to write, and I must get that mark out of my skirt. I've got plenty of little things to do this morning. You'd better go out by yourself.'

He perceived that she wanted to be rid of him, so that when she went upstairs, he took his hat and lounged out on to the cliffs, suppressedly angry.

Presently she too came out. She wore a hat with roses, and a long lace scarf hung over her white dress. Rather nervously, she put up her sunshade, and her face was half hidden in its coloured shadow. She went along the narrow track of flagstones that were worn hollow by the feet of the fishermen. She seemed to be avoiding her surroundings, as if she remained safe in the little obscurity of her parasol.

She passed the church, and went down the lane till she came to a high wall by the wayside. Under this she went slowly, stopping at length by an open doorway, which shone like a picture of light in the dark wall. There in the magic beyond the doorway, patterns of shadow lay on the sunny court, on the blue and white sea-pebbles of its paving, while a green lawn glowed beyond, where a bay tree glittered at the edges. She tiptoed nervously into the courtyard, glancing at the house that stood in shadow. The uncurtained windows looked black and soulless, the kitchen door stood open. Irresolutely she took a step forward, and again forward, leaning, yearning, towards the garden beyond.

She had almost gained the corner of the house when a heavy step came crunching through the trees. A gardener appeared before her. He held a wicker tray on which were rolling great, dark red gooseberries, over-ripe. He moved slowly.

'The garden isn't open to-day,' he said quietly to the attractive woman, who was poised for retreat.

For a moment she was silent with surprise. How should it be public at all?

'When is it open?' she asked, quick-witted.

'The rector lets visitors in on Fridays and Tuesdays.'

She stood still, reflecting. How strange to think of the rector opening his garden to the public!

'But everybody will be at church,' she said coaxingly to the man. 'There'll be nobody here, will there?'

He moved, and the big gooseberries rolled.

'The rector lives at the new rectory,' he said.

The two stood still. He did not like to ask her to go. At last she turned to him with a winning smile.

'Might I have *one* peep at the roses?' she coaxed, with pretty wilfulness.

'I don't suppose it would matter,' he said, moving aside; 'you won't stop long —'

She went forward, forgetting the gardener in a moment. Her face became strained, her movements eager. Glancing round, she saw all the windows giving on to the lawn were curtainless and dark. The house had a sterile appearance, as if it were still used, but not inhabited. A shadow seemed to go over her. She went across the lawn towards the garden, through an arch of crimson ramblers, a gate of colour. There beyond lay the soft blue sea within the bay, misty with morning, and the farthest headland of black rock jutting dimly out between blue and blue of the sky and water. Her face began to shine, transfigured with pain and joy. At her feet the garden fell steeply, all a confusion of flowers, and away below was the darkness of tree-tops covering the beck.

She turned to the garden that shone with sunny flowers around her. She knew the little corner where was the seat beneath the yew tree. Then there was the terrace where a great host of flowers shone, and from this, two paths went down, one at each side of the garden. She closed her sunshade and walked slowly among the many flowers. All round were rose bushes, big banks of roses, then roses hanging and tumbling from pillars, or roses balanced on the standard bushes. By the open earth were many other flowers. If she lifted her head, the sea was upraised beyond, and the Cape.

Slowly she went down one path, lingering, like one who has gone back into the past. Suddenly she was touching some heavy crimson roses that were soft as velvet, touching them thoughtfully, without knowing, as a mother sometimes fondles the hand of her child. She leaned slightly forward to catch the scent. Then she wandered on in abstraction. Sometimes a flame-coloured, scentless rose would hold her arrested. She stood gazing at it as if she could not understand it. Again the same softness of intimacy came over her, as she stood before a tumbling heap of pink petals. Then she wondered over the white rose, that was greenish, like ice, in the centre. So, slowly, like a white, pathetic butterfly, she drifted down the path, coming at last to a tiny terrace all full of roses. They seemed to fill the place, a sunny, gay throng. She was shy of them, they were so many and so bright. They seemed to be conversing and laughing. She felt herself in a strange crowd. It exhilarated her, carried her out of herself. She flushed with excitement. The air was pure scent.

Hastily, she went to a little seat among the white roses, and sat down.

Her scarlet sunshade made a hard blot of colour. She sat quite still, feeling her own existence lapse. She was no more than a rose, a rose that could not quite come into blossom, but remained tense. A little fly dropped on her knee, on her white dress. She watched it, as if it had fallen on a rose. She was not herself.

Then she started cruelly as a shadow crossed her and a figure moved into her sight. It was a man who had come in slippers, unheard. He wore a linen coat. The morning was shattered, the spell vanished away. She was only afraid of being questioned. He came forward. She rose. Then, seeing him, the strength went from her and she sank on the seat again.

He was a young man, military in appearance, growing slightly stout. His black hair was brushed smooth and bright, his moustache was waxed. But there was something rambling in his gait. She looked up, blanched to the lips, and saw his eyes. They were black, and stared without seeing. They were not a man's eyes. He was coming towards her.

He stared at her fixedly, made an unconscious salute, and sat down beside her on the seat. He moved on the bench, shifted his feet, saying, in a gentlemanly, military voice:

'I don't disturb you – do I?'

She was mute and helpless. He was scrupulously dressed in dark clothes and a linen coat. She could not move. Seeing his hands, with the ring she knew so well upon the little finger, she felt as if she were going dazed. The whole world was deranged. She sat unavailing. For his hands, her symbols of passionate love, filled her with horror as they rested now on his strong thighs.

'May I smoke?' he asked intimately, almost secretly, his hand going to his pocket.

She could not answer, but it did not matter, he was in another world. She wondered, craving, if he recognised her – if he could recognise her. She sat pale with anguish. But she had to go through it.

'I haven't got any tobacco,' he said thoughtfully.

But she paid no heed to his words, only she attended to him. Could he recognise her, or was it all gone? She sat still in a frozen kind of suspense.

'I smoke John Cotton,' he said, 'and I must economise with it, it is expensive. You know, I'm not very well off while these law-suits are going on.'

'No,' she said, and her heart was cold, her soul kept rigid.

He moved, made a loose salute, rose, and went away. She sat motionless. She could see his shape, the shape she had loved with all her passion: his compact, soldier's head, his fine figure now slackened. And it was not he. It only filled her with horror too difficult to know.

Suddenly he came again, his hand in his jacket pocket.

'Do you mind if I smoke?' he said. 'Perhaps I shall be able to see things more clearly.'

He sat down beside her again, filling a pipe. She watched his hands with the fine strong fingers. They had always inclined to tremble slightly. It had surprised her, long ago, in such a healthy man. Now they moved inaccurately, and the tobacco hung raggedly out of the pipe.

'I have legal business to attend to. Legal affairs are always so uncertain. I tell my solicitor exactly, precisely what I want, but I can never get it done.'

She sat and heard him talking. But it was not he. Yet those were the hands she had kissed, there were the glistening, strange black eyes that she had loved. Yet it was not he. She sat motionless with horror and silence. He dropped his tobacco-pouch, and groped for it on the ground. Yet she must wait to see if he would recognise her. Why could she not go! In a moment he rose.

'I must go at once,' he said. 'The owl is coming.' Then he added confidentially: 'His name isn't really the owl, but I call him that. I must go and see if he has come.'

She rose too. He stood before her, uncertain. He was a handsome, soldierly fellow, and a lunatic. Her eyes searched him, and searched him, to see if he would recognise her, if she could discover him.

'You don't know me?' she asked, from the terror of her soul, standing alone.

He looked back at her quizzically. She had to bear his eyes. They gleamed on her, but with no intelligence. He was drawing nearer to her.

'Yes, I do know you,' he said, fixed, intent, but mad, drawing his face nearer hers. Her horror was too great. The powerful lunatic was coming too near to her.

A man approached, hastening.

'The garden isn't open this morning,' he said.

The deranged man stopped and looked at him. The keeper went to the seat and picked up the tobacco-pouch left lying there.

'Don't leave your tobacco, sir,' he said, taking it to the gentleman in the linen coat.

'I was just asking this lady to stay to lunch,' the latter said politely. 'She is a friend of mine.'

The woman turned and walked swiftly, blindly, between the sunny roses, out from the garden, past the house with the blank, dark windows, through the sea-pebbled courtyard to the street. Hastening and blind, she went forward without hesitating, not knowing whither. Directly she came to the house she went upstairs, took off her hat, and sat down on the bed. It was as if some membrane had been torn in two in her, so that she was not an entity that could think and feel. She sat staring across at the window, where an ivy spray waved slowly up and down in the sea wind. There was some of the uncanny luminousness of the sunlit sea in the air. She sat perfectly still, without any being. She only felt she might be sick, and it might be blood that was loose in her torn entrails. She sat perfectly still and passive.

After a time she heard the hard tread of her husband on the floor below, and, without herself changing, she registered his movement. She heard his rather disconsolate footsteps go out again, then his voice speaking, answering, growing cheery, and his solid tread drawing near.

He entered, ruddy, rather pleased, an air of complacency about his alert, sturdy figure. She moved stiffly. He faltered in his approach.

'What's the matter?' he asked, a tinge of impatience in his voice. 'Aren't you feeling well?'

This was torture to her.

'Quite,' she replied.

His brown eyes became puzzled and angry.

'What is the matter?' he said.

'Nothing.'

He took a few strides, and stood obstinately, looking out of the window.

'Have you run up against anybody?' he asked.

'Nobody who knows me,' she said.

His hands began to twitch. It exasperated him, that she was no more sensible of him than if he did not exist. Turning on her at length, driven, he asked:

'Something has upset you, hasn't it?'

'No, why?' she said, neutral. He did not exist for her, except as an irritant.

His anger rose, filling the veins of his throat.

'It seems like it,' he said, making an effort not to show his anger, because there seemed no reason for it. He went away downstairs. She

215

sat still on the bed, and with the residue of feeling left to her, she disliked him because he tormented her. The time went by. She could smell the dinner being served, the smoke of her husband's pipe from the garden. But she could not move. She had no being. There was a tinkle of the bell. She heard him come indoors. And then he mounted the stairs again. At every step her heart grew tight in her. He opened the door.

'Dinner is on the table,' he said.

It was difficult for her to endure his presence, for he would interfere with her. She could not recover her life. She rose stiffly and went down. She could neither eat nor talk during the meal. She sat absent, torn, without any being of her own. He tried to go on as if nothing were the matter. But at last he became silent with fury. As soon as it was possible, she went upstairs again, and locked the bedroom door. She must be alone. He went with his pipe into the garden. All his suppressed anger against her who held herself superior to him filled and blackened his heart. Though he had not known it, yet he had never really won her, she had never loved him. She had taken him on sufferance. This had foiled him. He was only a labouring electrician in the mine, she was superior to him. He had always given way to her. But all the while, the injury and ignominy had been working in his soul because she did not hold him seriously. And now all his rage came up against her.

He turned and went indoors. The third time, she heard him mounting the stairs. Her heart stood still. He turned the catch and pushed the door – it was locked. He tried it again, harder. Her heart was standing still.

'Have you fastened the door?' he asked quietly, because of the landlady.

'Yes. Wait a minute.'

She rose and turned the lock, afraid he would burst in. She felt hatred towards him, because he did not leave her free. He entered, his pipe between his teeth, and she returned to her old position on the bed. He closed the door and stood with his back to it.

'What's the matter?' he asked determinedly.

She was sick with him. She could not look at him.

'Can't you leave me alone?' she replied, averting her face from him.

He looked at her quickly, fully, wincing with ignominy. Then he seemed to consider for a moment.

'There's something up with you, isn't there?' he asked definitely.

'Yes,' she said, 'but that's no reason why you should torment me.'

'I don't torment you. What's the matter?'

'Why should you know?' she cried, in hate and desperation.

Something snapped. He started and caught his pipe as it fell from his mouth. Then he pushed forward the bitten-off mouthpiece with his tongue, took it from off his lips, and looked at it. Then he put out his pipe, and brushed the ash from his waistcoat. After which he raised his head.

'I want to know,' he said. His face was greyish pale, and set uglily.

Neither looked at the other. She knew he was fired now. His heart was pounding heavily. She hated him, but she could not withstand him. Suddenly she lifted her head and turned on him.

'What right have you to know?' she asked.

He looked at her. She felt a pang of surprise for his tortured eyes and his fixed face. But her heart hardened swiftly. She had never loved him. She did not love him now.

But suddenly she lifted her head again swiftly, like a thing that tries to get free. She wanted to be free of it. It was not him so much, but it, something she had put on herself, that bound her so horribly. And having put the bond on herself, it was hardest to take it off. But now she hated everything and felt destructive. He stood with his back to the door, fixed, as if he would oppose her eternally, till she was extinguished. She looked at him. Her eyes were cold and hostile. His workman's hands spread on the panels of the door behind him.

'You know I used to live here?' she began, in a hard voice, as if wilfully to wound him. He braced himself against her, and nodded.

'Well, I was companion to Miss Birch of Torill Hall – she and the rector were friends, and Archie was the rector's son.' There was a pause. He listened without knowing what was happening. He stared at his wife. She was squatted in her white dress on the bed, carefully folding and re-folding the hem of her skirt. Her voice was full of hostility.

'He was an officer – a sub-lieutenant – then he quarrelled with his colonel and came out of the army. At any rate' – she plucked at her skirt hem, her husband stood motionless, watching her movements which filled his veins with madness – 'he was awfully fond of me, and I was of him – awfully.'

'How old was he?' asked the husband.

'When – when I first knew him? Or when he went away —?'

'When you first knew him.'

'When I first knew him, he was twenty-six – he's thirty-one – nearly thirty-two – because I'm twenty-nine, and he is nearly three years older —'

She lifted her head and looked at the opposite wall.

'And what then?' said her husband.

She hardened herself, and said callously:

'We were as good as engaged for nearly a year, though nobody knew – at least – they talked – but – it wasn't open. Then he went away —'

'He chucked you?' said the husband brutally, wanting to hurt her into contact with himself. Her heart rose wildly with rage. Then 'Yes,' she said, to anger him. He shifted from one foot to the other, giving a 'Pah!' of rage. There was silence for a time.

'Then,' she resumed, her pain giving a mocking note to her words, 'he suddenly went out to fight in Africa, and almost the very day I first met you, I heard from Miss Birch he'd got sunstroke – and two months after, that he was dead —'

'That was before you took on with me?' said the husband.

There was no answer. Neither spoke for a time. He had not understood. His eyes were contracted uglily.

'So you've been looking at your old courting places!' he said. 'That was what you wanted to go out by yourself for this morning.'

Still she did not answer him anything. He went away from the door to the window. He stood with his hands behind him, his back to her. She looked at him. His hands seemed gross to her, the back of his head paltry.

At length, almost against his will, he turned round, asking:

'How long were you carrying on with him?'

'What do you mean?' she replied coldly.

'I mean how long were you carrying on with him?'

She lifted her head, averting her face from him. She refused to answer. Then she said:

'I don't know what you mean, by carrying on. I loved him from the first days I met him – two months after I went to stay with Miss Birch.'

'And do you reckon he loved you?' he jeered.

'I know he did.'

'How do you know, if he'd have no more to do with you?'

There was a long silence of hate and suffering.

'And how far did it go between you?' he asked at length, in a frightened, stiff voice.

'I hate your not-straightforward questions,' she cried, beside herself with his baiting. 'We loved each other, and we *were* lovers – we were. I don't care what *you* think: what have you got to do with it? We were lovers before I knew you —'

'Lovers – lovers,' he said, white with fury. 'You mean you had your fling with an army man, and then came to me to marry you when you'd done —'

She sat swallowing her bitterness. There was a long pause.

'Do you mean to say you used to go – the whole hogger?' he asked, still incredulous.

'Why, what else do you think I mean?' she cried brutally.

He shrank, and became white, impersonal. There was a long, para-lysed silence. He seemed to have gone small.

'You never thought to tell me all this before I married you,' he said, with bitter irony, at last.

'You never asked me,' she replied.

'I never thought there was any need.'

'Well, then, you *should* think.'

He stood with expressionless, almost child-like set face, revolving many thoughts, whilst his heart was mad with anguish.

Suddenly she added:

'And I saw him to-day,' she said. 'He is not dead, he's mad.'

'Mad!' he said involuntarily.

'A lunatic,' she said. It almost cost her her reason to utter the word. There was a pause.

'Did he know you?' asked the husband, in a small voice.

'No,' she said.

He stood and looked at her. At last he had learned the width of the breach between them. She still squatted on the bed. He could not go near her. It would be violation to each of them to be brought into contact with the other. The thing must work itself out. They were both shocked so much, they were impersonal, and no longer hated each other. After some minutes he left her and went out.

219

GOOSE FAIR

I

THROUGH the gloom of evening, and the flare of torches of the night before the fair, through the still fogs of the succeeding dawn came paddling the weary geese, lifting their poor feet that had been dipped in tar for shoes, and trailing them along the cobble-stones into the town. Last of all, in the afternoon, a country girl drove in her dozen birds, disconsolate because she was so late. She was a heavily-built girl, fair, with regular features, and yet unprepossessing. She needed chiselling down, her contours were brutal. Perhaps it was weariness that hung her eyelids a little lower than was pleasant. When she spoke to her clumsily lagging birds it was in a snarling nasal tone. One of the silly things sat down in the gutter and refused to move. It looked very ridiculous, but also rather pitiful, squat there with its head up, refusing to be urged on by the ungentle toe of the girl. The latter swore heavily, then picked up the great complaining bird, and fronting her road stubbornly, drove on the lamentable eleven.

No one had noticed her. This afternoon the women were not sitting chatting on their doorsteps, seaming up the cotton hose, or swiftly passing through their fingers the piled white lace; and in the high dark house the song of the hosiery frames was hushed: 'Shackety-boom, Shackety-shackety-boom, Z – zzz!' As she dragged up Hollow Stone, people returning from the fair chaffed her and asked her what o'clock it was. She did not reply, her look was sullen. The Lace Market was quiet as the Sabbath: even the great brass plates on the doors were dull with neglect. There seemed an afternoon atmosphere of raw discontent. The girl stopped a moment before the dismal prospect of one of the great warehouses that had been gutted with fire. She looked at the lean, threatening walls, and watched her white flock waddling in reckless misery below, and she would have laughed out loud had the wall fallen flat upon them and relieved her of them. But the wall did not fall, so she crossed the road, and walking on the safe side, hurried after her charge. Her look was even more sullen. She remembered the state of trade – Trade, the invidious enemy; Trade, which thrust out its hand

220

and shut the factory doors, and pulled the stockingers off their seats, and left the web half-finished on the frame; Trade, which mysteriously choked up the sources of the rivulets of wealth, and blacker and more secret than a pestilence, starved the town. Through this morose atmosphere of bad trade, in the afternoon of the first day of the fair, the girl strode down to the Poultry with eleven sound geese and one lame one to sell.

The Frenchmen were at the bottom of it! So everybody said, though nobody quite knew how. At any rate, they had gone to war with the Prussians and got beaten, and trade was ruined in Nottingham!

A little fog rose up, and the twilight gathered around. Then they flared abroad their torches in the fair, insulting the night. The girl still sat in the Poultry, and her weary geese unsold on the stones, illuminated by the hissing lamp of a man who sold rabbits and pigeons and such-like assorted livestock.

II

In another part of the town, near Sneinton Church, another girl came to the door to look at the night. She was tall and slender, dressed with the severe accuracy which marks the girl of superior culture. Her hair was arranged with simplicity about the long, pale, cleanly cut face. She leaned forward very slightly to glance down the street, listening. She very carefully preserved the appearance of having come quite casually to the door, yet she lingered and lingered and stood very still to listen when she heard a footstep, but when it proved to be only a common man, she drew herself up proudly and looked with a small smile over his head. He hesitated to glance into the open hall, lighted so spaciously with a scarlet-shaded lamp, and at the slim girl in brown silk lifted up before the light. But she, she looked over his head. He passed on.

Presently she started and hung in suspense. Somebody was crossing the road. She ran down the steps in a pretty welcome, not effuse, saying in quick but accurately articulated words: 'Will! I began to think you'd gone to the fair. I came out to listen to it. I felt almost sure you'd gone. You're coming in, aren't you?' She waited a moment anxiously. 'We expect you to dinner, you know,' she added wistfully.

The man, who had a short face and spoke with his lip curling up on one side, in a drawling speech with ironically exaggerated intonation, replied after a short hesitation:

'I'm awfully sorry, I am, straight, Lois. It's a shame. I've got to go round to the biz. Man proposes – the devil disposes.' He turned aside with irony in the darkness.

'But surely, Will!' remonstrated the girl, keenly disappointed.

'Fact, Lois! – I feel wild about it myself. But I've got to go down to the works. They may be getting a bit warm down there, you know' – he jerked his head in the direction of the fair. 'If the Lambs get frisky! – they're a bit off about the work, and they'd just be in their element if they could set a lighted match to something —'

'Will, you don't think —!' exclaimed the girl, laying her hand on his arm in the true fashion of romance, and looking up at him earnestly.

'Dad's not sure,' he replied, looking down at her with gravity. They remained in this attitude for a moment, then he said:

'I might stop a bit. It's all right for an hour, I should think.'

She looked at him earnestly, then said in tones of deep disappointment and of fortitude: 'No, Will, you must go. You'd better go —'

'It's a shame!' he murmured, standing a moment at a loose end. Then, glancing down the street to see he was alone, he put his arm round her waist and said in a difficult voice: 'How goes it?'

She let him keep her for a moment, then he kissed her as if afraid of what he was doing. They were both uncomfortable.

'Well —!' he said at length.

'Good-night!' she said, setting him free to go.

He hung a moment near her, as if ashamed. Then 'Good-night,' he answered, and he broke away. She listened to his footsteps in the night, before composing herself to turn indoors.

'Helloa!' said her father, glancing over his paper as she entered the dining-room. 'What's up, then?'

'Oh, nothing,' she replied, in her calm tones. 'Will won't be here to dinner to-night.'

'What, gone to the fair?'

'No.'

'Oh! What's got him then?'

Lois looked at her father, and answered:

'He's gone down to the factory. They are afraid of the hands.'

Her father looked at her closely.

'Oh, aye!' he answered, undecided, and they sat down to dinner.

Lois retired very early. She had a fire in her bedroom. She drew the curtains and stood holding aside a heavy fold, looking out at the night. She could see only the nothingness of the fog; not even the glare of the fair was evident, though the noise clamoured small in the distance. In front of everything she could see her own faint image. She crossed to the dressing-table and there leaned her face to the mirror, and looked at herself. She looked a long time, then she rose, changed her dress for a dressing-jacket, and took up *Sesame and Lilies*.

Late in the night she was roused from sleep by a bustle in the house. She sat up and heard a hurrying to and fro and the sound of anxious voices. She put on her dressing-gown and went out to her mother's room. Seeing her mother at the head of the stairs, she said in her quick clean voice:

'Mother, what is it?'

'Oh, child, don't ask me! Go to bed, dear, do! I shall surely be worried out of my life.'

'Mother, what is it?' Lois was sharp and emphatic.

'I hope your father won't go. Now I do hope your father won't go. He's got a cold as it is.'

'Mother, tell me what it is?' Lois took her mother's arm.

'It's Selby's. I should have thought you would have heard the fire-engine, and Jack isn't in yet. I hope we're safe!' Lois returned to her bedroom and dressed. She coiled her plaited hair, and having put on a cloak, left the house.

She hurried along under the fog-dripping trees towards the meaner part of the town. When she got near, she saw a glare in the fog, and closed her lips tight. She hastened on till she was in the crowd. With peaked, noble face she watched the fire. Then she looked a little wildly over the fire-reddened faces in the crowd, and catching sight of her father, hurried to him.

'Oh, Dadda – is he safe? Is Will safe —?'

'Safe, aye, why not? You've no business here. Here, here's Sampson, he'll take you home. I've enough to bother me; there's my own place to watch. Go home now, I can't do with you here.'

'Have you seen Will?' she asked.

'Go home – Sampson, just take Miss Lois home – now!'

'You don't really know where he is – father?'

'Go home now – I don't want you here —' her father ordered per-emptorily.

The tears sprang to Lois' eyes. She looked at the fire and the tears were quickly dried by fear. The flames roared and struggled upward. The great wonder of the fire made her forget even her indignation at her father's light treatment of herself and of her lover. There was a crashing and bursting of timber, as the first floor fell in a mass into the blazing gulf, splashing the fire in all directions, to the terror of the crowd. She saw the steel of the machines growing white-hot and twist-ing like flaming letters. Piece after piece of the flooring gave way, and the machines dropped in red ruin as the wooden framework burned out. The air became unbreathable; the fog was swallowed up; sparks went rushing up as if they would burn the dark heavens; sometimes cards of lace went whirling into the gulf of the sky, waving with wings of fire. It was dangerous to stand near this great cup of roaring destruction.

Sampson, the grey old manager of Buxton and Co.'s, led her away as soon as she would turn her face to listen to him. He was a stout, irrit-able man. He elbowed his way roughly through the crowd, and Lois followed him, her head high, her lips closed. He led her for some dist-ance without speaking, then at last, unable to contain his garrulous irritability, he broke out:

'What do they expect? What can they expect? They can't expect to stand a bad time. They spring up like mushrooms as big as a house-side, but there's no stability in 'em. I remember William Selby when he'd run on my errands. Yes, there's some as can make much out of little, and there's some as can make much out of nothing, but they find it won't last. William Selby's sprung up in a day, and he'll vanish in a night. You can't trust to luck alone. Maybe he thinks it's a lucky thing this fire has come when things are looking black. But you can't get out of it as easy as that. There's been a few too many of 'em. No, indeed, a fire's the last thing I should hope to come to – the very last!'

Lois hurried and hurried, so that she brought the old manager pant-ing in distress up the steps of her home. She could not bear to hear him talking so. They could get no one to open the door for some time. When at last Lois ran upstairs, she found her mother dressed, but all un-buttoned again, lying back in the chair in her daughter's room, suffering from palpitation of the heart, with *Sesame and Lilies* crushed beneath her. Lois administered brandy, and her decisive words and movements helped largely to bring the good lady to a state of recovery sufficient to allow of her returning to her own bedroom.

Then Lois locked the door. She glanced at her fire-darkened face, and taking the flattened Ruskin out of the chair, sat down and wept. After a while she calmed herself, rose and sponged her face. Then once more on that fatal night she prepared for rest. Instead, however, of retiring, she pulled a silk quilt from her disordered bed, and wrapping it round her, sat miserably to think. It was two o'clock in the morning.

IV

The fire was sunk to cold ashes in the grate, and the grey morning was creeping through the half-opened curtains like a thing ashamed, when Lois awoke. It was painful to move her head: her neck was cramped. The girl awoke in full recollection. She sighed, roused herself and pulled the quilt closer about her. For a little while she sat and mused. A pale, tragic resignation fixed her face like a mask. She remembered her father's irritable answer to her question concerning her lover's safety – 'Safe, aye – why not?' She knew that he suspected the factory of having been purposely set on fire. But then, he had never liked Will. And yet – and yet – Lois' heart was heavy as lead. She felt her lover was guilty. And she felt she must hide her secret of his last communication to her. She saw herself being cross-examined – 'When did you last see this man?' But she would hide what he had said about watching at the works. How dreary it was – and how dreadful. Her life was ruined now, and nothing mattered any more. She must only behave with dignity, and submit to her own obliteration. For even if Will were never accused, she knew in her heart he was guilty. She knew it was over between them.

It was dawn among the yellow fog outside, and Lois, as she moved mechanically about her toilet, vaguely felt that all her days would arrive slowly struggling through a bleak fog. She felt an intense longing at this uncanny hour to slough the body's trammelled weariness and to issue at once into the new bright warmth of the far Dawn where a lover waited transfigured; it is so easy and pleasant in imagination to step out of the chill grey dampness of another terrestrial daybreak, straight into the sunshine of the eternal morning! And who can escape his hour? So Lois performed the meaningless routine of her toilet, which at last she made meaningful when she took her black dress, and fastened a black jet brooch at her throat.

Then she went downstairs and found her father eating a mutton chop. She quickly approached and kissed him on the forehead. Then she retreated to the other end of the table. Her father looked tired, even haggard.

'You are early,' he said, after a while. Lois did not reply. Her father continued to eat for a few moments, then he said:

'Have a chop – here's one! Ring for a hot plate. Eh, what? Why not?'

Lois was insulted, but she gave no sign. She sat down and took a cup of coffee, making no pretence to eat. Her father was absorbed, and had forgotten her.

'Our Jack's not come home yet,' he said at last.

Lois stirred faintly. 'Hasn't he?' she said.

'No.' There was silence for a time. Lois was frightened. Had something happened also to her brother? This fear was closer and more irksome.

'Selby's was cleaned out, gutted. We had a near shave of it —'

'You have no loss, Dadda?'

'Nothing to mention.' After another silence, her father said:

'I'd rather be myself than William Selby. Of course it may merely be bad luck – you don't know. But whatever it was, I wouldn't like to add one to the list of fires just now. Selby was at the "George" when it broke out – I don't know where the lad was —!'

'Father,' broke in Lois, 'why do you talk like that? Why do you talk as if Will had done it?' She ended suddenly. Her father looked at her pale, mute face.

'I don't talk as if Will had done it,' he said. 'I don't even think it.'

Feeling she was going to cry, Lois rose and left the room. Her father sighed, and leaning his elbows on his knees, whistled faintly into the fire. He was not thinking about her.

Lois went down to the kitchen and asked Lucy, the parlour-maid, to go out with her. She somehow shrank from going alone, lest people should stare at her overmuch: and she felt an overpowering impulse to go to the scene of the tragedy, to judge for herself.

The churches were chiming half-past eight when the young lady and the maid set off down the street. Nearer the fair, swarthy, thin-legged men were pushing barrels of water towards the market-place, and the gipsy women, with hard brows, and dressed in tight velvet bodices, hurried along the pavement with jugs of milk, and great brass water-ewers and loaves and breakfast parcels. People were just getting up, and in the poorer streets was a continual splash of tea-leaves, flung out on to the cobble-stones. A teapot came crashing down from an upper storey just behind Lois, and she, starting round and looking up, thought that the trembling, drink-bleared man at the upper window, who was stupidly staring after his pot, had had designs on her life; and she went on her way shuddering at the grim tragedy of life.

In the dull October morning the ruined factory was black and ghastly. The window-frames were all jagged, and the walls stood gaunt. Inside was a tangle of twisted débris, the iron, in parts red with bright rust, looking still hot; the charred wood was black and satiny; from dishevelled heaps, sodden with water, a faint smoke rose dimly. Lois stood and looked. If he had done that! He might even be dead there, burned to ash and lost for ever. It was almost soothing to feel so. He would be safe in the eternity which now she must hope in.

At her side the pretty, sympathetic maid chatted plaintively. Suddenly, from one of her lapses into silences, she exclaimed:

'Why if there isn't Mr. Jack!'

Lois turned suddenly and saw her brother and her lover approaching her. Both looked soiled, untidy and wan. Will had a black eye, some ten hours old, well coloured. Lois turned very pale as they approached. They were looking gloomily at the factory, and for a moment did not notice the girls.

'I'll be jiggered if there ain't our Lois!' exclaimed Jack, the reprobate, swearing under his breath.

'Oh, God!' exclaimed the other in disgust.

'Jack, where have you been?' said Lois sharply, in keen pain, not looking at her lover. Her sharp tone of suffering drove her lover to defend himself with an affectation of comic recklessness.

'In quod,' replied her brother, smiling sicklily.

'Jack!' cried his sister very sharply.

'Fact.'

Will Selby shuffled on his feet and smiled, trying to turn away his face so that she should not see his black eye. She glanced at him. He felt her boundless anger and contempt, and with great courage he looked straight at her, smiling ironically. Unfortunately his smile would not go over his swollen eye, which remained grave and lurid.

'Do I look pretty?' he inquired with a hateful twist of his lip.

'Very!' she replied.

'I thought I did,' he replied. And he turned to look at his father's ruined works, and he felt miserable and stubborn. The girl standing there so clean and out of it all! Oh, God, he felt sick. He turned to go home.

The three went together, Lois silent in anger and resentment. Her brother was tired and overstrung, but not suppressed. He chattered on, blindly.

'It was a lark we had! We met Bob Osborne and Freddy Mansell coming down Poultry. There was a girl with some geese. She looked a tanger sitting there, all like statues, her and the geese. It was Will who began it. He offered her threepence and asked her to begin the show. She called him a – she called him something, and then somebody poked an old gander to stir him up, and somebody squirted him in the eye. He upped and squawked and started off with his neck out. Laugh! We nearly killed ourselves, keeping back those old birds with squirts and teasers. Oh, Lum! Those old geese, oh, scrimmy, they didn't know where to turn, they fairly went off their dots, coming at us right an' left, and such a row – it was fun, you never knew! Then the girl she got up and knocked somebody over the jaw, and we were right in for it. Well, in the end, Bill here got hold of her round the waist —'

'Oh, dry it up!' exclaimed Will bitterly.

Jack looked at him, laughed mirthlessly, and continued: 'An' we said we'd buy her birds. So we got hold of one goose apiece – an' they took some holding, I can tell you – and off we set round the fair, Billy leading with the girl. The bloomin' geese squawked an' pecked. Laugh – I thought I should a' died. Well, then we wanted the girl to have her birds back – and then she fired up. She got some other chaps on her side, and there was a proper old row. The girl went tooth and nail for Will there – she was dead set against him. She gave him a black eye, by gum, and we went at it, I can tell you. It was a free fight, a beauty, an' we got run in. I don't know what became of the girl.'

Lois surveyed the two men. There was no glimmer of a smile on her face, though the maid behind her was sniggering. Will was very bitter. He glanced at his sweetheart and at the ruined factory.

'How's dad taken it?' he asked, in a biting, almost humble tone.

'I don't know,' she replied coldly. 'Father's in an awful way. I believe everybody thinks you set the place on fire.'

Lois drew herself up. She had delivered her blow. She drew herself up in cold condemnation and for a moment enjoyed her complete revenge. He was despicable, abject in his dishevelled, disfigured, unwashed condition.

'Aye, well, they made a mistake for once,' he replied, with a curl of the lip.

Curiously enough, they walked side by side as if they belonged to

228

each other. She was his conscience-keeper. She was far from forgiving him, but she was still farther from letting him go. And he walked at her side like a boy who has to be punished before he can be exonerated. He submitted. But there was a genuine bitter contempt in the curl of his lip.

THE WHITE STOCKING

I

'I'm getting up, Teddilinks,' said Mrs. Whiston, and she sprang out of bed briskly.

'What the Hanover's got you?' asked Whiston.

'Nothing. Can't I get up?' she replied animatedly.

It was about seven o'clock, scarcely light yet in the cold bedroom. Whiston lay still and looked at his wife. She was a pretty little thing, with her fleecy, short black hair all tousled. He watched her as she dressed quickly, flicking her small, delightful limbs, throwing her clothes about her. Her slovenliness and untidiness did not trouble him. When she picked up the edge of her petticoat, ripped off a torn string of white lace, and flung it on the dressing-table, her careless abandon made his spirit glow. She stood before the mirror and roughly scrambled together her profuse little mane of hair. He watched the quickness and softness of her young shoulders, calmly, like a husband, and appreciatively.

'Rise up,' she cried, turning to him with a quick wave of her arm – 'and shine forth.'

They had been married two years. But still, when she had gone out of the room, he felt as if all his light and warmth were taken away, he became aware of the raw, cold morning. So he rose himself, wondering casually what had roused her so early. Usually she lay in bed as late as she could.

Whiston fastened a belt round his loins and went downstairs in shirt and trousers. He heard her singing in her snatchy fashion. The stairs creaked under his weight. He passed down the narrow little passage, which she called a hall, of the seven and sixpenny house which was his first home.

He was a shapely young fellow of about twenty-eight, sleepy now and easy with well-being. He heard the water drumming into the kettle, and she began to whistle. He loved the quick way she dodged the supper cups under the tap to wash them for breakfast. She looked an untidy minx, but she was quick and handy enough.

230

'Teddilinks,' she cried.

'What?'

'Light a fire, quick.'

She wore an old, sack-like dressing-jacket of black silk pinned across her breast. But one of the sleeves, coming unfastened, showed some delightful pink upper-arm.

'Why don't you sew your sleeve up?' he said, suffering from the sight of the exposed soft flesh.

'Where?' she cried, peering round. 'Nuisance,' she said, seeing the gap, then with light fingers went on drying the cups.

The kitchen was of fair size, but gloomy. Whiston poked out the dead ashes.

Suddenly a thud was heard at the door down the passage.

'I'll go,' cried Mrs. Whiston, and she was gone down the hall.

The postman was a ruddy-faced man who had been a soldier. He smiled broadly, handing her some packages.

'They've not forgot you,' he said impudently.

'No – lucky for them,' she said, with a toss of the head. But she was interested only in her envelopes this morning. The postman waited inquisitively, smiling in an ingratiating fashion. She slowly, abstractedly, as if she did not know anyone was there, closed the door in his face, continuing to look at the addresses on her letters.

She tore open the thin envelope. There was a long, hideous, cartoon valentine. She smiled briefly and dropped it on the floor. Struggling with the string of a packet, she opened a white cardboard box, and there lay a white silk handkerchief packed neatly under the paper lace of the box, and her initial, worked in heliotrope, fully displayed. She smiled pleasantly, and gently put the box aside. The third envelope contained another white packet – apparently a cotton handkerchief neatly folded. She shook it out. It was a long white stocking, but there was a little weight in the toe. Quickly, she thrust down her arm, wriggling her fingers into the toe of the stocking, and brought out a small box. She peeped inside the box, then hastily opened a door on her left hand, and went into the little cold sitting-room. She had her lower lip caught earnestly between her teeth.

With a little flash of triumph, she lifted a pair of pearl ear-rings from the small box, and she went to the mirror. There, earnestly, she began to hook them through her ears, looking at herself sideways in the glass. Curiously concentrated and intent she seemed as she fingered the lobes of her ears, her head bent on one side.

Then the pearl ear-rings dangled under her rosy, small ears. She shook her head sharply, to see the swing of the drops. They went chill against her neck, in little, sharp touches. Then she stood still to look at herself, bridling her head in the dignified fashion. Then she simpered at herself. Catching her own eye, she could not help winking at herself and laughing.

She turned to look at the box. There was a scrap of paper with this posy:

> 'Pearls may be fair, but thou art fairer.
> Wear these for me, and I'll love the wearer.'

She made a grimace and a grin. But she was drawn to the mirror again, to look at her ear-rings.

Whiston had made the fire burn, so he came to look for her. When she heard him, she started round quickly, guiltily. She was watching him with intent blue eyes when he appeared.

He did not see much, in his morning-drowsy warmth. He gave her, as ever, a feeling of warmth and slowness. His eyes were very blue, very kind, his manner simple.

'What ha' you got?' he asked.

'Valentines,' she said briskly, ostentatiously turning to show him the silk handkerchief. She thrust it under his nose. 'Smell how good,' she said.

'Who's that from?' he replied, without smelling.

'It's a valentine,' she cried. 'How do I know who it's from?'

'I'll bet you know,' he said.

'Ted! – I don't!' she cried, beginning to shake her head, then stopping because of the ear-rings.

He stood still a moment, displeased.

'They've no right to send you valentines now,' he said.

'Ted! – Why not? You're not jealous, are you? I haven't the least idea who it's from. Look – there's my initial' – she pointed with an emphatic finger at the heliotrope embroidery —

> 'E for Elsie,
> Nice little gelsie,'

she sang.

'Get out,' he said. 'You know who it's from.'

'Truth, I don't,' she cried.

232

He looked round, and saw the white stocking lying on a chair.

'Is this another?' he said.

'No, that's a sample,' she said. 'There's only a comic.' And she fetched in the long cartoon.

He stretched it out and looked at it solemnly.

'Fools!' he said, and went out of the room.

She flew upstairs and took off the ear-rings. When she returned, he was crouched before the fire blowing the coals. The skin of his face was flushed, and slightly pitted, as if he had had small-pox. But his neck was white and smooth and goodly. She hung her arms round his neck as he crouched there, and clung to him. He balanced on his toes.

'This fire's a slow-coach,' he said.

'And who else is a slow-coach?' she said.

'One of us two, I know,' he said, and he rose carefully. She remained clinging round his neck, so that she was lifted off her feet.

'Ha! – swing me,' she cried.

He lowered his head, and she hung in the air, swinging from his neck, laughing. Then she slipped off.

'The kettle is singing,' she sang, flying for the teapot. He bent down again to blow the fire. The veins in his neck stood out, his shirt collar seemed too tight.

> *'Doctor Wyer,*
> *Blow the fire,*
> *Puff! puff! puff!'*

she sang, laughing.

He smiled at her.

She was so glad because of her pearl ear-rings.

Over the breakfast she grew serious. He did not notice. She became portentous in her gravity. Almost it penetrated through his steady good-humour to irritate him.

'Teddy!' she said at last.

'What?' he asked.

'I told you a lie,' she said, humbly tragic.

His soul stirred uneasily.

'Oh aye?' he said casually.

She was not satisfied. He ought to be more moved.

'Yes,' she said.

He cut a piece of bread.

233

'Was it a good one?' he asked.

She was piqued. Then she considered – *was* it a good one? Then she laughed.

'No,' she said, 'it wasn't up to much.'

'Ah!' he said easily, but with a steady strength of fondness for her in his tone. 'Get it out then.'

It became a little more difficult.

'You know that white stocking,' she said earnestly. 'I told you a lie. It wasn't a sample. It was a valentine.'

A little frown came on his brow.

'Then what did you invent it as a sample for?' he said. But he knew this weakness of hers. The touch of anger in his voice frightened her.

'I was afraid you'd be cross,' she said pathetically.

'I'll bet you were vastly afraid,' he said.

'I *was*, Teddy.'

There was a pause. He was resolving one or two things in his mind.

'And who sent it?' he asked.

'I can guess,' she said, 'though there wasn't a word with it – except —'

She ran to the sitting-room and returned with a slip of paper.

> *'Pearls may be fair, but thou art fairer.*
> *Wear these for me, and I'll love the wearer.*

He read it twice, then a dull red flush came on his face.

'And *who* do you guess it is?' he asked, with a ringing of anger in his voice.

'I suspect it's Sam Adams,' she said, with a little virtuous indignation.

Whiston was silent for a moment.

'Fool!' he said. 'An' what's it got to do with pearls? – and how can he say "wear these for me" when there's only one? He hasn't got the brain to invent a proper verse.'

He screwed the slip of paper into a ball and flung it into the fire.

'I suppose he thinks it'll make a pair with the one last year,' she said.

'Why, did he send one then?'

'Yes. I thought you'd be wild if you knew.'

His jaw set rather sullenly.

Presently he rose, and went to wash himself, rolling back his sleeves

234

and pulling open his shirt at the breast. It was as if his fine, clear-cut temples and steady eyes were degraded by the lower, rather brutal part of his face. But she loved it. As she whisked about, clearing the table, she loved the way in which he stood washing himself. He was such a man. She liked to see his neck glistening with water as he swilled it. It amused her and pleased her and thrilled her. He was so sure, so permanent, he had her so utterly in his power. It gave her a delightful, mischievous sense of liberty. Within his grasp, she could dart about excitingly.

He turned round to her, his face red from the cold water, his eyes fresh and very blue.

'You haven't been seeing anything of him, have you?' he asked roughly.

'Yes,' she answered, after a moment, as if caught guilty. 'He got into the tram with me, and he asked me to drink a coffee and a Benedictine in the Royal.'

'You've got it off fine and glib,' he said sullenly. 'And did you?'

'Yes,' she replied, with the air of a traitor before the rack.

The blood came up into his neck and face, he stood motionless, dangerous.

'It was cold, and it was such fun to go into the Royal,' she said.

'You'd go off with a nigger for a packet of chocolate,' he said, in anger and contempt, and some bitterness. Queer how he drew away from her, cut her off from him.

'Ted – how beastly!' she cried. 'You know quite well —' She caught her lip, flushed, and the tears came to her eyes.

He turned away, to put on his neck-tie. She went about her work, making a queer pathetic little mouth, down which occasionally dripped a tear.

He was ready to go. With his hat jammed down on his head, and his overcoat buttoned up to his chin, he came to kiss her. He would be miserable all the day if he went without. She allowed herself to be kissed. Her cheek was wet under his lip, and his heart burned. She hurt him so deeply. And she felt aggrieved, and did not quite forgive him.

In a moment she went upstairs to her ear-rings. Sweet they looked nestling in the little drawer – sweet! She examined them with voluptuous pleasure, she threaded them in her ears, she looked at herself, she posed and postured and smiled and looked sad and tragic and winning and appealing, all in turn before the mirror. And she was happy, and very pretty.

She wore her ear-rings all morning, in the house. She was self-conscious, and quite brilliantly winsome, when the baker came, wondering if he would notice. All the tradesmen left her door with a glow in them, feeling elated, and unconsciously favouring the delightful little creature, though there had been nothing to notice in her behaviour.

She was stimulated all the day. She did not think about her husband. He was the permanent basis from which she took these giddly little flights into nowhere. At night, like chickens and curses, she would come home to him, to roost.

Meanwhile Whiston, a traveller and confidential support of a small firm, hastened about his work, his heart all the while anxious for her, yearning for surety, and kept tense by not getting it.

II

She had been a warehouse girl in Adams's lace factory before she was married. Sam Adams was her employer. He was a bachelor of forty, growing stout, a man well dressed and florid, with a large brown moustache and thin hair. From the rest of his well-groomed, showy appearance, it was evident his baldness was a chagrin to him. He had a good presence, and some Irish blood in his veins.

His fondness for the girls, or the fondness of the girls for him, was notorious. And Elsie, quick, pretty, almost witty little thing – she *seemed* witty, although, when her sayings were repeated, they were entirely trivial – she had a great attraction for him. He would come into the warehouse dressed in a rather sporting reefer coat, of fawn colour, and trousers of fine black-and-white check, a cap with a big peak and scarlet carnation in his button-hole, to impress her. She was only half impressed. He was too loud for her good taste. Instinctively perceiving this, he sobered down to navy blue. Then a well-built man, florid, with large brown whiskers, smart navy blue suit, fashionable boots, and manly hat, he was the irreproachable. Elsie was impressed.

But meanwhile Whiston was courting her, and she made splendid little gestures, before her bedroom mirror, of the constant-and-true sort.

'True, true till death —'

That was her song. Whiston was made that way, so there was no need to take thought for him.

236

Every Christmas Sam Adams gave a party at his house, to which he invited his superior work-people – not factory hands and labourers, but those above. He was a generous man in his way, with a real warm feeling for giving pleasure.

Two years ago Elsie had attended this Christmas-party for the last time. Whiston had accompanied her. At that time he worked for Sam Adams.

She had been very proud of herself, in her close-fitting, full-skirted dress of blue silk. Whiston called for her. Then she tripped beside him, holding her large cashmere shawl across her breast. He strode with long strides, his trousers handsomely strapped under his boots, and her silk shoes bulging the pocket of his full-skirted overcoat.

They passed through the park gates, and her spirits rose. Above them the Castle Rock loomed grandly in the night, the naked trees stood still and dark in the frost, along the boulevard.

They were rather late. Agitated with anticipation, in the cloak-room she gave up her shawl, donned her silk shoes, and looked at herself in the mirror. The loose bunches of curls on either side her face danced prettily, her mouth smiled.

She hung a moment in the door of the brilliantly lighted room. Many people were moving within the blaze of lamps, under the crystal chandeliers, the full skirts of the women balancing and floating, the side-whiskers and white cravats of the men bowing above. Then she entered the light.

In an instant Sam Adams was coming forward, lifting both his arms in boisterous welcome. There was a constant red laugh on his face.

'Come late, would you,' he shouted, 'like royalty.'

He seized her hands and led her forward. He opened his mouth wide when he spoke, and the effect of the warm, dark opening behind the brown whiskers was disturbing. But she was floating into the throng on his arm. He was very gallant.

'Now then,' he said, taking her card to write down the dances, 'I've got *carte blanche*, haven't I?'

'Mr. Whiston doesn't dance,' she said.

'I am a lucky man!' he said, scribbling his initials. 'I was born with an *amourette* in my mouth.'

He wrote on, quietly. She blushed and laughed, not knowing what it meant.

'Why, what is that?' she said.

'It's you, even littler than you are, dressed in little wings,' he said.

'I should have to be pretty small to get in your mouth,' she said.

'You think you're too big, do you!' he said easily.

He handed her her card, with a bow.

'Now I'm set up, my darling, for this evening,' he said.

Then, quick, always at his ease, he looked over the room. She waited in front of him. He was ready. Catching the eye of the band, he nodded. In a moment, the music began. He seemed to relax, giving himself up.

'Now then, Elsie,' he said, with a curious caress in his voice that seemed to lap the outside of her body in a warm glow, delicious. She gave herself to it. She liked it.

He was an excellent dancer. He seemed to draw her close in to him by some male warmth of attraction, so that she became all soft and pliant to him, flowing to his form, whilst he united her with him and they lapsed along in one movement. She was just carried in a kind of strong, warm flood, her feet moved of themselves, and only the music threw her away from him, threw her back to him, to his clasp, in his strong form moving against her, rhythmically, deliciously.

When it was over, he was pleased and his eyes had a curious gleam which thrilled her and yet had nothing to do with her. Yet it held her. He did not speak to her. He only looked straight into her eyes with a curious, gleaming look that disturbed her fearfully and deliciously. But also there was in his look some of the automatic irony of the *roué*. It left her partly cold. She was not carried away.

She went, driven by an opposite, heavier impulse, to Whiston. He stood looking gloomy, trying to admit that she had a perfect right to enjoy herself apart from him. He received her with rather grudging kindliness.

'Aren't you going to play whist?' she asked.

'Aye,' he said. 'Directly.'

'I do wish you could dance.'

'Well, I can't,' he said. 'So you enjoy yourself.'

'But I should enjoy it better if I could dance with you.'

'Nay, you're all right,' he said. 'I'm not made that way.'

'Then you ought to be!' she cried.

'Well, it's my fault, not yours. You enjoy yourself,' he bade her. Which she proceeded to do, a little bit irked.

She went with anticipation to the arms of Sam Adams, when the time came to dance with him. It *was* so gratifying, irrespective of the man. And she felt a little grudge against Whiston, soon forgotten when

238

her host was holding her near to him, in a delicious embrace. And she watched his eyes, to meet the gleam in them, which gratified her.

She was getting warmed right through, the glow was penetrating into her, driving away everything else. Only in her heart was a little tightness, like conscience.

When she got a chance, she escaped from the dancing-room to the card-room. There, in a cloud of smoke, she found Whiston playing cribbage. Radiant, roused, animated, she came up to him and greeted him. She was too strong, too vibrant a note in the quiet room. He lifted his head, and a frown knitted his gloomy forehead.

'Are you playing cribbage? Is it exciting? How are you getting on?' she chattered.

He looked at her. None of these questions needed answering, and he did not feel in touch with her. She turned to the cribbage-board.

'Are you white or red?' she asked.

'He's red,' replied the partner.

'Then you're losing,' she said, still to Whiston. And she lifted the red peg from the board. 'One – two – three – four – five – six – seven – eight — Right up there you ought to jump —'

'Now put it back in its right place,' said Whiston.

'Where was it?' she asked gaily, knowing her transgression. He took the little red peg away from her and stuck it in its hole.

The cards were shuffled.

'What a shame you're losing,' said Elsie.

'You'd better cut for him,' said the partner.

She did so hastily. The cards were dealt. She put her hand on his shoulder, looking at his cards.

'It's good,' she cried, 'isn't it?'

He did not answer, but threw down two cards. It moved him more strongly than was comfortable, to have her hand on his shoulder, her curls dangling and touching his ears, whilst she was roused to another man. It made the blood flame over him.

At that moment Sam Adams appeared, florid and boisterous, intoxicated more with himself, with the dancing, than with wine. In his eye the curious, impersonal light gleamed.

'I thought I should find you here, Elsie,' he cried boisterously, a disturbing, high note in his voice.

'What made you think so?' she replied, the mischief rousing in her.

The florid, well-built man narrowed his eyes to a smile.

'I should never look for you among the ladies,' he said, with a kind of intimate, animal call to her. He laughed, bowed, and offered her his arm.

'Madam, the music waits.'

She went almost helplessly, carried along with him, unwilling, yet delighted.

That dance was an intoxication to her. After the first few steps, she felt herself slipping away from herself. She almost knew she was going, she did not even want to go. Yet she must have chosen to go. She lay in the arm of the steady, close man with whom she was dancing, and she seemed to swim away out of contact with the room, into him. She had passed into another, denser element of him, an essential privacy. The room was all vague around her, like an atmosphere, like under sea, with a flow of ghostly, dumb movements. But she herself was held real against her partner, and it seemed she was connected with him, as if the movements of his body and limbs were her own movements, yet not her own movements – and oh, delicious! He also was given up, oblivious, concentrated, into the dance. His eye was unseeing. Only his large, voluptuous body gave off a subtle activity. His fingers seemed to search into her flesh. Every moment, and every moment, she felt she would give way utterly, and sink molten: the fusion point was coming when she would fuse down into perfect unconsciousness at his feet and knees. But he bore her round the room in the dance, and he seemed to sustain all her body with his limbs, his body, and his warmth seemed to come closer into her, nearer, till it would fuse right through her, and she would be as liquid to him as an intoxication only.

It was exquisite. When it was over, she was dazed, and was scarcely breathing. She stood with him in the middle of the room as if she were alone in a remote place. He bent over her. She expected his lips on her bare shoulder, and waited. Yet they were not alone, they were not alone. It was cruel.

' 'Twas good, wasn't it, my darling?' he said to her, low and delighted. There was a strange impersonality about his low, exultant call that appealed to her irresistibly. Yet why was she aware of some part shut off in her? She pressed his arm, and he led her towards the door.

She was not aware of what she was doing, only a little grain of resistant trouble was in her. The man, possessed, yet with a superficial presence of mind, made way to the dining-room, as if to give her refreshment, cunningly working to his own escape with her. He was molten hot, filmed over with presence of mind, and bottomed with cold disbelief. In the dining-room was Whiston, carrying coffee to the plain, neglected ladies. Elsie saw him, but felt as if he could not see her. She was beyond his reach and ken. A sort of fusion existed between her and the large man at her side. She ate her custard, but an incomplete fusion all the while sustained and contained within the being of her employer.

But she was growing cooler. Whiston came up. She looked at him, and saw him with different eyes. She saw his slim, young man's figure real and enduring before her. That was he. But she was in the spell with the other man, fused with him, and she could not be taken away.

'Have you finished your cribbage?' she asked, with hasty evasion of him.

'Yes,' he replied. 'Aren't you getting tired of dancing?'

'Not a bit,' she said.

'Not she,' said Adams heartily. 'No girl with any spirit gets tired of dancing. Have something else, Elsie. Come – sherry. Have a glass of sherry with us, Whiston.'

Whilst they sipped the wine, Adams watched Whiston almost cunningly, to find his advantage.

'We'd better be getting back – there's the music,' he said. 'See the women get something to eat, Whiston, will you there's a good chap.'

And he began to draw away. Elsie was drifting helplessly with him. But Whiston put himself beside them, and went along with them. In silence they passed through to the dancing-room. There Adams hesitated, and looked round the room. It was as if he could not see.

A man came hurrying forward, claiming Elsie, and Adams went to his other partner. Whiston stood watching during the dance. She was conscious of him standing there observant of her, like a ghost, or a judgment, or a guardian angel. She was also conscious, much more intimately and impersonally, of the body of the other man moving somewhere in the room. She still belonged to him, but a feeling of distraction possessed her, and helplessness. Adams danced on, adhering to Elsie, waiting his time, with the persistence of cynicism.

The dance was over. Adams was detained. Elsie found herself beside Whiston. There was something shapely about him as he sat, about his knees and his distinct figure, that she clung to. It was as if he had enduring form. She put her hand on his knee.

'Are you enjoying yourself?' he asked.

'*Ever* so,' she replied, with a fervent, yet detached tone.

'It's going on for one o'clock,' he said.

'Is it?' she answered. It meant nothing to her.

'Should we be going?' he said.

She was silent. For the first time for an hour or more an inkling of her normal consciousness returned. She resented it.

'What for?' she said.

'I thought you might have had enough,' he said.

A slight soberness came over her, an irritation at being frustrated of her illusion.

'Why?' she said.

'We've been here since nine,' he said.

That was no answer, no reason. It conveyed nothing to her. She sat detached from him. Across the room Sam Adams glanced at her. She sat there exposed for him.

'You don't want to be too free with Sam Adams,' said Whiston cautiously, suffering. 'You know what he is.'

'How, free?' she asked.

'Why – you don't want to have too much to do with him.'

She sat silent. He was forcing her into consciousness of her position. But he could not get hold of her feelings, to change them. She had a curious, perverse desire that he should not.

'I like him,' she said.

'What do you find to like in him?' he said, with a hot heart.

'I don't know – but I like him,' she said.

She was immutable. He sat feeling heavy and dulled with rage. He was not clear as to what he felt. He sat there unliving whilst she danced. And she, distracted, lost to herself between the opposing forces of the two men, drifted. Between the dances, Whiston kept near to her. She was scarcely conscious. She glanced repeatedly at her card, to see when she would dance again with Adams, half in desire, half in dread. Sometimes she met his steady, glaucous eye as she passed him in the dance. Sometimes she saw the steadiness of his flank as he danced. And it was always as if she rested on his arm, were borne along, up-borne by him, away from herself. And always there was present the other's antagonism. She was divided.

The time came for her to dance with Adams. Oh, the delicious closing of contact with him, of his limbs touching her limbs, his arm supporting her. She seemed to resolve. Whiston had not made himself real to her. He was only a heavy place in her consciousness.

But she breathed heavily, beginning to suffer from the closeness of strain. She was nervous. Adams also was constrained. A tightness, a tension was coming over them all. And he was exasperated, feeling

242

something counteracting physical magnetism, feeling a will stronger with her than his own, intervening in what was becoming a vital necessity to him.

Elsie was almost lost to her own control. As she went forward with him to take her place at the dance, she stooped for her pocket handkerchief. The music sounded for quadrilles. Everybody was ready. Adams stood with his body near her, exerting his attraction over her. He was tense and fighting. She stooped for her pocket handkerchief, and shook it as she rose. It shook out and fell from her hand. With agony, she saw she had taken a white stocking instead of a handkerchief. For a second it lay on the floor, a twist of white stocking. Then, in an instant, Adams picked it up, with a little, surprised laugh of triumph.

'That'll do for me,' he whispered – seeming to take possession of her. And he stuffed the stocking in his trousers pocket, and quickly offered her his handkerchief.

The dance began. She felt weak and faint, as if her will were turned to water. A heavy sense of loss came over her. She could not help herself any more. But it was peace.

When the dance was over, Adams yielded her up. Whiston came to her.

'What was it as you dropped?' Whiston asked.

'I thought it was my handkerchief – I'd taken a stocking by mistake,' she said, detached and muted.

'And he's got it?'

'Yes.'

'What does he mean by that?'

She lifted her shoulders.

'Are you going to let him keep it?' he asked.

'I don't let him.'

There was a long pause.

'Am I to go and have it out with him?' he asked, his face flushed, his blue eyes going hard with opposition.

'No,' she said, pale.

'Why?'

'No – I don't want you to say anything about it.'

He sat exasperated and nonplussed.

'You'll let him keep it, then?' he asked.

She sat silent and made no form of answer.

'What do you mean by it?' he said, dark with fury. And he started up.

'No!' she cried. 'Ted!' And she caught hold of him, sharply detaining him.

It made him black with rage.

'Why?' he said.

The something about her mouth was pitiful to him. He did not understand, but he felt she must have her reasons.

'Then I'm not stopping here,' he said. 'Are you coming with me?'

She rose mutely, and they went out of the room. Adams had not noticed.

In a few moments they were in the street.

'What the hell do you mean?' he said, in a black fury.

She went at his side, in silence, neutral.

'That great hog, an' all,' he added.

Then they went a long time in silence through the frozen, deserted darkness of the town. She felt she could not go indoors. They were drawing near her house.

'I don't want to go home,' she suddenly cried in distress and anguish. 'I don't want to go home.'

He looked at her.

'Why don't you?' he said.

'I don't want to go home,' was all she could sob.

He heard somebody coming.

'Well, we can walk a bit farther,' he said.

She was silent again. They passed out of the town into the fields. He held her by the arm – they could not speak.

'What's a-matter?' he asked at length, puzzled.

She began to cry again.

At last he took her in his arms, to soothe her. She sobbed by herself, almost unaware of him.

'Tell me what's a-matter, Elsie,' he said. 'Tell me what's a-matter – my dear – tell me, then —'

He kissed her wet face, and caressed her. She made no response. He was puzzled and tender and miserable.

At length she became quiet. Then he kissed her, and she put her arms round him, and clung to him very tight, as if for fear and anguish. He held her in his arms, wondering.

'Ted!' she whispered, frantic. 'Ted!'

'What, my love?' he answered, becoming also afraid.

'Be good to me,' she cried. 'Don't be cruel to me.'

'No, my pet,' he said, amazed and grieved. 'Why?'

'Oh, be good to me,' she sobbed.

And he held her very safe, and his heart was white-hot with love for her. His mind was amazed. He could only hold her against his chest that was white-hot with love and belief in her. So she was restored at last.

III

She refused to go to her work at Adams's any more. Her father had to submit and she sent in her notice – she was not well. Sam Adams was ironical. But he had a curious patience. He did not fight.

In a few weeks, she and Whiston were married. She loved him with passion and worship, a fierce little abandon of love that moved him to the depths of his being, and gave him a permanent surety and sense of realness in himself. He did not trouble about himself any more: he felt he was fulfilled and now he had only the many things in the world to busy himself about. Whatever troubled him, at the bottom was surety. He had found himself in this love.

They spoke once or twice of the white stocking.

'Ah!' Whiston exclaimed. 'What does it matter?'

He was impatient and angry, and could not bear to consider the matter. So it was left unresolved.

She was quite happy at first, carried away by her adoration of her husband. Then gradually she got used to him. He always was the ground of her happiness, but she got used to him, as to the air she breathed. He never got used to her in the same way.

Inside of marriage she found her liberty. She was rid of the responsibility of herself. Her husband must look after that. She was free to get what she could out of her time.

So that, when, after some months, she met Sam Adams, she was not quite as unkind to him as she might have been. With a young wife's new and exciting knowledge of men, she perceived he was in love with her, she knew he had always kept an unsatisfied desire for her. And, sportive, she could not help playing a little with this, though she cared not one jot for the man himself.

When Valentine's day came, which was near the first anniversary of her wedding day, there arrived a white stocking with a little amethyst brooch. Luckily Whiston did not see it, so she said nothing of it to him. She had not the faintest intention of having anything to do with Sam

Adams, but once a little brooch was in her possession, it was hers, and she did not trouble her head for a moment how she had come by it. She kept it.

Now she had the pearl ear-rings. They were a more valuable and a more conspicuous present. She would have to ask her mother to give them to her, to explain their presence. She made a little plan in her head. And she was extraordinarily pleased. As for Sam Adams, even if he saw her wearing them, he would not give her away. What fun, if he saw her wearing his ear-rings! She would pretend she had inherited them from her grandmother, her mother's mother. She laughed to herself as she went down-town in the afternoon, the pretty drops dangling in front of her curls. But she saw no one of importance.

Whiston came home tired and depressed. All day the male in him had been uneasy, and this had fatigued him. She was curiously against him, inclined, as she sometimes was nowadays, to make mock of him and jeer at him and cut him off. He did not understand this, and it angered him deeply. She was uneasy before him.

She knew he was in a state of suppressed irritation. The veins stood out on the backs of his hands, his brow was drawn stiffly. Yet she could not help goading him.

'What did you do wi' that white stocking?' he asked, out of a gloomy silence, his voice strong and brutal.

'I put it in a drawer – why?' she replied flippantly.

'Why didn't you put it on the fire-back?' he said harshly. 'What are you hoarding it up for?'

'I'm not hoarding it up,' she said. 'I've got a pair.'

He relapsed into gloomy silence. She, unable to move him, ran away upstairs, leaving him smoking by the fire. Again she tried on the ear-rings. Then another little inspiration came to her. She drew on the white stockings, both of them.

Presently she came down in them. Her husband still sat immovable and glowering by the fire.

'Look!' she said. 'They'll do beautifully.'

And she picked up her skirts to her knees, and twisted round, looking at her pretty legs in the neat stockings.

He filled with unreasonable rage, and took the pipe from his mouth.

'Don't they look nice?' she said. 'One from last year and one from this, they just do. Save you buying a pair.'

And she looked over her shoulders at her pretty calves, and at the dangling frills of her knickers.

'Put your skirts down and don't make a fool of yourself,' he said.

'Why a fool of myself?' she asked.

And she began to dance slowly round the room, kicking up her feet half reckless, half jeering, in ballet-dancer's fashion. Almost fearful, yet in defiance, she kicked up her legs at him, singing as she did so. She resented him.

'You little fool, ha' done with it,' he said. 'And you'll backfire them stockings, I'm telling you.' He was angry. His face flushed dark, he kept his head bent. She ceased to dance.

'I shan't,' she said. 'They'll come in very useful.'

He lifted his head and watched her, with lighted, dangerous eyes.

'You'll put 'em on the fire-back, I tell you,' he said.

It was a war now. She bent forward, in a ballet-dancer's fashion, and put her tongue between her teeth.

'I shan't backfire them stockings,' she sang, repeating his words, 'I shan't, I shan't, I shan't.'

And she danced round the room doing a high kick to the tune of her words. There was a real biting indifference in her behaviour.

'We'll see whether you will or not,' he said, 'trollops! You'd like Sam Adams to know you was wearing 'em, wouldn't you? That's what would please you.'

'Yes, I'd like him to see how nicely they fit me, he might give me some more then.'

And she looked down at her pretty legs.

He knew somehow that she *would* like Sam Adams to see how pretty her legs looked in the white stockings. It made his anger go deep, almost to hatred.

'Yer nasty trolley,' he cried. 'Put yer petticoats down, and stop being so foul-minded.'

'I'm not foul-minded,' she said. 'My legs are my own. And why shouldn't Sam Adams think they're nice?'

There was a pause. He watched her with eyes glittering to a point.

'Have you been havin' owt to do with him?' he asked.

'I've just spoken to him when I've seen him,' she said. 'He's not as bad as you would make out.'

'Isn't he?' he cried, a certain wakefulness in his voice. 'Them who has anything to do wi' him is too bad for me, I tell you.'

'Why, what are you frightened of him for?' she mocked.

She was rousing all his uncontrollable anger. He sat glowering. Every one of her sentences stirred him up like a red-hot iron. Soon it would be too much. And she was afraid herself; but she was neither conquered nor convinced.

A curious little grin of hate came on his face. He had a long score against her.

'What am I frightened of him for?' he repeated automatically. 'What am I frightened of him for? Why, for you, you stray-running little bitch.'

She flushed. The insult went deep into her, right home.

'Well, if you're so dull —' she said, lowering her eyelids, and speaking coldly, haughtily.

'If I'm so dull I'll break your neck the first word you speak to him,' he said, tense.

'Pf!' she sneered. 'Do you think I'm frightened of you?' She spoke coldly, detached.

She was frightened, for all that, white round the mouth.

His heart was getting hotter.

'You *will* be frightened of me, the next time you have anything to do with him,' he said.

'Do you think *you'd* ever be told – ha!'

Her jeering scorn made him go white-hot, molten. He knew he was incoherent, scarcely responsible for what he might do. Slowly, unseeing, he rose and went out of doors, stifled, moved to kill her.

He stood leaning against the garden fence, unable either to see or hear. Below him, far off, fumed the lights of the town. He stood still, unconscious with a black storm of rage, his face lifted to the night.

Presently, still unconscious of what he was doing, he went indoors again. She stood, a small, stubborn figure with tight-pressed lips and big, sullen, childish eyes, watching him, white with fear. He went heavily across the floor and dropped into his chair.

There was a silence.

'You're not going to tell me everything I shall do, and everything I shan't,' she broke out at last.

He lifted his head.

'I tell you *this*,' he said, low and intense. 'Have anything to do with Sam Adams, and I'll break your neck.'

She laughed, shrill and false.

'How I hate your word "break your neck",' she said, with a grimace of the mouth. 'It sounds so common and beastly. Can't you say something else —'

There was a dead silence.

248

'And besides,' she said, with a queer chirrup of mocking laughter, 'what do you know about anything? He sent me an amethyst brooch and a pair of pearl ear-rings.'

'He what?' said Whiston, in a suddenly normal voice. His eyes were fixed on her.

'Sent me a pair of pearl ear-rings, and an amethyst brooch,' she repeated, mechanically, pale to the lips.

And her big, black, childish eyes watched him, fascinated, held in her spell.

He seemed to thrust his face and his eyes forward at her, as he rose slowly and came to her. She watched transfixed in terror. Her throat made a small sound, as she tried to scream.

Then, quick as lightning, the back of his hand struck her with a crash across the mouth, and she was flung back blinded against the wall. The shock shook a queer sound out of her. And then she saw him still coming on, his eyes holding her, his fist drawn back, advancing slowly. At any instant the blow might crash into her.

Mad with terror, she raised her hands with a queer clawing movement to cover her eyes and her temples, opening her mouth in a dumb shriek. There was no sound. But the sight of her slowly arrested him. He hung before her, looking at her fixedly, as she stood crouched against the wall with open, bleeding mouth, and wide-staring eyes, and two hands clawing over her temples. And his lust to see her bleed, to break her and destroy her, rose from an old source against her. It carried him. He wanted satisfaction.

But he had seen her standing there, a piteous, horrified thing, and he turned his face aside in shame and nausea. He went and sat heavily in his chair, and a curious ease, almost like sleep, came over his brain.

She walked away from the wall towards the fire, dizzy, white to the lips, mechanically wiping her small, bleeding mouth. He sat motionless. Then, gradually, her breath began to hiss, she shook, and was sobbing silently, in grief for herself. Without looking, he saw. It made his mad desire to destroy her come back.

At length he lifted his head. His eyes were glowing again, fixed on her.

'And what did he give them you for?' he asked, in a steady, unyielding voice.

Her crying dried up in a second. She also was tense.

'They came as valentines,' she replied, still not subjugated, even if beaten.

249

'When, to-day?'

'The pearl ear-rings to-day – the amethyst brooch last year.'

'You've had it a year?'

'Yes.'

She felt that now nothing would prevent him if he rose to kill her. She could not prevent him any more. She was yielded up to him. They both trembled in the balance, unconscious.

'What have you had to do with him?' he asked, in a barren voice.

'I've not had anything to do with him,' she quavered.

'You just kept 'em because they were jewellery?' he said.

A weariness came over him. What was the worth of speaking any more of it? He did not care any more. He was dreary and sick.

She began to cry again, but he took no notice. She kept wiping her mouth on her handkerchief. He could see it, the blood-mark. It made him only more sick and tired of the responsibility of it, the violence, the shame.

When she began to move about again, he raised his head once more from his dead, motionless position.

'Where are the things?' he said.

'They are upstairs,' she quavered. She knew the passion had gone down in him.

'Bring them down,' he said.

'I won't,' she wept, with rage. 'You're not going to bully me and hit me like that on the mouth.'

And she sobbed again. He looked at her in contempt and compassion and in rising anger.

'Where are they?' he said.

'They're in the little drawer under the looking-glass,' she sobbed.

He went slowly upstairs, struck a match, and found the trinkets. He brought them downstairs in his hand.

'These?' he said, looking at them as they lay in his palm.

She looked at them without answering. She was not interested in them any more.

He looked at the little jewels. They were pretty.

'It's none of their fault,' he said to himself.

And he searched round slowly, persistently, for a box. He tied the things up and addressed them to Sam Adams. Then he went out in his slippers to post the little package.

When he came back she was still sitting crying.

'You'd better go to bed,' he said.

She paid no attention. He sat by the fire. She still cried.

'I'm sleeping down here,' he said. 'Go you to bed.'

In a few moments she lifted her tear-stained, swollen face and looked at him with eyes all forlorn and pathetic. A great flash of anguish went over his body. He went over, slowly, and very gently took her in his hands. She let herself be taken. Then as she lay against his shoulder, she sobbed aloud:

'I never meant —'

'My love – my little love —' he cried, in anguish of spirit, holding her in his arms.

A SICK COLLIER

SHE was too good for him, everybody said. Yet still she did not regret marrying him. He had come courting her when he was only nineteen, and she twenty. He was in build what they call a tight little fellow; short, dark, with a warm colour, and that upright set of the head and chest, that flaunting way in movement recalling a mating bird, which denotes a body taut and compact with life. Being a good worker he had earned decent money in the mine, and having a good home had saved a little.

She was a cook at 'Uplands', a tall, fair girl, very quiet. Having seen her walk down the street, Horsepool had followed her from a distance. He was taken with her, he did not drink, and he was not lazy. So, although he seemed a bit simple, without much intelligence, but having a sort of physical brightness, she considered, and accepted him.

When they were married they went to live in Scargill Street, in a highly respectable six-roomed house which they had furnished between them. The street was built up the side of a long, steep hill. It was narrow and rather tunnel-like. Nevertheless, the back looked out over the adjoining pasture, across a wide valley of fields and woods, in the bottom of which the mine lay snugly.

He made himself gaffer in his own house. She was unacquainted with a collier's mode of life. They were married on a Saturday. On the Sunday night he said:

'Set th' table for my breakfast, an' put my pit-things afront o' th' fire. I s'll be gettin' up at ha'ef pas' five. Tha nedna shift thysen not till when ter likes.'

He showed her how to put a newspaper on the table for a cloth. When she demurred:

'I want none o' your white cloths i' th' mornin'. I like ter be able to slobber if I feel like it,' he said.

He put before the fire his moleskin trousers, a clean singlet, or sleeveless vest of thick flannel, a pair of stockings, and his pit-boots, arranging them all to be warm and ready for morning.

'Now tha sees. That wants doin' ivery night.'

252

Punctually at half-past five he left her, without any form of leave-taking, going downstairs in his shirt.

When he arrived home at four o'clock in the afternoon his dinner was ready to be dished up. She was startled when he came in, a short, sturdy figure, with a face indescribably black and streaked. She stood before the fire in her white blouse and white apron, a fair girl, the picture of a beautiful cleanliness. He 'clommaxed' in, in his heavy boots.

'Well, how 'as ter gone on?' he asked.

'I was ready for you to come home,' she replied tenderly. In his black face the whites of his brown eyes flashed at her.

'An' I wor ready for comin',' he said. He planked his tin bottle and snap-bag on the dresser, took off his coat and scarf and waistcoat, dragged his arm-chair nearer the fire and sat down.

'Let's ha'e a bit o' dinner, then – I'm about clammed,' he said.

'Aren't you goin' to wash yourself first?'

'What am I to wesh mysen for?'

'Well, you can't eat your dinner —'

'Oh, strike a daisy, Missis! Dunna I eat my snap i' th' pit wi'out weshin'? – forced to.'

She served the dinner and sat opposite him. His small bullet head was quite black, save for the whites of his eyes and his scarlet lips. It gave her a queer sensation to see him open his red mouth and bare his white teeth as he ate. His arms and hands were mottled black; his bare, strong neck got a little fairer as it settled towards his shoulders, reassuring her. There was the faint indescribable odour of the pit in the room, an odour of damp, exhausted air.

'Why is your vest so black on the shoulders?' she asked.

'My singlet? That's wi' th' watter droppin' on us from th' roof. This is a dry un as I put on afore I come up. They ha'e gre't clothes-'osses, an' we change us things, we put 'em on theer ter dry.'

When he washed himself, kneeling on the hearth-rug stripped to the waist, she felt afraid of him again. He was so muscular, he seemed so intent on what he was doing, so intensely himself, like a vigorous animal. And as he stood wiping himself, with his naked breast towards her, she felt rather sick, seeing his thick arms bulge their muscles.

They were nevertheless very happy. He was at a great pitch of pride because of her. The men in the pit might chaff him, they might try to entice him away, but nothing could reduce his self-assured pride because of her, nothing could unsettle his almost infantile satisfaction. In the evening he sat in his arm-chair chattering to her, or listening as she read the newspaper to him. When it was fine, he would go into the street, squat on his heels as colliers do, with his back against the wall of his parlour, and call to the passers-by, in greeting, one after another. If no one were passing, he was content just to squat and smoke, having such a fund of sufficiency and satisfaction in his heart. He was well married.

They had not been wed a year when all Brent and Wellwood's men came out on strike. Willy was in the Union, so with a pinch they scrambled through. The furniture was not all paid for, and other debts were incurred. She worried and contrived, he left it to her. But he was a good husband; he gave her all he had.

The men were out fifteen weeks. They had been back just over a year when Willy had an accident in the mine, tearing his bladder. At the pit head the doctor talked of the hospital. Losing his head entirely, the young collier raved like a madman, what with pain and fear of hospital.

'Tha s'lt go whoam, Willy, tha s'lt go whoam,' the deputy said.

A lad warned the wife to have the bed ready. Without speaking or hesitating she prepared. But when the ambulance came, and she heard him shout with pain at being moved, she was afraid lest she should sink down. They carried him in.

'Yo' should a' had a bed i' th' parlour, Missis,' said the deputy, 'then we shouldna' ha' had to hawkse 'im upstairs, an' it 'ud 'a' saved your legs.'

But it was too late now. They got him upstairs.

'They let me lie, Lucy,' he was crying, 'they let me lie two mortal hours on th' sleck afore they took me outer th' stall. Th' peen, Lucy, th' peen; oh, Lucy, th' peen, th' peen!'

'I know th' pain's bad, Willy, I know. But you must try an' bear it a bit.'

'Tha manna carry on in that form, lad, thy missis'll niver be able ter stan' it,' said the deputy.

'I canna 'elp it, it's th' peen, it's th' peen,' he cried again. He had never been ill in his life. When he had smashed a finger he could look at the wound. But this pain came from inside, and terrified him. At last he was soothed and exhausted.

It was some time before she could undress him and wash him. He would let no other woman do for him, having that savage modesty usual in such men.

For six weeks he was in bed, suffering much pain. The doctors were not quite sure what was the matter with him, and scarcely knew what to do. He could eat, he did not lose flesh, nor strength, yet the pain continued, and he could hardly walk at all.

In the sixth week the men came out in the national strike. He would get up quite early in the morning and sit by the window. On Wednesday, the second week of the strike, he sat gazing out on the street as usual, a bullet-headed young man, still vigorous-looking, but with a peculiar expression of hunted fear in his face.

'Lucy,' he called, 'Lucy!'

She, pale and worn, ran upstairs at his bidding.

'Gi'e me a han-kercher,' he said.

'Why, you've got one,' she replied, coming near.

'Tha nedna touch me,' he cried. Feeling his pocket, he produced a white handkerchief.

'I non want a white un, gi'e me a red un,' he said.

'An' if anybody comes to see you,' she answered, giving him a red handkerchief.

'Besides,' she continued, 'you needn't ha' brought me upstairs for that.'

'I b'lieve th' peen's commin' on again,' he said, with a little horror in his voice.

'It isn't, you know it isn't,' she replied. 'The doctor says you imagine it's there when it isn't.'

'Canna I feel what's inside me?' he shouted.

'There's a traction-engine coming downhill,' she said. 'That'll scatter them. – I'll just go an' finish your pudding.'

She left him. The traction-engine went by, shaking the houses. Then the street was quiet, save for the men. A gang of youths from fifteen to twenty-five years old were playing marbles in the middle of the road. Other little groups of men were playing on the pavement. The street was gloomy. Willy could hear the endless calling and shouting of men's voices.

'Tha'rt skinchin'!'

'I arena!'

'Come 'ere with that blood-alley.'

'Swop us four for't.'

'Shonna, gie's hold on't.'

He wanted to be out, he wanted to be playing marbles. The pain had weakened his mind, so that he hardly knew any self-control.

Presently another gang of men lounged up the street. It was pay morning. The Union was paying the men in the Primitive Chapel. They were returning with their half-sovereigns.

'Sorry!' bawled a voice. 'Sorry!'

The word is a form of address, corruption probably of 'Sirrah'. Willy started almost out of his chair.

'Sorry!' again bawled a great voice. 'Art goin' wi' me to see Notts play Villa?'

Many of the marble-players started up.

'What time is it? There's no treens, we s'll ha'e ter walk.'

The street was alive with men.

'Who's goin' ter Nottingham ter see th' match?' shouted the same big voice. A very large, tipsy man, with his cap over his eye, was calling.

'Com' on – aye, com' on!' came many voices. The street was full of the shouting of men. They split up in excited cliques and groups.

'Play up, Notts!' the big man shouted.

'Plee up, Notts!' shouted the youths and men. They were at kindling pitch. It only needed a shout to rouse them. Of this the careful authorities were aware.

'I'm goin', I'm goin'!' shouted the sick man at his window.

Lucy came running upstairs.

'I'm goin' ter see Notts play Villa on th' Meadows ground,' he declared.

'You – *you* can't go. There are no trains. You can't walk nine miles.'

'I'm goin' ter see th' match,' he declared, rising.

'You know you can't. Sit down now an' be quiet.'

She put her hand on him. He shook it off.

'Leave me alone, leave me alone. It's thee as ma'es th' peen come, it's thee. I'm goin' ter Nottingham to see th' football match.'

'Sit down – folks'll hear you, and what will they think?'

'Come off'n me. Com' off. It's her, it's her as does it. Com' off.'

He seized hold of her. His little head was bristling with madness, and he was strong as a lion.

'Oh, Willy!' she cried.

'It's 'er, it's 'er. Kill her!' he shouted, 'kill her.'

'Willy, folks'll hear you.'

'Th' peen's commin' on again, I tell yer. I'll kill her for it.'

He was completely out of his mind. She struggled with him to prevent his going to the stairs. When she escaped from him, who was

256

shouting and raving, she beckoned to her neighbour, a girl of twenty-four, who was cleaning the window across the road.

Ethel Mellor was the daughter of a well-to-do check-weighman. She ran across in fear to Mrs. Horsepool. Hearing the man raving, people were running out in the street and listening. Ethel hurried upstairs. Everything was clean and pretty in the young home.

Willy was staggering round the room, after the slowly retreating Lucy, shouting:

'Kill her! Kill her!'

'Mr. Horsepool!' cried Ethel, leaning against the bed, white as the sheets, and trembling. 'Whatever are you saying?'

'I tell yer it's 'er fault as th' pain comes on – I tell yer it is! Kill 'er – kill 'er!'

'Kill Mrs. Horsepool!' cried the trembling girl. 'Why, you're ever so fond of her, you know you are.'

'The peen – I ha'e such a lot o' peen – I want to kill 'er.'

He was subsiding. When he sat down his wife collapsed in a chair, weeping noiselessly. The tears ran down Ethel's face. He sat staring out of the window; then the old, hurt look came on his face.

'What 'ave I been sayin'?' he asked, looking piteously at his wife.

'Why!' said Ethel, 'you've been carrying on something awful, saying: "Kill her, kill her!"'

'Have I, Lucy?' he faltered.

'You didn't know what you were saying,' said his young wife gently but coldly.

His face puckered up. He bit his lips, then broke into tears, sobbing uncontrollably, with his face to the window.

There was no sound in the room but of three people crying bitterly, breath caught in sobs. Suddenly Lucy put away her tears and went over to him.

'You didn't know what you was sayin', Willy, I know you didn't. I knew you didn't, all the time. It doesn't matter, Willy. Only don't do it again.'

In a little while, when they were calmer, she went downstairs with Ethel.

'See if anybody is looking in the street,' she said.

Ethel went into the parlour and peeped through the curtains.

'Aye!' she said. 'You may back your life Lena an' Mrs. Severn'll be out gorping, and that clat-fartin' Mrs. Allsop.'

'Oh, I hope they haven't heard anything! If it gets about as he's out of his mind, they'll stop his compensation, I know they will.'

'They'd never stop his compensation for *that*,' protested Ethel.

'Well, they *have* been stopping some —'

'It'll not get about. I s'll tell nobody.'

'Oh, but if it does, whatever shall we do....?'

THE CHRISTENING

THE mistress of the British School stepped down from her school gate, and instead of turning to the left as usual, she turned to the right. Two women who were hastening home to scramble their husbands' dinners together – it was five minutes to four – stopped to look at her. They stood gazing after her for a moment; then they glanced at each other with a woman's little grimace.

To be sure, the retreating figure was ridiculous: small and thin, with a black straw hat, and a rusty cashmere dress hanging full all round the skirt. For so small and frail and rusty a creature to sail with slow, deliberate stride was also absurd. Hilda Rowbotham was less than thirty, so it was not years that set the measure of her pace; she had heart disease. Keeping her face, that was small with sickness, but not uncomely, firmly lifted and fronting ahead, the young woman sailed on past the market-place, like a black swan of mournful disreputable plumage.

She turned into Berryman's, the bakers. The shop displayed bread and cakes, sacks of flour and oatmeal, flitches of bacon, hams, lard, and sausages. The combination of scents was not unpleasing. Hilda Rowbotham stood for some minutes nervously tapping and pushing a large knife that lay on the counter, and looking at the tall, glittering brass scales. At last a morose man with sandy whiskers came down the step from the house-place.

'What is it?' he asked, not apologising for his delay.

'Will you give me sixpennyworth of assorted cakes and pastries – and put in some macaroons, please?' she asked, in remarkably rapid and nervous speech. Her lips fluttered like two leaves in a wind, and her words crowded and rushed like a flock of sheep at a gate.

'We've got no macaroons,' said the man churlishly.

He had evidently caught that word. He stood waiting.

'Then I can't have any, Mr. Berryman. Now I do feel disappointed. I like those macaroons, you know, and it's not often I treat myself. One gets so tired of trying to spoil oneself, don't you think? It's less profitable even than trying to spoil somebody else.' She laughed a quick little nervous laugh, putting her hand to her face.

'Then what'll you have?' asked the man, without the ghost of an answering smile. He evidently had not followed, so he looked more glum than ever.

'Oh, anything you've got,' replied the schoolmistress, flushing slightly. The man moved slowly about, dropping the cakes from various dishes one by one into a paper bag.

'How's that sister o' yours getting on?' he asked, as if he were talking to the flour-scoop.

'Whom do you mean?' snapped the schoolmistress.

'The youngest,' answered the stooping, pale-faced man, with a note of sarcasm.

'Emma! Oh, she's very well, thank you!' The schoolmistress was very red, but she spoke with sharp, ironical defiance. The man grunted. Then he handed her the bag, and watched her out of the shop without bidding her 'Good afternoon'.

She had the whole length of the main street to traverse, a half-mile of slow-stepping torture, with shame flushing over her neck. But she carried her white bag with an appearance of steadfast unconcern. When she turned into the field she seemed to droop a little. The wide valley opened out from her, with the far woods withdrawing into twilight, and away in the centre the great pit steaming its white smoke and chuffing as the men were being turned up. A full rose-coloured moon, like a flamingo flying low under the far, dusky east, drew out of the mist. It was beautiful, and it made her irritable sadness soften, diffuse.

Across the field, and she was at home. It was a new, substantial cottage, built with unstinted hand, such a house as an old miner could build himself out of his savings. In the rather small kitchen a woman of dark, saturnine complexion sat nursing a baby in a long white gown; a young woman of heavy, brutal cast stood at the table, cutting bread and butter. She had a downcast, humble mien that sat unnaturally on her, and was strangely irritating. She did not look round when her sister entered. Hilda put down the bag of cakes and left the room, not having spoken to Emma, nor to the baby, nor to Mrs. Carlin, who had come in to help for the afternoon.

Almost immediately the father entered from the yard with a dust-pan full of coals. He was a large man, but he was going to pieces. As he passed through, he gripped the door with his free hand to steady himself, but turning, he lurched and swayed. He began putting the coals on the fire, piece by piece. One lump fell from his hands and smashed on the white hearth. Emma Rowbotham looked round, and began in a

260

rough, loud voice of anger: 'Look at you!' Then she consciously moderated her tones. 'I'll sweep it up in a minute – don't you bother; you'll only be going head-first into the fire.'

Her father bent down nevertheless to clear up the mess he had made, saying, articulating his words loosely and slavering in his speech:

'The lousy bit of a thing, it slipped between my fingers like a fish.'

As he spoke he went tilting towards the fire. The dark-browed woman cried out; he put his hand on the hot stove to save himself; Emma swung round and dragged him off.

'Didn't I tell you!' she cried roughly. 'Now, have you burnt yourself?'

She held tight hold of the big man, and pushed him into his chair.

'What's the matter?' cried a sharp voice from the other room. The speaker appeared, a hard well-favoured woman of twenty-eight. 'Emma, don't speak like that to father.' Then, in a tone not so cold, but just as sharp: 'Now, father, what have you been doing?'

Emma withdrew to her table sullenly.

'It's nöwt,' said the old man, vainly protesting. 'It's nöwt at a'. Get on wi' what you're doin'.'

'I'm afraid 'e's burnt 'is 'and,' said the black-browed woman, speaking of him with a kind of hard pity, as if he were a cumbersome child. Bertha took the old man's hand and looked at it, making a quick tut-tutting noise of impatience.

'Emma, get that zinc ointment – and some white rag,' she commanded sharply. The younger sister put down her loaf with the knife in it, and went. To a sensitive observer, this obedience was more intolerable than the most hateful discord. The dark woman bent over the baby and made silent, gentle movements of motherliness to it. The little one smiled and moved on her lap. It continued to move and twist.

'I believe this child's hungry,' she said. 'How long is it since he had anything?'

'Just afore dinner,' said Emma dully.

'Good gracious!' exclaimed Bertha. 'You needn't starve the child now you've got it. Once every two hours it ought to be fed, as I've told you; and now it's three. Take him, poor little mite – I'll cut the bread.' She bent and looked at the bonny baby. She could not help herself: she smiled, and pressed its cheek with her finger, and nodded to it, making little noises. Then she turned and took the loaf from her sister. The woman rose and gave the child to its mother. Emma bent over the little sucking mite. She hated it when she looked at it, and saw it as a symbol, but when she felt it, her love was like fire in her blood.

'I should think 'e canna be comin',' said the father uneasily, looking up at the clock.

'Nonsense, father – the clock's fast! It's but half-past four! Don't fidget!' Bertha continued to cut the bread and butter.

'Open a tin of pears,' she said to the woman, in a much milder tone. Then she went into the next room. As soon as she was gone, the old man said again: 'I should ha'e thought he'd 'a' been 'ere by now, if he means comin'.'

Emma, engrossed, did not answer. The father had ceased to consider her, since she had become humbled.

' 'E'll come – 'e'll come!' assured the stranger.

A few minutes later Bertha hurried into the kitchen, taking off her apron. The dog barked furiously. She opened the door, commanded the dog to silence, and said: 'He will be quiet now, Mr. Kendal.'

'Thank you,' said a sonorous voice, and there was the sound of a bicycle being propped against a wall. A clergyman entered, a big-boned, thin, ugly man of nervous manner. He went straight to the father.

'Ah – how are you —' he asked musically, peering down on the great frame of the miner, ruined by locomotor ataxy.

His voice was full of gentleness, but he seemed as if he could not see distinctly, could not get things clear.

'Have you hurt your hand?' he said comfortingly, seeing the white rag.

'It wor nöwt but a pestered bit o' coal as dropped, an' I put my hand on th' hub. I thought tha worna commin'.'

The familiar 'tha', and the reproach, were unconscious retaliation on the old man's part. The minister smiled, half wistfully, half indulgently. He was full of vague tenderness. Then he turned to the young mother, who flushed sullenly because her dishonoured breast was uncovered.

'How are *you*?' he asked, very softly and gently, as if she were ill and he were mindful of her.

'I'm all right,' she replied, awkwardly taking his hand without rising, hiding her face and the anger that rose in her.

'Yes – yes' – he peered down at the baby, which sucked with distended mouth upon the firm breast. 'Yes, yes.' He seemed lost in a dim musing.

Coming to, he shook hands unseeingly with the woman.

Presently they all went into the next room, the minister hesitating to help his crippled old deacon.

'I can go by myself, thank yer,' testily replied the father.

Soon all were seated. Everybody was separated in feeling and isolated at table. High tea was spread in the middle kitchen, a large, ugly room kept for special occasions.

Hilda appeared last, and the clumsy, raw-boned clergyman rose to meet her. He was afraid of this family, the well-to-do old collier, and the brutal, self-willed children. But Hilda was queen among them. She was the clever one, and had been to college. She felt responsible for the keeping up of a high standard of conduct in all the members of the family. There *was* a difference between the Rowbothams and the common collier folk. Woodbine Cottage was a superior house to most – and was built in pride by the old man. She, Hilda, was a college-trained schoolmistress; she meant to keep up the prestige of her house in spite of blows.

She had put on a dress of green voile for this special occasion. But she was very thin; her neck protruded painfully. The clergyman, however, greeted her almost with reverence, and, with some assumption of dignity, she sat down before the tray. At the far end of the table sat the broken, massive frame of her father. Next to him was the youngest daughter, nursing the restless boy. The minister sat between Hilda and Bertha, hulking his bony frame uncomfortably.

There was a great spread on the table of tinned fruits and tinned salmon, ham and cakes. Miss Rowbotham kept a keen eye on everything: she felt the importance of the occasion. The young mother who had given rise to all this solemnity ate in sulky discomfort, snatching sullen little smiles at her child, smiles which came, in spite of her, when she felt its little limbs stirring vigorously on her lap. Bertha, sharp and abrupt, was chiefly concerned with the baby. She scorned her sister, and treated her like dirt. But the infant was a streak of light to her. Miss Rowbotham concerned herself with the function and the conversation. Her hands fluttered; she talked in little volleys, exceedingly nervous. Towards the end of the meal, there came a pause. The old man wiped his mouth with his red handkerchief, then, his blue eyes going fixed and staring, he began to speak, in a loose, slobbering fashion, charging his words at the clergyman.

'Well, mester – we'n axed you to come here ter christen this childt, an' you'n come, an' I'm sure we're very thankful. I can't see lettin' the poor blessed childt miss baptising, an' they aren't for goin' to church wi't —' He seemed to lapse into a muse. 'So,' he resumed, 'we'n axed you to come here to do the job. I'm not sayin' as it's not 'ard on us, it is. I'm breakin' up, an' mother's gone. I don't like leavin' a girl o' mine in a situation like 'ers is, but what the Lord's done, He's done, an' it's no matter murmuring. . . . There's one thing to be thankful for, an' we are thankful for it: they never need know the want of bread.'

Miss Rowbotham, the lady of the family, sat very stiff and pained during this discourse. She was sensitive to so many things that she was bewildered. She felt her young sister's shame, then a kind of swift protecting love for the baby, a feeling that included the mother; she was at a loss before her father's religious sentiment, and she felt and resented bitterly the mark upon the family, against which the common folk could lift their fingers. Still she winced from the sound of her father's words. It was a painful ordeal.

'It is hard for you,' began the clergyman in his soft, lingering, unworldly voice. 'It is hard for you to-day, but the Lord gives comfort in His time. A man child is born unto us, therefore let us rejoice and be glad. If sin has entered in among us, let us purify our hearts before the Lord. . . .'

He went on with his discourse. The young mother lifted the whimpering infant, till its face was hid in her loose hair. She was hurt, and a little glowering anger shone in her face. But nevertheless her fingers clasped the body of the child beautifully. She was stupefied with anger against this emotion let loose on her account.

Miss Bertha rose and went to the little kitchen, returning with water in a china bowl. She placed it there among the tea-things.

'Well, we're all ready,' said the old man, and the clergyman began to read the service. Miss Bertha was godmother, the two men godfathers. The old man sat with bent head. The scene became impressive. At last Miss Bertha took the child and put it in the arms of the clergyman. He, big and ugly, shone with a kind of unreal love. He had never mixed with life, and women were all unliving, Biblical things to him. When he asked for the name, the old man lifted his head fiercely. 'Joseph William, after me,' he said, almost out of breath.

'Joseph William, I baptise thee. . . .' resounded the strange, full, chanting voice of the clergyman. The baby was quite still.

'Let us pray!' It came with relief to them all. They knelt before their chairs, all but the young mother, who bent and hid herself over her baby. The clergyman began his hesitating, struggling prayer.

Just then heavy footsteps were heard coming up the path, ceasing at the window. The young mother, glancing up, saw her brother, black in his pit dirt, grinning in through the panes. His red mouth curved in a sneer; his fair hair shone above his blackened skin. He caught the eye of his sister and grinned. Then his black face disappeared. He had gone on into the kitchen. The girl with the child sat still and anger filled her heart. She herself hated now the praying clergyman and the whole emotional business; she hated her brother bitterly. In anger and bondage she sat and listened.

Suddenly her father began to pray. His familiar, loud, rambling voice made her shut herself up and become even insentient. Folks said his mind was weakening. She believed it to be true, and kept herself always disconnected from him.

'We ask Thee, Lord,' the old man cried, 'to look after this childt. Fatherless he is. But what does the earthly father matter before Thee? The childt is Thine, he is Thy childt. Lord, what father has a man but Thee? Lord, when a man says he is a father, he is wrong from the first word. For Thou art the Father, Lord, take away from us the conceit that our children are ours. Lord, Thou art Father of this childt as is fatherless here. O God, Thou bring him up. For I have stood between Thee and my children; I've had *my* way with them, Lord; I've stood between Thee and my children; I've cut 'em off from Thee because they were mine. And they've grown twisted, because of me. Who is their father, Lord, but Thee? But I put myself in the way, they've been plants under a stone, because of me. Lord, if it hadn't been for me, they might ha' been trees in the sunshine. Let me own it, Lord, I've done 'em mischief. It would ha' been better if they'd never known no father. No man is a father, Lord: only Thou art. They can never grow beyond Thee, but I hampered them. Lift 'em up again, and undo what I've done to my children. And let this young childt be like a willow tree beside the waters, with no father but Thee, O God. Aye, an' I wish it had been so with my children, that they'd had no father but Thee. For I've been like a stone upon them, and they rise up and curse me in their wickedness. But let me go, an' lift Thou them up, Lord . . .'

The minister, unaware of the feelings of a father, knelt in trouble, hearing without understanding the special language of fatherhood. Miss Rowbotham alone felt and understood a little. Her heart began to flutter; she was in pain. The two younger daughters kneeled unhearing, stiffened, and impervious. Bertha was thinking of the baby; and the young mother thought of the father of her child, whom she hated.

There was a clatter outside in the scullery. There the youngest son made as much noise as he could, pouring out the water for his wash, muttering in deep anger:

'Blortin', slaverin' old fool!'

And while the praying of his father continued, his heart was burning with rage. On the table was a paper bag. He picked it up and read: 'John Berryman – Bread, Pastries, etc.' Then he grinned with a grimace. The father of the baby was baker's man at Berryman's. The prayer went on in the middle kitchen. Laurie Rowbotham gathered together the mouth of the bag, inflated it, and burst it with his fist. There was a loud report. He grinned to himself. But he writhed at the same time with shame and fear of his father.

The father broke off from his prayer; the party shuffled to their feet. The young mother went into the scullery.

'What art doin', fool?' she said.

The collier youth tipped the baby under the chin, singing:

> *'Pat-a-cake, pat-a-cake, baker's man,*
> *Bake me a cake as fast as you can....'*

The mother snatched the child away. 'Shut thy mouth,' she said, the colour coming into her cheek.

> *'Prick it and stick it and mark it with P,*
> *And put it i' th' oven for baby an' me....'*

He grinned, showing a grimy, and jeering and unpleasant red mouth and white teeth.

'I s'll gi'e thee a dab ower th' mouth,' said the mother of the baby grimly. He began to sing again, and she struck out at him.

'Now what's to do?' said the father, staggering in.

The youth began to sing again. His sister stood sullen and furious.

'Why does *that* upset you?' asked the eldest Miss Rowbotham, sharply, of Emma the mother. 'Good gracious, it hasn't improved your temper.'

Miss Bertha came in, and took the bonny baby.

The father sat big and unheeding in his chair, his eyes vacant, his physique wrecked. He let them do as they would, he fell to pieces. And yet some power, involuntary, like a curse, remained in him. The very ruin of him was like a lodestone that held them in its control. The wreck of him still dominated the house, in his dissolution even he compelled their being. They had never lived; his life, his will had always been upon them and contained them. They were only half-individuals.

The day after the christening he staggered in at the doorway declaring, in a loud voice, with joy in life still: 'The daisies light up the earth, they clap their hands in multitudes, in praise of the morning.' And his daughters shrank, sullen.

ODOUR OF CHRYSANTHEMUMS

I

THE small locomotive engine, Number 4, came clanking, stumbling down from Selston with seven full wagons. It appeared round the corner with loud threats of speed, but the colt that it startled from among the gorse, which still flickered indistinctly in the raw afternoon, out-distanced it at a canter. A woman, walking up the railway line to Underwood, drew back into the hedge, held her basket aside, and watched the footplate of the engine advancing. The trucks thumped heavily past, one by one, with slow inevitable movements, as she stood insignificantly trapped between the jolting black wagons and the hedge; then they curved away towards the coppice where the withered oak leaves dropped noiselessly, while the birds, pulling at the scarlet hips beside the track, made off into the dusk that had already crept into the spinney. In the open, the smoke from the engine sank and cleaved to the rough grass. The fields were dreary and forsaken, and in the marshy strip that led to the whimsey, a reedy pit-pond, the fowls had already abandoned their run among the alders, to roost in the tarred fowl-house. The pit-bank looked up beyond the pond, flames like red sores licking its ashy sides, in the afternoon's stagnant light. Just beyond rose the tapering chimneys and the clumsy black headstocks of Brinsley Colliery. The two wheels were spinning fast up against the sky, and the winding engine rapped out its little spasms. The miners were being turned up.

The engine whistled as it came into the wide bay of railway lines beside the colliery, where rows of trucks stood in harbour.

Miners, single, trailing and in groups, passed like shadows diverging home. At the edge of the ribbed level of sidings squat a low cottage, three steps down from the cinder track. A large bony vine clutched at the house, as if to claw down the tiled roof. Round the bricked yard grew a few wintry primroses. Beyond, the long garden sloped down to a bush-covered brook course. There were some twiggy apple trees, winter-crack trees, and ragged cabbages. Beside the path hung dishevelled pink chrysanthemums, like pink cloths hung on bushes. A woman came stooping out of the felt-covered fowlhouse, half-way down the garden.

She closed and padlocked the door, then drew herself erect, having brushed some bits from her white apron.

She was a tall woman of imperious mien, handsome, with definite black eyebrows. Her smooth black hair was parted exactly. For a few moments she stood steadily watching the miners as they passed along the railway: then she turned towards the brook course. Her face was calm and set, her mouth was closed with disillusionment. After a moment she called:

'John!' There was no answer. She waited, and then said distinctly: 'Where are you?'

'Here!' replied a child's sulky voice from among the bushes. The woman looked piercingly through the dusk.

'Are you at that brook?' she asked sternly.

For answer the child showed himself before the raspberry-canes that rose like whips. He was a small, sturdy boy of five. He stood quite still, defiantly.

'Oh!' said the mother, conciliated. 'I thought you were down at that wet brook – and you remember what I told you —'

The boy did not move or answer.

'Come, come on in,' she said more gently, 'it's getting dark. There's your grandfather's engine coming down the line!'

The lad advanced slowly, with resentful, taciturn movement. He was dressed in trousers and waistcoat of cloth that was too thick and hard for the size of the garments. They were evidently cut down from a man's clothes.

As they went slowly towards the house he tore at the ragged wisps of chrysanthemums and dropped the petals in handfuls along the path.

'Don't do that – it does look nasty,' said his mother. He refrained, and she, suddenly pitiful, broke off a twig with three or four wan flowers and held them against her face. When mother and son reached the yard her hand hesitated, and instead of laying the flower aside, she pushed it in her apron-band. The mother and son stood at the foot of the three steps looking across the bay of lines at the passing home of the miners. The trundle of the small train was imminent. Suddenly the engine loomed past the house and came to a stop opposite the gate.

The engine-driver, a short man with round grey beard, leaned out of the cab high above the woman.

'Have you got a cup of tea?' he said in a cheery, hearty fashion.

It was her father. She went in, saying she would mash. Directly, she returned.

'I didn't come to see you on Sunday,' began the little grey-bearded man.

'I didn't expect you,' said his daughter.

The engine-driver winced; then, reassuming his cheery, airy manner, he said:

'Oh, have you heard then? Well, and what do you think —'

'I think it is soon enough,' she replied.

At her brief censure the little man made an impatient gesture, and said coaxingly, yet with dangerous coldness:

'Well, what's a man to do? It's no sort of life for a man of my years, to sit at my own hearth like a stranger. And if I'm going to marry again it may as well be soon as late – what does it matter to anybody?'

The woman did not reply, but turned and went into the house. The man in the engine-cab stood assertive, till she returned with a cup of tea and a piece of bread and butter on a plate. She went up the steps and stood near the footplate of the hissing engine.

'You needn't 'a' brought me bread an' butter,' said her father. 'But a cup of tea' – he sipped appreciatively – 'it's very nice.' He sipped for a moment or two, then: 'I hear as Walter's got another bout on,' he said.

'When hasn't he?' said the woman bitterly.

'I heerd tell of him in the "Lord Nelson" braggin' as he was going to spend that b—— afore he went: half a sovereign that was.'

'When?' asked the woman.

'A' Sat'day night – I know that's true.'

'Very likely,' she laughed bitterly. 'He gives me twenty-three shillings.'

'Aye, it's a nice thing, when a man can do nothing with his money but make a beast of himself!' said the grey-whiskered man. The woman turned her head away. Her father swallowed the last of his tea and handed her the cup.

'Aye,' he sighed, wiping his mouth. 'It's a settler, it is —'

He put his hand on the lever. The little engine strained and groaned, and the train rumbled towards the crossing. The woman again looked across the metals. Darkness was settling over the spaces of the railway and trucks: the miners, in grey sombre groups, were still passing home. The winding engine pulsed hurriedly, with brief pauses. Elizabeth Bates looked at the dreary flow of men, then she went indoors. Her husband did not come.

The kitchen was small and full of firelight; red coals piled glowing up the chimney mouth. All the life of the room seemed in the white, warm hearth and the steel fender reflecting the red fire. The cloth was laid for tea; cups glinted in the shadows. At the back, where the lowest stairs protruded into the room, the boy sat struggling with a knife and a piece of white wood. He was almost hidden in the shadow. It was half-past four. They had but to await the father's coming to begin tea. As the mother watched her son's sullen little struggle with the wood, she saw herself in his silence and pertinacity; she saw the father in her child's indifference to all but himself. She seemed to be occupied by her husband. He had probably gone past his home, slunk past his own door, to drink before he came in, while his dinner spoiled and wasted in waiting. She glanced at the clock, then took the potatoes to strain them in the yard. The garden and fields beyond the brook were closed in uncertain darkness. When she rose with the saucepan, leaving the drain steaming into the night behind her, she saw the yellow lamps were lit along the high road that went up the hill away beyond the space of the railway lines and the field.

Then again she watched the men trooping home, fewer now and fewer.

Indoors the fire was sinking and the room was dark red. The woman put her saucepan on the hob, and set a batter-pudding near the mouth of the oven. Then she stood unmoving. Directly, gratefully, came quick young steps to the door. Something hung on the latch a moment, then a little girl entered and began pulling off her outdoor things, dragging a mass of curls, just ripening from gold to brown, over her eyes with her hat.

Her mother chid her for coming late from school, and said she would have to keep her at home the dark winter days.

'Why, mother, it's hardly a bit dark yet. The lamp's not lighted, and my father's not home.'

'No, he isn't. But it's a quarter to five! Did you see anything of him?'

The child became serious. She looked at her mother with large, wistful blue eyes.

'No, mother, I've never seen him. Why? Has he come up an' gone past, to Old Brinsley? He hasn't, mother, 'cos I never saw him.'

'He'd watch that,' said the mother bitterly, 'he'd take care as you didn't see him. But you may depend upon it, he's seated in the "Prince o' Wales". He wouldn't be this late.'

The girl looked at her mother piteously.

'Let's have our teas, mother, should we?' said she.

The mother called John to table. She opened the door once more and looked out across the darkness of the lines. All was deserted: she could not hear the winding-engines.

'Perhaps,' she said to herself, 'he's stopped to get some ripping done.'

They sat down to tea. John, at the end of the table near the door, was almost lost in the darkness. Their faces were hidden from each other. The girl crouched against the fender slowly moving a thick piece of bread before the fire. The lad, his face a dusky mark on the shadow, sat watching her who was transfigured in the red glow.

'I do think it's beautiful to look in the fire,' said the child.

'Do you?' said her mother. 'Why?'

'It's so red, and full of little caves – and it feels so nice, and you can fair smell it.'

'It'll want mending directly,' replied her mother, 'and then if your father comes he'll carry on and say there never is a fire when a man comes home sweating from the pit. A public-house is always warm enough.'

There was silence till the boy said complainingly: 'Make haste, our Annie.'

'Well, I am doing! I can't make the fire do it no faster, can I?'

'She keeps wafflin' it about so's to make 'er slow,' grumbled the boy.

'Don't have such an evil imagination, child,' replied the mother.

Soon the room was busy in the darkness with the crisp sound of crunching. The mother ate very little. She drank her tea determinedly, and sat thinking. When she rose her anger was evident in the stern unbending of her head. She looked at the pudding in the fender, and broke out:

'It is a scandalous thing as a man can't even come home to his dinner! If it's crozzled up to a cinder I don't see why I should care. Past his very door he goes to get to a public-house, and here I sit with his dinner waiting for him —'

She went out. As she dropped piece after piece of coal on the red fire, the shadows fell on the walls, till the room was almost in total darkness.

'I canna see,' grumbled the invisible John. In spite of herself, the mother laughed.

'You know the way to your mouth,' she said. She set the dust-pan outside the door. When she came again like a shadow on the hearth, the lad repeated, complaining sulkily:

'I canna see.'

'Good gracious!' cried the mother irritably, 'you're as bad as your father if it's a bit dusk!'

Nevertheless, she took a paper spill from a sheaf on the mantelpiece and proceeded to light the lamp that hung from the ceiling in the middle of the room. As she reached up, her figure displayed itself just rounding with maternity.

'Oh, mother —!' exclaimed the girl.

'What?' said the woman, suspended in the act of putting the lamp-glass over the flame. The copper reflector shone handsomely on her, as she stood with uplifted arm, turning to face her daughter.

'You've got a flower in your apron!' said the child, in a little rapture at this unusual event.

'Goodness me!' exclaimed the woman, relieved. 'One would think the house was afire.' She replaced the glass and waited a moment before turning up the wick. A pale shadow was seen floating vaguely on the floor.

'Let me smell!' said the child, still rapturously, coming forward and putting her face to her mother's waist.

'Go along, silly!' said the mother, turning up the lamp. The light revealed their suspense so that the woman felt it almost unbearable. Annie was still bending at her waist. Irritably, the mother took the flowers out from her apron-band.

'Oh, mother – don't take them out!' Annie cried catching her hand and trying to replace the sprig.

'Such nonsense!' said the mother, turning away. The child put the pale chrysanthemums to her lips, murmuring:

'Don't they smell beautiful!'

Her mother gave a short laugh.

'No,' she said, 'not to me. It was chrysanthemums when I married him, and chrysanthemums when you were born, and the first time they ever brought him home drunk, he'd got brown chrysanthemums in his button-hole.'

She looked at the children. Their eyes and their parted lips were wondering. The mother sat rocking in silence for some time. Then she looked at the clock.

'Twenty minutes to six!' In a tone of fine bitter carelessness she continued: 'Eh, he'll not come now till they bring him. There he'll stick! But he needn't come rolling in here in his pit-dirt, for *I* won't wash him. He can lie on the floor — Eh, what a fool I've been, what a

273

fool! And this is what I came here for, to this dirty hole, rats and all, for him to slink past his very door. Twice last week – he's begun now —' She silenced herself, and rose to clear the table.

While for an hour or more the children played, subduedly intent, fertile of imagination, united in fear of the mother's wrath, and in dread of their father's home-coming, Mrs. Bates sat in her rocking-chair making a 'singlet' of thick cream-coloured flannel, which gave a dull wounded sound as she tore off the grey edge. She worked at her sewing with energy, listening to the children, and her anger wearied itself, lay down to rest, opening its eyes from time to time and steadily watching, its ears raised to listen. Sometimes even her anger quailed and shrank, and the mother suspended her sewing, tracing the footsteps that thudded along the sleepers outside; she would lift her head sharply to bid the children 'hush', but she recovered herself in time, and the footsteps went past the gate, and the children were not flung out of their play-world.

But at last Annie sighed, and gave in. She glanced at her wagon of slippers, and loathed the game. She turned plaintively to her mother.

'Mother!' – but she was inarticulate.

John crept out like a frog from under the sofa. His mother glanced up.

'Yes,' she said, 'just look at those shirt-sleeves!'

The boy held them out to survey them, saying nothing. Then somebody called in a hoarse voice away down the line, and suspense bristled in the room, till two people had gone by outside, talking.

'It is time for bed,' said the mother.

'My father hasn't come,' wailed Annie plaintively. But her mother was primed with courage.

'Never mind. They'll bring him when he does come – like a log.' She meant there would be no scene. 'And he may sleep on the floor till he wakes himself. I know he'll not go to work to-morrow after this!'

The children had their hands and faces wiped with a flannel. They were very quiet. When they had put on their nightdresses, they said their prayers, the boy mumbling. The mother looked down at them, at the brown silken bush of intertwining curls in the nape of the girl's neck, at the little black head of the lad, and her heart burst with anger at their father, who caused all three such distress. The children hid their faces in her skirts for comfort.

When Mrs. Bates came down, the room was strangely empty, with a tension of expectancy. She took up her sewing and stitched for some time without raising her head. Meantime her anger was tinged with fear.

II

The clock struck eight and she rose suddenly, dropping her sewing on her chair. She went to the stair-foot door, opened it, listening. Then she went out, locking the door behind her.

Something scuffled in the yard, and she started, though she knew it was only the rats with which the place was over-run. The night was very dark. In the great bay of railway lines, bulked with trucks, there was no trace of light, only away back she could see a few yellow lamps at the pit-top, and the red smear of the burning pit-bank on the night. She hurried along the edge of the track, then, crossing the converging lines, came to the stile by the white gates, whence she emerged on the road. Then the fear which had led her shrank. People were walking up to New Brinsley; she saw the lights in the houses; twenty yards farther on were the broad windows of the 'Prince of Wales', very warm and bright, and the loud voices of men could be heard distinctly. What a fool she had been to imagine that anything had happened to him! He was merely drinking over there at the 'Prince of Wales'. She faltered. She had never yet been to fetch him, and she never would go. So she continued her walk towards the long straggling line of houses, standing back on the highway. She entered a passage between the dwellings.

'Mr. Rigley? – Yes! Did you want him? No, he's not in at this minute.'

The raw-boned woman leaned forward from her dark scullery and peered at the other, upon whom fell a dim light through the blind of the kitchen window.

'Is it Mrs. Bates?' She asked in a tone tinged with respect.

'Yes. I wondered if your Master was at home. Mine hasn't come yet.'

' 'Asn't e! Oh, Jack's been 'ome an' 'ad 'is dinner an' gone out. 'E's just gone for 'alf an hour afore bed-time. Did you call at the "Prince of Wales"?'

'No —'

'No, you didn't like—! It's not very nice.' The other woman was indulgent. There was an awkward pause. 'Jack never said nothink about – about your Master,' she said.

275

'No! – I expect he's stuck in there!'

Elizabeth Bates said this bitterly, and with recklessness. She knew that the woman across the yard was standing at her door listening, but she did not care. As she turned:

'Stop a minute! I'll just go an' ask Jack if 'e knows anythink,' said Mrs. Rigley.

'Oh no – I wouldn't like to put —!'

'Yes, I will, if you'll just step inside an' see as th' childer doesn't come downstairs and set theirselves afire.'

Elizabeth Bates, murmuring a remonstrance, stepped inside. The other woman apologised for the state of the room.

The kitchen needed apology. There were little frocks and trousers and childish undergarments on the squab and on the floor, and a litter of playthings everywhere. On the black American cloth of the table were pieces of bread and cake, crusts, slops, and a teapot with cold tea.

'Eh, ours is just as bad,' said Elizabeth Bates, looking at the woman, not at the house. Mrs. Rigley put a shawl over her head and hurried out, saying:

'I shanna be a minute.'

The other sat, noting with faint disapproval the general untidiness of the room. Then she fell to counting the shoes of various sizes scattered over the floor. There were twelve. She sighed and said to herself: 'No wonder!' – glancing at the litter. There came the scratching of two pairs of feet on the yard, and the Rigleys entered. Elizabeth Bates rose. Rigley was a big man, with very large bones. His head looked particularly bony. Across his temple was a blue scar, caused by a wound got in the pit, a wound in which the coal-dust remained blue like tattooing.

''Asna 'e come whoam yit?' asked the man, without any form of greeting, but with deference and sympathy. 'I couldn'a say wheer he is – 'e's non ower theer!' – he jerked his head to signify the 'Prince of Wales'.

''E's 'appen gone up to th' "Yew",' said Mrs. Rigley.

There was another pause. Rigley had evidently something to get off his mind:

'Ah left 'im finishin' a stint,' he began. 'Loose-all 'ad bin gone about ten minutes when we com'n away, an' I shouted: "Are ter comin', Walt?" an' 'e said: "Go on, Ah shanna be but a'ef a minnit," so we com'n ter th' bottom, me an' Bowers, thinkin' as 'e wor just behint, an' 'ud come up i' the' next bantle —'

He stood perplexed, as if answering a charge of deserting his mate.

276

Elizabeth Bates, now again certain of disaster, hastened to reassure him:

'I expect 'e's gone up to th' "Yew Tree", as you say. It's not the first time. I've fretted myself into a fever before now. He'll come home when they carry him.'

'Ay, isn't it too bad!' deplored the other woman.

'I'll just step up to Dick's an' see if 'e *is* theer,' offered the man, afraid of appearing alarmed, afraid of taking liberties.

'Oh, I wouldn't think of bothering you that far,' said Elizabeth Bates, with emphasis, but he knew she was glad of his offer.

As they stumbled up the entry, Elizabeth Bates heard Rigley's wife run across the yard and open her neighbour's door. At this, suddenly all the blood in her body seemed to switch away from her heart.

'Mind!' warned Rigley. 'Ah've said many a time as Ah'd fill up them ruts in this entry, sumb'dy 'll be breakin' their legs yit.'

She recovered herself and walked quickly along with the miner.

'I don't like leaving the children in bed, and nobody in the house,' she said.

'No, you dunna!' he replied courteously. They were soon at the gate of the cottage.

'Well, I shanna be many minnits. Dunna you be frettin' now, 'e'll be all right,' said the butty.

'Thank you very much, Mr. Rigley,' she replied.

'You're welcome!' he stammered, moving away. 'I shanna be many minnits.'

The house was quiet. Elizabeth Bates took off her hat and shawl, and rolled back the rug. When she had finished, she sat down. It was a few minutes past nine. She was startled by the rapid chuff of the winding-engine at the pit, and the sharp whirr of the brakes on the rope as it descended. Again she felt the painful sweep of her blood, and she put her hand to her side, saying aloud: 'Good gracious! – it's only the nine o'clock deputy going down,' rebuking herself.

She sat still, listening. Half an hour of this, and she was wearied out.

'What am I working myself up like this for?' she said pitiably to herself. 'I s'll only be doing myself some damage.'

She took out her sewing again.

At a quarter to ten there were footsteps. One person! She watched for the door to open. It was an elderly woman, in a black bonnet and a black woollen shawl – his mother. She was about sixty years old, pale, with blue eyes, and her face all wrinkled and lamentable. She shut the door and turned to her daughter-in-law peevishly.

'Eh, Lizzie, whatever shall we do, whatever shall we do!' she cried.

Elizabeth drew back a little, sharply.

'What is it, mother?' she said.

The elder woman seated herself on the sofa.

'I don't know, child, I can't tell you!' – she shook her head slowly. Elizabeth sat watching her, anxious and vexed.

'I don't know,' replied the grandmother, sighing very deeply. 'There's no end to my troubles, there isn't. The things I've gone through, I'm sure it's enough —!' She wept without wiping her eyes, the tears running.

'But, mother,' interrupted Elizabeth, 'what do you mean? What is it?'

The grandmother slowly wiped her eyes. The fountains of her tears were stopped by Elizabeth's directness. She wiped her eyes slowly.

'Poor child! Eh, you poor thing!' she moaned. 'I don't know what we're going to do, I don't – and you as you are – it's a thing, it is indeed!'

Elizabeth waited.

'Is he dead?' she asked, and at the words her heart swung violently, though she felt a slight flush of shame at the ultimate extravagance of the question. Her words sufficiently frightened the old lady, almost brought her to herself.

'Don't say so, Elizabeth! We'll hope it's not as bad as that; no, may the Lord spare us that, Elizabeth. Jack Rigley came just as I was sittin' down to a glass afore going to bed, an' 'e said: " 'Appen you'll go down th' line, Mrs. Bates. Walt's had an accident. 'Appen you'll go an' sit wi' 'er till we can get him home." I hadn't time to ask him a word afore he was gone. An' I put my bonnet on an' come straight down, Lizzie. I thought to myself: "Eh, that poor blessed child, if anybody should come an' tell her of a sudden, there's no knowin' what'll 'appen to 'er." You mustn't let it upset you, Lizzie – or you know what to expect. How long is it, six months – or is it five, Lizzie? Ay!' – the old woman shook her head – 'time slips on, it slips on! Ay!'

Elizabeth's thoughts were busy elsewhere. If he was killed – would she be able to manage on the little pension and what she could earn? – she counted up rapidly. If he was hurt – they wouldn't take him to the hospital – how tiresome he would be to nurse! – but perhaps she'd be able to get him away from the drink and his hateful ways. She would –

278

while he was ill. The tears offered to come to her eyes at the picture. But what sentimental luxury was this she was beginning? She turned to consider the children. At any rate she was absolutely necessary for them. They were her business.

'Ay!' repeated the old woman, 'it seems but a week or two since he brought me his first wages. Ay – he was a good lad, Elizabeth, he was, in his way. I don't know why he got to be such a trouble, I don't. He was a happy lad at home, only full of spirits. But there's no mistake he's been a handful of trouble, he has! I hope the Lord'll spare him to mend his ways. I hope so, I hope so. You've had a sight o' trouble with him, Elizabeth, you have indeed. But he was a jolly enough lad wi' me, he was, I can assure you. I don't know how it is....'

The old woman continued to muse aloud, a monotonous irritating sound, while Elizabeth thought concentratedly, startled once, when she heard the winding-engine chuff quickly, and the brakes skirr with a shriek. Then she heard the engine more slowly, and the brakes made no sound. The old woman did not notice. Elizabeth waited in suspense. The mother-in-law talked, with lapses into silence.

'But he wasn't your son, Lizzie, an' it makes a difference. Whatever he was, I remember him when he was little, an' I learned to understand him and to make allowances. You've got to make allowances for them —'

It was half-past ten, and the old woman was saying: 'But it's trouble from beginning to end; you're never too old for trouble, never too old for that —' when the gate banged back, and there were heavy feet on the steps.

'I'll go, Lizzie, let me go,' cried the old woman, rising. But Elizabeth was at the door. It was a man in pit-clothes.

'They're bringin' 'im, Missis,' he said. Elizabeth's heart halted a moment. Then it surged on again, almost suffocating her.

'Is he – is it bad?' she asked.

The man turned away, looking at the darkness:

'The doctor says 'e'd been dead hours. 'E saw 'im i' th' lamp-cabin.'

The old woman, who stood just behind Elizabeth, dropped into a chair, and folded her hands crying: 'Oh, my boy, my boy!'

'Hush!' said Elizabeth, with a sharp twitch of a frown. 'Be still, mother, don't waken th' children: I wouldn't have them down for anything!'

The old woman moaned softly, rocking herself. The man was drawing away. Elizabeth took a step forward.

279

'How was it?' she asked.

'Well, I couldn't say for sure,' the man replied, very ill at ease. ' 'E wor finishin' a stint an' th' butties 'ad gone, an' a lot o' stuff come down atop 'n 'im.'

'And crushed him?' cried the widow, with a shudder.

'No,' said the man, 'it fell at th' back of 'im. 'E wor under th' face, an' it niver touched 'im. It shut 'im in. It seems 'e wor smothered.'

Elizabeth shrank back. She heard the old woman behind her cry:

'What? – what did 'e say it was?'

The man replied, more loudly: ' 'E wor smothered!'

Then the old woman wailed aloud, and this relieved Elizabeth.

'Oh, mother,' she said, putting her hand on the old woman, 'don't waken th' children, don't waken th' children.'

She wept a little, unknowing, while the old mother rocked herself and moaned. Elizabeth remembered that they were bringing him home, and she must be ready. 'They'll lay him in the parlour,' she said to herself, standing a moment pale and perplexed.

Then she lighted a candle and went into the tiny room. The air was cold and damp, but she could not make a fire, there was no fireplace. She set down the candle and looked round. The candlelight glittered on the lustre-glasses, on two vases that held some of the pink chrysanthemums, and on the dark mahogany. There was a cold, deathly smell of chrysanthemums in the room. Elizabeth stood looking at the flowers. She turned away, and calculated whether there would be room to lay him on the floor, between the couch and the chiffonier. She pushed the chairs aside. There would be room to lay him down and to step round him. Then she fetched the old red tablecloth, and another old cloth, spreading them down to save her bit of carpet. She shivered on leaving the parlour; so, from the dresser drawer she took a clean shirt and put it at the fire to air. All the time her mother-in-law was rocking herself in the chair and moaning.

'You'll have to move from there, mother,' said Elizabeth. 'They'll be bringing him in. Come in the rocker.'

The old mother rose mechanically, and seated herself by the fire, continuing to lament. Elizabeth went into the pantry for another candle, and there, in the little pent-house under naked tiles, she heard them coming. She stood still in the pantry doorway, listening. She heard them pass the end of the house, and come awkwardly down the three steps, a jumble of shuffling footsteps and muttering voices. The old woman was silent. The men were in the yard.

Then Elizabeth heard Matthews, the manager of the pit, say: 'You go in first, Jim. Mind!'

The door came open, and the two women saw a collier backing into the room, holding one end of a stretcher, on which they could see the nailed pit-boots of the dead man. The two carriers halted, the man at the head stooping to the lintel of the door.

'Wheer will you have him?' asked the manager, a short, white-bearded man.

Elizabeth roused herself and came from the pantry carrying the un-lighted candle.

'In the parlour,' she said.

'In there, Jim!' pointed the manager, and the carriers backed round into the tiny room. The coat with which they had covered the body fell off as they awkwardly turned through the two doorways, and the women saw their man, naked to the waist, lying stripped for work. The old woman began to moan in a low voice of horror.

'Lay th' stretcher at th' side,' snapped the manager, 'an' put 'im on th' cloths. Mind now, mind! Look you now —!'

One of the men had knocked off a vase of chrysanthemums. He stared awkwardly, then they set down the stretcher. Elizabeth did not look at her husband. As soon as she could get in the room, she went and picked up the broken vase and the flowers.

'Wait a minute!' she said.

The three men waited in silence while she mopped up the water with a duster.

'Eh, what a job, what a job, to be sure!' the manager was saying, rubbing his brow with trouble and perplexity. 'Never knew such a thing in my life, never! He'd no business to ha' been left. I never knew such a thing in my life! Fell over him clean as a whistle, an' shut him in. Not four foot of space, there wasn't – yet it scarce bruised him.'

He looked down at the dead man, lying prone, half naked, all grimed with coal-dust.

' " 'Sphyxiated," the doctor said. It *is* the most terrible job I've ever known. Seems as if it was done o' purpose. Clean over him, an' shut 'im in, like a mouse-trap' – he made a sharp, descending gesture with his hand.

The colliers standing by jerked aside their heads in hopeless com-ment.

The horror of the thing bristled upon them all.

Then they heard the girl's voice upstairs calling shrilly: 'Mother, mother – who is it? Mother, who is it?'

Elizabeth hurried to the foot of the stairs and opened the door:

'Go to sleep!' She commanded sharply. 'What are you shouting about? Go to sleep at once – there's nothing —'

Then she began to mount the stairs. They could hear her on the boards, and on the plaster floor of the little bedroom. They could hear her distinctly:

'What's the matter now? – what's the matter with you, silly thing?' – her voice was much agitated, with an unreal gentleness.

'I thought it was some men come,' said the plaintive voice of the child. 'Has he come?'

'Yes, they've brought him. There's nothing to make a fuss about. Go to sleep now, like a good child.'

They could hear her voice in the bedroom, they waited whilst she covered the children under the bedclothes.

'Is he drunk?' asked the girl, timidly, faintly.

'No! No – he's not! He's asleep.'

'Is he asleep downstairs?'

'Yes – and don't make a noise.'

There was silence for a moment, then the men heard the frightened child again:

'What's that noise?'

'It's nothing, I tell you, what are you bothering for?'

The noise was the grandmother moaning. She was oblivious of everything, sitting on her chair rocking and moaning. The manager put his hand on her arm and bade her 'Sh – sh!!'

The old woman opened her eyes and looked at him. She was shocked by this interruption, and seemed to wonder.

'What time is it?' the plaintive thin voice of the child, sinking back unhappily into sleep, asked this last question.

'Ten o'clock,' answered the mother more softly. Then she must have bent down and kissed the children.

Matthews beckoned to the men to come away. They put on their caps and took up the stretcher. Stepping over the body, they tiptoed out of the house. None of them spoke till they were far from the wakeful children.

When Elizabeth came down she found her mother alone on the parlour floor, leaning over the dead man, the tears dropping on him.

'We must lay him out,' the wife said. She put on the kettle, then returning knelt at the feet, and began to unfasten the knotted leather laces. The room was clammy and dim with only one candle, so that she had to bend her face almost to the floor. At last she got off the heavy boots and put them away.

'You must help me now,' she whispered to the old woman. Together they stripped the man.

When they arose, saw him lying in the naïve dignity of death, the women stood arrested in fear and respect. For a few moments they remained still, looking down, the old mother whimpering. Elizabeth felt countermanded. She saw him, how utterly inviolable he lay in himself. She had nothing to do with him. She could not accept it. Stooping, she laid her hand on him, in claim. He was still warm, for the mine was hot where he had died. His mother had his face between her hands, and was murmuring incoherently. The old tears fell in succession as drops from wet leaves; the mother was not weeping, merely her tears flowed. Elizabeth embraced the body of her husband, with cheek and lips. She seemed to be listening, inquiring, trying to get some connection. But she could not. She was driven away. He was impregnable.

She rose, went into the kitchen, where she poured warm water into a bowl, brought soap and flannel and a soft towel.

'I must wash him,' she said.

Then the old mother rose stiffly, and watched Elizabeth as she carefully washed his face, carefully brushing the big blond moustache from his mouth with the flannel. She was afraid with a bottomless fear, so she ministered to him. The old woman, jealous, said:

'Let me wipe him!' – and she kneeled on the other side drying slowly as Elizabeth washed, her big black bonnet sometimes brushing the dark head of her daughter-in-law. They worked thus in silence for a long time. They never forgot it was death, and the touch of the man's dead body gave them strange emotions, different in each of the women; a great dread possessed them both, the mother felt the lie was given to her womb, she was denied; the wife felt the utter isolation of the human soul, the child within her was a weight apart from her.

At last it was finished. He was a man of handsome body, and his face showed no traces of drink. He was blond, full-fleshed, with fine limbs. But he was dead.

'Bless him,' whispered his mother, looking always at his face, and speaking out of sheer terror. 'Dear lad – bless him!' She spoke in a faint, sibilant ecstasy of fear and mother love.

Elizabeth sank down again to the floor, and put her face against his neck, and trembled and shuddered. But she had to draw away again. He was dead, and her living flesh had no place against his. A great dread and weariness held her: she was so unavailing. Her life was gone like this.

'White as milk he is, clear as a twelve-month baby, bless him, the darling!' the old mother murmured to herself. 'Not a mark on him, clear and clean and white, beautiful as ever a child was made,' she murmured with pride. Elizabeth kept her face hidden.

'He went peaceful, Lizzie – peaceful as sleep. Isn't he beautiful, the lamb? Ay – he must ha' made his peace, Lizzie. 'Appen he made it all right, Lizzie, shut in there. He'd have time. He wouldn't look like this if he hadn't made his peace. The lamb, the dear lamb. Eh, but he had a hearty laugh. I loved to hear it. He had the heartiest laugh, Lizzie, as a lad —'

Elizabeth looked up. The man's mouth was fallen back, slightly open under the cover of the moustache. The eyes, half shut, did not show glazed in the obscurity. Life with its smoky burning gone from him, had left him apart and utterly alien to her. And she knew what a stranger he was to her. In her womb was ice of fear, because of this separate stranger with whom she had been living as one flesh. Was this what it all meant – utter, intact separateness, obscured by heat of living? In dread she turned her face away. The fact was too deadly. There had been nothing between them, and yet they had come together, exchanging their nakedness repeatedly. Each time he had taken her, they had been two isolated beings, far apart as now. He was no more responsible than she. The child was like ice in her womb. For as she looked at the dead man, her mind, cold and detached, said clearly: 'Who am I? What have I been doing? I have been fighting a husband who did not exist. *He* existed all the time. What wrong have I done? What was that I have been living with? There lies the reality, this man.' And her soul died in her for fear: she knew she had never seen him, and he had never seen her, they had met in the dark and had fought in the dark, not knowing whom they met nor whom they fought. And now she saw, and turned silent in seeing. For she had been wrong. She had said he was something he was not; she had felt familiar with him. Whereas he was apart all the while, living as she never lived, feeling as she never felt.

In fear and shame she looked at his naked body, that she had known falsely. And he was the father of her children. Her soul was torn from her body and stood apart. She looked at his naked body and was ashamed, as if she had denied it. After all, it was itself. It seemed awful

to her. She looked at his face, and she turned her own face to the wall.
For his look was other than hers, his way was not her way. She had
denied him what he was – she saw it now. She had refused him as
himself. And this had been her life, and his life. She was grateful to
death, which restored the truth. And she knew she was not dead.

And all the while her heart was bursting with grief and pity for him.
What had he suffered? What stretch of horror for this helpless man!
She was rigid with agony. She had not been able to help him. He had
been cruelly injured, this naked man, this other being, and she could
make no reparation. There were the children – but the children belonged to life. This dead man had nothing to do with them. He and she
were only channels through which life had flowed to issue in the children. She was a mother – but how awful she knew it now to have been
a wife. And he, dead now, how awful he must have felt it to be a husband. She felt that in the next world he would be a stranger to her. If
they met, there in the beyond, they would only be ashamed of what
had been before. The children had come, for some mysterious reason,
out of both of them. But the children did not unite them. Now he was
dead, she knew how eternally he was apart from her, how eternally he
had nothing more to do with her. She saw this episode of her life closed.
They had denied each other in life. Now he had withdrawn. An anguish
came over her. It was finished then: it had become hopeless between
them long before he died. Yet he had been her husband. But how little!

'Have you got his shirt, 'Lizabeth?'

Elizabeth turned without answering, though she strove to weep and
behave as her mother-in-law expected. But she could not, she was silenced. She went into the kitchen and returned with the garment.

'It is aired,' she said, grasping the cotton shirt here and there to try.
She was almost ashamed to handle him; what right had she or anyone
to lay hands on him; but her touch was humble on his body. It was hard
work to clothe him. He was so heavy and inert. A terrible dread gripped
her all the while: that he could be so heavy and utterly inert, unre-
sponsive, apart. The horror of the distance between them was almost
too much for her – it was so infinite a gap she must look across.

At last it was finished. They covered him with a sheet and left him
lying, with his face bound. And she fastened the door of the little
parlour, lest the children should see what was lying there. Then, with
peace sunk heavy on her heart, she went about making tidy the kitchen.
She knew she submitted to life, which was her immediate master. But
from death, her ultimate master, she winced with fear and shame.

285

ENGLAND, MY ENGLAND

HE was working on the edge of the common, beyond the small brook that ran in the dip at the bottom of the garden, carrying the garden path in continuation from the plank bridge on to the common. He had cut the rough turf and bracken, leaving the grey, dryish soil bare. But he was worried because he could not get the path straight, there was a pleat between his brows. He had set up his sticks, and taken the sights between the big pine trees, but for some reason everything seemed wrong. He looked again, straining his keen blue eyes, that had a touch of the Viking in them, through the shadowy pine trees as through a doorway, at the green-grassed garden path rising from the shadow of alders by the log bridge up to the sunlit flowers. Tall white and purple columbines, and the butt-end of the old Hampshire cottage that crouched near the earth amid flowers, blossoming in the bit of shaggy wildness round about.

There was a sound of children's voices calling and talking: high, childish, girlish voices, slightly didactic and tinged with domineering: 'If you don't come quick, nurse, I shall run out there to where there are snakes.' And nobody had the sang-froid to reply: 'Run then, little fool.' It was always: 'No, darling. Very well, darling. In a moment, darling. Darling, you *must* be patient.'

His heart was hard with disillusion: a continual gnawing and resistance. But he worked on. What was there to do but submit!

The sunlight blazed down upon the earth, there was a vividness of flamy vegetation, of fierce seclusion amid the savage peace of the commons. Strange how the savage England lingers in patches: as here, amid these shaggy gorse commons, and marshy, snake-infested places near the foot of the South Downs. The spirit of place lingering on primeval, as when the Saxons came, so long ago.

Ah, how he had loved it! The green garden path, the tufts of flowers, purple and white columbines, and great Oriental red poppies with their black chaps and mulleins tall and yellow: this flamy garden which had been a garden for a thousand years, scooped out in the little hollow among the snake-infested commons. He had made it flame with flowers, in a sun-cup under its hedges and trees. So old, so old a place! And yet he had re-created it.

The timbered cottage with its sloping, cloak-like roof was old and forgotten. It belonged to the old England of hamlets and yeomen. Lost all alone on the edge of the common, at the end of a wide, grassy, briar-entangled lane shaded with oak, it had never known the world of to-day. Not till Egbert came with his bride. And he had come to fill it with flowers.

The house was ancient and very uncomfortable. But he did not want to alter it. Ah, marvellous to sit there in the wide, black, time-old chimney, at night when the wind roared overhead, and the wood which he had chopped himself sputtered on the hearth! Himself on one side the angle, and Winifred on the other.

Ah, how he had wanted her: Winifred! She was young and beautiful and strong with life, like a flame in sunshine. She moved with a slow grace of energy like a blossoming, red-flowered bush in motion. She, too, seemed to come out of the old England, ruddy, strong, with a certain crude, passionate quiescence, and a hawthorn robustness. And he, he was tall and slim and agile, like an English archer with his long supple legs and fine movements. Her hair was nut-brown and all in energic curls and tendrils. Her eyes were nut-brown, too, like a robin's for brightness. And he was white-skinned with fine, silky hair that had darkened from fair, and a slightly arched nose of an old country family. They were a beautiful couple.

The house was Winifred's. Her father was a man of energy, too. He had come from the north poor. Now he was moderately rich. He had bought this fair stretch of inexpensive land, down in Hampshire. Not far from the tiny church of the almost extinct hamlet stood his own house, a commodious old farmhouse standing back from the road across a bare grassed yard. On one side of this quadrangle was the long, long barn or shed which he had made into a cottage for his youngest daughter Priscilla. One saw little blue-and-white check curtains at the long windows, and inside, overhead, the grand old timbers of the high-pitched shed. This was Prissy's house. Fifty yards away was the pretty little new cottage which he had built for his daughter Magdalen, with the vegetable garden stretching away to the oak copse. And then away beyond the lawns and rose trees of the house-garden went the track across a shaggy, wild grass space, towards the ridge of tall black pines that grew on a dyke-bank, through the pines and above the sloping little bog, under the wide, desolate oak trees, till there was Winifred's cottage crouching unexpectedly in front, so much alone, and so primitive.

It was Winifred's own house, and the gardens and the bit of common and the boggy slope were hers: her tiny domain. She had married just at the time when her father had bought the estate, about ten years before the war, so she had been able to come to Egbert with this for a marriage portion. And who was more delighted, he or she, it would be hard to say. She was only twenty at the time, and he was only twenty-one. He had about a hundred and fifty pounds a year of his own – and nothing else but his very considerable personal attractions. He had no profession: he earned nothing. But he talked of literature and music, he had a passion for old folk-music, collecting folk-songs and folk-dances, studying the Morris-dance and the old customs. Of course, in time he would make money in these ways.

Meanwhile youth and health and passion and promise. Winifred's father was always generous: but still, he was a man from the north with a hard head and a hard skin too, having received a good many knocks. At home he kept the hard head out of sight, and played at poetry and romance with his literary wife and his sturdy, passionate girls. He was a man of courage, not given to complaining, bearing his burdens by himself. No, he did not let the world intrude far into his home. He had a delicate, sensitive wife whose poetry won some fame in the narrow world of letters. He himself, with his tough old barbarian fighting spirit, had an almost child-like delight in verse, in sweet poetry, and in the delightful game of a cultured home. His blood was strong even to coarseness. But that only made the home more vigorous, more robust and Christmassy. There was also a touch of Christmas about him, now he was well off. If there was poetry after dinner, there were also chocolates, and nuts, and good little out-of-the-way things to be munching.

Well then, into this family came Egbert. He was made of quite a different paste. The girls and the father were strong-limbed, thick-blooded people, true English, as holly trees and hawthorn are English. Their culture was grafted on to them, as one might perhaps graft a common pink rose on to a thorn stem. It flowered oddly enough, but it did not alter their blood.

And Egbert was a born rose. The age-long breeding had left him with a delightful spontaneous passion. He was not clever, nor even 'literary'. No, but the intonation of his voice, and the movement of his supple, handsome body, and the fine texture of his flesh and his hair, the slight arch of his nose, the quickness of his blue eyes would easily take the place of poetry. Winifred loved him, loved him, this southerner, as a higher being. A *higher* being, mind you. Not a deeper. And as for him, he loved her in passion with every fibre of him. She was the very warm stuff of life to him.

Wonderful then, those days at Crockham Cottage, the first days, all alone save for the woman who came to work in the mornings. Marvellous days, when she had all his tall, supple, fine-fleshed youth to herself, for herself, and he had her like a ruddy fire into which he could cast himself for rejuvenation. Ah, that it might never end, this passion, this marriage! The flame of their two bodies burnt again into that old cottage, that was haunted already by so much bygone, physical desire. You could not be in the dark room for an hour without the influences coming over you. The hot blood-desire of bygone yeomen, there in this old den where they had lusted and bred for so many generations. The silent house, dark, with thick, timbered walls, and the big black chimney-place and the sense of secrecy. Dark, with low, little windows, sunk into the earth. Dark, like a lair where strong beasts had lurked and mated, lonely at night and lonely by day, left to themselves and their own intensity for so many generations. It seemed to cast a spell on the two young people. They became different. There was a curious secret glow about them, a certain slumbering flame hard to understand, that enveloped them both. They too felt that they did not belong to the London world any more. Crockham had changed their blood: the sense of the snakes that lived and slept even in their own garden, in the sun, so that he, going forward with the spade, would see a curious coiled brownish pile on the black soil, which suddenly would start up, hiss, and dazzle rapidly away, hissing. One day Winifred heard the strangest scream from the flower-bed under the low window of the living-room: ah, the strangest scream, like the very soul of the dark past crying aloud. She ran out, and saw a long brown snake on the flower-bed, and in its flat mouth the one hind leg of a frog was striving to escape, and screaming its strange, tiny, bellowing scream. She looked at the snake, and from its sullen flat head it looked at her, obstinately. She gave a cry, and it released the frog and slid angrily away.

That was Crockham. The spear of modern invention had not passed through it, and it lay there secret, primitive, savage as when the Saxons first came. And Egbert and she were caught there, caught out of the world.

He was not idle, nor was she. There were plenty of things to be done, the house to be put into final repair after the workmen had gone, cushions and curtains to sew, the paths to make, the water to fetch and attend to, and then the slope of the deep-soiled, neglected garden to level, to terrace with little terraces and paths, to fill with flowers. He worked away, in his shirt-sleeves, worked all day intermittently doing this thing and the other. And she, quiet and rich in herself, seeing him stooping and labouring away by himself, would come to help him, to be near him. He of course was an amateur – a born amateur. He worked so hard, and did so little, and nothing he ever did would hold together for long. If he terraced the garden, he held up the earth with a couple of long narrow planks that soon began to bend with the pressure from behind, and would not need many years to rot through and break and let the soil slither all down again in a heap towards the stream-bed. But there you are. He had not been brought up to come to grips with anything, and he thought it would do. Nay, he did not think there was anything else except little temporary contrivances possible, he who had such a passion for his old enduring cottage, and for the old enduring things of the bygone England. Curious that the sense of permanency in the past had such a hold over him, whilst in the present he was all amateurish and sketchy.

Winifred would not criticise him. Town-bred, everything seemed to her splendid, and the very digging and shovelling itself seemed romantic. But neither Egbert nor she yet realised the difference between work and romance.

Godfrey Marshall, her father, was at first perfectly pleased with the *ménage* down at Crockham Cottage. He thought Egbert was wonderful, the many things he accomplished, and he was gratified by the glow of physical passion between the two young people. To the man who in London still worked hard to keep steady his modest fortune, the thought of this young couple digging away and loving one another down at Crockham Cottage, buried deep among the commons and marshes, near the pale-showing bulk of the downs, was like a chapter of living romance. And they drew the sustenance for their fire of passion from him, from the old man. It was he who fed their flame. He triumphed secretly in the thought. And it was to her father that Winifred still turned, as the one source of all surety and life and support. She loved Egbert with passion. But behind her was the power of her father. It was the power of her father she referred to, whenever she needed to refer. It never occurred to her to refer to Egbert, if she were in difficulty or doubt. No, in all the *serious* matters she depended on her father.

For Egbert had no intention of coming to grips with life. He had no ambition whatsoever. He came from a decent family, from a pleasant country home, from delightful surroundings. He should, of course, have had a profession. He should have studied law or entered business in some way. But no – that fatal three pounds a week would keep him from starving as long as he lived, and he did not want to give himself into bondage. It was not that he was idle. He was always doing something, in his amateurish way. But he had no desire to give himself to the world, and still less had he any desire to fight his way in the world. No, no, the world wasn't worth it. He wanted to ignore it, to go his own way apart, like a casual pilgrim down the forsaken side-tracks. He loved his wife, his cottage and garden. He would make his life there, as a sort of epicurean hermit. He loved the past, the old music and dances and customs of old England. He would try and live in the spirit of these, not in the spirit of the world of business.

But often Winifred's father called her to London: for he loved to have his children round him. So Egbert and she must have a tiny flat in town, and the young couple must transfer themselves from time to time from the country to the city. In town Egbert had plenty of friends, of the same ineffectual sort as himself, tampering with the arts, literature, painting, sculpture, music. He was not bored.

Three pounds a week, however, would not pay for all this. Winifred's father paid. He liked paying. He made her only a very small allowance, but he often gave her ten pounds – or gave Egbert ten pounds. So they both looked on the old man as a mainstay. Egbert didn't mind being patronised and paid for. Only when he felt the family was a little *too* condescending, on account of money, he began to get huffy.

Then of course children came: a lovely little blonde daughter with a head of thistle-down. Everybody adored the child. It was the first exquisite blonde thing that had come into the family, a little mite with the white, slim, beautiful limbs of its father, and as it grew up the dancing, dainty movement of a wild little daisy-spirit. No wonder the Marshalls all loved the child: they called her Joyce. They themselves had their own grace, but it was slow, rather heavy. They had every one of them strong, heavy limbs and darkish skins, and they were short in stature. And now they had for one of their own this light little cowslip child. She was like a little poem in herself.

But nevertheless, she brought a new difficulty. Winifred must have a nurse for her. Yes, yes, there must be a nurse. It was the family decree. Who was to pay for the nurse? The grandfather – seeing the father himself earned no money. Yes, the grandfather would pay, as he had paid all the lying-in expenses. There came a slight sense of money-strain. Egbert was living on his father-in-law.

291

After the child was born, it was never quite the same between him and Winifred. The difference was at first hardly perceptible. But it was there. In the first place Winifred had a new centre of interest. She was not going to adore her child. But she had what the modern mother so often has in the place of spontaneous love: a profound sense of duty towards her child. Winifred appreciated her darling little girl, and felt a deep sense of duty towards her. Strange, that this sense of duty should go deeper than the love for her husband. But so it was. And so it often is. The responsibility of motherhood was the prime responsibility in Winifred's heart: the responsibility of wifehood came a long way second.

Her child seemed to link her up again in a circuit with her own family. Her father and mother, herself, and her child, that was the human trinity for her. Her husband—? Yes, she loved him still. But that was like play. She had an almost barbaric sense of duty and of family. Till she married, her first human duty had been towards her father: he was the pillar, the source of life, the everlasting support. Now another link was added to the chain of duty: her father, herself, and her child.

Egbert was out of it. Without anything happening, he was gradually, unconsciously excluded from the circle. His wife still loved him, physically. But, but – he was *almost* the unnecessary party in the affair. He could not complain of Winifred. She still did her duty towards him. She still had physical passion for him, that physical passion on which he had put all his life and soul. But – but —

It was for a long while an ever-recurring *but*. And then, after the second child, another blonde, winsome touching little thing, not so proud and flame-like as Joyce – after Annabel came, then Egbert began truly to realise how it was. His wife still loved him. But – and now the but had grown enormous – her physical love for him was of secondary importance to her. It became ever less important. After all, she had had it, this physical passion, for two years now. It was not this that one lived from. No, no – something sterner, realer.

She began to resent her own passion for Egbert – just a little she began to despise it. For after all there he was, he was charming, he was lovable, he was terribly desirable. But – but – oh, the awful looming cloud of that *but*! – he did not stand firm in the landscape of her life like a tower of strength, like a great pillar of significance. No, he was like a cat one has about the house, which will one day disappear and leave no trace. He was like a flower in the garden, trembling in the wind of life, and then gone, leaving nothing to show. As an adjunct, as an accessory, he was perfect. Many a woman would have adored to have him about her all her life, but the most beautiful and desirable of all her possessions. But Winifred belonged to another school.

The years went by, and instead of coming more to grips with life, he relaxed more. He was of a subtle, sensitive, passionate nature. But he simply *would* not give himself to what Winifred called life, *Work*. No, he would not go into the world and work for money. No, he just would not. If Winifred liked to live beyond their small income – well, it was her look-out.

And Winifred did not really want him to go out into the world to work for money. Money became, alas, a word like a firebrand between them, setting them both aflame with anger. But that is because we must talk in symbols. Winifred did not really care about money. She did not care whether he earned or did not earn anything. Only she knew she was dependent on her father for three-fourths of the money spent for herself and her children, that she let that be the *casus belli*, the drawn weapon between herself and Egbert.

What did she want – what did she want? Her mother once said to her, with that characteristic touch of irony: 'Well, dear, if it is your fate to consider the lilies, that toil not, neither do they spin, that is one destiny among many others, and perhaps not so unpleasant as most. Why do you take it amiss, my child?'

The mother was subtler than her children, they very rarely knew how to answer her. So Winifred was only more confused. It was not a question of lilies. At least, if it were a question of lilies, then her children were the little blossoms. They at least *grew*. Doesn't Jesus say: 'Consider the lilies *how they grow*.' Good then, she had her growing babies. But as for that other tall, handsome flower of a father of theirs, he was full grown already, so she did not want to spend her life considering him in the flower of his days.

No, it was not that he didn't earn money. It was not that he was idle. He was *not* idle. He was always doing something, always working away, down at Crockham, doing little jobs. But, oh dear, the little jobs – the garden paths – the gorgeous flowers – the chairs to mend, old chairs to mend!

It was that he stood for nothing. If he had done something unsuccessfully, and *lost* what money they had! If he had but striven with something. Nay, even if he had been wicked, a waster, she would have been more free. She would have had something to resist, at least. A waster stands for something, really. He says: 'No, I will not aid and abet society in this business of increase and hanging together, I will upset the apple-cart as much as I can, in my small way.' Or else he says: 'No, I will *not* bother about others. I have lusts, they are my own, and I prefer them to other people's virtues. So, a waster, a scamp, takes a sort of stand. He exposes himself to opposition and final castigation: at any rate in story-books.

But Egbert! What are you to do with a man like Egbert? He had no vices. He was really kind, nay, generous. And he was not weak. If he had been weak Winifred could have been kind to him. But he did not even give her that consolation. He was not weak, and he did not want her consolation or her kindness. No, thank you. He was of a fine passionate temper, and of a rarer steel than she. He knew it, and she knew it. Hence she was only the more baffled and maddened, poor thing. He, the higher, the finer, in his way the stronger, played with his garden, and his old folk-songs and Morris dances, just played, and let her support the pillars of the future on her own heart.

And he began to get bitter, and a wicked look began to come on his face. He did not give in to her; not he. There were seven devils inside his long, slim, white body. He was healthy, full of restrained life. Yes, even he himself had to lock up his own vivid life inside himself, now she would not take it from him. Or rather, now that she only took it occasionally. For she had to yield at times. She loved him so, she desired him so, he was so exquisite to her, the fine creature that he was, finer than herself. Yes, with a groan she had to give in to her own unquenched passion for him. And he came to her then – ah, terrible, ah, wonderful, sometimes she wondered how either of them could live after the terror of the passion that swept between them. It was to her as if pure lightning, flash after flash, went through every fibre of her, till extinction came.

But it is the fate of human beings to live on. And it is the fate of clouds that seem nothing but bits of vapour slowly to pile up, to pile up and fill the heavens and blacken the sun entirely.

So it was. The love came back, the lightning of passion flashed tremendously between them. And there was blue sky and gorgeousness for a little while. And then, as inevitably, as inevitably, slowly the clouds began to edge up again above the horizon, slowly, slowly to lurk about the heavens, throwing an occasional cold and hateful shadow: slowly, slowly to congregate, to fill the empyrean space.

And as the years passed, the lightning cleared the sky more and more rarely, less and less the blue showed. Gradually the grey lid sank down upon them, as if it would be permanent.

Why didn't Egbert do something, then? Why didn't he come to grips with life? Why wasn't he like Winifred's father, a pillar of society, even if a slender, exquisite column? Why didn't he go into harness of some sort? Why didn't he take *some* direction?

Well, you can bring an ass to the water, but you cannot make him drink. The world was the water and Egbert was the ass. And he wasn't having any. He couldn't: he just couldn't. Since necessity did not force him to work for his bread and butter, he would not work for work's sake. You can't make the columbine flowers nod in January, nor make the cuckoo sing in England at Christmas. Why? It isn't his season. He doesn't want to. Nay, he *can't* want to.

And there it was with Egbert. He couldn't link up with the world's work, because the basic desire was absent from him. Nay, at the bottom of him he had an even stronger desire: to hold aloof. To hold aloof. To do nobody any damage. But to hold aloof. It was not his season.

Perhaps he should not have married and had children. But you can't stop the waters flowing.

Which held true for Winifred, too. She was not made to endure aloof. Her family tree was a robust vegetation that had to be stirring and believing. In one direction or another her life *had* to go on. In her own home she had known nothing of this diffidence which she found in Egbert, and which she could not understand, and which threw her into such dismay. What was she to do, what was she to do, in face of this terrible diffidence?

It was all so different in her own home. Her father may have had his own misgivings, but he kept them to himself. Perhaps he had no very profound belief in this world of ours, this society which we had elaborated with so much effort, only to find ourselves elaborated to death at last. But Godfrey Marshall was of tough, rough fibre, not without a vein of healthy cunning through it all. It was for him a question of winning through, and leaving the rest to heaven. Without having many illusions to grace him, he still *did* believe in heaven. In a dark and unquestioning way, he had a sort of faith: an acrid faith like the sap of some not-to-be-exterminated tree. Just a blind acrid faith as sap is blind and acrid, and yet pushes on in growth and in faith. Perhaps he was unscrupulous, but only as a striving tree is unscrupulous, pushing its single way in a jungle of others.

In the end, it is only this robust, sap-like faith which keeps man going. He may live on for many generations inside the shelter of the social establishment which he has erected for himself, as pear trees and currant bushes would go on bearing fruit for many seasons, inside a walled garden, even if the race of man were suddenly exterminated. But bit by bit the wall fruit trees would gradually pull down the very walls that sustained them. Bit by bit every establishment collapses, unless it is renewed or restored by living hands, all the while.

Egbert could not bring himself to any more of this restoring or renewing business He was not aware of the fact: but awareness doesn't help much, anyhow. He just couldn't. He had the stoic and epicurean quality of his old, fine breeding. His father-in-law, however, though he was not one bit more of a fool than Egbert, realised that since we are here we may as well live. And so he applied himself to his own tiny section of the social work, and to doing the best for his family, and to leaving the rest to the ultimate will of heaven. A certain robustness of blood made him able to go on. But sometimes even from him spurted a sudden gall of bitterness against the world and its make-up. And yet – he had his own will-to-succeed, and this carried him through. He refused to ask himself what the success would amount to. It amounted to the estate down in Hampshire, and his children lacking for nothing, and himself of some importance in the world: *and basta!* – Basta! Basta!

Nevertheless, do not let us imagine that he was a common pusher. He was not. He knew as well as Egbert what disillusion meant. Perhaps in his soul he had the same estimation of success. But he had a certain acrid courage, and a certain will-to-power. In his own small circle he would emanate power, the single power of his own blind self. With all his spoiling of his children, he was still the father of the old English type. He was too wise to make laws and to domineer in the abstract. But he had kept, and all honour to him, a certain primitive dominion over the souls of his children, the old, almost magic prestige of paternity. There it was, still burning in him, the old smoky torch of paternal godhead.

And in the sacred glare of this torch his children had been brought up. He had given the girls every liberty, at last. But he had never really let them go beyond his power. And they, venturing out into the hard white light of our fatherless world, learned to see with the eyes of the world. They learned to criticise their father, even, from some effulgence of worldly white light, to see him as inferior. But this was all very well in the head. The moment they forgot their tricks of criticism, the old red glow of his authority came over them again. He was not to be quenched.

Let the psycho-analyst talk about father complex. It is just a word invented. Here was a man who had kept alive the old red flame of fatherhood, fatherhood that had even the right to sacrifice the child to God, like Isaac. Fatherhood that had life-and-death authority over the children: a great natural power. And till his children could be brought under some other great authority as girls; or could arrive at manhood and become themselves centres of the same power, continuing the same male mystery as men; until such time, willy-nilly, Godfrey Marshall would keep his children.

It had seemed as if he might lose Winifred. Winifred had *adored* her husband, and looked up to him as to something wonderful. Perhaps she had expected in him another great authority, a male authority greater, finer than her father's. For having once known the glow of male power, she would not easily turn to the cold white light of feminine independence. She would hunger, all her life for the warmth and shelter of true male strength.

And hunger she might, for Egbert's power lay in the abnegation of power. He was himself the living negative of power. Even of responsibility. For the negation of power at last means the negation of responsibility. As far as these things went, he would confine himself to himself. He would try to confine his own influence even to himself. He would try, as far as possible, to abstain from influencing his children by assuming any responsibility for them. 'A little child shall lead them —' His child should lead, then. He would try not to make it go in any direction whatever. He would abstain from influencing it. Liberty! —

Poor Winifred was like a fish out of water in this liberty, gasping for the denser element which should contain her. Till her child came. And then she knew that she must be responsible for it, that she must have authority over it.

But here Egbert, silently and negatively, stepped in. Silently, negatively, but fatally he neutralised her authority over her children.

There was a third little girl born. And after this Winifred wanted no more children. Her soul was turning to salt.

So she had charge of the children, they were her responsibility. The money for them had come from her father. She would do her very best for them, and have command over their life and death. But no! Egbert would not take the responsibility. He would not even provide the money. But he would not let her have her way. Her dark, silent, passionate authority he would not allow. It was a battle between them, the battle between liberty and the old blood-power. And of course he won.

The little girls loved him and adored him. 'Daddy! Daddy!' They could do as they liked with him. Their mother would have ruled them. She would have ruled them passionately, with indulgence, with the old dark magic of parental authority, something looming and unquestioned and, after all, divine: if we believe in divine authority. The Marshalls did, being Catholic.

And Egbert, he turned her old dark, Catholic blood-authority into a sort of tyranny. He would not leave her her children. He stole them from her, and yet without assuming responsibility for them. He stole them from her, in emotion and spirit, and left her only to command their behaviour. A thankless lot for a mother. And her children adored him, adored him, little knowing the empty bitterness they were preparing for themselves when they too grew up to have husbands: husbands such as Egbert, adorable and null.

Joyce, the eldest, was still his favourite. She was now a quicksilver little thing of six years old. Barbara, the youngest was a toddler of two years. They spent most of their time down at Crockham, because he wanted to be there. And even Winifred loved the place really. But now, in her frustrated and blinded state, it was full of menace for her children. The adders, the poison-berries, the brook, the marsh, the water that might not be pure – one thing and another. From mother and nurse it was a guerrilla gunfire of commands, and blithe, quicksilver disobedience from the three blonde, never-still little girls. Behind the girls was the father, against mother and nurse. And so it was.

'If you don't come quick, nurse, I shall run out there to where there are snakes.'

'Joyce, you *must* be patient. I'm just changing Annabel!'

There you are. There it was: always the same. Working away on the common across the brook he heard it. And he worked on, just the same.

Suddenly he heard a shriek, and he flung the spade from him and started for the bridge, looking up like a startled deer. Ah, there was Winifred – Joyce had hurt herself. He went on up the garden.

'What is it?'

The child was still screaming – now it was – 'Daddy! Daddy! Oh – oh, Daddy!' And the mother was saying:

'Don't be frightened, darling. Let mother look.'

But the child only cried:

'Oh, Daddy, Daddy, Daddy!'

She was terrified by the sight of the blood running from her own knee. Winifred crouched down, with her child of six in her lap, to examine the knee. Egbert bent over also.

'Don't make such a noise, Joyce,' he said irritably. 'How did she do it?'

'She fell on that sickle thing which you left lying about after cutting the grass,' said Winifred, looking into his face with bitter accusation as he bent near.

He had taken his handkerchief and tied it round the knee. Then he lifted the still sobbing child in his arms, and carried her into the house and upstairs to her bed. In his arms she became quiet. But his heart was burning with pain and with guilt. He had left the sickle there lying on the edge of the grass, and so his first-born child whom he loved so dearly had come to hurt. But then it was an accident – it was an accident. Why should he feel guilty? It would probably be nothing, better in two or three days. Why take it to heart, why worry? He put it aside.

The child lay on the bed in her little summer frock, her face very white now after the shock. Nurse had come carrying the youngest child: and little Annabel stood holding her skirt. Winifred, terribly serious and wooden-seeming, was bending over the knee, from which she had taken his blood-soaked handkerchief. Egbert bent forward, too, keeping more sang-froid in his face than in his heart. Winfred went all of a lump of seriousness, so he had to keep some reserve. The child moaned and whimpered.

The knee was still bleeding profusely – it was a deep cut right in the joint.

'You'd better go for the doctor, Egbert,' said Winifred bitterly.

'Oh no! Oh no!' cried Joyce in a panic.

'Joyce, my darling, don't cry!' said Winifred, suddenly catching the little girl to her breast in a strange tragic anguish, the *Mater Dolorata*. Even the child was frightened into silence. Egbert looked at the tragic figure of his wife with the child at her breast, and turned away. Only Annabel started suddenly to cry: 'Joycey, Joycey, don't have your leg bleeding!'

Egbert rode four miles to the village for the doctor. He could not help feeling that Winifred was laying it on rather. Surely the knee itself wasn't hurt! Surely not. It was only a surface cut.

The doctor was out. Egbert left the message and came cycling swiftly home, his heart pinched with anxiety. He dropped sweating off his bicycle and went into the house, looking rather small, like a man who is at fault. Winifred was upstairs sitting by Joyce, who was looking pale and important in bed, and was eating some tapioca pudding. The pale, small, scared face of his child went to Egbert's heart.

'Doctor Wing was out. He'll be here about half-past two,' said Egbert.

'I don't want him to come,' whimpered Joyce.

'Joyce, dear, you must be patient and quiet,' said Winifred. 'He won't hurt you. But he will tell us what to do to make your knee better quickly. That is why he must come.'

Winifred always explained carefully to her little girls: and it always took the words off their lips for the moment.

'Does it bleed yet?' said Egbert.

Winifred moved the bedclothes carefully aside.

'I think not,' she said.

Egbert stooped also to look.

'No, it doesn't,' he said. Then he stood up with a relieved look on his face. He turned to the child.

'Eat your pudding, Joyce,' he said. 'It won't be anything. You've only got to keep still for a few days.'

'You haven't had your dinner, have you, Daddy?'

'Not yet.'

'Nurse will give it to you,' said Winifred.

'You'll be all right, Joyce,' he said, smiling to the child and pushing the blonde hair aside off her brow. She smiled back winsomely into his face.

He went downstairs and ate his meal alone. Nurse served him. She liked waiting on him. All women liked him and liked to do things for him.

The doctor came – a fat country practitioner, pleasant and kind.

'What, little girl, been tumbling down, have you? There's a thing to be doing, for a smart little lady like you! What! And cutting your knee! Tut-tut-tut! That *wasn't* clever of you, now was it? Never mind, never mind, soon be better. Let us look at it. Won't hurt you. Not the least in life. Bring a bowl with a little warm water, nurse. Soon have it all right again, soon have it all right.'

Joyce smiled at him with a pale smile of faint superiority. This was *not* the way in which she was used to being talked to.

He bent down, carefully looking at the little, thin, wounded knee of the child. Egbert bent over him.

'Oh, dear, oh, dear! Quite a deep little cut. Nasty little cut. Nasty little cut. But, never mind. Never mind, little lady. What's your name?'

'My name is Joyce,' said the child distinctly.

'Oh, really!' he replied. 'Oh, really! Well, that's a fine name too, in my opinion. Joyce, eh? – And how old might Miss Joyce be? Can she tell me that?'

'I'm six,' said the child, slightly amused and very condescending.

'Six! There now. Add up and count as far as six, can you? Well, that's a clever little girl, a clever little girl. And if she had to drink a spoonful of medicine, she won't make a murmur, I'll be bound. Not like *some* little girls. What? Eh?'

'I take it if mother wishes me to,' said Joyce.

'Ah, there now! That's the style! That's what I like to hear from a little lady in bed because she's cut her knee. That's the style —'

The comfortable and prolix doctor dressed and bandaged the knee and recommended bed and a light diet for the little lady. He thought a week or a fortnight would put it right. No bones or ligatures damaged – fortunately. Only a flesh cut. He would come again in a day or two.

So Joyce was reassured and stayed in bed and had all her toys up. Her father often played with her. The doctor came the third day. He was fairly pleased with the knee. It was healing. It was healing – yes – yes. Let the child continue in bed. He came again after a day or two. Winifred was a trifle uneasy. The wound seemed to be healing on the top, but it hurt the child too much. It didn't look quite right. She said so to Egbert.

'Egbert, I'm sure Joyce's knee isn't healing properly.'

'I think it is,' he said. 'I think it's all right.'

'I'd rather Doctor Wing came again – I don't feel satisfied.'

'Aren't you trying to imagine it worse than it really is?'

'You would say so, of course. But I shall write a post-card to Doctor Wing now.'

The doctor came next day. He examined the knee. Yes, there was inflammation. Yes, there *might* be a little septic poisoning – there might. There might. Was the child feverish?

So a fortnight passed by, and the child *was* feverish, and the knee was more inflamed and grew worse and was painful, painful. She cried in the night, and her mother had to sit up with her. Egbert still insisted it was nothing, really – it would pass. But in his heart he was anxious.

Winifred wrote again to her father. On Saturday the elderly man appeared. And no sooner did Winifred see the thick, rather short figure in its grey suit than a great yearning came over her.

'Father, I'm not satisfied with Joyce. I'm not satisfied with Doctor Wing.'

'Well, Winnie, dear, if you're not satisfied we must have further advice, that is all.'

The sturdy, powerful, elderly man went upstairs, his voice sounding rather grating through the house, as if it cut upon the tense atmosphere.

'How are you, Joyce, darling?' he said to the child. 'Does your knee hurt you? Does it hurt you, dear?'

'It does sometimes.' The child was shy of him, cold towards him.

'Well, dear, I'm sorry for that. I hope you try to bear it, and not trouble mother too much.'

There was no answer. He looked at the knee. It was red and stiff.

'Of course,' he said, 'I think we must have another doctor's opinion. And if we're going to have it, we had better have it at once. Egbert, do you think you might cycle in to Bingham for Doctor Wayne? I found him *very* satisfactory for Winnie's mother.'

'I can go if you think it necessary,' said Egbert.

'Certainly I think it necessary. Even if there *is* nothing, we can have peace of mind. Certainly I think it necessary. I should like Doctor Wayne to come this evening if possible.'

So Egbert set off on his bicycle through the wind, like a boy sent on an errand, leaving his father-in-law a pillar of assurance, with Winifred.

Doctor Wayne came, and looked grave. Yes, the knee was certainly taking the wrong way. The child might be lame for life.

Up went the fire of fear and anger in every heart. Doctor Wayne came again the next day for a proper examination. And, yes, the knee had really taken bad ways. It should be X-rayed. It was very important.

Godfrey Marshall walked up and down the lane with the doctor, beside the standing motor-car: up and down, up and down in one of those consultations of which he had had so many in his life.

As a result he came indoors to Winifred.

'Well, Winnie, dear, the best thing to do is to take Joyce up to London, to a nursing home where she can have proper treatment. Of course this knee has been allowed to go wrong. And apparently there is a risk that the child may even lose her leg. What do you think, dear? You agree to our taking her up to town and putting her under the best care?'

'Oh, father, you *know* I would do anything on earth for her.'

'I know you would, Winnie darling. The pity is that there has been

302

this unfortunate delay already. I can't think what Doctor Wing was doing. Apparently the child is in danger of losing her leg. Well then, if you will have everything ready, we will take her up to town to-morrow. I will order the large car from Denley's to be here at ten. Egbert, will you take a telegram at once to Doctor Jackson? It is a small nursing home for children and for surgical cases, not far from Baker Street. I'm sure Joyce will be all right there.'

'Oh, father, can't I nurse her myself?'

'Well, darling, if she is to have proper treatment, she had best be in a home. The X-ray treatment, and the electric treatment, and whatever is necessary.'

'It will cost a great deal —' said Winifred.

'We can't think of cost, if the child's leg is in danger – or even her life. No use speaking of cost,' said the elder man impatiently.

And so it was. Poor Joyce, stretched out on a bed in the big closed motor-car – the mother sitting by her head, the grandfather in his short grey beard and bowler hat, sitting by her feet, thick, and implacable in his responsibility – they rolled slowly away from Crockham, and from Egbert, who stood there bareheaded and a little ignominious, left behind. He was to shut up the house and bring the rest of the family back to town, by train, the next day.

Followed a dark and bitter time. The poor child. The poor, poor child, how she suffered, an agony and a long crucifixion in that nursing home. It was a bitter six weeks which changed the soul of Winifred for ever. As she sat by the bed of her poor, tortured little child, tortured with the agony of the knee, and the still worse agony of these diabolic, but perhaps necessary modern treatments, she felt her heart killed and going cold in her breast. Her little Joyce, her frail, brave, wonderful, little Joyce, frail and small and pale as a white flower! Ah, how had she, Winifred, dared to be so wicked, so wicked, so careless, so sensual.

'Let my heart die! Let my woman's heart of flesh die! Saviour, let my heart die. And save my child. Let my heart die from the world and from the flesh. Oh, destroy my heart that is so wayward. Let my heart of pride die. Let my heart die.'

She prayed beside the bed of her child. And like the Mother with the seven swords in her breast, slowly her heart of pride and passion died in her breast, bleeding away. Slowly it died, bleeding away, and she turned to the Church for comfort, to Jesus, to the Mother of God, but most of all, to that great and enduring institution, the Roman Catholic Church. She withdrew into the shadow of the Church. She was a mother with three children. But in her soul she died, her heart of pride and passion and desire bled to death, her soul belonged to her Church, her body belonged to her duty as a mother.

Her duty as a wife did not enter. As a wife she had no sense of duty: only a certain bitterness towards the man with whom she had known such sensuality and distraction. She was purely the *Mater Dolorata*. To the man she was closed as a tomb.

Egbert came to see his child. But Winifred seemed to be always seated there, like the tomb of his manhood and his fatherhood. Poor Winifred: she was still young, still strong and ruddy and beautiful like a ruddy hard flower of the field. Strange – her ruddy, healthy face, so sombre, and her strong, heavy, full-blooded body, so still. She, a nun! Never. And yet the gates of her heart and soul had shut in his face with a slow, resonant clang, shutting him out for ever. There was no need for her to go into a convent. Her will had done it.

And between this young mother and this young father lay the crippled child, like a bit of pale silk floss on the pillow, and a little white pain-quenched face. He could not bear it. He just could not bear it. He turned aside. There was nothing to do but to turn aside. He turned aside, and went hither and thither, desultory. He was still attractive and desirable. But there was a little frown between his brow as if he had been cleft there with a hatchet: cleft right in, for ever, and that was the stigma.

The child's leg was saved: but the knee was locked stiff. The fear now was lest the lower leg should wither, or cease to grow. There must be long-continued massage and treatment, daily treatment, even when the child left the nursing home. And the whole of the expense was borne by the grandfather.

Egbert now had no real home. Winifred with the children and nurse was tied to the little flat in London. He could not live there: he could not contain himself. The cottage was shut up – or lent to friends. He went down sometimes to work in his garden and keep the place in order. Then with the empty house around him at night, all the empty rooms, he felt his heart go wicked. The sense of frustration and futility, like some slow, torpid snake, slowly bit right through his heart. Futility, futility, futility: the horrible marsh-poison went through his veins and killed him.

As he worked in the garden in the silence of day he would listen for a sound. No sound. No sound of Winifred from the dark inside of the cottage: no sound of children's voices from the air, from the common,

304

from the near distance. No sound, nothing but the old dark marsh-venomous atmosphere of the place. So he worked spasmodically through the day, and at night made a fire and cooked some food alone.

He was alone. He himself cleaned the cottage and made his bed. But his mending he did not do. His shirts were slit on the shoulders, when he had been working, and the white flesh showed through. He would feel the air and the spots of rain on his exposed flesh. And he would look again across the common, where the dark, tufted gorse was dying to seed, and the bits of cat-heather were coming pink in tufts, like a sprinkling of sacrificial blood.

His heart went back to the savage old spirit of the place: the desire for old gods, old, lost passions, the passion of the cold-blooded, darting snakes that hissed and shot away from him, the mystery of blood-sacrifices, all the lost, intense sensations of the primeval people of the place, whose passions seethed in the air still, from those long days before the Romans came. The seethe of a lost, dark passion, in the air. The presence of unseen snakes.

A queer, baffled, half-wicked look came on his face. He could not stay long at the cottage. Suddenly he must swing on to his bicycle and go – anywhere. Anywhere, away from the place. He would stay a few days with his mother in the old home. His mother adored him and grieved as a mother would. But the little, baffled, half-wicked smile curled on his face, and he swung away from his mother's solicitude as from everything else.

Always moving on – from place to place, friend to friend: and always swinging away from sympathy. As soon as sympathy, like a soft hand, was reached out to touch him, away he swerved, instinctively, as a harmless snake swerves and swerves and swerves away from an outstretched hand. Away he must go. And periodically he went back to Winifred.

He was terrible to her now, like a temptation. She had devoted herself to her children and her Church. Joyce was once more on her feet; but, alas! lame, with iron supports to her leg, and a little crutch. It was strange how she had grown into a long, pallid, wild little thing. Strange that the pain had not made her soft and docile, but had brought out a wild, almost mænad temper in the child. She was seven, and long and white and thin, but by no means subdued. Her blonde hair was darkening. She still had long sufferings to face, and, in her own childish consciousness, the stigma of her lameness to bear.

And she bore it. An almost mænad courage seemed to possess her, as

305

if she were a long, thin, young weapon of life. She acknowledged all her mother's care. She would stand by her mother for ever. But some of her father's fine-tempered desperation flashed in her.

When Egbert saw his little girl limping horribly – not only limping but lurching horribly in a crippled, childish way, his heart again hardened with chagrin, like steel that is tempered again. There was a tacit understanding between him and his little girl: not what we would call love, but a weapon-like kinship. There was a tiny touch of irony in his manner towards her, contrasting sharply with Winifred's heavy, unleavened solicitude and care. The child flickered back to him with an answering little smile of irony and recklessness: an odd flippancy which made Winifred only the more sombre and earnest.

The Marshalls took endless thought and trouble for the child, searching out every means to save her limb and her active freedom. They spared no effort and no money, they spared no strength of will. With all their slow, heavy power of will they willed that Joyce should have her liberty of movement, should win back her wild, free grace. Even if it took a long time to recover, it should be recovered.

So the situation stood. And Joyce submitted, week after week, month after month, to the tyranny and pain of the treatment. She acknowledged the honourable effort on her behalf. But her flamy reckless spirit was her father's. It was he who had all the glamour for her. He and she were like members of some forbidden secret society who know one another but may not recognise one another. Knowledge they had in common, the same secret of life, the father and the child. But the child stayed in the camp of her mother, honourably, and the father wandered outside like Ishmael, only coming sometimes to sit in the home for an hour or two, an evening or two beside the camp-fire, like Ishmael, in a curious silence and tension, with the mocking answer of the desert speaking out of his silence, and annulling the whole convention of the domestic home.

His presence was almost an anguish to Winifred. She prayed against it. That little cleft between his brow, that flickering, wicked little smile that seemed to haunt his face, and above all, the triumphant loneliness, the Ishmael quality. And then the erectness of his supple body, like a symbol. The very way he stood, so quiet, so insidious, like an erect, supple symbol of life, the living body, confronting her downcast soul, was torture to her. He was like a supple living idol moving before her eyes, and she felt if she watched him she was damned.

And he came and made himself at home in her little home. When he was there, moving in his own quiet way, she felt as if the whole great law of sacrifice, by which she had elected to live, were annulled. He annulled by his very presence the laws of her life. And what did he substitute? Ah, against that question she hardened herself in recoil.

It was awful to her to have to have him about – moving about in his shirt-sleeves, speaking in his tenor, throaty voice to the children. Annabel simply adored him, and he teased the little girl. The baby, Barbara, was not sure of him. She had been born a stranger to him. But even the nurse, when she saw his white shoulder of flesh through the slits of his torn shirt, thought it a shame.

Winifred felt it was only another weapon of his against her.

'You have other shirts – why do you wear that old one that is all torn, Egbert?' she said.

'I may as well wear it out,' he said subtly.

He knew she would not offer to mend it for him. She *could* not. And no, she would not. Had she not her own gods to honour? And could she betray them, submitting to his Baal and Ashtaroth? And it was terrible to her, his unsheathed presence, that seemed to annul her and her faith, like another revelation. Like a gleaming idol evoked against her, a vivid life-idol that might triumph.

He came and he went – and she persisted. And then the Great War broke out. He was a man who could not go to the dogs. He could not dissipate himself. He was pure-bred in his Englishness, and even when he would have liked to be vicious, he could not.

So when the war broke out his whole instinct was against it: against war. He had not the faintest desire to overcome any foreigners or to help in their death. He had no conception of Imperial England, and Rule Britannia was just a joke to him. He was a pure-blooded Englishman, perfect in his race, and when he was truly himself he could no more have been aggressive on the score of his Englishness than a rose can be aggressive on the score of its rosiness.

No, he had no desire to defy Germany and to exalt England. The distinction between German and English was not for him the distinction between good and bad. It was the distinction between blue water-flowers and red or white bush-blossoms: just difference. The difference between the wild boar and the wild bear. And a man was good or bad according to his nature, not according to his nationality.

Egbert was well-bred, and this was part of his natural understanding. It was merely unnatural to him to hate a nation *en bloc*. Certain individuals he disliked, and others he liked, and the mass he knew nothing about. Certain deeds he disliked, certain deeds seemed natural to him, and about most deeds he had no particular feeling.

He had, however, the one deepest pure-bred instinct. He recoiled inevitably from having his feelings dictated to him by the mass feeling. His feelings were his own, his understanding was his own, and he would never go back on either, willingly. Shall a man become inferior to his own true knowledge and self, just because the mob expects it of him?

What Egbert felt subtly and without question, his father-in-law felt also in a rough, more combative way. Different as the two men were, they were two real Englishmen, and their instincts were almost the same.

And Godfrey Marshall had the world to reckon with. There was German military aggression, and the English non-military idea of liberty and the 'conquests of peace' – meaning industrialism. Even if the choice between militarism and industrialism were a choice of evils, the elderly man asserted his choice of the latter, perforce. He whose soul was quick with the instinct of power.

Egbert just refused to reckon with the world. He just refused even to decide between German militarism and British industrialism. He chose neither. As for atrocities, he despised the people who committed them, as inferior criminal types. There was nothing national about crime.

And yet, war! War! Just war! Not right or wrong, but just war itself. Should he join? Should he give himself over to war? The question was in his mind for some weeks. Not because he thought England was right and Germany wrong. Probably Germany was wrong, but he refused to make a choice. Not because he felt inspired. No. But just – war.

The deterrent was the giving himself over into the power of other men, and into the power of the mob-spirit of a democratic army. Should he give himself over? Should he make over his own life and body to the control of something which he *knew* was inferior, in spirit, to his own self? Should he commit himself into the power of an inferior control? Should he? Should he betray himself?

He was going to put himself into the power of his inferiors, and he knew it. He was going to subjugate himself. He was going to be ordered about by petty *canaille* of non-commissioned officers – and even commissioned officers. He who was born and bred free. Should he do it?

He went to his wife, to speak to her.

'Shall I join up, Winifred?'

She was silent. Her instinct also was dead against it. And yet a certain profound resentment made her answer:

'You have three children dependent on you. I don't know whether you have thought of that.'

It was still only the third month of the war, and the old pre-war ideas were still alive.

'Of course. But it won't make much difference to them. I shall be earning a shilling a day, at least.'

'You'd better speak to father, I think,' she replied heavily.

Egbert went to his father-in-law. The elderly man's heart was full of resentment.

'I should say,' he said rather sourly, 'it is the best thing you could do.'

Egbert went and joined up immediately, as a private soldier. He was drafted into the light artillery.

Winifred now had a new duty towards him: the duty of a wife towards a husband who is himself performing his duty towards the world. She loved him still. She would always love him, as far as earthly love went. But it was duty she now lived by. When he came back to her in khaki, a soldier, she submitted to him as a wife. It was her duty. But to his passion she could never again fully submit. Something prevented her, for ever: even her own deepest choice.

He went back again to camp. It did not suit him to be a modern soldier. In the thick, gritty, hideous khaki his subtle physique was extinguished as if he had been killed. In the ugly intimacy of the camp his thoroughbred sensibilities were just degraded. But he had chosen, so he accepted. An ugly little look came on to his face, of a man who has accepted his own degradation.

In the early spring Winifred went down to Crockham to be there when primroses were out, and the tassels hanging on the hazel-bushes. She felt something like a reconciliation towards Egbert, now he was a prisoner in camp most of his days. Joyce was wild with delight at seeing the garden and the common again, after the eight or nine months of London and misery. She was still lame. She still had the irons up her leg. But she lurched about with a wild, crippled agility.

Egbert came for a week-end, in his gritty, thick, sandpaper khaki and puttees and the hideous cap. Nay, he looked terrible. And on his face a slightly impure look, a little sore on his lip, as if he had eaten too much or drunk too much or let his blood become a little unclean. He was almost uglily healthy, with the camp life. It did not suit him.

Winifred waited for him in a little passion of duty and sacrifice, willing to serve the soldier, if not the man. It only made him feel a little more ugly inside. The week-end was torment to him: the memory of the camp, the knowledge of the life he led there; even the sight of his own legs in that abhorrent khaki. He felt as if the hideous cloth went into his blood and made it gritty and dirty. Then Winifred so ready to serve the *soldier*, when she repudiated the man. And this made the grit worse between his teeth. And the children running around playing and calling in the rather mincing fashion of children who have nurses and governesses and literature in the family. And Joyce so lame! It had all become unreal to him, after the camp. It only set his soul on edge. He left at dawn on the Monday morning, glad to get back to the realness and vulgarity of the camp.

Winifred would never meet him again at the cottage – only in London, where the world was with them. But sometimes he came alone to Crockham, perhaps when friends were staying there. And then he would work a while in his garden. This summer still it would flame with blue anchusas and big red poppies, the mulleins would sway their soft, downy erections in the air: he loved mulleins: and the honeysuckle would stream out scent like memory, when the owl was whooing. Then he sat by the fire with the friends and with Winifred's sisters, and they sang the folk-songs. He put on thin civilian clothes and his charm and his beauty and the supple dominancy of his body glowed out again. But Winifred was not there.

At the end of the summer he went to Flanders, into action. He seemed already to have gone out of life, beyond the pale of life. He hardly remembered his life any more, being like a man who is going to take a jump from a height, and is only looking to where he must land.

He was twice slightly wounded, in two months. But not enough to put him off duty for more than a day or two. They were retiring again, holding the enemy back. He was in the rear – three machine-guns. The country was all pleasant, war had not yet trampled it. Only the air seemed shattered, and the land awaiting death. It was a small, unimportant action in which he was engaged.

The guns were stationed on a little bushy hillock just outside a village. But occasionally, it was difficult to say from which direction, came the sharp crackle of rifle-fire, and beyond, the far-off thud of cannon. The afternoon was wintry and cold.

A lieutenant stood on a little iron platform at the top of the ladders, taking the sights and giving the aim, calling in a high, tense mechanical voice. Out of the sky came the sharp cry of the directions, then the warning numbers, then 'Fire!' The shot went, the piston of the gun sprang back, there was a sharp explosion, and a very faint film of smoke in the air. Then the other two guns fired, and there was a lull. The officer was uncertain of the enemy's position. The thick clump of horse-chestnut trees below was without change. Only in the far distance the sound of heavy firing continued, so far off as to give a sense of peace.

The gorse bushes on either hand were dark, but a few sparks of flowers showed yellow. He noticed them almost unconsciously as he waited in the lull. He was in his shirt-sleeves, and the air came chill on his arms. Again his shirt was slit on the shoulders, and the flesh showed through. He was dirty and unkempt. But his face was quiet. So many things go out of consciousness before we come to the end of consciousness.

Before him, below, was the highroad, running between high banks of grass and gorse. He saw the whitish, muddy tracks and deep scores in the road, where the part of the regiment had retired. Now all was still. Sounds that came, came from the outside. The place where he stood was still silent, chill, serene: the white church among the trees beyond seemed like a thought only.

He moved into a lightning-like mechanical response at the sharp cry from the officer overhead. Mechanism, the pure mechanical action of obedience at the guns. Pure mechanical action at the guns. It left the soul unburdened, brooding in dark nakedness. In the end, the soul is alone, brooding on the face of the uncreated flux, as a bird on a dark sea.

Nothing could be seen but the road, and a crucifix knocked slanting and the dark, autumnal fields and woods. There appeared three horse-men on a little eminence, very small, on the crest of a ploughed field. They were our own men. Of the enemy, nothing.

The lull continued. Then suddenly came sharp orders, and a new direction of the guns, and an intense, exciting activity. Yet at the centre the soul remained dark and aloof, alone.

But even so, it was the soul that heard the new sound: the new, deep 'papp!' of a gun that seemed to touch right upon the soul. He kept up the rapid activity at the machine-gun, sweating. But in his soul was the echo of the new, deep sound, deeper than life.

And in confirmation came the awful faint whistling of a shell, ad-vancing almost suddenly into a piercing, tearing shriek that would tear through the membrane of life. He heard it in his ears, but he heard it also in his soul, in tension. There was relief when the thing had swung by and struck, away beyond. He heard the hoarseness of its explosion, and the voice of the soldier calling to the horses. But he did not turn round to look. He only noticed a twig of holly with red berries fall like a gift on to the road below.

Not this time, not this time. Whither you goest I will go. Did he say it to the shell, or to whom? Whither thou goest I will go. Then, the faint whistling of another shell dawned, and his blood became small and still to receive it. It drew nearer, like some horrible blast of wind; his blood lost consciousness. But in the second of suspension he saw the heavy shell swoop to earth, into the rocky bushes on the right, and earth and stones poured up into the sky. It was as if he heard no sound. The earth and stones and fragments of bush fell to earth again, and there was the same unchanging peace. The Germans had got the aim.

Would they move now? Would they retire? Yes. The officer was giving the last lightning-rapid orders to fire before withdrawing. A shell passed unnoticed in the rapidity of action. And then, into the silence, into the suspense where the soul brooded, finally crashed a noise and a darkness and a moment's flaming agony and horror. Ah, he had seen the dark bird flying towards him, flying home this time. In one instant life and eternity went up in a conflagration of agony, then there was a weight of darkness.

When faintly something began to struggle in the darkness, a consciousness of himself, he was aware of a great load and a clanging sound. To have known the moment of death! And to be forced, before dying, to review it. So, fate, even in death.

There was a resounding of pain. It seemed to sound from the outside of his consciousness: like a loud bell clanging very near. Yet he knew it was himself. He must associate himself with it. After a lapse and a new effort, he identified a pain in his hand, a large pain that clanged and resounded. So far he could identify himself with himself. Then there was a lapse.

After a time he seemed to wake up again, and waking, to know that he was at the front, and that he was killed. He did not open his eyes. Light was not yet his. The clanging pain in his head rang out the rest of his consciousness. So he lapsed away from consciousness, in unutterable sick abandon of life.

Bit by bit, like a doom, came the necessity to know. He was hit in the head. It was only a vague surmise at first. But in the swinging of the pendulum of pain, swinging ever nearer and nearer, to touch him into

312

an agony of consciousness and a consciousness of agony, gradually the knowledge emerged – he must be hit in the head – hit on the left brow; if so, there would be blood – was there blood? – could he feel blood in his left eye? Then the clanging seemed to burst the membrane of his brain, like death-madness.

Was there blood on his face? Was hot blood flowing? Or was it dry blood congealing down his cheek? It took him hours even to ask the question: time being no more than an agony in darkness, without measurement.

A long time after he had opened his eyes he realised he was seeing something – something, something, but the effort to recall what was too great. No, no; no recall!

Were they the stars in the dark sky? Was it possible it was stars in the dark sky? Stars? The world? Ah, no, he could not know it! Stars and the world were gone for him, he closed his eyes. No stars, no sky, no world. No, no! The thick darkness of blood alone. It should be one great lapse into the thick darkness of blood in agony.

Death, oh, death! The world all blood, and the blood all writhing with death. The soul like the tiniest little light out on a dark sea, the sea of blood. And the light guttering, beating, pulsing in a windless storm, wishing it could go out, yet unable.

There had been life. There had been Winifred and his children. But the frail death-agony effort to catch at straws of memory, straws of life from the past, brought on too great a nausea. No, no! No Winifred, no children. No world, no people. Better the agony of dissolution ahead than the nausea of the effort backwards. Better the terrible work should go forward, the dissolving into the black sea of death, in the extremity of dissolution, than that there should be any reaching back towards life. To forget! To forget! Utterly, utterly to forget, in the great forgetting of death. To break the core and the unit of life, and to lapse out on the great darkness. Only that. To break the clue, and mingle and commingle with the one darkness, without afterwards or forwards. Let the black sea of death itself solve the problem of futurity. Let the will of man break and give up.

What was that? A light! A terrible light! Was it figures? Was it legs of a horse colossal – colossal above him: huge, huge?

The Germans heard a slight noise, and started. Then, in the glare of a light-bomb, by the side of the heap of earth thrown up by the shell, they saw the dead face.

313

TICKETS, PLEASE

THERE is in the Midlands a single-line tramway system which boldly leaves the county town and plunges off into the black, industrial countryside, up hill and down dale, through the long ugly villages of workmen's houses, over canals and railways, past churches perched high and nobly over the smoke and shadows, through stark, grimy cold little market-places, tilting away in a rush past cinemas and shops down to the hollow where the collieries are, then up again, past a little rural church, under the ash trees, on in a rush to the terminus, the last little ugly place of industry, the cold little town that shivers on the edge of the wild, gloomy country beyond. There the green and creamy coloured tram-cars seems to pause and purr with curious satisfaction. But in a few minutes – the clock on the turret of the Co-operative Wholesale Society's shops gives the time – away it starts once more on the adventure. Again there are the reckless swoops downhill, bouncing the loops: again the chilly wait in the hill-top market-place: again the breathless slithering round the precipitous drop under the church: again the patient halts at the loops, waiting for the outcoming car: so on and on, for two long hours, till at last the city looms beyond the fat gas-works, the narrow factories draw near, we are in the sordid streets of the great town, once more we sidle to a standstill at our terminus, abashed by the great crimson and cream coloured city cars, but still perky, jaunty, somewhat dare-devil, green as a jaunty sprig of parsley out of a black colliery garden.

To ride on these cars is always an adventure. Since we are in war-time, the drivers are men unfit for active service: cripples and hunch-backs. So they have the spirit of the devil in them. The ride becomes a steeplechase. Hurray! we have leapt in a clear jump over the canal bridge – now for the four-lane corner. With a shriek and a trail of sparks we are clear again. To be sure, a tram often leaps the rails – but what matter! It sits in a ditch till other trams come to haul it out. It is quite common for a car, parked with one solid mass of living people, to come to a dead halt in the midst of unbroken blackness, the heart of nowhere on a dark night, and for the driver and the girl conductor to call: 'All get off – car's on fire!' Instead, however, of rushing out in a panic, the passengers stolidly reply: 'Get on – get on! We're not coming out. We're stopping where we are. Push on, George.' So till flames actually appear.

The reason for this reluctance to dismount is that the nights are howlingly cold, black, and windswept, and a car is a haven of refuge. From village to village the miners travel, for a change of cinema, of girl, of pub. The trams are desperately packed. Who is going to risk himself in the black gulf outside, to wait perhaps an hour for another tram, then to see the forlorn notice 'Depôt Only', because there is something wrong! Or to greet a unit of three bright cars all so tight with people that they sail past with a howl of derision. Trams that pass in the night.

This, the most dangerous tram-service in England, as the authorities themselves declare, with pride, is entirely conducted by girls, and driven by rash young men, a little crippled, or by delicate young men, who creep forward in terror. The girls are fearless young hussies. In their ugly blue uniform, skirts up to their knees, shapeless old peaked caps on their heads, they have all the sang-froid of an old non-commissioned officer. With a tram packed with howling colliers, roaring hymns downstairs and a sort of antiphony of obscenities upstairs, the lasses are perfectly at their ease. They pounce on the youths who try to evade their ticket-machine. They push off the men at the end of their distance. They are not going to be done in the eyes – not they. They fear nobody – and everybody fears them.

'Hello, Annie!'

'Hello, Ted!'

'Oh, mind my corn, Miss Stone. It's my belief you've got a heart of stone, for you've trod on it again.'

'You should keep it in your pocket,' replies Miss Stone, and she goes sturdily upstairs in her high boots.

'Tickets, please.'

She is peremptory, suspicious, and ready to hit first. She can hold her own against ten thousand. The step of that tram-car is her Thermopylæ.

Therefore, there is a certain wild romance aboard these cars – and in the sturdy bosom of Annie herself. The time for soft romance is in the morning, between ten o'clock and one, when things are rather slack: that is, except market-day and Saturday. Thus Annie has time to look about her. Then she often hops off her car and into a shop where she has spied something, while the driver chats in the main road. There is very good feeling between the girls and the drivers. Are they not companions in peril, shipments aboard this careering vessel of a tram-car, for ever rocking on the waves of a stormy land.

Then, also, during the easy hours, the inspectors are most in evidence. For some reason, everybody employed in this tram-service is young: there are no grey heads. It would not do. Therefore the inspectors are of the right age, and one, the chief, is also good-looking. See him stand on a wet, gloomy morning, in his long oilskin, his peaked cap well down over his eyes, waiting to board a car. His face ruddy, his small brown moustache is weathered, he had a faint impudent smile. Fairly tall and agile, even in his waterproof, he springs aboard a car and greets Annie.

'Hello, Annie! Keeping the wet out?'

'Trying to.'

There are only two people in the car. Inspecting is soon over. Then for a long and impudent chat on the foot-board, a good, easy, twelve-mile chat.

The inspector's name is John Thomas Raynor – always called John Thomas, except sometimes, in malice, Coddy. His face sets in fury when he is addressed, from a distance, with this abbreviation. There is considerable scandal about John Thomas in half a dozen villages. He flirts with the girl conductors in the morning, and walks out with them in the dark night, when they leave their tram-car at the depôt. Of course, the girls quit the service frequently. Then he flirts and walks out with the newcomer: always providing she is sufficiently attractive, and that she will consent to walk. It is remarkable, however, that most of the girls are quite comely, they are all young, and this roving life aboard the car gives them a sailor's dash and recklessness. What matter how they behave when the ship is in port? To-morrow they will be aboard again.

Annie, however, was something of a Tartar, and her sharp tongue had kept John Thomas at arm's length for many months. Perhaps, therefore, she liked him all the more: for he always came up smiling, with impudence. She watched him vanquish one girl, then another. She could tell by the movement of his mouth and eyes, when he flirted with her in the morning, that he had been walking out with this lass, or the other, the night before. A fine cock-of-the-walk he was. She could sum him up pretty well.

In this subtle antagonism they knew each other like old friends, they were as shrewd with one another almost as man and wife. But Annie had always kept him sufficiently at arm's length. Besides, she had a boy of her own.

The Statutes fair, however, came in November, at Bestwood. It happened that Annie had the Monday night off. It was a drizzling ugly night, yet she dressed herself up and went to the fair-ground. She was alone, but she expected soon to find a pal of some sort.

The roundabouts were veering round and grinding out their music, the side-shows were making as much commotion as possible. In the coconut shies there was no coconuts, but artificial war-time substitutes, which the lads declared were fastened into the irons. There was a sad decline in brilliance and luxury. None the less, the ground was muddy as ever, there was the same crush, the press of faces lighted up by the flares and the electric lights, the same smell of naphtha and a few potatoes, and of electricity.

Who should be the first to greet Miss Annie on the showground but John Thomas. He had a black overcoat buttoned up to his chin, and a tweed cap pulled down over his brows, his face between was ruddy and smiling and handy as ever. She knew so well the way his mouth moved.

She was very glad to have a 'boy'. To be at the Statutes without a fellow was no fun. Instantly, like the gallant he was, he took her on the Dragons, grim-toothed, roundabout switchbacks. It was not nearly so exciting as a tram-car actually. But, then, to be seated in a shaking, green dragon, uplifted above the sea of bubble faces, careering in a rickety fashion in the lower heavens, whilst John Thomas leaned over her, his cigarette in his mouth, was after all the right style. She was a plump, quick, alive little creature. So she was quite excited and happy.

John Thomas made her stay on for the next round. And therefore she could hardly for shame repulse him when he put his arm around her and drew her a little nearer to him, in a very warm and cuddly manner. Besides, he was fairly discreet, he kept his movement as hidden as possible. She looked down, and saw that his red, clean hand was out of sight of the crowd. And they knew each other so well. So they warmed up to the fair.

After the dragons they went on the horses. John Thomas paid each time, so she could but be complaisant. He, of course, sat astride on the outer horse – named 'Black Bess' – and she sat sideways, towards him, on the inner horse – named 'Wildfire'. But of course John Thomas was not going to sit discreetly on 'Black Bess', holding the brass bar. Round they spun and heaved, in the light. And round he swung on his wooden steed, flinging one leg across her mount, and perilously tipping up and down, across the space, half lying back, laughing at her. He was perfectly happy; she was afraid her hat was on one side, but she was excited.

He threw quoits on a table, and won for her two large, pale blue hatpins. And then, hearing the noise of the cinema, announcing another performance, they climbed the boards and went in.

Of course, during these performances pitch darkness falls from time to time, when the machine goes wrong. Then there is a wild whooping, and a loud smacking of simulated kisses. In these moments John Thomas drew Annie towards him. After all, he had a wonderfully warm, cosy way of holding a girl with his arm, he seemed to make such a nice fit. And, after all, it was pleasant to be so held: so very comforting and cosy and nice. He leaned over her and she felt his breath on her hair; she knew he wanted to kiss her on the lips. And, after all, he was so warm and she fitted in to him so softly. After all, she wanted him to touch her lips.

But the light sprang up; she also started electrically, and put her hat straight. He left his arm lying nonchalantly behind her. Well, it was fun, it was exciting to be at the Statutes with John Thomas.

When the cinema was over they went for a walk across the dark, damp fields. He had all the arts of love-making. He was especially good at holding a girl, when he sat with her on a stile in the black, drizzling darkness. He seemed to be holding her in space, against his own warmth and gratification. And his kisses were soft and slow and searching.

So Annie walked out with John Thomas, though she kept her own boy dangling in the distance. Some of the tram-girls chose to be huffy. But there, you must take things as you find them, in this life.

There was no mistake about it, Annie liked John Thomas a good deal. She felt so rich and warm in herself whenever he was near. And John Thomas really liked Annie, more than usual. The soft, melting way in which she could flow into a fellow, as if she melted into his very bones, was something rare and good. He fully appreciated this.

But with a developing acquaintance there began a developing intimacy. Annie wanted to consider him a person, a man: she wanted to take an intelligent interest in him, and to have an intelligent response. She did not want a mere nocturnal presence, which was what he was so far. And she prided herself that he could not leave her.

Here she made a mistake. John Thomas intended to remain a nocturnal presence; he had no idea of becoming an all-round individual to her.

318

When she started to take an intelligent interest in him and his life and his character, he sheered off. He hated intelligent interest. And he knew that the only way to stop it was to avoid it. The possessive female was aroused in Annie. So he left her.

It is no use saying she was not surprised. She was at first startled, thrown out of her count. For she had been so *very* sure of holding him. For a while she was staggered, and everything became uncertain to her. Then she wept with fury, indignation, desolation, and misery. Then she had a spasm of despair. And then, when he came, still impudently, on to her car, still familiar, but letting her see by the movement of his head that he had gone away to somebody else for the time being, and was enjoying pastures new, then she determined to have her own back.

She had a very shrewd idea what girls John Thomas had taken out. She went to Nora Purdy. Nora was a tall, rather pale, but well-built girl, with beautiful yellow hair. She was rather secretive.

'Hey!' said Annie, accosting her; then softly: 'Who's John Thomas on with now?'

'I don't know,' said Nora.

'Why, tha does,' said Annie, ironically lapsing into dialect. 'Tha knows as well as I do.'

'Well, I do, then,' said Nora. 'It isn't me, so don't bother.'

'It's Cissy Meakin, isn't it?'

'It is, for all I know.'

'Hasn't he got a face on him!' said Annie. 'I don't half like his cheek. I could knock him off the foot-board when he comes round at me.'

'He'll get dropped on one of these days,' said Nora.

'Ay, he will, when somebody makes up their mind to drop it on him. I should like to see him taken down a peg or two, shouldn't you?'

'I shouldn't mind,' said Nora.

'You've got quite as much cause as I have,' said Annie. 'But we'll drop on him one of these days, my girl. What? Don't you want to?'

'I don't mind,' said Nora.

But as a matter of fact, Nora was much more vindictive than Annie.

One by one Annie went the round of the old flames. It so happened that Cissy Meakin left the tramway service in quite a short time. Her mother made her leave. Then John Thomas was on the *qui vive*. He cast his eyes over his old flock. And his eyes lighted on Annie. He thought she would be safe now. Besides, he liked her.

She arranged to walk home with him on Sunday night. It so happened that her car would be in the depôt at half-past nine: the last car would come in at 10.15. So John Thomas was to wait for her there.

At the depôt the girls had a little waiting-room of their own. It was quite rough, but cosy, with a fire and an oven and a mirror, and table and wooden chairs. The half-dozen girls who knew John Thomas only too well had arranged to take service this Sunday afternoon. So, as the cars began to come in, early, the girls dropped into the waiting-room. And instead of hurrying off home, they sat around the fire and had a cup of tea. Outside was the darkness and lawlessness of war-time.

John Thomas came on the car after Annie, at about a quarter to ten. He poked his head easily into the girls' waiting-room.

'Prayer-meeting?' he asked.

'Ay,' said Laura Sharp. 'Ladies only.'

'That's me!' said John Thomas. It was one of his favourite exclamations.

'Shut the door, boy,' said Muriel Baggaley.

'Oh, which side of me?' said John Thomas.

'Which tha likes,' said Polly Birkin.

He had come in and closed the door behind him. The girls moved in their circle, to make a place for him near the fire. He took off his great-coat and pushed back his hat.

'Who handles the teapot?' he said.

Nora Purdy silently poured him out a cup of tea.

'Want a bit o' my bread and drippin'?' said Muriel Baggaley to him.

'Ay, give us a bit.'

And he began to eat his piece of bread.

'There's no place like home, girls,' he said.

They all looked at him as he uttered this piece of impudence. He seemed to be sunning himself in the presence of so many damsels.

'Especially if you're not afraid to go home in the dark,' said Laura Sharp.

'Me! By myself I am.'

They sat till they heard the last tram come in. In a few minutes Emma Houselay entered.

'Come on, my old duck!' cried Polly Birkin.

'It *is* perishing,' said Emma, holding her fingers to the fire.

'But – I'm afraid to, go home in, the dark,' sang Laura Sharp, the tune having got into her mind.

'Who're you going with to-night, John Thomas?' asked Muriel Baggaley coolly.

'To-night?' said John Thomas. 'Oh, I'm going home by myself to-night – all on my lonely-o.'

'That's me!' said Nora Purdy, using his own ejaculation.

The girls laughed shrilly.

'Me as well, Nora,' said John Thomas.

'Don't know what you mean,' said Laura.

'Yes, I'm toddling,' said he, rising and reaching for his overcoat.

'Nay,' said Polly. 'We're all here waiting for you.'

'We've got to be up in good time in the morning,' he said, in the benevolent official manner.

They all laughed.

'Nay,' said Muriel. 'Don't leave us all lonely, John Thomas. Take one!'

'I'll take the lot, if you like,' he responded gallantly.

'That you won't, either,' said Muriel. 'Two's company; seven's too much of a good thing.'

'Nay – take one,' said Laura. 'Fair and square, all above board and say which.'

'Ay,' cried Annie, speaking for the first time. 'Pick, John Thomas; let's hear thee.'

'Nay,' he said. 'I'm going home quiet to-night. Feeling good, for once.'

'Whereabouts?' said Annie. 'Take a good 'un, then. But tha's got to take one of us!'

'Nay, how can I take one,' he said, laughing uneasily. 'I don't want to make enemies.'

'You'd only make *one*,' said Annie.

'The chosen *one*,' added Laura.

'Oh, my! Who said girls!' exclaimed John Thomas, again turning, as if to escape. 'Well – good-night.'

'Nay, you've got to make your pick,' said Muriel. 'Turn your face to the wall, and say which one touches you. Go on – we shall only just touch your back – one of us. Go on – turn your face to the wall, and don't look, and say which one touches you.'

He was uneasy, mistrusting them. Yet he had not the courage to break away. They pushed him to a wall and stood him there with his face to it. Behind his back they all grimaced, tittering. He looked so comical. He looked around uneasily.

'Go on!' he cried.

'You're looking – you're looking!' they shouted.

He turned his head away. And suddenly, with a movement like a swift cat, Annie went forward and fetched him a box on the side of the head that sent his cap flying and himself staggering. He started round.

But at Annie's signal they all flew at him, slapping him, pinching him, pulling his hair, though more in fun than in spite or anger. He, however, saw red. His blue eyes flamed with strange fear as well as fury, and he butted through the girls to the door. It was locked. He wrenched at it. Roused, alert, the girls stood round and looked at him. He faced them, at bay. At that moment they were rather horrifying to him, as they stood in their short uniforms. He was distinctly afraid.

'Come on, John Thomas! Come on! Choose!' said Annie.

'What are you after? Open the door,' he said.

'We shan't – not till you've chosen!' said Muriel.

'Chosen what?' he said.

'Chosen the one you're going to marry,' she replied.

He hesitated a moment.

'Open the blasted door,' he said, 'and get back to your senses.' He spoke with official authority.

'You've got to choose!' cried the girls.

'Come on!' cried Annie, looking him in the eye. 'Come on! Come on!'

He went forward, rather vaguely. She had taken off her belt, and swinging it, she fetched him a sharp blow over the head with the buckle end. He sprang and seized her. But immediately the other girls rushed upon him, pulling and tearing and beating him. Their blood was now thoroughly up. He was their sport now. They were going to have their own back, out of him. Strange, wild creatures, they hung on him and rushed at him to bear him down. His tunic was torn right up the back, Nora had hold at the back of his collar, and was actually strangling him. Luckily the button burst. He struggled in a wild frenzy of fury and terror, almost mad terror. His tunic was simply torn off his back, his shirt-sleeves were torn away, his arms were naked. The girls rushed at him, clenched their hands on him and pulled at him: or they rushed at him and pushed him, butted him with all their might: or they struck him wild blows. He ducked and cringed and struck sideways. They became more intense.

At last he was down. They rushed on him, kneeling on him. He had neither breath nor strength to move. His face was bleeding with a long scratch, his brow was bruised.

Annie knelt on him, the other girls knelt and hung on to him. Their faces were flushed, their hair wild, their eyes were all glittering strangely. He lay at last quite still, with face averted, as an animal lies when it is defeated and at the mercy of the captor. Sometimes his eye glanced back at the wild faces of the girls. His breast rose heavily, his wrists were torn.

'Now, then, my fellow!' gasped Annie at length. 'Now then – now —'

At the sound of her terrifying, cold triumph, he suddenly started to struggle as an animal might, but the girls threw themselves upon him with unnatural strength and power, forcing him down.

'Yes – now, then!' gasped Annie at length.

And there was a dead silence, in which the thud of heart-beating was to be heard. It was a suspense of pure silence in every soul.

'Now you know where you are,' said Annie.

The sight of his white, bare arm maddened the girls. He lay in a kind of trance of fear and antagonism. They felt themselves filled with supernatural strength.

Suddenly Polly started to laugh – to giggle wildly – helplessly – and Emma and Muriel joined in. But Annie and Nora and Laura remained the same, tense, watchful, with gleaming eyes. He winced away from these eyes.

'Yes,' said Annie, in a curious low tone, secret and deadly. 'Yes! You've got it now. You know what you've done, don't you? You know what you've done.'

He made no sound nor sign, but lay with bright, averted eyes, and averted, bleeding face.

'You ought to be *killed*, that's what you ought,' said Annie, tensely. 'You ought to be *killed*.' And there was a terrifying lust in her voice.

Polly was ceasing to laugh, and giving long-drawn Oh-h-hs and sighs as she came to herself.

'He's got to choose,' she said vaguely.

'Oh, yes, he has,' said Laura, with vindictive decision.

'Do you hear – do you hear?' said Annie. And with a sharp movement, that made him wince, she turned his face to her.

'Do you hear?' she repeated, shaking him.

But he was quite dumb. She fetched him a sharp slap on the face. He started, and his eyes widened. Then his face darkened with defiance, after all.

'Do you hear?' she repeated.

He only looked at her with hostile eyes.

'Speak!' she said, putting her face devilishly near his.

'What?' he said, almost overcome. 'You've got to *choose*!' she cried, as if it were some terrible menace, and as if it hurt her that she could not exact more.

'What?' he said, in fear.

'Choose your girl, Coddy. You've got to choose her now. And you'll get your neck broken if you play any more of your tricks, my boy. You're settled now.'

There was a pause. Again he averted his face. He was cunning in his overthrow. He did not give in to them really – no, not if they tore him to bits.

'All right, then,' he said, 'I choose Annie.' His voice was strange and full of malice. Annie let go of him as if he had been a hot coal.

'He's chosen Annie!' said the girls in chorus.

'Me!' cried Annie. She was still kneeling, but away from him. He was still lying prostrate, with averted face. The girls grouped uneasily around.

'Me!' repeated Annie, with a terrible bitter accent.

Then she got up, drawing away from him with strange disgust and bitterness.

'I wouldn't touch him,' she said.

But her face quivered with a kind of agony, she seemed as if she would fall. The other girls turned aside. He remained lying on the floor, with his torn clothes and bleeding, averted face.

'Oh, if he's chosen —' said Polly.

'I don't want him – he can choose again,' said Annie, with the same rather bitter hopelessness.

'Get up,' said Polly, lifting his shoulder. 'Get up.'

He rose slowly, a strange, ragged, dazed creature. The girls eyed him from a distance, curiously, furtively, dangerously.

'Who wants him?' cried Laura, roughly.

'Nobody,' they answered, with contempt. Yet each one of them waitied for him to look at her, hoped he would look at her. All except Annie, and something was broken in her.

He, however, kept his face closed and averted from them all. There was a silence of the end. He picked up the torn pieces of his tunic, without knowing what to do with them. The girls stood about uneasily, flushed, panting, tidying their hair and their dress unconsciously, and watching him. He looked at none of them. He espied his cap in a corner, and went and picked it up. He put it on his head, and one of the girls burst into a shrill, hysteric laugh at the sight he presented. He, however, took no heed, but went straight to where his overcoat hung on a peg. The girls moved away from contact with him as if he had been an electric wire. He put on his coat and buttoned it down. Then he rolled his tunic-rags into a bundle, and stood before the locked door, dumbly.

'Open the door, somebody,' said Laura.

'Annie's got the key,' said one.

Annie silently offered the key to the girls. Nora unlocked the door.

'Tit for tat, old man,' she said. 'Show yourself a man, and don't bear a grudge.'

But without a word or sign he had opened the door and gone, his face closed, his head dropped.

'That'll learn him,' said Laura.

'Coddy!' said Nora.

'Shut up, for God's sake!' cried Annie fiercely, as if in torture.

'Well, I'm about ready to go, Polly. Look sharp!' said Muriel.

The girls were all anxious to be off. They were tidying themselves hurriedly, with mute stupefied faces.

THE BLIND MAN

Isabel Pervin was listening for two sounds – for the sound of wheels on the drive outside and for the noise of her husband's footsteps in the hall. Her dearest and oldest friend, a man who seemed almost indispensable to her living, would drive up in the rainy dusk of the closing November day. The trap had gone to fetch him from the station. And her husband, who had been blinded in Flanders, and who had a disfiguring mark on his brow, would be coming in from the out-houses.

He had been home for a year now. He was totally blind. Yet they had been very happy. The Grange was Maurice's own place. The back was a farmstead, and the Wernhams, who occupied the rear premises, acted as farmers. Isabel lived with her husband in the handsome rooms in front. She and he had been almost entirely alone together since he was wounded. They talked and sang and read together in a wonderful and unspeakable intimacy. Then she reviewed books for a Scottish newspaper, carrying on her old interest, and he occupied himself a good deal with the farm. Sightless, he could still discuss everything with Wernham, and he could also do a good deal of work about the place – menial work, it is true, but it gave him satisfaction. He milked the cows, carried in the pails, turned the separator, attended to the pigs and horses. Life was still very full and strangely serene for the blind man, peaceful with the almost incomprehensible peace of immediate contact in darkness. With his wife he had a whole world, rich and real and invisible.

They were newly and remotely happy. He did not even regret the loss of his sight in these times of dark, palpable joy. A certain exultance swelled his soul.

But as time wore on, sometimes the rich glamour would leave them. Sometimes, after months of this intensity, a sense of burden overcame Isabel, a weariness, a terrible ennui, in that silent house approached between a colonnade of tall-shafted pines. Then she felt she would go mad, for she could not bear it. And sometimes he had devastating fits of depression, which seemed to lay waste his whole being. It was worse than depression – a black misery, when his own life was a torture to him, and when his presence was unbearable to his wife. The dread went down to the roots of her soul as these black days recurred. In a kind of

326

panic she tried to wrap herself up still further in her husband. She forced the old spontaneous cheerfulness and joy to continue. But the effort it cost her was almost too much. She knew she could not keep it up. She felt she would scream with the strain, and would give anything, anything, to escape. She longed to possess her husband utterly; it gave her inordinate joy to have him entirely to herself. And yet, when again he was gone in a black and massive misery, she could not bear him, she could not bear herself; she wished she could be snatched away off the earth altogether, anything rather than live at this cost.

Dazed, she schemed for a way out. She invited friends, she tried to give him some further connection with the outer world. But it was no good. After all their joy and suffering, after their dark, great year of blindness and solitude and unspeakable nearness, other people seemed to them both shallow, prattling, rather impertinent. Shallow prattle seemed presumptuous. He became impatient and irritated, she was wearied. And so they lapsed into their solitude again. For they preferred it.

But now, in a few weeks' time, her second baby would be born. The first had died, an infant, when her husband first went out to France. She looked with joy and relief to the coming of the second. It would be her salvation. But also she felt some anxiety. She was thirty years old, her husband was a year younger. They both wanted the child very much. Yet she could not help feeling afraid. She had her husband on her hands, a terrible joy to her, and a terrifying burden. The child would occupy her love and attention. And then, what of Maurice? What would he do? If only she could feel that he, too, would be at peace and happy when the child came! She did so want to luxuriate in a rich, physical satisfaction of maternity. But the man, what would he do? How could she provide for him, how avert those shattering black moods of his, which destroyed them both?

She sighed with fear. But at this time Bertie Reid wrote to Isabel. He was her old friend, a second or third cousin, a Scotsman, as she was a Scotswoman. They had been brought up near to one another, and all her life he had been her friend, like a brother, but better than her own brothers. She loved him – though not in the marrying sense. There was a sort of kinship between them, an affinity. They understood one another instinctively. But Isabel would never have thought of marrying Bertie. It would have seemed like marrying in her own family.

Bertie was a barrister and a man of letters, a Scotsman of the intellectual type, quick, ironical, sentimental, and on his knees before the women he adored but did not want to marry. Maurice Pervin was different. He came of a good old country family – the Grange was not a very great distance from Oxford. He was passionate, sensitive, perhaps over-sensitive, wincing – a big fellow with heavy limbs and a forehead that flushed painfully. For his mind was slow, as if drugged by the strong provincial blood that beat in his veins. He was very sensitive to his own mental slowness, his feelings being quick and acute. So that he was just the opposite to Bertie, whose mind was much quicker than his emotions, which were not so very fine.

From the first the two men did not like each other. Isabel felt that they *ought* to get on together. But they did not. She felt that if only each could have the clue to the other there would be such a rare understanding between them. It did not come off, however. Bertie adopted a slightly ironical attitude, very offensive to Maurice, who returned the Scotch irony with English resentment, a resentment which deepened sometimes into stupid hatred.

This was a little puzzling to Isabel. However, she accepted it in the course of things. Men were made freakish and unreasonable. Therefore, when Maurice was going out to France for the second time, she felt that, for her husband's sake, she must discontinue her friendship with Bertie. She wrote to the barrister to this effect. Bertram Reid simply replied that in this, as in all other matters, he must obey her wishes, if these were indeed her wishes.

For nearly two years nothing had passed between the two friends. Isabel rather gloried in the fact; she had no compunction. She had one great article of faith, which was, that husband and wife should be so important to one another, that the rest of the world simply did not count. She and Maurice were husband and wife. They loved one another. They would have children. Then let everybody and everything else fade into insignificance outside this connubial felicity. She professed herself quite happy and ready to receive Maurice's friends. She was happy and ready: the happy wife, the ready woman in possession. Without knowing why, the friends retired abashed, and came no more. Maurice, of course, took as much satisfaction in this connubial absorption as Isabel did.

He shared in Isabel's literary activities, she cultivated a real interest in agriculture and cattle-raising. For she, being at heart perhaps an emotional enthusiast, always cultivated the practical side of life, and prided herself on her mastery of practical affairs. Thus the husband and wife had spent the five years of their married life. The last had been one of blindness and unspeakable intimacy. And now Isabel felt a great indifference coming over her, a sort of lethargy. She wanted to be allowed to bear her child in peace, to nod by the fire and drift vaguely, physically, from day to day. Maurice was like an ominous thundercloud. She had to keep waking up to remember him.

When a little note came from Bertie, asking if he were to put up a tombstone to their dead friendship, and speaking of the real pain he felt on account of her husband's loss of sight, she felt a pang, a fluttering agitation of re-awakening. And she read the letter to Maurice.

'Ask him to come down,' he said.

'Ask Bertie to come here!' she re-echoed.

'Yes – if he wants to.'

Isabel paused for a few moments.

'I know he wants to – he'd only be too glad,' she replied. 'But what about you, Maurice? How would you like it?'

'I should like it.'

'Well – in that case —— But I thought you didn't care for him —'

'Oh, I don't know. I might think differently of him now,' the blind man replied. It was rather abstruse to Isabel.

'Well, dear,' she said, 'if you're quite sure —'

'I'm sure enough. Let him come,' said Maurice.

So Bertie was coming, coming this evening, in the November rain and darkness. Isabel was agitated, racked with her old restlessness and indecision. She had always suffered from this pain of doubt, just an agonising sense of uncertainty. It had begun to pass off, in the lethargy of maternity. Now it returned, and she resented it. She struggled as usual to maintain her calm, composed, friendly bearing, a sort of mask she wore over all her body.

A woman had lighted a tall lamp beside the table, and spread the cloth. The long dining-room was dim, with its elegant but rather severe pieces of old furniture. Only the round table glowed softly under the light. It had a rich, beautiful effect. The white cloth glistened and dropped its heavy, pointed lace corners almost to the carpet, the china was old and handsome, creamy-yellow, with a blotched pattern of harsh red and deep blue, the cups large and bell-shaped, the teapot gallant. Isabel looked at it with superficial appreciation.

Her nerves were hurting her. She looked automatically again at the high, uncurtained windows. In the last dusk she could just perceive outside a huge fir tree swaying its boughs: it was as if she thought it rather than saw it. The rain came flying on the window panes. Ah, why had she no peace? These two men, why did they tear at her? Why did they not come – why was there this suspense?

She sat in a lassitude that was really suspense and irritation. Maurice, at least, might come in – there was nothing to keep him out. She rose to her feet. Catching sight of her reflection in a mirror, she glanced at herself with a slight smile of recognition, as if she were an old friend to herself. Her face was oval and calm, her nose a little arched. Her neck made a beautiful line down to her shoulder. With hair knotted loosely behind, she had something of a warm, maternal look. Thinking this of herself, she arched her eyebrows and her rather heavy lids, with a little flicker of a smile, and for a moment her grey eyes looked amused and wicked, a little sardonic, out of her transfigured Madonna face.

Then, resuming her air of womanly patience – she was really fatally self-determined – she went with a little jerk towards the door. Her eyes were slightly reddened.

She passed down the wide hall, and through a door at the end. Then she was in the farm premises. The scent of dairy, and of farm-kitchen, and of farmyard and of leather almost overcame her: but particularly the scent of dairy. They had been scalding out the pans. The flagged passage in front of her was dark, puddled and wet. Light came out from the open kitchen door. She went forward and stood in the doorway. The farm-people were at tea, seated at a little distance from her, round a long, narrow table, in the centre of which stood a white lamp. Ruddy faces, ruddy hands holding food, red mouths working, heads bent over the tea-cups: men, land-girls, boys: it was tea-time, feeding-time. Some faces caught sight of her. Mrs. Wernham, going round behind the chairs with a large black teapot, halting slightly in her walk, was not aware of her for a moment. Then she turned suddenly.

'Oh, is it Madame!' she exclaimed. 'Come in, then, come in! We're at tea.' And she dragged forward a chair.

'No, I won't come in,' said Isabel. 'I'm afraid I interrupt your meal.'

'No – no – not likely, Madame, not likely.'

'Hasn't Mr. Pervin come in, do you know?'

'I'm sure I couldn't say! Missed him, have you, Madame?'

'No, I only wanted him to come in,' laughed Isabel, as if shyly.

'Wanted him, did ye? Get up, boy – get up, now —'

Mrs. Wernham knocked one of the boys on the shoulder. He began to scrape to his feet, chewing largely.

'I believe he's in top stable,' said another face from the table.

'Ah! No, don't get up. I'm going myself,' said Isabel.

'Don't you go out of a dirty night like this. Let the lad go. Get along wi' ye, boy,' said Mrs. Wernham.

'No, no,' said Isabel, with a decision that was always obeyed. 'Go on with your tea, Tom. I'd like to go across to the stable, Mrs. Wernham.'

'Did ever you hear tell!' exclaimed the woman.

'Isn't the trap late?' asked Isabel.

'Why, no,' said Mrs. Wernham, peering into the distance at the tall, dim clock. 'No, Madame – we can give it another quarter or twenty minutes yet, good – yes, every bit of a quarter.'

'Ah! It seems late when darkness falls so early,' said Isabel.

'It do, that it do. Bother the days, that they draw in so,' answered Mrs. Wernham. 'Proper miserable!'

'They are,' said Isabel, withdrawing.

She pulled on her over-shoes, wrapped a large tartan shawl around her, put on a man's felt hat, and ventured out along the causeways of the first yard. It was very dark. The wind was roaring in the great elms behind the out-houses. When she came to the second yard the darkness seemed deeper. She was unsure of her footing. She wished she had brought a lantern. Rain blew against her. Half she liked it, half she felt unwilling to battle.

She reached at last the just visible door of the stable. There was no sign of a light anywhere. Opening the upper half, she looked in: into a simple well of darkness. The smell of horses, ammonia, and of warmth was startling to her, in that full night. She listened with all her ears, but could hear nothing save the night, and the stirring of a horse.

'Maurice!' she called, softly and musically, though she was afraid. 'Maurice – are you there?'

Nothing came from the darkness. She knew the rain and wind blew in upon the horses, the hot animal life. Feeling it wrong, she entered the stable, and draw the lower half of the door shut, holding the upper part close. She did not stir, because she was aware of the presence of the dark hindquarters of the horses, though she could not see them, and she was afraid. Something wild stirred in her heart.

She listened intensely. Then she heard a small noise in the distance – far away, it seemed – the chink of a pan, and a man's voice speaking a brief word. It would be Maurice, in the other part of the stable. She stood motionless, waiting for him to come through the partition door. The horses were so terrifyingly near to her, in the invisible.

The loud jarring of the inner door-latch made her start; the door was opened. She could hear and feel her husband entering and invisibly passing among the horses near to her, in darkness as they were, actively intermingled. The rather low sound of his voice as he spoke to the horses came velvety to her nerves. How near he was, and how invisible! The darkness seemed to be in a strange swirl of violent life, just upon her. She turned giddy.

Her presence of mind made her call, quietly and musically:

'Maurice! Maurice – dea-ar!'

'Yes,' he answered. 'Isabel?'

She saw nothing, and the sound of his voice seemed to touch her.

'Hello!' she answered cheerfully, straining her eyes to see him. He was still busy, attending to the horses near her, but she saw only darkness. It made her almost desperate.

'Won't you come in, dear?' she said.

'Yes, I'm coming. Just half a minute. *Stand over – now!* Trap's not come, has it?'

'Not yet,' said Isabel.

His voice was pleasant and ordinary, but it had a slight suggestion of the stable to her. She wished he would come away. While he was so utterly invisible she was afraid of him.

'How's the time,' he asked.

'Not yet six,' she replied. She disliked to answer into the dark. Presently he came very near to her, and she retreated out of doors.

'The weather blows in here,' he said, coming steadily forward, feeling for the doors. She shrank away. At last she could dimly see him.

'Bertie won't have much of a drive,' he said, as he closed the doors.

'He won't indeed!' said Isabel calmly, watching the dark shape at the door.

'Give me your arm, dear,' she said.

She pressed his arm close to her, as she went. But she longed to see him, to look at him. She was nervous. He walked erect, with face rather lifted, but with a curious tentative movement of his powerful, muscular legs. She could feel the clever, careful, strong contact of his feet with the earth, as she balanced against him. For a moment he was a tower of darkness to her, as if he rose out of the earth.

In the house-passage he wavered, and went cautiously, with a curious look of silence about him as he felt for the bench. Then he sat down heavily. He was a man with rather sloping shoulders, but with heavy limbs, powerful legs that seemed to know the earth. His head was small, usually carried high and light. As he bent down to unfasten his gaiters and boots he did not look blind. His hair was brown and crisp, his hands were large, reddish, intelligent, the veins stood out in the wrists; and his thighs and knees seemed massive. When he stood up his face and neck were surcharged with blood, the veins stood out on his temples. She did not look at his blindness.

Isabel was always glad when they had passed through the dividing door into their own regions of repose and beauty. She was a little afraid of him, out there in the animal grossness of the back. His bearing also changed, as he smelt the familiar, indefinable odour that pervaded his wife's surroundings, a delicate, refined scent, very faintly spicy. Perhaps it came from the pot-pourri bowls.

He stood at the foot of the stairs, arrested, listening. She watched him, and her heart sickened. He seemed to be listening to fate.

'He's not here yet,' he said. 'I'll go up and change.'

'Maurice,' she said, 'you're not wishing he wouldn't come, are you?'

'I couldn't quite say,' he answered. 'I feel myself rather on the *qui vive*.'

'I can see you are,' she answered. And she reached up and kissed his cheek. She saw his mouth relax into a slow smile.

'What are you laughing at?' she said roguishly.

'You consoling me,' he answered.

'Nay,' she answered. 'Why should I console you? You know we love each other – you know *how* married we are! What does anything else matter?'

'Nothing at all, my dear.'

He felt for her face, and touched it, smiling.

'*You're* all right, aren't you?' he asked, anxiously.

'I'm wonderfully all right, love,' she answered. 'It's you I am a little troubled about, at times.'

'Why me?' he said, touching her cheeks delicately with the tips of his fingers. The touch had an almost hypnotising effect on her.

He went away upstairs. She saw him mount into the darkness, unseeing and unchanging. He did not know that the lamps on the upper corridor were unlighted. He went on into the darkness with unchanging step. She heard him in the bathroom.

Pervin moved about almost unconsciously in his familiar surroundings, dark though everything was. He seemed to know the presence of objects before he touched them. It was a pleasure to him to rock thus through a world of things, carried on the flood in a sort of blood-prescience. He did not think much or trouble much. So long as he kept this sheer immediacy of blood-contact with the substantial world he was happy, he wanted no intervention of visual consciousness. In this state there was a certain rich positivity, bordering sometimes on rapture. Life seemed to move in him like a tide lapping, lapping, and advancing, enveloping all things darkly. It was a pleasure to stretch forth the hand and meet the unseen object, clasp it, and possess it in pure contact. He did not try to remember, to visualise. He did not want to. The new way of consciousness substituted itself in him.

The rich suffusion of this state generally kept him happy, reaching its culmination in the consuming passion for his wife. But at times the flow would seem to be checked and thrown back. Then it would beat inside him like a tangled sea, and he was tortured in the shattered chaos of his own blood. He grew to dread this arrest, this throw-back, this chaos inside himself, when he seemed merely at the mercy of his own powerful and conflicting elements. How to get some measure of control or surety, this was the question. And when the question rose maddening in him, he would clench his fists as if he would *compel* the whole universe to submit to him. But it was in vain. He could not even compel himself.

To-night, however, he was still serene, though little tremors of un-reasonable exasperation ran through him. He had to handle the razor very carefully, as he shaved, for it was not at one with him, he was afraid of it. His hearing also was too much sharpened. He heard the woman lighting the lamps on the corridor, and attending to the fire in the visitor's room. And then, as he went to his room he heard the trap arrive. Then came Isabel's voice, lifted and calling, like a bell ringing:

'Is it you, Bertie? Have you come?'

And a man's voice answered out of the wind:

'Hullo, Isabel! There you are.'

'Have you had a miserable drive? I'm so sorry we couldn't send a closed carriage. I can't see you at all, you know.'

'I'm coming. No, I liked the drive – it was like Perthshire. Well, how are you? You're looking fit as ever, as far as I can see.'

'Oh, yes,' said Isabel. 'I'm wonderfully well. How are you? Rather thin, I think—'

'Worked to death – everybody's old cry. But I'm all right, Ciss. How's Pervin? – isn't he here?'

'Oh, yes, he's upstairs changing. Yes, he's awfully well. Take off your wet things; I'll send them to be dried.'

'And how are you both, in spirits? He doesn't fret?'

'No – no, not at all. No, on the contrary, really. We've been wonderfully happy, incredibly. It's more than I can understand – so wonderful: the nearness, and the peace —'

'Ah! Well, that's awfully good news —'

They moved away. Pervin heard no more. But a childish sense of desolation had come over him, as he heard their brisk voices. He seemed shut out – like a child that is left out. He was aimless and excluded, he did not know what to do with himself. The helpless desolation came over him. He fumbled nervously as he dressed himself, in a state almost of childishness. He disliked the Scotch accent in Bertie's speech, and the slight response it found on Isabel's tongue. He disliked the slight purr of complacency in the Scottish speech. He disliked intensely the glib way in which Isabel spoke of their happiness and nearness. It made him recoil. He was fretful and beside himself like a child, he had almost a childish nostalgia to be included in the life circle. And at the same time he was a man, dark and powerful and infuriated by his own weakness. By some fatal flaw, he could not be by himself, he had to depend on the support of another. And this very dependence enraged him. He hated Bertie Reid, and at the same time he knew the hatred was nonsense, he knew it was the outcome of his own weakness.

He went downstairs. Isabel was alone in the dining-room. She watched him enter, head erect, his feet tentative. He looked so strong-blooded and healthy, and, at the same time, cancelled. Cancelled – that was the word that flew across her mind. Perhaps it was his scars suggested it.

'You heard Bertie come, Maurice?' she said.

'Yes – isn't he here?'

'He's in his room. He looks very thin and worn.'

'I suppose he works himself to death.'

A woman came in with a tray – and after a few minutes Bertie came down. He was a little dark man, with a very big forehead, thin, wispy hair, and sad, large eyes. His expression was inordinately sad – almost funny. He had odd, short legs.

Isabel watched him hesitate under the door and glance nervously at her husband. Pervin heard him and turned.

'Here you are, now,' said Isabel. 'Come, let us eat.'

Bertie went across to Maurice.

'How are you, Pervin?' he said, as he advanced.

The blind man stuck his hand out into space, and Bertie took it.

'Very fit. Glad you've come,' said Maurice.

335

Isabel glanced at them, and glanced away, as if she could not bear to see them.

'Come,' she said. 'Come to table. Aren't you both awfully hungry? I am, tremendously.'

'I'm afraid you waited for me,' said Bertie, as they sat down.

Maurice had a curious monolithic way of sitting in a chair, erect and distant. Isabel's heart always beat when she caught sight of him thus.

'No,' she replied to Bertie. 'We're very little later than usual. We're having a sort of high tea, not dinner. Do you mind? It gives us such a nice long evening uninterrupted.'

'I like it,' said Bertie.

Maurice was feeling, with curious little movements, almost like a cat kneading her bed, for his place, his knife and his fork, his napkin. He was getting the whole geography of his cover into his consciousness. He sat erect and inscrutable, remote-seeming. Bertie watched the static figure of the blind man, the delicate tactile discernment of the large, ruddy hands, and the curious mindless silence of the brow, above the scar. With difficulty he looked away, and without knowing what he did, picked up a little crystal bowl of violets from the table, and held them to his nose.

'They are sweet-scented,' he said. 'Where do they come from?'

'From the garden – under the windows,' said Isabel.

'So late in the year – and so fragrant! Do you remember the violets under Aunt Bell's south wall?'

The two friends looked at each other and exchanged a smile, Isabel's eyes lighting up.

'Don't I?' she replied. *'Wasn't* she queer!'

'A curious old girl,' laughed Bertie. 'There's a streak of freakishness in the family, Isabel.'

'Ah – but not in you and me, Bertie,' said Isabel. 'Give them to Maurice, will you?' she added, as Bertie was putting down the flowers. 'Have you smelled the violets, dear? Do! – they are so scented.'

Maurice held out his hand, and Bertie placed the tiny bowl against his large, warm-looking fingers. Maurice's hand closed over the thin white fingers of the barrister. Bertie carefully extricated himself. Then the two watched the blind man smelling the violets. He bent his head and seemed to be thinking. Isabel waited.

'Aren't they sweet, Maurice?' she said at last, anxiously.

'Very,' he said. And he held out the bowl. Bertie took it. Both he and Isabel were a little afraid, and deeply disturbed.

The meal continued. Isabel and Bertie chatted spasmodically. The blind man was silent. He touched his food repeatedly, with quick, delicate touches of his knife-point, then cut irregular bits. He could not bear to be helped. Both Isabel and Bertie suffered: Isabel wondered why. She did not suffer when she was alone with Maurice. Bertie made her conscious of a strangeness.

After the meal the three drew their chairs to the fire, and sat down to talk. The decanters were put on a table near at hand. Isabel knocked the logs on the fire, and clouds of brilliant sparks went up the chimney. Bertie noticed a slight weariness in her bearing.

'You will be glad when your child comes now, Isabel?' he said.

She looked up to him with a quick wan smile.

'Yes, I shall be glad,' she answered. 'It begins to seem long. Yes, I shall be very glad. So will you, Maurice, won't you?' she added.

'Yes, I shall,' replied her husband.

'We are both looking forward so much to having it, she said.

'Yes, of course,' said Bertie.

He was a bachelor, three or four years older than Isabel. He lived in beautiful rooms overlooking the river, guarded by a faithful Scottish manservant. And he had his friends amongst the fair sex – not lovers, friends. So long as he could avoid any danger of courtship or marriage, he adored a few good women with constant and unfailing homage, and he was chivalrously fond of quite a number. But if they seemed to encroach on him, he withdrew and detested them.

Isabel knew him very well, knew his beautiful constancy, and kindness, also his incurable weakness, which made him unable ever to enter into close contact of any sort. He was ashamed of himself, because he could not marry, could not approach women physically. He wanted to do so. But he could not. At the centre of him he was afraid, helplessly and even brutally afraid. He had given up hope, had ceased to expect any more that he could escape his own weakness. Hence he was a brilliant and successful barrister, also *littérateur* of high repute, a rich man, and a great social success. At the centre he felt himself neuter, nothing.

Isabel knew him well. She despised him even while she admired him. She looked at his sad face, his little short legs, and felt contempt of him. She looked at his dark grey eyes, with their uncanny, almost childlike intuition, and she loved him. He understood amazingly – but she had no fear of his understanding. As a man she patronised him.

And she turned to the impassive, silent figure of her husband. He sat leaning back, with folded arms, and face a little uptilted. His knees were straight and massive. She sighed, picked up the poker, and again began to prod the fire, to rouse the clouds of soft, brilliant sparks.

'Isabel tells me,' Bertie began suddenly, 'that you have not suffered unbearably from the loss of sight.'

Maurice straightened himself to attend, but kept his arms folded.

'No,' he said, 'not unbearably. Now and again one struggles against it, you know. But there are compensations.'

'They say it is much worse to be stone deaf,' said Isabel.

'I believe it is,' said Bertie. 'Are there compensations?' he added, to Maurice.

'Yes. You cease to bother about a great many things.' Again Maurice stretched his figure, stretched the strong muscles of his back, and leaned backwards, with uplifted face.

'And that is a relief,' said Bertie. 'But what is there in place of the bothering? What replaces the activity?'

There was a pause. At length the blind man replied, as out of a negligent, unattentive thinking:

'Oh, I don't know. There's a good deal when you're not active.'

'Is there?' said Bertie. 'What, exactly? It always seems to me that when there is no thought and no action, there is nothing.'

Again Maurice was slow in replying.

'There is something,' he replied. 'I couldn't tell you what it is.'

And the talk lapsed once more, Isabel and Bertie chatting gossip and reminiscence, the blind man silent.

At length Maurice rose restlessly, a big, obtrusive figure. He felt tight and hampered. He wanted to go away.

'Do you mind,' he said, 'if I go and speak to Wernham?'

'No – go along, dear,' said Isabel.

And he went out. A silence came over the two friends. At length Bertie said:

'Nevertheless, it is a great deprivation, Cissie.'

'It is, Bertie. I know it is.'

'Something lacking all the time,' said Bertie.

'Yes, I know. And yet – and yet – Maurice is right. There is something else, something *there*, which you never knew was there, and which you can't express.'

'What is there?' asked Bertie.

'I don't know – it's awfully hard to define it – but something strong and immediate. There's something strange in Maurice's presence – indefinable – but I couldn't do without it. I agree that it seems to put

338

one's mind to sleep. But when we're alone I miss nothing; it seems awfully rich, almost splendid, you know.'

'I'm afraid I don't follow,' said Bertie.

They talked desultorily. The wind blew loudly outside, rain chattered on the window-panes, making a sharp drum-sound, because of the closed, mellow-golden shutters inside. The logs burned slowly, with hot, almost invisible small flames. Bertie seemed uneasy, there were dark circles round his eyes. Isabel, rich with her approaching maternity, leaned looking into the fire. Her hair curled in odd, loose strands, very pleasing to the man. But she had a curious feeling of old woe in her heart, old, timeless night-woe.

'I suppose we're all deficient somewhere,' said Bertie.

'I suppose so,' said Isabel wearily.

'Damned, sooner or later.'

'I don't know,' she said, rousing herself. 'I feel quite all right, you know. The child coming seems to make me indifferent to everything, just placid. I can't feel that there's anything to trouble about, you know.'

'A good thing, I should say,' he replied slowly.

'Well, there it is. I suppose it's just Nature. If only I felt I needn't trouble about Maurice, I should be perfectly content —'

'But you feel you must trouble about him?'

'Well — I don't know —' She even resented this much effort.

The evening passed slowly. Isabel looked at the clock. 'I say,' she said. 'It's nearly ten o'clock. Where can Maurice be? I'm sure they're all in bed at the back. Excuse me a moment.'

She went out, returning almost immediately.

'It's all shut up and in darkness,' she said. 'I wonder where he is. He must have gone out to the farm —'

Bertie looked at her.

'I suppose he'll come in,' he said.

'I suppose so,' she said. 'But it's unusual for him to be out now.'

'Would you like me to go out and see?'

'Well — if you wouldn't mind. I'd go, but —' She did not want to make the physical effort.

Bertie put on an old overcoat and took a lantern. He went out from the side door. He shrank from the wet and roaring night. Such weather had a nervous effect on him: too much moisture everywhere made him feel almost imbecile. Unwilling, he went through it all. A dog barked violently at him. He peered in all the buildings. At last, he opened the upper door of a sort of intermediate barn, he heard a grinding noise, and looking in, holding up his lantern, saw Maurice, in his shirt-sleeves, standing listening, holding the handle of a turnip-pulper. He had been pulping sweet roots, a pile of which lay dimly heaped in a corner behind him.

'That you, Wernham?' said Maurice, listening.

'No, it's me,' said Bertie.

A large, half-wild grey cat was rubbing at Maurice's leg. The blind man stooped to rub its sides. Bertie watched the scene, then unconsciously entered and shut the door behind him. He was in a high sort of barn-place, from which, right and left, ran off the corridors in front of the stalled cattle. He watched the slow, stooping motion of the other man, as he caressed the great cat.

Maurice straightened himself.

'You came to look for me?' he said.

'Isabel was a little uneasy,' said Bertie.

'I'll come in. I like messing about doing these jobs.'

The cat had reared her sinister, feline length against his leg, clawing at his thigh affectionately. He lifted her claws out of his flesh.

'I hope I'm not in your way at all at the Grange here,' said Bertie, rather shy and stiff.

'My way? No, not a bit. I'm glad Isabel had somebody to talk to. I'm afraid it's I who am in the way. I know I'm not very lively company. Isabel's all right, don't you think? She's not unhappy, is she?'

'I don't think so.'

'What does she say?'

'She says she's very content – only a little troubled about you.'

'Why me?'

'Perhaps afraid that you might brood,' said Bertie cautiously.

'She needn't be afraid of that.' He continued to caress the flattened grey head of the cat with his fingers. 'What I am a bit afraid of,' he resumed, 'is that she'll find me a dead weight, always along with me down here.'

'I don't think you need think that,' said Bertie, though this was what he feared himself.

'I don't know,' said Maurice. 'Sometimes I feel it isn't fair that she's saddled with me.' Then he dropped his voice curiously. 'I say,' he asked, secretly struggling, 'is my face much disfigured? Do you mind telling me?'

340

'There is the scar,' said Bertie, wondering. 'Yes, it is a disfigurement. But more pitiable than shocking.'

'A pretty bad scar, though,' said Maurice.

'Oh yes.'

There was a pause.

'Sometimes I feel I am horrible,' said Maurice, in a low voice, talking as if to himself. And Bertie actually felt a quiver of horror.

'That's nonsense,' he said.

Maurice again straightened himself, leaving the cat.

'There's no telling,' he said. Then again, in an odd tone, he added: 'I don't really know you, do I?'

'Probably not,' said Bertie.

'Do you mind if I touch you?'

The lawyer shrank away instinctively. And yet, out of very philanthropy, he said, in a small voice: 'Not at all.'

But he suffered as the blind man stretched out a strong, naked hand to him. Maurice accidentally knocked off Bertie's hat.

'I thought you were taller,' he said, starting. Then he laid his hand on Bertie Reid's head, closing the dome of the skull in a soft, firm grasp, gathering it, as it were; then, shifting his grasp and softly closing again, with a fine, close pressure, till he had covered the skull and the face of the smaller man, tracing the brows, and touching the full, closed eyes, touching the small nose and the nostrils, the rough, short moustache, the mouth, the rather strong chin. The hand of the blind man grasped the shoulder, the arm, the hand of the other man. He seemed to take him, in the soft, travelling grasp.

'You seem young,' he said quietly, at last.

The lawyer stood almost annihilated, unable to answer.

'Your head seems tender, as if you were young,' Maurice repeated. 'So do your hands. Touch my eyes, will you? – touch my scar.'

Now Bertie quivered with revulsion. Yet he was under the power of the blind man, as if hypnotised. He lifted his hand, and laid the fingers on the scar, on the scarred eyes. Maurice suddenly covered them with his own hand, pressed the fingers of the other man upon his disfigured eye-sockets, trembling in every fibre, and rocking slightly, slowly, from side to side. He remained thus for a minute or more, whilst Bertie stood as if in a swoon, unconscious, imprisoned.

Then suddenly Maurice removed the hand of the other man from his brow, and stood holding it in his own.

'Oh, my God,' he said, 'we shall know each other now, shan't we? We shall know each other now.'

Bertie could not answer. He gazed mute and terror-struck, overcome by his own weakness. He knew he could not answer. He had an unreasonable fear, lest the other man should suddenly destroy him. Whereas Maurice was actually filled with hot, poignant love, the passion of friendship. Perhaps it was this very passion of friendship which Bertie shrank from most.

'We're all right together now, aren't we?' said Maurice. 'It's all right now, as long as we live, so far as we're concerned.'

'Yes,' said Bertie, trying by any means to escape.

Maurice stood with head lifted, as if listening. The new delicate fulfilment of mortal friendship had come as a revelation and surprise to him, something exquisite and unhoped-for. He seemed to be listening to hear if it were real.

Then he turned for his coat.

'Come,' he said, 'we'll go Isabel.'

Bertie took the lantern and opened the door. The cat disappeared. The two men went in silence along the causeways. Isabel, as they came, thought their footsteps sounded strange. She looked up pathetically and anxiously for their entrance. There seemed a curious elation about Maurice. Bertie was haggard, with sunken eyes.

'What is it?' she asked.

'We've become friends,' said Maurice, standing with his feet apart, like a strange colossus.

'Friends!' re-echoed Isabel. And she looked again at Bertie. He met her eyes with a furtive, haggard look; his eyes were as if glazed with misery.

'I'm so glad,' she said, in sheer perplexity.

'Yes,' said Maurice.

He was indeed so glad. Isabel took his hand with both hers, and held it fast.

'You'll be happier now, dear,' she said.

But she was watching Bertie. She knew that he had one desire – to escape from this intimacy, this friendship, which had been thrust upon him. He could not bear it that he had been touched by the blind man, his insane reserve broken in. He was like a mollusc whose shell is broken.

MONKEY NUTS

At first Joe thought the job O.K. He was loading hay on the trucks, along with Albert, the corporal. The two men were pleasantly billeted in a cottage not far from the station: they were their own masters, for Joe never thought of Albert as a master. And the little sidings of the tiny village station was as pleasant a place as you could wish for. On one side, beyond the line, stretched the woods: on the other, the near side, across the green smooth field, red houses were dotted among flowering apple trees. The weather being sunny, work being easy, Albert, a real good pal, what life could be better! After Flanders, it was heaven itself.

Albert, the corporal, was a clean-shaven, shrewd-looking fellow of about forty. He seemed to think his one aim in life was to be full of sun and nonsense. In repose, his face looked a little withered, old. He was a very good pal to Joe, steady, decent and grave under all his 'mischief'; for his mischief was only his laborious way of skirting his own ennui.

Joe was much younger than Albert – only twenty-three. He was a tallish, quiet youth, pleasant-looking. He was of a slightly better class than his corporal, more personable. Careful about his appearance, he shaved every day. 'I haven't got much of a face,' said Albert. 'If I was to shave every day like you, Joe, I should have none.'

There was plenty of life in the little goods-yard: three porter youths, a continual come and go of farm wagons bringing hay, wagons with timber from the woods, coal-carts loading at the trucks. The black coal seemed to make the place sleepier, hotter. Round the big white gate the station-master's children played and his white chickens walked, whilst the station-master himself, a young man getting too fat, helped his wife to peg out the washing on the clothes-line in the meadow.

The great boat-shaped wagons came up from Playcross with the hay. At first the farm-men wagoned it. On the third day one of the land-girls appeared with the first load, drawing to a standstill easily at the head of her two great horses. She was a buxom girl, young, in linen overalls and gaiters. Her face was ruddy, she had large blue eyes.

'Now that's the wagoner for us, boys,' said the corporal loudly.

'Whoa!' she said to her horses; and then to the corporal: 'Which boys do you mean?'

343

'We are the pick of the bunch. That's Joe, my pal. Don't you let on that my name's Albert,' said the corporal to his private. 'I'm the corporal.'

'And I'm Miss Stokes,' said the land-girl coolly, 'if that's all the boys you are.'

'You know you couldn't want more, Miss Stokes,' said Albert politely. Joe, who was bare-headed, whose grey flannel sleeves were rolled up to the elbow, and whose shirt was open at the breast, looked modestly aside as if he had no part in the affair.

'Are you on this job regular then?' said the corporal to Miss Stokes.

'I don't know for sure,' she said, pushing a piece of hair under her hat, and attending to her splendid horses.

'Oh, make it a certainty,' said Albert.

She did not reply. She turned and looked over the two men coolly. She was pretty, moderately blonde, with crisp hair, a good skin, and large blue eyes. She was strong, too, and the work went on leisurely and easily.

'Now!' said the corporal, stopping as usual to look round, 'pleasant company makes work a pleasure – don't hurry it, boys.' He stood on the truck surveying the world. That was one of his great and absorbing occupations: to stand and look out on things in general. Joe, also standing on the truck, also turned round to look what was to be seen. But he could not become blankly absorbed, as Albert could.

Miss Stokes watched the two men from under her broad felt hat. She had seen hundreds of Alberts, khaki soldiers standing in loose attitudes, absorbed in watching nothing in particular. She had seen also a good many Joes, quiet, good-looking young soldiers with half-averted faces. But there was something in the turn of Joe's head, and something in his quiet, tender-looking form, young and fresh – which attracted her eye. As she watched him closely from below, he turned as if he felt her, and his dark-blue eye met her straight, light-blue gaze. He faltered and turned aside again and looked as if he were going to fall off the truck. A slight flush mounted under the girl's full, ruddy face. She liked him.

Always, after this, when she came into the sidings with her team, it was Joe she looked for. She acknowledged to herself that she was sweet on him. But Albert did all the talking. He was so full of fun and nonsense. Joe was a very shy bird, very brief and remote in his answers. Miss Stokes was driven to indulge in repartee with Albert, but she fixed her magnetic attention on the younger fellow. Joe would talk with Albert, and laugh at his jokes. But Miss Stokes could get little out of

344

him. She had to depend on her silent forces. They were more effective than might be imagined.

Suddenly, on Saturday afternoon, at about two o'clock, Joe received a bolt from the blue – a telegram: 'Meet me Belbury Station 6.00 p.m. to-day. M.S.' He knew at once who M.S. was. His heart melted, he felt weak as if he had had a blow.

'What's the trouble, boy?' asked Albert anxiously.

'No – no trouble – it's to meet somebody.' Joe lifted his dark, blue eyes in confusion towards his corporal.

'Meet somebody!' repeated the corporal, watching his young pal with keen blue eyes.'It's all right, then; nothing wrong?'

'No – nothing wrong. I'm not going,' said Joe.

Albert was old and shrewd enough to see that nothing more should be said before the housewife. He also saw that Joe did not want to take him into confidence. So he held his peace, though he was piqued.

The two soldiers went into town, smartened up. Albert knew a fair number of the boys round about; there would be plenty of gossip in the market-place, plenty of lounging in groups on the Bath Road, watching the Saturday evening shoppers. Then a modest drink or two, and the movies. They passed an agreeable, casual, nothing-in-particular evening, with which Joe was quite satisfied. He thought of Belbury Station, and of M.S. waiting there He had not the faintest intention of meeting her. And he had not the faintest intention of telling Albert.

And yet, when the two men were in their bedroom, half undressed, Joe suddenly held out the telegram to his corporal, saying: 'What d'you think of that?'

Albert was just unbuttoning his braces. He desisted, took the telegram form, and turned towards the candle to read it.

'*Meet me Belbury Station 6.00 p.m. to-day. M.S.*,' he read, *sotto voce*. His face took on its fun-and-nonsense look.

'Who's M.S.?' he asked, looking shrewdly at Joe.

'You know as well as I do,' said Joe, non-committal.

'*M.S.*,' repeated Albert. 'Blamed if I know, boy. Is it a woman?'

The conversation was carried on in tiny voices, for fear of disturbing the householders.

'I don't know,' said Joe, turning. He looked full at Albert, the two men looked straight into each other's eyes. There was a lurking grin in each of them.

'Well, I'm – *blamed*!' said Albert at last, throwing the telegram down emphatically on the bed.

'Wha-at?' said Joe, grinning rather sheepishly, his eyes clouded, none the less.

Albert sat on the bed and proceeded to undress, nodding his head with mock gravity all the while. Joe watched him foolishly.

'What?' he repeated faintly.

Albert looked up at him with a knowing look.

'If that isn't coming it quick, boy!' he said. 'What the blazes! What ha' you bin doing?'

'Nothing!' said Joe.

Albert slowly shook his head as he sat on the side of the bed.

'Don't happen to me when *I've* bin doin' nothing,' he said. And he proceeded to pull off his stockings.

Joe turned away, looking at himself in the mirror as he unbuttoned his tunic.

'You didn't want to keep the appointment?' Albert asked, in a changed voice, from the bedside.

Joe did not answer for a moment. Then he said:

'I made no appointment.'

'I'm not saying you did, boy. Don't be nasty about it. I mean you didn't want to answer the – unknown person's summons – shall I put it that way?'

'No,' said Joe.

'What was the deterring motive?' asked Albert, who was now lying on his back in bed.

'Oh,' said Joe, suddenly looking round rather haughtily. 'I didn't want to.' He had a well-balanced head, and could take on a sudden distant bearing.

'Didn't want to – didn't cotton on, like. Well – *they be artful, the women*—' he mimicked his landlord. 'Come on into bed, boy. Don't loiter about as if you'd lost something.'

Albert turned over, to sleep.

On Monday Miss Stokes turned up as usual, striding beside her team. Her 'whoa!' was resonant and challenging, she looked up at the truck as her steeds came to a standstill. Joe had turned aside, and had his face averted from her. She glanced him over – save for his slender succulent tenderness she would have despised him. She sized him up in a steady look. Then she turned to Albert, who was looking down at her and smiling in his mischievous turn. She knew his aspects by now. She looked straight back at him, though her eyes were hot. He saluted her.

'Beautiful morning, Miss Stokes.'

'Very!' she replied.

'Handsome is as handsome looks,' said Albert.

Which produced no response.

'Now, Joe, come on here,' said the corporal. 'Don't keep the ladies waiting – it's the sign of a weak heart.'

Joe turned and the work began. Nothing more was said for the time being. As the week went on all parties became more comfortable. Joe remained silent, averted, neutral, a little on his dignity. Miss Stokes was off-hand and masterful. Albert was full of mischief.

The great theme was a circus, which was coming to the market town on the following Saturday.

'You'll go to the circus, Miss Stokes?' said Albert.

'I may go. Are you going?'

'Certainly. Give us the pleasure of escorting you.'

'No, thanks.'

'That's what I call a flat refusal – what, Joe? You din't mean that you have no liking for our company, Miss Stokes?'

'Oh, I don't know,' said Miss Stokes. 'How many are there of you?'

'Only me and Joe.'

'Oh, is that all?' she said satirically.

Albert was a little nonplussed.

'Isn't that enough for you?' he asked.

'Too many by half,' blurted out Joe, jeeringly, in a sudden fit of uncouth rudeness that made both the others stare.

'Oh, I'll stand out of the way, boy, if that's it,' said Albert to Joe. Then he turned mischievously to Miss Stokes. 'He wants to know what M. stands for,' he said confidentially.

'Monkeys,' she replied, turning to her horses.

'What's M.S.?' said Albert.

'Monkey-nuts,' she retorted, leading off her team.

Albert looked after her a little discomfited. Joe had flushed dark, and cursed Albert in his heart.

On the Saturday afternoon the two soldiers took the train into town. They would have to walk home. They had tea at six o'clock, and lounged about till half-past seven. The circus was in a meadow near the river – a great red-and-white striped tent. Caravans stood at the side. A great crowd of people was gathered round the ticket-caravan.

Inside the tent the lamps were lighted, shining on a ring of faces, a great circular bank of faces round the green grassy centre. Along with some comrades, the two soldiers packed themselves on a thin plank seat,

347

rather high. They were delighted with the flaring lights, the wild effect. But the circus performance did not affect them deeply. They admired the lad in black velvet with rose-purple legs who leapt so neatly on to the galloping horse; they watched the feats of strength, and laughed at the clown. But they felt a little patronising, they missed the sensational drama of the cinema.

Half-way through the performance Joe was electrified to see the face of Miss Stokes not very far from him. There she was, in her khaki and her felt hat, as usual; he pretended not to see her. She was laughing at the clown; she also pretended not to see him. It was a blow to him, and it made him angry. He would not even mention it to Albert. Least said, soonest mended. He liked to believe she had not seen him. But he knew, fatally, that she had.

When they came out of it was nearly eleven o'clock; a lovely night, with a moon and tall, dark, noble trees: a magnificent May night. Joe and Albert laughed and chaffed with the boys. Joe looked round frequently to see if he were safe from Miss Stokes. It seemed so.

But there were six miles to walk home. At last the two soldiers set off, swinging their canes. The road was white between tall hedges, other stragglers were passing out of the town towards the villages; the air was full of pleased excitement.

They were drawing near to the village when they saw a dark figure ahead. Joe's heart sank with pure fear. It was a figure wheeling a bicycle; a land-girl; Miss Stokes. Albert was ready with his nonsense. Miss Stokes had a puncture.

'Let me wheel the rattler,' said Albert.

'Thank you,' said Miss Stokes. 'You *are* kind.'

'Oh, I'd be kinder than that, if you'd show me how,' said Albert.

'Are you sure?' said Miss Stokes.

'Doubt my words?' said Albert. 'That's cruel of you, Miss Stokes.'

Miss Stokes walked between them, close to Joe.

'Have you been to the circus?' she asked him.

'Yes,' he replied mildly.

'Have *you* been?' Albert asked her.

'Yes. I didn't see you,' she replied.

'What! – you say so! Didn't see us! Didn't think us worth looking at,' began Albert. 'Aren't as I handsome as the clown, now? And you didn't as much as glance in our direction? I call it a downright oversight.'

'I never *saw* you,' reiterated Miss Stokes. 'I didn't know you saw me.'

'That makes it worse,' said Albert.

The road passed through a belt of dark pine-wood. The village, and the branch road, was very near. Miss Stokes put out her fingers and felt for Joe's hand as it swung at his side. To say he was staggered is to put it mildly. Yet he allowed her softly to clasp his fingers for a few moments. But he was a mortified youth.

At the cross-road they stopped – Miss Stokes should turn off. She'd have another mile to go.

'You'll let us see you home,' said Albert.

'Do me a kindness,' she said. 'Put my bike in your shed, and take it to Baker's on Monday, will you?'

'I'll sit up all night and mend it for you, if you like.'

'No, thanks. And Joe and I'll walk on.'

'Oh – ho! Oh – ho!' said Albert. 'Joe! Joe! What do you say to that, boy? Aren't you in luck's way? And I get the bloomin' old bike for my pal. Consider it again, Miss Stokes.'

Joe turned aside his face, and did not speak.

'Oh, well! I wheel the grid, do I? I leave you, boy —'

'I'm not keen on going any farther,' barked out Joe, in an uncouth voice. 'She bain't my choice.'

The girl stood silent, and watched the two men.

'There now!' said Albert. 'Think o' that! If it was *me* now —' But he was uncomfortable. 'Well, Miss Stokes, have me,' he added.

Miss Stokes stood quite still, neither moved nor spoke. And so the three remained for some time at the lane end. At last Joe began kicking the ground – then he suddenly lifted his face. At that moment Miss Stokes was at his side. She put her arm delicately round his waist.

'Seems I'm the one extra, don't you think?' Albert inquired of the high bland moon.

Joe had dropped his head and did not answer. Miss Stokes stood with her arm lightly round his waist. Albert bowed, saluted, and bade goodnight. He walked away, leaving the two standing.

Miss Stokes put a light pressure on Joe's waist, and drew him down the road. They walked in silence. The night was full of scent – wild cherry, the first bluebells. Still they walked in silence. A nightingale was singing. They approached nearer and nearer, till they stood close by his dark bush. The powerful notes sounded from the cover, almost like flashes of light – then the interval of silence – then the moaning notes, almost like a dog faintly howling, followed by the long, rich trill, and flashing notes. Then a short silence again.

Miss Stokes turned at last to Joe. She looked up at him, and in the moonlight he saw her faintly smiling. He felt maddened, but helpless. Her arm was round his waist, she drew him closely to her with a soft pressure that made all his bones rotten.

Meanwhile Albert was waiting at home. He put on his overcoat, for the fire was out, and he had had malarial fever. He looked fitfully at the *Daily Mirror* and the *Daily Sketch*, but he saw nothing. It seemed a long time. He began to yawn widely, even to nod. At last Joe came in.

Albert looked at him keenly. The young man's brow was black, his face sullen.

'All right, boy?' asked Albert.

Joe merely grunted for a reply. There was nothing more to be got out of him. So they went to bed.

Next day Joe was silent, sullen. Albert could make nothing of him. He proposed a walk after tea.

'I'm going somewhere,' said Joe.

'Where – Monkey-nuts?' asked the corporal. But Joe's brow only became darker.

So the days went by. Almost every evening Joe went off alone, returning late. He was sullen, taciturn and had a hang-dog look, a curious way of dropping his head and looking dangerously from under his brows. And he and Albert did not get on so well any more with one another. For all his fun and nonsense, Albert was really irritable, soon made angry. And Joe's stand-offish sulkiness and complete lack of confidence riled him, got on his nerves. His fun and nonsense took a biting, sarcastic turn, at which Joe's eyes glittered occasionally, though the young man turned unheeding aside. Then again Joe would be full of odd, whimsical fun, out-shining Albert himself.

Miss Stokes still came to the station with the wain: Monkey-nuts. Albert called her, though not to her face. For she was very clear and good-looking, almost she seemed to gleam. And Albert was a tiny bit afraid of her. She very rarely addressed Joe whilst the hay-loading was going on, and that young man always turned his back to her. He seemed thinner, and his limber figure looked more slouching. But still it had the tender, attractive appearance, especially from behind. His tanned face, a little thinned and darkened, took a handsome, slightly sinister look.

'Come on, Joe!' the corporal urged sharply one day. 'What're you doing, boy? Looking for beetles on the bank?'

Joe turned round swiftly, almost menacing, to work.

350

'He's a different fellow these days, Miss Stokes,' said Albert to the young woman. 'What's got him? Is it Monkey-nuts that don't suit him, do you think?'

'Choked with chaff, more like,' she retorted. 'It's as bad as feeding a threshing machine, to have to listen to some folks.'

'As bad as what?' said Albert. 'You don't mean *me*, do you, Miss Stokes?'

'No,' she cried. 'I don't mean you.'

Joe's face became dark red during these sallies, but he said nothing. He would eye the young woman curiously, as she swung so easily at the work, and he had some of the look of a dog which is going to bite.

Albert, with his nerves on edge, began to find the strain rather severe. The next Saturday evening, when Joe came in more black-browed than ever, he watched him, determined to have it out with him.

When the boy went upstairs to bed, the corporal followed him. He closed the door behind him carefully, sat on the bed and watched the younger man undressing. And for once he spoke in a natural voice, neither chaffing nor commanding.

'What's gone wrong, boy?'

Joe stopped a moment as if he had been shot. Then he went on unwinding his puttees, and did not answer or look up.

'You can hear, can't you?' said Albert, nettled.

'Yes, I can hear,' said Joe, stooping over his puttees till his face was purple.

'Then why don't you answer?'

Joe sat up. He gave a long, sideways look at the corporal. Then he lifted his eyes and stared at the crack in the ceiling.

The corporal watched these movements shrewdly.

'And *then* what?' he asked ironically.

Again Joe turned and stared him in the face. The corporal smiled very slightly, but kindly.

'There'll be murder done one of these days,' said Joe, in a quiet unimpassioned voice.

'So long as it's by daylight —' replied Albert. Then he went over, sat down by Joe, put his hand on his shoulder affectionately, and continued: 'What is it, boy? What's gone wrong? You can trust me, can't you?'

Joe turned and looked curiously at the face so near to his.

'It's nothing, that's all,' he said laconically.

Albert frowned.

'Then who's going to be murdered? – and who's going to do the murdering? – me or you – which is it, boy?' He smiled gently at the stupid youth, looking straight at him all the while, into his eyes. Gradually the stupid, hunted, glowering look died out of Joe's eyes. He turned his head aside, gently, as one rousing from a spell.

'I don't want her,' he said, with fierce resentment.

'Then you needn't have her,' said Albert. 'What do you go for, boy?'

But it wasn't as simple as all that. Joe made no remark.

'She's a smart-looking girl. What's wrong with her, my boy? I should have thought you were a lucky chap, myself.'

'I don't want 'er,' Joe barked, with ferocity and resentment.

'Then tell her so and have done,' said Albert. He waited a while. There was no response. 'Why don't you?' he added.

'Because I don't,' confessed Joe sulkily.

Albert pondered – rubbed his head.

'You're too soft-hearted, that's where it is, boy. You want your mettle dipping in cold water, to temper it. You're too soft-hearted —'

He laid his arm affectionately across the shoulders of the younger man. Joe seemed to yield a little towards him.

'When are you going to see her again?' Albert asked. For a long time there was no answer.

'When is it, boy?' persisted the softened voice of the corporal.

'To-morrow,' confessed Joe.

'Then let me go,' said Albert. 'Let me go, will you?'

The morrow was Sunday, a sunny day, but a cold evening. The sky was grey, the new foliage very green, but the air was chill and depressing. Albert walked briskly down the white road towards Beeley. He crossed a larch plantation, and followed a narrow by-road, where blue speedwell flowers fell from the banks into the dust. He walked swinging his cane, with mixed sensations. Then having gone a certain length, he turned and began to walk in the opposite direction.

So he saw a young woman approaching him. She was wearing a wide hat of grey straw, and a loose, swinging dress of nigger-grey velvet. She walked with slow inevitability. Albert faltered a little as he approached her. Then he saluted her, and his roguish, slightly withered skin flushed. She was staring straight into his face.

He fell in by her side, saying impudently:

'Not so nice for a walk as it was, is it?'

She only stared at him. He looked back at her.

'You've seen me before, you know,' he said, grinning slightly. 'Perhaps you never noticed me. Oh, I'm quite nice-looking, in a quiet way, you know. What —?'

But Miss Stokes did not speak: she only stared with large, icy blue eyes at him. He became self-conscious, lifted up his chin, walked with his nose in the air, and whistled at random. So they went down the quiet, deserted grey lane. He was whistling the air: 'I'm Gilbert, the filbert, the colonel of the nuts.'

At last she found her voice:

'Where's Joe?'

'He thought you'd like a change: they say variety's the salt of life — that's why I'm mostly in pickle.'

'Where is he?'

'Am I my brother's keeper? He's gone his own ways.'

'Where?'

'Nay, how am I to know? Not so far but he'll be back for supper.'

She stopped in the middle of the lane. He stopped facing her.

'Where's Joe?' she asked.

He struck a careless attitude, looked down the road this way and that, lifted his eyebrows, pushed his khaki cap on one side, and answered:

'He is not conducting the service to-night: he asked me if I'd offici-ate.'

'Why hasn't he come?'

'Didn't want to, I expect. *I* wanted to.'

She stared him up and down, and he felt uncomfortable in his spine, but maintained his air of nonchalance. Then she turned slowly on her heel, and started to walk back. The corporal went at her side.

'You're not going back, are you?' he pleaded. 'Why, me and you, we should get on like a house on fire.'

She took no heed, but walked on. He went uncomfortably at her side, making his funny remarks from time to time. But she was as if stone deaf. He glanced at her, and to his dismay saw the tears running down her cheeks. He stopped suddenly, and pushed back his cap.

'I say, you know —' he began.

But she was walking on like an automaton, and he had to hurry after her.

She never spoke to him. At the gate of her farm she walked straight in, as if he were not there. He watched her disappear. Then he turned on his heel, cursing silently, puzzled, lifting off his cap to scratch his head.

That night, when they were in bed, he remarked:

353

'Say, Joe, boy; strikes me you're well off without Monkey-nuts. Gord love us, beans ain't in it.'

So they slept in amity. But they waited with some anxiety for the morrow.

It was a cold morning, a grey sky shifting in a cold wind, and threatening rain. They watched the wagon come up the road and through the yard gates. Miss Stokes was with her team as usual; her 'Whoa!' rang out like a war-whoop.

She faced up at the truck where the two men stood.

'Joe!' she called, to the averted figure which stood up in the wind.

'What?' he turned unwillingly.

She made a queer movement, lifting her head slightly in a sipping, half-inviting, half-commanding gesture. And Joe was crouching already to jump off the truck to obey her, when Albert put his hand on his shoulder.

'Half a minute, boy! Where are you off? Work's work, and nuts is nuts. You stop here.'

Joe slowly straightened himself.

'Joe?' came the woman's clear call from below.

Again Joe looked at her. But Albert's hand was on his shoulder, detaining him. He stood half averted, with his tail between his legs.

'Take your hand off him, you!' said Miss Stokes.

'Yes, Major,' retorted Albert satirically.

She stood and watched.

'Joe!' Her voice rang for the third time.

Joe turned and looked at her, and a slow, jeering smile gathered on his face.

'Monkey-nuts!' he replied, in a tone mocking her call.

She turned white – dead white. The men thought she would fall. Albert began yelling to the porters up the line to come and help with the load. He could yell like any non-commissioned officer upon occasion.

Some way or other the wagon was unloaded, the girl was gone. Joe and his corporal looked at one another and smiled slowly. But they had a weight on their minds, they were afraid.

They were reassured, however, when they found that Miss Stokes came no more with the hay. As far as they were concerned, she had vanished into oblivion. And Joe felt more relieved even than he had felt when he heard the firing cease, after the news had come that the armistice was signed.

WINTRY PEACOCK

THERE was thin, crisp snow on the ground, the sky was blue, the wind very cold, the air clear. Farmers were just turning out the cows for an hour or so in the midday, and the smell of cowsheds was unendurable as I entered Tible. I noticed the ash-twigs up in the sky were pale and luminous, passing into the blue. And then I saw the peacocks. There they were in the road before me, three of them, and tailless, brown, speckled birds, with dark-blue necks and ragged crests. They stepped archly over the filigree snow, and their bodies moved with slow motion, like small, light, flat-bottomed boats. I admired them, they were curious. Then a gust of wind caught them, heeled them over as if they were three frail boats, opening their feathers like ragged sails. They hopped and skipped with discomfort, to get out of the draught of the wind. And then, in the lee of the walls, they resumed their arch, wintry motion, light and unballasted now their tails were gone, indifferent. They were indifferent to my presence. I might have touched them. They turned off to the shelter of an open shed.

As I passed the end of the upper house, I saw a young woman just coming out of the back door. I had spoken to her in the summer. She recognised me at once, and waved to me. She was carrying a pail, wearing a white apron that was longer than her preposterously short skirt, and she had on the cotton bonnet. I took off my hat to her and was going on. But she put down her pail and darted with a swift, furtive movement after me.

'Do you mind waiting a minute?' she said. 'I'll be out in a minute.'

She gave me a slight, odd smile, and ran back. Her face was long and sallow and her nose rather red. But her gloomy black eyes softened caressively to me for a moment, with that momentary humility which makes a man lord of the earth.

I stood in the road, looking at the fluffy, dark-red young cattle that mooed and seemed to bark at me. They seemed happy, frisky cattle, a little impudent, and either determined to go back into the warm shed, or determined not to go back. I could not decide which.

Presently the woman came forward again, her head rather ducked.

355

But she looked up at me and smiled, with that odd, immediate intimacy, something witch-like and impossible.

'Sorry to keep you waiting,' she said. 'Shall we stand in this cart-shed – it will be more out of the wind.'

So we stood among the shafts of the open cart-shed that faced the road. Then she looked down at the ground, a little sideways, and I noticed a small black frown on her brows. She seemed to brood for a moment. Then she looked straight into my eyes, so that I blinked and wanted to turn my face aside. She was searching me for something and her look was too near. The frown was still on her keen, sallow brow.

'Can you speak French?' she asked me abruptly.

'More or less,' I replied.

'I was supposed to learn it at school,' she said. 'But I don't know a word.' She ducked her head and laughed, with a slightly ugly grimace and a rolling of her black eyes.

'No good keeping your mind full of scraps,' I answered.

But she had turned aside her sallow, long face, and did not hear what I said. Suddenly again she looked at me. She was searching. And at the same time she smiled at me, and her eyes looked softly, darkly, with infinite trustful humility into mine. I was being cajoled.

'Would you mind reading a letter for me, in French,' she said, her face immediately black and bitter-looking. She glanced at me, frowning.

'Not at all,' I said.

'It's a letter to my husband,' she said, still scrutinising.

I looked at her, and didn't quite realise. She looked too far into me, my wits were gone. She glanced round. Then she looked at me shrewdly. She drew a letter from her pocket, and handed it to me. It was addressed from France to Lance-Corporal Goyte, at Tible. I took out the letter and began to read it, as mere words. *'Mon cher* Alfred' – it might have been a bit of a torn newspaper. So I followed the script: the trite phrases of a letter from a French-speaking girl to an English soldier. 'I think of you always, always. Do you think sometimes of me?' And then I vaguely realised that I was reading a man's private correspondence. And yet, how could one consider these trivial, facile French phrases private! Nothing more trite and vulgar in the world, than such a love-letter – no newspaper more obvious.

Therefore I read with a callous heart the effusions of the Belgian damsel. But then I gathered my attention. For the letter went on: *'Notre cher petit bébé* – our dear little baby was born a week ago.

Almost I died, knowing you were far away, and perhaps forgetting the fruit of our perfect love. But the child comforted me. He has the smiling eyes and virile air of his English father. I pray to the Mother of Jesus to send me the dear father of my child, that I may see him with my child in his arms, and that we may be united in holy family love. Ah, my Alfred, can I tell you how I miss you, how I weep for you. My thoughts are with you always, I think of nothing but you, I live for nothing but you and our dear baby. If you do not come back to me soon, I shall die, and our child will die. But no, you cannot come back to me. But I can come to you, come to England with our child. If you do not wish to present me to your good mother and father, you can meet me in some town, some city, for I shall be so frightened to be alone in England with my child, and no one to take care of us. Yet I must come to you, I must bring my child, my little Alfred to his father, the big, beautiful Alfred that I love so much. Oh, write and tell me where I shall come. I have some money, I am not a penniless creature. I have money for myself and my dear baby —'

I read to the end. It was signed: 'Your very happy and still more unhappy Elise.' I suppose I must have been smiling.

'I can see it makes you laugh,' said Mrs. Goyte, sardonically. I looked up at her.

'It's a love-letter, I know that,' she said. 'There's too many "Alfreds" in it.'

'One too many,' I said.

'Oh, yes — And what does she say – Eliza? We know her name's Eliza, that's another thing.' She grimaced a little, looking up at me with a mocking laugh.

'Where did you get this letter?' I said.

'Postman gave it me last week.'

'And is your husband at home?'

'I expect him home to-night. He's been wounded, you know, and we've been applying for him home. He was home about six weeks ago – he's been in Scotland since then. Oh, he was wounded in the leg. Yes, he's all right, a great strapping fellow. But he's lame, he limps a bit. He expects he'll get his discharge – but I don't think he will. We married? We've been married six years – and he joined up the first day of the war. Oh, he thought he'd like the life. He's been through the South African War. No, he was sick of it, fed up. I'm living with his father and mother – I've no home of my own now. My people had a big farm – over a thousand acres – in Oxfordshire. Not like here – no. Oh,

357

they're very good to me, his father and mother. Oh, yes, they couldn't be better. They think more of me than of their own daughters. But it's not like being in a place of your own, is it? You can't *really* do as you like. No, there's only me and his father and mother at home. Before the war? Oh, he was anything. He had a good education – but he liked the farming better. Then he was a chauffeur. That's how he knew French. He was driving in France for a long time —'

At this point the peacocks came round the corner on a puff of wind.

'Hello, Joey!' she called, and one of the birds came forward, on delicate legs. Its grey speckled back was very elegant, it rolled its full, dark-blue neck as it moved to her. She crouched down. 'Joey, dear,' she said, in an odd, saturnine caressive voice, 'you're bound to find me, aren't you?' She put her face forward, and the bird rolled his neck, almost touching her face with his beak, as if kissing her.

'He loves you,' I said.

She twisted her face up at me with a laugh.

'Yes,' she said, 'he loves me, Joey does,' – then, to the bird – 'and I love Joey, don't I. I *do* love Joey.' And she smoothed his feathers for a moment. Then she rose, saying: 'He's an affectionate bird.'

I smiled at the roll of her 'bir-rrd'.

'Oh, yes, he is,' she protested. 'He came with me from my home seven years ago. Those others are his descendants – but they're not like Joey – *are they, dee-urr?*' Her voice rose at the end with a witch-like cry.

Then she forgot the bird in the cart-shed and turned to business again.

'Won't you read that letter?' she said. 'Read it, so that I know what it says.'

'It's rather behind his back,' I said.

'Oh, never mind him,' she cried. 'He's been behind my back long enough – all these four years. If he never did no worse things behind my back than I do behind his, he wouldn't have cause to grumble. You read me what it says.'

Now I felt a distinct reluctance to do as she bid, and yet I began – 'My dear Alfred.'

'I guessed that much,' she said. 'Eliza's dear Alfred.' She laughed. 'How do you say it in French? *Eliza?*'

I told her, and she repeated the name with great contempt – *Elise*.

'Go on,' she said. 'You're not reading.'

So I began – 'I have been thinking of you sometimes – have you been thinking of me —?'

'Of several others as well, beside her, I'll wager,' said Mrs. Goyte.

'Probably not,' said I, and continued. 'A dear little baby was born here a week ago. Ah, can I tell you my feelings when I take my darling little brother into my arms —'

'I'll bet it's *his*,' cried Mrs. Goyte.

'No,' I said. 'It's her mother's.'

'Don't you believe it,' she cried. 'It's a blind. You mark it's her own right enough – and his.'

'No,' I said, 'it's her mother's.' 'He has sweet smiling eyes, but not like your beautiful English eyes —'

She suddenly struck her hand on her skirt with a wild motion, and bent down, doubled with laughter. Then she rose and covered her face with her hand.

'I'm forced to laugh at the beautiful English eyes,' she said.

'Aren't his eyes beautiful?' I asked.

'Oh, yes – *very*! Go on! – *Joey, dear, dee-urr, Joey!*' – this to the peacock.

– 'Er – We miss you very much. We all miss you. We wish you were here to see the darling baby. Ah, Alfred, how happy we were when you stayed with us. We all loved you so much. My mother will call the baby Alfred so that we shall never forget you —'

'Of course it's his right enough,' cried Mrs. Goyte.

'No,' I said. 'It's the mother's.' 'Er – My mother is very well. My father came home yesterday – on leave. He is delighted with his son, my little brother, and wishes to have him named after you, because you were so good to us all in that terrible time, which I shall never forget. I must weep now when I think of it. Well, you are far away in England, and perhaps I shall never see you again. How did you find your dear mother and father? I am so happy that your wound is better, and that you can nearly walk —'

'How did he find his dear *wife*?' cried Mrs. Goyte. 'He never told her he had one. Think of taking the poor girl in like that!'

'We are so pleased when you write to us. Yet now you are in England you will forget the family you served so well —'

'A bit too well – eh, *Joey*?' cried the wife.

'If it had not been for you we should not be alive now, to grieve and to rejoice in this life, that is so hard for us. But we have recovered some of our losses, and no longer feel the burden of poverty. The little Alfred

359

is a great comfort to me. I hold him to my breast and think of the big, good Alfred, and I weep to think that those times of suffering were perhaps the times of a great happiness that is gone for ever.'

'Oh, but isn't it a shame, to take a poor girl in like that!' cried Mrs. Goyte. 'Never to let on that he was married, and raise her hopes – I call it beastly, I do.'

'You don't know,' I said. 'You know how anxious women are to fall in love, wife or no wife. How could he help it, if she was determined to fall in love with him?'

'He could have helped it if he'd wanted.'

'Well,' I said, 'we aren't all heroes.'

'Oh, but that's different! The big, good Alfred! – did ever you hear such tommy-rot in your life! Go on – what does she say at the end?'

'Er – We shall be pleased to hear of your life in England. We all send many kind regards to your good parents. I wish you all happiness for your future days. Your very affectionate and ever-grateful, Elise.'

There was silence for a moment, during which Mrs. Goyte remained with her head dropped, sinister and abstracted. Suddenly she lifted her face, and her eyes flashed.

'Oh, but I call it beastly, I call it mean, to take a girl in like that.'

'Nay,' I said. 'Probably he hasn't taken her in at all. Do you think those French girls are such poor innocent things? I guess she's a great deal more downy than he.'

'Oh, he's one of the biggest fools that ever walked,' she cried.

'There you are!' said I.

'But it's his child right enough,' she said.

'I don't think so,' said I.

'I'm sure of it.'

'Oh, well,' I said, 'if you prefer to think that way.'

'What other reason has she for writing like that —?'

I went out into the road and looked at the cattle.

'Who is this driving the cows?' I said. She too came out.

'It's the boy from the next farm,' she said.

'Oh, well,' said I, 'those Belgian girls! You never know where their letters will end. And, after all, it's his affair – you needn't bother.'

'Oh —!' she cried with scorn – 'it's not *me* that bothers. But it's the nasty meanness of it – me writing him such loving letters' – she put her hand before her face and laughed malevolently – 'and sending him parcels all the time. You bet he fed that gurrl on my parcels – I know he did. It's just like him. I'll bet they laughed together over my letters. I'll bet anything they did —'

'Nay,' said I. 'He'd burn your letters for fear they'd give him away.'

There was a black look on her yellow face. Suddenly a voice was heard calling. She poked her head out of the shed, and answered coolly:

'All right!' Then turning to me: 'That's his mother looking after me.'

She laughed into my face, witch-like, and we turned down the road.

When I awoke, the morning after this episode, I found the house darkened with deep, soft snow, which had blown against the large west windows, covering them with a screen. I went outside, and saw the valley all white and ghastly below me, the trees beneath black and thin-looking like wire, the rock-faces dark between the glistening shroud, and the sky above sombre, heavy, yellowish-dark, much too heavy for this world below of hollow bluey whiteness figured with black. I felt I was in a valley of the dead. And I sensed I was a prisoner, for the snow was everywhere deep, and drifted in places. So all the morning I remained indoors, looking up the drive at the shrubs so heavily plumed with snow, at the gate-posts raised high with a foot or more of extra whiteness. Or I looked down into the white-and-black valley that was utterly motionless and beyond life, a hollow sarcophagus.

Nothing stirred the whole day – no plume fell off the shrubs, the valley was as abstracted as a grove of death. I looked over at the tiny, half-buried farms away on the bare uplands beyond the valley hollow, and I thought of Tible in the snow, of the black witch-like little Mrs. Goyte. And the snow seemed to lay me bare to influences I wanted to escape.

In the faint glow of the half-clear light that came about four o'clock in the afternoon, I was roused to see a motion in the snow away below, near where the thorn trees stood very black and dwarfed, like a little savage group, in the dismal white. I watched closely. Yes, there was a flapping and a struggle – a big bird, it must be, labouring in the snow. I wondered. Our biggest birds, in the valley, were the large hawks that often hung flickering opposite my windows, level with me, but high above some prey on the steep valley-side. This was much too big for a hawk – too big for any known bird. I searched in my mind for the largest English wild bird, geese, buzzards.

Still it laboured and strove, then was still, a dark spot, then struggled again. I went out of the house and down the steep slope, at risk of breaking my leg between the rocks. I knew the ground so well – and yet I got well shaken before I drew near the thorn trees.

Yes, it was a bird. It was Joey. It was the grey-brown peacock with a blue neck. He was snow-wet and spent.

'Joey – Joey, de-urr!' I said, staggering unevenly towards him. He looked so pathetic, rowing and struggling in the snow, too spent to rise, his blue neck stretching out and lying sometimes on the snow, his eye closing and opening quickly, his crest all battered.

'Joey dee-urr!' I said caressingly to him. And at last he lay still, blinking, in the surged and furrowed snow, whilst I came near and touched him, stroked him, gathering him under my arm. He stretched his long, wetted neck away from me as I held him, none the less he was quiet in my arm, too tired, perhaps, to struggle. Still he held his poor, crested head away from me, and seemed sometimes to droop, to wilt, as if he might suddenly die.

He was not so heavy as I expected, yet it was a struggle to get up to the house with him again. We set him down, not too near the fire, and gently wiped him with cloths. He submitted, only now and then stretched his soft neck away from us, avoiding us helplessly. Then we set warm food by him. I put it to his beak, tried to make him eat. But he ignored it. He seemed to be ignorant of what we were doing, recoiled inside himself inexplicably. So we put him in a basket with cloths, and left him crouching oblivious. His food we put near him. The blinds were drawn, the house was warm, it was night. Sometimes he stirred, but mostly he huddled still leaning his queer crested head on one side. He touched no food, and took no heed of sounds or movements. We talked of brandy or stimulants. But I realised we had best leave him alone.

In the night, however, we heard him thumping about. I got up anxiously with a candle. He had eaten some food, and scattered more, making a mess. And he was perched on the back of a heavy arm-chair. So I concluded he was recovered, or recovering.

The next day was clear, and the snow had frozen, so I decided to carry him back to Tible. He consented, after various flappings, to sit in a big fish-bag with his battered head peeping out with wild uneasiness. And so I set off with him slithering down into the valley, making good progress down in the pale shadow beside the rushing waters, then climbing painfully up the arrested white valley-side, plumed with clusters of young pine trees, into the paler white radiance of the snowy, upper regions, where the wind cut fine. Joey seemed to watch all the time with wide, anxious, unseeing eye, brilliant and inscrutable. As I drew near to Tible township he stirred violently in the bag, though I do not know if he recognised the place. Then, as I came to the sheds, he looked sharply from side to side, and stretched his neck out long. I was a little afraid of him. He gave a loud, vehement yell, opening his sinister beak, and I stood still, looking at him as he struggled in the bag, shaken myself by his struggles, yet not thinking to release him.

Mrs. Goyte came darting past the end of the house, her head sticking forward in sharp scrutiny. She saw me, and came forward.

'Have you got Joey?' she cried sharply, as if I were a thief.

I opened the bag, and he flopped out, flapping as if he hated the touch of the snow now. She gathered him up, and put her lips to his beak. She was flushed and handsome, her eyes bright, her hair slack, thick, but more witch-like than ever. She did not speak.

She had been followed by a grey-haired woman with a round, rather sallow face and a slightly hostile bearing.

'Did you bring him with you, then?' she asked sharply. I answered that I had rescued him the previous evening.

From the background slowly approached a slender man with a grey moustache and large patches on his trousers.

'You've got 'im back 'gain, ah see,' he said to his daughter-in-law. His wife explained how I had found Joey.

'Ah,' went on the grey man. 'It wor our Alfred scarred him off, back your life. He must'a flyed ower t'valley. Tha ma' thank thy stars as 'e wor fun, Maggie. 'E'd a bin froze. They a bit nesh, you know,' he concluded to me.

'They are,' I answered. 'This isn't their country.'

'No, it isna,' replied Mr. Goyte. He spoke very slowly and deliberately, quietly, as if the soft pedal were always down in his voice. He looked at his daughter-in-law as she crouched, flushed and dark, before the peacock, which would lay its long blue neck for a moment along her lap. In spite of his grey moustache and thin grey hair, the elderly man had a face young and almost delicate, like a young man's. His blue eyes twinkled with some inscrutable source of pleasure, his skin was fine and tender, his nose delicately arched. His grey hair being slightly ruffled, he had a debonair look, as of a youth who is in love.

'We mun tell 'im it's come,' he said slowly, and turning he called: 'Alfred – Alfred! Wheer's ter gotten to?'

Then he turned again to the group.

'Get up then, Maggie, lass, get up wi' thee. Tha ma'es too much o' th' bod.'

A young man approached, wearing rough khaki and knee-breeches. He was Danish-looking, broad at the loins.

'I's come back then,' said the father to the son; 'leastwise, he's bin browt back, flyed ower the Griff Low.'

The son looked at me. He had a devil-may-care bearing, his cap on one side, his hands stuck in the front pockets of his breeches. But he said nothing.

'Shall you come in a minute, Master,' said the elderly woman, to me.

'Ay, come in an' ha'e a cup o' tea or summat. You'll do wi' summat, carrin' that bod. Come on, Maggie wench, let's go in.'

So we went indoors, into the rather stuffy, overcrowded living-room, that was too cosy, and too warm. The son followed last, standing in the doorway. The father talked to me. Maggie put out the tea-cups. The mother went into the dairy again.

'Tha'lt rouse thysen up a bit again, now, Maggie,' the father-in-law said – and then to me: ' 'Ers not bin very bright sin' Alfred come whoam, an' the bod flyed awee. 'E come whoam a Wednesday night, Alfred did. But ay, you knowed, didna yer. Ay, 'e comed 'a Wednesday – an' I reckon there wor a bit of a to-do between 'em worn't there, Maggie?'

He twinkled maliciously to his daughter-in-law, who flushed, brilliant and handsome.

'Oh, be quiet, father. You're wound up, by the sound of you,' she said to him, as if crossly. But she could never be cross with him.

' 'Ers got 'er colour back this mornin',' continued the father-in-law slowly. 'It's bin heavy weather wi' 'er this last two days. Ay – 'er's bin north-east sin' 'er seed you a Wednesday.'

'Father, do stop talking. You'd wear the leg off an iron pot. I can't think where you've found your tongue, all of a sudden,' said Maggie, with caressive sharpness.

'Ah've found it wheer I lost it. Aren't goin' ter come in an' sit thee down, Alfred?'

But Alfred turned and disappeared.

' 'E's got th' monkey on 'is back ower this letter job,' said the father secretly to me. 'Mother, 'er knows nowt about it. Lot o' tom-foolery, isn't it? Ay! What's good o' makkin' a peck o' trouble over what's far enough off, an' ned niver come no nigher. No – not a smite o' use.'

364

That's what I tell 'er. 'Er should ta'e no notice on't. Ty, what can y' expect.'

The mother came in again, and the talk became general. Maggie flashed her eyes at me from time to time, complacent and satisfied, moving among the men. I paid her little compliments, which she did not seem to hear. She attended to me with a kind of sinister witch-like graciousness, her dark head ducked between her shoulders, at once humble and powerful. She was happy as a child attending to her father-in-law and to me. But there was something ominous between her eye-brows, as if a dark moth were settled there – and something ominous in her bent, hulking bearing.

She sat on a low stool by the fire, near her father-in-law. Her head was dropped, she seemed in a state of abstraction. From time to time she would suddenly recover, and look up at us, laughing and chatting. Then she would forget again. Yet in her hulked black forgetting she seemed very near to us.

The door having been opened, the peacock came slowly in, prancing calmly. He went near to her and crouched down, coiling his blue neck. She glanced at him, but almost as if she did not observe him. The bird sat silent, seeming to sleep, and the woman also sat hulked and silent, seemingly oblivious. Then once more there was a heavy step, and Al-fred entered. He looked at his wife, and he looked at the peacock crouching by her. He stood large in the doorway, his hands stuck in front of him, in his breeches pockets. Nobody spoke. He turned on his heel and went out again.

I rose to go. Maggie started as if coming to herself.

'Must you go?' she asked, rising and coming near to me, standing in front of me, twisting her head sideways and looking up at me. 'Can't you stop a bit longer? We can all be cosy to-day, there's nothing to do outdoors.' And she laughed, showing her teeth oddly. She had a long chin.

I said I must go. The peacock uncoiled and coiled again his long blue neck, as he lay on the hearth. Maggie still stood close in front of me, so that I was acutely aware of my waistcoat buttons.

'Oh, well,' she said, 'you'll come again, won't you? Do come again.'

I promised.

'Come to tea one day – yes, do!'

I promised – one day.

The moment I went out of her presence I ceased utterly to exist for her – as utterly as I ceased to exist for Joey. With her curious abstractedness she forgot me again immediately. I knew it as I left her. Yet she seemed almost in physical contact with me while I was with her.

The sky was all pallid again, yellowish. When I went out there was no sun; the snow was blue and cold. I hurried away down the hill, musing on Maggie. The road made a loop down the sharp face of the slope. As I went crunching over the laborious snow I became aware of a figure striding down the steep scarp to intercept me. It was a man with his hands in front of him, half stuck in his breeches pockets, and his shoulders square – a real farmer of the hills; Alfred, of course. He waited for me by the stone fence.

'Excuse me,' he said as I came up.

I came to a halt in front of him and looked into his sullen blue eyes. He had a certain odd haughtiness on his brows. But his blue eyes stared insolently at me.

'Do you know anything about a letter – in French – that my wife opened – a letter of mine —?'

'Yes,' said I. 'She asked me to read it to her.'

He looked square at me. He did not know exactly how to feel.

'What was there in it?' he asked.

'Why?' I said. 'Don't you know?'

'She makes out she's burnt it,' he said.

'Without showing it you?' I asked.

He nodded slightly. He seemed to be meditating as to what line of action he should take. He wanted to know the contents of the letter: he must know: and therefore he must ask me, for evidently his wife had taunted him. At the same time, no doubt, he would like to wreak untold vengeance on my unfortunate person. So he eyed me, and I eyed him, and neither of us spoke. He did not want to repeat his requests to me. And yet I only looked at him, and considered.

Suddenly he threw back his head and glanced down the valley. Then he changed his position – he was a horse-soldier. Then he looked at me more confidentially.

'She burnt the blasted thing before I saw it,' he said.

'Well,' I answered slowly, 'she doesn't know herself what was in it.'

He continued to watch me narrowly. I grinned to myself. 'I didn't like to read her out what there was in it,' I continued.

He suddenly flushed so that the veins in his neck stood out, and he stirred again uncomfortably.

366

'The Belgian girl said her baby had been born a week ago, and that they were going to call it Alfred,' I told him.

He met my eyes. I was grinning. He began to grin, too.

'Good luck to her,' he said.

'Best of luck,' said I.

'And what did you tell *her*?' he asked.

'That the baby belonged to the old mother – that it was brother to your girl, who was writing to you as a friend of the family.'

He stood smiling, with the long, subtle malice of a farmer.

'And did she take it in?' he asked.

'As much as she took anything else.'

He stood grinning fixedly. Then he broke into a short laugh.

'Good for *her*!' he exclaimed cryptically.

And then he laughed aloud once more, evidently feeling he had won a big move in his contest with his wife.

'What about the other woman?' I asked.

'Who?'

'Elise.'

'Oh' – he shifted uneasily – 'she was all right —'

'You'll be getting back to her,' I said.

He looked at me. Then he made a grimace with his mouth.

'Not me,' he said. 'Back your life it's a plant.'

'You don't think the *cher petit bébé* is a little Alfred?'

'It might be,' he said.

'Only might?'

'Yes – an' there's lots of mites in a pound of cheese.' He laughed boisterously but uneasily.

'What did she say, exactly?' he asked.

I began to repeat, as well as I could, the phrases of the letter:

'*Mon cher Alfred – Figure-toi comme je suis désolée —*'

He listened with some confusion. When I had finished all I could remember, he said:

'They know how to pitch you out a letter, those Belgian lasses.'

'Practice,' said I.

'They get plenty,' he said.

There was a pause.

'Oh, well,' he said. 'I've never got that letter, anyhow.'

The wind blew fine and keen, in the sunshine, across the snow. I blew my nose and prepared to depart.

'And *she* doesn't know anything?' he continued, jerking his head up the hill in the direction of Tible.

'She knows nothing but what I've said – that is, if she really burnt the letter.'

'I believe she burnt it,' he said, 'for spite. She's a little devil, she is. But I shall have it out with her.' His jaw was stubborn and sullen. Then suddenly he turned to me with a new note.

'Why?' he said. 'Why didn't you wring that b—— peacock's neck – that b—— Joey?'

'Why?' I said. 'What for?'

'I hate the brute,' he said. 'I had a shot at him —'

I laughed. He stood and mused.

'Poor little Elise,' he murmured.

'Was she small – petite?' I asked. He jerked up his head.

'No,' he said. 'Rather tall.'

'Taller than your wife, I suppose.'

Again he looked into my eyes. And then once more he went into a loud burst of laughter that made the still, snow-deserted valley clap again.

'God, it's a knock-out!' he said, thoroughly amused. Then he stood at ease, one foot out, his hands in his breeches pockets, in front of him, his head thrown back, a handsome figure of a man.

'But I'll do that blasted Joey in —' he mused.

I ran down the hill, shouting with laughter.

YOU TOUCHED ME

THE Pottery House was a square, ugly, brick house girt in by the wall that enclosed the whole grounds of the pottery itself. To be sure, a privet hedge partly masked the house and its ground from the pottery-yard and works: but only partly. Through the hedge could be seen the desolate yard, and the many-windowed, factory-like pottery, over the hedge could be seen the chimneys and the outhouses. But inside the hedge, a pleasant garden and lawn sloped down to a willow pool, which had once supplied the works.

The Pottery itself was now closed, the great doors of the yard permanently shut. No more the great crates with yellow straw showing through stood in stacks by the packing-shed. No more the drays drawn by great horses rolled down the hill with a high load. No more the pottery-lasses in their clay-coloured overalls, their faces and hair splashed with grey fine mud, shrieked and larked with the men. All that was over.

'We like it much better – oh, much better – quieter,' said Matilda Rockley.

'Oh, yes,' assented Emmie Rockley, her sister.

'I'm sure you do,' agreed the visitor.

But whether the two Rockley girls really like it better, or whether they only imagined they did, is a question. Certainly their lives were much more grey and dreary now that the grey clay had ceased to spatter its mud and silt its dust over the premises. They did not quite realise how they missed the shrieking, shouting lasses, whom they had known all their lives and disliked so much.

Matilda and Emmie were already old maids. In a thorough industrial district, it is not easy for the girls who have expectations above the common to find husbands. The ugly industrial town was full of men, young men who were ready to marry. But they were all colliers or pottery-hands, mere workmen. The Rockley girls would have about ten thousand pounds each when their father died: ten thousand pounds' worth of profitable house-property. It was not to be sneezed at: they felt so themselves, and refrained from sneezing away such a fortune on any mere member of the proletariat. Consequently, bank-clerks or nonconformist clergymen or even school-teachers having failed to come forward, Matilda had begun to give up all idea of ever leaving the Pottery House.

Matilda was a tall, thin, graceful, fair girl with a rather large nose. She was the Mary to Emmie's Martha: that is, Matilda loved painting and music, and read a good many novels, whilst Emmie looked after the housekeeping. Emmie was shorter, plumper than her sister, and she had no accomplishments. She looked up to Matilda, whose mind was naturally refined and sensible.

In their quiet, melancholy way, two girls were happy. Their mother was dead. Their father was ill also. He was an intelligent man who had had some education, but preferred to remain as if he were one with the rest of the working people. He had a passion for music and played the violin pretty well. But now he was getting old, he was very ill, dying of a kidney disease. He had been rather a heavy whisky-drinker.

This quiet household, with one servant-maid, lived on year after year in the Pottery House. Friends came in, the girls went out, the father drank himself more and more ill. Outside in the street there was a continual racket of the colliers and their dogs and children. But inside the pottery wall was a deserted quiet.

In all this ointment there was one little fly. Ted Rockley, the father of the girls, had had four daughters, and no son. As his girls grew, he felt angry at finding himself always in a household of women. He went off to London and adopted a boy out of a Charity Institution. Emmie was fourteen years old, and Matilda sixteen, when their father arrived home with his prodigy, the boy of six, Hadrian.

Hadrian was just an ordinary boy from a Charity Home, with ordinary brownish hair and ordinary bluish eyes and of ordinary rather Cockney speech. The Rockley girls – there were three at home at the time of his arrival – had resented his being sprung on them. He, with his watchful, charity-institution instinct, knew this at once. Though he was only six years old, Hadrian had a subtle, jeering look on his face when he regarded the three young women. They insisted he should address them as Cousin: Cousin Flora, Cousin Matilda, Cousin Emmie. He complied, but there seemed a mockery in his tone.

The girls, however, were kind-hearted by nature. Flora married and left home. Hadrian did very much as he pleased with Matilda and Emmie, though they had certain strictnesses. He grew up in the Pottery House and about the Pottery premises, went to an elementary school, and was invariably called Hadrian Rockley. He regarded Cousin Matilda and Cousin Emmie with a certain laconic indifference, was quiet and reticent in his ways. The girls called him sly, but that was unjust. He was merely cautious, and without frankness. His uncle, Ted Rockley, understood him tacitly, their natures were somewhat akin. Hadrian and the elderly man had a real but unemotional regard for one another.

When he was thirteen years old the boy was sent to a High School in the County town. He did not like it. His Cousin Matilda had longed to make a little gentleman of him, but he refused to be made. He would give a little contemptuous curve to his lip, and take on a shy, charity-boy grin, when refinement was thrust upon him. He played truant from the High School, sold his books, his cap with its badge, even his very scarf and pocket-handkerchief, to his school-fellows, and went raking off heaven knows where with the money. So he spent two very unsatisfactory years.

When he was fifteen he announced that he wanted to leave England to go to the Colonies. He had kept touch with the Home. The Rockleys knew that, when Hadrian made a declaration, in his quiet, half-jeering manner, it was worse than useless to oppose him. So at last the boy departed, going to Canada under the protection of the Institution to which he had belonged. He said good-bye to the Rockleys, without a word of thanks, and parted, it seemed, without a pang. Matilda and Emmie wept often to think of how he left them: even on their father's face a queer look came. But Hadrian wrote fairly regularly from Canada. He had entered some electricity works near Montreal, and was doing well.

At last, however, the war came. In his turn, Hadrian joined up and came to Europe. The Rockleys saw nothing of him. They lived on, just the same, in the Pottery House. Ted Rockley was dying of a sort of dropsy, and in his heart he wanted to see the boy. When the Armistice was signed, Hadrian had a long leave, and wrote that he was coming home to the Pottery House.

The girls were terribly fluttered. To tell the truth, they were a little afraid of Hadrian. Matilda, tall and thin, was frail in her health, both girls were worn with nursing their father. To have Hadrian, a young man of twenty-one in the house with them, after he had left them so coldly five years before, was a trying circumstance.

They were in a flutter. Emmie persuaded her father to have his bed made finally in the morning-room downstairs, whilst his room upstairs was prepared for Hadrian. This was done, and preparations were going on for the arrival, when, at ten o'clock in the morning, the young man suddenly turned up, quite unexpectedly. Cousin Emmie, with her hair bobbed up in absurd little bobs round her forehead, was busily polishing the stair-rods, while Cousin Matilda was in the kitchen washing the drawing-room ornaments in a lather, her sleeves rolled back on her thin arms, and her head tied up oddly and coquettishly in a duster.

Cousin Matilda blushed deep with mortification when the self-possessed young man walked in with his kit-bag, and put his cap on the sewing-machine. He was little and self-confident, with a curious neatness about him that still suggested the Charity Institution. His face was brown, he had a small moustache, he was vigorous enough in his smallness.

'*Well*, is it Hadrian!' exclaimed Cousin Matilda, wringing the lather off her hand. 'We didn't expect you till to-morrow.'

'I got off Monday night,' said Hadrian, glancing round the room.

'Fancy!' said Cousin Matilda. Then, having dried her hands, she went forward, held out her hand, and said:

'How are you?'

'Quite well, thank you,' said Hadrian.

'You're quite a man,' said Cousin Matilda.

Hadrian glanced at her. She did not look her best: so thin, so large-nosed, with that pink-and-white checked duster tied round her head. She felt her disadvantage. But she had had a good deal of suffering and sorrow, she did not mind any more.

The servant entered – one that did not know Hadrian.

'Come and see my father,' said Cousin Matilda.

In the hall they roused Cousin Emmie like a partridge from cover. She was on the stairs pushing the bright stair-rods into place. Instinctively her hand went to the little knobs, her front hair bobbed on her forehead.

'Why!' she exclaimed, crossly. 'What have you come to-day for?'

'I got off a day earlier,' said Hadrian, and his man's voice so deep and unexpected was like a blow to Cousin Emmie.

'Well, you've caught us in the midst of it,' she said, with resentment. Then all three went into the middle room.

Mr. Rockley was dressed – that is, he had on his trousers and socks – but he was resting on the bed, propped up just under the window, from whence he could see his beloved and resplendent garden, where tulips and apple trees were ablaze. He did not look as ill as he was, for the water puffed him up, and his face kept its colour. His stomach was much swollen.

He glanced round swiftly, turning his eyes without turning his head. He was the wreck of a handsome, well-built man.

Seeing Hadrian, a queer, unwilling smile went over his face. The young man greeted him sheepishly.

'You wouldn't make a life-guardsman,' he said. 'Do you want something to eat?'

Hadrian looked round – as if for the meal.

'I don't mind,' he said.

'What shall you have – egg and bacon?' asked Emmie shortly.

'Yes, I don't mind,' said Hadrian.

The sisters went down to the kitchen, and sent the servant to finish the stairs.

'Isn't he *altered*?' said Matilda, *sotto voce*.

'Isn't he!' said Cousin Emmie. '*What* a little man!'

They both made a grimace, and laughed nervously.

'Get the frying-pan,' said Emmie to Matilda.

'But he's as cocky as ever,' said Matilda, narrowing her eyes and shaking her head knowingly, as she handed the frying-pan.

'Mannie!' said Emmie sarcastically. Hadrian's new-fledged, cocksure manliness evidently found no favour in her eyes.

'Oh, he's not bad,' said Matilda. 'You don't want to be prejudiced against him.'

'I'm not prejudiced against him, I think he's all right for looks,' said Emmie, 'but there's too much of the little mannie about him.'

'Fancy catching us like this,' said Matilda.

'They've no thought for anything,' said Emmie with contempt. 'You go up and get dressed, our Matilda. I don't care about him. I can see to things, and you can talk to him. I shan't.'

'He'll talk to my father,' said Matilda, meaningful.

'*Sly* —!' exclaimed Emmie, with a grimace.

The sisters believed that Hadrian had come hoping to get something out of their father – hoping for a legacy. And they were not at all sure he would not get it.

Matilda went upstairs to change. She had thought it all out how she would receive Hadrian, and impress him. And he had caught her with her head tied up in a duster, and her thin arms in a basin of lather. But she did not care. She now dressed herself most scrupulously, carefully folded her long, beautiful, blonde hair, touched her pallor with a little rouge, and put her long string of exquisite crystal beads over her soft

373

green dress. Now she looked elegant, like a heroine in a magazine illustration, and almost as unreal.

She found Hadrian and her father talking away. The young man was short of speech as a rule, but he could find his tongue with his 'uncle'. They were both sipping a glass of brandy, and smoking, and chatting like a pair of old cronies. Hadrian was telling about Canada. He was going back there when his leave was up.

'You wouldn't like to stop in England, then?' said Mr. Rockley.

'No, I wouldn't stop in England,' said Hadrian.

'How's that? There's plenty of electricians here,' said Mr. Rockley.

'Yes. But there's too much difference between the men and the employers over here – too much of that for me,' said Hadrian.

The sick man looked at him narrowly, with oddly smiling eyes.

'That's it, is it?' he replied.

Matilda heard and understood. 'So that's your big idea, is it, my little man,' she said to herself. She had always said of Hadrian that he had no proper *respect* for anybody or anything, that he was sly and *common*. She went down to the kitchen for a *sotto voce* confab with Emmie.

'He thinks a rare lot of himself!' she whispered.

'He's somebody, he is!' said Emmie with contempt.

'He thinks there's too much difference between masters and men over here,' said Matilda.

'Is it any different in Canada?' asked Emmie.

'Oh yes – democratic,' replied Matilda. 'He thinks they're all on a level over there.'

'Ay, well, he's over here now,' said Emmie dryly, 'so he can keep his place.'

As they talked they saw the young man sauntering down the garden, looking casually at the flowers. He had his hands in his pockets, and his soldier's cap neatly on his head. He looked quite at his ease, as if in possession. The two women, fluttered, watched him through the window.

'We know what he's come for,' said Emmie, churlishly. Matilda looked a long time at the neat khaki figure. It had something of the charity-boy about it still; but now it was a man's figure, laconic, charged with plebeian energy. She thought of a derisive passion in his voice as he had declaimed against the propertied classes, to her father.

'You don't know, Emmie. Perhaps he's not come for that,' she rebuked her sister. They were both thinking of the money.

They were still watching the young soldier. He stood away at the bottom of the garden, with his back to them, his hands in his pockets, looking into the water of the willow pond. Matilda's dark blue eyes had a strange, full look in them, the lids, with the faint blue veins showing, dropped rather low. She carried her head light and high, but she had a look of pain. The young man at the bottom of the garden turned and looked up the path. Perhaps he saw them through the window. Matilda moved into shadow.

That afternoon their father seemed weak and ill. He was easily exhausted. The doctor came, and told Matilda that the sick man might die suddenly at any moment – but then he might not. They must be prepared.

So the day passed, and the next. Hadrian made himself at home. He went about in the morning in his brownish jersey and his khaki trousers, collarless, his bare neck showing. He explored the pottery premises, as if he had some secret purpose in so doing, he talked with Mr. Rockley, when the sick man had strength. The two girls were always angry when the two men sat talking together like cronies. Yet it was chiefly a kind of politics they talked.

On the second day after Hadrian's arrival, Matilda sat with her father in the evening. She was drawing a picture which she wanted to copy. It was very still, Hadrian was gone out somewhere, no one knew where, and Emmie was busy. Mr. Rockley reclined on his bed, looking out in silence over his evening-sunny garden.

'If anything happens to me, Matilda,' he said, 'you won't sell this house – you'll stop here —'

Matilda's eyes took their slightly haggard look as she stared at her father.

'Well, we couldn't do anything else,' she said.

'You don't know what you might do,' he said. 'Everything is left to you and Emmie, equally. You do as you like with it – only don't sell this house, don't part with it.'

'No,' she said.

'And give Hadrian my watch and chain, and a hundred pounds out of what's in the bank – and help him if he ever wants helping. I haven't put his name in the will.'

'Your watch and chain, and a hundred pounds – yes. But you'll be here when he goes back to Canada, father.'

'You never know what'll happen,' said her father.

Matilda sat and watched him, with her full, haggard eyes, for a long

375

time, as if tranced. She saw that he knew he must go soon – she saw like a clairvoyant.

Later on she told Emmie what her father had said about the watch and chain and the money.

'What right has *he* – *he*' – meaning Hadrian – 'to my father's watch and chain – what has it to do with him? Let him have the money, and get off,' said Emmie. She loved her father.

That night Matilda sat late in her room. Her heart was anxious and breaking, her mind seemed entranced. She was too much entranced even to weep, and all the time she thought of her father, only her father. At last she felt she must go to him.

It was near midnight. She went along the passage and to his room. There was a faint light from the moon outside. She listened at his door. Then she softly opened and entered. The room was faintly dark. She heard a movement on the bed.

'Are you asleep?' she said softly, advancing to the side of the bed.

'Are you asleep?' she repeated gently, as she stood at the side of the bed. And she reached her hand in the darkness to touch his forehead. Delicately, her fingers met the nose and the eyebrows, she laid her fine, delicate hand on his brow. It seemed fresh and smooth – very fresh and smooth. A sort of surprise stirred her, in her entranced state. But it could not waken her. Gently, she leaned over the bed and stirred her fingers over the low-growing hair on his brow.

'Can't you sleep to-night?' she said.

There was a quick stirring in the bed. 'Yes, I can,' a voice answered. It was Hadrian's voice. She started away. Instantly she was wakened from her late-at-night trance. She remembered that her father was downstairs, that Hadrian had his room. She stood in the darkness as if stung.

'Is it you, Hadrian?' she said. 'I thought it was my father.' She was so startled, so shocked, that she could not move. The young man gave an uncomfortable laugh, and turned in his bed.

At last she got out of the room. When she was back in her own room, in the light, and her door was closed, she stood holding up her hand that had touched him, as if it were hurt. She was almost too shocked, she could not endure.

'Well,' said her calm and weary mind, 'it was only a mistake, why take any notice of it.'

But she could not reason her feelings so easily. She suffered, feeling herself in a false position. Her right hand, which she had laid so gently on his face, on his fresh skin, ached now, as if it were really injured. She could not forgive Hadrian for the mistake: it made her dislike him deeply.

Hadrian too slept badly. He had been awakened by the opening of the door, and had not realised what the question meant. But the soft, straying tenderness of her hand on his face startled something out of his soul. He was a charity-boy, aloof and more or less at bay. The fragile exquisiteness of her caress startled him most, revealed unknown things to him.

In the morning she could feel the consciousness in his eyes, when she came downstairs. She tried to bear herself as if nothing at all had happened, and she succeeded. She had the calm self-control, self-indifference, of one who has suffered and borne her suffering. She looked at him from her darkish, almost drugged blue eyes, she met the spark of consciousness in his eyes, and quenched it. And with her long, fine hand she put the sugar in his coffee.

But she could not control him as she thought she could. He had a keen memory stinging his mind, a new set of sensations working in his consciousness. Something new was alert in him. At the back of his reticent, guarded mind he kept his secret alive and vivid. She was at his mercy, for he was unscrupulous, his standard was not her standard.

He looked at her curiously. She was not beautiful, her nose was too large, her chin was too small, her neck was too thin. But her skin was clear and fine, she had a high-bred sensitiveness. This queer, brave, high-bred quality she shared with her father. The charity-boy could see it in her tapering fingers, which were white and ringed. The same glamour that he knew in the elderly man he now saw in the woman. And he wanted to possess himself of it, he wanted to make himself master of it. As he went about through the old pottery-yard, his secretive mind schemed and worked. To be master of that strange soft delicacy such as he had felt in her hand upon his face – this was what he set himself towards. He was secretly plotting.

He watched Matilda as she went about, and she became aware of his attention, as of some shadow following her. But her pride made her ignore it. When he sauntered near her, his hands in his pockets, she received him with that same common-place kindliness which mastered him more than any contempt. Her superior breeding seemed to control him. She made herself feel towards him exactly as she had always felt: he was a young boy who lived in the house with them, but he was a stranger. Only, she dared not remember his face under her hand. When she remembered that, she was bewildered. Her hand had offended her, she wanted to cut it off. And she wanted, fiercely, to cut off the memory in him. She assumed she had done so.

One day, when he sat talking with his 'uncle', he looked straight into the eyes of the sick man, and said:

'But I shouldn't like to live and die here in Rawsley.'

'No – well – you needn't,' said the sick man.

'Do you think Cousin Matilda likes it?'

'I should think so.'

'I don't call it much of a life,' said the youth. 'How much older is she than me, Uncle?'

The sick man looked at the young soldier.

'A good bit,' he said.

'Over thirty?' said Hadrian.

'Well, not so much. She's thirty-two.'

Hadrian considered a while.

'She doesn't look it,' he said.

Again the sick father looked at him.

'Do you think she'd like to leave here?' said Hadrian.

'Nay, I don't know,' replied the father, restive.

Hadrian sat still, having his own thoughts. Then in a small, quiet voice, as if he were speaking from inside himself, he said:

'I'd marry her if you wanted me to.'

The sick man raised his eyes suddenly and stared. He stared for a long time. The youth looked inscrutably out of the window.

'*You!*' said the sick man, mocking, with some contempt. Hadrian turned and met his eyes. The two men had an inexplicable understanding.

'If you wasn't against it,' said Hadrian.

'Nay,' said the father, turning aside, 'I don't think I'm against it. I've never thought of it. But – but Emmie's the youngest.'

He had flushed, and looked suddenly more alive. Secretly he loved the boy.

'You might ask her,' said Hadrian.

The elder man considered.

'Hadn't you better ask her yourself?' he said.

'She'd take more notice of you,' said Hadrian.

They were both silent. Then Emmie came in.

For two days Mr. Rockley was excited and thoughtful. Hadrian went about quietly, secretly, unquestioning. At last the father and daughter

378

were alone together. It was very early morning, the father had been in much pain. As the pain abated, he lay still thinking.

'Matilda!' he said suddenly, looking at his daughter.

'Yes, I'm here,' she said.

'Ay! I want you to do something —'

She rose in anticipation.

'Nay, sit still. I want you to marry Hadrian —'

She thought he was raving. She rose, bewildered and frightened.

'Nay, sit you still, sit you still. You hear what I tell you.'

'But you don't know what you're saying, father.'

'Ay, I know well enough. I want you to marry Hadrian, I tell you.'

She was dumbfounded. He was a man of few words.

'You'll do what I tell you,' he said.

She looked at him slowly.

'What put such an idea in your mind?' she said proudly.

'He did.'

Matilda almost looked her father down, her pride was so offended.

'Why, it's disgraceful,' she said.

'Why?'

She watched him slowly.

'What do you ask me for?' she said. 'It's disgusting.'

'The lad's sound enough,' he replied testily.

'You'd better tell him to clear out,' she said coldly.

He turned and looked out of the window. She sat flushed and erect for a long time. At length her father turned to her, looking really malevolent.

'If you won't,' he said, 'you're a fool, and I'll make you pay for your foolishness, do you see?'

Suddenly a cold fear gripped her. She could not believe her senses. She was terrified and bewildered. She stared at her father, believing him to be delirious, or mad, or drunk. What could she do?

'I tell you,' he said. 'I'll send for Whittle to-morrow. If you don't. You shall neither of you have anything of mine.'

Whittle was the solicitor. She understood her father well enough: he would send for his solicitor, and make a will leaving all his property to Hadrian: neither she nor Emmie should have anything. It was too much. She rose and went out of the room, up to her own room, where she locked herself in.

She did not come out for some hours. At last, late at night, she confided in Emmie.

'The sliving demon, he wants the money,' said Emmie. 'My father's out of his mind.'

The thought that Hadrian merely wanted the money was another blow to Matilda. She did not love the impossible youth – but she had not yet learned to think of him as a thing of evil. He now became hideous to her mind.

Emmie had a little scene with her father next day.

'You don't mean what you said to our Matilda yesterday, do you, father?' she asked aggressively.

'Yes,' he replied.

'What, that you'll alter your will?'

'Yes.'

'You won't,' said his angry daughter.

But he looked at her with a malevolent little smile.

'Annie!' he shouted. 'Annie!'

He had still power to make his voice carry. The servant maid came in from the kitchen.

'Put your things on, and go down to Whittle's office, and say I want to see Mr. Whittle as soon as he can, and will he bring a will-form.'

The sick man lay back a little – he could not lie down. His daughter sat as if she had been struck. Then she left the room.

Hadrian was pottering about in the garden. She went straight down to him.

'Here,' she said. 'You'd better get off. You'd better take your things and go from here, quick.'

Hadrian looked slowly at the infuriated girl.

'Who says so?' he asked.

'*We* say so – get off, you've done enough mischief and damage.'

'Does Uncle say so?'

'Yes, he does.'

'I'll go and ask him.'

But like a fury Emmie barred his way.

'No, you needn't. You needn't ask him nothing at all. We don't want you, so you can go.'

'Uncle's boss here.'

'A man that's dying, and you crawling round and working on him for his money! – you're not fit to live.'

'Oh!' he said. 'Who says I'm working for his money?'

'I say. But my father told our Matilda, and *she* knows what you are.

She knows what you're after. So you might as well clear out, for all you'll get – guttersnipe!'

He turned his back on her, to think. It had occurred to him that they would think he was after the money. He *did* want the money – badly. He badly wanted to be an employer himself, not one of the employed. But he knew, in his subtle, calculating way, that it was not for money he wanted Matilda. He wanted both the money and Matilda. But he told himself the two desires were separate, not one. He could not do with Matilda, *without* the money. But he did not want her *for* the money.

When he got this clear in his mind, he sought for an opportunity to tell it, lurking and watching. But she avoided him. In the evening the lawyer came. Mr. Rockley seemed to have a new access of strength – a will was drawn up, making the previous arrangements wholly conditional. The old will held good, if Matilda would consent to marry Hadrian. If she refused then at the end of six months the whole property passed to Hadrian.

Mr. Rockley told this to the young man, with malevolent satisfaction. He seemed to have a strange desire, quite unreasonable, for revenge upon the women who had surrounded him for so long, and served him so carefully.

'Tell her in front of me,' said Hadrian.

So Mr. Rockley sent for his daughters.

At last they came, pale, mute, stubborn. Matilda seemed to have retired far off, Emmie seemed like a fighter ready to fight to the death. The sick man reclined on the bed, his eyes bright, his puffed hand trembling. But his face had again some of its old, bright handsomeness. Hadrian sat quiet, a little aside: the indomitable, dangerous charity boy.

'There's the will,' said their father, pointing them to the paper.

The two women sat mute and immovable, they took no notice.

'Either you marry Hadrian, or he has everything,' said the father with satisfaction.

'Then let him have everything,' said Matilda coldly.

'He's not! He's not!' cried Emmie fiercely. 'He's not going to have it. The guttersnipe!'

An amused look came on her father's face.

'You hear that, Hadrian,' he said.

'I didn't offer to marry Cousin Matilda for the money,' said Hadrian, flushing and moving on his seat.

Matilda looked at him slowly, with her dark blue, drugged eyes. He seemed a strange little monster to her.

'Why, you liar, you know you did,' cried Emmie.

The sick man laughed. Matilda continued to gaze strangely at the young man.

'She knows I didn't,' said Hadrian.

He too had his courage, as a rat has indomitable courage in the end. Hadrian had some of the neatness, the reserve, the underground quality of the rat. But he had perhaps the ultimate courage, the most unquenched courage of all.

Emmie looked at her sister.

'Oh, well,' she said. 'Matilda – don't you bother. Let him have everything, we can look after ourselves.'

'I know he'll take everything,' said Matilda, abstractedly.

Hadrian did not answer. He knew in fact that if Matilda refused him he would take everything, and go off with it.

'A clever little mannie — !' said Emmie, with a jeering grimace.

The father laughed noiselessly to himself. But he was tired. . . .

'Go on, then,' he said. 'Go on, let me be quiet.'

Emmie turned and looked at him.

'You deserve what you've got,' she said to her father bluntly.

'Go on,' he answered mildly. 'Go on.'

Another night passed – a night nurse sat up with Mr. Rockley. Another day came. Hadrian was there as ever, in his woollen jersey and coarse khaki trousers and bare neck. Matilda went about, frail and distant, Emmie black-browed in spite of her blondeness. They were all quiet, for they did not intend the mystified servant to learn anything.

Mr. Rockley had very bad attacks of pain, he could not breathe. The end seemed near. They all went about quiet and stoical, all unyielding. Hadrian pondered within himself. If he did not marry Matilda he would go to Canada with twenty thousand pounds. This was itself a very satisfactory prospect. If Matilda consented he would have nothing – she would have her own money.

Emmie was the one to act. She went off in search of the solicitor and brought him home with her. There was an interview, and Whittle tried to frighten the youth into withdrawal – but without avail. The clergyman and relatives were summoned – but Hadrian stared at them and took no notice. It made him angry, however.

He wanted to catch Matilda alone. Many days went by, and he was not successful: she avoided him. At last, lurking, he surprised her one day as she came to pick gooseberries, and he cut off her retreat. He came to the point at once.

'You don't want me, then?' he said, in his subtle, insinuating voice.

'I don't want to speak to you,' she said, averting her face.

'You put your hand on me, though,' he said. 'You shouldn't have done that, and then I should never have thought of it. You shouldn't have touched me.'

'If you were anything decent, you'd know that was a mistake, and forget it,' she said.

'I know it was a mistake – but I shan't forget it. If you wake a man up, he can't go to sleep again because he's told to.'

'If you had any decent feeling in you, you'd have gone away,' she replied.

'I didn't want to,' he replied.

She looked away into the distance. At last she asked:

'What do you persecute me for, if it isn't for the money? I'm old enough to be your mother. In a way I've been your mother.'

'Doesn't matter,' he said. 'You've been no mother to me. Let us marry and go out to Canada – you might as well – you've touched me.'

She was white and trembling. Suddenly she flushed with anger.

'It's so *indecent*,' she said.

'How?' he retorted. 'You touched me.'

But she walked away from him. She felt as if he had trapped her. He was angry and depressed, he felt again despised.

That same evening she went into her father's room.

'Yes,' she said suddenly, 'I'll marry him.'

Her father looked up at her. He was in pain, and very ill.

'You like him now, do you?' he said, with a faint smile.

She looked down into his face, and saw death not far off. She turned and went coldly out of the room.

The solicitor was sent for, preparations were hastily made. In all the interval Matilda did not speak to Hadrian, never answered him if he addressed her. He approached her in the morning.

'You've come round to it, then?' he said, giving her a pleasant look from his twinkling, almost kindly eyes. She looked down at him and turned aside. She looked down on him both literally and figuratively. Still he persisted, and triumphed.

Emmie raved and wept, the secret flew abroad. But Matilda was silent and unmoved, Hadrian was quiet and satisfied, and nipped with fear also. But he held out against his fear. Mr. Rockley was very ill, but unchanged.

On the third day the marriage took place. Matilda and Hadrian drove straight home from the registrar, and went straight into the room of the dying man. His face lit up with a clear twinkling smile.

'Hadrian – you've got her?' he said, a little hoarsely.

'Yes,' said Hadrian, who was pale round the gills.

'Ay, my lad, I'm glad you're mine,' replied the dying man. Then he turned his eyes closely on Matilda.

'Let's look at you, Matilda,' he said. Then his voice went strange and unrecognisable. 'Kiss me,' he said.

She stooped and kissed him. She had never kissed him before, not since she was a tiny child. But she was quiet, very still.

'Kiss him,' the dying man said.

Obediently, Matilda put forward her mouth and kissed the young husband.

'That's right! That's right!' murmured the dying man.

SAMSON AND DELILAH

A MAN got down from the motor-omnibus that runs from Penzance to St. Just-in-Penwith, and turned northwards, uphill towards the Pole-star. It was only half-past six, but already the stars were out, a cold little wind was blowing from the sea, and the crystalline, three-pulse flash of the lighthouse below the cliffs beat rhythmically in the first darkness.

The man was alone. He went his way unhesitating, but looked from side to side with cautious curiosity. Tall, ruined power-houses of tin-mines loomed in the darkness from time to time, like remnants of some by-gone civilisation. The lights of many miners' cottages scattered on the hilly darkness twinkled desolate in their disorder, yet twinkled with the lonely homeliness of the Celtic night.

He tramped steadily on, always watchful with curiosity. He was a tall, well-built man, apparently in the prime of life. His shoulders were square and rather stiff, he leaned forwards a little as he went, from the hips, like a man who must stoop to lower his height. But he did not stoop his shoulders: he bent his straight back from the hips.

Now and again short, stumpy, thick-legged figures of Cornish miners passed him, and he invariably gave them good-night, as if to insist that he was on his own ground. He spoke with the West Cornish intonation. And as he went along the dreary road, looking now at the lights of the dwellings on land, now at the lights away to sea, vessels veering round in sight of the Longships Lighthouse, the whole of the Atlantic Ocean in darkness and space between him and America, he seemed a little excited and pleased with himself, watchful, thrilled, veering along in a sense of mastery and of power in conflict.

The houses began to close on the road, he was entering the strag-gling, formless, desolate mining village, that he knew of old. On the left was a little space set back from the road, and cosy lights of an inn. There it was. He peered up at the sign: 'The Tinners' Rest'. But he could not make out the name of the proprietor. He listened. There was excited talking and laughing, a woman's voice laughing shrilly among the men's.

Stooping a little, he entered the warmly-lit bar. The lamp was burning, a buxom woman rose from the white-scrubbed deal table where the black and white and red cards were scattered, and several men, miners, lifted their faces from the game.

The stranger went to the counter, averting his face. His cap was pulled down over his brow.

'Good evening!' said the landlady, in her rather ingratiating voice.

'Good evening. A glass of ale.'

'A glass of ale,' repeated the landlady suavely. 'Cold night – but bright.'

'Yes,' the man assented, laconically. Then he added, when nobody expected him to say any more: 'Seasonable weather.'

'Quite seasonable, quite,' said the landlady. 'Thank you.'

The man lifted his glass straight to his lips, and emptied it. He put it down again on the zinc counter with a click.

'Let's have another,' he said.

The woman drew the beer, and the man went away with his glass to the second table, near the fire. The woman, after a moment's hesitation, took her seat again at the table with the card-players. She had noticed the man: a big fine fellow, well dressed, a stranger.

But he spoke with that Cornish–Yankee accent she accepted as the natural twang among the miners.

The stranger put his foot on the fender and looked into the fire. He was handsome, well coloured, with well-drawn Cornish eyebrows, and the usual dark, bright, mindless Cornish eyes. He seemed abstracted in thought. Then he watched the card-party.

The woman was buxom and healthy, with dark hair and small, quick brown eyes. She was bursting with life and vigour, the energy she threw into the game of cards excited all the men, they shouted, and laughed, and the woman held her breast, shrieking with laughter.

'Oh, my, it'll be the death o' me,' she panted. 'Now, come on, Mr. Trevorrow, play fair. Play fair, I say, or I s'll put the cards down.'

'Play fair! Why, who's played unfair?' ejaculated Mr. Trevorrow. 'Do you mean t'accuse me, as I haven't played fair, Mrs. Nankervis?'

'I do. I say it, and I mean it. Haven't you got the Queen of Spades? Now, come on, no dodging round me. *I* know you've got that Queen, as well as I know my name's Alice.'

'Well – if your name's Alice, you'll have to have it —'

'Ay, now – what did I say? Did ever you see such a man? My word, but your missus must be easy took in, by the looks of things.'

And off she went into peals of laughter. She was interrupted by the entrance of four men in khaki, a short, stumpy sergeant of middle age, a young corporal, and two young privates. The woman leaned back in her chair.

'Oh, my!' she cried. 'If there isn't the boys back: looking perished, I believe —'

'Perished, Ma!' exclaimed the sergeant. 'Not yet.'

'Near enough,' said a young private uncouthly.

The woman got up.

'I'm sure you are, my dears. You'll be wanting your suppers, I'll be bound.'

'We could do with 'em.'

'Let's have a wet first,' said the sergeant.

The woman bustled about getting the drinks. The soldiers moved to the fire, spreading out their hands.

'Have your suppers in here, will you?' she said. 'Or in the kitchen?'

'Let's have it here,' said the sergeant. 'More cosier – *if* you don't mind.'

'You shall have it where you like, boys, where you like.'

She disappeared. In a minute a girl of about sixteen came in. She was tall and fresh, with dark, young, expressionless eyes, and well-drawn brows, and the immature softness and mindlessness of the sensuous Celtic type.

'Ho, Maryann! Evenin', Maryann! How's Maryann, now?' came the multiple greeting.

She replied to everybody in a soft voice, a strange, soft aplomb that was very attractive. And she moved round with rather mechanical, attractive movements, as if her thoughts were elsewhere. But she had always this dim far-awayness in her bearing: a sort of modesty. The strange man by the fire watched her curiously. There was an alert, inquisitive, mindless curiosity on his well-coloured face.

'I'll have a bit of supper with you, if I might,' he said.

She looked at him with her clear, unreasoning eyes, just like the eyes of some non-human creature.

'I'll ask mother,' she said. Her voice was soft-breathing, gently sing-song.

When she came in again:

'Yes,' she said, almost whispering. 'What will you have?'

'What have you got?' he said, looking up into her face.

'There's cold meat —'

'That's for me, then.'

The stranger sat at the end of the table, and ate with the tired, quiet soldiers. Now the landlady was interested in him. Her brow was knit rather tense, there was a look of panic in her large, healthy face, but her small brown eyes were fixed most dangerously. She was a big woman, but her eyes were small and tense. She drew near the stranger. She wore a rather loud-patterned flannelette blouse and a dark skirt.

'What will you have to drink with your supper?' she asked, and there was a new, dangerous note in her voice.

He moved uneasily.

'Oh, I'll go on with ale.'

She drew him another glass. Then she sat down on the bench at the table with him and the soldiers, and fixed him with her attention.

'You've come from St. Just, have you?' she said.

He looked at her with those clear, dark, inscrutable Cornish eyes, and answered at length:

'No, from Penzance.'

'Penzance! – but you're not thinking of going back there to-night?'

'No – no.'

He still looked at her with those wide, clear eyes that seemed like very bright agate. Her anger began to rise. It was seen on her brow. Yet her voice was still suave and deprecating.

'I *thought* not – but you're not living in these parts, are you?'

'No – no, I'm not living here.' He was always slow in answering, as if something intervened between him and any outside question.

'Oh, I see,' she said. 'You've got relations down here.'

Again he looked straight into her eyes, as if looking her into silence.

'Yes,' he said.

He did not say any more. She rose with a flounce. The anger was tight on her brow. There was no more laughing and card-playing that evening, though she kept up her motherly, suave, good-humoured way with the men. But they knew her, they were all afraid of her.

The supper was finished, the table cleared, the stranger did not go. Two of the young soldiers went off to bed, with their cheery:

'Good-night, Ma. Good-night, Maryann.'

The stranger talked a little to the sergeant about the war, which was in its first year, about the new army, a fragment of which was quartered in this district, about America.

The landlady darted looks at him from her small eyes, minute by minute the electric storm welled in her bosom, as still he did not go. She was quivering with suppressed, violent passion, something frightening and abnormal. She could not sit still for a moment. Her heavy form seemed to flash with sudden, involuntary movements as the minutes passed by, and still he sat there, and the tension on her heart grew unbearable. She watched the hands of the clock move on. Three of the soldiers had gone to bed, only the crop-headed, terrier-like old sergeant remained.

The landlady sat behind the bar fidgeting spasmodically with the newspaper. She looked again at the clock. At last it was five minutes to ten.

'Gentlemen – the enemy!' she said in her diminished, furious voice. 'Time, please. Time, my dears. And good-night, all!'

The men began to drop out, with a brief good-night. It was a minute to ten. The landlady rose.

'Come,' she said. 'I'm shutting the door.'

The last of the miners passed out. She stood, stout and menacing, holding the door. Still the stranger sat on by the fire, his black overcoat opened, smoking.

'We're closed now, sir,' came the perilous, narrowed voice of the landlady.

The little, dog-like, hard-headed sergeant touched the arm of the stranger.

'Closing time,' he said.

The stranger turned round in his seat, and his quick-moving, dark, jewel-like eyes went from the sergeant to the landlady.

'I'm stopping here to-night,' he said, in his laconic Cornish–Yankee accent.

The landlady seemed to tower. Her eyes lifted strangely, frightening.

'Oh, indeed!' she cried. 'Oh, indeed! And whose orders are those, may I ask?'

He looked at her again.

'My orders,' he said.

Involuntarily she shut the door, and advanced like a great, dangerous bird. Her voice rose, there was a touch of hoarseness in it.

'And what might *your* orders be, if you please?' she cried. 'Who might *you* be, to give orders, in the house?'

He sat still, watching her.

'You know who I am,' he said. 'At least, I know who you are.'

'Oh, do you? Oh, do you? And who am *I* then, if you'll be so good as to tell me?'

389

He stared at her with his bright, dark eyes.

'You're my Missis, you are,' he said. 'And you know it, as well as I do.'

She started as if something had exploded in her.

Her eyes lifted and flared madly.

'*Do* I know it, indeed!' she cried. 'I know no such thing! I know no such thing! Do you think a man's going to walk into this bar, and tell me off-hand I'm his Missis, and I'm going to believe him? I say to you, whoever you may be, you're mistaken. I know myself for no Missis of yours, and I'll thank you to go out of this house, this minute, before I get those that will put you out.'

The man rose to his feet, stretching his head towards her a little. He was a handsomely built Cornishman in the prime of life.

'What you say, eh? You don't know me?' he said in his sing-song voice, emotionless, but rather smothered and pressing: it reminded one of the girl's. 'I should know you anywhere, you see. I should! I shouldn't have to look twice to know you, you see. You see, now, don't you?'

The woman was baffled.

'So you may say,' she replied, staccato. 'So you may say. That's easy enough. My name's known, and respected, by most people for ten miles round. But I don't know *you.*'

Her voice ran to sarcasm. 'I can't say I know *you.* You're a *perfect* stranger to me, and I don't believe I've ever set eyes on you before to-night.'

Her voice was very flexible and sarcastic.

'Yes, you have,' replied the man, in his reasonable way. 'Yes, you have. Your name's my name, and that girl Maryann is my girl; she's my daughter. You're my Missis right enough. As sure as I'm Willie Nankervis.'

He spoke as if it were an accepted fact. His face was handsome, with a strange, watchful alertness and a fundamental fixity of intention that maddened her.

'You villain!' she cried. 'You villain, to come to this house and dare to speak to me. You villain, you downright rascal!'

He looked at her.

'Ay,' he said, unmoved. 'All that.' He was uneasy before her. Only he was not afraid of her. There was something impenetrable about him, like his eyes, which were as bright as agate.

She towered, and drew near to him menacingly.

'You're going out of this house, aren't you?' She stamped her foot in sudden madness. '*This minute!*'

He watched her. He knew she wanted to strike him.

'No,' he said, with suppressed emphasis. 'I've told you, I'm stopping here.'

He was afraid of her personality, but it did not alter him. She wavered. Her small, tawny-brown eyes concentrated in a point of vivid, sightless fury, like a tiger's. The man was wincing, but he stood his ground. Then she bethought herself. She would gather her forces.

'We'll see whether you're stopping here,' she said. And she turned, with a curious, frightening lifting of her eyes, and surged out of the room. The man, listening, heard her go upstairs, heard her tapping at a bedroom door, heard her saying: 'Do you mind coming down a minute, boys? I want you. I'm in trouble.'

The man in the bar took off his cap and his black overcoat, and threw them on the seat behind him. His black hair was short and touched with grey at the temples. He wore a well-cut, well-fitting suit of dark grey, American in style, and a turn-down collar. He looked well-to-do, a fine, solid figure of a man. The rather rigid look of the shoulders came from his having had his collar-bone twice broken in the mines.

The little terrier of a sergeant, in dirty khaki, looked at him furtively.

'She's your Missis?' he asked, jerking his head in the direction of the departed woman.

'Yes, she is,' barked the man. 'She's that, sure enough.'

'Not seen her for a long time, haven't ye?'

'Sixteen years come March month.'

'Hm!'

And the sergeant laconically resumed his smoking.

The landlady was coming back, followed by the three young soldiers, who entered rather sheepishly, in trousers and shirt and stocking-feet. The woman stood histrionically at the end of the bar, and exclaimed:

'That man refuses to leave the house, claims he's stopping the night here. You know very well I have no bed, don't you? And this house doesn't accommodate travellers. Yet he's going to stop in spite of all! But not while I've a drop of blood in my body, that I declare with my dying breath. And not if you men are worth the name of men, and will help a woman as has no one to help her.'

Her eyes sparkled, her face was flushed pink. She was drawn up like an Amazon.

391

The young soldiers looked on in delight, the sergeant smoked, looked at the man, they looked at the sergeant, one of them looked down and fastened his braces on the second button.

'What say, sergeant?' asked one whose face twinkled for a little devilment.

'Man says he's husband to Mrs. Nankervis,' said the sergeant.

'He's no husband of mine. I declare I never set eyes on him before this night. It's a dirty trick, nothing else, it's a dirty trick.'

'Why, you're a liar, saying you never set eyes on me before,' barked the man near the hearth. 'You're married to me, and that girl Maryann you had by me – well enough you know it.'

The young soldiers looked on in delight, the sergeant smoked imperturbed.

'Yes,' sang the landlady, slowly shaking her head in supreme sarcasm, 'it sounds very pretty, doesn't it? But you see we don't believe a word of it, and *how* are you going to prove it?' She smiled nastily.

The man watched in silence for a moment, then he said:

'It wants no proof.'

'Oh, yes, but it does! Oh, yes, but it does, sir, it wants a lot of proving!' sang the lady's sarcasm. 'We're not such gulls as all that, to swallow your words whole.'

But he stood unmoved near the fire. She stood with one hand resting on the zinc-covered bar, the sergeant sat with legs crossed, smoking, on the seat half-way between them, the three young soldiers in their shirts and braces stood wavering in the gloom behind the bar. There was silence.

'Do you know anything of the whereabouts of your husband, Mrs. Nankervis? Is he still living?' asked the sergeant, in his judicious fashion.

Suddenly the landlady began to cry, great scalding tears, that left the young men aghast.

'I know nothing of him,' she sobbed, feeling for her pocket handkerchief. 'He left me when Maryann was a baby, went mining to America, and after about six months never wrote a line nor sent me a penny bit. I can't say whether he's alive or dead, the villain. All I've heard of him's the bad – and I've heard nothing for years an' all, now.' She sobbed violently.

The golden-skinned, handsome man near the fire watched her as she wept. He was frightened, he was troubled, he was bewildered, but none of his emotions altered him underneath.

There was no sound in the room but the violent sobbing of the land-lady. The men, one and all, were overcome.

'Don't you think as you'd better go, for to-night?' said the sergeant to the man, with sweet reasonableness. 'You'd better leave it a bit, and arrange something between you. You can't have much claim on a woman, I should imagine, if it's how she says. And you've come down on her a bit too sudden-like.'

The landlady sobbed heart-brokenly. The man watched her large breasts shaken. They seemed to cast a spell over his mind.

'How I've treated her, that's no matter,' he replied. 'I've come back, and I'm going to stop in my own home – for a bit, anyhow. There you've got it.'

'A dirty action,' said the sergeant, his face flushing dark. 'A dirty action, to come, after deserting a woman for that number of years, and want to force yourself on her! A dirty action – as isn't allowed by the law.'

The landlady wiped her eyes.

'Never you mind about law or nothing,' cried the man, in a strange, strong voice. 'I'm not moving out of this public to-night.'

The woman turned to the soldiers behind her, and said in a wheed-ling, sarcastic tone:

'Are we going to stand it, boys? Are we going to be done like this, Sergeant Thomas, by a scoundrel and a bully as has led a life beyond *mention* in those American mining-camps, and then wants to come back and make havoc of a poor woman's life and savings, after having left her with a baby in arms to struggle as best she might? It's a crying shame if nobody will stand up for me – a crying shame —!'

The soldiers and the little sergeant were bristling. The woman stooped and rummaged under the counter for a minute. Then, unseen to the man away near the fire, she threw out a plaited grass rope, such as is used for binding bales, and left it lying near the feet of the young soldiers, in the gloom at the back of the bar.

Then she rose and fronted the situation.

'Come now,' she said to the man, in a reasonable, coldly-coaxing tone, 'put your coat on and leave us alone. Be a man, and not worse than a brute of a German. You can get a bed easy enough in St. Just, and if you've nothing to pay for it, sergeant would lend you a couple of shillings, I'm sure he would.'

All eyes were fixed on the man. He was looking down at the woman like a creature spell-bound or possessed by some devil's own intention.

'I've got money of my own,' he said. 'Don't you be frightened for your money, I've plenty of that, for the time.'

'Well, then,' she coaxed, in a cold, almost sneering propitiation, 'put your coat on and go where you're wanted – be a *man*, not a brute of a German.'

She had drawn quite near to him, in her challenging coaxing intentness. He looked down at her with his bewitched face.

'No, I shan't,' he said. 'I shan't do no such thing. *You'll* put me up for to-night.'

'Shall I?' she cried. And suddenly she flung her arms round him, hung on to him with all her powerful weight, calling to the soldiers: 'Get the rope, boys, and fasten him up. Alfred – John, quick now —'

The man reared, looked round with maddened eyes, and heaved his powerful body. But the woman was powerful also, and very heavy, and was clenched with the determination of death. Her face, with its exulting, horribly vindictive look, was turned up to him from his own breast; he reached back his head frantically, to get away from it. Meanwhile the young soldiers, after having watched this frightful Laocoon swaying for a moment, stirred, and the malicious one darted swiftly with the rope. It was tangled a little.

'Give me the end here,' cried the sergeant.

Meanwhile the big man heaved and struggled, swung the woman round against the seat and the table, in his convulsive effort to get free. But she pinned down his arms like a cuttle-fish wreathed heavily upon him. And he heaved and swayed, and they thrashed about the room, the soldiers hopping, the furniture bumping.

The young soldier had got the rope once round, the brisk sergeant helping him. The woman sank heavily lower, they got the rope round several times. In the struggle the victim fell over against the table. The ropes tightened till they cut his arms. The woman clung to his knees. Another soldier ran in a flash of genius, and fastened the strange man's feet with the pair of braces. Seats had crashed over, the table was thrown against the wall, but the man was bound, his arms pinned against his sides, his feet tied. He lay half-fallen, sunk against the table, still for a moment.

The woman rose, and sank, faint, on to the seat against the wall. Her breast heaved, she could not speak, she thought she was going to die. The bound man lay against the overturned table, his coat all twisted and pulled up beneath the ropes, leaving the loins exposed. The soldiers stood around, a little dazed, but excited with the row.

The man began to struggle again, heaving instinctively against the ropes, taking great, deep breaths. His face, with its golden skin, flushed dark and surcharged. He heaved again. The great veins in his neck stood out. But it was no good, he went relaxed. Then again, suddenly, he jerked his feet.

'Another pair of braces, William,' cried the excited soldier. He threw himself on the legs of the bound man, and managed to fasten the knees. Then again there was stillness. They could hear the clock tick.

The woman looked at the prostrate figure, the strong, straight limbs, the strong back bound in subjection, the wide-eyed face that reminded her of a calf tied in a sack in a cart, only its head stretched dumbly backwards. And she triumphed.

The bound-up body began to struggle again. She watched fascinated the muscles working, the shoulders, the hips, the large, clean thighs. Even now he might break the ropes. She was afraid. But the lively young soldier sat on the shoulders of the bound man, and after a few perilous moments, there was stillness again.

'Now,' said the judicious sergeant to the bound man, 'if we untie you, will you promise to go off and make no more trouble?'

'You'll not untie him in here,' cried the woman. 'I wouldn't trust him as far as I could blow him.'

There was silence.

'We might carry him outside, and undo him there,' said the soldier. 'Then we could get the policeman, if he made any more bother.'

'Yes,' said the sergeant. 'We could do that.' Then again, in an altered, almost severe tone, to the prisoner: 'If we undo you outside, will you take your coat and go without creating any more disturbance?'

But the prisoner would not answer, he only lay with wide, dark, bright eyes, like a bound animal. There was a space of perplexed silence.

'Well, then, do as you say,' said the woman irritably. 'Carry him out amongst you, and let us shut up the house.'

They did so. Picking up the bound man, the four soldiers staggered clumsily into the silent square in front of the inn, the woman following with the cap and the overcoat. The young soldiers quickly unfastened the braces from the prisoner's legs, and they hopped indoors. They were in their stocking-feet, and outside the stars flashed cold. They stood in the doorway watching. The man lay quite still on the cold ground.

'Now,' said the sergeant, in a subdued voice, 'I'll loosen the knot, and he can work himself free, if you go in, Missis.'

She gave a last look at the dishevelled, bound man, as he sat on the ground. Then she went indoors, followed quickly by the sergeant. Then they were heard locking and barring the door.

The man seated on the ground outside worked and strained at the rope. But it was not so easy to undo himself even now. So, with hands bound, making an effort, he got on his feet, and went and worked the cord against the rough edge of an old wall. The rope, being of a kind of plaited grass, soon frayed and broke, and he freed himself. He had various contusions. His arms were hurt and bruised from the bonds. He rubbed them slowly. Then he pulled his clothes straight, stooped, put on his cap, struggled into his overcoat, and walked away.

The stars were very brilliant. Clear as crystal, the beam from the lighthouse under the cliffs struck rhythmically on the night. Dazed, the man walked along the road past the churchyard. Then he stood leaning up against a wall, for a long time.

He was roused because his feet were so cold. So he pulled himself together, and turned again in the silent night, back towards the inn.

The bar was in darkness. But there was a light in the kitchen. He hesitated. Then very quietly he tried the door.

He was surprised to find it open. He entered, and quietly closed it behind him. Then he went down the step past the bar-counter, and through to the lighted doorway of the kitchen. There sat his wife, planted in front of the range, where a furze fire was burning. She sat in a chair full in front of the range, her knees wide apart on the fender. She looked over her shoulder at him as he entered, but she did not speak. Then she stared in the fire again.

It was a small, narrow kitchen. He dropped his cap on the table that was covered with yellowish American cloth, and took a seat with his back to the wall, near the oven. His wife still sat with her knees apart, her feet on the steel fender and stared into the fire, motionless. Her skin was smooth and rosy in the firelight. Everything in the house was very clean and bright. The man sat silent, too, his head dropped. And thus they remained.

It was a question who would speak first. The woman leaned forward and poked the ends of the sticks in between the bars of the range. He lifted his head and looked at her.

'Others gone to bed, have they?' he asked.

But she remained closed in silence.

' 'S a cold night, out,' he said, as if to himself.

And he laid his large, yet well-shapen workman's hand on the top of the stove, that was polished black and smooth as velvet. She would not look at him, yet she glanced out of the corners of her eyes.

His eyes were fixed brightly on her, the pupils large and electric like those of a cat.

'I should have picked you out among thousands,' he said. 'Though you're bigger than I'd have believed. Fine flesh you've made.'

She was silent for some time. Then she turned in her chair upon him.

'What do you think of yourself,' she said, 'coming back on me like this after over fifteen year? You don't think I've not heard of you, neither, in Butte City and elsewhere?'

He was watching her with his clear, translucent, unchallenged eyes.

'Yes,' he said. 'Chaps comes an' goes – I've heard tell of you from time to time.'

She drew herself up.

'And what lies have you heard about *me*?' she demanded superbly.

'I dunno as I've heard any lies at all – 'cept as you was getting on very well, like.'

His voice ran warily and detached. Her anger stirred again in her violently. But she subdued it, because of the danger there was in him, and more, perhaps, because of the beauty of his head and his level drawn brows, which she could not bear to forfeit.

'That's more than I can say of *you*,' she said. 'I've heard more harm than good about *you*.'

'Ay, I dessay,' he said looking in the fire. It was a long time since he had seen the furze burning, he said to himself. There was a silence, during which she watched his face.

'Do you call yourself a *man*?' she said, more in contemptuous reproach than in anger. 'Leave a woman as you've left me, you don't care to what! – and then to turn up in *this* fashion, without a word to say for yourself.'

He stirred in his chair, planted his feet apart, and resting his arms on his knees, looked steadily into the fire without answering. So near to her was his head, and the close black hair, she could scarcely refrain from starting away, as if it would bite her.

'Do you call that the action of a *man*?' she repeated.

'No,' he said, reaching and poking the bits of wood into the fire with his fingers. 'I didn't call it anything, as I know of. It's no good calling things by any names whatsoever, as I know of.'

She watched him in his actions. There was a longer and longer pause between each speech, though neither knew it.

'I *wonder* what you think of yourself!' she exclaimed, with vexed emphasis. 'I *wonder* what sort of fellow you take yourself to be!' She was really perplexed as well as angry.

'Well,' he said, lifting his head to look at her, 'I guess I'll answer for my own faults, if everybody else'll answer for theirs.'

Her heart beat fiery hot as he lifted his face to her. She breathed heavily, averting her face, almost losing her self-control.

'And what do you take *me* to be?' she cried, in real helplessness.

His face was lifted, watching her soft, averted face. And the softly heaving mass of her breasts.

'I take you,' he said, with that laconic truthfulness which exercised such power over her, 'to be the deuce of a fine woman – darn me if you're not as fine a built woman as I've seen, handsome with it as well. I shouldn't have expected you to put on such handsome flesh: 'struth I shouldn't.'

Her heart beat fiery hot, as he watched her with those bright agate eyes, fixedly.

'Been very handsome to *you*, for fifteen years, my sakes!' she replied.

He made no answer to this, but sat with his bright, quick eyes upon her.

Then he rose. She started involuntarily. But he only said, in his laconic, measured way:

'It's warm in here now.'

And he pulled off his overcoat, throwing it on the table. She sat as if slightly cowed, whilst he did so.

'Them ropes has given my arms something, by Ga-ard,' he drawled, feeling his arms with his hands.

Still she sat in her chair before him, slightly cowed.

'You was sharp, wasn't you, to catch me like that, eh?' he smiled slowly. 'By Ga-ard, you had me fixed proper, proper you had. Darn me, you fixed me up proper – proper, you did.'

He leaned forwards in his chair towards her.

'I don't think no worse of you for it, no, darned if I do. Fine pluck in a woman's what I admire. That I do, indeed.'

She only gazed into the fire.

'We fet from the start, we did. And, my word, you begin again quick the minute you see me, you did. Darn me, you was too sharp for me. A darn fine woman, puts up a darn good fight. Darn me if I could find a woman in all the darn States as could get me down like that. Wonderful fine woman you be, truth to say, at this minute.'

She only sat glowering into the fire.

'As grand a pluck as a man could wish to find in a woman, true as I'm here,' he said, reaching forward his hand and tentatively touching her between her full, warm breasts, quietly.

She started, and seemed to shudder. But his hand insinuated itself between her breasts, as she continued to gaze in the fire.

'And don't you think I've come back here a-begging,' he said. 'I've more than *one* thousand pounds to my name, I have. And a bit of a fight for a how-de-do pleases me, that it do. But that doesn't mean as you're going to deny as you're my Missis ...'

THE PRIMROSE PATH

A YOUNG man came out of the Victoria station, looking undecidedly at the taxi-cabs, dark red and black, pressing against the kerb under the glass roof. Several men in greatcoats and brass buttons jerked themselves erect to catch his attention, at the same time keeping an eye on the other people as they filtered through the open doors of the station. Berry, however, was occupied by one of the men, a big, burly fellow whose blue eyes glared back and whose red-brown moustache bristled in defiance.

'Do you *want* a cab, sir?' the man asked, in a half-mocking, challenging voice.

Berry hesitated still.

'Are you Daniel Sutton?' he asked.

'Yes,' replied the other defiantly, with uneasy conscience.

'Then you are my uncle,' said Berry.

They were alike in colour, and somewhat in features, but the taxi driver was a powerful, well-fleshed man who glared at the world aggressively, being really on the defensive against his own heart. His nephew, of the same height, was thin, well-dressed, quiet and indifferent in his manner. And yet they were obviously kin.

'And who the devil are you?' asked the taxi driver.

'I'm Daniel Berry,' replied the nephew.

'Well, I'm damned – never saw you since you were a kid.'

Rather awkwardly at this late hour the two shook hands. 'How are you, lad?'

'All right. I thought you were in Australia.'

'Been back three months – bought a couple of these damned things' – he kicked the tyre of his taxi-cab in affectionate disgust. There was a moment's silence.

'Oh, but I'm going back out there I can't stand this cankering, rotten-hearted hell of a country any more; you want to come out to Sydney with me, lad. That's the place for you – beautiful place, oh, you could wish for nothing better. And money, in it, too. How's your mother?'

'She died at Christmas,' said the young man.

'Dead! What! – our Anna!' The big man's eyes stared, and he recoiled in fear. 'God, lad,' he said, 'that's three of 'em gone!'

The two men looked away at the people passing along the pale grey pavements, under the wall of Trinity Church.

'Well, strike me lucky!' said the taxi driver at last, out of breath. 'She wor th' best o' th' bunch of 'em. I see nowt nor hear nowt from any of 'em – they're not worth it, I'll be damned if they are – our sermon-lapping Adela and Maud,' he looked scornfully at his nephew. 'But she was the best of 'em, our Anna was, that's a fact.'

He was talking because he was afraid.

'An' after a hard life like she'd had. How old was she, lad?'

'Fifty-five.'

'Fifty-five . . .' He hesitated. Then, in a rather hushed voice, he asked the question that frightened him: 'And what was it, then?'

'Cancer.'

'Cancer again, like Julia! I never knew there was cancer in our family. Oh, my good God, our poor Anna, after the life she'd had! What, lad, do you see any God at the back of that? I'm damned if I do.'

He was glaring, very blue-eyed and fierce, at his nephew. Berry lifted his shoulders slightly.

'God?' went on the taxi driver, in a curious intense tone. 'You've only to look at the folk in the street to know there's nothing keeps it going but gravitation. Look at 'em. Look at him!' A mongrel-looking man was nosing past. 'Wouldn't *he* murder you for your watch-chain, but that he's afraid of society? He's got it *in* him. . . . Look at 'em.'

Berry watched the townspeople go by, and, sensitively feeling his uncle's antipathy, it seemed he was watching a sort of *danse macabre* of ugly criminals.

'Did you ever see such a God-forsaken crew creeping about! It gives you the very horrors to look at 'em. I sit in this damned car and watch 'em till, I can tell you, I feel like running the cab amuck among 'em, and running myself to kingdom come —'

Berry wondered at this outburst. He knew his uncle was the black sheep, the youngest, the darling of his mother's family. He knew him to be at outs with respectability, mixing with the looser, sporting type, all betting and drinking and showing dogs and birds, and racing. As a critic of life, however, he did not know him. But the young man felt curiously understanding. 'He uses words like I do, he talks nearly as I talk, except that I shouldn't say those things. But I might feel like that, in myself, if I went a certain road.'

401

'I've got to go to Watmore,' he said. 'Can you take me?'

'When d'you want to go?' asked the uncle fiercely.

'Now.'

'Come on, then. What d'yer stand gassin' on th' causeway for?'

The nephew took his seat beside the driver. The cab began to quiver, then it started forward with a whirr. The uncle, his hands and feet acting mechanically, kept his blue eyes fixed on the high road into whose traffic the car was insinuating its way. Berry felt curiously as if he were sitting beside an older development of himself. His mind went back to his mother. She had been twenty years older than this brother of hers, whom she had loved so dearly. 'He was one of the most affectionate little lads, and such a curly head! I could never have believed he would grow into the great, coarse bully he is – for he's nothing else. My father made a god of him – well, it's a good thing his father is dead. He got in with that sporting gang, that's what did it. Things were made too easy for him, and so he thought of no one but himself, and this is the result.'

Not that 'Joky' Sutton was so very black a sheep. He had lived idly till he was eighteen, then he had suddenly married a young, beautiful girl with clear brows and dark-grey eyes, a factory girl. Having taken her to live with his parents he, lover of dogs and pigeons, went on to the staff of a sporting paper. But his wife was without uplift or warmth. Though they made money enough, their house was dark and cold and uninviting. He had two or three dogs, and the whole attic was turned into a great pigeon-house. He and his wife lived together roughly, with no warmth, no refinement, no touch of beauty anywhere, except that she was beautiful. He was a blustering, impetuous man, she was rather cold in her soul, did not care about anything very much, was rather capable and close with money. And she had a common accent in her speech. He outdid her a thousand times in coarse language, and yet that cold twang in her voice tortured him with shame that he stamped down in bullying and in becoming more violent in his own speech.

Only his dogs adored him, and to them, and to his pigeons, he talked with rough, yet curiously tender caresses while they leaped and fluttered for joy.

After he and his wife had been married for seven years a little girl was born to them, then later, another. But the husband and wife drew no nearer together. She had an affection for her children almost like a cool governess. He had an emotional man's fear of sentiment, which helped to nip his wife from putting out any shoots. He treated his children roughly, and pretended to think it a good job when one was adopted by a well-to-do maternal aunt. But in his soul he hated his wife that she could give away one of his children. For after her cool fashion, she loved him. With a chaos of a man such as he, she had no chance of being anything but cold and hard, poor thing. For she did love him.

In the end he fell absurdly and violently in love with a rather sentimental young woman who read Browning. He made his wife an allowance and established a new *ménage* with the young lady, shortly after emigrating with her to Australia. Meanwhile his wife had gone to live with a publican, a widower, with whom she had had one of those curious, tacit understandings of which quiet women are capable, something like an arrangement for provision in the future.

This was as much as the nephew knew. He sat beside his uncle, wondering how things stood at the present. They raced lightly out past the cemetery and along the boulevard, then turned into the rather grimy country. The mud flew out on either side, there was a fine mist of rain which blew in their faces. Berry covered himself up.

In the lanes the high hedges shone black with rain. The silvery-grey sky, faintly dappled, spread wide over the low, green land. The elder man glanced fiercely up the road, then turned his red face to his nephew.

'And how're you going on, lad?' he said loudly. Berry noticed that his uncle was slightly uneasy of him. It made him also uncomfortable. The elder man had evidently something pressing on his soul.

'Who are you living with in town?' asked the nephew. 'Have you gone back to Aunt Maud?'

'No,' barked the uncle. 'She wouldn't have me. I offered to – I wanted to – but she wouldn't.'

'You're alone, then?'

'No, I'm not alone.'

He turned and glared with his fierce blue eyes at his nephew, but said no more for some time. The car ran on through the mud, under the wet wall of the park.

'That other devil tried to poison me,' suddenly shouted the elder man. 'The one I went to Australia with.' At which, in spite of himself, the younger smiled in secret.

'How was that?' he asked.

'Wanted to get rid of me. She got in with another fellow on the ship. . . . By Jove, I was bad.'

403

'Where – on the ship?'

'No,' bellowed the other. 'No. That was in Wellington, New Zealand. I was bad, and got lower an' lower – couldn't think what was up. I could hardly crawl about. As certain as I'm here, she was poisoning me, to get to th' other chap – I'm certain of it.'

'And what did you do?'

'I cleared out – went to Sydney —'

'And left her?'

'Yes, I thought begod I'd better clear out if I wanted to live.'

'And you were all right in Sydney?'

'Better in no time – I *know* she was putting poison in my coffee.'

'Hm!'

There was a glum silence. The driver stared at the road ahead, fixedly, managing the car as if it were a live thing. The nephew felt that his uncle was afraid, quite stupefied with fear, fear of life, of death, of himself.

'You're in rooms, then?' asked the nephew.

'No, I'm in a house of my own,' said the uncle defiantly, 'wi' th' best little woman in th' Midlands. She's a marvel. Why don't you come and see us?'

'I will. Who is she?'

'Oh, she's a good girl – a beautiful little thing. I was clean gone on her first time I saw her. An' she was on me. Her mother lives with us – respectable girl, none o' your . . .'

'And how old is she?'

'How old is she? She's twenty-one.'

'Poor thing.'

'*She's* right enough.'

'You'd marry her – getting a divorce —?'

'I shall marry her.'

There was a little antagonism between the two men.

'Where's Aunt Maud?' asked the younger.

'She's at the "Railway Arms" – we passed it, just against Rollin's Mill Crossing. . . . They sent me a note this morning to go an' see her when I can spare time. She's got consumption.'

'Good Lord! Are you going?'

'Yes —'

But again Berry felt that his uncle was afraid.

The young man got through his commission in the village, had a drink with his uncle at the inn, and the two were returning home. The elder man's subject of conversation was Australia. As they drew near the town they grew silent, thinking both of the public-house. At last they saw the gates of the railway crossing were closed before them.

'Shan't you call?' asked Berry, jerking his head in the direction of the inn, which stood at the corner between two roads, its sign hanging under a bare horse-chestnut tree in front.

'I might as well. Come in an' have a drink,' said the uncle.

It had been raining all the morning, so shallow pools of water lay about. A brewer's wagon, with wet barrels and warm-smelling horses, stood near the door of the inn. Everywhere seemed silent, but for the rattle of trains at the crossing. The two men went uneasily up the steps and into the bar. The place was paddled with wet feet, empty. As the barman was heard approaching, the uncle asked, his usual bluster slightly hushed by fear:

'What yer goin' ta have, lad? Same as last time?'

A man entered, evidently the proprietor. He was good-looking, with a long, heavy face and quick, dark eyes. His glance at Sutton was swift, a start, a recognition, and withdrawal, into heavy neutrality.

'How are yer, Dan?' he said, scarcely troubling to speak.

'Are yer, George?' replied Sutton, hanging back. 'My nephew, Dan Berry. Give us Red Seal, George.'

The publican nodded to the younger man, and set the glasses on the bar. He pushed forward the two glasses, then leaned back in the dark corner behind the door, his arms folded, evidently prefering to get back from the watchful eyes of the nephew.

'——'s luck,' said Sutton.

The publican nodded in acknowledgment. Sutton and his nephew drank.

'Why the hell don't you get that road mended in Cinder Hill —' said Sutton fiercely, pushing back his driver's cap and showing his short-cut, bristling hair.

'They can't find it in their hearts to pull it up,' replied the publican, laconically.

'Find in their hearts! They want settin' in barrows an' runnin' up an' down it till they cried for mercy.'

Sutton put down his glass. The publican renewed it with a sure hand, at ease in whatsoever he did. Then he leaned back against the bar. He wore no coat. He stood with arms folded, his chin on his chest, his long moustache hanging. His back was round and slack, so that the lower part of his abdomen stuck forward, though he was not stout. His cheek

405

was healthy, brown-red, and he was muscular. Yet there was about him this physical slackness, a reluctance in his slow, sure movements. His eyes were keen under his dark brows, but reluctant also, as if he were gloomily apathetic.

There was a halt. The publican evidently would say nothing. Berry looked at the mahogany bar-counter, slopped with beer, at the whisky-bottles on the shelves. Sutton, his cap pushed back, showing a white brow above a weather-reddened face, rubbed his cropped hair uneasily.

The publican glanced round suddenly. It seemed that only his dark eyes moved.

'Going up?' he asked.

And something, perhaps his eyes, indicated the unseen bed-chamber.

'Ay – that's what I came for,' replied Sutton, shifting nervously from one foot to the other. 'She's been asking for me?'

'This morning,' replied the publican, neutral.

Then he put up a flap of the bar, and turned away through the dark doorway behind. Sutton, pulling off his cap, showing a round, short-cropped head which now was ducked forward, followed after him, the buttons holding the strap of his greatcoat behind glittering for a moment.

They climbed the dark stairs, the husband placing his feet carefully, because of his big boots. Then he followed down the passage, trying vaguely to keep a grip on his bowels, which seemed to be melting away, and definitely wishing for a neat brandy. The publican opened a door. Sutton, big and burly in his greatcoat, went past him.

The bedroom seemed light and warm after the passage. There was a red eiderdown on the bed. Then, making an effort, Sutton turned his eyes to see the sick woman. He met her eyes direct, dark, dilated. It was such a shock he almost started away. For a second he remained in torture, as if some invisible flame were playing on him to reduce his bones and fuse him down. Then he saw the sharp white edge of her jaw, and the black hair beside the hollow cheek. With a start he went towards the bed.

'Hello, Maud!' he said. 'Why, what ye been doin'?'

The publican stood at the window with his back to the bed. The husband, like one condemned but on the point of starting away, stood by the bedside staring in horror at his wife, whose dilated grey eyes, nearly all black now, watched him wearily, as if she were looking at something a long way off.

Going exceedingly pale, he jerked up his head and stared at the wall over the pillows. There was a little coloured picture of a bird perched on a bell, and a nest among ivy leaves beneath. It appealed to him, made him wonder, roused a feeling of childish magic in him. They were wonderfully fresh, green ivy leaves, and nobody had seen the nest among them save him.

Then suddenly he looked down again at the face on the bed, to try and recognise it. He knew the white brow and the beautiful clear eyebrows. That was his wife, with whom he had passed his youth, flesh of his flesh, his, himself. Then those tired eyes, which met his again from a long way off, disturbed him until he did not know where he was. Only the sunken cheeks and the mouth that seemed to protrude now were foreign to him, and filled him with horror. It seemed he lost his identity. He was the young husband of the woman with the clear brows; he was the married man fighting with her whose eyes watched him, a little indifferently, from a long way off; and he was a child in horror of that protruding mouth.

There came a crackling sound of her voice. He knew she had consumption of the throat, and braced himself hard to bear the noise.

'What was it, Maud?' he asked in panic.

Then the broken, crackling voice came again. He was too terrified of the sound of it to hear what was said. There was a pause.

'You'll take Winnie?' the publican's voice interpreted from the window.

'Don't you bother, Maud, I'll take her,' he said, stupefying his mind so as not to understand.

He looked curiously round the room. It was not a bad bedroom, light and warm. There were many medicine bottles aggregated in a corner of the washstand – and a bottle of Three Star brandy, half full. And there were also photographs of strange people on the chest of drawers. It was not a bad room.

Again he started as if he were shot. She was speaking. He bent down, but did not look at her.

'Be good to her,' she whispered.

When he realised her meaning, that he should be good to their child when the mother was gone, a blade went through his flesh.

'I'll be good to her, Maud, don't you bother,' he said, beginning to feel shaky.

He looked again at the picture of the bird. It perched cheerfully under the blue sky, with robust, jolly ivy leaves near. He was gathering his courage to depart. He looked down, but struggled hard not to take in the sight of his wife's face.

'I s'll come again, Maud,' he said. 'I hope you'll go on all right. Is there anything as you want?'

There was an almost imperceptible shake of the head from the sick woman, making his heart melt swiftly again. Then, dragging his limbs, he got out of the room and down the stairs.

The landlord came after him.

'I'll let you know if anything happens,' the publican said, still laconic, but with his eyes dark and swift.

'Ay, a' right,' said Sutton blindly. He looked round for his cap, which he had all the time in his hand. Then he got out of doors.

In a moment the uncle and nephew were in the car jolting on the level crossing. The elder man seemed as if something tight in his brain made him open his eyes wide, and stare. He held the steering-wheel firmly. He knew he could steer accurately, to a hair's breadth. Glaring fixedly ahead, he let the car go, till it bounded over the uneven road. There were three coal-carts in a string. In an instant the car grazed past them, almost biting the kerb on the other side. Sutton aimed his car like a projectile, staring ahead. He did not want to know, to think, to realise, he wanted to be only the driver of that quick taxi.

The town drew near suddenly. There were allotment-gardens, with dark-purple twiggy fruit trees and wet alleys between the hedges. Then suddenly the streets of dwelling-houses whirled close, and the car was climbing the hill, with an angry whirr – up – up – till they rode out on to the crest and could see the tramcars, dark red and yellow, threading their way round the corner below, and all the traffic roaring between the shops.

'Got anywhere to go?' asked Sutton of his nephew.

'I was going to see one or two people.'

'Come an' have a bit o' dinner with us,' said the other.

Berry knew that his uncle wanted to be distracted, so that he should not think nor realise. The big man was running hard away from the horror of realisation.

'All right,' Berry agreed.

The car went quickly through the town. It ran up a long street nearly into the country again. Then it pulled up at a house that stood alone, below the road.

'I s'll be back in ten minutes,' said the uncle.

The car went on to the garage. Berry stood curiously at the top of the stone stairs that led from the high-road down to the level of the house, an old stone place. The garden was dilapidated. Broken fruit trees leaned at a sharp angle down the steep bank. Right across the dim grey atmosphere, in a kind of valley on the edge of the town, new suburb-patches showed pinkish on the dark earth. It was a kind of unresolved borderland.

Berry went down the steps. Through the broken black fence of the orchard, long grass showed yellow. The place seemed deserted. He knocked, then knocked again. An elderly woman appeared. She looked like a housekeeper. At first she said suspiciously that Mr. Sutton was not in.

'My uncle just put me down. He'll be in in ten minutes,' replied the visitor.

'Oh, are you the Mr. Berry who is related to him?' exclaimed the elderly woman. 'Come in – come in.'

She was at once kindly and a little bit servile. The young man entered. It was an old house, rather dark, and sparsely furnished. The elderly woman sat nervously on the edge of one of the chairs in a drawing-room that looked as if it were furnished from dismal relics of dismal homes, and there was a little straggling attempt at conversation. Mrs. Greenwell was evidently a working-class woman unused to service or to any formality.

Presently she gathered up courage to invite her visitor into the dining-room. There from the table under the window rose a tall, slim girl with a cat in her arms. She was evidently a little more lady-like than was habitual to her, but she had a gentle, delicate, small nature. Her brown hair almost covered her ears, her dark lashes came down in shy awkwardness over her beautiful blue eyes. She shook hands in a frank way, yet she was shrinking. Evidently she was not sure how her position would affect her visitor. And yet she was assured in herself, shrinking and timid as she was.

'She must be a good deal in love with him,' thought Berry.

Both women glanced shamefacedly at the roughly laid table. Evidently they ate in a rather rough and ready fashion.

Elaine – she had this poetic name – fingered her cat timidly, not knowing what to say or to do, unable even to ask her visitor to sit down. He noticed how her skirt hung almost flat on her hips. She was young, scarce developed, a long, slender thing. Her clothing was warm and exquisite.

The elder woman bustled out to the kitchen. Berry fondled the terrier dogs that had come curiously to his heels, and glanced out of the window at the wet, deserted orchard.

This room, too, was not well furnished, and rather dark. But there was a big red fire.

'He always has fox-terriers,' he said.

'Yes,' she answered, showing her teeth in a smile.

'Do you like them, too?'

'Yes' – she glanced down at the dogs. 'I like Tam better than Sally —'

Her speech always tailed off into an awkward silence.

'We've been to see Aunt Maud,' said the nephew.

Her eyes, blue and scared and shrinking, met his.

'Dan had a letter,' he explained. 'She's very bad.'

'Isn't it horrible!' she exclaimed, her face crumbling up with fear.

The old woman, evidently a hard-used, rather down-trodden workman's wife, came in with two soup-plates. She glanced anxiously to see how her daughter was progressing with the visitor.

'Mother, Dan's been to see Maud,' said Elaine, in a quiet voice full of fear and touble.

The old woman looked up anxiously, in question.

'I think she wanted him to take the child. She's very bad, I believe,' explained Berry.

'Oh, we should take Winnie!' cried Elaine. But both women seemed uncertain, wavering in their position. Already Berry could see that his uncle had bullied them, as he bullied everybody. But they were used to unpleasant men, and seemed to keep at a distance.

'Will you have some soup?' asked the mother humbly.

She evidently did the work. The daughter was to be a lady, more or less, always dressed and nice for when Sutton came in.

They heard him heavily running down the steps outside. The dogs got up. Elaine seemed to forget the visitor. It was as if she came into life. Yet she was nervous and afraid. The mother stood as if ready to exculpate herself.

Sutton burst open the door. Big, blustering, wet in his immense grey coat, he came into the dining-room.

'Hello!' he said to his nephew, 'making yourself at home?'

'Oh yes,' replied Berry.

'Hello, Jack,' he said to the girl. 'Got owt to grizzle about?'

'What for?' she asked, in a clear, half-challenging voice, that had that

410

peculiar twang, almost petulant, so female and so attractive. Yet she was defiant like a boy.

'It's a wonder if you haven't,' growled Sutton. And, with a really intimate movement, he stooped down and fondled his dogs, though paying no attention to them. Then he stood up, and remained with feet apart on the hearth-rug, his head ducked forward, watching the girl. He seemed abstracted, as if he could only watch her. His greatcoat hung open, so that she could see his figure, simple and human in the great husk of cloth. She stood nervously with her hands behind her, glancing at him, unable to see anything else. And he was scarcely conscious but of her. His eyes were still strained and staring, and as they followed the girl, when, long-limbed and languid, she moved away, it was as if he saw in her something impersonal, the female, not the woman.

'Had your dinner?' he asked.

'We were just going to have it,' she replied, with the same curious little vibration in her voice, like the twang of a string.

The mother entered, bringing a saucepan from which she ladled soup into three plates.

'Sit down, lad,' said Sutton. 'You sit down, Jack, an' give me mine here.'

'Oh, aren't you coming to table?' she complained.

'No, I tell you,' he snarled, almost pretending to be disagreeable. But she was slightly afraid even of the pretence, which pleased and relieved him. He stood on the hearth-rug eating his soup noisily.

'Aren't you going to take your coat off?' she said. 'It's filling the place full of steam.'

He did not answer, but, with his head bent forward over the plate, he ate his soup hastily, to get it done with. When he put down his empty plate, she rose and went to him.

'Do take your coat off, Dan,' she said, and she took hold of the breast of his coat, trying to push it back over his shoulder. But she could not. Only the stare in his eyes changed to a glare as her hand moved over his shoulder. He looked down into her eyes. She became pale, rather frightened-looking, and she turned her face away, and it was drawn slightly with love and fear and misery. She tried again to put off his coat, her thin wrists pulling at it. He stood solidly planted, and did not look at her, but stared straight in front. She was playing with passion, afraid of it, and really wretched because it left her, the person, out of count. Yet she continued. And there came into his bearing, into his eyes, the curious smile of passion, pushing away even the death-horror. It was life stronger than death in him. She stood close to his breast. Their eyes met, and she was carried away.

'Take your coat off, Dan,' she said coaxingly, in a low tone meant for no one but him. And she slid her hands on his shoulder, and he yielded, so that the coat was pushed back. She had flushed, and her eyes had grown very bright. She got hold of the cuff of his coat. Gently, he eased himself, so that she drew it off. Then he stood in a thin suit, which revealed his vigorous, almost mature form.

'What a weight!' she exclaimed, in a peculiar penetrating voice, as she went out hugging the overcoat. In a moment she came back.

He stood still in the same position, a frown over his fiercely staring eyes. The pain, the fear, the horror in his breast were all burning away in the new, fiercest flame of passion.

'Get your dinner,' he said roughly to her.

'I've had all I want,' she said. 'You come an' have yours.'

He looked at the table as if he found it difficult to see things.

'I want no more,' he said.

She stood close to his chest. She wanted to touch him and to comfort him. There was something about him now that fascinated her. Berry felt slightly ashamed that she seemed to ignore the presence of others in the room.

The mother came in. She glanced at Sutton, standing planted on the hearth-rug, his head ducked, the heavy frown hiding his face. There was a peculiar braced intensity about him that made the elder woman afraid. Suddenly he jerked his head round to his nephew.

'Get on wi' your dinner, lad,' he said, and he went to the door. The dogs, which had continually lain down and got up again, uneasy, now rose and watched. The girl went after him, saying, clearly:

'What did you want, Dan?'

Her slim, quick figure was gone, the door was closed behind her.

There was silence. The mother, still more slave-like in her movement, sat down in a low chair. Berry drank some beer.

'That girl will leave him,' he said to himself. 'She'll hate him like poison. And serve him right. Then she'll go off with somebody else.'

And she did.

412

THE HORSE DEALER'S DAUGHTER

'WELL, Mabel, and what are you going to do with yourself?' asked Joe, with foolish flippancy. He felt quite safe himself. Without listening for an answer, he turned aside, worked a grain of tobacco to the tip of his tongue, and spat it out. He did not care about anything, since he felt safe himself.

The three brothers and the sister sat round the desolate breakfast-table, attempting some sort of desultory consultation. The morning's post had given the final tap to the family fortunes, and all was over. The dreary dining-room itself, with its heavy mahogany furniture, looked as if it were waiting to be done away with.

But the consultation amounted to nothing. There was a strange air of ineffectuality about the three men, as they sprawled at table, smoking and reflecting vaguely on their own condition. The girl was alone, a rather short, sullen-looking young woman of twenty-seven. She did not share the same life as her brothers. She would have been good-looking, save for the impressive fixity of her face, 'bull-dog', as her brothers called it.

There was a confused tramping of horses' feet outside. The three men all sprawled round in their chairs to watch. Beyond the dark holly bushes that separated the strip of lawn from the high-road, they could see a cavalcade of shire horses swinging out of their own yard, being taken for exercise. This was the last time. These were the last horses that would go through their hands. The young men watched with critical, callous look. They were all frightened at the collapse of their lives, and the sense of disaster in which they were involved left them no inner freedom.

Yet they were three fine, well-set fellows enough. Joe, the eldest, was a man of thirty-three, broad and handsome in a hot, flushed way. His face was red, he twisted his black moustache over a thick finger, his eyes were shallow and restless. He had a sensual way of uncovering his teeth when he laughed, and his bearing was stupid. Now he watched the horses with a glazed look of helplessness in his eyes, a certain stupor of downfall.

The great draught-horses swung past. They were tied head to tail,

413

four of them, and they heaved along to where a lane branched off from the high-road, planting their great hoofs floutingly in the fine black mud, swinging their great rounded haunches sumptuously, and trotting a few sudden steps as they were led into the lane, round the corner. Every movement showed a massive, slumbrous strength, and a stupidity which held them in subjection. The groom at the head looked back, jerking the leading rope. And the cavalcade moved out of sight up the lane, the tail of the last horse, bobbed up tight and stiff, held out taut from the swinging great haunches as they rocked behind the hedges in a motion-like sleep.

Joe watched with glazed hopeless eyes. The horses were almost like his own body to him. He felt he was done for now. Luckily he was engaged to a woman as old as himself, and therefore her father, who was steward of a neighbouring estate, would provide him with a job. He would marry and go into harness. His life was over, he would be a subject animal now.

He turned uneasily aside, the retreating steps of the horses echoing in his ears. Then, with foolish restlessness, he reached for the scraps of bacon-rind from the plates, and making a faint whistling sound, flung them to the terrier that lay against the fender. He watched the dog swallow them, and waited till the creature looked into his eyes. Then a faint grin came on his face, and in a high, foolish voice he said:

'You won't get much more bacon, shall you, you little b——?'

The dog faintly and dismally wagged its tail, then lowered its haunches, circled round, and lay down again.

There was another helpless silence at the table. Joe sprawled uneasily in his seat, not willing to go till the family conclave was dissolved. Fred Henry, the second brother, was erect, clean-limbed, alert. He had watched the passing of the horses with more sang-froid. If he was an animal, like Joe, he was an animal which controls, not one which is controlled. He was master of any horse, and he carried himself with a well-tempered air of mastery. But he was not master of the situations of life. He pushed his coarse brown moustache upwards, off his lip, and glanced irritably at his sister, who sat impassive and inscrutable.

'You'll go and stop with Lucy for a bit, shan't you?' he asked. The girl did not answer.

'I don't see what else you can do,' persisted Fred Henry.

'Go as a skivvy,' Joe interpolated laconically.

The girl did not move a muscle.

'If I was her, I should go in for training for a nurse,' said Malcolm, the youngest of them all. He was the baby of the family, a young man of twenty-two, with a fresh, jaunty *museau*.

But Mabel did not take any notice of him. They had talked at her and round her for so many years, that she hardly heard them at all.

The marble clock on the mantelpiece softly chimed the half-hour, the dog rose uneasily from the hearth-rug and looked at the party at the breakfast-table. But still they sat on in ineffectual conclave.

'Oh, all right,' said Joe suddenly, apropos of nothing. 'I'll get a move on.'

He pushed back his chair, straddled his knees with a downward jerk, to get them free, in horsey fashion, and went to the fire. Still, he did not go out of the room; he was curious to know what the others would do or say. He began to charge his pipe, looking down at the dog and saying in a high, affected voice:

'Going wi' me? Going wi' me are ter? Tha'rt goin' further than tha counts on just now, dost hear?'

The dog faintly wagged its tail, the man stuck out his jaw and covered his pipe with his hands, and puffed intently, losing himself in the tobacco, looking down all the while at the dog with an absent brown eye. The dog looked up at him in mournful distrust. Joe stood with his knees stuck out, in real horsey fashion.

'Have you had a letter from Lucy?' Fred Henry asked of his sister.

'Last week,' came the neutral reply.

'And what does she say?'

There was no answer.

'Does she *ask* you to go and stop there?' persisted Fred Henry.

'She says I can if I like.'

'Well, then, you'd better. Tell her you'll come on Monday.'

This was received in silence.

'That's what you'll do then, is it?' said Fred Henry, in some exasperation.

But she made no answer. There was a silence of futility and irritation in the room. Malcolm grinned fatuously.

'You'll have to make up your mind between now and next Wednesday,' said Joe loudly, 'or else find yourself lodgings on the kerbstone.'

The face of the young woman darkened, but she sat on immutable.

'Here's Jack Fergusson!' exclaimed Malcolm, who was looking aimlessly out of the window.

'Where?' exclaimed Joe loudly.

'Just gone past.'

'Coming in?'

Malcolm craned his neck to see the gate.

'Yes,' he said.

There was a silence. Mabel sat on like one condemned, at the head of the table. Then a whistle was heard from the kitchen. The dog got up and barked sharply. Joe opened the door and shouted:

'Come on.'

After a moment a young man entered. He was muffled up in overcoat and a purple woollen scarf, and his tweed cap, which he did not remove, was pulled down on his head. He was of medium height, his face was rather long and pale, his eyes looked tired.

'Hello, Jack! Well, Jack!' exclaimed Malcolm and Joe. Fred Henry merely said: 'Jack.'

'What's doing?' asked the newcomer, evidently addressing Fred Henry.

'Same. We've got to be out by Wednesday. Got a cold?'

'I have – got it bad, too.'

'Why don't you stop in?'

'*Me* stop in? When I can't stand on my legs, perhaps I shall have a chance.' The young man spoke huskily. He had a slight Scotch accent.

'It's a knock-out, isn't it,' said Joe, boisterously, 'if a doctor goes round croaking with a cold. Looks bad for the patients, doesn't it?'

The young doctor looked at him slowly.

'Anything the matter with *you*, then?' he asked sarcastically.

'Not as I know of. Damn your eyes, I hope not. Why?'

'I thought you were very concerned about the patients, wondered if you might be one yourself.'

'Damn it, no, I've never been patient to no flaming doctor, and hope I never shall be,' returned Joe.

At this point Mabel rose from the table, and they all seemed to become aware of her existence. She began putting the dishes together. The young doctor looked at her, but did not address her. He had not greeted her. She went out of the room with the tray, her face impassive and unchanged.

'When are you off then, all of you?' asked the doctor.

'I'm catching the eleven-forty,' replied Malcolm. 'Are you goin' down wi' th' trap, Joe?'

'Yes, I've told you I'm going down wi' th' trap, haven't I?'

'We'd better be getting her in then. So long, Jack, if I don't see you before I go,' said Malcolm, shaking hands.

416

He went out, followed by Joe, who seemed to have his tail between his legs.

'Well, this is the devil's own,' exclaimed the doctor, when he was left alone with Fred Henry. 'Going before Wednesday, are you?'

'That's the orders,' replied the other.,

'Where, to Northampton?'

'That's it.'

'The devil!' exclaimed Fergusson, with quiet chagrin.

And there was silence between the two.

'All settled up, are you?' asked Fergusson.

'About.'

There was another pause.

'Well, I shall miss yer, Freddy, boy,' said the young doctor.

'And I shall miss thee, Jack,' returned the other.

'Miss you like hell,' mused the doctor.

Fred Henry turned aside. There was nothing to say. Mabel came in again, to finish clearing the table.

'What are *you* going to do, then, Miss Pervin?' asked Fergusson. 'Going to your sister's, are you?'

Mabel looked at him with her steady, dangerous eyes, that always made him uncomfortable, unsettling his superficial ease.

'No,' she said.

'Well, what in the name of fortune *are* you going to do? Say what you mean to do,' cried Fred Henry, with futile intensity.

But she only averted her head, and continued her work. She folded the white table-cloth, and put on the chenille cloth.

'The sulkiest bitch that ever trod!' muttered her brother.

But she finished her task with perfectly impassive face, the young doctor watching her interestedly all the while. Then she went out.

Fred Henry stared after her, clenching his lips, his blue eyes fixing in sharp antagonism, as he made a grimace of sour exasperation.

'You could bray her into bits, and that's all you'd get out of her,' he said, in a small, narrowed tone.

The doctor smiled faintly.

'What's she *going* to do, then?' he asked.

'Strike me if *I* know!' returned the other.

There was a pause. Then the doctor stirred.

'I'll be seeing you to-night, shall I?' he said to his friend.

'Ay – where's it to be? Are we going over to Jessdale?'

'I don't know. I've got such a cold on me. I'll come round to the "Moon and Stars", anyway.'

'Let Lizzie and May miss their night for once, eh?'

'That's it – if I feel as I do now.'

'All's one —'

The two young men went through the passage and down to the back door together. The house was large, but it was servantless now, and desolate. At the back was a small bricked house-yard and beyond that a big square, gravelled fine and red, and having stables on two sides. Sloping, dank, winter-dark fields stretched away on the open sides.

But the stables were empty. Joseph Pervin, the father of the family, had been a man of no education, who had become a fairly large horse dealer. The stables had been full of horses, there was a great turmoil and come-and-go of horses and of dealers and grooms. Then the kitchen was full of servants. But of late things had declined. The old man had married a second time, to retrieve his fortunes. Now he was dead and everything was gone to the dogs, there was nothing but debt and threatening.

For months, Mabel had been servantless in the big house, keeping the home together in penury for her ineffectual brothers. She had kept house for ten years. But previously it was with unstinted means. Then, however brutal and coarse everything was, the sense of money had kept her proud, confident. The men might be foul-mouthed, the women in the kitchen might have bad reputations, her brothers might have illegitimate children. But so long as there was money, the girl felt herself established, and brutally proud, reserved.

No company came to the house, save dealers and coarse men. Mabel had no associates of her own sex, after her sister went away. But she did not mind. She went regularly to church, she attended to her father. And she lived in the memory of her mother, who had died when she was fourteen, and whom she had loved. She had loved her father, too, in a different way, depending upon him, and feeling secure in him, until at the age of fifty-four he married again. And then she had set hard against him. Now he had died and left them all hopelessly in debt.

She had suffered badly during the period of poverty. Nothing, however, could shake the curious, sullen, animal pride that dominated each member of the family. Now, for Mabel, the end had come. Still she would not cast about her. She would follow her own way just the same. She would always hold the keys of her own situation. Mindless and persistent, she endured from day to day. Why should she think? Why should she answer anybody? It was enough that this was the end, and there was no way out. She need not pass any more darkly along the main street of the small town, avoiding every eye. She need not demean herself any more, going into the shops and buying the cheapest food. This was at an end. She thought of nobody, not even of herself. Mindless and persistent, she seemed in a sort of ecstasy to be coming nearer to her fulfilment, her own glorification, approaching her dead mother, who was glorified.

In the afternoon she took a little bag, with shears and sponge and a small scrubbing-brush, and went out. It was a grey, wintry day, with saddened, dark green fields and an atmosphere blackened by the smoke of foundries not far off. She went quickly, darkly along the causeway, heeding nobody, through the town to the churchyard.

There she always felt secure, as if no one could see her, although as a matter of fact she was exposed to the stare of everyone who passed along under the churchyard wall. Nevertheless, once under the shadow of the great looming church, among the graves, she felt immune from the world, reserved within the thick churchyard wall as in another country.

Carefully she clipped the grass from the grave, and arranged the pinky white, small chrysanthemums in the tin cross. When this was done, she took an empty jar from a neighbouring grave, brought water, and carefully, most scrupulously sponged the marble headstone and the coping-stone.

It gave her sincere satisfaction to do this. She felt in immediate contact with the world of her mother. She took minute pains, went through the park in a state bordering on pure happiness, as if in performing this task she came into a subtle, intimate connection with her mother. For the life she followed here in the world was far less real than the world of death she inherited from her mother.

The doctor's house was just by the church. Fergusson, being a mere hired assistant, was slave to the country-side. As he hurried now to attend to the out-patients in the surgery, glancing across the graveyard with his quick eye, he saw the girl at her task at the grave. She seemed so intent and remote, it was like looking into another world. Some mystical element was touched in him. He slowed down as he walked, watching her as if spellbound.

She lifted her eyes, feeling him looking. Their eyes met. And each looked again at once, each feeling, in some way, found out by the other. He lifted his cap and passed on down the road. There remained distinct

419

in his consciousness, like a vision, the memory of her face, lifted from the tombstone in the churchyard, and looking at him with slow, large, portentous eyes. It *was* portentous, her face. It seemed to mesmerise him. There was a heavy power in her eyes which laid hold of his whole being, as if he had drunk some powerful drug. He had been feeling weak and done before. Now the life came back into him, he felt delivered from his own fretted, daily self.

He finished his duties at the surgery as quickly as might be, hastily filling up the bottles of the waiting people with cheap drugs. Then, in perpetual haste, he set off again to visit several cases in another part of his round, before tea-time. At all times he preferred to walk if he could, but particularly when he was not well. He fancied the motion restored him.

The afternoon was falling. It was grey, deadened, and wintry, with a slow, moist, heavy coldness sinking in and deadening all the faculties. But why should he think or notice? He hastily climbed the hill and turned across the dark green fields, following the black cinder-track. In the distance, across a shallow dip in the country, the small town was clustered like smouldering ash, a tower, a spire, a heap of low, raw, extinct houses. And on the nearest fringe of the town, sloping into the dip, was Oldmeadow, the Pervins' house. He could see the stables and the outbuildings distinctly, as they lay towards him on the slope. Well, he would not go there many more times! Another resource would be lost to him, another place gone: the only company he cared for in the alien, ugly little town he was losing. Nothing but work, drudgery, constant hastening from dwelling to dwelling among the colliers and the iron-workers. It wore him out, but at the same time he had a craving for it. It was a stimulant to him to be in the homes of the working people, moving, as it were, through the innermost body of their life. His nerves were excited and gratified. He could come so near, into the very lives of the rough, inarticulate, powerfully emotional men and women. He grumbled, he said he hated the hellish hole. But as a matter of fact it excited him, the contact with the rough, strongly-feeling people was a stimulant applied direct to his nerves.

Below Oldmeadow, in the green, shallow, soddened hollow of fields, lay a square, deep pond. Roving across the landscape, the doctor's quick eye detected a figure in black passing through the gate of the field, down towards the pond. He looked again. It would be Mabel Pervin. His mind suddenly became alive and attentive.

Why was she going down there? He pulled up on the path on the slope above, and stood staring. He could just make sure of the small black figure moving in the hollow of the failing day. He seemed to see her in the midst of such obscurity, that he was like a clairvoyant, seeing rather with the mind's eye than with ordinary sight. Yet he could see her positively enough, whilst he kept his eye attentive. He felt, if he looked away from her, in the thick, ugly falling dusk, he would lose her altogether.

He followed her minutely as she moved, direct and intent, like something transmitted rather than stirring in voluntary activity, straight down the field towards the pond. There she stood on the bank for a moment. She never raised her head. Then she waded slowly into the water.

He stood motionless as the small black figure walked slowly and deliberately towards the centre of the pond, very slowly, gradually moving deeper into the motionless water, and still moving forward as the water got up to her breast. Then he could see her no more in the dusk of the dead afternoon.

'There!' he exclaimed. 'Would you believe it?'

And he hastened straight down, running over the wet, soddened fields, pushing through the hedges, down into the depression of callous wintry obscurity. It took him several minutes to come to the pond. He stood on the bank, breathing heavily. He could see nothing. His eyes seemed to penetrate the dead water. Yes, perhaps that was the dark shadow of her black clothing beneath the surface of the water.

He slowly ventured into the pond. The bottom was deep, soft clay, he sank in, and the water clasped dead cold round his legs. As he stirred he could smell the cold, rotten clay that fouled up into the water. It was objectionable in his lungs. Still, repelled and yet not heeding, he moved deeper into the pond. The cold water rose over his thighs, over his loins, upon his abdomen. The lower part of his body was all sunk in the hideous cold element. And the bottom was so deeply soft and uncertain, he was afraid of pitching with his mouth underneath. He could not swim, and was afraid.

He crouched a little, spreading his hands under the water and moving them round, trying to feel for her. The dead cold pond swayed upon his chest. He moved again, a little deeper, and again, with his hands underneath, he felt all around under the water. And he touched her clothing. But it evaded his fingers. He made a desperate effort to grasp it.

And so doing he lost his balance and went under, horribly, suffocating in the foul earthy water, struggling madly for a few moments. At last, after what seemed an eternity, he got his footing, rose again into the air and looked around. He gasped, and knew he was in the world. Then he looked at the water. She had risen near him. He grasped her clothing, and drawing her nearer, turned to take his way to land again.

He went very slowly, carefully, absorbed in the slow process. He rose higher, climbing out of the pond. The water was now only about his legs; he was thankful, full of relief to be out of the clutches of the pond. He lifted her and staggered on to the bank, out of the horror of wet, grey clay.

He laid her down on the bank. She was quite unconscious and running with water. He made the water come from her mouth, he worked to restore her. He did not have to work very long before he could feel the breathing begin again in her; she was breathing naturally. He worked a little longer. He could feel her live beneath his hands; she was coming back. He wiped her face, wrapped her in his overcoat, looked round into the dim, dark grey world, then lifted her and staggered down the bank and across the fields.

It seemed an unthinkably long way, and his burden so heavy he felt he would never get to the house. But at last he was in the stable-yard, and then in the house-yard. He opened the door and went into the house. In the kitchen he laid her down on the hearth-rug and called. The house was empty. But the fire was burning in the grate.

Then again he kneeled to attend to her. She was breathing regularly, her eyes were wide open and as if conscious, but there seemed something missing in her look. She was conscious in herself, but unconscious of her surroundings.

He ran upstairs, took blankets from a bed, and put them before the fire to warm. Then he removed her saturated, earthy-smelling clothing, rubbed her dry with a towel, and wrapped her naked in the blankets. Then he went into the dining-room, to look for spirits. There was a little whisky. He drank a gulp himself, and put some into her mouth.

The effect was instantaneous. She looked full into his face, as if she had been seeing him for some time, and yet had only just become conscious of him.

'Dr. Fergusson?' she said.

'What?' he answered.

He was divesting himself of his coat, intending to find some dry clothing upstairs. He could not bear the smell of the dead, clayey water, and he was mortally afraid for his own health.

'What did I do?' she asked.

'Walked into the pond,' he replied. He had begun to shudder like one sick, and could hardly attend to her. Her eyes remained full on him, he seemed to be going dark in his mind, looking back at her helplessly. The shuddering became quieter in him, his life came back to him, dark and unknowing, but strong again.

'Was I out of my mind?' she asked, while her eyes were fixed on him all the time.

'Maybe, for the moment,' he replied. He felt quiet, because his strength had come back. The strange fretful strain had left him.

'Am I out of my mind now?' she asked.

'Are you?' he reflected a moment. 'No,' he answered truthfully, 'I don't see that you are.' He turned his face aside. He was afraid now, because he felt dazed, and felt dimly that her power was stronger than his, in this issue. And she continued to look at him fixedly all the time. 'Can you tell me where I shall find some dry things to put on?' he asked.

'Did you dive into the pond for me?' she asked.

'No,' he answered. 'I walked in. But I went in overhead as well.'

There was silence for a moment. He hesitated. He very much wanted to go upstairs to get into dry clothing. But there was another desire in him. And she seemed to hold him. His will seemed to have gone to sleep, and left him, standing there slack before her. But he felt warm inside himself. He did not shudder at all, though his clothes were sodden on him.

'Why did you?' she asked.

'Because I didn't want you to do such a foolish thing,' he said.

'It wasn't foolish,' she said, still gazing at him as she lay on the floor, with a sofa cushion under her head. 'It was the right thing to do. *I* knew best, then.'

'I'll go and shift these wet things,' he said. But still he had not the power to move out of her presence, until she sent him. It was as if she had the life of his body in her hands, and he could not extricate himself. Or perhaps he did not want to.

Suddenly she sat up. Then she became aware of her own immediate condition. She felt the blankets about her, she knew her own limbs. For a moment it seemed as if her reason were going. She looked round, with wild eye, as if seeking something. He stood still with fear. She saw her clothing lying scattered.

'Who undressed me?' she asked, her eyes resting full and inevitable on his face.

423

'I did,' he replied, 'to bring you round.'

For some moments she sat and gazed at him awfully, her lips parted. 'Do you love me, then?' she asked.

He only stood and stared at her, fascinated. His soul seemed to melt.

She shuffled forward on her knees, and put her arms round him, round his legs, as he stood there, pressing her breasts against his knees and thighs, clutching him with strange, convulsive certainty, pressing his thighs against her, drawing him to her face, her throat, as she looked up at him with flaring, humble eyes and transfiguration, triumphant in first possession.

'You love me,' she murmured, in strange transport, yearning and triumphant and confident. 'You love me. I know you love me, I know.'

And she was passionately kissing his knees, through the wet clothing, passionately and indiscriminately kissing his knees, his legs, as if unaware of everything.

He looked down at the tangled wet hair, the wild, bare, animal shoulders. He was amazed, bewildered, and afraid. He had never thought of loving her. He had never wanted to love her. When he rescued her and restored her, he was a doctor, and she was a patient. He had had no single personal thought of her. Nay, this introduction of the personal element was very distasteful to him, a violation of his professional honour. It was horrible to have her there embracing his knees. It was horrible. He revolted from it, violently. And yet – and yet – he had not the power to break away.

She looked at him again, with the same supplication of powerful love, and that same transcendent, frightening light of triumph. In view of the delicate flame which seemed to come from her face like a light, he was powerless. And yet he had never intended to love her. He had never intended. And something stubborn in him could not give way.

'You love me,' she repeated, in a murmur of deep, rhapsodic assurance. 'You love me.'

Her hands were drawing him, drawing him down to her. He was afraid, even a little horrified. For he had, really, no intention of loving her. Yet her hands were drawing him towards her. He put out his hand quickly to steady himself, and grasped her bare shoulder. A flame seemed to burn the hand that grasped her soft shoulder. He had no intention of loving her: his whole will was against his yielding. It was horrible. And yet wonderful was the touch of her shoulders, beautiful the shining of her face. Was she perhaps mad? He had a horror of yielding to her. Yet something in him ached also.

He had been staring away at the door, away from her. But his hand remained on her shoulder. She had gone suddenly very still. He looked down at her. Her eyes were now wide with fear, with doubt, the light was dying from her face, a shadow of terrible greyness was returning. He could not bear the touch of her eyes' question upon him, and the look of death behind the question.

With an inward groan he gave way, and let his heart yield towards her. A sudden gentle smile came on his face. And her eyes, which never left his face, slowly, slowly filled with tears. He watched the strange water rise in her eyes, like some slow fountain coming up. And his heart seemed to burn and melt away in his breast.

He could not bear to look at her any more. He dropped on his knees and caught her head with his arms and pressed her face against his throat. She was very still. His heart, which seemed to have broken, was burning with a kind of agony in his breast. And he felt her slow, hot tears wetting his throat. But he could not move.

He felt the hot tears wet his neck and the hollows of his neck, and he remained motionless, suspended through one of man's eternities. Only now it had become indispensable to him to have her face pressed close to him; he could never let her go again. He could never let her head go away from the close clutch of his arm. He wanted to remain like that for ever, with his heart hurting him in a pain that was also life to him. Without knowing, he was looking down on her damp, soft brown hair.

Then, as it were suddenly, he smelt the horrid stagnant smell of that water. And at the same moment she drew away from him and looked at him. Her eyes were wistful and unfathomable. He was afraid of them, and he fell to kissing her, not knowing what he was doing. He wanted her eyes not to have that terrible, wistful, unfathomable look.

When she turned her face to him again, a faint delicate flush was glowing, and there was again dawning that terrible shining of joy in her eyes, which really terrified him, and yet which he now wanted to see, because he feared the look of doubt still more.

'You love me?' she said, rather faltering.

'Yes.' The word cost him a painful effort. Not because it wasn't true. But because it was too newly true, the *saying* seemed to tear open again his newly-torn heart. And he hardly wanted it to be true, even now.

She lifted her face to him, and he bent forward and kissed her on the mouth, gently, with the one kiss that is an eternal pledge. And as he kissed her his heart strained again in his breast. He never intended to love her. But now it was over. He had crossed over the gulf to her, and all that he had left behind had shrivelled and become void.

After the kiss, her eyes again slowly filled with tears. She sat still, away from him, with her face drooped aside, and her hands folded in her lap. The tears fell very slowly. There was complete silence. He too sat there motionless and silent on the hearth-rug. The strange pain of his heart that was broken seemed to consume him. That he should love her? That this was love! That he should be ripped open in this way! Him, a doctor! How they would all jeer if they knew! It was agony to him to think they might know.

In the curious naked pain of the thought he looked again to her. She was sitting there drooped into a muse. He saw a tear fall, and his heart flared hot. He saw for the first time that one of her shoulders was quite uncovered, one arm bare, he could see one of her small breasts; dimly, because it had become almost dark in the room.

'Why are you crying?' he asked, in an altered voice.

She looked up at him, and behind her tears the consciousness of her situation for the first time brought a dark look of shame to her eyes.

'I'm not crying, really,' she said, watching him, half frightened.

He reached his hand, and softly closed it on her bare arm.

'I love you! I love you!' he said in a soft, low vibrating voice, unlike himself.

She shrank, and dropped her head. The soft, penetrating grip of his hand on her arm distressed her. She looked up at him.

'I want to go,' she said. 'I want to go and get you some dry things.'

'Why?' he said. 'I'm all right.'

'But I want to go,' she said. 'And I want you to change your things.'

He released her arm, and she wrapped herself in the blanket, looking at him rather frightened. And still she did not rise.

'Kiss me,' she said wistfully.

He kissed her, but briefly, half in anger.

Then, after a second, she rose nervously, all mixed up in the blanket. He watched her in her confusion as she tried to extricate herself and wrap herself up so that she could walk. He watched her relentlessly, as she knew. And as she went, the blanket trailing, and as he saw a glimpse of her feet and her white leg, he tried to remember her as she was when he had wrapped her in the blanket. But then he didn't want to remember, because she had been nothing to him then, and his nature revolted from remembering her as she was when she was nothing to him.

426

A tumbling, muffled noise from within the dark house startled him. Then he heard her voice: 'There are clothes.' He rose and went to the foot of the stairs, and gathered up the garments she had thrown down. Then he came back to the fire, to rub himself down and dress. He grinned at his own appearance when he had finished.

The fire was sinking, so he put on coal. The house was now quite dark, save for the light of a street-lamp that shone in faintly from beyond the holly trees. He lit the gas with matches he found on the mantelpiece. Then he emptied the pockets of his own clothes, and threw all his wet things in a heap into the scullery. After which he gathered up her sodden clothes, gently, and put them in a separate heap on the copper-top in the scullery.

It was six o'clock on the clock. His own watch had stopped. He ought to go back to the surgery. He waited, and still she did not come down. So he went to the foot of the stairs and called:

'I shall have to go.'

Almost immediately he heard her coming down. She had on her best dress of black voile, and her hair was tidy, but still damp. She looked at him – and in spite of herself, smiled.

'I don't like you in those clothes,' she said.

'Do I look a sight?' he answered.

They were shy of one another.

'I'll make you some tea,' she said.

'No, I must go.'

'Must you?' And she looked at him again with the wide, strained, doubtful eyes. And again, from the pain of his breast, he knew how he loved her. He went and bent to kiss her, gently, passionately, with his heart's painful kiss.

'And my hair smells so horrible,' she murmured in distraction. 'And I'm so awful, I'm so awful! Oh no, I'm too awful.' And she broke into bitter, heart-broken sobbing. 'You can't want to love me, I'm horrible.'

'Don't be silly, don't be silly,' he said, trying to comfort her, kissing her, holding her in his arms. 'I want you, I want to marry you, we're going to be married, quickly, quickly – to-morrow if I can.'

But she only sobbed terribly, and cried:

'I feel awful. I feel awful. I feel I'm horrible to you.'

'No, I want you, I want you,' was all he answered, blindly, with that terrible intonation which frightened her almost more than her horror lest he should *not* want her.

FANNY AND ANNIE

FLAME-LURID his face as he turned among the throng of flame-lit and dark faces upon the platform. In the light of the furnace she caught sight of his drifting countenance, like a piece of floating fire. And the nostalgia, the doom of home-coming went through her veins like a drug. His eternal face, flame-lit now! The pulse and darkness of red fire from the furnace towers in the sky, lighting the desultory, industrial crowd on the wayside station, lit him and went out.

Of course he did not see her. Flame-lit and unseeing! Always the same, with his meeting eyebrows, his common cap, and his red-and-black scarf knotted round his throat. Not even a collar to meet her! The flames had sunk, there was shadow.

She opened the door of her grimy, branch-line carriage, and began to get down her bags. The porter was nowhere, of course, but there was Harry, obscure, on the outer edge of the little crowd, missing her, of course.

'Here! Harry!' she called, waving her umbrella in the twilight. He hurried forward.

'Tha's come, has ter?' he said, in a sort of cheerful welcome. She got down, rather flustered, and gave him a peck of a kiss.

'Two suit-cases!' she said.

Her soul groaned within her, as he clambered into the carriage after her bags. Up shot the fire in the twilight sky, from the great furnace behind the station. She felt the red flame go across her face. She had come back, she had come back for good. And her spirit groaned dismally. She doubted if she could bear it.

There, on the sordid little station under the furnaces, she stood, tall and distinguished, in her well-made coat and skirt and her broad grey velour hat. She held her umbrella, her bead chatelaine, and a little leather case in her grey-gloved hands, while Harry staggered out of the ugly little train with her bags.

'There's a trunk at the back,' she said in her bright voice. But she was not feeling bright. The twin black cones of the iron foundry blasted their sky-high fires into the night. The whole scene was lurid. The train

428

waited cheerfully. It would wait another ten minutes. She knew it. It was all so deadly familiar.

Let us confess it at once. She was a lady's maid, thirty years old, come back to marry her first-love, a foundry worker: after having kept him dangling off and on, for a dozen years. Why had she come back? Did she love him? No. She didn't pretend to. She had loved her brilliant and ambitious cousin, who had jilted her, and who had died. She had had other affairs which had come to nothing. So here she was, come back suddenly to marry her first-love, who had waited – or remained single – all these years.

'Won't a porter carry these?' she said, as Harry strode with his workman's stride down the platform towards the guard's van.

'I can manage,' he said.

And with her umbrella, her chatelaine, and her little leather case, she followed him.

The trunk was there.

'We'll get Heather's greengrocer's cart to fetch it up,' he said.

'Isn't there a cab?' said Fanny, knowing dismally enough that there wasn't.

'I'll just put it aside o' the penny-in-the-slot, and Heather's greengrocers'll fetch it about half-past eight,' he said.

He seized the box by its two handles and staggered with it across the level-crossing, bumping his legs against it as he waddled. Then he dropped it by the red sweetmeats machine.

'Will it be safe there?' she said.

'Ay – safe as houses,' he answered. He returned for the two bags. Thus laden, they started to plod up the hill, under the great long black building of the foundry. She walked beside him – workman of workmen he was, trudging with that luggage. The red lights flared over the deepening darkness. From the foundry came the horrible, slow clang clang, clang of iron, a great noise, with an interval just long enough to make it unendurable.

Compare this with the arrival at Gloucester: the carriage for her mistress, the dog-cart for herself with the luggage! the drive out past the river, the pleasant trees of the carriage-approach; and herself sitting beside Arthur, everybody so polite to her.

She had come home – for good! Her heart nearly stopped beating as she trudged up that hideous and interminable hill, beside the laden figure. What a come-down! What a come-down! She could not take it with her usual bright cheerfulness. She knew it all too well. It is easy to bear up against the unusual, but the deadly familiarity of an old stale past!

He dumped the bags down under a lamp-post, for a rest. There they stood, the two of them, in the lamp-light. Passers-by stared at her, and gave good-night to Harry. Her they hardly knew, she had become a stranger.

'They're too heavy for you, let me carry one,' she said.

'They begin to weigh a bit by the time you've gone a mile,' he answered.

'Let me carry the little one,' she insisted.

'Tha can ha'e it for a minute, if ter's a mind,' he said, handing over the valise.

And thus they arrived in the streets of shops of the little ugly town on top of the hill. How everybody stared at her; my word, how they stared! And the cinema was just going in, and the queues were tailing down the road to the corner. And everybody took full stock of her. 'Night, Harry!' shouted the fellows, in an interested voice.

However, they arrived at her aunt's – a little sweet-shop in a side street. They 'pinged' the door-bell, and her aunt came running forward out of the kitchen.

'There you are, child! Dying for a cup of tea, I'm sure. How are you?'

Fanny's aunt kissed her, and it was all Fanny could do to refrain from bursting into tears, she felt so low. Perhaps it was her tea she wanted.

'You've had a drag with that luggage,' said Fanny's aunt to Harry.

'Ay – I'm not sorry to put it down,' he said, looking at his hand which was crushed and cramped by the bag handle.

Then he departed to see about Heather's greengrocery cart.

When Fanny sat at tea, her aunt, a grey-haired, fair-faced little woman, looked at her with an admiring heart, feeling bitterly sore for her. For Fanny was beautiful: tall, erect, finely coloured, with her delicately arched nose, her rich brown hair, her large lustrous-grey eyes. A passionate woman – a woman to be afraid of. So proud, so inwardly violent! She came of a violent race.

It needed a woman to sympathise with her. Men had not the courage. Poor Fanny! She was such a lady, and so straight and magnificent. And yet everything seemed to do her down. Every time she seemed to be doomed to humiliation and disappointment, this handsome, brilliantly sensitive woman, with her nervous, over-wrought laugh.

'So you've really come back, child?' said her aunt.

'I really have, Aunt,' said Fanny.

'Poor Harry! I'm not sure, you know, Fanny, that you're not taking a bit of an advantage of him.'

'Oh, Aunt, he's waited so long, he may as well have what he's waited for.' Fanny laughed grimly.

'Yes, child, he's waited so long, that I'm not sure it isn't a bit hard on him. You know, I *like* him, Fanny – though as you know quite well, I don't think he's good enough for you. And I think he thinks so himself, poor fellow.'

'Don't you be so sure of that, Aunt. Harry is common, but he's not humble. He wouldn't think the Queen was any too good for him, if he's a mind to her.'

'Well – it's as well if he has a proper opinion of himself.'

'It depends what you call proper,' said Fanny. 'But he's got his good points —'

'Oh, he's a nice fellow, and I like him, I do like him. Only, as I tell you, he's not good enough for you.'

'I've made up my mind, Aunt,' said Fanny, grimly.

'Yes,' mused the aunt. 'They say all things come to him who waits —'

'More than he's bargained, for, eh, Aunt?' laughed Fanny rather bitterly.

The poor aunt, this bitterness grieved her for her niece.

They were interrupted by the ping of the shop-bell, and Harry's call of 'Right!' But as he did not come in at once, Fanny, feeling solicitous for him presumably at the moment, rose and went into the shop. She saw a cart outside, and went to the door.

And the moment she stood in the doorway, she heard a woman's common vituperative voice crying from the darkness of the opposite side of the road:

'Tha'rt theer, are ter? I'll shame thee, Mester. I'll shame thee, see if I dunna.'

Startled, Fanny started across the darkness, and saw a woman in a black bonnet go under one of the lamps up the side street.

Harry and Bill Heather had dragged the trunk off the little dray, and she retreated before them as they came up the shop step with it.

'Wheer shal ha'e it?' asked Harry.

'Best take it upstairs,' said Fanny.

She went up first to light the gas.

When Heather had gone, and Harry was sitting down having tea and pork-pie, Fanny asked:

'Who was that woman shouting?'

'Nay, I canna tell thee. To somebody, I s'd think,' replied Harry. Fanny looked at him, but asked no more.

He was a fair-haired fellow of thirty-two, with a fair moustache. He was broad in his speech, and looked like a foundry-hand, which he was. But women always liked him. There was something of a mother's lad about him – something warm and playful and really sensitive.

He had his attractions even for Fanny. What she rebelled against so bitterly was that he had no sort of ambition. He was a moulder, but of very commonplace skill. He was thirty-two years old, and hadn't saved twenty pounds. She would have to provide the money for the home. He didn't care. He just didn't care. He had no initiative at all. He had no vices – no obvious ones. But he was just indifferent, spending as he went, and not caring. Yet he did not look happy. She remembered his face in the fire-glow: something haunted, abstracted about it. As he sat there eating his pork-pie, bulging his cheek out, she felt he was like a doom to her. And she raged against the doom of him. It wasn't that he was gross. His *way* was common, almost on purpose. But he himself wasn't really common. For instance, his food was not particularly important to him, he was not greedy. He had a charm, too, particularly for women, with his blondness and his sensitiveness and his way of making a woman feel that she was a higher being. But Fanny knew him, knew the peculiar obstinate limitedness of him, that would nearly send her mad.

He stayed till about half-past nine. She went to the door with him.

'When are you coming up?' he said, jerking his head in the direction, presumably, of his own home.

'I'll come to-morrow afternoon,' she said brightly. Between Fanny and Mrs. Goodall, his mother, there was naturally no love lost.

Again she gave him an awkward little kiss, and said good-night.

'You can't wonder, you know, child, if he doesn't seem so very keen,' said her aunt, 'It's your own fault.'

'Oh, Aunt, I couldn't stand him when he was keen. I can do with him a lot better as he is.'

The two women sat and talked far into the night. They understood each other. The aunt, too, had married as Fanny was marrying: a man who was no companion to her, a violent man, brother of Fanny's father. He was dead, Fanny's father was dead.

Poor Aunt Lizzie, she cried woefully over her bright niece, when she had gone to bed.

Fanny paid the promised visit to his people the next afternoon. Mrs. Goodall was a large woman with smooth-parted hair, a common, obstinate woman, who had spoiled her four lads and her one vixen of a married daughter. She was one of those old-fashioned powerful natures that couldn't do with looks or education or any form of showing-off. She fairly hated the sound of correct English. She *thee'd* and *tha'd* her prospective daughter-in-law, and said:

'I'm none as ormin' as I look, seest ta.'

Fanny did not think her prospective mother-in-law looked at all orming, so the speech was unnecessary.

'I towd him mysen,' said Mrs. Goodall, ' 'Er's held back all this long, let 'er stop as 'er is. 'E'd none ha' had thee for *my* tellin' – tha hears. No, 'e's a fool, an' I know it. I says to him: "Tha looks a man, doesn't ter, at thy age, goin' an' openin' to her when ter hears her scrat' at th' gate, after she's done gallivantin' round wherever she's a mind. That looks rare an' soft." But it's no use o' any talking: he answered that letter o' thine and made his own bad bargain.'

But in spite of the old woman's anger, she was also flattered at Fanny's coming back to Harry. For Mrs. Goodall was impressed by Fanny – a woman of her own match. And more than this, everybody knew that Fanny's Aunt Kate had left her two hundred pounds: this apart from the girl's savings.

So there was high tea in Princes Street when Harry came home black from work, and a rather acrid odour of cordiality, the vixen Jinny darting in to say vulgar things. Of course Jinny lived in a house whose garden end joined the paternal garden. They were a clan who stuck together, these Goodalls.

It was arranged that Fanny should come to tea again on the Sunday, and the wedding was discussed. It should take place in a fortnight's time at Morley Chapel. Morley was a hamlet on the edge of the real country, and in its little Congregational Chapel Fanny and Harry had first met.

What a creature of habit he was! He was still in the choir of Morley Chapel – not very regular. He belonged just because he had a tenor voice, and enjoyed singing. Indeed, his solos were only spoilt to local fame because when he sang he handled his aitches so hopelessly.

'And I saw 'eaven hopened
And be'old, a wite 'orse —'

433

This was one of Harry's classics, only surpassed by the fine outburst of his heaving:

'*Hangels – hever bright an' fair —*'

It was a pity, but it was unalterable. He had a good voice, and he sang with a certain lacerating fire, but his pronunciation made it all funny. And *nothing* could alter him.

So he was never heard save at cheap concerts and in the little, poorer chapels. The other scoffed.

Now the month was September, and Sunday was Harvest Festival at Morley Chapel, and Harry was singing solos. So that Fanny was to go to service, and come home to a grand spread of Sunday tea with him. Poor Fanny! One of the most wonderful afternoons had been a Sunday afternoon service, with her cousin Luther at her side, Harvest Festival in Morley Chapel. Harry had sung solos then – ten years ago. She remembered his pale-blue tie, and the purple asters and the great vegetable marrows in which he was famed, and her cousin Luther at her side, young, clever, come down from London, where he was getting on well, learning his Latin and his French and German so brilliantly.

However, once again it was Harvest Festival at Morley Chapel, and once again, as ten years before, a soft, exquisite September day, with the last roses pink in the cottage gardens, the last dahlias crimson, the last sunflowers yellow. And again the little old chapel was a bower, with its famous sheaves of corn and corn-plaited pillars, its great bunches of grapes, dangling like tassels from the pulpit corners, its marrows and potatoes and pears and apples and damsons, its purple asters and yellow Japanese sunflowers. Just as before, the red dahlias round the pillars were dropping, weak-headed among the oats. The place was crowded and hot, the plates of tomatoes seemed balanced perilous on the gallery front, the Rev. Enderby was weirder than ever to look at, so long and emaciated and hairless.

The Rev. Enderby, probably forewarned, came and shook hands with her and welcomed her, in his broad northern, melancholy sing-song before he mounted the pulpit. Fanny was handsome in a gauzy dress and a beautiful lace hat. Being a little late, she sat in a chair in the side-aisle wedged in, right in front of the chapel. Harry was in the gallery above, and she could only see him from the eyes upwards. She noticed again how his eyebrows met, blond and not very marked, over his nose. He was attractive, too: physically lovable, very. If only – if only her *pride* had not suffered! She felt he dragged her down.

> *'Come, ye thankful people, come,*
> *Raise the song of harvest-home.*
> *All is safely gathered in*
> *Ere the winter storms begin —'*

Even the hymn was a falsehood, as the season had been wet, and half the crops were still out, and in a poor way.

Poor Fanny! She sang little, and looked beautiful through that inappropriate hymn. Above her stood Harry – mercifully in a dark suit and a dark tie, looking almost handsome. And his lacerating, pure tenor sounded well, when the words were drowned in the general commotion. Brilliant she looked, and brilliant she felt, for she was hot and angrily miserable and inflamed with a sort of fatal despair. Because there was about him a physical attraction which she really hated, but which she could not escape from. He was the first man who had ever kissed her. And his kisses, even while she rebelled from them, had lived in her blood and sent roots down into her soul. After all this time she had come back to them. And her soul groaned, for she felt dragged down, dragged down to earth, as a bird which some dog has got down in the dust. She knew her life would be unhappy. She knew that what she was doing was fatal. Yet it was her doom. She had to come back to him.

He had to sing two solos this afternoon: one before the 'address' from the pulpit and one after. Fanny looked in him, and wondered he was not too shy to stand up there in front of all the people. But no, he was not shy. He had even a kind of assurance on his face as he looked down from the choir gallery at her: the assurance of a common man deliberately entrenched in his commonness. Oh, such a rage went through her veins as she saw the air of triumph, laconic, indifferent triumph which sat so obstinately and recklessly on his eyelids as he looked down at her. Ah, she despised him! But there he stood up in that choir gallery like Balaam's ass in front of her, and she could not get beyond him. A certain winsomeness also about him. A certain physical winsomeness, and as if his flesh were new and lovely to touch. The thorn of desire rankled bitterly in her heart.

He, it goes without saying, sang like a canary, this particular afternoon, with a certain defiant passion which pleasantly crisped the blood of the congregation. Fanny felt the crisp flames go through her veins as she listened. Even the curious loud-mouthed vernacular had a certain fascination. But, oh, also, it was so repugnant. He would triumph over

435

her, obstinately he would drag her right back into the common people:
a doom, a vulgar doom.

The second performance was an anthem, in which Harry sang the
solo parts. It was clumsy, but beautiful, with lovely words.

> *'They that sow in tears shall reap in joy,*
> *He that goeth forth and weepeth, bearing precious seed*
> *Shall doubtless come again rejoicing, bring his sheaves with*
> *   him —'*

'*Shall doubtless come, Shall doubtless come* —' softly intoned the
altos – '*Bringing his she-e-eaves with him,*' the trebles flourished
brightly, and then again began the half-wistful solo:

> *'They that sow in tears shall reap in joy —'*

Yes, it was effective and moving.

But at the moment when Harry's voice sank carelessly down to his
close, and the choir, standing behind him, were opening their mouths
for the final triumphant outburst, a shouting female voice rose up from
the body of the congregation. The organ gave one startled trump, and
went silent; the choir stood transfixed.

'You look well standing there, singing in God's holy house,' came the
loud, angry female shout. Everybody turned electrified. A stoutish, red-
faced woman in a black bonnet was standing up denouncing the soloist.
Almost fainting with shock, the congregation realised it. 'You look
well, don't you, standing there singing solos in God's holy house, you,
Goodall. But I said I'd shame on you. You look well, bringing your
young woman here with you, don't you? I'll let her know who she's
dealing with. A scamp as won't take the consequences of what he's
done.' The hard-faced, frenzied woman turned in the direction of
Fanny. '*That's* what Harry Goodall is, if you want to know.'

And she sat down again in her seat. Fanny, startled like all the
rest, had turned to look. She had gone white, and then a burning red,
under the attack. She knew the woman: a Mrs. Nixon, a devil of a
woman, who beat her pathetic, drunken, red-nosed second husband,
Bob, and her two lanky daughters, grown-up as they were. A notorious
character. Fanny turned round again, and sat motionless as eternity in
her seat.

There was a minute of perfect silence and suspense. The audience
was open-mouthed and dumb; the choir stood like Lot's wife; and

Harry, with his music-sheet, stood there uplifted, looking down with a dumb sort of indifference on Mrs. Nixon, his face naïve and faintly mocking. Mrs. Nixon sat defiant in her seat, braving them all.

Then a rustle, like a wood when the wind suddenly catches the leaves. And then the tall, weird minister got to his feet, and in his strong, bell-like, beautiful voice – the only beautiful thing about him – he said with infinite mournful pathos:

'Let us unite in singing the last hymn on the hymn-sheet; the last hymn on the hymn-sheet, number eleven.

> *"Fair waved the golden corn*
> *In Canaan's pleasant land."* '

The organ tuned up promptly. During the hymn the offertory was taken. And after the hymn, the prayer.

Mr. Enderby came from Northumberland. Like Harry, he had never been able to conquer his accent, which was very broad. He was a little simple, one of God's fools, perhaps, an odd bachelor soul, emotional, ugly, but very gentle.

'And if, O our dear Lord, beloved Jesus, there should fall a shadow of sin upon our harvest, we leave it to Thee to judge, for Thou art judge. We lift our spirits and our sorrow, Jesus, to Thee, and our mouths are dumb. O Lord, keep us from forward speech, restrain us from foolish words and thoughts, we pray Thee, Lord Jesus, who knowest all and judgest all.'

Thus the minister said in his sad, resonant voice, washed his hands before the Lord. Fanny bent forward open-eyed during the prayer. She could see the roundish head of Harry, also bent forward. His face was inscrutable and expressionless. The shock left her bewildered. Anger perhaps was her dominating emotion.

The audience began to rustle to its feet, to ooze slowly and excitedly out of the chapel, looking with wildly interested eyes at Fanny, at Mrs. Nixon, and at Harry. Mrs. Nixon, shortish, stood defiant in her pew, facing the aisle, as if announcing that, without rolling her sleeves up, she was ready for anybody. Fanny sat quite still. Luckily the people did not have to pass her. And Harry, with red ears, was making his way sheepishly out of the gallery. The loud noise of the organ covered all the downstairs commotion of exit.

The minister sat silent and inscrutable in his pulpit, rather like a death's-head, while the congregation filed out. When the last lingerers had unwillingly departed, craning their necks to stare at the still seated Fanny, he rose, stalked in his hooked fashion down the little country chapel and fastened the door. Then he returned and sat down by the silent young woman.

'This is most unfortunate, most unfortunate!' he moaned. 'I am so sorry, I am so sorry, indeed, indeed, ah, indeed!' he sighed himself to a close.

'It's a sudden surprise, that's one thing,' said Fanny brightly.

'Yes – yes – indeed. Yes, a surprise, yes. I don't know the woman, I don't know her.'

'I know her,' said Fanny. 'She's a bad one.'

'Well! Well!' said the minister. 'I don't know her. I don't understand. I don't understand at all. But it is to be regretted, it is very much to be regretted. I am very sorry.'

Fanny was watching the vestry door. The gallery stairs communicated with the vestry, not with the body of the chapel. She knew the choir members had been peeping for information.

At last Harry came – rather sheepishly – with his hat in his hand.

'Well!' said Fanny, rising to her feet.

'We've had a bit of an extra,' said Harry.

'I should think so,' said Fanny.

'A most unfortunate circumstance – a most *unfortunate* circumstance. Do you understand it, Harry? I don't understand it at all.'

'Ay, I understand it. The daughter's goin' to have a childt, an' 'er lays it to me.'

'And has she no occasion to?' asked Fanny, rather censorious.

'It's no more mine than it is some other chap's,' said Harry, looking aside.

There was a moment of pause.

'Which girl is it?' asked Fanny.

'Annie – the young one —'

There followed another silence.

'I don't think I know them, do I?' asked the minister.

'I shouldn't think so. Their name's Nixon – mother married old Bob for her second husband. She's a tanger, she's driven the gel to what she is. They live in Manners Road.'

'Why, what's amiss with the girl?' asked Fanny sharply. 'She was all right when I knew her.'

'Ay – she's all right. But she's always in an' out o' th' pubs, wi' th' fellows,' said Harry.

438

'A nice thing!' said Fanny.

Harry glanced towards the door. He wanted to get out.

'Most distressing, indeed!' the minister slowly shook his head.

'What about to-night, Mr. Enderby?' asked Harry, in rather a small voice. 'Shall you want me?'

Mr. Enderby looked up painedly, and put his hand to his brow. He studied Harry for some time, vacantly. There was the faintest sort of a resemblance between the two men.

'Yes,' he said. 'Yes, I think. I think we must take no notice and cause as little remark as possible.'

Fanny hesitated. Then she said to Harry:

'But *will* you come?'

He looked at her.

'Ay, I s'll come,' he said.

Then he turned to Mr. Enderby.

'Well, good afternoon, Mr. Enderby,' he said.

'Good afternoon, Harry, good afternoon,' replied the mournful minister. Fanny followed Harry to the door, and for some time they walked in silence through the late afternoon.

'And it's yours as much as anybody else's?' she said.

'Ay,' he answered shortly.

And they went without another word, for the long mile or so, till they came to the corner of the street where Harry lived. Fanny hesitated. Should she go on to her aunt's? Should she? It would mean leaving all this, for ever. Harry stood silent.

Some obstinacy made her turn with him along the road to his own home. When they entered the house-place, the whole family was there, mother and father and Jinny, with Jinny's husband and children and Harry's two brothers.

'You've been having your ears warmed, they tell me,' said Mrs. Goodall grimly.

'Who told thee?' asked Harry shortly.

'Maggie and Luke's both been in.'

'You look well, don't you!' said interfering Jinny.

Harry went and hung his hat up, without replying.

'Come upstairs and take your hat off,' said Mrs. Goodall to Fanny, almost kindly. It would have annoyed her very much if Fanny had dropped her son at this moment.

'What's 'er say, then?' asked the father secretly of Harry, jerking his head in the direction of the stairs whence Fanny had disappeared.

'Nowt yet,' said Harry.

'Serve you right if she chucks you now,' said Jinny. 'I'll bet it's right about Annie Nixon an' you.'

'Tha bets so much,' said Harry.

'Yi – but you can't deny it,' said Jinny.

'I can if I've a mind.'

His father looked at him inquiringly.

'It's no more mine than it is Bill Bower's, or Ted Slaney's, or six or seven on 'em,' said Harry to his father.

And the father nodded silently.

'That'll not get you out of it, in court,' said Jinny.

Upstairs Fanny evaded all the thrusts made by his mother, and did not declare her hand. She tidied her hair, washed her hands, and put the tiniest bit of powder on her face, for coolness, there in front of Mrs. Goodall's indignant gaze. It was like a declaration of independence. But the old woman said nothing.

They came down to Sunday tea, with sardines and tinned salmon and tinned peaches, besides tarts and cakes. The chatter was general. It concerned the Nixon family and the scandal.

'Oh, she's a foul-mouthed woman,' said Jinny of Mrs. Nixon. 'She may well talk about God's holy house, *she* had. It's first time she's set foot in it, ever since she dropped off from being converted. She's a devil and she always was one. Can't you remember how she treated Bob's children, mother, when we lived down in the Buildings? I can remember when I was a little girl she used to bathe them in the yard, in the cold, so that they shouldn't splash the house. She'd half kill them if they made a mark on the floor, and the language she'd use! And one Saturday I can remember Garry, that was Bob's own girl, she ran off when her stepmother was going to bathe her – ran off without a rag of clothes on – can you remember, mother? And she hid in Smedley's closes – it was the time of mowing-grass – and nobody could find her. She hid out there all night, didn't she, mother? Nobody could find her. My word, there was a talk. They found her on Sunday morning —'

'Fred Coutts threatened to break every bone in the woman's body, if she touched the children again,' put in the father.

'Anyhow, they frightened her,' said Jinny. 'But she was nearly as bad with her own two. And anybody can see that she'd driven old Bob till he's gone soft.'

'Ah, soft as mush,' said Jack Goodall. ''E'd never addle a week's wages, nor yet a day's, if th' chaps didn't make it up to him.'

'My word, if he didn't bring her a week's wage, she'd pull his head off,' said Jinny.

'But a clean woman, and respectable, except for her foul mouth,' said Mr. Goodall. 'Keeps to herself like a bulldog. Never lets anybody come near the house, and neighbours with nobody.'

'Wanted it thrashed out of her,' said Mr. Goodall, a silent, evasive sort of man.

'Where Bob gets the money for his drink from is a mystery,' said Jinny.

'Chaps treats him,' said Harry.

'Well, he's got the pair of frightenedest rabbit-eyes you'd wish to see,' said Jinny.

'Ay, with a drunken man's murder in them, *I* think,' said Mrs. Goodall.

So the talk went on after tea, till it was practically time to start off to the chapel again.

'You'll have to be getting ready, Fanny,' said Mrs. Goodall.

'I'm not going to-night,' said Fanny abruptly. And there was a sudden halt in the family. 'I'll stop with *you* to-night, mother,' she added.

'Best you had, my gel,' said Mrs. Goodall, flattered and assured.

THE PRINCESS

To her father, she was The Princess. To her Boston aunts and uncles she was just *Dollie Urquhart, poor little thing*.

Colin Urquhart was just a bit mad. He was of an old Scottish family, and he claimed royal blood. The blood of Scottish kings flowed in his veins. On this point, his American relatives said, he was just a bit 'off'. They could not bear any more to be told *which* royal blood of Scotland blued his veins. The whole thing was rather ridiculous, and a sore point. The only fact they remembered was that it was not Stuart.

He was a handsome man, with a wide-open blue eye that seemed sometimes to be looking at nothing, soft black hair brushed rather low on his low, broad brow, and a very attractive body. Add to this a most beautiful speaking voice, usually rather hushed and diffident, but sometimes resonant and powerful like bronze, and you have the sum of his charms. He looked like some old Celtic hero. He looked as if he should have worn a greyish kilt and a sporran, and shown his knees. His voice came direct out of the hushed Ossianic past.

For the rest, he was one of those gentlemen of sufficient but not excessive means who fifty years ago wandered vaguely about, never arriving anywhere, never doing anything, and never definitely being anything, yet well received in the good society of more than one country.

He did not marry till he was nearly forty, and then it was a wealthy Miss Prescott, from New England. Hannah Prescott at twenty-two was fascinated by the man with the soft black hair not yet touched by grey, and the wide, rather vague blue eyes. Many women had been fascinated before her. But Colin Urquhart, by his very vagueness, had avoided any decisive connection.

Mrs. Urquhart lived three years in the mist and glamour of her husband's presence. And then it broke her. It was like living with a fascinating spectre. About most things he was completely, even ghostly oblivious. He was always charming, courteous, perfectly gracious in that hushed, musical voice of his. But absent. When all came to all, he just wasn't there. 'Not all there,' as the vulgar say.

He was the father of the little girl she bore at the end of the first year. But this did not substantiate him the more. His very beauty and his haunting musical quality became dreadful to her after the first few months. The strange echo: he was like a living echo! His very flesh, when you touched it, did not seem quite the flesh of a real man.

Perhaps it was that he was a little bit mad. She thought it definitely the night her baby was born.

'Ah, so my little princess has come at last!' he said, in his throaty, singing Celtic voice, like a glad chant, swaying absorbed.

It was a tiny, frail baby, with wide, amazed blue eyes. They christened it Mary Henrietta. She called the little thing *My Dollie*. He called it always *My Princess*.

It was useless to fly at him. He just opened his wide blue eyes wider, and took a child-like, silent dignity there was no getting past.

Hannah Prescott had never been robust. She had no great desire to live. So when the baby was two years old she suddenly died.

The Prescotts felt a deep but unadmitted resentment against Colin Urquhart. They said he was selfish. Therefore they discontinued Hannah's income, a month after her burial in Florence, after they had urged the father to give the child over to them, and he had courteously, musically, but quite finally refused. He treated the Prescotts as if they were not of his world, not realities to him: just casual phenomena, or gramophones, talking-machines that had to be answered. He answered them. But of their actual existence he was never once aware.

They debated having him certified unsuitable to be guardian of his own child. But that would have created a scandal. So they did the simplest thing, after all – washed their hands of him. But they wrote scrupulously to the child, and sent her modest presents of money at Christmas, and on the anniversary of the death of her mother.

To The Princess her Boston relatives were for many years just a nominal reality. She lived with her father, and he travelled continually, though in a modest way, living on his moderate income. And never going to America. The child changed nurses all the time. In Italy it was a contadina; in India she had an ayah; in Germany she had a yellow-haired peasant girl.

Father and child were inseparable. He was not a recluse. Wherever he went he was to be seen paying formal calls going out to luncheon or to tea, rarely to dinner. And always with the child. People called her Princess Urquhart, as if that were her christened name.

She was a quick, dainty little thing with dark gold hair that went a soft brown, and wide, slightly prominent blue eyes that were at once so candid and so knowing. She was always grown up; she never really grew up. Always strangely wise, and always childish.

It was her father's fault.

'My little Princess must never take too much notice of people and the things they say and do,' he repeated to her. 'People don't know what they are doing and saying. They chatter-chatter, and they hurt one another, and they hurt themselves very often, till they cry. But don't take any notice, my little Princess. Because it is all nothing. Inside everybody there is another creature, a demon which doesn't care at all. You peel away all the things they say and do and feel, as cook peels away the outside of the onions. And in the middle of everybody there is a green demon which you can't peel away. And this green demon never changes, and it doesn't care at all about all the things that happen to the outside leaves of the person, all the chatter-chatter, and all the husbands and wives and children, and troubles and fusses. You peel everything away from people, and there is a green, upright demon in every man and woman; and this demon is a man's real self, and a woman's real self. It doesn't really care about anybody, it belongs to the demons and the primitive fairies, who never care. But, even so, there are big demons and mean demons, and splendid demonish fairies, and vulgar ones. But there are no royal fairy women left. Only you, my little Princess. You are the last of the royal race of the old people; the last, my Princess. There are no others. You and I are the last. When I am dead there will be only you. And that is why, darling, you will never care for any of the people in the world very much. Because their demons are all dwindled and vulgar. They are not royal. Only you are royal, after me. Always remember that. And always remember, it is a *great secret*. If you tell people, they will try to kill you, because they will envy you for being a Princess. It is our great secret, darling. I am a prince, and you a princess, of the old, old blood. And we keep our secret between us, all alone. And so, darling, you must treat all people very politely, because *noblesse oblige*. But you must never forget that you alone are the last of Princesses, and that all other are less than you are, less noble, more vulgar. Treat them politely and gently and kindly, darling. But you are the Princess, and they are commoners. Never try to think of them as if they were like you. They are not. You will find, always, that they are lacking, lacking in the royal touch, which only you have —'

The Princess learned her lesson early – the first lesson, of absolute reticence, the impossibility of intimacy with any other than her father;

the second lesson, of naïve, slightly benevolent politeness. As a small child, something crystallised in her character, making her clear and finished, and as impervious as crystal.

'Dear child!' her hostesses said of her. 'She is so quaint and old-fashioned; such a lady, poor little mite!'

She was erect, and very dainty. Always small, nearly tiny in physique, she seemed like a changeling beside her big, handsome, slightly mad father. She dressed very simply, usually in blue or delicate greys, with little collars of old Milan point, or very finely-worked linen. She had exquisite little hands, that made the piano sound like a spinet when she played. She was rather given to wearing cloaks and capes, instead of coats, out of doors, and little eighteenth-century sort of hats. Her complexion was pure apple-blossom.

She looked as if she had stepped out of a picture. But no one, to her dying day, ever knew exactly the strange picture her father had framed her in and from which she never stepped.

Her grandfather and grandmother and her Aunt Maud demanded twice to see her, once in Rome and once in Paris. Each time they were charmed, piqued, and annoyed. She was so exquisite and such a little virgin. At the same time so knowing and so oddly assured. That odd, assured touch of condescension, and the inward coldness, infuriated her American relations.

Only she really fascinated her grandfather. He was spellbound; in a way, in love with the little faultless thing. His wife would catch him brooding, musing over his grandchild, long months after the meeting, and craving to see her again. He cherished to the end the fond hope that she might come to live with him and her grandmother.

'Thank you so much, grandfather. You are so very kind. But Papa and I are such an old couple, you see, such a crochety old couple, living in a world of our own.'

Her father let her see the world – from the outside. And he let her read. When she was in her teens she read Zola and Maupassant, and with the eyes of Zola and Maupassant she looked on Paris. A little later she read Tolstoi and Dostoevsky. The latter confused her. The others, she seemed to undertand with a very shrewd, canny understanding, just as she understood the Decameron stories as she read them in their old Italian, or the Nibelung poems. Strange and *uncanny*, she seemed to understand things in a cold light perfectly, with all the flush of fire absent. She was something like a changeling, not quite human.

This earned her, also, strange antipathies. Cabmen and railway porters, especially in Paris and Rome, would suddenly treat her with brutal rudeness, when she was alone. They seemed to look on her with sudden violent antipathy. They sensed in her curious impertinence, an easy, sterile impertinence towards the things *they* felt most. She was so assured, and her flower of maidenhood was so scentless. She could look at a lusty, sensual Roman cabman as if he were a sort of grotesque, to make her smile. She knew all about him, in Zola. And the peculiar condescension with which she would give him her order, as if she, frail, beautiful thing, were the only reality, and he, coarse monster, was a sort of Caliban floundering in the mud on the margin of the pool of the perfect lotus, would suddenly enrage the fellow, the real Mediterranean who prided himself on his *beauté male*, and to whom the phallic mystery was still the only mystery. And he would turn a terrible face on her, bully her in a brutal, coarse fashion – hideous. For to him she had only the blasphemous impertinence of her own sterility.

Encounters like these made her tremble, and made her know she must have support from the outside. The power of her spirit did not extend to these low people, and they had all the physical power. She realised an implacability of hatred in their turning on her. But she did not lose her head. She quietly paid out money and turned away.

Those were dangerous moments, though, and she learned to be prepared for them. The Princess she was, and the fairy from the North, and could never understand the volcanic phallic rage with which coarse people could turn on her in a paroxysm of hatred. They never turned on her father like that. And quite early she decided it was the New England mother in her whom they hated. Never for one minute could she see with the old Roman eyes, see herself as sterility, the barren flower taking on airs and an intolerable impertinence. This was what the Roman cabman saw in her. And he longed to crush the barren blossom. Its sexless beauty and its authority put him in a passion of brutal revolt.

When she was nineteen her grandfather died, leaving her a considerable fortune in the safe hands of responsible trustees. They would deliver her her income, but only on condition that she resided for six months in the year in the United States.

'Why should they make me conditions?' she said to her father. 'I refuse to be imprisoned six months in the year in the United States. We will tell them to keep their money.'

'Let us be wise, my little Princess, let us be wise. No, we are almost poor, and we are never safe from rudeness. I cannot allow anybody to be rude to me. I hate it, I hate it!' His eyes flamed as he said it. 'I could kill any man or woman who is rude to me. But we are in exile in the world. We are powerless. If we were really poor, we should be quite powerless, and then I should die. No, my Princess. Let us take their money, then they will not dare to be rude to us. Let us take it, as we put on clothes, to cover ourselves from their aggressions.'

There began a new phase, when the father and daughter spent their summers on the Great Lakes or in California, or in the South-West. The father was something of a poet, the daughter something of a painter. He wrote poems about the lakes or the redwood trees, and she made dainty drawings. He was physically a strong man, and he loved the out-of-doors. He would go off with her for days, paddling in a canoe and sleeping by a camp-fire. Frail little Princess, she was always undaunted, always undaunted. She would ride with him on horseback over the mountain trails till she was so tired she was nothing but a bodiless consciousness sitting astride her pony. But she never gave in. And at night he folded her in her blanket on a bed of balsam pine twigs, and she lay and looked at the stars unmurmuring. She was fulfilling her rôle.

People said to her as the years passed, and she was a woman of twenty-five, then a woman of thirty, and always the same virgin dainty Princess, 'knowing' in a dispassionate way, like an old woman, and utterly intact:

'Don't you ever think what you will do when your father is no longer with you?'

She looked at her interlocutor with that cold, elfin detachment of hers:

'No, I never think of it,' she said.

She had a tiny, but exquisite little house in London, and another small perfect house in Connecticut, each with a faithful housekeeper. Two homes, if she chose. And she knew many interesting literary and artistic people. What more?

So the years passed imperceptibly. And she had that quality of the sexless fairies, she did not change. At thirty-three she looked twenty-three.

Her father, however, was ageing, and becoming more and more queer. It was now her task to be his guardian in his private madness. He spent the last three years of life in the house in Connecticut. He was very much estranged, sometimes had fits of violence which almost killed the little Princess. Physical violence was horrible to her; it seemed to shatter her heart. But she found a woman a few years younger than herself, well-educated and sensitive, to be a sort of nurse-companion to the mad old man. So the fact of madness was never openly admitted. Miss Cummins, the companion, had a passionate loyalty to the Princess, and a curious affection, tinged with love, for the handsome, white-haired, courteous old man, who was never at all aware of his fits of violence once they had passed.

The princess was thirty-eight years old when her father died. And quite unchanged. She was still tiny, and like a dignified, scentless flower. Her soft brownish hair, almost the colour of beaver fur, was bobbed, and fluffed softly round her apple-blossom face, that was modelled with an arched nose like a proud old Florentine portrait. In her voice, manner and bearing she was exceedingly still, like a flower that has blossomed in a shadowy place. And from her blue eyes looked out the Princess's eternal laconic challenge, that grew almost sardonic as the years passed. She was the Princess, and sardonically she looked out on the princeless world.

She was relieved when her father died, and at the same time, it was as if everything had evaporated around her. She had lived in a sort of hot-house, in the aura of her father's madness. Suddenly the hot-house had been removed from around her, and she was in the raw, vast, vulgar open air.

Quoi faire? What was she to do? She seemed faced with absolute nothingness. Only she had Miss Cummins, who shared with her the secret, and almost the passion for her father. In fact, the Princess felt that her passion for her mad father had in some curious way transferred itself largely to Charlotte Cummins during the last years. And now Miss Cummins was the vessel that held the passion for the dead man. She herself, the Princess, was an empty vessel.

An empty vessel in the enormous warehouse of the world.

Quoi faire? What was she to do? She felt that, since she could not evaporate into nothingness, like alcohol from an unstoppered bottle, she must *do* something. Never before in her life had she felt the incumbency. Never, never had she felt she must *do* anything. That was left to the vulgar.

Now her father was dead, she found herself on the *fringe* of the vulgar crowd, sharing their necessity to *do* something. It was a little humiliating. She felt herself becoming vulgarised. At the same time she found herself looking at men with a shrewder eye: an eye to marriage. Not that she felt any sudden interest in men, or attraction towards them. No. She was still neither interested nor attracted towards men vitally. But *marriage*, that peculiar abstraction, had imposed a sort of spell on her. She thought that *marriage*, in the blank abstract, was the thing she ought to *do*. That *marriage* implied a man she also knew. She knew all the facts. But the man seemed a property of her own mind rather than a thing in himself, another thing.

Her father died in the summer, the month after her thirty-eighth birthday. When all was over, the obvious thing to do, of course, was to travel. With Miss Cummins. The two women knew each other intimately, but they were always Miss Urquhart and Miss Cummins to one another, and a certain distance was instinctively maintained. Miss Cummins, from Philadelphia, of scholastic stock, and intelligent but untravelled, four years younger than the Princess, felt herself immensely the junior of her 'lady'. She had a sort of passionate veneration for the Princess, who seemed to her ageless, timeless. She could not see the rows of tiny, dainty, exquisite shoes in the Princess's cupboard without feeling a stab at the heart, a stab of tenderness and reverence, almost of awe.

Miss Cummins also was virginal, but with a look of puzzled surprise in her brown eyes. Her skin was pale and clear, her features well modelled, but there was a certain blankness in her expression, where the Princess had an odd touch of Renaissance grandeur. Miss Cummins's voice was also hushed almost to a whisper; it was the inevitable effect of Colin Urquhart's room. But the hushedness had a hoarse quality.

The Princess did not want to go to Europe. Her face seemed turned west. Now her father was gone, she felt she would go west, westwards, as if for ever. Following, no doubt, the March of Empire, which is brought up rather short on the Pacific coast, among swarms of wallowing bathers.

No, not the Pacific coast. She would stop short of that. The South-West was less vulgar. She would go to New Mexico.

She and Miss Cummins arrived at the Rancho del Cerro Gordo towards the end of August, when the crowd was beginning to drift back east. The ranch lay by a stream on the desert some four miles from the foot of the mountains, a mile away from the Indian pueblo of San Cristobal. It was a ranch for the rich; the Princess paid thirty dollars a day for herself and Miss Cummins. But then she had a little cottage to herself, among the apple trees of the orchard, with an excellent cook. She and Miss Cummins, however, took dinner at evening in the large guest-house. For the Princess still entertained the idea of *marriage*.

The guests at the Rancho del Cerro Gordo were of all sorts, except

449

the poor sort. They were practically all rich, and many were romantic. Some were charming, others were vulgar, some were movie people, quite quaint and not unattractive in their vulgarity, and many were Jews. The Princess did not care for Jews, though they were usually the most interesting to *talk* to. So she talked a good deal with the Jews, and painted with the artists, and rode with the young men from college, and had altogether quite a good time. And yet she felt something of a fish out of water, or a bird in the wrong forest. And *marriage* remained still completely in the abstract. No connecting it with any of these young men, even the nice ones.

The Princess looked just twenty-five. The freshness of her mouth, the hushed, delicate-complexioned virginity of her face gave her not a day more. Only a certain laconic look in her eyes was disconcerting. When she was *forced* to write her age, she put twenty-eight, making the figure *two* rather badly, so that it just avoided being a three.

Men hinted marriage at her. Especially boys from college suggested it from a distance. But they all failed before the look of sardonic ridicule in the Princess's eyes. It always seemed to her rather preposterous, quite ridiculous, and a tiny bit impertinent on their part.

The only man that intrigued her at all was one of the guides, a man called Romero – Domingo Romero. It was he who had sold the ranch itself to the Wilkiesons, ten years before, for two thousand dollars. He had gone away, then reappeared at the old place. For he was the son of the old Romero, the last of the Spanish family that had owned miles of land around San Cristobal. But the coming of the white man and the failure of the vast flocks of sheep, and the fatal inertia which overcomes all men, at last, on the desert near the mountains, had finished the Romero family. The last descendants were just Mexican peasants.

Domongo, the heir, had spent his two thousand dollars, and was working for white people. He was now about thirty years old, a tall, silent fellow, with a heavy closed mouth and black eyes that looked across at one almost sullenly. From behind he was handsome, with a strong, natural body, and the back of his neck very dark and well-shapen, strong with life. But his dark face was long and heavy, almost sinister, with that peculiar heavy meaningless in it, characteristic of the Mexicans of his own locality. They are strong, they seem healthy. They laugh and joke with one another. But their physique and their natures seem static, as if there were nowhere, nowhere at all for their energies to go, and their faces, degenerating to misshapen heaviness, seem to have no *raison d'être*, no radical meaning. Waiting either to die or to be aroused into passion and hope. In some of the black eyes a queer, haunting mystic quality, sombre and a bit gruesome, the skull-and-cross-bones look of the Penitentes. They had found their *raison d'être* in self-torture and death-worship. Unable to wrest a *positive* significance for themselves from the vast, beautiful, but vindictive landscape they were born into, they turned on their own selves, and worshipped death through self-torture. The mystic gloom of this showed in their eyes.

But as a rule the dark eyes of the Mexicans were heavy and half alive, sometimes hostile, sometimes kindly, often with the fatal Indian glaze on them, or the fatal Indian glint.

Domingo Romero was *almost* a typical Mexican to look at, with the typical heavy, dark, long face, clean-shaven, with an almost brutally heavy mouth. His eyes were black and Indian-looking. Only, at the centre of their hopelessness was a spark of pride, or self-confidence, or dauntlessness. Just a spark in the midst of the blackness of static despair.

But this spark was the difference between him and the mass of men. It gave a certain alert sensitiveness to his bearing and a certain beauty to his appearance. He wore a low-crowned black hat, instead of the ponderous headgear of the usual Mexican, and his clothes were thinnish and graceful. Silent, aloof, almost imperceptible in the landscape, he was an admirable guide, with a startling quick intelligence that anticipated difficulties about to rise. He could cook, too, crouching over the camp-fire and moving his lean deft brown hands. The only fault he had was that he was not forthcoming, he wasn't chatty and cosy.

'Oh, don't send Romero with us,' the Jews would say. 'One can't get any response from him.'

Tourists come and go, but they rarely *see* anything, inwardly. None of them ever saw the spark at the middle of Romero's eye; they were not alive enough to see it.

The Princess caught it one day, when she had him for a guide. She was fishing for trout in the canyon, Miss Cummins was reading a book, the horses were tied under the trees, Romero was fixing a proper fly on her line. He fixed the fly and handed her the line, looking up at her. And at that moment she caught the spark in his eye. And instantly she knew that he was a gentleman, that his 'demon', as her father would have said, was a fine demon. And instantly her manner towards him changed.

He had perched her on a rock over a quiet pool, beyond the cotton-wood trees. It was early September, and the canyon already cool, but

451

the leaves of the cottonwoods were still green. The Princess stood on her rock, a small but perfectly-formed figure, wearing a soft, close grey sweater and neatly-cut grey riding-breeches, with tall black boots, her fluffy brown hair straggling from under a little grey felt hat. A woman? Not quite. A changeling of some sort, perched in outline there on the rock, in the bristling wild canyon. She knew perfectly well how to handle a line. Her father had made a fisherman of her.

Romero, in a black shirt and with loose black trousers pushed into wide black riding-boots, was fishing a little farther down. He had put his hat on a rock behind him; his dark head head was bent a little forward, watching the water. He had caught three trout. From time to time he glanced up-stream at the Princess, perched there so daintily. He saw she had caught nothing.

Soon he quietly drew in his line and came up to her. His keen eye watched her line, watched her position. Then, quietly, he suggested certain changes to her, putting his sensitive brown hand before her. And he withdrew a little, and stood in silence, leaning against a tree, watching her. He was helping her across the distance. She knew it, and thrilled. And in a moment she had a bite. In two minutes she landed a good trout. She looked round at him quickly, her eyes sparkling, the colour heightened in her cheeks. And as she met his eyes a smile of greeting went over his dark face, very sudden, with an odd sweetness.

She knew he was helping her. And she felt in his presence a subtle, insidious male *kindliness* she had never known before waiting upon her. Her cheek flushed, and her blue eyes darkened.

After this, she always looked for him, and for that curious dark beam of a man's kindliness which he could give her, as it were, from his chest, from his heart. It was something she had never known before.

A vague, unspoken intimacy grew up between them. She liked his voice, his appearance, his presence. His natural language was Spanish; he spoke English like a foreign language, rather slow, with a slight hesitation, but with a sad, plangent sonority lingering over from his Spanish. There was a certain subtle correctness in his appearance; he was always perfectly shaved; his hair was thick and rather long on top, but always carefully groomed behind. And his fine black cashmere shirt, his wide leather belt, his well-cut, wide black trousers going into the embroidered cowboy boots had a certain inextinguishable elegance. He wore no silver rings or buckles. Only his boots were embroidered and decorated at the top with an inlay of white *suède*. He seemed elegant, slender, yet he was very strong.

And at the same time, curiously, he gave her the feeling that death was not far from him. Perhaps he too was half in love with death. However that may be, the sense she had that death was not far from him made him 'possible' to her.

Small as she was, she was quite a good horsewoman. They gave her at the ranch a sorrel mare, very lovely in colour, and well-made, with a powerful broad neck and the hollow back that betokens a swift runner. Tansy, she was called. Her only fault was the usual mare's failing, she was inclined to be hysterical.

So that every day the Princess set off with Miss Cummins and Romero, on horseback, riding into the mountains. Once they went camping for several days, with two more friends in the party.

'I think I like it better,' the Princess said to Romero, 'when we three go alone.'

And he gave her one of his quick, transfiguring smiles.

It was curious no white man had ever showed her this capacity for subtle gentleness, this power to *help* her in silence across a distance, if she were fishing without success, or tired of her horse, or if Tansy suddenly got scared. It was as if Romero could send her *from his heart* a dark beam of succour and sustaining. She had never known this before, and it was very thrilling.

Then the smile that suddenly creased his dark face, showing the strong white teeth. It creased his face almost into a savage grotesque. And at the same time there was in it something so warm, such a dark flame of kindliness for her, she was elated into her true Princess self.

Then that vivid, latent spark in his eye, which she had seen, and which she knew he was aware she had seen. It made an inter-recognition between them, silent and delicate. Here he was delicate as a woman in this subtle inter-recognition.

And yet his presence only put to flight in her the *idée fixe* of 'marriage'. For some reason, in her strange little brain, the idea of *marrying* him could not enter. Not for any definite reason. He was in himself a gentleman, and she had plenty of money for two. There was no actual obstacle. Nor was she conventional.

No, now she came down to it, it was as if their two 'dæmons' could marry, were perhaps married. Only their two *selves*, Miss Urquhart and Señor Domingo Romero, were for some reason incompatible. There was a peculiar subtle intimacy of inter-recognition between them. But she did not see in the least how it would lead to marriage. Almost she could more easily marry one of the nice boys from Harvard or Yale.

453

The time passed, and she let it pass. The end of September came, with aspens going yellow on the mountain heights, and oak-scrub going red. But as yet the cottonwoods in the valley and canyons had not changed.

'When will you go away?' Romero asked her, looking at her fixedly, with a blank black eye.

'By the end of October,' she said. 'I have promised to be in Santa Barbara at the beginning of November.'

He was hiding the spark in his eye from her. But she saw the peculiar sullen thickening of his heavy mouth.

She had complained to him many times that one never saw any wild animals, except chipmunks and squirrels, and perhaps a skunk and a porcupine. Never a deer, or a bear, or a mountain lion.

'Are there no bigger animals in these mountains?' she asked, dissatisfied.

'Yes,' he said. 'There are deer – I see their tracks. And I saw the tracks of a bear.'

'But why can one never see the animals themselves?' She looked dissatisfied and wistful like a child.

'Why, it's pretty hard for you to see them. They won't let you come close. You have to keep still, in a place where they come. Or else you have to follow their tracks a long way.'

'I can't bear to go away till I've seen them: a bear, or a deer —'

The smile came suddenly on his face, indulgent.

'Well, what do you want? Do you want to go up into the mountains to some place, to wait till they come?'

'Yes,' she said, looking up at him with a sudden naïve impulse of recklessness.

And immediately his face became sombre again, responsible.

'Well,' he said, with slight irony, a touch of mockery of her. 'You will have to find a house. It's very cold at night now. You would have to stay all night in a house.'

'And there are no houses up there?' she said.

'Yes,' he replied. 'There is a little shack that belongs to me, that a miner built a long time ago, looking for gold. You can go there and stay one night, and maybe you see something. Maybe! I don't know. Maybe nothing come.'

'How much chance is there?'

'Well, I don't know. Last time when I was there I see three deer come down to drink at the water, and I shot two raccoons. But maybe this time we don't see anything.'

'Is there water there?' she asked.

'Yes, there is a little round pond, you know, below the spruce trees. And the water from the snow runs into it.'

'Is it far away?' she asked.

'Yes, pretty far. You see that ridge there' – and turning to the mountains he lifted his arm in the gesture which is somehow so moving, out in the West, pointing to the distance – 'that ridge where there are no trees, only rock' – his black eyes were focussed on the distance, his face impassive, but as if in pain – 'you go round that ridge, and along, then you come down through the spruce trees to where that cabin is. My father bought that placer claim from a miner who was broke, but nobody ever found any gold or anything, and nobody ever goes there. Too lonesome!'

The Princess watched the massive, heavy-sitting, beautiful bulk of the Rocky Mountains. It was early in October, and the aspens were already losing their gold leaves; high up, the spruce and pine seemed to be growing darker; the great flat patches of oak scrub on the heights were red like gore.

'Can I go over there?' she asked, turning to him and meeting the spark in his eye.

His face was heavy with responsibility.

'Yes,' he said, 'you can go. But there'll be snow over the ridge, and it's awful cold, and awful lonesome.'

'I should like to go,' she said, persistent.

'All right,' he said. 'You can go if you want to.'

She doubted, though, if the Wilkiesons would let her go; at least alone with Romero and Miss Cummins.

Yet an obstinacy characteristic of her nature, an obstinacy tinged perhaps with madness, had taken hold of her. She wanted to look over the mountains into their secret heart. She wanted to descend to the cabin below the spruce trees, near the tarn of bright green water. She wanted to see the wild animals move about in their wild unconsciousness.

'Let us say to the Wilkiesons that we want to make the trip round the Frijoles canyon,' she said.

The trip round the Frijoles canyon was a usual thing. It would not be strenuous, nor cold, nor lonely: they could sleep in the log house that was called an hotel.

Romero looked at her quickly.

'If you want to say that,' he replied, 'you can tell Mrs. Wilkieson. Only I know she'll be mad with me if I take you up in the mountains to that place. And I've got to go there first with a pack-horse, to take lots of blankets and some bread. Maybe Miss Cummins can't stand it. Maybe not. It's a hard trip.'

He was speaking, and thinking, in the heavy, disconnected Mexican fashion.

'Never mind!' The Princess was suddenly very decisive and stiff with authority. 'I want to do it. I will arrange with Mrs. Wilkieson. And we'll go on Saturday.'

He shook his head slowly.

'I've got to go up on Sunday with a pack-horse and blankets,' he said. 'Can't do it before.'

'Very well!' she said, rather piqued. 'Then we'll start on Monday.'

She hated being thwarted even the tiniest bit.

He knew that if he started with the pack on Sunday at dawn he would not be back until late at night. But he consented that they should start on Monday morning at seven. The obedient Miss Cummins was told to prepare for the Frijoles trip. On Sunday Romero had his day off. He had not put in an appearance when the Princess retired on Sunday night, but on Monday morning, as she was dressing, she saw him bringing in the three horses from the corral. She was in high spirits.

The night had been cold. There was ice at the edges of the irrigation ditch, and the chipmunks crawled into the sun and lay with wide, dumb, anxious eyes, almost too numb to run.

'We may be away two or three days,' said the Princess.

'Very well. We won't begin to be anxious about you before Thursday, then,' said Mrs. Wilkieson, who was young and capable: from Chicago. 'Anyway,' she added, 'Romero will see you through. He's so trustworthy.'

The sun was already on the desert as they set off towards the mountains, making the greasewood and the sage pale as pale-grey sands, luminous the great level around them. To the right glinted the shadows of the adope pueblo, flat and almost invisible on the plain, earth of its earth. Behind lay the ranch and the tufts of tall, plumy cottonwoods, whose summits were yellowing under the perfect blue sky.

Autumn breaking into colour in the great spaces of the South-West.

But the three trotted gently along the trail, towards the sun that sparkled yellow just above the dark bulk of the ponderous mountains. Side-slopes were already gleaming yellow, flaming with a second light, under coldish blue of the pale sky. The front slopes were in shadow, with submerged lustre of red oak scrub and dull-gold aspens, blue-black pines and grey-blue rock. While the canyon was full of a deep blueness.

They rode single file, Romero first, on a black horse. Himself in black, made a flickering black spot in the delicate pallor of the great landscape, where even pine trees at a distance take a film of blue paler than their green. Romero rode on in silence past the tufts of furry greasewood. The Princess came next, on her sorrel mare. And Miss Cummins, who was not quite happy on horseback, came last, in the pale dust that the others kicked up. Sometimes her horse sneezed, and she started.

But on they went at a gentle trot. Romero never looked round. He could hear the sound of the hoofs following, and that was all he wanted.

For the rest, he held ahead. And the Princess, with that black, unheeding figure always travelling away from her, felt strangely helpless, withal elated.

They neared the pale, round foot-hills, dotted with the round dark piñon and cedar shrubs. The horses clinked and trotted among the stones. Occasionally a big round greasewood held out fleecy tufts of flowers, pure gold. They wound into blue shadow, then up a steep stony slope, with the world lying pallid away behind and below. Then they dropped into the shadow of the San Cristobal canyon.

The stream was running full and swift. Occasionally the horses snatched at a tuft of grass. The trail narrowed and became rocky; the rocks closed in; it was dark and cool as the horses climbed and climbed upwards, and the tree trunks crowded in the shadowy, silent tightness of the canyon. They were among cottonwood trees than ran straight up and smooth and round to an extraordinary height. Above, the tips were gold, and it was sun. But away below, where the horses struggled up the rocks and wound among the trunks, there was still blue shadow by the sound of waters and an occasional grey festoon of old man's beard, and here and there a pale, dripping crane's-bill flower among the tangle and the débris of the virgin place. And again the chill entered the Princess's heart as she realised what a tangle of decay and despair lay in the virgin forests.

They scrambled downwards, splashed across stream, up rocks and along the trail of the other side. Romero's black horse stopped, looked down quizzically at the fallen trees, then stepped over lightly. The

Princess's sorrel followed, carefully. But Miss Cummins's buckskin made a fuss, and had to be got round.

In the same silence, save for the clinking of horses and the splashing as the trail crossed stream, they worked their way upwards in the tight, tangled shadow of the canyon. Sometimes, crossing stream the Princess would glance upwards, and then always her heart caught in her breast. For high up, away in heaven, the mountain heights shone yellow, dappled with dark spruce firs, clear almost as speckled daffodils against the pale turquoise blue lying high and serene above the dark-blue shadow where the Princess was. And she would snatch at the blood-red leaves of the oak as her horse crossed a more open slope, not knowing what she felt.

They were getting fairly high, occasionally lifted above the canyon itself, in the low groove below the speckled, gold-sparkling heights which towered beyond. Then again they dipped and crossed stream, the horses stepping gingerly across a tangle of fallen, frail aspen stems, then suddenly floundering in a mass of rocks. The black emerged ahead, his black tail waving. The Princess let her mare find her own footing; then she too emerged from the clatter. She rode on after the black. Then came a great frantic rattle of the buckskin behind. The Princess was aware of Romero's dark face looking round, with a strange, demon-like watchfulness, before she herself looked round, to see the buckskin scrambling rather lamely beyond the rocks, with one of his pale buff knees already red with blood.

'He almost went down!' called Miss Cummins.

But Romero was already out of the saddle and hastening down the path. He made quiet little noises to the buckskin, and began examining the cut knee.

'Is he hurt?' cried Miss Cummins anxiously, and she climbed hastily down.

'Oh, my goodness!' she cried, as she saw the blood running down the slender buff leg of the horse in a thin trickle. 'Isn't that *awful*?' She spoke in a stricken voice, and her face was white.

Romero was still carefully feeling the knee of the busksin. Then he made him walk a few paces. And at last he stood up straight and shook his head.

'Not very bad!' he said. 'Nothing broken.'

Again he bent and worked at the knee. Then he looked up at the Princess.

'He can go on,' he said. 'It's not bad.'

The Princess looked down at the dark face in silence.

'What, go on right up here?' cried Miss Cummins. 'How many hours?'

'About five!' said Romero simply.

'Five hours!' cried Miss Cummins. 'A horse with a lame knee! And a steep mountain! Why-y!'

'Yes, it's pretty steep up there,' said Romero, pushing back his hat and staring fixedly at the bleeding knee. The buckskin stood in a stricken sort of dejection. 'But I think he'll make it all right,' the man added.

'Oh!' cried Miss Cummins, her eyes bright with sudden passion of unshed tears. 'I wouldn't think of it. I wouldn't ride him up there, not for any money.'

'Why wouldn't you?' asked Romero.

'It *hurts* him.'

Romero bent down again to the horse's knee.

'Maybe it hurts him a little,' he said. 'But he can make it all right, and his leg won't get stiff.'

'What! Ride him five hours up the steep mountains?' cried Miss Cummins. 'I couldn't. I just couldn't do it. I'll lead him a little way and see if he can go. But I *couldn't* ride him again. I couldn't. Let me walk.'

'But Miss Cummins, dear, if Romero says he'll be all right?' said the Princess.

'I know it hurts him. Oh, I just couldn't hear it.'

There was no doing anything with Miss Cummins. The thought of a hurt animal always put her into a sort of hysterics.

They walked forward a little, leading the buckskin. He limped rather badly. Miss Cummins sat on a rock.

'Why, it's agony to see him!' she cried. 'It's *cruel*!'

'He won't limp after a bit, if you take no notice of him,' said Romero. 'Now he plays up, and limps very much, because he wants to make you see.'

'I don't think there can be much playing up,' said Miss Cummins bitterly. 'We can *see* how it must hurt him.'

'It don't hurt much,' said Romero.

But now Miss Cummins was silent with antipathy.

It was a deadlock. The party remained motionless on the trail, the Princess in the saddle, Miss Cummins seated on a rock, Romero standing black and remote near the drooping buckskin.

'Well!' said the man suddenly at last. 'I guess we go back, then.'

And he looked up swiftly at his horse, which was cropping at the mountain herbage and treading on the trailing reins.

'No!' cried the Princess. 'Oh no!' Her voice rang with a great wail of disappointment and anger. Then she checked herself.

Miss Cummins rose with energy.

'Let me lead the buckskin home,' she said, with cold dignity, 'and you two go on.'

This was received in silence. The Princess was looking down at her with a sardonic, almost cruel gaze.

'We've only come about two hours,' said Miss Cummins. 'I don't mind a bit leading him home. But I *couldn't* ride him. I *couldn't* have him ridden with that knee.'

This again was received in dead silence. Romero remained impassive, almost inert.

'Very well, then,' said the Princess. 'You lead him home. You'll be quite all right. Nothing can happen to you, possibly. And say to them that we have gone on and shall be home tomorrow – or the day after.'

She spoke coldly and distinctly. For she could not bear to be thwarted.

'Better all go back, and come again another day,' said Romero – non-committal.

'There will never *be* another day,' cried the Princess. 'I want to go on.'

She looked at him square in the eyes, and met the spark in his eye.

He raised his shoulders slightly.

'If you want it,' he said. 'I'll go on with you. But Miss Cummins can ride my horse to the end of the canyon, and I lead the buckskin. Then I come back to you.'

It was arranged so. Miss Cummins had her saddle put on Romero's black horse, Romero took the buckskin's bridle, and they started back. The Princess rode very slowly on upwards, alone. She was at first so angry with Miss Cummins that she was blind to everything else. She just let her mare follow her own inclinations.

The peculiar spell of anger carried the Princess on, almost unconscious, for an hour or so. And by this time she was beginning to climb pretty high. Her horse walked steadily all the time. They emerged on a bare slope, and the trail wound through frail aspen stems. Here a wind swept, and some of the aspen were already bare. Others were fluttering their discs of pure, solid yellow leaves, so *nearly* like petals, while the slope ahead was one soft, glowing fleece of daffodil yellow; fleecy like a golden foxskin, and yellow as daffodils alive in the wind and the high mountain sun.

She paused and looked back. The near great slopes were mottled with gold and the dark hue of spruce, like some unsinged eagle, and the light lay gleaming upon them. Away through the gap of the canyon she could see the pale blue of the egg-like desert, with the crumpled dark crack of the Rio Grande Canyon. And far, far off, the blue mountains like a fence of angels on the horizon.

And she thought of her adventure. She was going on alone with Romero. But then she was very sure of herself, and Romero was not the kind of man to do anything to her against her will. This was her first thought. And she just had a fixed desire to go over the brim of the mountains, to look into the inner chaos of the Rockies. And she wanted to go with Romero, because he had some peculiar kinship with her; there was some peculiar link between the two of them. Miss Cummins anyhow would have been only a discordant note.

She rode on, and emerged at length in the lap of the summit. Beyond her was a great concave of stone and stark, dead-grey trees, where the mountain ended against the sky. But nearer was the dense black, bristling spruce, and at her feet was the lap of the summit, a flat little valley of sere grass and quiet-standing yellow aspens, the stream trickling like a thread across.

It was a little valley or shell from which the stream was gently poured into the lower rocks and trees of the canyon. Around her was a fairy-like gentleness, the delicate sere grass, the groves of delicate-stemmed aspens dropping their flakes of bright yellow. And the delicate, quick little stream threading through the wild, sere grass.

Here one might expect deer and fawns and wild things, as in a little paradise. Here she was to wait for Romero, and they were to have lunch.

She unfastened her saddle and pulled it to the ground with a crash, letting her horse wander with a long rope. How beautiful Tansy looked, sorrel, among the yellow leaves that lay like a patina on the sere ground. The Princess herself wore a fleecy sweater of a pale, sere buff, like the grass, and riding-breeches of a pure orange-tawny colour. She felt quite in the picture.

From her saddle-pouches she took the packages of lunch, spread a little cloth, and sat to wait for Romero. Then she made a little fire.

Then she ate a devilled egg. Then she ran after Tansy, who was straying across-stream. Then she sat in the sun, in the stillness near the aspens, and waited.

The sky was blue. Her little alp was soft and delicate as fairy-land. But beyond and up jutted the great slopes, dark with the pointed feathers of spruce, bristling with grey dead trees among grey rock, or dappled with dark and gold. The beautiful, but fierce, heavy cruel mountains, with their moments of tenderness.

She saw Tansy start, and begin to run. Two ghost-like figures on horseback emerged from the black of the spruce across the stream. It was two Indians on horseback, swathed like seated mummies in their pale-grey cotton blankets. Their guns jutted beyond the saddles. They rode straight towards her, to her thread of smoke.

As they came near, they unswathed themselves and greeted her, looking at her curiously from their dark eyes. Their black hair was somewhat untidy, the long rolled plaits on their shoulders were soiled. They looked tired.

They got down from their horses near her little fire – a camp was a camp – swathed their blankets round their hips, pulled the saddles from their ponies and turned them loose, then sat down. One was a young Indian whom she had met before, the other was an older man.

'You all alone?' said the younger man.

'Romero will be here in a minute,' she said, glancing back along the trail.

'Ah, Romero! You with him? Where are you going?'

'Round the ridge,' she said. 'Where are you going?'

'We going down to Pueblo.'

'Been out hunting? How long have you been out?'

'Yes. Been out five days.' The young Indian gave a little meaningless laugh.

'Got anything?'

'No. We see tracks of two deer – but not got nothing.'

The Princess noticed a suspicious-looking bulk under one of the saddles – surely a folded-up deer. But she said nothing.

'You must have been cold,' she said.

'Yes, very cold in the night. And hungry. Got nothing to eat since yesterday. Eat it all up.' And again he laughed his little meaningless laugh. Under their dark skins, the two men looked peaked and hungry. The Princess rummaged for food among the saddle-bags. There was a lump of bacon – the regular stand-back – and some bread. She gave

462

them this, and they began toasting slices of it on long sticks at the fire. Such was the little camp Romero saw as he rode down the slope: the Princess in her orange breeches, her head tied in a blue-and-brown silk kerchief, sitting opposite the two dark-headed Indians across the camp-fire, while one of the Indians was leaning forward toasting bacon, his two plaits of braid-hair dangling as if wearily.

Romero rode up, his face expressionless. The Indians greeted him in Spanish. He unsaddled his horse, took food from the bags, and sat down at the camp to eat. The Princess went to the stream for water, and to wash her hands.

'Got coffee?' asked the Indians.

'No coffee this outfit,' said Romero.

They lingered an hour or more in the warm midday sun. Then Romero saddled the horses. The Indians still squatted by the fire. Romero and the Princess rode away, calling *Adios!* to the Indians over the stream and into the dense spruce whence two strange figures had emerged.

When they were alone, Romero turned and looked at her curiously, in a way she could not understand, with such a hard glint in his eyes. And for the first time she wondered if she was rash.

'I hope you don't mind going alone with me,' she said.

'If you want it,' he replied.

They emerged at the foot of the great bare slope of rocky summit, where dead spruce trees stood sparse and bristling like bristles on a grey dead hog. Romero said the Mexicans, twenty years back, had fired the mountains, to drive out the whites. This grey concave slope of summit was corpse-like.

The trail was almost invisible. Romero watched for the trees which the Forest Service had blazed. And they climbed the stark corpse slope, among dead spruce, fallen and ash-grey, into the wind. The wind came rushing from the west, up the funnel of the canyon, from the desert. And there was the desert, like a vast mirage tilting slowly upwards towards the west, immense and pallid, away beyond the funnel of the canyon. The Princess could hardly look.

For an hour their horses rushed the slope, hastening with a great working of the haunches upwards, and halting to breathe, scrambling again, and rowing their way up length by length, on the livid, slanting wall. While the wind blew like some vast machine.

After an hour they were working their way on the incline, no longer forcing straight up. All was grey and dead around them; the horses

463

picked their way over the silver-grey corpses of the spruce. But they were near the top, near the ridge.

Even the horses made a rush for the last bit. They had worked round to a scrap of spruce forest near the very top. They hurried in, out of the huge, monstrous, mechanical wind, that whistled inhumanly and was palely cold. So, stepping through the dark screens of trees, they emerged over the crest.

In front now was nothing but mountains, ponderous, massive, down-sitting mountains, in a huge and intricate knot, empty of life or soul. Under the bristling black feathers of spruce near-by lay patches of white snow. The lifeless valleys were concaves of rock and spruce, the rounded summits and the hog-backed summits of grey rock crowded one behind the other like some monstrous herd in arrest.

It frightened the Princess, it was *so* inhuman. She had not thought it could be so inhuman, so, as it were, anti-life. And yet now one of her desires was fulfilled. She had seen it, the massive, gruesome, repellent core of the Rockies. She saw it there beneath her eyes, in its gigantic, heavy gruesomeness.

And she wanted to go back. At this moment she wanted to turn back. She had looked down into the intestinal knot of these mountains. She was frightened. She wanted to go back.

But Romero was riding on, on the lee side of the spruce forest, above the concaves of the inner mountains. He turned round to her and pointed at the slope with a dark hand.

'Here a miner has been trying for gold,' he said. It was a grey scratched-out heap near a hole – like a great badger hole. And it looked quite fresh.

'Quite lately?' said the Princess.

'No, long ago – twenty, thirty years.' He had reined in his horse and was looking at the mountains. 'Look!' he said. 'There goes the Forest Service trail – along those ridges, on the top, way over there till it comes to Lucytown, where is the Government road. We go down there – no trail – see behind that mountain – you see the top, no trees, and some grass?'

His arm was lifted, his brown hand pointing, his dark eyes piercing into the distance, as he sat on his black horse twisting round to her. Strange and ominous, only the demon of himself, he seemed to her. She was dazed and a little sick, at that height, and she could not see any more. Only she saw an eagle turning in the air beyond, and the light from the west showed the pattern on him underneath.

'Shall I ever be able to go so far?' asked the Princess faintly, petulantly.

'Oh yes! All easy now. No more hard places.'

They worked along the ridge, up and down, keeping on the lee side, the inner side, in the dark shadow. It was cold. Then the trail laddered up again, and they emerged on a narrow ridge-track, with the mountain slipping away enormously on either side. The Princess was afraid. For one moment she looked out, and saw the desert, the desert ridges, more desert, more blue ridges, shining pale and very vast, far below, vastly palely tilting to the western horizon. It was ethereal and terrifying in its gleaming, pale, half-burnished immensity, tilted at the west. She could not bear it. To the left was the ponderous, involved mass of mountains all kneeling heavily.

She closed her eyes and let her consciousness evaporate away. The mare followed the trail. So on and on, in the wind again.

They turned their backs to the wind, facing inwards to the mountains. She thought they had left the trail; it was quite invisible.

'No,' he said, lifting his hand and pointing. 'Don't you see the blazed trees?'

And making an effort of consciousness, she was able to perceive on a pale-grey dead spruce stem the old marks where an axe had chipped a piece away. But with the height, the cold, the wind, her brain was numb.

They turned again and began to descend; he told her they had left the trail. The horses slithered in the loose stones, picking their way downward. It was afternoon, the sun stood obtrusive and gleaming in the lower heavens – about four o'clock. The horses went steadily, slowly, but obstinately onwards. The air was getting colder. They were in among the lumpish peaks and steep concave valleys. She was barely conscious at all of Romero.

He dismounted and came to help her from her saddle. She tottered, but would not betray her feebleness.

'We must slide down here,' he said. 'I can lead the horses.'

They were on a ridge, and facing a steep bare slope of pallid, tawny mountain grass on which the western sun shone full. It was steep and concave. The Princess felt she might start slipping, and go down like a toboggan into the great hollow.

But she pulled herself together. Her eye blazed up again with excitement and determination. A wind rushed past her; she could hear the shriek of spruce trees far below. Bright spots came on her cheeks as her hair blew across. She looked a wild, fairy-like little thing.

'No,' she said. 'I will take my horse.'

'Then mind she doesn't slip down on top of you,' said Romero. And away he went, nimbly dropping down the pale, steep incline, making from rock to rock, down the grass, and following any little slanting groove. His horse hopped and slithered after him, and sometimes stopped dead, with forefeet pressed back, refusing to go farther. He, below his horse, looked up and pulled the reins gently, and encouraged the creature. Then the horse once more dropped his forefeet with a jerk, and the descent continued.

The Princess set off in blind, reckless pursuit, tottering and yet nimble. And Romero, looking constantly back to see how she was faring, saw her fluttering down like some queer little bird, her orange breeches twinkling like the legs of some duck, and her head, tied in the blue and buff kerchief, bound round and round like the head of some blue-topped bird. The sorrel mare rocked and slipped behind her. But down came the Princess in a reckless intensity, a tiny, vivid spot on the great hollow flank of the tawny mountain. So tiny! Tiny as a frail bird's egg. It made Romero's mind go blank with wonder.

But they had to get down, out of that cold and dragging wind. The spruce trees stood below, where a tiny stream emerged in stones. Away plunged Romero, zigzagging down. And away behind, up the slope, fluttered the tiny, bright-coloured Princess, holding the end of the long reins, and leading the lumbering, four-footed, sliding mare.

At last they were down. Romero sat in the sun, below the wind, beside some squaw-berry bushes. The Princess came near, the colour flaming in her cheeks, her eyes dark blue, much darker than the kerchief on her head, and glowing unnaturally.

'We make it,' said Romero.

'Yes,' said the Princess, dropping the reins and subsiding on to the grass, unable to speak, unable to think.

But, thank heaven, they were out of the wind and in the sun.

In a few minutes her consciousness and her control began to come back. She drank a little water. Romero was attending to the saddles. Then they set off again, leading the horses still a little farther down the tiny stream-bed. Then they could mount.

They rode down a bank and into a valley grove dense with aspens. Winding through the thin, crowding, pale-smooth stems, the sun shone flickering beyond them, and the disc-like aspen leaves, waving queer mechanical signals, seemed to be splashing the gold light before her eyes. She rode on in a splashing dazzle of gold.

Then they entered shadow and the dark, resinous spruce trees. The fierce boughs alway wanted to sweep her off her horse. She had to twist and squirm past.

But there was a semblance of an old trail. And all at once they emerged in the sun on the edge of the spruce grove, and there was a little cabin, and the bottom of a small, naked valley with grey rock and heaps of stones, and a round pool of intense green water, dark green. The sun was just about to leave it.

Indeed, as she stood, the shadow came over the cabin and over herself; they were in the lower gloom, a twilight. Above, the heights still blazed.

It was a little hole of a cabin, near the spruce trees, with an earthen floor and an unhinged door. There was a wooden bed-bunk, three old sawn-off log-lengths to sit on as stools, and a sort of fireplace; no room for anything else. The little hole would hardly contain two people. The roof had gone – but Romero had laid on thick spruce boughs.

The strange squalor of the primitive forest pervaded the place, the squalor of animals and their droppings, the squalor of the wild. The Princess knew the peculiar repulsiveness of it. She was tired and faint.

Romero hastily got a handful of twigs, set a little fire going in the stove grate, and went out to attend to the horses. The Princess vaguely, mechanically, put sticks on the fire, in a sort of stupor, watching the blaze, stupefied and fascinated. She could not make much fire – it would set the whole cabin alight. And smoke oozed out of the dilapidated mud-and-stone chimney.

When Romero came in with the saddle-pouches and saddles, hanging the saddles on the wall, there sat the little Princess on her stump of wood in front of the dilapidated fire-grate, warming her tiny hands at the blaze, while her orange breeches glowed almost like another fire. She was in a sort of stupor.

'You have some whisky now, or some tea? Or wait for some soup?' he asked.

She rose and looked at him with bright, dazed eyes, half comprehendingly; the colour glowing hectic in her cheeks.

'Some tea,' she said, 'with a little whisky in it. Where's the kettle?'

'Wait,' he said. 'I'll bring the things.'

She took her cloak from the back of her saddle, and followed him into the open. It was a deep cup of shadow. But above the sky was still shining, and the heights of the mountains were blazing with aspen like fire blazing.

Their horses were cropping the grass among the stones. Romero clambered up a heap of grey stones and began lifting away logs and rocks, till he had opened the mouth of one of the miner's little old workings. This was his cache. He brought out bundles of blankets, pans for cooking, a little petrol camp-stove, an axe, the regular camp outfit. He seemed so quick and energetic and full of force. This quick force dismayed the Princess a little.

She took a saucepan and went down the stones to the water. It was very still and mysterious, and of a deep green colour, yet pure, transparent as glass. How cold the place was! How mysterious and fearful.

She crouched in her dark cloak by the water, rinsing the saucepan, feeling the cold heavy above her, the shadow like a vast weight upon her, bowing her down. The sun was leaving the mountain-tops, departing, leaving her under profound shadow. Soon it would crush her down completely.

Sparks? Or eyes looking at her across the water? She gazed, hypnotised. And with her sharp eyes she made out in the dusk the pale form of a bob-cat crouching by the water's edge, pale as the stones amongst which it crouched, opposite. And it was watching her with cold, electric eyes of strange intentness, a sort of cold, icy wonder and fearlessness. She saw its *museau* pushed forward, its tufted ears pricking intensely up. It was watching her with cold, animal curiosity, something demonish and conscienceless.

She made a swift movement, spilling her water. And in a flash the creature was gone, leaping like a cat that is escaping; but strange and soft in its motion, with its little bob-tail. Rather fascinating. Yet that cold, intent, demonish watching! She shivered with cold and fear. She knew well enough the dread and repulsiveness of the wild.

Romero carried in the bundles of bedding and the camp outfit. The windowless cabin was already dark inside. He lit a lantern, and then went out again with the axe. She heard him chopping wood as she fed sticks to the fire under her water. When he came in with an armful of oak-scrub faggots, she had just thrown the tea into the water.

'Sit down,' she said, 'and drink tea.'

He poured a little bootleg whisky into the enamel cups, and in the silence the two sat on the log-ends, sipping the lot liquid and coughing occasionally from the smoke.

'We burn these oak sticks,' he said. 'They don't make hardly any smoke.'

Curious and remote he was, saying nothing except what had to be said. And she, for her part, was as remote from him. They seemed far, far apart, worlds apart, now they were so near.

He unwrapped one bundle of bedding, and spread the blankets and the sheepskin in the wooden bunk.

'You lie down and rest,' he said, 'and I make the supper.'

She decided to do so. Wrapping her cloak round her, she lay down in the bunk, turning her face to the wall. She could hear him preparing supper over the little petrol stove. Soon she could smell the soup he was heating; and soon she heard the hissing of fried chicken in a pan.

'You eat your supper now?' he said.

With a jerky, despairing movement, she sat up in the bunk, tossing back her hair. She felt cornered.

'Give it me here,' she said.

He handed her first the cupful of soup. She sat among the blankets, eating it slowly. She was hungry. Then he gave her an enamel plate with pieces of fried chicken and currant jelly, butter and bread. It was very good. As they ate the chicken he made the coffee. She said never a word. A certain resentment filled her. She was cornered.

When supper was over he washed the dishes, dried them, and put everything away carefully, else there would have been no room to move in the hole of a cabin. The oak-wood gave out a good bright heat.

He stood for a few moments at a loss. Then he asked her:

'You want to go to bed soon?'

'Soon,' she said. 'Where are you going to sleep?'

'I make my bed here —' he pointed to the floor along the wall. 'Too cold out of doors.'

'Yes,' she said. 'I suppose it is.'

She sat immobile, her cheeks hot, full of conflicting thoughts. And she watched him while he folded the blankets on the floor, a sheepskin underneath. Then she went out into the night.

The stars were big. Mars sat on the edge of a mountain, for all the world like the blazing eye of a crouching mountain lion. But she herself was deep, deep below in a pit of shadow. In the intense silence she seemed to hear the spruce forest crackling with electricity and cold. Strange, foreign stars floated on that unmoving water. The night was going to freeze. Over the hills came the far sobbing-singing howling of the coyotes. She wondered how the horses would be.

Shuddering a little, she turned to the cabin. Warm light showed through its chinks. She pushed at the rickety, half-opened door.

'What about the horses?' she said.

'My black, he won't go away. And your mare will stay with him. You want to go to bed now?'

'I think I do.'

'All right. I feed the horses some oats.'

And he went out into the night.

He did not come back for some time. She was lying wrapped up tight in the bunk.

He blew out the lantern, and sat down on his bedding to take off his clothes. She lay with her back turned. And soon, in the silence, she was asleep.

She dreamed it was snowing and the snow was falling on her through the roof, softly, softly, helplessly, and she was going to be buried alive. She was growing colder and colder, the snow was weighing down on her. The snow was going to absorb her.

She awoke with a sudden convulsion, like pain. She was really very cold; pehaps the heavy blankets had numbed her. Her heart seemed unable to beat, she felt she could not move.

With another convulsion she sat up. It was intensely dark. There was not even a spark of fire, the light wood had burned right away. She sat in thick oblivious darkness. Only through a chink she could see a star.

What did she want? Oh, what did she want? She sat in bed and rocked herself woefully. She could hear the steady breathing of the sleeping man. She was shivering with cold; her heart seemed as if it could not beat. She wanted warmth, protection, she wanted to be taken away from herself. And at the same time, perhaps more deeply than anything, she wanted to keep herself intact, intact, untouched, that no one should have any power over her, or rights to her. It was a wild necessity in her that no one, particularly no man, should have any rights or power over her, that no one and nothing should possess her.

Yet that other thing! And she was so cold, so shivering, and her heart could not beat. Oh, would not someone help her heart to beat?

She tried to speak, and could not. Then she cleared her throat.

'Romero,' she said strangely, 'it is so cold.'

Where did her voice come from, and whose voice was it, in the dark?

She heard him at once sit up, and his voice, startled, with a resonance that seemed to vibrate against her, saying:

470

'You want me to make you warm?'

'Yes.'

As soon as he had lifted her in his arms, she wanted to scream to him not to touch her. She stiffened herself. Yet she was dumb.

And he was warm, but with a terrible animal warmth that seemed to annihilate her. He panted like an animal with desire. And she was given over to this thing.

She had never, never wanted to be given over to this. But she had *willed* that it should happen to her. And according to her will, she lay and let it happen. But she never wanted it. She never wanted to be thus assailed and handled, and mauled. She wanted to keep herself to herself.

However, she had willed it to happen, and it had happened. She panted with relief when it was over.

Yet even now she had to lie within the hard, powerful clasp of this other creature, this man. She dreaded to struggle to go away. She dreaded almost too much the icy cold of that other bunk.

'Do you want to go away from me?' asked his strange voice. Oh, if it could have been a thousand miles away from her! Yet she had willed to have it thus close.

'No,' she said.

And she could feel a curious joy and pride surging up again in him: at her expense. Because he had got her. She felt like a victim there. And he was exulting in his power over her, his possession, his pleasure.

When dawn came, he was fast asleep. She sat up suddenly.

'I want a fire,' she said.

He opened his brown eyes wide, and smiled with a curious tender luxuriousness.

'I want you to make a fire,' she said.

He glanced at the chinks of light. His brown face hardened to the day.

'All right,' he said, 'I'll make it.'

She did her face while he dressed. She could not bear to look at him. He was so suffused with pride and luxury. She hid her face almost in despair. But feeling the cold blast of air as he opened the door, she wriggled down into the warm place where he had been. How soon the warmth ebbed, when he had gone!

He made a fire and went out, returning after a while with water.

'You stay in bed till the sun comes,' he said. 'It very cold.'

471

'Hand me my cloak.'

She wrapped the cloak fast round her, and sat up among the blankets. The warmth was already spreading from the fire.

'I suppose we will start back as soon as we've had breakfast?'

He was crouching at his camp-stove making scrambled eggs. He looked up suddenly, transfixed, and his brown eyes, so soft and luxuriously widened, looked straight at her.

'You want to?' he said.

'We'd better get back as soon as possible,' she said, turning aside from his eyes.

'You want to get away from me?' he asked, repeating the question of the night in a sort of dread.

'I want to get away from here,' she said decisively. And it was true. She wanted supremely to get away, back to the world of people.

He rose slowly to his feet, holding the aluminium frying-pan.

'Don't you like last night?' he asked.

'Not really,' she said. 'Why? Do you?'

He put down the frying-pan and stood staring at the wall. She could see she had given him a cruel blow. But she did not relent. She was getting her own back. She wanted to regain possession of all herself, and in some mysterious way she felt that he possessed some part of her still.

He looked round at her slowly, his face greyish and heavy.

'You Americans,' he said, 'you always want to do a man down.'

'I am not American,' she said. 'I am British. And I don't want to do any man down. I only want to go back now.'

'And what will you say about me, down there?'

'That you were very kind to me, and very good.'

He crouched down again, and went on turning the eggs. He gave her her plate, and her coffee, and sat down to his own food.

But again he seemed not to be able to swallow. He looked up at her.

'You don't like last night?' he asked.

'Not really,' she said, though with some difficulty. 'I don't care for that kind of thing.'

A blank sort of wonder spread over his face at these words, followed immediately by a black look of anger, and then a stony, sinister despair.

'You don't?' he said, looking her in the eyes.

'Not really,' she replied, looking back with steady hostility into his eyes.

472

Then a dark flame seemed to come from his face.

'I make you,' he said, as if to himself.

He rose and reached her clothes, that hung on a peg: the fine linen underwear, the orange breeches, the fleecy jumper, the blue-and-bluff kerchief; then he took up her riding-boots and her bead moccasins. Crushing everything in his arms, he opened the door. Sitting up, she saw him stride down to the dark green pool in the frozen shadow of that deep cup of a valley. He tossed the clothing and the boots out on the pool. Ice had formed. And on the pure, dark green mirror, in the slaty shadow, the Princess saw her things lying, the white linen, the orange breeches, the black boots, the blue moccasins, a tangled heap of colour. Romero picked up rocks and heaved them out at the ice, till the surface broke and the fluttering clothing disappeared in the rattling water, while the valley echoed and shouted again with the sound.

She sat in despair among the blankets, hugging tight her pale-blue cloak. Romero strode straight back to the cabin.

'Now you stay here with me,' he said.

She was furious. Her blue eyes met his. They were like two demons watching one another. In his face, beyond a sort of unrelieved gloom, was a demonish desire for death.

He saw her looking round the cabin, scheming. He saw her eyes on his rifle. He took the gun and went out with it. Returning, he pulled out her saddle, carried it to the tarn, and threw it in. Then he fetched his own saddle, and did the same.

'Now will you go away?' he said, looking at her with a smile.

She debated within herself whether to coax him and wheedle him. But she knew he was already beyond it. She sat among her blankets in a frozen sort of despair, hard as hard ice with anger.

He did the chores, and disappeared with the gun. She got up in her blue pyjamas, huddled in her cloak, and stood in the doorway. The dark-green pool was motionless again, the stony slopes were pallid and frozen. Shadow still lay, like an after-death, deep in this valley. Always in the distance she saw the horses feeding. If she could catch one! The brilliant yellow sun was half-way down the mountain. It was nine o'clock.

All day she was alone, and she was frightened. What she was frightened of she didn't know. Perhaps the crackling in the dark spruce wood. Perhaps just the savage, heartless wildness of the mountains. But all day she sat in the sun in the doorway of the cabin, watching, watching for hope. And all the time her bowels were cramped with fear.

473

She saw a dark spot that probably was a bear, roving across the pale grassy slope in the far distance, in the sun.

When, in the afternoon, she saw Romero approaching, with silent suddenness, carrying his gun and a dead deer, the cramp in her bowels relaxed, then became colder. She dreaded him with a cold dread.

'There is deer-meat,' he said, throwing the dead doe at her feet.

'You don't want to go away from here,' he said. 'This is a nice place.'

She shrank into the cabin.

'Come into the sun,' he said, following her. She looked up at him with hostile, frightened eyes.

'Come into the sun,' he repeated, taking her gently by the arm, in a powerful grasp.

She knew it was useless to rebel. Quietly he led her out, and seated himself in the doorway, holding her still by the arm.

'In the sun it is warm,' he said. 'Look, this is a nice place. You are such a pretty white woman, why do you want to act mean to me? Isn't this a nice place? Come! Come here! It is sure warm here.'

He drew her to him, and in spite of her stony resistance, he took her cloak from her, holding her in her thin blue pyjamas.

'You sure are a pretty little white woman, small and pretty,' he said. 'You sure won't act mean to me – you don't want to, I know you don't.'

She, stony and powerless, had to submit to him. The sun shone on her white, delicate skin.

'I sure don't mind hell fire,' he said. 'After this.'

A queer, luxurious good humour seemed to possess him again. But though outwardly she was powerless, inwardly she resisted him, absolutely and stonily.

When later he was leaving her again, she said to him suddenly:

'You think you can conquer me this way. But you can't. You can never conquer me.'

He stood arrested, looking back at her, with many emotions conflicting in his face – wonder, surprise, a touch of horror, and an unconscious pain that crumpled his face till it was like a mask. Then he went out without saying a word, hung the dead deer on a bough, and started to flay it. While he was at this butcher's work, the sun sank and cold night came on again.

'You see,' he said to her as he crouched, cooking the supper, 'I ain't going to let you go. I reckon you called to me in the night, and I've

474

some right. If you want to fix it up right now with me, and say you want to be with me, we'll fix it up now and go down to the ranch tomorrow and get married or whatever you want. But you've got to say you want to be with me. Else I shall stay right here, till something happens.'

She waited a while before she answered:

'I don't want to be with anybody against my will. I don't dislike you; at least, I didn't, till you tried to put your will over mine. I won't have anybody's will put over me. You can't succeed. Nobody could. You can never get me under your will. And you won't have long to try, because soon they will send someone to look for me.'

He pondered this last, and she regretted having said it. Then, sombre, he bent to the cooking again.

He could not conquer her, however much he violated her. Because her spirit was hard and flawless as a diamond. But he could shatter her. This she knew. Much more, and she would be shattered.

In a sombre, violent excess he tried to expend his desire for her. And she was racked with an agony, and felt each time she would die. Because, in some peculiar way, he had got hold of her, some unrealised part of her which she never wished to realise. Racked with a burning, tearing anguish, she felt that the thread of her being would break, and she would die. The burning heat that racked her inwardly.

If only, only she could be alone again, cool and intact! If only she could recover herself again, cool and intact! Would she ever, ever, ever be able to bear herself again?

Even now she did not hate him. It was beyond that. Like some racking, hot doom. Personally he hardly existed.

The next day he would not let her have any fire, because of attracting attention with the smoke. It was a grey day, and she was cold. He stayed round, and heated soup on the petrol stove. She lay motionless in the blankets.

And in the afternoon she pulled the clothes over her head and broke into tears. She had never really cried in her life. He dragged the blankets away and looked to see what was shaking her. She sobbed in helpless hysterics. He covered her over again and went outside, looking at the mountains, where clouds were dragging and leaving a little snow. It was a violent, windy, horrible day, the evil of winter rushing down.

She cried for hours. And after this a great silence came between them. They were two people who had died. He did not touch her any more. In the night she lay and shivered like a dying dog. She felt that her very shivering would rupture something in her body, and she would die.

At last she had to speak.

'Could you make a fire? I am so cold,' she said, with chattering teeth.

'Want to come over here?' came his voice.

'I would rather you made me a fire,' she said, her teeth knocking together and chopping the words in two.

He got up and kindled a fire. At last the warmth spread, and she could sleep.

The next day was still chilly, with some wind. But the sun shone. He went about in silence, with a dead-looking face. It was now so dreary and so like death she wished he would do anything rather than continue in this negation. If now he asked her to go down with him to the world and marry him, she would do it. What did it matter? Nothing mattered any more.

But he would not ask her. His desire was dead and heavy like ice within him. He kept watch around the house.

On the fourth day as she sat huddled in the doorway in the sun, hugged in a blanket, she saw two horsemen come over the crest of the grassy slope – small figures. She gave a cry. He looked up quickly and saw the figures. The men had dismounted. They were looking for the trail.

'They are looking for me,' she said.

'*Muy bien,*' he answered in Spanish.

He went and fetched his gun, and sat with it across his knees.

'Oh!' she said. 'Don't shoot!'

He looked across at her.

'Why?' he said. 'You like staying with me?'

'No,' she said. 'But don't shoot.'

'I ain't going to Pen,' he said.

'You won't have to go to Pen,' she said. 'Don't shoot!'

'I'm going to shoot,' he muttered.

And straightaway he kneeled and took very careful aim. The Princess sat on in an agony of helplessness and hopelessness.

The shot rang out. In an instant she saw one of the horses on the pale grassy slope rear and go rolling down. The man had dropped in the grass, and was invisible. The second man clambered on his horse, and on that precipitous place went at a gallop in a long swerve towards the

476

nearest spruce tree cover. Bang! Bang! went Romero's shots. But each time he missed, and the running horse leaped like a kangaroo towards cover.

It was hidden. Romero now got behind a rock; tense silence, in the brilliant sunshine. The Princess sat on the bunk inside the cabin, crouching, paralysed. For hours, it seemed, Romero knelt behind this rock, in his black shirt, bare-headed, watching. He had a beautiful, alert figure. The Princess wondered why she did not feel sorry for him. But her spirit was hard and cold, her heart could not melt. Though now she would have called him to her, with love.

But no, she did not love him. She would never love any man. Never! It was fixed and sealed in her, almost vindictively.

Suddenly she was so startled she almost fell from the bunk. A shot rang out quite close from behind the cabin. Romero leaped straight into the air, his arms fell outstretched, turning as he leaped. And even while he was in the air, a second shot rang out, and he fell with a crash, squirming, his hands clutching the earth towards the cabin door.

The Princess sat absolutely motionless, transfixed, staring at the prostrate figure. In a few moments the figure of a man in the Forest Service appeared close to the house; a young man in a broad-brimmed Stetson hat, dark flannel shirt, and riding-boots, carrying a gun. He strode over to the prostrate figure.

'Got you, Romero!' he said aloud. And he turned the dead man over. There was already a little pool of blood where Romero's breast had been.

'H'm!' said the Forest Service man. 'Guess I got you nearer than I thought.'

And he squatted there, staring at the dead man.

The distant calling of his comrade aroused him. He stood up.

'Hullo, Bill!' he shouted. 'Yep! Got him! Yep! Done him in, apparently.'

The second man rode out of the forest on a grey horse. He had a ruddy, kind face, and round brown eyes, dilated with dismay.

'He's not passed out?' he asked anxiously.

'Looks like it,' said the first young man coolly.

The second dismounted and bent over the body. Then he stood up again, and nodded.

'Yea-a!' he said. 'He's done in all right. It's him all right, boy! It's Domingo Romero.'

'Yep! I know it!' replied the other.

Then in perplexity he turned and looked into the cabin, where the Princess squatted, staring with big owl eyes from her red blanket.

'Hello!' he said, coming towards the hut. And he took his hat off. Oh, the sense of ridicule she felt! Though he did not mean any.

But she could not speak, no matter what she felt.

'What'd this man start firing for?' he asked.

She fumbled for words, with numb lips.

'He had gone out of his mind!' she said, with solemn, stammering conviction.

'Good Lord! You mean to say he'd gone out of his mind? Whew! That's pretty awful! That explains it then. H'm!'

He accepted the explanation without more ado.

With some difficulty they succeeded in getting the Princess down to the ranch. But she, too, was not a little mad.

'I'm not quite sure where I am,' she said to Mrs. Wilkieson, as she lay in bed. 'Do you mind explaining?'

Mrs. Wilkieson explained tactfully.

'Oh yes!' said the Princess. 'I remember. And I had an accident in the mountains, didn't I? Didn't we meet a man who'd gone mad, and who shot my horse from under me?'

'Yes, you met a man who had gone out of his mind.'

The real affair was hushed up. The Princess departed east in a fortnight's time, in Miss Cummins's care. Apparently she had recovered herself entirely. She was the Princess, and a virgin intact.

But her bobbed hair was grey at the temples, and her eyes were a little mad. She was slightly crazy.

'Since my accident in the mountains, when a man went mad and shot my horse from under me, and my guide had to shoot him dead, I have never felt quite myself.'

So she put it.

Later, she married an elderly man, and seemed pleased.

TWO BLUE BIRDS

THERE was a woman who loved her husband, but she could not live with him. The husband, on his side, was sincerely attached to his wife, yet he could not live with her. They were both under forty, both handsome and both attractive. They had the most sincere regard for one another, and felt, in some odd way, eternally married to one another. They knew one another more intimately than they knew anybody else, they felt more known to one another than to any other person.

Yet they could not live together. Usually, they kept a thousand miles apart, geographically. But when he sat in the greyness of England, at the back of his mind, with a certain grim fidelity, he was aware of his wife, her strange yearning to be loyal and faithful, having her gallant affairs away in the sun, in the south. And she, as she drank her cocktail on the terrace over the sea, and turned her grey, sardonic eyes on the heavy dark face of her admirer, whom she really liked quite a lot, she was actually preoccupied with the clear-cut features of her handsome young husband, thinking of how he would be asking his secretary to do something for him, asking in that good-natured, confident voice of a man who knows that his request will be only too gladly fulfilled.

The secretary, of course, adored him. She was *very* competent, quite young, and quite good-looking. She adored him. But then all his servants always did, particularly his women-servants. His men-servants were likely to swindle him.

When a man has an adoring secretary, and you are the man's wife, what are you to do? Not that there was anything 'wrong' – if you know what I mean! – between them. Nothing you could call adultery, to come down to brass tacks. No, no! They were just the young master and his secretary. He dictated to her, she slaved for him and adored him, and the whole thing went on wheels.

He didn't 'adore' her. A man doesn't need to adore his secretary. But he depended on her. 'I simply rely on Miss Wrexall.' Whereas he could never rely on his wife. The one thing he knew finally about *her* was that she didn't intend to be relied on.

So they remained friends, in the awful unspoken intimacy of the once-married. Usually each year they went away together for a holiday, and, if they had not been man and wife, they would have found a great deal of fun and stimulation in one another. The fact that they were married, had been married for the last dozen years, and couldn't live together for the last three or four, spoilt them for one another. Each had a private feeling of bitterness about the other.

However, they were awfully kind. He was the soul of generosity, and held her in real tender esteem, no matter how many gallant affairs she had. Her gallant affairs were part of her modern necessity. 'After all, I've got to *live*. I can't turn into a pillar of salt in five minutes just because you and I can't live together! It takes years for a woman like me to turn into a pillar of salt. At least I hope so!'

'Quite!' he replied. 'Quite! By all means put them in pickle, make pickled cucumbers of them, before you crystallise out. That's my advice.'

He was like that: so awfully clever and enigmatic. She could more or less fathom the idea of the pickled cucumbers, but the 'crystallising out' – what did that signify?

And did he mean to suggest that he himself had been well pickled and that further immersion was for him unnecessary, would spoil his flavour? Was that what he meant? And herself, was she the brine and the vale of tears?

You never knew how catty a man was being, when he was really clever and engimatic, withal a bit whimsical. He was adorably whimsical, with a twist of his flexible, vain mouth, that had a long upper lip, so fraught with vanity! But then a handsome, clear-cut, histrionic young man like that, how could he help being vain? The women made him so.

Ah, the women! How nice men would be if there were no other women!

And how nice the women would be if there were no other men! That's the best of a secretary. She may have a husband, but a husband is the mere shred of a man, compared to a boss, a chief, a man who dictates to you and whose words you faithfully write down and then transcribe. Imagine a wife writing down anything her husband said to her! But a secretary! Every *and* and *but* of his she preserves for ever. What are candied violets in comparison!

Now it is all very well having gallant affairs under the southern sun, when you know there is a husband whom you adore dictating to a secretary whom you are too scornful to hate yet whom you rather despise, though you allow she has her good points, away north in the

480

place you ought to regard as home. A gallant affair isn't much good when you've got a bit of grit in your eye. Or something at the back of your mind.

What's to be done? The husband, of course, did not send his wife away.

'You've got your secretary and your work,' she said. 'There's no room for me.'

'There's a bedroom and a sitting-room exclusively for you,' he replied. 'And a garden and half a motor-car. But please yourself entirely. Do what gives you most pleasure.'

'In that case,' she said, 'I'll just go south for the winter.'

'Yes, do!' he said. 'You always enjoy it.'

'I always do,' she replied.

They parted with a certain relentlessness that had a touch of wistful sentiment behind it. Off she went to her gallant affairs, that were like the curate's egg, palatable in parts. And he settled down to work. He said he hated working, but he never did anything else. Ten or eleven hours a day. That's what it is to be your own master!

So the winter wore away, and it was spring, when the swallows homeward fly, or northward, in this case. This winter, one of a series similar, had been rather hard to get through. The bit of grit in the gallant lady's eye had worked deeper in the more she blinked. Dark faces might be dark, and icy cocktails might lend a glow; she blinked her hardest to blink that bit of grit away, without success. Under the spicy balls of the mimosa she thought of that husband of hers in his library, and of that neat, competent but *common* little secretary of his, for ever taking down what he said!

'How a man can *stand* it! How *she* can stand it, common little thing as she is, I don't know!' the wife cried to herself. She meant this dictating business, this ten hours a day intercourse, *à deux*, with nothing but a pencil between them, and a flow of words.

What was to be done? Matters, instead of improving, had grown worse. The little secretary had brought her mother and sister into the establishment. The mother was a sort of cook-housekeeper, the sister was a sort of upper maid – she did the fine laundry, and looked after 'his' clothes, and valeted him beautifully. It was really an excellent arrangement. The old mother was a splendid plain cook, the sister was all that could be desired as a valet de chambre, a fine laundress, an upper parlour-maid, and a table-waiter. And all economical to a degree. They knew his affairs by heart. His secretary flew to town when a creditor became dangerous, and she *always* smoothed over the financial crisis.

'He', of course, had debts, and he was working to pay them off. And if he had been a fairy prince who could call the ants to help him, he would not have been more wonderful than in securing this secretary and her family. They took hardly any wages. And they seemed to perform the miracle of loaves and fishes daily.

'She', of course, was the wife who loved her husband, but helped him into debt, and she still was an expensive item. Yet when she appeared at her 'home', the secretarial family received her with most elaborate attentions and deference. The knight returning from the Crusades didn't create a greater stir. She felt like Queen Elizabeth at Kenilworth, a sovereign paying a vist to her faithful subjects. But perhaps there lurked always this hair in her soup! Won't they be glad to be rid of me again!

But they protested No! No! They had been waiting and hoping and praying she would come. They had been pining for her to be there, in charge: the mistress, 'his' wife. Ah, 'his' wife!

'His' wife! His halo was like a bucket over her head.

The cook-mother was 'of the people', so it was the upper-maid daughter who came for orders.

'What will you order for to-morrow's lunch and dinner, Mrs. Gee?'

'Well, what do you usually have?'

'Oh, we want *you* to say.'

'No, what do you *usually* have?'

'We don't have anything fixed. Mother goes out and chooses the best she can find, that is nice and fresh. But she thought you would tell her now what to get.'

'Oh, I don't know! I'm not very good at that sort of thing. Ask her to go on just the same; I'm quite sure she knows best.'

'Perhaps you'd like to suggest a sweet?'

'No, I don't care for sweets – and you know Mr. Gee doesn't. So don't make one for me.'

Could anything be more impossible! They had the house spotless and running like a dream; how could an incompetent and extravagant wife dare to interfere, when she saw their amazing and almost inspired economy! But they ran the place on simply nothing!

Simply marvellous people! And the way they strewed palm branches under her feet!

But that only made her feel ridiculous.

'Don't you think the family manage very well?' he asked her tentatively.

'Awfully well! Almost romantically well!' she replied. 'But I suppose you're perfectly happy?'

'I'm perfectly comfortable,' he replied.

'I can see you are,' she replied. 'Amazingly so! I never knew such comfort! Are you sure it isn't bad for you?'

She eyed him stealthily. He looked very well, and extremely handsome, in his histrionic way. He was shockingly well-dressed and valeted. And he had that air of easy aplomb and good humour which is so becoming to a man, and which he only acquires when he is cock of his own little walk, made much of by his own hens.

'No!' he said, taking his pipe from his mouth and smiling whimsically round at her. 'Do I look as if it were bad for me?'

'No, you don't,' she replied promptly: thinking, naturally, as a woman is supposed to think nowadays, of his health and comfort, the foundation, apparently, of all happiness.

Then, of course, away she went on the back-wash.

'Perhaps for your work, though, it's not so good as it is for *you*,' she said in a rather small voice. She knew he couldn't bear it if she mocked at his work for one moment. And he knew that rather small voice of hers.

'In what way?' he said, bristles rising.

'Oh, I don't know,' she answered indifferently. 'Perhaps it's not good for a man's work if he is too comfortable.'

'I don't know about *that*!' he said, taking a dramatic turn round the library and drawing at his pipe. 'Considering I work, actually, by the clock, for twelve hours a day, and for ten hours when it's a short day, I don't think you can say I am deteriorating from easy comfort.'

'No, I suppose not,' she admitted.

Yet she did think it, nevertheless. His comfortableness didn't consist so much in good food and a soft bed, as in having nobody, absolutely nobody and nothing to contradict him. 'I do like to think he's got nothing to aggravate him,' the secretary had said to the wife.

'Nothing to aggravate him!' What a position for a man! Fostered by women who would let nothing 'aggravate' him. If anything would aggravate his wounded vanity, this would!

So thought the wife. But what was to be done about it? In the silence of midnight she heard his voice in the distance, dictating away, like the voice of God to Samuel, alone and monotonous, and she imagined the little figure of the secretary busily scribbling shorthand. Then in the sunny hours of morning, while he was still in bed – he never rose till noon – from another distance came that sharp insect noise of the typewriter, like some immense grasshopper chirping and rattling. It was the secretary, poor thing, typing out his notes.

That girl – she was only twenty-eight – really slaved herself to skin and bone. She was small and neat, but she was actually worn out. She did far more work than he did, for she had not only to take down all those words he uttered, she had to type them out, make three copies, while he was still resting.

'What on earth she gets out of it,' thought the wife, 'I don't know. She's simply worn to the bone, for a very poor salary, and he's never kissed her, and never will, if I know anything about him.'

Whether his never kissing her – the secretary, that is – made it worse or better, the wife did not decide. He never kissed anybody. Whether she herself – the wife, that is – wanted to be kissed by him, even that she was not clear about. She rather thought she didn't.

What on earth did she want then? She was his wife. What on earth did she want of him?

She certainly didn't want to take him down in shorthand, and type out again all those words. And she didn't really want him to kiss her; she knew him too well. Yes, she knew him too well. If you know a man too well, you don't want him to kiss you.

What then? What did she want? Why had she such an extraordinary hang-over about him? Just because she was his wife? Why did she rather 'enjoy' other men – and she was relentless about enjoyment – without ever taking them seriously? And why must she take him so damn seriously, when she never really 'enjoyed' him?

Of course she *had* had good times with him, in the past, before – ah! before a thousand things, all amounting really to nothing. But she enjoyed him no more. She never even enjoyed being with him. There was a silent, ceaseless tension between them, that never broke, even when they were a thousand miles apart.

Awful! That's what you call being married! What's to be done about it? Ridiculous, to know it all and not to do anything about it!

She came back once more, and there she was, in her own house, a sort of super-guest, even to him. And the secretarial family devoting their lives to him.

Devoting their lives to him! But actually! Three women pouring out

484

their lives for him day and night! And what did they get in return? Not one kiss! Very little money, because they knew all about his debts, and had made it their life business to get them paid off! No expectations! Twelve hours' work a day! Comparative isolation, for he saw nobody!

And beyond that? Nothing! Perhaps a sense of uplift and importance because they saw his name and photograph in the newspaper sometimes. But would anybody believe that it was good enough?

Yet they adored it! They seemed to get a deep satisfaction out of it, like people with a mission. Extraordinary!

Well, if they did, let them. They were, of course, rather common, 'of the people'; there might be a sort of glamour in it for them.

But it was bad for him. No doubt about it. His work was getting diffuse and poor in quality – and what wonder! His whole tone was going down – becoming commoner. Of course it was bad for him.

Being his wife, she felt she ought to do something to save him. But how could she? That perfectly devoted, marvellous secretarial family, how could she make an attack on them? Yet she'd love to sweep them into oblivion. Of course they were bad for him: ruining his work, ruining his reputation as a writer, ruining his life. Ruining him with their slavish service.

Of course she ought to make an onslaught on them! But how *could* she? Such devotion! And what had she herself to offer in their place? Certainly not slavish devotion to him, nor to his flow of words! Certainly not!

She imagined him stripped once more naked of secretary and secretarial family, and she shuddered. It was like throwing the naked baby in the dust-bin. Couldn't do that!

Yet something must be done. She felt it. She was almost tempted to get into debt for another thousand pounds, and send in the bill, or have it sent in to him, as usual.

But no! Something more drastic, or perhaps more gentle. She wavered between the two. And wavering, she first did nothing, came to no decision, dragged vacantly on from day to day, waiting for sufficient energy to take her departure once more.

It was spring! What a fool she had been to come up in spring! And she was forty! What an idiot of a woman to go and be forty!

She went down the garden in the warm afternoon, when birds were whistling loudly from the cover, the sky being low and warm, and she had nothing to do. The garden was full of flowers: he loved them for

485

their theatrical display. Lilac and snowball bushes, and laburnum and red may, tulips and anemones and coloured daisies. Lots of flowers! Borders of forget-me-nots! Bachelor's buttons! What absurd names flowers had! She would have called them blue dots and yellow blobs and white frills. Not so much sentiment, after all!

There is a certain nonsense, something showy and stagey about spring, with its pushing leaves and chorus-girl flowers, unless you have something corresponding inside you. Which she hadn't.

Oh, heaven! Beyond the hedge she heard a voice, a steady rather theatrical voice. Oh, heaven! He was dictating to his secretary in the garden. Good God, was there nowhere to get away from it!

She looked around: there was indeed plenty of escape. But what was the good of escaping? He would go on and on. She went quietly towards the hedge, and listened.

He was dictating a magazine article about the modern novel. 'What the modern novel lacks is architecture.' Good God! Architecture! He might just as well say: What the modern novel lacks is whalebone, or a teaspoon, or a tooth stopped.

Yet the secretary took it down, took it down, took it down! No, this could not go on! It was more than flesh and blood could bear.

She went quietly along the hedge, somewhat wolf-like in her prowl, a broad, strong woman in an expensive mustard-coloured silk jersey and cream-coloured pleated skirt. Her legs were long and shapely, and her shoes were expensive.

With a curious wolf-like stealth she turned the hedge and looked across at the small, shaded lawn where the daisies grew impertinently. 'He' was reclining in a coloured hammock under the pink-flowering horse-chestnut tree, dressed in white serge with a fine yellow-coloured linen shirt. His elegant hand dropped over the side of the hammock and beat a sort of vague rhythm to his words. At a little wicker table the little secretary, in a green knitted frock, bent her dark head over her note-book, and diligently made those awful shorthand marks. He was not difficult to take down, as he dictated slowly, and kept a sort of rhythm, beating time with his dangling hand.

'In every novel there must be one outstanding character with which we always sympathise – with *whom* we always sympathise – even though we recognise it – even when we are most aware of the human frailties —'

Every man his own hero, thought the wife grimly, forgetting that every woman is intensely her own heroine.

But what did startle her was a blue bird dashing about near the feet of the absorbed, shorthand-scribbling little secretary. At least it was a blue-tit, blue with grey and some yellow. But to the wife it seemed blue, that juicy spring day, in the translucent afternoon. The blue bird, fluttering round the pretty but rather *common* little feet of the little secretary.

The blue bird! The blue bird of happiness! Well, I'm blest, – thought the wife. Well, I'm blest!

And as she was being blest, appeared another blue bird – that is another blue-tit – and began to wrestle with the first blue-tit. A couple of blue birds of happiness, having a fight over it! Well, I'm blest!

She was more or less out of sight of the human preoccupied pair. But 'he' was disturbed by the fighting blue birds, whose little feathers began to float loose.

'Get out!' he said to them mildly, waving a dark-yellow handkerchief at them. 'Fight your little fight, and settle your private affairs elsewhere, my dear little gentlemen.'

The little secretary looked up quickly, for she had already begun to write it down. He smiled at her his twisted whimsical smile.

'No, don't take that down,' he said affectionately. 'Did you see those two tits laying into one another?'

'No!' said the little secretary, gazing brightly round, her eyes half-blinded with work.

But she saw the queer, powerful, elegant, wolf-like figure of the wife, behind her, and terror came into her eyes.

'I did!' said the wife, stepping forward with those curious, shapely, she-wolf legs of hers, under the very short skirt.

'Aren't they extraordinarily vicious little beasts?' said he.

'Extraordinarily!' she re-echoed, stooping and picking up a little breast-feather. 'Extraordinarily! See how the feathers fly!'

And she got the feather on the tip of her finger, and looked at it. Then she looked at the secretary, then she looked at him. She had a queer, were-wolf expression between her brows.

'I think,' he began, 'these are the loveliest afternoons, when there's no direct sun, but all the sounds and the colours and the scents are sort of dissolved, don't you know, in the air, and the whole thing is steeped, steeped in spring. It's like being on the inside; you know how I mean, like being inside the egg and just ready to chip the shell.'

'Quite like that!' she assented, without conviction.

487

There was a little pause. The secretary said nothing. They were waiting for the wife to depart again.

'I suppose,' said the latter, 'you're awfully busy, as usual?'

'Just about the same,' he said, pursing his mouth deprecatingly.

Again the blank pause, in which he waited for her to go away again.

'I know I'm interrupting you,' she said.

'As a matter of fact,' he said, 'I was just watching those two blue-tits.'

'Pair of little demons!' said the wife, blowing away the yellow feather from her finger-tip.

'Absolutely!' he said.

'Well, I'd better go, and let you get on with your work,' she said.

'No hurry!' he said, with benevolent nonchalance. 'As a matter of fact, I don't think it's a great success, working out of doors.'

'What made you try it?' said the wife. "You know you never could do it.'

'Miss Wrexall suggested it might make a change. But I don't think it altogether helps, do you, Miss Wrexall?'

'I'm sorry,' said the little secretary.

'Why should *you* be sorry?' said the wife, looking down at her as a wolf might look down half-benignly at a little black-and-tan mongrel. 'You only suggested it for his good, I'm sure!'

'I thought the air might be good for him,' the secretary admitted.

'Why do people like you never think about yourselves?' the wife asked.

The secretary looked her in the eye.

'I suppose we do, in a different way,' she said.

'A *very* different way!' said the wife ironically. 'Why don't you make *him* think about *you*?' she added, slowly, with a sort of drawl. 'On a soft spring afternoon like this, you ought to have him dictating poems to you, about the blue-birds of happiness fluttering round your dainty little feet. I know *I* would, if I were his secretary.'

There was a dead pause. The wife stood immobile and statuesque, in an attitude characteristic of her, half turning back to the little secretary, half averted. She half turned her back on everything.

The secretary looked at him.

'As a matter of fact,' he said, 'I was doing an article on the Future of the Novel.'

'I know that,' said the wife. 'That's what's so awful! Why not something lively in the life of the novelist?'

There was a prolonged silence, in which he looked pained, and somewhat remote, statuesque. The little secretary hung her head. The wife sauntered slowly away.

'Just where were we, Miss Wrexall?' came the sound of his voice.

The little secretary started. She was feeling profoundly indignant. Their beautiful relationship, his and hers, to be so insulted!

But soon she was veering down-stream on the flow of his words, too busy to have any feelings, except one of elation at being so busy.

Tea-time came; the sister brought out the tea-tray into the garden. And immediately, the wife appeared. She had changed, and was wearing a chicory-blue dress of fine cloth. The little secretary had gathered up her papers and was departing, on rather high heels.

'Don't go, Miss Wrexall,' said the wife.

The little secretary stopped short, then hesitated.

'Mother will be expecting me,' she said.

'Tell her you're not coming. And ask your sister to bring another cup. I want you to have tea with us.'

Miss Wrexall looked at the man, who was reared on one elbow in the hammock, and was looking enigmatical, Hamletish.

He glanced at her quickly, then pursed his mouth in a boyish negligence.

'Yes, stay and have tea with us for once,' he said. 'I see strawberries, and I know you're the bird for them.'

She glanced at him, smiled wanly, and hurried away to tell her mother. She even stayed long enough to slip on a silk dress.

'Why, how smart you are!' said the wife, when the little secretary reappeared on the lawn, in chicory-blue silk.

'Oh, don't look at my dress, compared to yours!' said Miss Wrexall. They were of the same colour, indeed!

'At least you earned yours, which is more than I did mine,' said the wife, as she poured tea. 'You like it strong?'

She looked with her heavy eyes at the smallish, birdy, blue-clad, overworked young woman, and her eyes seemed to speak many inexplicable dark volumes.

'Oh, as it comes, thank you,' said Miss Wrexall, leaning nervously forward.

'It's coming pretty black, if you want to ruin your digestion,' said the wife.

'Oh, I'll have some water in it, then.'

'Better, I should say.'

489

'How'd the work go – all right?' asked the wife, as they drank tea, and the two women looked at each other's blue dresses.

'Oh!' he said. 'As well as you can expect. It was a piece of pure flummery. But it's what they want. Awful rot, wasn't it, Miss Wrexall?'

Miss Wrexall moved uneasily on her chair.

'It interested me,' she said, 'though not so much as the novel.'

'The novel? Which novel?' said the wife. 'Is there another new one?'

Miss Wrexall looked at him. Not for worlds would she give away any of his literary activities.

'Oh, I was just sketching out an idea to Miss Wrexall,' he said.

'Tell us about it!' said the wife. 'Miss Wrexall, *you* tell us what it's about.'

She turned on her chair, and fixed the little secretary.

'I'm afraid' – Miss Wrexall squirmed – 'I haven't got it very clearly myself, yet.'

'Oh, go along! Tell us what you *have* got then!'

Miss Wrexall sat dumb and very vexed. She felt she was being baited. She looked at the blue pleatings of her skirt.

'I'm afraid I can't,' she said.

'Why are you afraid you can't? You're so *very* competent. I'm sure you've got it all at your finger-ends. I expect you write a good deal of Mr. Gee's books for him, really. He gives you the hint, and you fill it all in. Isn't that how you do it?' She spoke ironically, and as if she were teasing a child. And then she glanced down at the fine pleatings of her own blue skirt, very fine and expensive.

'Of course you're not speaking seriously?' said Miss Wrexall, rising on her mettle.

'Of course I am! I've suspected for a long time – at least, for some time – that you write a good deal of Mr. Gee's books for him, from his hints.'

It was said in a tone of raillery, but it was cruel.

'I should be terribly flattered,' said Miss Wrexall, straightening herself, 'if I didn't know you were only trying to make me feel a fool.'

'Make you feel a fool? My dear child! – why, nothing could be farther from me! You're twice as clever, and a million times as competent as I am. Why, my dear child, I've the greatest admiration for you! I wouldn't do what you do, not for all the pearls in India. I *couldn't* anyhow —'

Miss Wrexall closed up and was silent.

'Do you mean to say my books read as if —' he began, rearing up and speaking in a harrowed voice.

'I do!' said the wife. '*Just* as if Miss Wrexall had written them from your hints. I *honestly* thought she did – when you were too busy —'

'How very clever of you!' he said.

'Very!' she said. 'Especially if I was wrong!'

'Which you were,' he said.

'How very extraordinary!' she cried. 'Well, I am once more mistaken!'

There was a complete pause.

It was broken by Miss Wrexall, who was nervously twisting her fingers.

'You want to spoil what there is between me and him, I can see that,' she said bitterly.

'My dear, but what *is* there between you and him?' asked the wife.

'I was *happy* working with him, working for him! I was *happy* working for him!' cried Miss Wrexall, tears of indignant anger and chagrin in her eyes.

'My dear child!' cried the wife, with simulated excitement, 'go *on* being happy working with him, go on being happy while you can! If it makes you happy, why then, enjoy it! Of course! Do you think I'd be so cruel as to want to take it away from you? – working with him? *I* can't do shorthand and typewriting and double-entrance book-keeping, or whatever it's called. I tell you, I'm utterly incompetent. I never earn anything. I'm the parasite of the British oak, like the mistletoe. The blue bird doesn't flutter round my feet. Perhaps they're too big and trampling.'

She looked down at her expensive shoes.

'If I *did* have a word of criticism to offer,' she said turning to her husband, 'it would be to you, Cameron, for taking so much from her and giving her nothing.'

'But he gives me everything, everything!' cried Miss Wrexall. 'He gives me everything!'

'What do you mean by everything?' said the wife, turning on her sternly.

Miss Wrexall pulled up short. There was a snap in the air, and a change of currents.

'I mean nothing that *you* need begrudge me,' said the little secretary rather haughtily. 'I've never made myself cheap.'

491

There was a blank pause.

'My God!' said the wife. 'You don't call that being cheap? Why, I should say you got nothing out of him at all, you only give! And if you don't call that making yourself cheap – my God!'

'You see, we see things different,' said the secretary.

'I should say we do! – *thank God!*' rejoined the wife.

'On whose behalf are you thanking God?' he asked sarcastically.

'Everybody's, I suppose! Yours, because you get everything for nothing, and Miss Wrexall's, because she seems to like it, and mine because I'm well out of it all.'

'You *needn't* be out of it all,' cried Miss Wrexall magnanimously, 'if you didn't *put* yourself out of it all.'

'Thank you, my dear, for your offer,' said the wife, rising, 'but I'm afraid no man can expect *two* blue birds of happiness to flutter round his feet, tearing out their little feathers!'

With which she walked away.

After a tense and desperate interim, Miss Wrexall cried:

'And *really*, need any woman be jealous of *me*?'

'Quite!' he said.

And that was all he did say.

SUN

I

'TAKE her away, into the sun,' the doctors said.

She herself was sceptical of the sun, but she permitted herself to be carried away, with her child, and a nurse, and her mother, over the sea.

The ship sailed at midnight. And for two hours her husband stayed with her, while the child was put to bed, and the passengers came on board. It was a black night, the Hudson swayed with heavy blackness, shaken over with spilled dribbles of light. She leaned on the rail, and looking down thought: This is the sea; it is deeper than one imagines, and fuller of memories. At that moment the sea seemed to heave like the serpent of chaos that has lived for ever.

'These partings are no good, you know,' her husband was saying, at her side. 'They're no good. I don't like them.'

His tone was full of apprehension, misgiving, and there was a certain note of clinging to the last straw of hope.

'No, neither do I,' she responded in a flat voice.

She remembered how bitterly they had wanted to get away from one another, he and she. The emotion of parting gave a slight tug at her emotions, but only caused the iron that had gone into her soul to gore deeper.

So, they looked at their sleeping son, and the father's eyes were wet. But it is not the wetting of the eyes which counts, it is the deep iron rhythm of habit, the year-long, life-long habits; the deep-set stroke of power.

And in their two lives the stroke of power was hostile, his and hers. Like two engines running at variance, they shattered one another.

'All ashore! All ashore!'

'Maurice, you must go!'

And she thought to herself: For him it is *All Ashore!* For me it is *Out to sea!*

Well, he waved his hanky on the midnight dreariness of the pier as the boat inched away; one among the crowd. One among a crowd! *C'est ça!*

The ferry-boats, like great dishes piled with rows of lights, were still slanting across the Hudson. That black mouth must be the Lackawanna Station.

The ship ebbed on, the Hudson seemed interminable. But at last they were round the bend, and there was the poor harvest of lights at the Battery. Liberty flung up her torch in a tantrum. There was the wash of the sea.

And though the Atlantic was grey as lava, she did come at last into the sun. Even she had a house above the bluest of seas, with a vast garden, or vineyard, all vines and olives steeply, terrace after terrace, to the strip of coast-plain; and the garden full of secret places, deep groves of lemon far down in the cleft of the earth, and hidden, pure green reservoirs of water; then a spring issuing out of a little cavern, where the old Sicules had drunk before the Greeks came; and a grey goat bleating, stabled in an ancient tomb, with all the niches empty. There was the scent of mimosa, and beyond the snow of the volcano.

She saw it all, and in a measure it was soothing. But it was all external. She didn't really care about it. She was herself, just the same, with all her anger and frustration inside her, and her incapacity to feel anything real. The child irritated her, and preyed on her peace of mind. She felt so horribly, ghastly responsible for him: as if she must be responsible for every breath he drew. And that was torture to her, to the child, and to everybody else concerned.

'You know, Juliet, the doctor told you to lie in the sun, without your clothes. Why don't you?' said the mother.

'When I am fit to do so, I will. Do you want to kill me?' Juliet flew at her.

'To kill you, no! Only to do you good.'

'For God's sake, leave off wanting to do me good.'

The mother at last was so hurt and incensed, she departed. The sea went white – and then invisible. Pouring rain fell. It was cold, in the house built for the sun.

Again a morning when the sun lifted himself naked and molten, sparkling over the sea's rim. The house faced south-west. Juliet lay in her bed and watched him rise. It was as if she had never seen the sun rise before. She had never seen the naked sun stand up pure upon the sea-line, shaking the night off himself.

So the desire sprang secretly in her to go naked in the sun. She cherished her desire like a secret.

But she wanted to go away from the house – away from people. And it is not easy, in a country where every olive tree has eyes, and every slope is seen from afar, to go hidden.

But she found a place: a rocky bluff, shoved out to the sea and sun and overgrown with large cactus, the flat-leaved cactus called prickly pear. Out of this blue-grey knoll of cactus rose one cypress tree, with a pallid, thick trunk, and a tip that leaned over, flexible, up in the blue. It stood like a guardian looking to sea; or a low, silvery candle whose huge flame was darkness against light: earth sending up her proud tongue of gloom.

Juliet sat down by the cypress trees and took off her clothes. The contorted cactus made a forest, hideous yet fascinating, about her. She sat and offered her bosom to the sun, sighing, even now, with a certain hard pain, against the cruelty of having to give herself.

But the sun marched in blue heaven and sent down his rays as he went. She felt the soft air of the sea on her breasts, that seemed as if they would never ripen. But she hardly felt the sun. Fruits that would wither and not mature, her breasts.

Soon, however, she felt the sun inside them, warmer than ever love had been, warmer than milk or the hands of her baby. At last, at last her breasts were like long white grapes in the hot sun.

She slid off all her clothes and lay naked in the sun, and as she lay she looked up through her fingers at the central sun, his blue pulsing roundness, whose outer edges streamed brilliance. Pulsing with marvellous blue, and alive, and streaming white fire from his edges, the sun! He faced down to her with his look of blue fire, and enveloped her breasts and her face, her throat, her tired belly, her knees, her thighs and her feet.

She lay with shut eyes, the colour of rosy flame through her lids. It was too much. She reached and put leaves over her eyes. Then she lay again, like a long white gourd in the sun, that must ripen to gold.

She could feel the sun penetrating even into her bones; nay, farther, even into her emotions and her thoughts. The dark tensions of her emotion began to give way, the cold dark clots of her thoughts began to dissolve. She was beginning to feel warm right through. Turning over, she let her shoulders dissolve in the sun, her loins, the backs of her thighs, even her heels. And she lay half stunned with wonder at the thing that was happening to her. Her weary, chilled heart was melting, and, in melting, evaporating.

When she was dressed again she lay once more and looked up at the cypress tree, whose crest, a flexible filament, fell this way and that in the breeze. Meanwhile, she was conscious of the great sun roaming in heaven.

So, dazed, she went home, only half-seeing, sun-blinded and sun-dazed. And her blindness was like a richness to her, and her dim, warm, heavy half-consciousness was like wealth.

'Mummy! Mummy!' her child came running towards her, calling in that peculiar bird-like little anguish of want, always wanting her. She was surprised that her drowsed heart for once felt none of the anxious love-anguish in return. She caught the child up in her arms, but she thought: He should not be such a lump! If he were in the sun, he would spring up.

She resented, rather, his little hands clutching at her, especially at her neck. She pulled her throat away. She did not want to be touched. She put the child gently down.

'Run!' she said. 'Run in the sun!'

And there and then she took off his clothes and set him naked on the warm terrace.

'Play in the sun!' she said.

He was frightened and wanted to cry. But she, in the warm indolence of her body, and the complete indifference of her heart, rolled him an orange across the red tiles, and with his soft, unformed little body he toddled after it. Then immediately he had it, he dropped it because it felt strange against his flesh. And he looked back at her, querulous, wrinkling his face to cry, frightened because he was stark.

'Bring me the orange,' she said, amazed at her own deep indifference to his trepidation. 'Bring Mummy the orange.'

'He shall not grow up like his father,' she said to herself. 'Like a worm that the sun has never seen.'

II

She had had the child so much on her mind, in a torment of responsibility, as if, having borne him, she had to answer for his whole existence. Even if his nose were running, it had been repulsive and a goad in her vitals, as if she must say to herself: Look at the thing you brought forth!

Now a change took place. She was no longer vitally interested in the child, she took the strain of her anxiety and her will from off him. And he thrived all the more for it.

She was thinking inside herself, of the sun in his splendour, and her mating with him. Her life was now a whole ritual. She lay always awake, before dawn, watching for the grey to colour to pale gold, to know if cloud lay on the sea's edge. Her joy was when he rose all molten in his nakedness, and threw off blue-white fire, into the tender heaven.

But sometimes he came ruddy, like a big, shy creature. And sometimes slow and crimson red, with a look of anger, slowly pushing and shouldering. Sometimes again she could not see him, only the level cloud threw down gold and scarlet from above, as he moved behind the wall.

She was fortunate. Weeks went by, and though the dawn was sometimes clouded, and afternoon was sometimes grey, never a day passed sunless, and most days, winter though it was, streamed radiant. Then thin little wild crocuses came up mauve and striped, the wild narcissi hung their winter stars.

Every day she went down to the cypress tree, among the cactus grove on the knoll with yellowish cliffs at the foot. She was wiser and subtler now, wearing only a dove-grey wrapper, and sandals. So that in an instant, in any hidden niche, she was naked to the sun. And the moment she was covered again she was grey and invisible.

Every day, in the morning towards noon, she lay at the foot of the powerful, silver-pawed cypress tree, while the sun rode jovial in heaven. By now she knew the sun in every thread of her body, there was not a cold shadow left. And her heart, that anxious, straining heart, had disappeared altogether, like a flower that falls in the sun, and leaves only a ripe seed-case.

She knew the sun in heaven, blue-molten with his white fire edges, throwing off fire. And though he shone on all the world, when she lay unclothed he focussed on her. It was one of the wonders of the sun, he could shine on a million people and still be the radiant, splendid, unique sun, focussed on her alone.

With her knowledge of the sun, and her conviction that the sun *knew* her, in the cosmic carnal sense of the word, came over her a feeling of detachment from people, and a certain contempt for human beings altogether. They were so un-elemental, so unsunned. They were so like graveyard worms.

Even the peasants passing up the rocky, ancient little road with their donkeys, sun-blackened as they were, were not sunned right through. There was a little soft white core of fear, like a snail in a shell, where the soul of the men cowered in fear of death, and in fear of the natural blaze of life. He dared not quite emerge: always innerly cowed. All men were like that.

Why admit men!

With her indifference to people, to men, she was not now so cautious about being unseen. She had told Marinina, who went shopping for her in the village, that the doctor had ordered sun-baths. Let that suffice.

Marinina was a woman over sixty, tall, thin, erect, with curling dark grey hair, and dark grey eyes that had the shrewdness of thousands of years in them, with the laugh that underlies all long experience. Tragedy is lack of experience.

'It must be beautiful to go unclothed in the sun,' said Marinina, with a shrewd laugh in her eyes, as she looked keenly at the other woman. Juliet's fair, bobbed hair curled in a little cloud at her temple. Marinina was a woman of Magna Græcia, and had far memories. She looked again at Juliet. 'But you have to be beautiful yourself, if you're not going to give offence to the sun? Isn't it so?' she added, with that queer, breathless little laugh of the women of the past.

'Who knows if I am beautiful?' said Juliet.

But beautiful or not, she felt that by the sun she was appreciated. Which is the same.

When, out of the sun at noon, sometimes she stole down over the rocks and past the cliff-edge, down to the deep gully where the lemons hung in cool eternal shadow, and in the silence slipped off her wrapper to wash herself quickly at one of the deep, clear green basins, she would notice, in the bare green twilight under the lemon leaves, that all her body was rosy, rosy and turning to gold. She was like another person. She was another person.

So she remembered that the Greeks had said, a white, unsunned body was fishy and unhealthy.

And she would rub a little olive oil in her skin, and wander a moment in the dark underworld of the lemons, balancing a lemon flower in her navel, laughing to herself. There was just a chance some peasant might see her. But if he did he would be more afraid of her than she of him. She knew the white core of fear in the clothed bodies of men.

She knew it even in her little son. How he mistrusted her, now that she laughed at him, with the sun in her face! She insisted on his toddling naked in the sunshine every day. And now his little body was pink, too, his blond hair was pushed thick from his brow, his cheeks had a pomegranate scarlet, in the delicate gold of the sunny skin. He was bonny and healthy, and the servants, loving his red and gold and blue, called him an angel from heaven.

But he mistrusted his mother: she laughed at him. And she saw in his wide blue eyes, under the little frown, that centre of fear, misgiving, which she believed was at the centre of all male eyes now. She called it fear of the sun.

'He fears the sun,' she would say to herself, looking down into the eyes of the child.

And as she watched him toddling, swaying, tumbling in the sunshine, making his little, bird-like noises, she saw that he held himself tight and hidden from the sun, inside himself. His spirit was like a snail in a shell, in a damp, cold crevice inside himself. It made her think of his father. She wished she could make him come forth, break out in a gesture of recklessness and salutation.

She determined to take him with her, down to the cypress tree among the cactus. She would have to watch him, because of the thorns. But surely in that place he would come forth from that little shell, deep inside him. That little civilised tension would disappear off his brow.

She spread a rug for him and sat him down. Then she slid off her wrapper and lay down herself, watching a hawk high in the blue, and the tip of the cypress hanging over.

The boy played with stones on the rug. When he got up to toddle away, she sat up too. He turned and looked at her. Almost, from his blue eyes, it was the challenging, warm look of the true male. And he was handsome, with the scarlet in the golden blond of his skin. He was not really white. His skin was gold-dusky.

'Mind the thorns, darling,' she said.

'Thorns!' re-echoed the child, in a birdy chirp, still looking at her over his shoulder, like some naked cherub in a picture, doubtful.

'Nasty prickly thorns.'

' 'Ickly thorns!'

He staggered in his little sandals over the stones, pulling at the dry, wild mint. She was quick as a serpent, leaping to him, when he was going to fall against the prickles. It surprised even herself. 'What a wild cat I am, really!' she said to herself.

She brought him every day, when the sun shone, to the cypress tree.

'Come!' she said. 'Let us go to the cypress tree.'

And if there was a cloudy day, with the tramontana blowing, so that she could not go down, the child would chirp incessantly: 'Cypress tree! Cypress tree!'

He missed it as much as she did.

It was not just taking sunbaths. It was much more than that. Something deep inside her unfolded and relaxed, and she was given. By some mysterious power inside her, deeper than her known consciousness and will, she was put into connection with the sun, and the stream flowed of itself, from her womb. She herself, her conscious self, was secondary, a secondary person, almost an onlooker. The true Juliet was this dark flow from her deep body to the sun.

She had always been mistress of herself, aware of what she was doing, and held tense for her own power. Now she felt inside her quite another sort of power, something greater than herself, flowing by itself. Now she was vague, but she had a power beyond herself.

III

The end of February was suddenly very hot. Almond blossom was falling like pink snow, in the touch of the smallest breeze. The mauve, silky little anemonies were out, the asphodels tall in bud, and the sea was cornflower blue.

Juliet had ceased to trouble about anything. Now, most of the day, she and the child were naked in the sun, and it was all she wanted. Sometimes she went down to the sea to bathe: often she wandered in the gullies where the sun shone in, and she was out of sight. Sometimes she saw a peasant with an ass, and he saw her. But she went so simply and quietly with her child; and the fame of the sun's healing power, for the soul as well as for the body, had already spread among the people; so that there was no excitement.

The child and she were now both tanned with a rosy-golden tan all over. 'I am another being!' she said to herself, as she looked at her red-gold breasts and thighs.

The child, too, was another creature, with a peculiar, quiet, sun-darkened absorption. Now he played by himself in silence, and she hardly need notice him. He seemed no longer to know when he was alone.

There was a breeze, and the sea was ultramarine. She sat by the great silver paw of the cypress tree, drowsed in the sun, but her breasts alert, full of sap. She was becoming aware that an activity was rousing in her, an activity which would carry her into a new way of life. Still she did not want to be aware. She knew well enough the vast cold apparatus of civilisation, so difficult to evade.

500

The child had gone a few yards down the rocky path, round the great sprawling of a cactus. She had seen him, a real gold-brown infant of the winds, with burnt gold hair and red cheeks, collecting the speckled pitcher-flowers and laying them in rows. He could balance now, and was quick for his own emergencies, like an absorbed young animal playing silent.

Suddenly she heard him speaking: '*Look, Mummy! Mummy, look!*' A note in his bird-like voice made her lean forward sharply.

Her heart stood still. He was looking over his naked little shoulder at her, and pointing with a loose little hand at a snake which had reared itself up a yard away from him, and was opening its mouth so that its forked, soft tongue flickered black like a shadow, uttering a short hiss.

'Look, Mummy!'

'Yes, darling, it's a snake!' came the slow, deep voice.

He looked at her, his wide blue eyes uncertain whether to be afraid or not. Some stillness of the sun in her reassured him.

'Snake!' he chirped.

'Yes, darling! Don't touch it, it can bite.'

The snake had sunk down, and was reaching away from the coils in which it had been basking asleep, and slowly was easing its long, gold-brown body into the rocks, with slow curves. The boy turned and watched it in silence. Then he said:

'Snake going!'

'Yes! Let it go. It likes to be alone.'

He still watched the slow, easing length as the creature drew itself apathetic out of sight.

'Snake gone back,' he said.

'Yes, it's gone back. Come to Mummy a moment.'

He came and sat with his plump, naked little body on her naked lap, and she smoothed his burnt, bright hair. She said nothing, feeling that everything was passed. The curious soothing power of the sun filled her, filled the whole place like a charm, and the snake was part of the place, along with her and the child.

Another day, in the dry stone wall of one of the olive terraces, she saw a black snake horizontally creeping.

'Marinina,' she said, 'I saw a black snake. Are they harmful?'

'Ah, the black snakes, no! But the yellow ones, yes! If the yellow ones bite you, you die. But they frighten me, they frighten me, even the black ones, when I see one.'

Juliet still went to the cypress tree with the child. But she always

501

looked carefully round before she sat down, examining everywhere where the child might go. Then she would lie and turn to the sun again, her tanned, pear-shaped breasts pointing up. She would take no thought for the morrow. She refused to think outside her garden, and she could not write letters. She would tell the nurse to write.

IV

It was March, and the sun was growing very powerful. In the hot hours she would lie in the shade of the trees, or she would even go down to the depths of the cool lemon grove. The child ran in the distance, like a young animal absorbed in life.

One day she was sitting in the sun on the steep slope of the gully, having bathed in one of the great tanks. Below, under the lemons, the child was wading among the yellow oxalis flowers of the shadow, gathering fallen lemons, passing with his tanned little body into flecks of light, moving all dappled.

Suddenly, high over the land's edge, against the full-lit pale blue sky, Marinina appeared, a black cloth tied round her head, calling quietly: '*Signora! Signora Giulietta!*'

Juliet faced round, standing up. Marinina paused a moment, seeing the naked woman standing alert, her sun-faded fair hair in a little cloud. Then the swift old woman came on down the slant of the steep track.

She stood a few steps, erect, in front of the sun-coloured woman, and eyed her shrewdly.

'But how beautiful you are, you!' she said coolly, almost cynically. 'There is your husband.'

'My husband!' cried Juliet.

The old woman gave a shrewd bark of a little laugh, the mockery of the women of the past.

'Haven't you got one, a husband, you?' she taunted.

'But where is he?' cried Juliet.

The old woman glanced over her shoulder.

'He was following me,' she said. 'But he will not have found the path.' And she gave another little bark of a laugh.

The paths were all grown high with grass and flowers and nepitella, till they were like bird-trails in an eternally wild place. Strange, the vivid wildness of the old places of civilisation, a wildness that is not gaunt.

502

Juliet looked at her serving-woman with meditating eyes.

'Oh, very well!' she said at last. 'Let him come.'

'Let him come here? Now?' asked Marinina, her laughing, smoke-grey eyes looking with mockery into Juliet's. Then she gave a little jerk of her shoulders.

'All right, as you wish. But for him it is a rare one!'

She opened her mouth in a laugh of noiseless joy. Then she pointed down to the child, who was heaping lemons against his little chest. 'Look how beautiful the child is! That, certainly, will please him, poor thing. Then I'll bring him.'

'Bring him,' said Juliet.

The old woman scrambled rapidly up the track again. Maurice was standing grey-faced, in his grey felt hat and his dark grey suit, at a loss among the vine terraces. He looked pathetically out of place, in that resplendent sunshine and the grace of the old Greek world; like a blot of ink on the pale, sun-glowing slope.

'Come!' said Marinina to him. 'She is down here.'

And swiftly she led the way, striding with a rapid stride, making her way through the grasses. Suddenly she stopped on the brow of the slope. The tops of the lemon trees were dark, away below.

'You, you go down here,' she said to him, and he thanked her, looking up at her swiftly.

He was a man of forty, clean-shaven, grey-faced, very quiet and really shy. He managed his own business carefully, without startling success, but efficiently. And he confided in nobody. The old woman of Magna Græcia saw him at a glance: he is good, she said to herself, but not a man, poor thing.

'Down there is the Signora!' said Marinina, pointing like one of the Fates.

And again he said. 'Thank you! Than you!' without a twinkle, and stepped carefully into the track. Marinina lifted her chin with a joyful wickedness. Then she strode off towards the house.

Maurice was watching his step through the tangle of Mediterranean herbage, so he did not catch sight of his wife till he came round a little bend, quite near her. She was standing erect and nude by the jutting rock, glistening with the sun and with warm life. Her breasts seemed to be lifting up, alert, to listen, her thighs looked brown and fleet. Her glance on him, as he came like ink on blotting paper, was swift and nervous.

Maurice, poor fellow, hesitated, and glanced away from her. He turned his face aside.

'Hello, Julie!' he said, with a little nervous cough – 'Splendid! Splendid!'

He advanced with his face averted, shooting further glances at her, as she stood with the peculiar satiny gleam of the sun on her tanned skin. Somehow she did not seem so terribly naked. It was the golden-rose tan of the sun that clothed her.

'Hello, Maurice!' she said, hanging back from him. 'I wasn't expecting you so soon.'

'No,' he said. 'No! I managed to slip away a little earlier.'

And again he coughed awkwardly.

They stood several yards away from one another, and there was silence.

'Well!' he said, 'er – this is splendid, splendid! You are – er – splendid! Where is the boy?'

'There he is,' she said, pointing down to where a naked urchin in the deep shade was piling fallen lemons together.

The father gave an odd little laugh.

'Ah, yes, there he is! So there's the little man! Fine!' he said. He really was thrilled in his suppressed nervous soul. 'Hello, Johnny!' he called, and it sounded rather feeble. 'Hello, Johnny!'

The child looked up, spilling lemons from his chubby arms, but did not respond.

'I guess we'll go down to him,' said Juliet, as she turned and went striding down the path. Her husband followed, watching the rosy, fleet-looking lifting and sinking of her quick hips, as she swayed a little in the socket of her waist. He was dazed with admiration, but also, at a deadly loss. What should he do with himself? He was utterly out of the picture, in his dark grey suit and pale grey hat, and his grey, monastic face of a shy business man.

'He looks all right, doesn't he,' said Juliet, as they came through the deep sea of yellow-flowering oxalis, under the lemon trees.

'Ah! – yes! yes! Splendid! Splendid! Hello, Johnny! Do you know Daddy? Do you know Daddy, Johnny?'

He crouched down and held out his hands.

'Lemons!' said the child, birdily chirping. 'Two lemons!'

'Two lemons!' replied the father. 'Lots of lemons.'

The infant came and put a lemon in each of his father's open hands. Then he stood back to look.

504

'Two lemons!' repeated the father. 'Come, Johnny! Come and say "Hello" to Daddy.'

'Daddy going back?' said the child.

'Going back? Well – well – not to-day.'

And he gathered his son in his arms.

'Take a coat off! Daddy take a coat off!' said the boy, squirming debonair away from the cloth.

'All right, son! Daddy take a coat off!'

He took off his coat and laid it carefully aside, then again took his son in his arms. The naked woman looked down at the naked infant in the arms of the man in his shirt-sleeves. The boy had pulled off the father's hat, and Juliet looked at the sleek, black-and-grey hair of her husband, not a hair out of place. And utterly, utterly indoors. She was silent for a long time, while the father talked to the child, who was fond of his Daddy.

'What are you going to do about it, Maurice?' she said suddenly.

He looked at her swiftly, sideways.

'Er – about what, Julie?'

'Oh, everything! About this! I can't go back into East Forty-Seventh.'

'Er —' he hesitated, 'no, I suppose not – not just now at least.'

'Never,' she said, and there was a silence.

'Well – er – I don't know,' he said.

'Do you think you can come out here?' she said.

'Yes, I can stay for a month. I think I can manage a month,' he hesitated. Then he ventured a complicated, shy peep at her, and hid his face again.

She looked down at him, her alert breasts lifted with a sigh, as if a breeze of impatience shook them.

'I can't go back,' she said slowly. 'I can't go back on this sun. If you can't come here —'

She ended on an open note. He glanced at her again and again, furtively, but with growing admiration and lessening confusion.

'No!' he said. 'This kind of thing suits you. You are splendid! No, I don't think you can go back.'

He was thinking of her in the New York flat, pale, silent, oppressing him terribly. He was the soul of gentle timidity, in his human relations, and her silent, awful hostility after the baby was born, had frightened him deeply. Because he had realised she couldn't help it. Women were like that. Their feelings took a reverse direction, even against their own

505

selves, and it was awful – awful! Awful, awful to live in the house with a woman like that, whose feelings were reversed even against herself! He had felt himself ground down under the millstone of her helpless enmity. She had ground even herself down to the quick, and the child as well. No, anything rather than that.

'But what about *you*?' she asked.

'I? Oh, I! I can carry on the business, and – er – come over here for the holidays – as long as you like to stay. You stay as long as you wish.' He looked a long time down at the earth, then glanced up at her with a touch of supplication in his uneasy eyes.

'Even for ever?'

'Well – er – yes, if you like. For ever is a long time. One can't set a date.'

'And I can do anything I like?' She looked him straight in the eyes, challenging. And he was powerless against her rosy, wind-hardened nakedness.

'Er – yes! I suppose so! So long as you don't make yourself unhappy – or the boy.'

Again he looked up at her with a complicated, uneasy appeal – thinking of the child, but hoping for himself.

'I won't,' she said quickly.

'No!' he said. 'No! I don't think you will.'

There was a pause. The bells of the village were hastily clanging midday. That meant lunch.

She slipped into her grey crêpe kimono, and fastened a broad green sash round her waist. Then she slipped a little blue shirt over the boy's head, and they went up to the house.

At table she watched her husband, his grey city face, his fixed, black-grey hair, his very precise table manners, and his extreme moderation in eating and drinking. Sometimes he glanced at her, furtively, from under his black lashes. He had the gold-grey eyes of an animal that has been caught young, and reared completely in captivity.

They went on to the balcony for coffee. Below, beyond, on the next podere across the steep little gully, a peasant and his wife were sitting under an almond tree, near the green wheat, eating their midday meal from a little white cloth spread on the ground. There was a huge piece of bread, and glasses with dark wine.

Juliet put her husband with his back to this picture; she sat facing. Because, the moment she and Maurice had come out on the balcony, the peasant had glanced up.

506

V

She knew him, in the distance, perfectly. He was a rather fat, very broad fellow of about thirty-five, and he chewed large mouthfuls of bread. His wife was stiff and dark-faced, handsome, sombre. They had no children. So much Juliet had learned.

The peasant worked a great deal alone, on the opposite podere. His clothes were always very clean and cared-for, white trousers and a coloured shirt, and an old straw hat. Both he and his wife had that air of quiet superiority which belongs to individuals, not to a class.

His attraction was in his vitality, the peculiar quick energy which gave a charm to his movements, stout and broad as he was. In the early days before she took to the sun, Juliet had met him suddenly, among the rocks, when she had scrambled over to the next podere. He had been aware of her before she saw him, so that when she did look up, he took off his hat, gazing at her with shyness and pride, from his big blue eyes. His face was broad, sunburnt, he had a cropped brown moustache, and thick brown eyebrows, nearly as thick as his moustache, meeting under his low, wide brow.

'Oh!' she said. 'Can I walk here?'

'Surely!' he replied with that peculiar hot haste which characterised his movement. 'My padrone would wish you to walk wherever you like on his land.'

And he pressed back his head in the quick, vivid, shy generosity of his nature. She had gone on quickly. But instantly she had recognised the violent generosity of his blood, and the equally violent *farouche* shyness.

Since then she had seen him in the distance every day, and she came to realise that he was one who lived a good deal to himself, like a quick animal, and that his wife loved him intensely, with a jealousy that was almost hate; because, probably, he wanted to give himself still, still further, beyond where she could take him.

One day, when a group of peasants sat under a tree, she had seen him dancing quick and gay with a child – his wife watching darkly.

Gradually Juliet and he had become intimate, across the distance. They were aware of one another. She knew, in the morning, the moment he arrived with his ass. And the moment she went out on the balcony he turned to look. But they never saluted. Yet she missed him when he did not come to work on the podere.

Once, in the hot morning when she had been walking naked, deep in the gully between the two estates, she had came upon him, as he was bending down, with his powerful shoulders, picking up wood to pile on his motionless, waiting donkey. He saw her as he lifted his flushed face, and she was backing away. A flame went over his eyes, and a flame flew over her body, melting her bones. But she backed away behind the bushes, silently, and retreated whence she had come. And she wondered a little resentfully over the silence in which he could work, hidden in the bushy places. He had that wild animal faculty.

Since then there had been a definite pain of consciousness in the body of each of them, though neither would admit it, and they gave no sign of recognition. But the man's wife was instinctively aware.

And Juliet had thought: Why shouldn't I meet this man for an hour, and bear his child? Why should I have to identify my life with a man's life? Why not meet him for an hour, as long as the desire lasts, and no more? There is already the spark between us.

But she had never made any sign. And now she saw him looking up, from where he sat by the white cloth, opposite his black-clad wife, looking up at Maurice. The wife turned and looked, too, saturnine.

And Juliet felt a grudge come over her. She would have to bear Maurice's child again. She had seen it in her husband's eyes. And she knew it from his answer, when she spoke to him.

'Will you walk about in the sun, too, without your clothes?' she asked him.

'Why – er – yes! Yes, I should like to, while I'm here – I suppose it's quite private?'

There was a gleam in his eyes, a desperate kind of courage of his desire, and a glance at the alert lifting of her breasts in her wrapper. In this way, he was a man, too, he faced the world and was not entirely quenched in his male courage. He would dare to walk in the sun, even ridiculously.

But he smelled of the world, and all its fetters and its mongrel cowering. He was branded with the brand that is not a hall-mark.

Ripe now, and brown-rosy all over with the sun, and with a heart like a fallen rose, she had wanted to go down to the hot, shy peasant and bear his child. Her sentiments had fallen like petals. She had seen the flushed blood in the burnt face, and the flame in the southern blue eyes, and the answer in her had been a gush of fire. He would have been a procreative sun-bath to her, and she wanted it.

Nevertheless, her next child would be Maurice's. The fatal chain of continuity would cause it.

THE WOMAN WHO RODE AWAY

SHE had thought that this marriage, of all marriages, would be an adventure. Not that the man himself was exactly magical to her. A little, wiry, twisted fellow, twenty years older than herself, with brown eyes and greying hair, who had come to America a scrap of a wastrel, from Holland, years ago, as a tiny boy, and from the gold-mines of the west had been kicked south into Mexico, and now was more or less rich, owning silver-mines in the wilds of the Sierra Madre: it was obvious that the adventure lay in his circumstances, rather than his person. But he was still a little dynamo of energy, in spite of accidents survived, and what he had accomplished he had accomplished alone. One of those human oddments there is no accounting for.

When she actually *saw* what he had accomplished, her heart quailed. Great green-covered, unbroken mountain-hills, and in the midst of the lifeless isolation, the sharp pinkish mounds of the dried mud from the silver-works. Under the nakedness of the works, the walled-in, one-storey adobe house, with its garden inside, and its deep inner veranda with tropical climbers on the sides. And when you looked up from this shut-in flowered patio, you saw the huge pink cone of the silver-mud refuse, and the machinery of the extracting plant against heaven above. No more.

To be sure, the great wooden doors were often open. And then she could stand outside, in the vast open world. And see great, void, tree-clad hills piling behind one another, from nowhere into nowhere. They were green in autumn-time. For the rest, pinkish, stark, dry, and abstract.

And in his battered Ford car her husband would take her into the dead, thrice-dead little Spanish town forgotten among the mountains. The great, sun-dried dead church, the dead portales, the hopeless covered market-place, where, the first time she went, she saw a dead dog lying between the meat-stalls and the vegetable array, stretched out as if for ever, nobody troubling to throw it away. Deadness within deadness.

Everybody feebly talking silver, and showing bits of ore. But silver was at a standstill. The great war came and went. Silver was a dead market. Her husband's mines were closed down. But she and he lived on in the abode house under the works, among the flowers that were never very flowery to her.

She had two children, a boy and a girl. And her eldest, the boy, was nearly ten years old before she aroused from her stupor of subjected amazement. She was now thirty-three, a large, blue-eyed, dazed woman, beginning to grow stout. Her little, wiry, tough, twisted, brown-eyed husband was fifty-three, a man as tough as wire, tenacious as wire, still full of energy, but dimmed by the lapse of silver from the market, and by some curious inaccessibility on his wife's part.

He was a man of principles, and a good husband. In a way, he doted on her. He never quite got over his dazzled admiration of her. But essentially, he was still a bachelor. He had been thrown out on the world, a little bachelor, at the age of ten. When he married he was over forty, and had enough money to marry on. But his capital was all a bachelor's. He was boss of his own works, and marriage was the last and most intimate bit of his own works.

He admired his wife to extinction, he admired her body, all her points. And she was to him always the rather dazzling Californian girl from Berkeley, whom he had first known. Like any sheikh, he kept her guarded among those mountains of Chihuahua. He was jealous of her as he was of his silver-mine: and that is saying a lot.

At thirty-three she really was still the girl from Berkeley, in all but physique. Her conscious development had stopped mysteriously with her marriage, completely arrested. Her husband had never become real to her, neither mentally nor physically. In spite of his late sort of passion for her, he never meant anything to her, physically. Only morally he swayed her, downed her, kept her in an invincible slavery.

So the years went by, in the adobe house strung round the sunny patio, with the silver-works overhead. Her husband was never still. When the silver went dead, he ran a ranch lower down, some twenty miles away, and raised pure-bred hogs, splendid creatures. At the same time, he hated pigs. He was a squeamish waif of an idealist, and really hated the physical side of life. He loved work, work, work, and making things. His marriage, his children, were something he was making, part of his business, but with a sentimental income this time.

Gradually her nerves began to go wrong: she must get out. She must

510

get out. So he took her to El Paso for three months. And at least it was the United States.

But he kept his spell over her. The three months ended: back she was, just the same, in her adobe house among those eternal green or pinky-brown hills, void as only the undiscovered is void. She taught her children, she supervised the Mexican boys who were her servants. And sometimes her husband brought visitors, Spaniards or Mexicans or occasionally white men.

He really loved to have white men staying on the place. Yet he had not a moment's peace when they were there. It was as if his wife were some peculiar secret vein of ore in his mines, which no one must be aware of except himself. And she was fascinated by the young gentlemen, mining engineers, who were his guests at times. He, too, was fascinated by a real gentleman. But he was an old-timer miner with a wife, and if a gentleman looked at his wife, he felt as if his mind were being looted, the secrets of it pried out.

It was one of these young gentlemen who put the idea into her mind. They were all standing outside the great wooden doors of the patio, looking at the outer world. The eternal, motionless hills were all green, it was September, after the rains. There was no sign of anything, save the deserted mine, the deserted works, and a bunch of half-deserted miners' dwellings.

'I wonder,' said the young man, 'what there is behind those great blank hills.'

'More hills,' said Lederman. 'If you go that way, Sonora and the coast. This way is the desert – you came from there – and the other way, hills and mountains.'

'Yes, but what *lives* in the hills and the mountains? *Surely* there is something wonderful? It looks *so* like nowhere on earth: like being on the moon.'

'There's plenty of game, if you want to shoot. And Indians, if you call *them* wonderful.'

'Wild ones?'

'Wild enough.'

'But friendly?'

'It depends. Some of them are quite wild, and they don't let anybody near. They kill a missionary at sight. And where a missionary can't get, nobody can.'

'But what does the government say?'

'They're so far from everywhere, the government leaves 'em alone.

And they're wily; if they think there'll be trouble, they send a delega-
tion to Chihuahua and make a formal submission. The government is
glad to leave it at that.'

'And do they live quite wild, with their own savage customs and
religion?'

'Oh yes. They use nothing but bows and arrows. I've seen them in
town, in the Plaza, with funny sort of hats with flowers round them,
and a bow in one hand, quite naked except for a sort of shirt, even in
cold weather – striding round with their savage's bare legs.'

'But don't you suppose it's wonderful, up there in their secret villages?'

'No. What would there be wonderful about it? Savages are savages,
and all savages behave more or less alike: rather low-down and dirty,
unsanitary, with a few cunning tricks, and struggling to get enough to
eat.'

'But surely they have old, old religions and mysteries – it *must* be
wonderful, surely it must.'

'I don't know about mysteries – howling and heathen practices more
or less indecent. No, I see nothing wonderful in that kind of stuff. And
I wonder that you should, when you have lived in London or Paris or
New York—'

'Ah, *everybody* lives in London or Paris or New York' – said the
young man, as if this were an argument.

And this particular vague enthusiasm for unknown Indians found a
full echo in the woman's heart. She was overcome by a foolish romanti-
cism more unreal than a girl's. She felt it was her destiny to wander
into the secret haunts of these timeless, mysterious, marvellous Indians
of the mountains.

She kept her secret. The young man was departing, her husband was
going with him down to Torreon, on business: would be away for some
days. But before the departure, she made her husband talk about the
Indians: about the wandering tribes, resembling the Navajo, who were
still wandering free; and the Yaquis of Sonora: and the different
groups in the different valleys of Chihuahua State.

There was supposed to be one tribe, the Chilchuis, living in a high
valley to the south, who were the sacred tribe of all the Indians. The
descendants of Montezuma and the old Aztec or Totonac kings still
lived among them, and the old priests still kept up the ancient religion,
and offered human sacrifices – so it was said. Some scientists had been
to the Chilchui country, and had come back gaunt and exhausted with

512

hunger and bitter privation, bringing various curious, barbaric objects of worship, but having seen nothing extraordinary in the hungry, stark village of savages.

Though Lederman talked in this off-hand way, it was obvious he felt some of the vulgar excitement at the idea of ancient and mysterious savages.

'How far away are they?' she asked.

'Oh – three days on horseback – past Cuchitee and a little lake there is up there.'

Her husband and the young man departed. The woman made her crazy plans. Of late, to break the monotony of her life, she had harassed her husband into letting her go riding with him, occasionally, on horseback. She was never allowed to go out alone. The country truly was not safe, lawless and crude.

But she had her own horse, and she dreamed of being free as she had been as a girl, among the hills of California.

Her daughter, nine years old, was now in a tiny convent in the little half-deserted Spanish mining-town five miles away.

'Manuel,' said the woman to her house-servant, 'I'm going to ride to the convent to see Margarita, and take her a few things. Perhaps I shall stay the night in the convent. You look after Freddy and see everything is all right till I come back.'

'Shall I ride with you on the master's horse, or shall Juan?' asked the servant.

'Neither of you. I shall go alone.'

The young man looked her in the eyes, in protest. Absolutely impossible that the woman should ride alone!

'I shall go alone,' repeated the large, placid-seeming, fair-complexioned woman, with peculiar overbearing emphasis. And the man silently, unhappily yielded.

'Why are you going alone, mother?' asked her son, as she made up parcels of food.

'Am I *never* to be let alone? Not one moment of my life?' she cried, with sudden explosion of energy. And the child, like the servant, shrank into silence.

She set off without a qualm, riding astride on her strong roan horse, and wearing a riding-suit of coarse linen, a riding-skirt over her linen breeches, a scarlet neck-tie over her white blouse, and a black felt hat on her head. She had food in her saddle-bags, an army canteen with water, and a large, native blanket tied on behind the saddle. Peering into the distance, she set off from her home. Manuel and the little boy stood in the gateway to watch her go. She did not even turn to wave them farewell.

But when she had ridden about a mile, she left the wild road and took a small trail to the right, that led into another valley, over steep places and past great trees, and through another deserted mining settlement. It was September, the water was running freely in the little stream that had fed the now-abandoned mine. She got down to drink, and let the horse drink too.

She saw natives coming through the trees, away up the slope. They had seen her, and were watching her closely. She watched in turn. The three people, two women and a youth, were making a wide detour, so as not to come too close to her. She did not care. Mounting, she trotted ahead up the silent valley, beyond the silver-works, beyond any trace of mining. There was still a rough trail that led over rocks and loose stones into the valley beyond. This trail she had already ridden, with her husband. Beyond that she knew she must go south.

Curiously she was not afraid, although it was a frightening country, the silent, fatal-seeming mountain slopes, the occasional distant, suspicious, elusive natives among the trees, the great carrion birds occasionally hovering, like great flies, in the distance, over some carrion or some ranch-house or some group of huts.

As she climbed, the trees shrank and the trail ran through a thorny scrub, that was trailed over with blue convolvulus and an occasional pink creeper. Then these flowers lapsed. She was nearing the pine trees.

She was over the crest, and before her another silent, void, green-clad valley. It was past midday. Her horse turned to a little runlet of water, so she got down to eat her midday meal. She sat in silence looking at the motionless, unliving valley, and at the sharp-peaked hills, rising higher to rock and pine trees, southwards. She rested two hours in the heat of the day, while the horse cropped around her.

Curious that she was neither afraid nor lonely. Indeed, the loneliness was like a drink of cold water to one who is very thirsty. And a strange elation sustained her from within.

She travelled on, and camped at night in a valley beside a stream, deep among the bushes. She had seen cattle and had crossed several trails. There must be a ranch not far off. She heard the strange wailing shriek of a mountain-lion, and the answer of dogs. But she sat by her small camp-fire in a secret hollow place and was not really afraid. She was buoyed up always by the curious, bubbling elation within her.

It was very cold before dawn. She lay wrapped in her blanket looking at the stars, listening to her horse shivering, and feeling like a woman who has died and passed beyond. She was not sure that she had not heard, during the night, a great crash at the centre of herself, which was the crash of her own death. Or else it was a crash at the centre of the earth, and meant something big and mysterious.

With the first peep of light she got up, numb with cold, and made a fire. She ate hastily, gave her horse some pieces of oil-seed cake, and set off again. She avoided any meeting – and since she met nobody, it was evident that she in turn was avoided. She came at last in sight of the village of Cuchitee, with its black houses with their reddish roofs, a sombre, dreary little cluster below another silent, long-abandoned mine. And beyond, a long, great mountain-side, rising up green and light to the darker, shaggier green of pine trees. And beyond the pine trees stretches of naked rock against the sky, rock slashed already and brindled with white stripes of snow. High up, the new snow had already begun to fall.

And now, as she neared, more or less, her destination, she began to go vague and disheartened. She had passed the little lake among yellowing aspen trees whose white trunks were round and suave like the white round arms of some woman. What a lovely place! In California she would have raved about it. But here she looked and saw that it was lovely, but she didn't care. She was weary and spent with her two nights in the open, afraid of the coming night. She didn't know where she was going, or what she was going for. Her horse plodded dejectedly on, towards that immense and forbidding mountain-slope, following a stony little trail. And if she had had any will of her own left, she would have turned back, to the village, to be protected and sent home to her husband.

But she had no will of her own. Her horse splashed through a brook, and turned up a valley, under immense yellowing cottonwood trees. She must have been near nine thousand feet above sea-level, and her head was light with the altitude and with weariness. Beyond the cottonwood trees she could see, on each side, the steep sides of mountain-slopes hemming her in, sharp-plumaged with overlapping aspen, and, higher up, with sprouting, pointed spruce and pine tree. Her horse went on automatically. In this tight valley, on this slight trail, there was nowhere to go but ahead, climbing.

Suddenly her horse jumped, and three men in dark blankets were on the trail before her.

'*Adios!*' came the greeting, in the full, restrained Indian voice.

'*Adios!*' she replied, in her assured, American woman's voice.

'Where are you going?' came the quiet question, in Spanish.

The men in the dark sarapes had come closer, and were looking up at her.

'On ahead,' she replied coolly, in her hard, Saxon Spanish.

These were just natives to her: dark-faced, strongly-built men in dark sarapes and straw hats. They would have been the same as the men who worked for her husband, except, strangely, for the long black hair that fell over their shoulders. She noted this long black hair with a certain distaste. These must be the wild Indians she had come to see.

'Where do you come from?' the same man asked. It was always the one man who spoke. He was young, with quick, large, bright black eyes that glanced sideways at her. He had a soft black moustache on his dark face, and a sparse tuft of beard, loose hairs on his chin. His long black hair, full of life, hung unrestrained on his shoulders. Dark as he was, he did not look as if he had washed lately.

His two companions were the same, but older men, powerful and silent. One had a thin black line of moustache, but was beardless. The other had the smooth cheeks and the sparse dark hairs marking the lines of his chin with the beard characteristic of the Indians.

'I come from far away,' she replied, with half-jocular evasion.

This was received in silence.

'But where do you live?' asked the young man, with that same quiet insistence.

'In the north,' she replied airily.

Again there was a moment's silence. The young man conversed quietly, in Indian, with his two companions.

'Where do you want to go, up this way?' he asked suddenly, with challenge and authority, pointing briefly up the trail.

'To the Chilchui Indians,' answered the woman laconically.

The young man looked at her. His eyes were quick and black, and inhuman. He saw, in the full evening light, the faint sub-smile of assurance on her rather large, calm, fresh-complexioned face; the weary, bluish lines under her large blue eyes; and in her eyes, as she looked down at him, a half-childish, half-arrogant confidence in her own female power. But in her eyes also, a curious look of trance.

'*Usted es Señora?* You are a lady?' the Indian asked her.

'Yes, I am a lady,' she replied complacently.

'With a family?'

'With a husband and two children, boy and girl,' she said.

The Indian turned to his companion and translated, in the low, gurgling speech, like hidden water running. They were evidently at a loss.

'Where is your husband?' asked the young man.

'Who knows?' she replied airily. 'He has gone away on business for a week.'

The black eyes watched her shrewdly. She, for all her weariness, smiled faintly in the pride of her own adventure and the assurance of her own womanhood, and the spell of the madness that was on her.

'And what do *you* want to do?' the Indian asked her.

'I want to visit the Chilchui Indians – to see their houses and to know their gods,' she replied.

The young man turned and translated quickly, and there was a silence almost of consternation. The grave elder men were glancing at her sideways, with strange looks, from under their decorated hats. And they said something to the young man, in deep chest voices.

The latter still hesitated. Then he turned to the woman.

'Good!' he said. 'Let us go. But we cannot arrive until to-morrow. We shall have to make a camp to-night.'

'Good!' she said. 'I can make a camp.'

Without more ado, they set off at a good speed up the stony trail. The young Indian ran alongside her horse's head, the other two ran behind. One of them had taken a thick stick, and occasionally he struck her horse a resounding blow on the haunch, to urge him forward. This made the horse jump, and threw her back in the saddle, which, tired as she was, made her angry.

'Don't do that!' she cried, looking round angrily at the fellow. She met his black, large, bright eyes, and for the first time her spirit really quailed. The man's eyes were not human to her, and they did not see her as a beautiful white woman. He looked at her with a black, bright inhuman look, and saw no woman in her at all. As if she were some strange, unaccountable *thing*, incomprehensible to him, but inimical. She sat in her saddle in wonder, feeling once more as if she had died. And again he struck her horse, and jerked her badly in the saddle.

All the passionate anger of the spoilt white woman rose in her. She pulled her horse to a standstill, and turned with blazing eyes to the man at her bridle.

'Tell that fellow not to touch my horse again,' she cried.

She met the eyes of the young man, and in their bright black inscrutability she saw a fine spark, as in a snake's eye, of derision. He spoke to

517

his companion in the rear, in the low tones of the Indian. The man with the stick listened without looking. Then, giving a strange low cry to the horse, he struck it again on the rear, so that it leaped forward spasmodically up the stony trail, scattering the stones, pitching the weary woman in her seat.

The anger flew like a madness into her eyes, she went white at the gills. Fiercely she reined in her horse. But before she could turn, the young Indian had caught the reins under the horse's throat, jerked them forward, and was trotting ahead rapidly, leading the horse.

The woman was powerless. And along with her supreme anger there came a slight thrill of exultation. She knew she was dead.

The sun was setting, a great yellow light flooded the last of the aspens, flared on the trunks of the pine trees, the pine needles bristled and stood out with dark lustre, the rocks glowed with unearthly glamour. And through the effulgence the Indian at her horse's head trotted unweariedly on, his dark blanket swinging, his bare legs glowing with a strange transfigured ruddiness in the powerful light, and his straw hat with its half-absurd decorations of flowers and feathers shining showily above his river of long black hair. At times he would utter a low call to the horse, and then the other Indian, behind, would fetch the beast a whack with the stick.

The wonder-light faded off the mountains, the world began to grow dark, a cold air breathed down. In the sky, half a moon was struggling against the glow in the west. Huge shadows came down from steep rocky slopes. Water was rushing. The woman was conscious only of her fatigue, her unspeakable fatigue, and the old wind from the heights. She was not aware how moonlight replaced daylight. It happened while she travelled unconscious with weariness.

For some hours they travelled by moonlight. Then suddenly they came to a standstill. The men conversed in low tones for a moment.

'We camp here,' said the young man.

She waited for him to help her down. He merely stood holding the horse's bridle. She almost fell from the saddle, so fatigued.

They had chosen a place at the foot of rocks that still gave off a little warmth of the sun. One man cut pine boughs, another erected little screens of pine boughs against the rock for shelter, and put boughs of balsam pine for beds. The third made a small fire, to heat tortillas. They worked in silence.

The woman drank water. She did not want to eat – only to lie down. 'Where do I sleep?' she asked.

The young man pointed to one of the shelters. She crept in and lay inert. She did not care what happened to her, she was so weary, and so beyond everything. Through the twigs of spruce she could see the three men squatting round the fire on their hams, chewing the tortillas they picked from the ashes with their dark fingers, and drinking water from a gourd. They talked in low, muttering tones, with long intervals of silence. Her saddle and saddle-bags lay not far from the fire, unopened, untouched. The men were not interested in her nor her belongings. There they squatted with their hats on their heads, eating, eating mechanically, like animals, the dark sarape with its fringe falling to the ground before and behind, the powerful dark legs naked and squatting like an animal's showing the dirty white shirt and the sort of loin-cloth which was the only other garment, underneath. And they showed no more sign of interest in her than if she had been a piece of venison they were bringing home from the hunt, and had hung inside a shelter.

After a while they carefully extinguished the fire, and went inside their own shelter. Watching through the screen boughs, she had a moment's thrill of fear and anxiety, seeing the dark forms cross and pass silently in the moonlight. Would they attack her now?

But no! They were as if oblivious to her. Her horse was hobbled; she could hear it hopping wearily. All was silent, mountain-silent, cold, deathly. She slept and woke and slept in a semi-conscious numbness of cold and fatigue. A long, long night, icy and eternal, and she aware that she had died.

II

Yet when there was a stirring, and a clink of flint and steel, and the form of a man crouching like a dog over a bone, at a red splutter of fire, and she knew it was morning coming, it seemed to her the night had passed too soon.

When the fire was going, she came out of her shelter with one real desire left: for coffee. The men were warming more tortillas.

'Can we make coffee?' she asked.

The young man looked at her, and she imagined the same faint spark of derision in his eyes. He shook his head.

'We don't take it,' he said. 'There is no time.'

And the elder men, squatting on their haunches, look up at her in the terrible paling dawn, and there was not even derision in their eyes.

Only that intense, yet remote, inhuman glitter which was terrible to her. They were inaccessible. They could not see her as a woman at all. As if she *were* not a woman. As if, perhaps, her whiteness took away all her womanhood, and left her as some giant, female white ant. That was all they could see in her.

Before the sun was up, she was in the saddle again, and they were climbing steeply, in the icy air. The sun came, and soon she was very hot, exposed to the glare in the bare places. It seemed to her they were climbing to the roof of the world. Beyond against heaven were slashes of snow.

During the course of the morning, they came to a place where the horse could not go farther. They rested for a time with a great slant of living rock in front of them, like the glossy breast of some earth-beast. Across this rock, along a wavering crack, they had to go. It seemed to her that for hours she went in torment, on her hands and knees, from crack to crevice, along the slanting face of this pure rock-mountain. An Indian in front and an Indian behind walked slowly erect, shod with sandals of braided leather. But she in her riding-boots dared not stand erect.

Yet what she wondered, all the time, was why she persisted in clinging and crawling along these mile-long sheets of rock. Why she did not hurl herself down, and have done! The world was below her.

When they emerged at last on a stony slope, she looked back, and saw the third Indian coming carrying her saddle and saddle-bags on his back, the whole hung from a band across his forehead. And he had his hat in his hand, as he stepped slowly, with the slow, soft, heavy tread of the Indian, unwavering in the chinks of rock, as if along a scratch in the mountain's iron shield.

The stony slope led downwards. The Indians seemed to grow excited. One ran ahead at a slow trot, disappearing round the curve of stones. And the track curved round and down, till at last in the full blaze of the mid-morning sun, they could see a valley below them, between walls of rock, as in a great wide chasm let in the mountains. A green valley, with a river, and trees, and clusters of low flat sparkling houses. It was all tiny and perfect, three thousand feet below. Even the flat bridge over the stream, and the square with the houses around it, the bigger buildings piled up at opposite ends of the square, the tall cottonwood trees, the pastures and stretches of yellow-sere maize, the patches of brown sheep or goats in the distance, on the slopes, the railed enclosures by the stream-side. There it was, all small and perfect, looking magical, as any place will look magical seen from the mountains above. The unusual thing was that the low houses glittered white, white-washed, looking like crystals of salt, or silver. This frightened her.

They began the long, winding descent at the head of the barranca, following the stream that rushed and fell. At first it was all rocks; then the pine trees began, and soon the silver-limbed aspens. The flowers of autumn, big daisy-like flowers, and white ones, and many yellow flowers, were in profusion. But she had to sit down and rest, she was so weary. And she saw the bright flowers shadowily, as pale shadows hovering, as one who is dead must see them.

At length came grass and pasture-slopes between mingled aspen and pine trees. A shepherd, naked in the sun save for his hat and his cotton loin-cloth, was driving his brown sheep away. In a grove of trees they sat and waited, she and the young Indian. The one with the saddle had also gone forward.

They heard a sound of someone coming. It was three men, in the fine sarapes of red and orange and yellow and black, and with brilliant feather head-dresses. The oldest had his grey hair braided with fur, and his red and orange-yellow sarape was covered with curious black markings, like a leopard-skin. The other two were not grey-haired, but they were elders too. Their blankets were in stripes, and their head-dresses not so elaborate.

The young Indian addressed the elders in a few quiet words. They listened without answering or looking at him or at the woman, keeping their faces averted and their eyes turned to the ground, only listening. And at length they turned and looked at the woman.

The old chief, or medicine-man, whatever he was, had a deeply wrinkled and lined face of dark bronze, with a few sparse grey hairs round the mouth. Two long braids of grey hair, braided with fur and coloured feather, hung on his shoulders. And yet, it was only his eyes that mattered. They were black and of extraordinary piercing strength, without a qualm of misgiving in their demonish, dauntless power. He looked into the eyes of the white woman with a long piercing look, seeking she knew not what. She summoned all her strength to meet his eyes and keep up her guard. But it was no good. He was not looking at her as one human being looks at another. He never even perceived her resistance or her challenge, but looked past them both, into she knew not what.

She could see it was hopeless to expect a human communication with this old being.

He turned and said a few words to the young Indian.

'He asks what do you seek here?' said the young man in Spanish.

'I? Nothing! I only came to see what it was like.'

This was again translated, and the old man turned his eyes on her once more. Then he spoke again, in his low muttering tone, to the young Indian.

'He says, why does she leave her house with the white men? Does she want to bring the white man's God to the Chilchui?'

'No,' she replied, foolhardy. 'I came away from the white man's God myself. I came to look for the God of the Chilchui.'

Profound silence followed, when this was translated. Then the old man spoke again, in a small voice almost of weariness.

'Does the white woman seek the gods of the Chilchui because she is weary of her own God?' came the question.

'Yes, she does. She is tired of the white man's God,' she replied, thinking that was what they wanted her to say. She would like to serve the gods of the Chilchui.

She was aware of an extraordinary thrill of triumph and exultance passing through the Indians, in the tense silence that followed when this was translated. Then they all looked at her with piercing black eyes, in which a steely covetous intent glittered incomprehensible. She was the more puzzled, as there was nothing sensual or sexual in the look. It had a terrible glittering purity that was beyond her. She was afraid, she would have been paralysed with fear, had not something died within her, leaving her with a cold, watchful wonder only.

The elders talked a little while, then the two went away, leaving her with the young man and the oldest chief. The old man now looked at her with a certain solicitude.

'He says are you tired?' asked the young man.

'Very tired,' she said.

'The men will bring you a carriage,' said the young Indian.

The carriage, when it came, proved to be a litter consisting of a sort of hammock of dark woollen frieze, slung on to a pole which was borne on the shoulders of two long-haired Indians. The woollen hammock was spread on the ground, she sat down on it, and the two men raised the pole to their shoulders. Swinging rather as if she were in a sack, she was carried out of the grove of trees, following the old chief, whose leopard-spotted banket moved curiously in the sunlight.

They had emerged in the valley-head. Just in front were the maize-fields, with ripe ears of maize. The corn was not very tall, in this high altitude. The well-worn path went between it, and all she could see was the erect form of the old chief, in the flame and black sarape, stepping soft and heavy and swift, his head forward, looking neither to right nor left. Her bearers followed, stepping rhythmically, the long blue-black hair glistening like a river down the naked shoulders of the man in front.

They passed the maize, and came to a big wall or earthwork made of earth and adobe bricks. The wooden doors were open. Passing on, they were in a network of small gardens, full of flowers and herbs and fruit trees, each garden watered by a tiny ditch of running water. Among each cluster of trees and flowers was a small, glittering white house, windowless, and with closed door. The place was a network of little paths, small streams, and little bridges among square, flowering gardens.

Following the broadest path – a soft narrow track between leaves and grass, a path worn smooth by centuries of human feet, no hoof of horse nor any wheel to disfigure it – they came to the little river of swift bright water, and crossed on a log bridge. Everything was silent – there was not a human being anywhere. The road went on under magnificent cottonwood trees. It emerged suddenly outside the central plaza or square of the village.

This was a long oblong of low white houses with flat roofs, and two bigger buildings, having as it were little square huts piled on top of bigger long huts, stood at either end of the oblong, facing each other rather askew. Every little house was a dazzling white, save for the great round beam-ends which projected under the flat eaves, and for the flat roofs. Round each of the bigger buildings, on the outside of the square, was a stockyard fence, inside which was garden with trees and flowers, and various small houses.

Not a soul was in sight. They passed silently between the houses into the central square. This was quite bare and arid, the earth trodden smooth by endless generations of passing feet, passing across from door to door. All the doors of the windowless houses gave on to this blank square, but all doors were closed. The firewood lay near the threshold, a clay oven was still smoking, but there was no sign of moving life.

The old man walked straight across the square to the big house at the end, where the two upper storeys, as in a house of toy bricks, stood each one smaller than the lower one. A stone staircase, outside, led up to the roof of the first storey.

At the foot of this staircase the litter-bearers stood still, and lowered the woman to the ground.

'You will come up,' said the young Indian who spoke Spanish.

She mounted the stone stairs to the earthen roof of the first house, which formed a platform round the wall of the second storey. She followed around this platform to the back of the big house. There they descended again, into the garden at the rear.

So far they had seen no one. But now two men appeared, bare-headed, with long braided hair, and wearing a sort of white shirt gathered into a loin-cloth. These went along with the three newcomers, across the garden where red flowers and yellow flowers were blooming, to a long, low white house. There they entered without knocking.

It was dark inside. There was a low murmur of men's voices. Several men were present, their white shirts showing in the gloom, their dark faces invisible. They were sitting on a great log of smooth old wood, that lay along the far wall. And save for this log, the room seemed empty. But no, in the dark at one end was a couch, a sort of bed, and someone lying there, covered with furs.

The old Indian in the spotted sarape, who had accompanied the woman, now took off his hat and his blanket and his sandals. Laying them aside, he approached the couch, and spoke in a low voice. For some moments there was no answer. Then an old man with the snow-white hair hanging round his darkly-visible face roused himself like a vision, and leaned on one elbow, looking vaguely at the company, in tense silence.

The grey-haired Indian spoke again, and then the young Indian, taking the woman's hand, led her forward. In her linen riding-habit, and black boots and hat, and her pathetic bit of a red tie, she stood there beside the fur-covered bed of the old, old man, who sat reared up, leaning on one elbow, remote as a ghost, his white hair streaming in disorder, his face almost black, yet with a far-off intentness, not of this world, leaning forward to look at her.

His face was so old, it was like dark glass, and the few curling hairs that sprang white from his lips and chin were quite incredible. The long white locks fell unbraided and disorderly on either side of the glassy dark face. And under a faint powder of white eyebrows, the black eyes of the old chief looked at her as if from the far, far dead, seeing something that was never to be seen.

At last he spoke a few deep, hollow words, as if to the dark air.

'He says, do you bring your heart to the god of the Chilchui?' translated the young Indian.

'Tell him yes,' she said, automatically.

There was a pause. The old Indian spoke again, as if to the air. One of the men present went out. There was a silence as if of eternity in the dim room that was lighted only through the open door.

The woman looked round. Four old men with grey hair sat on the log by the wall facing the door. Two other men, powerful and impassive, stood near the door. They all had long hair, and wore white shirts gathered into a loin-cloth. Their powerful legs were naked and dark. There was a silence like eternity.

At length the man returned, with white and dark clothing on his arm. The young Indian took them, and holding them in front of the woman, said:

'You must take off your clothes, and put these on.'

'If all you men will go out,' she said.

'No one will hurt you,' he said quietly.

'Not while you men are here,' she said.

He looked at the two men by the door. They came quickly forward, and suddenly gripped her arms as she stood, without hurting her, but with great power. Then two of the old men came, and with curious skill slit her boots down with keen knives, and drew them off, and slit her clothing so that it came away from her. In a few moments she stood there white and uncovered. The old man on the bed spoke, and they turned her round for him to see. He spoke again, and the young Indian deftly took the pins and comb from her fair hair, so that it fell over her shoulders in a bunchy tangle.

Then the old man spoke again. The Indian led her to the bedside. The white-haired, glassy-dark old man moistened his finger-tips at his mouth, and most delicately touched her on the breasts and on the body, then on the back. And she winced strangely each time, as the finger-tips drew along her skin, as if Death itself were touching her.

And she wondered, almost sadly, why she did not feel shamed in her nakedness. She only felt sad and lost. Because nobody felt ashamed. The elder men were all dark and tense with some other deep, gloomy, incomprehensible emotion, which suspended all her agitation, while the young Indian had a strange look of ecstasy on his face. And she, she was only utterly strange and beyond herself, as if her body were not her own.

They gave her the new clothing: a long white cotton shift, that came to her knees: then a tunic of thick blue woollen stuff, embroidered with scarlet and green flowers. It was fastened over one shoulder only, and belted with a braid sash of scarlet and black wool.

When she was thus dressed, they took her away, barefoot, to a little house in the stockaded garden. The young Indian told her she might have what she wanted. She asked for water to wash herself. He brought it in a jar, together with a long wooden bowl. Then he fastened the gate-door of her house, and left her a prisoner. She could see through the bars of the gate-door of her house, the red flowers of the garden, and a humming-bird. Then from the roof of the big house she heard the long, heavy sound of a drum, unearthly to her in its summons, and an up-lifted voice calling from the house-top in a strange language, with a far-away emotionless intonation, delivering some speech or message. And she listened as if from the dead.

But she was very tired. She lay down on a couch of skins, pulling over her the blanket of dark wool, and she slept, giving up every-thing.

When she woke it was late afternoon, and the young Indian was entering with a basket-tray containing food, tortillas, and corn-mush with bits of meat, probably mutton, and a drink made of honey, and some fresh plums. He brought her also a long garland of red and yellow flowers with knots of blue buds at the end. He sprinkled the garland with water from a jar, then offered it to her, with a smile. He seemed very gentle and thoughtful, and on his face and in his dark eyes was a curious look of triumph and ecstasy, that frightened her a little. The glitter had gone from the black eyes, with their curving dark lashes, and he would look at her with this strange soft glow of ecstasy that was not quite human, and terribly impersonal, and which made her uneasy.

'Is there anything you want?' he said, in his low, slow, melodious voice, that aways seemed withheld, as if he were speaking aside to somebody else, or as if he did not want to let the sound come out to her.

'Am I going to be kept a prisoner here?' she asked.

'No, you can walk in the garden to-morrow,' he said softly. Always this curious solicitude.

'Do you like that drink?' he said, offering her a little earthenware cup. 'It is very refreshing.'

She sipped the liquor curiously. It was made with herbs and sweet-ened with honey, and had a strange, lingering flavour. The young man watched her with gratification.

'It has a peculiar taste,' she said.

'It is very refreshing,' he replied, his black eyes resting on her always with that look of gratified ecstasy. Then he went away. And presently she began to be sick, and to vomit violently, as if she had no control over herself.

Afterwards she felt a great soothing languor steal over her, her limbs felt strong and loose and full of languor, and she lay on her couch listening to the sounds of the village, watching the yellowing sky, smelling the scent of burning cedar wood, or pine wood. So distinctly she heard the yapping of tiny dogs, the shuffle of far-off feet, the murmur of voices, so keenly she detected the smell of smoke, and flowers, and evening falling, so vividly she saw the one bright star infinitely remote, stirring above the sunset, that she felt as if all her senses were diffused on the air, that she could distinguish the sound of evening flowers unfolding, and the actual crystal sound of the heavens, as the vast belts of the world-atmosphere slid past one another, and as if the moisture ascending and the moisture descending in the air resounded like some harp in the cosmos.

She was a prisoner in her house, and in the stockaded garden, but she scarcely minded. And it was days before she realised that she never saw another woman. Only the men, the elderly men of the big house, that she imagined must be some sort of temple, and the men priests of some sort. For they always had the same colours, red, orange, yellow, and black, and the same grave, abstracted demeanour.

Sometimes an old man would come and sit in her room with her, in absolute silence. None spoke any language but Indian, save the one younger man. The older men would smile at her, and sit with her for an hour at a time, sometimes smiling at her when she spoke in Spanish, but never answering save with this slow, benevolent-seeming smile. And they gave off a feeling of almost fatherly solicitude. Yet their dark eyes, brooding over her, had something away in their depths that was awesomely ferocious and relentless. They would cover it with a smile, at once, if they felt her looking. But she had seen it.

Always they treated her with this curious impersonal solicitude, this utterly impersonal gentleness, as an old man treats a child. But underneath it she felt there was something else, something terrible. When her old visitor had gone away, in his silent, insidious, fatherly fashion, a shock of fear would come over her; though of what she knew not.

The young Indian would sit and talk with her freely, as if with great candour. But with him, too, she felt that everything real was unsaid. Perhaps it was unspeakable. His big dark eyes would rest on her almost cherishingly, touched with ecstasy, and his beautiful, slow, languorous voice would trail out its simple, ungrammatical Spanish. He told her he

527

was the grandson of the old, old man, son of the man in the spotted sarape: and they were caciques, kings from the old, old days, before even the Spaniards came. But he himself had been in Mexico City, and also in the United States. He had worked as a labourer, building the roads in Los Angeles. He had travelled as far as Chicago.

'Don't you speak English, then?' she asked.

His eyes rested on her with a curious look of duplicity and conflict, and he mutely shook his head.

'What did you do with your long hair, when you were in the United States?' she asked. 'Did you cut it off?'

Again, with the look of torment in his eyes, he shook his head.

'No,' he said, in a low, subdued voice, 'I wore a hat, and a handkerchief tied round my head.'

And he relapsed into silence, as if of tormented memories.

'Are you the only man of your people who has been to the United States?' she asked him.

'Yes. I am the only one who has been away from here for a long time. The others come back soon, in one week. They don't stay away. The old men don't let them.'

'And why did you go?'

'The old men want me to go – because I shall be the cacique —'

He talked always with the same naïveté, and almost childish candour. But she felt that this was perhaps just the effect of his Spanish. Or perhaps speech altogether was unreal to him. Anyhow, she felt that all the real things were kept back.

He came and sat with her a good deal – sometimes more than she wished – as if he wanted to be near her. She asked him if he was married. He said he was – with two children.

'I should like to see your children,' she said.

But he answered only with that smile, a sweet, almost ecstatic smile, above which the dark eyes hardly change from their enigmatic abstraction.

It was curious, he would sit with her by the hour, without ever making her self-conscious, or sex-conscious. He seemed to have no sex, as he sat there so still and gentle and apparently submissive with his head bent a little forward, and the river of glistening black hair streaming maidenly over his shoulders.

Yet when she looked again, she saw his shoulders broad and powerful, his eyebrows black and level, the short, curved, obstinate black lashes over his lowered eyes, the small, fur-like line of moustache above his blackish, heavy lips, and the strong chin, and she knew that in some other mysterious way he was darkly and powerfully male. And he, feeling her watching him, would glance up at her swiftly with a dark lurking look in his eyes, which immediately he veiled with that half-sad smile.

The days and the weeks went by, in a vague kind of contentment. She was uneasy sometimes, feeling she had lost the power over herself. She was not in her own power, she was under the spell of some other control. And at times she had moments of terror and horror. But then these Indians would come and sit with her, casting their insidious spell over her by their very silent presence, their silent, sexless, powerful physical presence. As they sat they seemed to take her will away, and leaving her will-less and victim to her own indifference. And the young man would bring her sweetened drink, often the same emetic drink, but sometimes other kinds. And after drinking, the languor filled her heavy limbs, her senses seemed to float in the air, listening, hearing. They had brought her a little female dog, which she called Flora. And once, in the trance of her senses, she felt she *heard* the little dog conceive, in her tiny womb, and begin to be complex, with young. And another day she could hear the vast sound of the earth going round, like some immense arrow-string booming.

But as the days grew shorter and colder, when she was cold, she would get a sudden revival of her will, and a desire to go out, to go away. And she insisted to the young man, she wanted to go out.

So one day, they let her climb to the topmost roof of the big house where she was, and look down the square. It was the day of the big dance, but not everybody was dancing. Women with babies in their arms stood in their doorways, watching. Opposite, at the other end of the square, there was a throng before the other big house, and a small, brilliant group on the terrace roof of the first storey, in front of wide open doors of the upper storey. Through these wide open doors she could see fire glinting in darkness and priests in head-dresses of black and yellow and scarlet feathers, wearing robe-like blankets of black and red and yellow, with long green fringes, were moving about. A big drum was beating slowly and regularly, in the dense, Indian silence. The crowd below waited.

Then a drum started on a high beat, and there came the deep, powerful burst of men singing a heavy, savage music, like a wind roaring in some timeless forest, many mature men singing in one breath, like the wind; and long lines of dancers walked out from under the big house.

Men with naked, golden-bronze bodies and streaming black hair, tufts of red and yellow feathers on their arms, and kilts of white frieze with a bar of heavy red and black and green embroidery round their waists, bending slightly forward and stamping the earth in their absorbed, monotonous stamp of the dance, a fox-fur, hung by the nose from their belt behind, swaying with the sumputous swaying of a beautiful fox-fur, the tip of the tail writhing above the dancer's heels. And after each man, a woman with a strange elaborate head-dress of feathers and sea-shells, and wearing a short black tunic, moving erect, holding up tufts of feathers in each hand, swaying her wrists rythmically and subtly beating the earth with her bare feet.

So, the long line of the dance unfurling from the big house opposite. And from the big house beneath her, strange scent of incense, strange tense silence, then the answering burst of inhuman male singing, and the long line of the dance unfurling.

It went on all day, the insistence of the drum, the cavernous, roaring, storm-like sound of male singing, the incessant swinging of the fox-skins behind the powerful, gold-bronze, stamping legs of the men, the autumn sun from a perfect blue heaven pouring on the rivers of black hair, men's and women's, the valley all still, the walls of rock beyond, the awful huge bulking of the mountain against the pure sky, its snow seething with sheer whiteness.

For hours and hours she watched, spellbound, and as if drugged. And in all the terrible persistence of the drumming and the primeval, rushing deep singing, and the endless stamping of the dance of fox-tailed men, the tread of heavy, bird-erect women in their black tunics, she seemed at last to feel her own death; her own obliteration. As if she were to be obliterated from the field of life again. In the strange towering symbols on the heads of the changeless, absorbed women she seemed to read once more the *Mene Mene Tekel Upharsin*. Her kind of womanhood, intensely personal and individual, was to be obliterated again, and the great primeval symbols were to tower once more over the fallen individual independence of woman. The sharpness and the quivering nervous consciousness of the highly-bred white woman was to be destroyed again, womanhood was to be cast once more into the great stream of impersonal sex and impersonal passion. Strangely, as if clairvoyant, she saw the immense sacrifice prepared. And she went back to her little house in a trance of agony.

After this, there was always a certain agony when she heard the drums at evening, and the strange uplifted savage sound of men singing round the drum, like wild creatures howling to the invisible gods of the moon and the vanished sun. Something of the chuckling, sobbing cry of the coyote, something of the exultant bark of the fox, the far-off wild melancholy exultance of the howling wolf, the torment of the puma's scream, and the insistence of the ancient fierce human male, with his lapses of tenderness and his abiding ferocity.

Sometimes she would climb the high roof after nightfall, and listen to the dim cluster of young men round the drum on the bridge just beyond the square, singing by the hour. Sometimes there would be a fire, and in the fire-glow, men in their white shirts or naked save for a loin-cloth, would be dancing and stamping like spectres, hour after hour in the dark cold air, within the fire-glow, forever dancing and stamping like turkeys, or dropping squatting by the fire to rest, throwing their blankets round them.

'Why do you all have the same colours?' she asked the young Indian. 'Why do you all have red and yellow and black, over your white shirts? And the women have black tunics?'

He looked into her eyes, curiously, and the faint, evasive smile came on to his face. Behind the smile lay a soft, strange malignancy.

'Because our men are the fire and the day-time, and our women are the spaces between the stars at night,' he said.

'Aren't the women even stars?' she said.

'No. We say they are the spaces between the stars, that keep the stars apart.'

He looked at her oddly, and again the touch of derision came into his eyes.

'White people,' he said, 'they know nothing. They are like children, always with toys. We know the sun, and we know the moon. And we say, when a white woman sacrifice herself to our gods, then our gods will begin to make the world again, and the white man's gods will fall to pieces.'

'How sacrifice herself?' she asked quickly.

And he, as quickly covered, covered himself with a subtle smile.

'She sacrifice her own gods and come to our gods, I mean that,' he said soothingly.

But she was not reassured. An icy pang of fear and certainty was at her heart.

'The sun he is alive at one end of the sky,' he continued, 'and the moon lives at the other end. And the man all the time have to keep the sun happy in his side of the sky, and the woman have to keep the moon quiet at her side of the sky. All the time she have to work at this. And the sun can't ever go into the house of the moon, and the moon can't ever go into the house of the sun, in the sky. So the woman, she asks the moon to come into her cave, inside her. And the man, he draws the sun down till he has the power of the sun. All the time he do this. Then when the man gets a woman, the sun goes into the cave of the moon, and that is how everything in the world starts.'

She listened, watching him closely, as one enemy watches another who is speaking with double meaning.

'Then,' she said, 'why aren't you Indians masters of the white men?'

'Because,' he said, 'the Indian got weak, and lost his power with the sun, so the white men stole the sun. But they can't keep him – they don't know how. They got him, but they don't know what to do with him, like a boy who catches a big grizzly bear, and can't kill him, and can't run away from him. The grizzly bear eats the boy that catch him, when he want to run away from him. White men don't know what they are doing with the sun, and white women don't know what they do with the moon. The moon she got angry with white women, like a puma when someone kills her little ones. The moon, she bites white women – here inside,' and he pressed his side. 'The moon, she is angry in a white woman's cave. The Indian can see it. And soon,' he added, 'the Indian women get the moon back and keep her quiet in their house. And the Indian men get the sun, and the power over all the world. White men don't know what the sun is. They never know.'

He subsided into a curious exultant silence.

'But,' she faltered, 'why do you hate us so? Why do you hate me?'

He looked up suddenly with a light on his face, and a startling flame of a smile.

'No, we don't hate,' he said softly, looking with a curious glitter into her face.

'You do,' she said, forlorn and hopeless.

And after a moment's silence, he rose and went away.

III

Winter had now come, in the high valley, with snow that melted in the day's sun, and nights that were bitter cold. She lived on, in a kind of daze, feeling her power ebbing more and more away from her, as if her will was leaving her. She felt always in the same relaxed, confused,

532

victimised state, unless the sweetened herb drink would numb her mind altogether, and release her senses into a sort of heightened, mystic acuteness and a feeling as if she were diffusing out deliciously into the harmony of things. This at length became the only state of consciousness she really recognised: this exquisite sense of bleeding out into the higher beauty and harmony of things. Then she could actually hear the great stars in heaven, which she saw through her door, speaking from their motion and brightness, saying things perfectly to the cosmos, as they trod in perfect ripples, like bells on the floor of heaven, passing one another and grouping in the timeless dance, with the spaces of dark between. And she could hear the snow on a cold, cloudy day twittering and faintly whistling in the sky, like birds that flock and fly away in autumn, suddenly calling farewell to the invisible moon, and slipping out of the plains of the air, releasing peaceful warmth. She herself would call to the arrested snow to fall from the upper air. She would call to the unseen moon to cease to be angry, to make peace again with the unseen sun like a woman who ceases to be angry in her house. And she would smell the sweetness of the moon relaxing to the sun in the wintry heaven, when the snow fell in a faint, cold-perfumed relaxation, as the peace of the sun mingled again in a sort of unison with the peace of the moon.

She was aware too of the sort of shadow that was on the Indians of the valley, a deep stoical disconsolation, almost religious in its depth.

'We have lost our power over the sun, and we are trying to get him back. But he is wild with us, and shy like a horse that has got away. We have to go through a lot.' So the young Indian said to her, looking into her eyes with a strained meaning. And she, as if bewitched, replied:

'I hope you will get him back.'

The smile of triumph flew over his face.

'Do you hope it?' he said.

'I do,' she answered fatally.

'Then all right,' he said. 'We shall get him.'

And he went away in exultance.

She felt she was drifting on some consummation, which she had no will to avoid, yet which seemed heavy and finally terrible to her.

It must have been almost December, for the days were short when she was taken again before the aged man, and stripped of her clothing, and touched with the old finger-tips.

The aged cacique looked her in the eyes, with his eyes of lonely, far-off, black intentness, and murmured something to her.

'He wants you to make the sign of peace,' the young man translated, showing her the gesture. 'Peace and farewell to him.'

She was fascinated by the black, glass-like, intent eyes of the old cacique, that watched her without blinking, like a basilisk's, overpowering her. In their depths also she saw a certain fatherly compassion, and pleading. She put her hand before her face, in the required manner, making the sign of peace and farewell. He made the sign of peace back again to her, then sank among his furs. She thought he was going to die, and that he knew it.

There followed a day of ceremonial, when she was brought out before all the people, in a blue blanket with white fringe, and holding blue feathers in her hands. Before an altar of one house she was perfumed with incense and sprinkled with ash. Before the altar of the opposite house she was fumigated again with incense by the gorgeous, terrifying priests in yellow and scarlet and black, their faces painted with scarlet paint. And then they threw water on her. Meanwhile she was faintly aware of the fire on the altar, the heavy, heavy sound of a drum, the heavy sound of men beginning powerfully, deeply, savagely to sing, the swaying of the crowd of faces in the plaza below, and the formation for a sacred dance.

But at this time her commonplace consciousness was numb, she was aware of her immediate surroundings as shadows, almost immaterial. With refined and heightened senses she could hear the sound of the earth winging on its journey, like a shot arrow, the ripple-rustling of the air, and the boom of the great arrow-string. And it seemed to her there were two great influences in the upper air, one golden towards the sun, and one invisible silver; the first travelling like rain ascending to the gold presence sunwards, the second like rain silverily descending the ladders of space towards the hovering, lurking clouds over the snowy mountain-top. Then between them, another presence, waiting to shake himself free of moisture, of heavy white snow that had mysteriously collected about him. And in summer, like a scorched eagle, he would wait to shake himself clear of the weight of heavy sunbeams. And he was coloured like fire. And he was always shaking himself clear, of snow or of heavy heat, like an eagle rustling.

Then there was a still stranger presence, standing watching from the blue distance, always watching. Sometimes running in upon the wind, or shimmering in the heat-waves. The blue wind itself, rushing, as it were, out of the holes into the sky, rushing out of the sky down upon the earth. The blue wind, the go-between, the invisible ghost that belonged to two worlds, that played upon the ascending and the descending chords of the rains.

More and more her ordinary personal consciousness had left her, she had gone into that other state of passional cosmic consciousness, like one who is drugged. The Indians, with their heavy religious natures, had made her succumb to their vision.

Only one personal question she asked the young Indian:

'Why am I the only one that wears blue?'

'It is the colour of the wind. It is the colour of what goes away and is never coming back, but which is always here, waiting like death among us. It is the colour of the dead. And it is the colour that stands away off, looking at us from the distance, that cannot come near to us. When we go near, it goes farther. It can't be near. We are all brown and yellow and black hair, and white teeth and red blood. We are the ones that are here. You with blue eyes, you are the messengers from the far-away, you cannot stay, and now it is time for you to go back.'

'Where to?' she asked.

'To the way-off things like the sun and the blue mother of rain, and tell them that we are the people on the world again, and we can bring the sun to the moon again, like a red horse to a blue mare; we are the people. The white women have driven back the moon in the sky, won't let her come to the sun. So the sun is angry. And the Indian must give the moon to the sun.'

'How?' she said.

'The white woman got to die and go like a wind to the sun, tell him the Indians will open the gate to him. And the Indian women will open the gate to the moon. The white women don't let the moon come down out of the blue coral. The moon used to come down among the Indian women, like a white goat among the flowers. And the sun want to come down to the Indian men, like an eagle to the pine trees. The sun, he is shut out behind the white man, and the moon she is shut out behind the white woman, and they can't get away. They are angry, everything in the world gets angrier. The Indian says he will give the white woman to the sun, so the sun will leap over the white man and come to the Indian again. And the moon will be surprised, she will see the gate open, and she not know which way to go. But the Indian woman will call to the moon: *Come! Come! Come back into my grasslands. The wicked white woman can't harm you any more.* Then the sun will look over the heads of the white men, and see the moon in the pastures of our women, with the Red Men standing around like pine trees. Then he will leap

535

over the heads of the white men, and come running past to the Indians through the spruce trees. And we, who are red and black and yellow, we who stay, we shall have the sun on our right hand and the moon on our left. So we can bring the rain down out of the blue meadows, and up out of the black; and we can call the wind that tells the corn to grow, when we ask him, and we shall make the clouds to break, and the sheep to have twin lambs. And we shall be full of power, like a spring day. But the white people will be a hard winter, without snow —'

'But,' said the white woman, 'I don't shut out the moon – how can I?'

'Yes,' he said, 'you shut the gate, and then laugh, think you have it all your own way.'

She could never quite understand the way he looked at her. He was always so curiously gentle, and his smile was so soft. Yet there was such a glitter in his eyes, and an unrelenting sort of hate came out of his words, a strange, profound, impersonal hate. Personally he liked her, she was sure. He was gentle with her, attracted by her in some strange, soft, passionless way. But impersonally he hated her with a mystic hatred. He would smile at her, winningly. Yet if, the next moment, she glanced round at him unawares, she would catch that gleam of pure after-hate in his eyes.

'Have I got to die and be given to the sun?' she asked.

'Some time,' he said, laughing evasively. 'Some time we all die.'

They were gentle with her, and very considerate with her. Strange men, the old priests and the young cacique alike, they watched over her and cared for her like women. In their soft, insidious understanding, there was something womanly. Yet their eyes, with that strange glitter, and their dark, shut mouths that would open to the broad jaw, the small, strong, white teeth, had something very primitively male and cruel.

One wintry day, when snow was falling, they took her to a great dark chamber in the big house. The fire was burning in a corner on a high raised dais under a sort of hood or canopy of adobe-work. She saw in the fire-glow the glowing bodies of the almost naked priests, and strange symbols on the roof and walls of the chamber. There was no door or window in the chamber, they had descended by a ladder, from the roof. And the fire of pinewood danced continually, showing walls painted with strange devices, which she could not understand, and a ceiling of poles making a curious pattern of black and red and yellow, and alcoves or niches in which were curious objects she could not discern.

The older priests were going through some ceremony near the fire, in silence, intense Indian silence. She was seated on a low projection of the wall, opposite the fire, two men seated beside her. Presently they gave her a drink from a cup, which she took gladly, because of the semitrance it would induce.

In the darkness and in the silence she was accurately aware of everything that happened to her: how they took off her clothes, and, standing her before a great, weird device on the wall, coloured blue and white and black, washed her all over with water and the amole infusion; washed even her hair, softly, carefully, and dried it on white cloths, till it was soft and glistening. Then they laid her on a couch under another great indecipherable image of red and black and yellow, and now rubbed all her body with sweet-scented oil, and massaged all her limbs, and her back, and her sides, with a long, strange, hypnotic massage. Their dark hands were incredibly powerful, yet soft with a watery softness she could not understand. And the dark faces, leaning near her white body, she saw were darkened with red pigment, with lines of yellow round the cheeks. And the dark eyes glittered absorbed, as the hands worked upon the soft white body of the woman.

They were so impersonal, absorbed in something that was beyond her. They never saw her as a personal woman: she could tell that. She was some mystic object to them, some vehicle of passions too remote for her to grasp. Herself in a state of trance, she watched their faces bending over her, dark, strangely glistening with the transparent red paint, and lined with bars of yellow. And in this weird, luminous-dark mask of living face, the eyes were fixed with an unchanging steadfast gleam, and the purplish-pigmented lips were closed in a full, sinister, sad grimness. The immense fundamental sadness, the grimness of ultimate decision, the fixity of revenge, and the nascent exultance of those that are going to triumph – these things she could read in their faces, as she lay and was rubbed into a misty glow by their uncanny dark hands. Her limbs, her flesh, her very bones at last seemed to be diffusing into a roseate sort of mist, in which her consciousness hovered like some sungleam in a flushed cloud.

She knew the gleam would fade, the cloud would go grey. But at present she did not believe it. She knew she was a victim; that all this elaborate work upon her was the work of victimising her. But she did not mind. She wanted it.

Later, they put a short blue tunic on her and took her to the upper terrace, and presented her to the people. She saw the plaza below her full of dark faces and of glittering eyes. There was no pity: only the curious hard exultance. The people gave a subdued cry when they saw her, and she shuddered. But she hardly cared.

Next day was the last. She slept in a chamber of the big house. At dawn they put on her a big blue blanket with a fringe, and led her out into the plaza, among the throng of silent, dark-blanketed people. There was pure white snow on the ground, and the dark people in their dark-brown blankets looked like inhabitants of another world.

A large drum was slowly pounding, and an old priest was declaiming from a house-top. But it was not till noon that a litter came forth, and the people gave that low, animal cry which was so moving. In the sack-like litter sat the old, old cacique, his white hair braided with black braid and large turquoise stones. His face was like a piece of obsidian. He lifted his hand in token, and the litter stopped in front of her. Fixing her with his old eyes, he spoke to her for a few moments, in his hollow voice. No one translated.

Another litter came, and she was placed in it. Four priests moved ahead, in their scarlet and yellow and black, with plumed head-dresses. Then came the litter of the old cacique. Then the light drums began, and two groups of singers burst simultaneously into song, male and wild. And the golden-red, almost naked men, adorned with ceremonial feathers and kilts, the rivers of black hair down their backs, formed into two files and began to tread the dance. So they threaded out of the snowy plaza, in two long, sumptuous lines of dark red-gold and black and fur, swaying with a faint tinkle of bits of shell and flint, winding over the snow between the two bee-clusters of men who sang around the drums.

Slowly they moved out, and her litter, with its attendance of feathered, lurid dancing priests, moved after. Everybody danced the tread of the dance-step, even, subtly, the litter-bearers. And out of the plaza they went, past smoking ovens, on the trail to the great cottonwood trees, that stood like grey-silver lace against the blue sky, bare and exquisite above the snow. The river, diminished, rushed among fangs of ice. The chequer-squares of gardens within fences were all snowy, and the white houses now looked yellowish.

The whole valley glittered intolerably with pure snow, away to the walls of the standing rock. And across the flat cradle of snow-bed wound the long thread of the dance, shaking slowly and sumptuously in its orange and black motion. The high drums thudded quickly, and on the crystalline frozen air the swell and roar of the chant of savages was like an obsession.

She sat looking out of her litter with big, transfixed blue eyes, under which were the wan markings of her drugged weariness. She knew she was going to die, among the glisten of this snow, at the hands of this savage, sumptuous people. And as she stared at the blaze of the blue sky above the slashed and ponderous mountain, she thought: 'I am dead already. What difference does it make, the transition from the dead I am to the dead I shall be, very soon!' Yet her soul sickened and felt wan.

The strange procession trailed on, in perpetual dance, slowly across the plain of snow, and then entered the slopes between the pine trees. She saw the copper-dark men dancing the dance-tread, onwards, between the copper-pale tree trunks. And at last, she, too, in her swaying litter, entered the pine trees.

They were travelling on and on, upwards, across the snow under the trees, past superb shafts of pale, flaked copper, the rustle and shake and tread of the threading dance, penetrating into the forest, into the mountain. They were following a stream-bed: but the stream was dry, like summer, dried up by the frozenness of the head-waters. There were dark, red-bronze willow bushes with wattles like wild hair, and pallid aspen trees looking cold flesh again the snow. Then jutting dark rocks.

At last she could tell that the dancers were moving forward no more. Nearer and nearer she came upon the drums, as to a lair of mysterious animals. Then through the bushes she emerged into a strange amphitheatre. Facing was a great wall of hollow rock, down the front of which hung a great, dripping, fang-like spoke of ice. The ice came pouring over the rock from the precipice above, and then stood arrested, dripping out of high heaven, almost down to the hollow stones where the stream-pool should be below. But the pool was dry.

On either side the dry pool the lines of dancers had formed, and the dance was continuing without intermission, against a background of bushes.

But what she felt was that fanged inverted pinnacle of ice, hanging from the lip of the dark precipice above. And behind the great rope of ice she saw the leopard-like figures of priests climbing the hollow cliff face, to the cave that like a dark socket bored a cavity, an orifice, half-way up the crag.

Before she could realise, her litter-bearers were staggering in the footholds, climbing the rock. She, too, was behind the ice. There it hung, like a curtain that is not spread, but hangs like a great fang. And near above her was the orifice of the cave sinking dark into the rock. She watched it as she swayed upwards.

On the platform of the cave stood the priests, waiting in all their gorgeousness of feathers and fringed robes, watching her ascent. Two of them stooped to help her litter-bearer. And at length she was on the platform of the cave, far in behind the shaft of ice, above the hollow amphitheatre among the bushes below, where men were dancing, and the whole populace of the village was clustered in silence.

The sun was sloping down the afternoon sky, on the left. She knew that this was the shortest day of the year, and the last day of her life. They stood her facing the iridescent column of ice, which fell down marvellously arrested, away in front of her.

Some signal was given, and the dance below stopped. There was now absolute silence. She was given a little to drink, then two priests took off her mantle and her tunic, and in her strange pallor she stood there, between the lurid robes of the priests, beyond the pillar of ice, beyond and above the dark-faced people. The throng below gave the low, wild cry. Then the priest turned her round, so she stood with her back to the open world, her long blonde hair to the people below. And they cried again.

She was facing the cave, inwards. A fire was burning and flickering in the depths. Four priests had taken off their robes, and were almost as naked as she was. They were powerful men in the prime of life, and they kept their dark, painted faces lowered.

From the fire came the old, old priest, with an incense-pan. He was naked and in a state of barbaric ecstasy. He fumigated his victim, reciting at the same time in a hollow voice. Behind him came another robe-less priest, with two flint knives.

When she was fumigated, they laid her on a large flat stone, the four powerful men holding her by the outstretched arms and legs. Behind stood the aged man, like a skeleton covered with dark glass, holding a knife and transfixedly watching the sun; and behind him again was another naked priest, with a knife.

She felt little sensation, though she knew all that was happening. Turning to the sky, she looked at the yellow sun. It was sinking. The shaft of ice was like a shadow between her and it. And she realised that the yellow rays were filling half the cave, though they had not reached the altar where the fire was, at the far end of the funnel-shaped cavity.

540

Yes, the rays were creeping round slowly. As they grew ruddier, they penetrated farther. When the red sun was about to sink, he would shine full through the shaft of ice deep into the hollow of the cave, to the innermost.

She understood now that this was what the men were waiting for. Even those that held her down were bent and twisted round, their black eyes watching the sun with a glittering eagerness, and awe, and craving. The black eyes of the aged cacique were fixed like black mirrors on the sun, as if sightless, yet containing some terrible answer to the reddening winter planet. And all the eyes of the priests were fixed and glittering on the sinking orb, in the reddening, icy silence of the winter afternoon.

They were anxious, terribly anxious, and fierce. Their ferocity wanted something, and they were waiting for the moment. And their ferocity was ready to leap out into a mystic exultance, of triumph. But they were anxious.

Only the eyes of the oldest man were not anxious. Black, and fixed, and as if sightless, they watched the sun, seeing beyond the sun. And in their black, empty concentration there was power, power intensely abstract and remote, but deep, deep to the heart of the earth, and the heart of the sun. In absolute motionlessness he watched till the red sun should send his ray through the column of ice. Then the old man would strike, and strike home, accomplish the sacrifice and achieve the power.

The mastery that man must hold, and that passes from race to race.

SMILE

HE had decided to sit up all night, as a kind of penance. The telegram had simply said: 'Ophelia's condition critical.' He felt, under the circumstances, that to go to bed in the *wagon-lit* would be frivolous. So he sat wearily in the first-class compartment as night fell over France.

He ought, of course, to be sitting by Ophelia's bedside. But Ophelia didn't want him. So he sat up in the train.

Deep inside him was a black and ponderous weight: like some tumour filled with sheer gloom, weighing down his vitals. He had always taken life seriously. Seriousness now overwhelmed him. His dark, handsome, clean-shaven face would have done for Christ on the Cross, with the thick black eyebrows tilted in the dazed agony.

The night in the train was like an inferno: nothing was real. Two elderly Englishwomen opposite him had died long ago, perhaps even before he had. Because, of course, he was dead himself.

Slow, grey dawn came in the mountains of the frontier, and he watched it with unseeing eyes. But his mind repeated:

> 'And when the dawn came, dim and sad
> And chill with early showers,
> Her quiet eyelids closed: she had
> Another morn than ours.'

And his monk's changeless, tormented face showed no trace of the contempt he felt, even self-contempt, for this bathos, as his critical mind judged it.

He was in Italy: he looked at the country with faint aversion. Not capable of much feeling any more, he had only a tinge of aversion as he saw the olives and the sea. A sort of poetic swindle.

It was night again when he reached the home of the Blue Sisters, where Ophelia had chosen to retreat. He was ushered into the Mother Superior's room, in the palace. She rose and bowed to him in silence, looking at him along her nose. Then she said in French:

'It pains me to tell you. She died this afternoon.'

He stood stupefied, not feeling much, anyhow, but gazing at nothingness from his handsome, strong-featured monk's face.

The Mother Superior softly put her white, handsome hand on his arm and gazed up into his face, leaning to him.

'Courage!' she said softly. 'Courage, no?'

He stepped back. He was always scared when a woman leaned at him like that. In her voluminous skirts, the Mother Superior was very womanly.

'Quite!' he replied in English. 'Can I see her?'

The Mother Superior rang a bell, and a young sister appeared. She was rather pale, but there was something naïve and mischevious in her hazel eyes. The elder woman murmured an introduction, the young woman demurely made a slight reverence. But Matthew held out his hand, like a man reaching for the last straw. The young nun unfolded her white hands and shyly slid one into his, passive as a sleeping bird.

And out of the fathomless Hades of his gloom he thought: 'What a nice hand!'

They went along a handsome but cold corridor, and tapped at a door. Matthew, walking in far-off Hades, still was aware of the soft, fine voluminousness of the women's black skirts, moving with soft, fluttered haste in front of him.

He was terrified when the door opened, and he saw the candles burning round the white bed, in the lofty, noble room. A sister sat beside the candles, her face dark and primitive, in the white coif, as she looked up from her breviary. Then she rose, a sturdy woman, and made a little bow, and Matthew was aware of creamy-dusky hands twisting a black rosary, against the rich, blue silk of her bosom.

The three sisters flocked silent, yet fluttered and very feminine, in their volumes of silky black skirts, to the bed-head. The Mother Superior leaned, and with utmost delicacy lifted the veil of white lawn from the dead face.

Matthew saw the dead, beautiful composure of his wife's face, and instantly, something leaped like laughter in the depths of him, he gave a little grunt, and an extraordinary smile came over his face.

The three nuns, in the candle glow that quivered warm and quick like a Christmas tree, were looking at him with heavily compassionate eyes, from under their coif-bands. They were like a mirror. Six eyes suddenly started with a little fear, then changed, puzzled, into wonder. And over the three nuns' faces, helplessly facing him in the candle-glow, a strange, involuntary smile began to come. In the three faces, the same smile growing so differently, like three subtle flowers opening. In the pale young nun, it was almost pain, with a touch of mischievous ecstasy. But the dark Ligurian face of the watching sister, a mature, level-browed woman, curled with a pagan smile, slow, infinitely subtle in its archaic humour. It was the Etruscan smile, subtle and unabashed, and unanswerable.

The Mother Superior, who had a large-featured face something like Matthew's own, tried hard not to smile. But he kept his humorous, malevolent chin uplifted at her, and she lowered her face as the smile grew, grew and grew over her face.

The young, pale sister suddenly covered her face with her sleeve, her body shaking. The Mother Superior put her arm over the girl's shoulder, murmuring with Italian emotion: 'Poor little thing! Weep, then, poor little thing!' But the chuckle was still there, under the emotion. The sturdy dark sister stood unchanging, clutching the black beads, but the noiseless smile immovable.

Matthew suddenly turned to the bed, to see if his dead wife had observed him. It was a movement of fear.

Ophelia lay so pretty and so touching, with her peaked, dead little nose sticking up, and her face of an obstinate child fixed in the final obstinacy. The smile went away from Matthew and the look of super-martyrdom took its place. He did not weep: he just gazed without meaning. Only, on his face deepened the look: I knew this martyrdom was in store for me!

She was so pretty, so childlike, so clever, so obstinate, so worn – and so dead! He felt so blank about it all.

They had been married ten years. He himself had not been perfect – no, no, not by any means! But Ophelia had always wanted her own will. She had loved him, and grown obstinate, and left him, and grown wistful, or contemptuous, or angry, a dozen times, and a dozen times come back to him.

They had no children. And he, sentimentally, had always wanted children. He felt very largely sad.

Now she would never come back to him. This was the thirteenth time, and she was gone for ever.

But was she? Even as he thought it, he felt her nudging him somewhere in the ribs, to make him smile. He writhed a little, and an angry frown came on his brow. He was not *going* to smile! He set his square, naked jaw, and bared his big teeth, as he looked down at the infinitely provoking dead woman. 'At it again' – he wanted to say to her, like the man in Dickens.

He himself had not been perfect. He was going to dwell on his own imperfections.

He turned suddenly to the three women, who had faded backwards beyond the candles, and now hovered, in the white frames of their coifs, between him and nowhere. His eyes glared, and he bared his teeth.

'*Mea culpa! Mea culpa!*' he snarled.

'*Macchè!*' exclaimed the daunted Mother Superior, and her two hands flew apart, then together again, in the density of the sleeves, like birds nesting in couples.

Matthew ducked his head and peered round, prepared to bolt. The Mother Superior, in the background, softly intoned a Pater Noster, and her beads dangled. The pale young sister faded farther back. But the black eyes of the sturdy, black-avised sister twinkled like eternally humorous stars upon him, and he felt the smile digging him in the ribs again.

'Look here!' he said to the women, in expostulation, 'I'm awfully upset. I'd better go.'

They hovered in fascinating bewilderment. He ducked for the door. But even as he went, the smile began to come on his face, caught by the tail of the sturdy sister's black eye, with its everlasting twink. And, he was secretly thinking, he wished he could hold both her creamy-dusky hands, that were folded like mating birds, voluptuously.

But he insisted on dwelling upon his own imperfections. *Mea culpa!* he howled at himself. And even as he howled it, he felt something nudge him in the ribs, saying to him: *Smile!*

The three women left behind in the lofty room looked at one another, and their hands flew up for a moment, like six birds flying suddenly out of the foliage, then settling again.

'Poor thing!' said the Mother Superior, compassionately.

'Yes! Yes! Poor thing!' cried the young sister, with naïve, shrill impulsiveness.

'Già!' said the dark-avised sister.

The Mother Superior noiselessly moved to the bed, and leaned over the dead face.

'She seems to know, poor soul!' she murmured. 'Don't you think so?'

The three coifed heads leaned together. And for the first time they

545

saw the faint ironical curl at the corners of Ophelia's mouth. They looked in fluttering wonder.

'She has seen him!' whispered the thrilling young sister.

The Mother Superior delicately laid the fine-worked veil over the cold face. Then they murmured a prayer for the anima, fingering their beads. Then the Mother Superior set two of the candles straight upon their spikes, clenching the thick candle with firm, soft grip, and pressing it down.

The dark-faced, sturdy sister sat down again with her little holy book. The other two rustled softly to the door, and out into the great white corridor. There softly, noiselessly sailing in all their dark drapery, like dark swans down a river, they suddenly hesitated. Together they had seen a forlorn man's figure, in a melancholy overcoat, loitering in the cold distance at the corridor's end. The Mother Superior suddenly pressed her pace into an appearance of speed.

Matthew saw them bearing down on him, these voluminous figures with framed faces and lost hands. The young sister trailed a little behind.

'*Pardon, ma Mère!*' he said, as if in the street. 'I left my hat somewhere. . . .'

He made a desperate, moving sweep with his arm, and never was man more utterly smileless.

THE BORDER LINE

KATHERINE FARQUHAR was a handsome woman of forty, no longer slim, but attractive in her soft, full feminine way. The French porters ran round her, getting a voluptuous pleasure from merely carrying her bags. And she gave them ridiculously high tips, because, in the first place, she had never really known the value of money, and secondly, she had a morbid fear of underpaying anyone, but particularly a man who was eager to serve her.

It was really a joke to her, how eagerly these Frenchmen – all sorts of Frenchmen – ran round her, and *Madame*'d her. Their voluptuous obsequiousness. Because, after all, she was Boche. Fifteen years of marriage to an Englishman – or rather to two Englishmen – had not altered her racially. Daughter of a German baron she was, and remained in her own mind and body, although England had become her life-home. And surely she looked German, with her fresh complexion and her strong, full figure. But, like most people in the world, she was a mixture, with Russian blood and French blood also in her veins. And she had lived in one country and another, till she was somewhat indifferent to her surroundings. So that perhaps the Parisian men might be excused for running round her so eagerly, and getting a voluptuous pleasure from calling a taxi for her, or giving up a place in the omnibus to her, or carrying her bags, or holding the menu card before her. Nevertheless, it amused her. And she had to confess she liked them, these Parisians. They had their own kind of manliness, even if it wasn't an English sort; and if a woman looked pleasant and soft-fleshed, and a wee bit helpless, they were ardent and generous. Katherine understood so well that Frenchmen were rude to the dry, hard-seeming, competent Englishwoman or American. She sympathised with the Frenchman's point of view; too much obvious capacity to help herself is a disagreeable trait in a woman.

At the Gare de l'Est, of course, everybody was expected to be Boche, and it was almost a convention, with the porters, to assume a certain small-boyish superciliousness. Nevertheless, there was the same voluptuous scramble to escort Katherine Farquhar to her seat in the first-class carriage. *Madame* was travelling alone.

547

She was going to Germany via Strasburg, meeting her sister in Baden-Baden. Philip, her husband, was in Germany, collecting some sort of evidence for his newspaper. Katherine felt a little weary of newspapers, and of the sort of 'evidence' that is extracted out of nowhere to feed them. However, Philip was quite clever, he was a little somebody in the world.

Her world, she had realised, consisted almost entirely of little somebodies. She was outside the sphere of the nobodies, always had been. And the Somebodies with a capital 'S' were all safely dead. She knew enough of the world to-day to know that it is not going to put up with any great Somebody; but many little nobodies and a sufficient number of little somebodies. Which, after all, is as it should be, she felt.

Sometimes she had vague misgivings.

Paris, for example, with its Louvre and its Luxembourg and its cathedral, seemed intended for Somebody. In a ghostly way it called for some supreme Somebody. But all its little men, nobodies and somebodies, were as sparrows twittering for crumbs, and dropping their little droppings on the palace cornices.

To Katherine, Paris brought back again her first husband, Alan Anstruther, that red-haired fighting Celt, father of her two grown-up children. Alan had had a weird innate conviction that he was beyond ordinary judgment. Katherine could never quite see where it came in. Son of a Scottish baronet, and captain in a Highland regiment did not seem to her stupendous. As for Alan himself, he was handsome in uniform, with his kilt swinging and his blue eye glaring. Even stark naked and without any trimmings, he had a bony, dauntless, overbearing manliness of his own. The one thing Katherine could *not quite* appreciate was his silent, indomitable assumption that he was actually first-born, a born lord. He was a clever man, too, ready to assume that General This or Colonel That might really be his superior. Until he actually came into contact with General This or Colonel That. Whereupon his over-weening blue eye arched in his bony face, and a faint tinge of contempt infused itself into his homage.

Lordly or not, he wasn't much of a success in the worldly sense. Katherine had loved him, and he had loved her: that was indisputable. But when it came to innate conviction of lordliness, it was a question which of them was worse. For she, in her amiable, queen-bee self, thought that ultimately hers was the right to the last homage.

Alan had been too unyielding and haughty to say much. But sometimes he would stand and look at her in silent rage, wonder, and indignation. The wondering indignation had been *almost* too much for her. What did the man think he was?

He was one of the hard, clever Scotsmen, with a philosophic tendency, but without sentimentality. His contempt of Nietzsche, whom she adored, was intolerable. Alan just asserted himself like a pillar of rock, and expected the tides of the modern world to recede around him. They didn't.

So he concerned himself with astronomy, gazing through a telescope and watching the worlds beyond worlds. Which seemed to give him relief.

After ten years they had ceased to live together, passionate as they both were. They were too proud and unforgiving to yield to one another, and much too haughty to yield to any outsider.

Alan had a friend, Philip, also a Scotsman, and a university friend. Philip, trained for the Bar, had gone into journalism, and had made himself a name. He was a little black Highlander of the insidious sort, clever and *knowing*. This look of knowing in his dark eyes, and the feeling of secrecy that went with his dark little body, made him interesting to women. Another thing he could do was to give off a great sense of warmth and offering, like a dog when it loves you. He seemed to be able to do this at will. And Katherine, after feeling cool about him and rather despising him for years, at last fell under the spell of the dark, insidious fellow.

'You!' she said to Alan, whose over-weening masterfulness drove her wild. 'You don't even know that a woman exists. And that's where Philip Farquhar is more than you are. He *does* know something of what a woman *is*.'

'Bah! the little —' said Alan, using an obscene word of contempt.

Nevertheless, the friendship endured, kept up by Philip, who had an almost uncanny love for Alan. Alan was mostly indifferent. But he was used to Philip, and habit meant a great deal to him.

'Alan really is an amazing man!' Philip would say to Katherine. 'He is the only real man, what I call a real man, that I have ever met.'

'But why is he the only real man?' she asked. 'Don't you call yourself a real man?'

'Oh, *I* – I'm different! My strength lies in giving in – and then recovering myself. I do let myself be swept away. But, so far, I've always managed to get myself back again. Alan —' and Philip even had a half-reverential, half-envious way of uttering the word – 'Alan *never* lets himself be swept away. And he's the only man I know who doesn't.'

'Yah!' she said. 'He is fooled by plenty of things. You can fool him through his vanity.'

'No,' said Philip. 'Never altogether. You *can't* deceive him right through. When a thing really touches Alan, it is tested once and for all. You know if it's false or not. He's the only man I ever met who *can't help* being real.'

'Ha! You over-rate his reality,' said Katherine, rather scornfully.

And later, when Alan shrugged his shoulders with that mere indifferent tolerance, at the mention of Philip, she got angry.

'You are a poor friend,' she said.

'Friend!' he answered. 'I never was Farquhar's friend! If he asserts that he's mine, that's his side of the question. I never positively cared for the man. He's too much over the wrong side of the border for me.'

'Then,' she answered, 'you've no business to let him *consider* he is your friend. You've no right to let him think so much of you. You should tell him you don't like him.'

'I've told him a dozen times. He seems to enjoy it. It seems part of his game.'

And he went away to his astronomy.

Came the war, and the departure of Alan's regiment for France.

'There!' he said. 'Now you have to pay the penalty of having married a soldier. You find him fighting your own people. So it is.'

She was too much struck by this blow even to weep.

'Good-bye!' he said, kissing her gently, lingeringly. After all, he had been a husband to her.

And as he looked back at her, with the gentle, protective husband knowledge in his blue eyes, and at the same time that other quiet realisation of destiny, her consciousness fluttered into incoherence. She only wanted to alter everything, to alter the past, to alter all the flow of history – the terrible flow of history. Secretly somewhere inside herself she felt that with her queen-bee love, and queen-bee will, she *could* divert the whole flow of history – nay, even reverse it.

But in the remote, realising look that lay at the back of his eyes, behind all his changeless husband-care, she saw that it could never be so. That the whole of her womanly, motherly concentration could never put back the great flow of human destiny. That, as he said, only the cold strength of a man, accepting the destiny of destruction, could see the human flow through the chaos and beyond to a new outlet. But the chaos first, and the long rage of destruction.

550

For an instant her will broke. Almost her soul seemed broken. And then he was gone. And as soon as he was gone she recovered the core of her assurance.

Philip was a great consolation to her. He asserted that the war was monstrous, that it should never have been, and that men should refuse to consider it as anything but a colossal, disgraceful accident.

She, in her German soul, knew that it was no accident. It was inevitable, and even necessary. But Philip's attitude soothed her enormously, restored her to herself.

Alan never came back. In the spring of 1915 he was missing. She had never mourned for him. She had never really considered him dead. In a certain sense she had triumphed. The queen-bee had recovered her sway, as queen of the earth; the woman, the mother, the female with the ear of corn in her hand, as against the man with the sword.

Philip had gone through the war as a journalist, always throwing his weight on the side of humanity, and human truth and peace. He had been an inexpressible consolation. And in 1921 she had married him.

The thread of fate might be spun, it might even be measured out, but the hand of Lachesis had been stayed from cutting it through.

At first it was wonderfully pleasant and restful and voluptuous, especially for a woman of thirty-eight, to be married to Philip. Katherine felt he caressed her senses, and soothed her, and gave her what she wanted.

Then, gradually, a curious sense of degradation started in her spirit. She felt unsure, uncertain. It was almost like having a disease. Life became dull and unreal to her, as it had never been before. She did not even struggle and suffer. In the numbness of her flesh she could feel no reactions. Everything was turning into mud.

Then again, she would recover, and *enjoy* herself wonderfully. And after a while, the suffocating sense of nullity and degradation once more. Why, why, why did she feel degraded, in her secret soul? *Never*, of course, outwardly.

The memory of Alan came back into her. She still thought of him and his relentlessness with an arrested heart, but without the angry hostility she used to feel. A little awe of him, of his memory, stole back into her spirit. She resisted it. She was not used to feeling awe.

She realised, however, the difference between being married to a soldier, a ceaseless born fighter, a sword not to be sheathed, and this other man, this cunning civilian, this subtle equivocator, this adjuster of the scales of truth.

551

Philip was cleverer than she was. He set her up, the queen-bee, the mother, the woman, the female judgment, and he served her with subtle, cunning homage. He put the scales, the balance in her hand. But also, cunningly, he blindfolded her, and manipulated the scales when she was sightless.

Dimly she had realised all this. But only dimly, confusedly, because she was blindfolded. Philip had the subtle, fawning power that could keep her always blindfolded.

Sometimes she gasped and gasped from her oppressed lungs. And sometimes the bony, hard, masterful, but honest face of Alan would come back, and suddenly it would seem to her that she was all right again, that the strange, voluptuous suffocation, which left her soul in mud, was gone, and she could breathe the air of the open heavens once more. Even fighting air.

It came to her on the boat crossing the Channel. Suddenly she seemed to feel Alan at her side again, as if Philip had never existed. As if Philip had never meant anything more to her than the shop assistant measuring off her orders. And escaping, as it were, by herself across the cold, wintry Channel, she suddenly deluded herself into feeling as if Philip had never existed, only Alan had ever been her husband. He was her husband still. And she was going to meet him.

This gave her her blitheness in Paris, and made the Frenchmen so nice to her. For the Latins love to feel a woman is really enveloped in the spell of some man. Beyond all race is the problem of man and woman.

Katherine now sat dimly, vaguely excited and almost happy in the railway carriage on the East railway. It was like the old days when she was going home to Germany. Or even more like the old days when she was coming back to Alan. Because, in the past, when he was her husband, feel as she might towards him, she could never get over the sensation that the wheels of the railway carriage had wings, when they were taking her back to him. Even when she knew that he was going to be awful to her, hard and relentless and destructive, still the motion went on wings.

Whereas towards Philip she moved with a strange, disintegrating reluctance. She decided not to think of him.

As she looked unseeing out of the carriage window, suddenly, with a jolt, the wintry landscape realised itself in her consciousness. The flat, grey, wintry landscape, ploughed fields of greyish earth that looked as if they were compounded of the clay of dead men. Pallid, stark, thin trees

552

stood like wire beside straight, abstract roads. A ruined farm between a few more trees. And a dismal village filed past, with smashed houses like rotten teeth between the straight rows of the village street.

With sudden horror she realised that she must be in the Marne country, the ghastly Marne country, century after century digging the corpses of frustrated men into its soil. The border country, where the Latin races and the Germanic neutralise one another into horrid ash.

Perhaps even the corpse of her own man among that grey clay.

It was too much for her. She sat ashy herself with horror, wanting to escape.

'If I had only known,' she said. 'If only I had known, I would have gone by Basle.'

The train drew up at Soissons; name ghastly to her. She simply tried to make herself unreceptive to everything. And mercifully luncheon was served. She went down to the restaurant-car, and sat opposite to a little French officer in horizon-blue uniform, who suggested anything but war. He looked so naïve, rather child-like and nice, with the certain innocence that so many French people preserve under their so-called wickedness, that she felt really relieved. He bowed to her with an odd, shy little bow when she returned him his half-bottle of red wine, which had slowly jigged its way the length of the table, owing to the motion of the train. How nice he was! And how he would give himself to a woman, if she would only find real pleasure in the male that he was.

Nevertheless, she herself felt very remote from this business of male and female, and giving and taking.

After luncheon, in the heat of the train and the flush of her half-bottle of white wine, she went to sleep again, her feet grilling uncomfortably on the iron plate of the carriage floor. And as she slept, life, as she had known it, seemed all to turn artificial to her, the sunshine of the world an artificial light, with smoke above, like the light of torches, and things artificially growing, in a night that was lit up artificially with such intensity that it gave the illusion of day. It had been an illusion, her life-day, as a ballroom evening is an illusion. Her love and her emotions, her very panic of love, had been an illusion. She realised how love had become panic-stricken inside her during the war.

And now even this panic of love was an illusion. She had run to Philip to be saved. And now, both her panic-love and Philip's salvation were an illusion.

What remained then? Even panic-stricken love, the intensest thing, perhaps, she had ever felt, was only an illusion. What was left? The grey shadows of death?

When she looked out again it was growing dark, and they were at Nancy. She used to know this country as a girl. At half-past seven she was in Strasburg, where she must stay the night as there was no train over the Rhine till morning.

The porter, a blond, hefty fellow, addressed her at once in Alsatian German. He insisted on escorting her safely to her hotel – a German hotel – keeping guard over her like an appointed sentinel, very faithful and competent, so different from Frenchmen.

It was a cold, wintry night, but she wanted to go out after dinner to see the minster. She remembered it all so well, in that other life.

The wind blew icily in the street. The town seemed empty, as if its spirit had left it. The few squat, hefty foot-passengers were all talking the harsh Alsatian German. Shop-signs were in French, often with a little concession to German underneath. And the shops were full of goods, glutted with goods from the once-German factories of Mulhausen and other cities.

She crossed the night-dark river, where the wash-houses of the washerwomen were anchored along the stream, a few odd women still kneeling over the water's edge, in the dim electric light, rinsing their clothes in the grim, cold water. In the big square the icy wind was blowing, and the place seemed a desert. A city once more conquered.

After all she could not remember her way to the cathedral. She saw a French policeman in his blue cape and peaked cap, looking a lonely, vulnerable, silky specimen in this harsh Alsatian city. Crossing over to him, she asked him in French where was the cathedral.

He pointed out to her, the first turning on the left. He did not seem hostile; nobody seemed really hostile. Only the great frozen weariness of winter in a conquered city, on a weary everlasting border-line.

And the Frenchmen seemed far more weary, and also more sensitive, than the crude Alsatians.

She remembered the little street, the old, overhanging houses with black timbers and high gables. And like a great ghost, a reddish flush in its darkness, the uncanny cathedral breasting the oncomer, standing gigantic, looking down in darkness out of darkness, on the pigmy humanness of the city. It was built of reddish stone, that had a flush in the night, like dark flesh. And vast, an incomprehensibly tall, strange thing, it looked down out of the night. The great rose window, poised high, seemed like a breast of the vast Thing, and prisms and needles of stone shot up, as if it were plumage, dimly, half visible in heaven.

There it was in the upper darkness of the ponderous winter night, like a menace. She remembered her spirit used in the past to soar aloft with it. But now, looming with a faint rust of blood out of the upper black heavens, the Thing stood suspended, looking down with vast, demonish menace, calm and implacable.

Mystery and dim, ancient fear came over the woman's soul. The cathedral looked so strange and demonish-heathen. And an ancient, indomitable blood seemed to stir in it. It stood there like some vast silent beast with teeth of stone, waiting, and wondering when to stoop against this pallid humanity.

And dimly she realised that behind all the ashy pallor and sulphur of our civilisation, lurks the great blood-creature waiting, implacable and eternal, ready at last to crush our white brittleness and let the shadowy blood move erect once more, in a new implacable pride and strength. Even out of the lower heavens looms the great blood-dusky Thing, blotting out the Cross it was supposed to exalt.

The scroll of the night sky seemed to roll back, showing a huge, blood-dusky presence looming enormous, stooping, looking down, awaiting its moment.

As she turned to go away, to move away from the closed wings of the minster, she noticed a man standing on the pavement, in the direction of the post office which functions obscurely in the Cathedral Square. Immediately, she knew that that man, standing dark and motionless, was Alan. He was alone, motionless, remote.

He did not move towards her. She hesitated, then went in his direction, as if going to the post office. He stood perfectly motionless, and her heart died as she drew near. Then, as she passed, he turned suddenly, looking down on her.

It was he, though she could hardly see his face, it was so dark, with a dusky glow in the shadow.

'Alan!' she said.

He did not speak, but laid his hand detainingly on her arm, as he used in the early days, with strange, silent authority. And turning her with a faint pressure on her arm, he went along with her, leisurely, through the main street of the city, under the arcade where the shops were still lighted up.

She glanced at his face; it seemed much more dusky, and duskily ruddy, than she had known him. He was a stranger: and yet it was he, no other. He said nothing at all. But that was also in keeping. His mouth was closed, his watchful eyes seemed changeless, and there was a shadow of silence around him, impenetrable, but not cold. Rather aloof and gentle, like the silence that surrounds a wild animal.

She knew that she was walking with his spirit. But that even did not trouble her. It seemed natural. And there came over her again the feeling she had forgotten, the restful, thoughtless pleasure of a woman who moves in the aura of the man to whom she belongs. As a young woman she had had this unremarkable, yet very precious feeling, when she was with her husband. It had been a full contentment; and perhaps the fullness of it had made her unconscious of it. Later, it seemed to her she had almost wilfully destroyed it, this soft flow of contentment which she, a woman, had from him as a man.

Now, afterwards, she realised it. And as she walked at his side through the conquered city, she realised that it was the one enduring thing a woman can have, the intangible soft flood of contentment that carries her along at the side of the man she is married to. It is her perfection and her highest attainment.

Now, in the afterwards, she knew it. Now the strife was gone. And dimly she wondered why, why, why she had ever fought against it. No matter what the man does or is, as a person, if a woman can move at his side in this dim, full flood of contentment, she has the highest of him, and her scratching efforts at getting more than this, are her ignominious efforts at self-nullity.

Now she knew it, and she submitted. Now that she was walking with a man who came from the halls of death, to her, for her relief. The strong, silent kindliness of him towards her, even now, was able to wipe out the ashy, nervous horror of the world from her body. She went at his side, still and released, like one newly unbound, walking in the dimness of her own contentment.

At the bridge-head he came to a standstill, and drew his hand from her arm. She knew he was going to leave her. But he looked at her from under his peaked cap, darkly but kindly, and he waved his hand with a slight, kindly gesture of farewell, and of promise, as if in farewell he promised never to leave her, never to let the kindliness go out in his heart, to let it stay here always.

She hurried over the bridge with tears running down her cheeks, and on to her hotel. Hastily she climbed to her room. And as she undressed, she avoided the sight of her own face in the mirror. She must not rupture the spell of his presence.

Now, in the afterwards she realised *how* careful she must be, not to break the mystery that enveloped her. Now that she knew he had come back to her from the dead, she was aware how precious and how fragile the coming was. He had come back with his heart dark and kind, wanting her even in the afterwards. And not in any sense must she go against him. The warm, powerful, silent ghost had come back to her. It was he. She must not even try to think about him definitely, not to realise him or to understand. Only in her own woman's soul could she silently ponder him, darkly, and know him present in her, without even staring at him or trying to find him out. Once she tried to lay hands on him, to *have* him, to *realise* him, he would be gone for ever, and gone for ever this last precious flood of her woman's peace.

'Ah, no!' she said to herself. 'If he leaves his peace with me, I must ask no questions whatsoever.'

And she repented, silently, of the way she had questioned and demanded answers, in the past. What were the answers, when she had got them? Terrible ash in the mouth.

She now knew the supreme modern terror of a world all ashy and nerve-dead. If a man could come back out of death to save her from this, she would not ask questions of him, but be humble, and beyond tears grateful.

In the morning, she went out into the icy wind, under the grey sky, to see if he would be there again. Not that she *needed* him: his presence was still about her. But he might be waiting.

The town was stony and cold. The people looked pale, chilled through, and doomed in some way. Very far from her they were. She felt a sort of pity for them, but knew she could do nothing, nothing in time or eternity. And they looked at her, and looked quickly away again, as if they were uneasy in themselves.

The cathedral reared its great reddish-grey façade in the stark light; but it did not loom as in the night. The cathedral square was hard and cold. Inside, the church was cold and repellent, in spite of the glow of stained glass. And he was nowhere to be found.

So she hastened away to her hotel and to the station, to catch the 10.30 train into Germany.

It was a lonely, dismal train, with a few forlorn souls waiting to cross the Rhine. Her Alsatian porter looked after her with the same dogged care as before. She got into the first-class carriage that was going through to Prague – she was the only passenger travelling first. A real French porter, in blouse and moustache, and swagger, tried to say something a bit jeering to her, in his few words of German. But she only looked at him, and he subsided. He didn't really want to be rude. There was a certain hopelessness even about that.

The train crept slowly, disheartened, out of town. She saw the weird humped-up creature of the cathedral in the distance, pointing its one finger above the city. Why, oh, why had the old Germanic races put it there like that!

Slowly the country disintegrated into the Rhine flats and marshes, the canals, the willow trees, the overflow streams, the wet places frozen but not flooded. Weary the place all seemed. And old Father Rhine flowing in greenish volume, implacable, separating the races now weary of race struggle, but locked in the toils as in the coils of a great snake, unable to escape. Cold, full, green, and utterly disheartening the river came along under the wintry sky, passing beneath the bridge of iron.

There was a long wait in Kehl, where the German officials and the French observed a numb, dreary kind of neutrality. Passport and customs examination was soon over. But the train waited and waited, as if unable to get away from that point of pure negation, where the two races neutralised one another, and no polarity was felt, no life – no principle dominated.

Katherine Farquhar just sat still in the suspended silence of her husband's return. She heeded neither French nor German, spoke one language or the other at need, hardly knowing. She waited while the hot train steamed and hissed, arrested at the perfect neutral point of the new border-line, just across the Rhine.

And at last a little sun came out, and the train silently drew away, nervously, from the neutrality.

In the great flat field of the Rhine plain, the shallow flood water was frozen, the furrows ran straight towards nowhere, the air seemed frozen, too, but the earth felt strong and barbaric, it seemed to vibrate, with its straight furrows, in a deep, savage undertone. There was the frozen, savage thrill in the air also, something wild and unsubdued, pre-Roman.

This part of the Rhine Valley, even on the right bank in Germany, was occupied by the French; hence the curious vacancy, the suspense, as if no men lived there, but some spirit was watching, watching over the vast, empty, straight-furrowed fields and the water-meadows. Stillness, emptiness, suspense, and a sense of something still impending.

A long wait in the station of Appenweier, on the main line of the

Right-bank railway. The station was empty. Katherine remembered its excited, thrilling bustle in pre-war days.

'Yes,' said the German guard to the stationmaster, 'what do they hurry us out of Strasburg for, if they are only going to keep us so long here?'

The heavy Badisch German! The sense of resentful impotence in the Germans! Katherine smiled to herself. She realised that here the train left the occupied territory.

At last they set off, northwards, free for the moment, in Germany. It was the land beyond the Rhine, Germany of the pine forests. The very earth seemed strong and unsubdued, bristling with a few reeds and bushes, like savage hair. There was the same silence, and waiting, and the old barbaric undertone of the white-skinned north, under the waning civilisation. The audible overtone of our civilisation seemed to be wearing thin, the old, low, pine forest hum and roar of the ancient north seemed to be sounding through. At least, in Katherine's inner ear.

And there were the ponderous hills of the Black Forest, heaped and waiting sullenly, as if guarding the inner Germany. Black round hills, black with forest, save where white snow-patches of field had been cut out. Black and white, waiting there in the near distance, in sullen guard.

She knew the country so well. But not in this present mood, the emptiness, the sullenness, the heavy, recoiled waiting.

Steinbach! Then she was nearly there! She would have to change in Oos for Baden-Baden, her destination. Probably Philip would be there to meet her, in Oos; he would have come down from Heidelberg.

Yes, there he was! And at once she thought he looked ill, yellowish. His figure hollow and defeated.

'Aren't you well?' she asked, as she stepped out of the train on to the empty station.

'I'm so frightfully cold,' he said. 'I can't get warm.'

'And the train was so hot,' she said.

At last a porter came to carry her bags across to the little connecting train.

'How are you?' he said, looking at her with a certain pinched look in his face, and fear in his eyes.

'All right! It all feels very queer,' she said.

'I don't know how it is,' he said, 'but Germany freezes my inside, and does something to my chest.'

'We needn't stay long,' she said easily.

559

He was watching the bright look in her face. And she was thinking how queer and *chétif* he looked! Extraordinary! As she looked at him she felt for the first time, with curious clarity, that it was humiliating to be married to him, even in name. She was humiliated even by the fact that her name was Katherine Farquhar. Yet she used to think it a nice name!

'Just think of me married to that little man!' she thought to herself. 'Think of my having his name!'

It didn't fit. She thought of her own name: Katherine von Todtnau; or of her married name: Katherine Anstruther. The first seemed most fitting. But the second was her second nature. The third, Katherine Farquhar, wasn't her at all.

'Have you seen Marianne?' she asked.

'Oh yes!'

He was very brief. What was the matter with him?

'You'll have to be careful with your cold,' she said politely.

'I am careful!' he cried petulantly.

Marianne, her sister, was at the station, and in two minutes they were rattling away in German, and laughing and crying and exploding with laughter again. Philip quite ignored. In these days of frozen economy, there was no taxi. A porter would wheel up the luggage on a trolley, the new arrivals walked to their little hotel, through the half-deserted town.

'But the little one is quite nice!' said Marianne deprecatingly.

'Isn't he!' cried Katherine in the same tone.

And both sisters stood still and laughed in the middle of the street. 'The little one' was Philip.

'The other was more a man,' said Marianne. 'But I'm sure this one is easier. *The little one!* Yes, he *should* be easier,' and she laughed in her mocking way.

'The stand-up-mannikin!' said Katherine, referring to those little toy men weighed at the base with lead, that always stand up again.

Philip was very unhappy in this atmosphere. His strength was in his weakness, his appeal, his clinging dependence. He quite cunningly got his own way almost every time: but always by seeming to give in. In every emergency he bowed as low as need be and let the storm pass over him. Then he rose again, the same as ever, sentimental, on the side of the angels, offering defiance to nobody. The defiant men had been killed off during the war. He had seen it and secretly smiled. When the lion is shot, the dog gets the spoil. So he had come in for Katherine,

560

Alan's lioness. A live dog is better than a dead lion. And so the little semi-angelic journalist exulted in the triumph of his weakness.

But in Germany, in weird post-war Germany, he seemed snuffed out again. The air was so cold and vacant, all feeling seemed to have gone out of the country. Emotion, even sentiment, was numbed quite dead, as in a frost-bitten limb. And if the sentiment were numbed out of him, he was truly dead.

'I'm most frightfully glad you've come, Kathy,' he said. 'I could hardly have held out another day here, without you. I feel you're the only thing on earth that remains real.'

'You don't seem very real to me,' she said.

'I'm not real! I'm *not*! – not when I'm alone. But when I'm with you I'm the most real man alive. I know it!'

This was the sort of thing that had fetched her in the past, thrilled her through and through in her womanly conceit, even made her fall in love with the little creature who could so generously admit such pertinent truths. So different from the lordly Alan, who expected a woman to bow down to him!

Now, however, some of the coldness of numbed Germany seemed to have got into her breast too. She felt a cruel derision of the whimpering little beast who claimed reality only through a woman. She did not answer him, but looked out at the snow falling between her and the dark trees. Another world! When the snow left off, how bristling and ghostly the cold fir trees looked, tall, conical creatures crowding darkly and half whitened with snow! So tall, so wolfish!

Philip shivered and looked yellower. There was shortage of fuel, shortage of food, shortage of everything. He wanted Katherine to go to Paris with him. But she would stay at least two weeks near her people. The shortage she would put up with. She saw at evening the string of decent townsfolk waiting in the dark – the town was not half lighted – to fill their hot-water bottles at the hot spring outside the Kurhaus, silent, spectral, unable to afford fire to heat their own water. And she felt quite cold about Philip's shivering. Let him shiver.

The snow was crisp and dry, she walked out in the forest, up the steep slopes. The world was curiously vacant, gone wild again. She realised how very quickly the world would go wild if catastrophes overtook mankind. Philip, yellow and hollow, would trudge stumbling and reeling beside her: ludicrous. He was a man who never would walk firm on his legs. Now he just flopped. She could feel Alan among the trees, the thrill and vibration of him. And sometimes she would glance with beating heart at a great round fir-trunk that stood so alive and potent, so physical, bristling all its vast drooping greenness above the snow. She could feel him, Alan, in the tree's potent presence. She wanted to go and press herself against the trunk. But Philip would sit down on the snow, saying:

'Look here, Kathy, I can't go any farther. I've simply got no strength left!'

She stood on the path, proud, contemptuous, but silent, looking away towards where the dull, reddish rocks cropped out. And there, among the rocks, she was sure, Alan was waiting for her. She felt fierce and overbearing. Yet she took the stumbling Philip home.

He was really ill. She put him to bed, and he stayed in bed. The doctor came. But Philip was in a state of panic, afraid of everything. Katherine would walk out by herself, into the forest. She was expecting Alan, and was tingling to meet him. Then Philip would lie in bed half-conscious, and when she came back he would say, his big eyes glowing:

'You must have been *very far*!' And on the last two words he would show his large front teeth in a kind of snarl.

'Not very far,' she said.

One day Alan came to her from out of the dull reddish rocks in the forest. He was wearing a kilt that suited him so: but a khaki tunic. And he had no cap on. He came walking towards her, his knees throwing the kilt in the way she knew so well. He came triumphantly, rather splendid, and she waited trembling. He was always utterly silent. But he led her away with his arm round her, and she yielded in a complete yielding she had never known before. And among the rocks he made love to her, and took her in the silent passion of a husband, took a complete possession of her.

Afterwards she walked home in a muse, to find Philip seriously ill. She could see, he really might die. And she didn't care a bit. But she tended him, and stayed with him, and he seemed to be better.

The next day, however, she wanted to go out in the afternoon, she must! She could feel her husband waiting, and the call was imperative. She must go. But Philip became almost hysterical when she wanted to leave him.

'I assure you I shall die while you are out! I assure you I shall die if you leave me now!' He rolled his eyes wildly, and looked so queer, she felt it was true. So she stayed, sullen and full of resentment, her consciousness away among the rocks.

The afternoon grew colder and colder. Philip shivered in bed, under the greast bolster.

'But it's a murderous cold! It's murdering me!' he said.

She did not mind it. She sat abstracted, remote from him, her spirit going out into the frozen evening. A very powerful flow seemed to envelop her in another reality. It was Alan calling to her, holding her. And the hold seemed to grow stronger every hour.

She slept in the same room as Philip. But she had decided not to go to bed. He was really very weak. She would sit up with him. Towards midnight he roused, and said faintly:

'Katherine, I can't bear it!' – and his eyes rolled up showing only the whites.

'What? What can't you bear?' she said, bending over him.

'I can't bear it! I can't bear it! Hold me in your arms. Hold me! Hold me!' he whispered in pure terror of death.

Curiously reluctant, she began to push her hand under his shoulders, to raise him. As she did so, the door opened, and Alan came in, bareheaded, and a frown on his face. Philip lifted feeble hands, and put them round Katherine's neck, moaning faintly. Silent, bareheaded, Alan came over to the bed and loosened the sick man's hands from his wife's neck, and put them down on the sick man's own breast.

Philip unfurled his lips and showed his big teeth in a ghastly grin of death. Katherine felt his body convulse in strange throes under the hand, then go inert. He was dead. And on his face was a sickly grin of a thief caught in the very act.

But Alan drew her away, drew her to the other bed, in the silent passion of a husband come back from a very long journey.

JIMMY AND THE DESPERATE WOMAN

'HE is very fine and strong somewhere, but he does need a level-headed woman to look after him.'

That was the *friendly* feminine verdict upon him. It flattered him, it pleased him, it galled him.

Having divorced a very charming and clever wife, who had held this opinion for ten years, and at last had got tired of the level-headed protective game, his gall was uppermost.

'I want to throw Jimmy out on the world, but I know the poor little man will go and fall on some woman's bosom. That's the worst of him. If he could only stand alone for ten minutes. But he can't. At the same time, there *is* something fine about him, something rare.'

This had been Clarissa's summing-up as she floated away in the arms of the rich young American. The rich young American got rather angry when Jimmy's name was mentioned. Clarissa was now *his* wife. But she did sometimes talk as if she were still married to Jimmy.

Not in Jimmy's estimation, however. That worm had turned. Gall was uppermost. Gall and wormwood. He knew exactly what Clarissa thought – and said – about him. And the 'something fine, something rare, something strong' which he was supposed to have 'about him' was utterly outbalanced, in his feelings at least, by the 'poor little man' nestled upon 'some woman's bosom', which he was supposed to *be*.

'I am not,' he said to himself, 'a poor little man nestled upon some woman's bosom. If I could only find the right sort of woman, she should nestle on mine.'

Jimmy was now thirty-five, and this point, to nestle or to be nestled, was the emotional crux and turning-point.

He imagined to himself some really womanly woman, to whom he should be *only* 'fine and strong', and not for one moment 'the poor little man'. Why not some simple uneducated girl, some Tess of the D'Urbervilles, some wistful Gretchen, some humble Ruth gleaning an aftermath? Why not? Surely the world was full of such!

The trouble was he never met them. He only met sophisticated women. He really never had a chance of meeting 'real' people. So few of us ever do. Only the people we *don't* meet are the 'real' people, the simple, genuine, direct, spontaneous, unspoilt souls. All the simple, genuine, unspoilt people we *don't* meet! What a tragedy it is!

Because, of course, they must be there! Somewhere! Only we never come across them.

Jimmy was terribly handicapped by his position. It brought him into contact with so many people. Only never the right sort. Never the 'real' people: the simple, genuine, unspoilt, etc., etc.

He was editor of a high-class, rather high-brow, rather successful magazine, and his rather personal, very candid editorials brought him shoals, swarms, hosts of admiring acquaintances. Realise that he was handsome, and could be extraordinarily 'nice', when he liked, and was really very clever, in his own critical way, and you see how many chances he had of being adored and protected.

In the first place his good looks: the fine, clean lines of his face, like the face of the laughing faun in one of the faun's unlaughing, moody moments. The long, clean, lines of the cheeks, the strong chin and the slightly arched, full nose, the beautiful dark-grey eyes with long lashes, and the thick black brows. In his mocking moments, when he seemed most himself, it was a pure Pan face, with thick black eyebrows cocked up, and grey eyes with a sardonic goaty gleam, and nose and mouth curling with satire. A good-looking, smooth-skinned satyr. That was Jimmy at his best. In the opinion of his men friends.

In his own opinion, he was a sort of Martyred Saint Sebastian, at whom the wicked world shot arrow after arrow – Mater Dolorosa nothing to him – and he counted the drops of blood as they fell: when he could keep count. Sometimes – as for instance when Clarissa said she was really departing with the rich young American, and should she divorce Jimmy, or was Jimmy going to divorce her? – then the arrows assailed him like a flight of starlings, flying straight at him, jabbing at him, and the drops of martyred blood simply spattered down, he couldn't keep count.

So, naturally, he divorced Clarissa.

In the opinion of his men friends, he was, or should be, a consistently grinning faun, satyr, or Pan-person. In his own opinion, he was a Martyred Saint Sebastian with the mind of a Plato. In the opinion of his woman friends, he was a fascinating little man with a profound understanding of life and the capacity really to understand a woman and to make a woman feel a queen; which of course was to make a woman feel her *real* self....

He might, naturally, have made rich and resounding marriages, especially after the divorce. He didn't. The reason was, secretly, his resolve never to make any woman feel a queen any more. It was the turn of the women to make him feel a king.

Some unspoilt, unsophisticated, wild-blooded woman, to whom he would be a sort of Solomon of wisdom, beauty, and wealth. She would need to be in reduced circumstances to appreciate his wealth, which amounted to the noble sum of three thousand pounds and a little week-ending cottage in Hampshire. And to be unsophisticated she would have to be a woman of the people. Absolutely.

At the same time, not just the 'obscure vulgar simplican'.

He received many letters, many, many, many, enclosing poems, stories, articles, or more personal unbosomings. He read them all: like a solemn rook pecking and scratching among the litter.

And one – not one letter, but one correspondent – might be *the* one – Mrs. Emilia Pinnegar, who wrote from a mining village in Yorkshire. She was, of course, unhappily married.

Now Jimmy had always had a mysterious feeling about these dark and rather dreadful mining villages in the north. He himself had scarcely set foot north of Oxford. He felt that these miners up there must be the real stuff. And Pinnegar was a name, surely! And Emilia!

She wrote a poem, with a brief little note, that, if the editor of the *Commentator* thought the verses of no value, would he simply destroy them. Jimmy, as editor of the *Commentator*, thought the verses quite good and admired the brevity of the note. But he wasn't sure about printing the poem. He wrote back: Had Mrs. Pinnegar nothing else to submit?

Then followed a correspondence. And at length, upon request, this from Mrs. Pinnegar:

'You ask me about myself, but what shall I say? I am a woman of thirty-one, with one child, a girl of eight, and I am married to a man who lives in the same house with me, but goes to another woman. I try to write poetry, if it is poetry, because I have no other way of expressing myself at all, and even if it doesn't matter to anybody besides myself, I feel I must and will express myself, if only to save myself from developing cancer or some disease that women have. I was a schoolteacher before I was married, and I got my certificates at Rotherham College. If I could, I would teach again, and live alone. But married women teachers can't get jobs any more, they aren't allowed —'

566

THE COAL-MINER
By his Wife

The donkey-engine's beating noise
And the rattle, rattle of the sorting screens
Come down on me like the beat of his heart,
And mean the same as his breathing means.

The burning big pit-hill with fumes
Fills the air like the presence of that fair-haired man.
And the burning fire burning deeper and deeper
Is his will insisting since time began.

As he breathes the chair goes up and down
In the pit-shaft; he lusts as the wheel-fans spin
The sucking air: he lives in the coal
Underground: and his soul is a strange engine.

That is the manner of man he is.
I married him and I should know.
The mother earth from bowels of coal
Brought him forth for the overhead woe.

This was the poem that the editor of the *Commentator* hesitated about. He reflected, also, that Mrs. Pinnegar didn't sound like one of the nestling unsophisticated rustic type. It was something else that still attracted him: something desperate in a woman, something tragic.

THE NEXT EVENT

If at evening, when the twilight comes,
    You ask me what the day has been,
I shall not know. The distant drums
    Of some newcomer intervene

Between me and the day that's been
    Some strange man leading long columns
Of unseen soldiers through the green
    Sad twilight of these smoky slums.

And as the darkness slowly numbs
   My senses, everything I've seen
Or heard the daylight through, becomes
   Rubbish behind an opaque screen.

Instead, the sound of muffled drums
   Inside myself: I have to lean
And listen as my strength succumbs,
   To hear what these oncomings mean.

Perhaps the Death-God striking his thumbs
   On the drums in a deadly rat-ta-ta-plan.
Or a strange man marching slow as he strums
   The tune of a new weird hope in Man.

What does it matter! The day that began
   In coal-dust is ending the same, in crumbs
Of darkness like coal. I live if I can;
   If I can't then I welcome whatever comes.

This poem sounded so splendidly desperate, the editor of the *Commentator* decided to print it, and, moreover, to see the authoress. He wrote: Would she care to see him, if he happened to be in her neighbourhood? He was going to lecture in Sheffield. She replied: Certainly.

He gave his afternoon lecture, on *Men in Books and Men in Life*. Naturally, men in books came first. Then he caught a train to reach the mining village where the Pinnegars lived.

It was February, with gruesome patches of snow. It was dark when he arrived at Mill Valley, a sort of thick, turgid darkness full of menace, where men speaking in a weird accent went past like ghosts, dragging their heavy feet and emitting the weird scent of the coal-mine underworld. Weird and a bit gruesome it was.

He knew he had to walk uphill to the little market-place. As he went, he looked back and saw the black valleys with bunches of light, like camps of demons it seemed to him. And the demonish smell of sulphur and coal in the air, in the heavy, pregnant, clammy darkness.

They directed him to New London Lane, and down he went down another hill. His skin crept a little. The place felt uncanny and hostile, hard as if iron and minerals breathed into the black air. Thank goodness he couldn't see much, or be seen. When he had to ask his way the people treated him in a 'heave-half-a-brick-at-him' fashion.

After much weary walking and asking, he entered a lane between trees, in the cold slushy mud of the unfrozen February. The mines, apparently, were on the outskirts of the town, in some mud-sunk country. He could see the red, sore fires of the burning pit-hill through the trees, and he smelt the sulphur. He felt like some modern Ulysses wandering in the realms of Hecate. How much more dismal and horrible, a modern Odyssey among mines and factories, than any Sirens, Scyllas, or Charybdises.

So he mused to himself as he waded through icy black mud, in a black lane, under black trees that moaned an accompaniment to the sound of the coal-mine's occasional hissing and chuffing, under a black sky that quenched even the electric sparkle of the colliery. And the place seemed uninhabited like a cold black jungle.

At last he came in sight of a glimmer. Apparently, there were dwellings. Yes, a new little street, with one street-lamp, and the houses all apparently dark. He paused. Absolute desertion. Then three children.

They told him the house, and he stumbled up a dark passage. There was light on the little back-yard. He knocked, in some trepidation. A rather tall woman, looking down at him with a 'Who are you?' look, from the step above.

'Mrs. Pinnegar?'

'Oh, is it you, Mr. Frith? Come in.'

He stumbled up the step into the glaring light of the kitchen. There stood Mrs. Pinnegar, a tall woman with a face like a mask of passive anger, looking at him coldly. Immediately he felt his own shabbiness and smallness. In utter confusion, he stuck out his hand.

'I had an awful time getting here,' he said. 'I'm afraid I shall make a frightful mess of your house.' He looked down at his boots.

'That's all right,' she said. 'Have you had your tea?'

'No – but don't you bother about me.'

There was a little girl with fair hair in a fringe over her forehead, troubled blue eyes under the fringe, and two dolls. He felt easier.

'Is this your little girl?' he asked. 'She's awfully nice. What is her name?'

'Jane.'

'How are you, Jane?' he said. But the child only stared at him with the baffled, bewildered, pained eyes of a child who lives with hostile parents.

Mrs. Pinnegar set his tea, bread, and butter, jam, and buns. Then she sat opposite him. She was handsome, dark, straight brows and grey eyes

569

with yellow grains in them, and a way of looking straight at you as if she were used to holding her own. Her eyes were the nicest part of her. They had a certain kindliness, mingled, like the yellow grains among the grey, with a relentless, unyielding feminine will. Her nose and mouth were straight, like a Greek mask, and the expression was fixed. She gave him at once the impression of a woman who has made a mistake, who knows it, but who will not change: who cannot now change.

He felt very uneasy. Being a rather small, shambling man, she made him aware of his physical inconspicuousness. And she said not a word, only looked down on him, as he drank his tea, with that changeless look of a woman who is holding her own against Man and Fate. While, from the corner across the kitchen, the little girl with her fair hair and her dolls, watched him also in absolute silence, from her hot blue eyes.

'This seems a pretty awful place,' he said to her.

'It is. It's absolutely awful,' the woman said.

'You ought to get away from it,' he said.

But she received this in dead silence.

It was exceedingly difficult to make any headway. He asked about Mr. Pinnegar. She glanced at the clock.

'He comes up at nine,' she said.

'Is he down the mine?'

'Yes. He's on the afternoon shift.'

There was never a sound from the little girl.

'Doesn't Jane ever talk?' he asked.

'Not much,' said the mother, glancing round.

He talked a little about his lectures, about Sheffield, about London. But she was not really interested. She sat there rather distant, very laconic, looking at him with those curious unyielding eyes. She looked to him like a woman who has had her revenge, and is left stranded on the reefs where she wrecked her opponent. Still unrelenting, unregretting, unyielding, she seemed rather undecided as to what her revenge had been, and what it had all been about.

'You ought to get away from here,' he said to her.

'Where to?' she asked.

'Oh' – he made a vague gesture – 'anywhere, so long as it is *quite* away.'

She seemed to ponder this, under her portentous brow.

'I don't see what difference it would make,' she said. Then glancing round at her child: 'I don't see what difference anything would make, except getting out of the world altogether. But there's *her* to consider.' And she jerked her head in the direction of the child.

Jimmy felt definitely frightened. He wasn't used to this sort of grimness. At the same time he was excited. This handsome, laconic woman, with her soft brown hair and her unflinching eyes with their gold flecks, seemed to be challenging him to something. There was a touch of challenge in her remaining gold-flecked kindness. Somewhere, she had a heart. But what had happened to it? And why?

What had gone wrong with her? In some way, she must have gone against herself.

'Why don't you come and live with me?' he said, like the little gambler he was.

The queer, conflicting smile was on his face. He had taken up her challenge, like a gambler. The very sense of a gamble, in which he could not lose desperately, excited him. At the same time, he was scared of her, and determined to get beyond his scare.

She sat and watched him, with the faintest touch of a grim smile on her handsome mouth.

'How do you mean, live with you?' she said.

'Oh – I mean what it usually means,' he said, with a little puff of self-conscious laughter.

'You're evidently not happy here. You're evidently in the wrong circumstances altogether. You're obviously *not* just an ordinary woman. Well, then, break away. When I say, Come and live with me, I mean just what I say. Come to London and live with me as my wife, if you like, and then if we want to marry, when you get a divorce, why, we can do it.'

Jimmy made this speech more to himself than to the woman. That was how he was. He worked out all his things inside himself, as if it were all merely an interior problem of his own. And while he did so, he had an odd way of squinting his left eye and wagging his head loosely, like a man talking absolutely to himself, and turning his eyes inwards.

The woman watched him in a sort of wonder. This was something she was *not* used to. His extraordinary manner, and his extraordinary bald proposition, roused her from her own tense apathy.

'Well!' she said. 'That's got to be thought about. What about *her*?' – and again she jerked her head towards the round-eyed child in the corner. Jane sat with a completely expressionless face, her little red mouth fallen a little open. She seemed in a sort of trance: as if she understood like a grown-up person, but, as a child, sat in a trance, unconscious.

The mother wheeled round in her chair and stared at her child. The little girl stared back at her mother, with hot, troubled, almost guilty blue eyes. And neither said a word. Yet they seemed to exchange worlds of meaning.

'Why, of course,' said Jimmy, twisting his head again; 'she'd come, too.'

The woman gave a last look at her child, then turned to him, and started watching *him* with that slow, straight stare.

'It's not' – he began, stuttering – 'it's not anything *sudden* and un-considered on my part. I've been considering it for quite a long time – ever since I had the first poem, and your letter.'

He spoke still with his eyes turned inwards, talking to himself. And the woman watched him unflinchingly.

'Before you ever saw me?' she asked, with a queer irony.

'Oh, of course. Of course before I ever saw you. Or else I never *should* have seen you. From the very first, I had a definite feeling —'

He made odd, sharp gestures, like a drunken man, and he spoke like a drunken man, his eyes turned inward, talking to himself. The woman was no more than a ghost moving inside his own consciousness, and he was addressing her there.

The actual woman sat outside looking on in a sort of wonder. This was really something new to her.

'And now you see me, do you want me, really, to come to London?'

She spoke in a dull tone of incredulity. The thing was just a little preposterous to her. But why not? It would have to be something a little preposterous, to get her out of the tomb she was in.

'Of course I do!' he cried, with another scoop of his head and scoop of his hand. '*Now* I do *actually* want you, now I actually see you.' He never looked at her. His eyes were still turned in. He was still talking to himself in a sort of drunkenness with himself.

To her, it was something extraordinary. But it roused her from apathy.

He became aware of the hot blue eyes of the hot-cheeked little girl fixed upon him from the distant corner. And he gave a queer little giggle.

'Why, it's more than I could ever have hoped for,' he said, 'to have you and Jane to live with me! Why, it will mean *life* to me.' He spoke in an odd, strained voice, slightly delirious. And for the first time he looked up at the woman and, apparently, *straight* at her. But, even as he seemed to look straight at her, the curious cast was in his eye, and he was only looking at himself, inside himself, at the shadows inside his own consciousness.

'And when would you like me to come?' she asked, rather coldly.

'Why, as soon as possible. Come back with me to-morrow, if you will. I've got a little house in St. John's Wood, *waiting* for you. Come with me to-morrow. That's the simplest.'

She watched him for some time, as he sat with ducked head. He looked like a man who is drunk – drunk with himself. He was going bald at the crown, his rather curly black hair was thin.

'I couldn't come to-morrow. I should need a few days,' she said.

She wanted to see his face again. It was as if she could not remember what his face was like, this strange man who had appeared out of no-where, with such a strange proposition.

He lifted his face, his eyes still cast in that inturned, blind look. He looked now like a Mephistopheles who has gone blind. With his black brows cocked up, Mephistopheles, Mephistopheles blind and begging in the street.

'Why, of course it's wonderful that it's happened like this for me,' he said, with odd, pouting emphasis, pushing out his lips. 'I was finished, absolutely finished. I was finished while Clarissa was with me. But after she'd gone, I was *absolutely* finished. And I thought there was no chance for me in the world again. It seems to me perfectly marvellous that this has happened – that I've come across you —' he lifted his face sightlessly – 'and Jane – Jane – why, she's *really* too good to be true.' He gave a slight hysterical laugh. 'She really is.'

The woman, and Jane, watched him with some embarrassment.

'I shall have to settle up here with Mr. Pinnegar,' she said, rather coldly musing. 'Do you want to see him?'

'Oh, I —' he said, with a deprecating gesture, 'I don't *care*. But if you think I'd better – why, certainly —'

'I do think you'd better,' she said.

'Very well, then, I *will*. I'll see him whenever you like.'

'He comes in soon after nine,' she said.

'All right, I'll see him then. Much better. But I suppose I'd better see about finding a place to sleep first. Better not leave it too late.'

'I'll come with you and ask for you.'

'Oh, you'd better not, really. If you tell me where to go —'

He had taken on a protective tone: he was protecting her against

573

herself and against scandal. It was his manner, his rather Oxfordy manner, more than anything else, that went beyond her. She wasn't used to it.

Jimmy plunged out into the gulfing blackness of the Northern night, feeling how horrible it was, but pressing his hat on his brow in a sense of strong adventure. He was going through with it.

At the baker's shop, where she had suggested he should ask for a bed, they would have none of him. Absolutely they didn't like the looks of him. At the Pub, too, they shook their heads: didn't want to have anything to do with him. But, in a voice more expostulatingly Oxford than ever, he said:

'But look here – you can't ask a man to sleep under one of these hedges. Can't I see the landlady?'

He persuaded the landlady to promise to let him sleep on the big, soft settee in the parlour, where the fire was burning brightly. Then, saying he would be back about ten, he returned through mud and drizzle up New London Lane.

The child was in bed, a saucepan was boiling by the fire. Already the lines had softened a little in the woman's face.

She spread a cloth on the table. Jimmy sat in silence, feeling that she was hardly aware of his presence. She was absorbed, no doubt, in the coming of her husband. The stranger merely sat on the sofa, and waited. He felt himself wound up tight. And once he was really wound up, he could go through with anything.

They heard the nine o'clock whistle at the mine. The woman then took the saucepan from the fire and went into the scullery. Jimmy could smell the smell of potatoes being strained. He sat quite still. There was nothing for him to do or to say. He was wearing his big black-rimmed spectacles, and his face, blank and expressionless in the suspense of waiting, looked like the death-mask of some sceptical philosopher, who could wait through the ages, and who could hardly distinguish life from death at any time.

Came the heavy-shod tread up the house entry, and the man entered, rather like a blast of wind. The fair moustache stuck out from the blackish, mottled face, and the fierce blue eyes rolled their whites in the coal-blackened sockets.

'This gentleman is Mr. Frith,' said Emily Pinnegar.

Jimmy got up, with a bit of an Oxford wriggle, and held out his hand, saying: 'How do you do?'

His grey eyes, behind the spectacles, had an uncanny whitish gleam.

'My hand's not fit to shake hands,' said the miner. 'Take a seat.'

'Oh, nobody minds coal-dust,' said Jimmy, subsiding on to the sofa. 'It's clean dirt.'

'They say so,' said Pinnegar.

He was a man of medium height, thin, but energetic in build.

Mrs. Pinnegar was running hot water into a pail from the bright brass tap of the stove, which had a boiler to balance the oven. Pinnegar dropped heavily into a wooden arm-chair, and stooped to pull off his ponderous grey pit-boots. He smelled of the strange, stale underground. In silence he pulled on his slippers, then rose, taking his boots into the scullery. His wife followed with the pail of hot water. She returned and spread a coarse roller-towel on the steel fender. The man could be heard washing in the scullery in the semi-dark. Nobody said anything. Mrs. Pinnegar attended to her husband's dinner.

After a while, Pinnegar came running in, naked to the waist, and squatted plumb in front of the big red fire, on his heels. His head and face and the front part of his body were all wet. His back was grey and unwashed. He seized the towel from the fender and began to rub his face and head with a sort of brutal vigour, while his wife brought a bowl, and with a soapy flannel silently washed his back, right down to the loins, where the trousers were rolled back. The man was entirely oblivious of the stranger – this washing was part of the collier's ritual, and nobody existed for the moment. The woman, washing her husband's back, stooping there as he kneeled with knees wide apart, squatting on his heels on the rag hearth-rug, had a peculiar look on her strong, handsome face, a look sinister and derisive. She was deriding something or somebody; but Jimmy could not make out whom or what.

It was a new experience for him to sit completely and brutally excluded from a personal ritual. The collier vigorously rubbed his own fair short hair, till it all stood on end, then he stared into the red-hot fire, oblivious, while the red colour burned in his cheeks. Then again he rubbed his breast and his body with the rough towel, brutally, as if his body were some machine he was cleaning, while his wife, with a peculiar slow movement, dried his back with another towel.

She took away the towel and bowl. The man was dry. He still squatted with his hands on his knees, gazing abstractedly, blankly into the fire. That, too, seemed part of his daily ritual. The colour flushed in his cheeks, his fair moustache was rubbed on end. But his hot blue eyes stared hot and vague into the red coals, while the red glare of the coal fell on his breast and naked body.

He was a man of about thirty-five, in his prime, with a pure smooth skin and no fat on his body. His muscles were not large, but quick, alive with energy. And as he squatted bathing abstractedly in the glow of the fire, he seemed like some pure-moulded engine that sleeps between its motions, with incomprehensible eyes of dark iron-blue.

He looked round, always averting his face from the stranger on the sofa, shutting him out of consciousness. The wife took out a bundle from the dresser cupboard, and handed it to the outstretched, work-scarred hand of the man on the hearth. Curious, that big, horny, work-battered clean hand, at the end of the suave, thin, naked arm.

Pinnegar unrolled his shirt and undervest in front of the fire, warmed them for a moment in the glow, vaguely, sleepily, then pulled them over his head. And then at last he rose, with his shirt hanging over his trousers, and in the same abstract, sleepy way, shutting the world out of his consciousness, he went out again to the scullery, pausing at the same dresser cupboard to take out his rolled-up day trousers.

Mrs. Pinnegar took away the towels and set the dinner on the table – rich, oniony stew out of a hissing brown stew-jar, boiled potatoes, and a cup of tea. The man returned from the scullery in his clean flannelette shirt and black trousers, his fair hair neatly brushed. He planked his wooden arm-chair beside the table, and sat heavily down, to eat.

Then he looked at Jimmy, as one wary, probably hostile man looks at another.

'You're a stranger in these parts, I gather?' he said. There was something slightly formal, even a bit pompous, in his speech.

'An absolute stranger,' replied Jimmy, with a slight aside grin.

The man dabbed some mustard on his plate, and glanced at his food to see if he would like it.

'Come from a distance, do you?' he asked, as he began to eat. As he ate, he seemed to become oblivious again of Jimmy, bent his head over his plate, and ate. But probably he was ruminating something all the time, with barbaric wariness.

'From London,' said Jimmy warily.

'London!' said Pinnegar, without looking from his plate.

Mrs. Pinnegar came and sat, in ritualistic silence, in her tall-backed rocking-chair under the light.

'What brings you this way, then?' asked Pinnegar, stirring his tea.

'Oh!' Jimmy writhed a little on the sofa. 'I came to see Mrs. Pinnegar.'

The miner took a hasty gulp of tea.

576

'You're acquainted then, are you?' he said, still without looking round. He sat with his side face to Jimmy.

'Yes, we are *now*,' explained Jimmy. 'I didn't know Mrs. Pinnegar till this evening. As a matter of fact, she sent me some poems for the *Commentator* – I'm the editor – and I thought they were good, so I wrote and told her so. Then I felt I wanted to come and see her, and she was willing, so I came.'

The man reached out, cut himself a piece of bread, and swallowed a large mouthful.

'You thought her poetry was good?' he said, turning at last to Jimmy and looking straight at him, with a stare something like the child's, but aggressive. 'Are you going to put it in your magazine?'

'Yes, I think I am,' said Jimmy.

'I never read but one of her poems – something about a collier she knew all about, because she'd married him,' he said, in his peculiar harsh voice, that had a certain jeering clang in it, and a certain indomitableness.

Jimmy was silent. The other man's harsh, fighting voice made him shrink.

'I could never get on with the *Commentator* myself,' said Pinnegar, looking round for his pudding, pushing his meat-plate aside. 'Seems to me to go a long way round to get nowhere.'

'Well, probably it *does*,' said Jimmy, squirming a little. 'But so long as the *way* is interesting! I don't see that anything gets anywhere at present – certainly no periodical.'

'I don't know,' said Pinnegar. 'There's some facts in the *Liberator* – and there's some ideas in the *Janus*. I can't see the use myself of all these feelings folk say they have. They get you nowhere.'

'But,' said Jimmy, with a slight pouf of laughter, 'where do you *want* to get? It's all very well talking about getting somewhere, but where, where in the world to-day do you *want* to get? In general, I mean. If you want a better job in the mine – all right, go ahead and get it. But when you begin to talk about getting somewhere in *life* – why, you've got to know what you're talking about.'

'I'm a man, aren't I?' said the miner, going very still and hard.

'But what do you *mean* when you say you're a man?' snarled Jimmy, really exasperated. 'What do you mean? Yes, you *are* a man. But what about it?'

'Haven't I the right to say I won't be made use of?' said the collier, slow, harsh, and heavy.

'You've got a right to *say* it,' retorted Jimmy, with a pouf of laughter. 'But it doesn't *mean* anything. We're all made use of from King George downwards. We have to be. When you eat your pudding you're making use of hundreds of people – including your wife.'

'I know it. I know it. It makes no difference, though. I'm not going to be made use of.'

Jimmy shrugged his shoulders.

'Oh, all right!' he said. 'That's just a phrase, like any other.'

The miner sat very still in his chair, his face going hard and remote. He was evidently thinking over something that was stuck like a barb in his consciousness, something he was trying to harden over, as the skin sometimes hardens over a steel splinter in the flesh.

'I'm nothing but made use of,' he said, now talking hard and final to himself, and staring out into space. 'Down the pit, I'm made use of, and they give me a wage, such as it is. At the house, I'm made use of, and my wife sets the dinner on the table as if I was a customer in a shop.'

'But what do you *expect*?' cried Jimmy, writhing in his chair.

'Me? What do I expect? I expect nothing. But I tell you what —' he turned and looked straight and hard into Jimmy's eyes – 'I'm not going to put up with anything, either.'

Jimmy saw the hard finality in the other man's eyes, and squirmed away from it.

'If you *know* what you're not going to put up with —' he said.

'I don't want my wife writing poetry! And sending it to a parcel of men she's never seen. *I* don't want my wife sitting like Queen Boadicea, when I come home, and a face like a stone wall with holes in it. I don't know what's wrong with her. She doesn't know herself. But she does as she likes. Only, mark you, I do the same.'

'Of course!' cried Jimmy, though there was no of course about it.

'She's told you I've got another woman?'

'Yes.'

'And I'll tell you for why. If I give in to the coal face, and go down the mine every day to eight hours' slavery, more or less, somebody's got to give in to me.'

'Then,' said Jimmy, after a pause, 'if you mean you want your wife to submit to you – well, that's the problem. You have to marry the woman who *will* submit.'

It was amazing, this from Jimmy. He sat there and lectured the collier like a Puritan Father, completely forgetting the disintegrating flutter of Clarissa, in his own background.

'I want a wife who'll please me, who'll want to please me,' said the collier.

'Why should *you* be pleased, any more than anybody else?' asked the wife coldly.

'My child, my little girl wants to please me – if her mother would let her. But the women hang together. I tell you' – and here he turned to Jimmy, with a blaze in his dark blue eyes – 'I want a woman to please me, a woman who's anxious to please me. And if I can't find her in my own home, I'll find her out of it.'

'I hope she pleases you,' said the wife, rocking slightly.

'Well,' said the man, 'she does.'

'Then why don't you go and live with her altogether?' she said.

He turned and looked at her.

'Why don't I?' he said. 'Because I've got my home. I've got my house, I've got my wife, let her be what she may, as a woman to live with. And I've got my child. Why should I break it all up?'

'And what about me?' she asked, coldly and fiercely.

'You? You've got a home. You've got a child. You've got a man who works for you. You've got what you want. You do as you like —'

'Do I?' she asked, with intolerable sarcasm.

'Yes. Apart from the bit of work in the house, you do as you like. If you want to go, you can go. But while you live in my house, you must respect it. You bring no men here, you see.'

'Do *you* respect your home?' she said.

'Yes! I do! If I get another woman – who pleases me – I deprive you of nothing. All I ask of you is to do your duty as a housewife.'

'Down to washing your back!' she said, heavily sarcastic; and, Jimmy thought, a trifle vulgar.

'Down to washing my back, since it's got to be washed,' he said.

'What about the other woman? Let her do it.'

'This is my home.'

The wife gave a strange movement, like a mad woman.

Jimmy sat rather pale and frightened. Behind the collier's quietness he felt the concentration of almost cold anger and an unchanging will. In the man's lean face he could see the bones, the fixity of the male bones, and it was as if the human soul, or spirit, had gone into the living skull and skeleton, almost invulnerable.

Jimmy, for some strange reason, felt a wild anger against this bony and logical man. It was the hard-driven coldness, fixity, that he could not bear.

579

'Look here!' he cried in a resonant Oxford voice, his eyes glaring and casting inwards behind his spectacles. 'You say Mrs. Pinnegar is *free* – free to do as she pleases. In that case, you have no objection if she comes with me right away from here.'

The collier looked at the pale, strange face of the editor in wonder. Jimmy kept his face slightly averted, and sightless, seeing nobody. There was a Mephistophelian tilt about the eyebrows, and a Martyred Sebastian straightness about the mouth.

'Does she *want* to?' asked Pinnegar, with devastating incredulity. The wife smiled faintly, grimly. She could see the vanity of her husband in his utter inability to believe that she could prefer the other man to him.

'That,' said Jimmy, 'you must ask her yourself. But it's what I came here for: to ask her to come and live with me, and bring the child.'

'You came without having seen her, to ask her that?' said the husband, in growing wonder.

'Yes,' said Jimmy vehemently, nodding his head with drunken emphasis. 'Yes! Without ever having seen her!'

'You've caught a funny fish this time, with your poetry,' he said, turning with curious husband-familiarity to his wife. She hated this off-hand husband-familiarity.

'What sort of fish have *you* caught?' she retorted. 'And what did you catch *her* with?'

'Bird-lime!' he said, with a faint, quick grin.

Jimmy was sitting in suspense. They all three sat in suspense for some time.

'And what are you saying to him?' said the collier at length.

Jimmy looked up, and the malevolent half-smile on his face made him rather handsome again, a mixture of faun and Mephisto. He glanced curiously, invitingly, at the woman who was watching him from afar.

'I say yes!' she replied, in a cool voice.

The husband became very still, sitting erect in his wooden arm-chair and staring into space. It was as if he were fixedly watching something fly away from him, out of his own soul. But he was not going to yield at all to any emotion.

He could not now believe that this woman should *want* to leave him. Yet she did.

'I'm sure it's all for the best,' said Jimmy, in his Puritan Father voice. 'You don't mind, really' – he drawled uneasily – 'if she brings the child. I give you my word I'll do my very best for it.'

The collier looked at him as if he were very far away. Jimmy quailed under the look. He could see that the other man was relentlessly killing the emotion in himself, stripping himself, as it were, of his own flesh, stripping himself to the hard unemotional bone of the human male.

'I give her a blank cheque,' said Pinnegar, with numb lips. 'She does as she pleases.'

'So much for fatherly love, compared with selfishness,' she said.

He turned and looked at her with that curious power of remote anger. And immediately she became still, quenched.

'I give you a blank cheque, as far as I'm concerned,' he repeated abstractedly.

'It *is* blank indeed!' she said, with her first touch of bitterness.

Jimmy looked at the clock. It was growing late: he might be shut out of the public-house. He rose to go, saying he would return in the morning. He was leaving the next day, at noon, for London.

He plunged into the darkness and mud of that black, night-ridden country. There was a curious elation in his spirits, mingled with fear. But then he always needed an element of fear, really, to elate him. He thought with terror of those two human beings left in that house together. The frightening state of tension! He himself could never bear an extreme tension. He always had to compromise, to become apologetic and pathetic. He would be able to manage Mrs. Pinnegar that way. Emily! He must get used to saying it. Emily! The Emilia was absurd. He had never known an Emily.

He felt really scared, and really elated. He was doing something big. It was not that he was in *love* with the woman. But, my God, he wanted to take her away from that man. And he wanted the adventure of her. Absolutely the adventure of her. He felt really elated, really himself, really manly.

But in the morning he returned rather sheepishly to the collier's house. It was another dark, drizzling day, with black trees, black road, black hedges, blackish brick houses, and the smell of the sound of collieries under a skyless day. Like living in some weird underground.

Unwillingly he went up that passage-entry again, and knocked at the back door, glancing at the miserable little back garden with its cabbage-stalks and its ugly sanitary arrangements.

The child opened the door to him: with her fair hair, flushed cheeks, and hot, dark-blue eyes.

'Hello, Jane!' he said.

The mother stood tall and square by the table, watching him with portentous eyes as he entered. She was handsome, but her skin was not very good: as if the battle had been too much for her health. Jimmy glanced up at her smiling his slow, ingratiating smile, that always brought a glow of success into a woman's spirit. And as he saw her gold-flecked eyes searching in his eyes, without a bit of kindliness, he thought to himself: 'My God, however am I going to sleep with that woman!' His will was ready, however, and he would manage it somehow.

And when he glanced at the motionless, bony head and lean figure of the collier seated in the wooden arm-chair by the fire, he was the more ready. He must triumph over that man.

'What train are you going by?' asked Mrs. Pinnegar.

'By the 12.30.' He looked up at her as he spoke, with the wide, shining, childlike, almost coy eyes that were his peculiar asset. She looked down at him in a sort of interested wonder. She seemed almost fascinated by his childlike, shining, inviting dark-grey eyes, with their long lashes: such an absolute change from that resentful unyielding that looked out always from the back of her husband's blue eyes. Her husband always seemed like a menace to her, in his thinness, his concentration, his eternal unyielding. And this man looked at one with the wide, shining, fascinating eyes of a young Persian kitten, something at once bold and shy and coy and strangely inviting. She fell at once under their spell.

'You'll have dinner before you go,' she said.

'No!' he cried in panic, unwilling indeed to eat before that other man. 'No, I ate a fabulous breakfast. I will get a sandwich when I change in Sheffield: *really!*'

She had to go out shopping. She said she would go out to the station with him when she got back. It was just after eleven.

'But look here,' he said, addressing also the thin abstracted man who sat unnoticing, with a newspaper, 'we've got to get this thing settled. I *want* Mrs. Pinnegar to come and live with me, her and the child. And she's coming! So don't you think, now, it would be better if she came right along with me to-day! Just put a few things in a bag and come along. Why drag the thing out?'

'I tell you,' replied the husband, 'she has a blank cheque from me to do as she likes.'

'All right, then! Won't you do that? Won't you come along with me now?' said Jimmy, looking up at her exposedly, but casting his eyes a bit inwards. Throwing himself with deliberate impulsiveness on her mercy.

'I can't!' she said decisively. 'I can't come to-day.'

'But why not – really? Why not, while I'm here? You have that blank cheque, you can do as you please —'

'The blank cheque won't get me far,' she said rudely. 'I can't come to-day, anyhow.'

'When can you come, then?' he said, with that queer, petulant pleading. 'The sooner the better, surely.'

'I can come on Monday,' she said abruptly.

'Monday!' He gazed up at her in a kind of panic, through his spectacles. Then he set his teeth again and nodded his head up and down. 'All right, then! To-day is Saturday. Then Monday!'

'If you'll excuse me,' she said, 'I've got to go out for a few things. I'll walk to the station with you when I get back.'

She bundled Jane into a little sky-blue coat and bonnet, put on a heavy black coat and black hat herself, and went out.

Jimmy sat very uneasily opposite the collier, who also wore spectacles to read. Pinnegar put down the newspaper and pulled the spectacles off his nose, saying something about a Labour Government.

'Yes,' said Jimmy. 'After all, best be logical. If you *are* democratic, the only logical thing is a Labour Government. Though, personally, one government is as good as another to me.'

'Maybe so!' said the collier. 'But *something's* got to come to an end, sooner or later.'

'Oh, a great deal!' said Jimmy, and they lapsed into silence.

'Have you been married before?' asked Pinnegar, at length.

'Yes. My wife and I are divorced.'

'I suppose you want me to divorce *my* wife?' said the collier.

'Why – yes! – that would be best —'

'It's the same to me,' said Pinnegar; 'divorce or no divorce. I'll *live* with another woman, but I'll never *marry* another. Enough is as good as a feast. But if she wants a divorce, she can have it.'

'It would certainly be best,' said Jimmy.

There was a long pause. Jimmy wished the woman would come back.

'I look on you as an instrument,' said the miner. 'Something had to break. You are the instrument that breaks it.'

It was strange to sit in the room with this thin, remote, wilful man. Jimmy was a bit fascinated by him. But, at the same time, he hated him because he could not be in the same room with him without being under his spell. He felt himself dominated. And he hated it.

'My wife,' said Pinnegar, looking up at Jimmy with a peculiar, almost humorous, teasing grin, 'expects to see me go to the dogs when she leaves me. It is her last hope.'

Jimmy ducked his head and was silent, not knowing what to say. The other man sat still in his chair, like a sort of infinitely patient prisoner, looking away out of the window and waiting.

'She thinks,' he said again, 'that she has some wonderful future awaiting her somewhere, and you're going to open the door.'

And again the same amused grin was in his eyes.

And again Jimmy was fascinated by the man. And again he hated the spell of this fascination. For Jimmy wanted to be, in his own mind, the strongest man among men, but particularly among women. And this thin, peculiar man could dominate him. He knew it. The very silent unconsciousness of Pinnegar dominated the room, wherever he was.

Jimmy hated this.

At last Mrs. Pinnegar came back, and Jimmy set off with her. He shook hands with the collier.

'Good-bye!' he said.

'Good-bye!' said Pinnegar, looking down at him with those amused blue eyes, which Jimmy knew he would never be able to get beyond.

And the walk to the station was almost a walk of conspiracy against the man left behind, between the man in spectacles and the tall woman. They arranged the details for Monday. Emily was to come by the nine o'clock train: Jimmy would meet her at Marylebone, and install her in his house in St. John's Wood. Then, with the child, they would begin a new life. Pinnegar would divorce his wife, or she would divorce him: and then, another marriage.

Jimmy got a tremendous kick out of it all on the journey home. He felt he had really done something desperate and adventurous. But he was in too wild a flutter to analyse any results. Only, as he drew near London, a sinking feeling came over him. He was desperately tired after all, almost too tired to keep up.

Nevertheless, he went after dinner and sprang it all on Severn.

'You damn fool!' said Severn, in consternation. 'What did you do it for?'

'Well,' said Jimmy, writhing. 'Because I *wanted* to.'

'Good God! The woman sounds like the head of Medusa. You're a hero of some stomach, I must say! Remember Clarissa?'

'Oh,' writhed Jimmy. 'But this is different.'

'Ay, her name's Emma, or something of that sort, isn't it?'

'Emily!' said Jimmy briefly.

'Well, you're a fool, anyway, so you may as well keep on acting in character. I've no doubt, by playing weeping-willow, you'll outlive all the female storms you ever prepare for yourself. I never yet did see a weeping-willow uprooted by a gale, so keep on hanging your harp on it, and you'll be all right. Here's luck! But for a man who was looking for a little Gretchen to adore him, you're a corker!'

Which was all that Severn had to say. But Jimmy went home with his knees shaking. On Sunday morning he wrote an anxious letter. He didn't know how to begin it: *Dear Mrs. Pinnegar* and *Dear Emily* seemed either too late in the day or too early. So he just plunged in, without dear anything.

'I want you to have this before you come. Perhaps we have been precipitate. I only beg you to decide *finally*, for yourself, before you come. Don't come, please, unless you are absolutely sure of yourself. If you are *in the least* unsure, wait a while, wait till you are quite certain, one way or the other.

'For myself, if you don't come I shall understand. But please send me a telegram. If you do come, I shall welcome both you and the child. Yours ever – J.F.'

He paid a man his return fare, and three pounds extra, to go on the Sunday and deliver this letter.

The man came back in the evening. He had delivered the letter. There was no answer.

Awful Sunday night: tense Monday morning!

A telegram: *'Arrive Marylebone 12.50 with Jane. Yours ever. Emily.'*

Jimmy set his teeth and went to the station. But when he felt her looking at him, and so met her eyes: and after that saw her coming slowly down the platform, holding the child by the hand, her slow cat's eyes smouldering under her straight brows, smouldering at him: he almost swooned. A sickly grin came over him as he held out his hand. Nevertheless, he said:

'I'm *awfully* glad you came.'

And as he sat in the taxi, a perverse but intense desire for her came over him, making him almost helpless. He could feel, so strongly, the presence of that other man about her, and this went to his head like neat spirits. That other man! In some subtle, inexplicable way, he was actu-

585

ally bodily present, the husband. The woman moved in his aura. She was hopelessly married to him.

And this went to Jimmy's head like neat whisky. Which of the two would fall before him with a greater fall – the woman or the man, her husband?

THE LAST LAUGH

THERE was a little snow on the ground, and the church clock had just struck midnight. Hampstead in the night of winter for once was looking pretty, with clean white earth and lamps for moon, and dark sky above the lamps.

A confused little sound of voices, a gleam of hidden yellow light. And then the garden door of a tall, dark Georgian house suddenly opened, and three people confusedly emerged. A girl in a dark blue coat and fur turban, very erect: a fellow with a little dispatch-case, slouching: a thin man with a red beard, bareheaded, peering out of the gateway down the hill that swung in a curve downwards towards London.

'Look at it! A new world!' cried the man in the beard, ironically, as he stood on the step and peered out.

'No, Lorenzo! It's only white-wash!' cried the young man in the overcoat. His voice was handsome, resonant, plangent, with a weary sardonic touch. As he turned back his face was dark in shadow.

The girl with the erect, alert head, like a bird, turned back to the two men.

'What was that?' she asked, in her quick, quiet voice.

'Lorenzo says it's a new world. I say it's only white-wash,' cried the man in the street.

She stood still and lifted her woolly, gloved finger. She was deaf and was taking it in.

Yes, she had got it. She gave a quick, chuckling laugh, glanced very quickly at the man in the bowler hat, then back at the man in the stucco gateway, who was grinning like a satyr and waving good-bye.

'Good-bye, Lorenzo!' came the resonant, weary cry of the man in the bowler hat.

'Good-bye!' came the sharp, night-bird call of the girl.

The green gate slammed, then the inner door. The two were alone in the street, save for the policeman at the corner. The road curved steeply downhill.

'You'd better mind how you *step*!' shouted the man in the bowler hat, leaning near the erect, sharp girl, and slouching in his walk. She paused a moment, to make sure what he had said.

587

'Don't mind me, I'm quite all right. Mind yourself!' she said quickly. At that very moment he gave a wild lurch on the slippery snow, but managed to save himself from falling. She watched him, on tiptoes of alertness. His bowler hat bounced away in the thin snow. They were under a lamp near the curve. As he ducked for his hat he showed a bald spot, just like a tonsure, among his dark, thin, rather curly hair. And when he looked up at her, with his thick black brows sardonically arched, and his rather hooked nose self-derisive, jamming his hat on again, he seemed like a satanic young priest. His face had beautiful lines, like a faun, and a doubtful martyred expression. A sort of faun on the Cross, with all the malice of the complication.

'Did you hurt yourself?' she asked in her quick, cool, unemotional way.

'No!' he shouted derisively.

'Give me the machine, won't you?' she said, holding out her woolly hand. 'I believe I'm safer.'

'Do you *want* it?' he shouted.

'Yes, I'm sure I'm safer.'

He handed her the little brown dispatch-case, which was really a Marconi listening machine for her deafness. She marched erect as ever. He shoved his hands deep in his overcoat pockets and slouched along beside her, as if he wouldn't make his legs firm. The road curved down in front of them, clean and pale with snow under the lamps. A motor-car came churning up. A few dark figures slipped away into the dark recesses of the houses, like fishes among rocks above a sea-bed of white sand. On the left was a tuft of trees sloping upwards into the dark.

He kept looking around, pushing out his finely shaped chin and his hooked nose as if he were listening for something. He could still hear the motor-car climbing on to the Heath. Below was the yellow, foul-smelling glare of the Hampstead Tube Station. On the right the trees.

The girl, with her alert pink-and-white face, looked at him sharply, inquisitively. She had an odd nymph-like inquisitiveness, sometimes like a bird, sometimes a squirrel, sometimes a rabbit: never quite like a woman. At last he stood still, as if he would go no farther. There was a curious, baffled grin on his smooth, cream-coloured face.

'James,' he said loudly to her, leaning towards her ear. 'Do you hear somebody *laughing*?'

'Laughing?' she retorted quickly. 'Who's laughing?'

'I don't know. *Somebody*!' he shouted, showing his teeth at her in a very odd way.

'No, I hear nobody,' she announced.

'But it's most *extraordinary*!' he cried, his voice slurring up and down. 'Put on your machine.'

'Put it on?' she retorted. 'What for?'

'To see if you can *hear* it,' he cried.

'Hear what?'

'The *laughing*. Somebody laughing. It's most *extraordinary*.'

She gave her odd little chuckle and handed him her machine. He held it while she opened the lid and attached the wires, putting the band over her head and the receivers at her ears, like a wireless operator. Crumbs of snow fell down the cold darkness. She switched on: little yellow lights in glass tubes shone in the machine. She was connected, she was listening. He stood with his head ducked, his hands shoved down in his overcoat pockets.

Suddenly he lifted his face and gave the weirdest, slightly neighing laugh, uncovering his strong, spaced teeth, and arching his black brows, and watching her with queer, gleaming, goat-like eyes.

She seemed a little dismayed.

'There!' he said. 'Didn't you hear it?'

'I heard *you*!' she said, in a tone which conveyed that *that* was enough.

'But didn't you hear *it*!' he cried, unfurling his lips oddly again.

'No!' she said.

He looked at her vindictively, and stood again with ducked head. She remained erect, her fur hat in her hand, her fine bobbed hair banded with the machine-band and catching crumbs of snow, her odd, bright-eyed, deaf nymph's face lifted with blank listening.

'There!' he cried, suddenly jerking up his gleaming face. 'You mean to tell me you can't —' He was looking at her almost diabolically. But something else was too strong for him. His face wreathed with a startling, peculiar smile, seeming to gleam, and suddenly the most extraordinary laugh came bursting out of him, like an animal laughing. It was a strange, neighing sound, amazing in her ears. She was startled, and switched her machine quieter.

A large form loomed up: a tall, clean-shaven young policeman.

'A radio?' he asked laconically.

'No, it's my machine. I'm deaf!' said Miss James quickly and distinctly. She was not the daughter of a peer for nothing.

The man in the bowler hat lifted his face and glared at the fresh-faced young policeman with a peculiar white glare in his eyes.

'Look here!' he said distinctly. 'Did you hear someone laughing?'

'Laughing? I heard you, sir.'

'No, *not* me.' He gave an impatient jerk of his arm, and lifted his face again. His smooth, creamy face seemed to gleam, there were subtle curves of derisive triumph in all its lines. He was careful not to look directly at the young policeman. 'The most extraordinary laughter I ever heard,' he added, and the same touch of derisive exultation sounded in his tones.

The policeman looked down on him cogitatingly.

'It's perfectly all right,' said Miss James coolly. 'He's not drunk. He just hears something that we don't hear.'

'Drunk!' echoed the man in the bowler hat, in profoundly amused derision. 'If I were merely drunk —' And off he went again in the wild, neighing, animal laughter, while his averted face seemed to flash.

At the sound of the laughter something roused in the blood of the girl and of the policeman. They stood nearer to one another, so that their sleeves touched and they looked wonderingly across at the man in the bowler hat. He lifted his black brows at them.

'Do you mean to say you heard nothing?' he asked.

'Only you,' said Miss James.

'Only you, sir!' echoed the policeman.

'What was it like?' asked Miss James.

'Ask me to *describe* it!' retorted the young man, in extreme contempt. 'It's the most marvellous sound in the world.'

And truly he seemed wrapped up in a new mystery.

'Where does it come from?' asked Miss James, very practical.

'Apparently,' it answered in contempt, 'from over there.' And he pointed to the trees and bushes inside the railings over the road.

'Well, let's go and see!' she said. 'I can carry my machine and go on listening.'

The man seemed relieved to get rid of the burden. He shoved his hands in his pockets again and sloped off across the road. The policeman, a queer look flickering on his fresh young face, put his hand round the girl's arm carefully and subtly, to help her. She did not lean at all on the support of the big hand, but she was interested, so she did not resent it. Having held herself all her life intensely aloof from physical contact, and never having let any man touch her, she now, with a certain nymph-like voluptuousness, allowed the large hand of the young policeman to support her as they followed the quick wolf-like figure of the other man across the road uphill. And she could feel the presence of the young policeman, through all the thickness of his dark-blue uniform, as something young and alert and bright.

When they came up to the man in the bowler hat, he was standing with his head ducked, his ears pricked, listening beside the iron rail inside which grew big black holly trees tufted with snow, and old, ribbed, silent English elms.

The policeman and the girl stood waiting. She was peering into the bushes with the sharp eyes of a deaf nymph, deaf to the world's noises. The man in the bowler hat listened intensely. A lorry rolled downhill, making the earth tremble.

'There!' cried the girl, as the lorry rumbled darkly past. And she glanced round with flashing eyes at her policeman, her fresh soft face gleaming with startled life. She glanced straight into the puzzled, amused eyes of the young policeman. He was just enjoying himself.

'Don't you see?' she said, rather imperiously.

'What is it, Miss?' answered the policeman.

'I mustn't point,' she said. 'Look where I look.'

And she looked away with brilliant eyes, into the dark holly bushes. She must see something, for she smiled faintly, with subtle satisfaction, and she tossed her erect head in all the pride of vindication. The policeman looked at her instead of into the bushes. There was a certain brilliance of triumph and vindication in all the poise of her slim body.

'I always knew I should see him,' she said triumphantly to herself.

'Whom do you see?' shouted the man in the bowler hat.

'Don't you see him too?' she asked, turning round her soft, arch, nymph-like face anxiously. She was anxious for the little man to see.

'No, I see nothing. What do you see, James?' cried the man in the bowler hat, insisting.

'A man.'

'Where?'

'There. Among the holly bushes.'

'Is he there now?'

'No! He's gone.'

'What sort of a man?'

'I don't know.'

'What did he look like?'

'I can't tell you.'

But at that instant the man in the bowler hat turned suddenly, and the arch, triumphant look flew to his face.

'Why, he must be *there*!' he cried, pointing up the grove. 'Don't you hear him laughing? He must be behind those trees.'

And his voice, with curious delight, broke into a laugh again, as he stood and stamped his feet on the snow, and danced to his own laughter, ducking his head. Then he turned away and ran swiftly up the avenue lined with old trees.

He slowed down as a door at the end of a garden path, white with untouched snow, suddenly opened, and a woman in a long-fringed black shawl stood in the light. She peered out into the night. Then she came down to the low garden gate. Crumbs of snow still fell. She had dark hair and a tall dark comb.

'Did you knock at my door?' she asked of the man in the bowler hat.

'I? No!'

'Somebody knocked at my door.'

'Did they? Are you sure? They can't have done. There are no foot-marks in the snow.'

'Nor are there!' she said. 'But somebody knocked and called some-thing.'

'That's very curious,' said the man. 'Were you expecting someone?'

'No. Not exactly expecting anyone. Except that one is always expect-ing Somebody, you know.' In the dimness of the snow-lit night he could see her making big, dark eyes at him.

'Was it someone laughing?' he said.

'No. It was no one laughing, exactly. Someone knocked, and I ran to open, hoping as one always hopes, you know —'

'What?'

'Oh – that something wonderful is going to happen.'

He was standing close to the low gate. She stood on the opposite side. Her hair was dark, her face seemed dusky, as she looked up at him with her dark, meaningful eyes.

'Did you wish someone would come?' he asked.

'Very much,' she replied, in her plangent Jewish voice. She must be a Jewess.

'No matter who?' he said, laughing.

'So long as it was a man I could like,' she said, in a low, meaningful, falsely shy voice.

'Really!' he said. 'Perhaps after all it was I who knocked – without knowing.'

'I think it was,' she said. 'It must have been.'

'Shall I come in?' he asked, putting his hand on the little gate.

'Don't you think you'd better?' she replied.

He bent down, unlatching the gate. As he did so the woman in the black shawl turned, and, glancing over her shoulder, hurried back to the house, walking unevenly in the snow, on her high-heeled shoes. The man hurried after her, hastening like a hound to catch up.

Meanwhile the girl and the policeman had come up. The girl stood still when she saw the man in the bowler hat going up the garden walk after the woman in the black shawl with the fringe.

'Is he going in?' she asked quickly.

'Looks like it, doesn't it?' said the policeman.

'Does he know that woman?'

'I can't say. I should say he soon will,' replied the policeman.

'But who is she?'

'I couldn't say who she is.'

The two dark, confused figures entered the lighted doorway, then the door closed on them.

'He's gone,' said the girl outside on the snow. She hastily began to pull off the band of her telephone receiver, and switched off her machine. The tubes of secret light disappeared, she packed up the little leather case. Then, pulling on her soft fur cap, she stood once more ready.

The slightly martial look which her long dark-blue military-seeming coat gave her was intensified, while the slightly anxious, bewildered look on her face had gone. She seemed to stretch herself, to stretch her limbs free. And the inert look had left her full soft cheeks. Her cheeks were alive with the glimmer of pride and a new dangerous surety.

She looked quickly at the tall young policeman. He was clean-shaven, fresh-faced, smiling oddly under his helmet, waiting in subtle patience, a few yards away. She saw that he was a decent young man, one of the waiting sort.

The second of ancient fear was followed at once in her by a blithe, unaccustomed sense of power.

'Well!' she said. 'I should say it's no use waiting.' She spoke decisively.

'You don't have to wait for him, do you?' asked the policeman.

'Not at all. He's much better where he is.' She laughed an odd, brief laugh. Then glancing over her shoulder, she set off down the hill, carrying her little case. Her feet felt lighter, her legs felt long and strong. She glanced over her shoulder again. The young policeman was following her, and she laughed to herself. Her limbs felt so lithe and so strong, if she wished she could easily run faster than he. If she wished she could easily kill him, even with her hands.

So it seemed to her. But why kill him? He was a decent young fellow. She had in front of her eyes the dark face among the holly bushes, with the brilliant, mocking eyes. Her breast felt full of power, and her legs felt long and strong and wild. She was surprised herself at the strong, bright, throbbing sensation beneath her breasts, a sensation of triumph and rosy anger. Her hands felt keen on her wrists. She who had always declared she had not a muscle in her body! Even now, it was not muscle, it was a sort of flame.

Suddenly it began to snow heavily, with fierce frozen puffs of wind. The snow was small, in frozen grains, and hit sharp on her face. It seemed to whirl round her as if she herself were whirling in a cloud. But she did not mind. There was a flame in her, her limbs felt flamey and strong, amid the whirl.

And the whirling snowy air seemed full of presences, full of strange unheard voices. She was used to the sensation of noises taking place which she could not hear. This sensation became very strong. She felt something was happening in the wild air.

The London air was no longer heavy and clammy, saturated with ghosts of the unwilling dead. A new, clean tempest swept down from the Pole, and there were noises.

Voices were calling. In spite of her deafness she could hear someone, several voices, calling and whistling, as if many people were hallooing through the air:

'He's come back! Aha! He's come back!'

There was a wild, whistling, jubilant sound of voices in the storm of snow. Then obscured lightning winked through the snow in the air.

'Is that thunder and lightning?' she asked of the young policeman, as she stood still, waiting for his form to emerge through the veil of whirling snow.

'Seems like it to me,' he said.

And at that very moment the lightning blinked again, and the dark, laughing face was near her face, it almost touched her cheek.

She started back, but a flame of delight went over her.

'There!' she said. 'Did you see that?'

'It lightened,' said the policeman.

She was looking at him almost angrily. But then the clean, fresh animal look of his skin, and the tame-animal look in his frightened eyes

594

amused her, she laughed her low, triumphant laugh. He was obviously afraid, like a frightened dog that sees something uncanny.

The storm suddenly whistled louder, more violently, and, with a strange noise like castanets, she seemed to hear voices clapping and crying:

'He is here! He's come back!'

She nodded her head gravely.

The policeman and she moved on side by side. She lived alone in a little stucco house in a side street down the hill. There was a church and a grove of trees and then the little old row of houses. The wind blew fiercely, thick with snow. Now and again a taxi went by, with its lights showing weirdly. But the world seemed empty, uninhabited save by snow and voices.

As the girl and the policeman turned past the grove of trees near the church, a great whirl of wind and snow made them stand still, and in the wild confusion they heard a whirling of sharp, delighted voices, something like seagulls, crying:

'He's here! He's here!'

'Well, I'm jolly glad he's back,' said the girl calmly.

'What's that?' said the nervous policeman, hovering near the girl.

The wind let them move forward. As they passed along the railings it seemed to them the doors of the church were open, and the windows were out, and the snow and the voices were blowing in a wild career all through the church.

'How extraordinary that they left the church open!' said the girl.

The policeman stood still. He could not reply.

And as they listened to the wind and the church full of whirling voices all calling confusedly.

'*Now* I hear the laughing,' she said suddenly.

It came from the church: a sound of low, subtle, endless laughter, a strange, naked sound.

'Now I hear it!' she said.

But the policeman did not speak. He stood cowed, with his tail between his legs, listening to the strange noises in the church.

The wind must have blown out one of the windows, for they could see the snow whirling in volleys through the black gap, and whirling inside the church like a dim light. There came a sudden crash, followed by a burst of chuckling, naked laughter. The snow seemed to make a queer light inside the building, like ghosts moving, big and tall.

There was more laughter, and a tearing sound. On the wind, pieces of paper, leaves of books, came whirling among the snow through the dark window. Then a white thing, soaring like a crazy bird, rose up on the wind as if it had wings, and lodged on a black tree outside, struggling. It was the altar-cloth.

There came a bit of gay, trilling music. The wind was running over the organ-pipes like pan-pipes, quickly up and down. Snatches of wild, gay, trilling music, and bursts of the naked low laughter.

'Really!' said the girl. 'This is most extraordinary. Do you hear the music and the people laughing?'

'Yes, I hear somebody on the organ!' said the policeman.

'And do you get the puff of warm wind? Smelling of spring. Almond blossom, that's what it is! A most marvellous scent of almond blossom. *Isn't* it an extraordinary thing!'

She went on triumphantly past the church, and came to the row of little old houses. She entered her own gate in the little railed entrance.

'Here I am!' she said finally. 'I'm home now. Thank you very much for coming with me.'

She looked at the young policeman. His whole body was white as a wall with snow, and in the vague light of the arc-lamp from the street his face was humble and frightened.

'Can I come in and warm myself a bit?' he asked humbly. She knew it was fear rather than cold that froze him. He was in mortal fear.

'Well!' she said. 'Stay down in the sitting-room if you like. But don't come upstairs, because I am alone in the house. You can make up the fire in the sitting-room, and you can go when you are warm.'

She left him on the big, low couch before the fire, his face bluish and blank with fear. He rolled his blue eyes after her as she left the room. But she went up to her bedroom and fastened her door.

In the morning she was in her studio upstairs in her little house, looking at her own paintings and laughing to herself. Her canaries were talking and shrilly whistling in the sunshine that followed the storm. The cold snow outside was still clean, and the white glare in the air gave the effect of much stronger sunshine than actually existed.

She was looking at her own paintings, and chuckling to herself over their comicalness. Suddenly they struck her as absolutely absurd. She quite enjoyed looking at them, they seemed to her so grotesque. Especially her self-portrait, with its nice brown hair and its slightly opened rabbit-mouth and its baffled uncertain rabbit-eyes. She looked at the painted face and laughed in a long, rippling laugh, till the yellow canaries like faded daffodils almost went mad in an effort to sing louder. The girl's long, rippling laugh sounded through the house uncannily.

The house-keeper, a rather sad-faced young woman of a superior sort – nearly all people in England are of the superior sort, superiority being an English ailment – came in with an inquiring and rather disapproving look.

'Did you call, Miss James?' she asked loudly.

'No. No, I didn't call. Don't shout, I can hear quite well,' replied the girl.

The housekeeper looked at her again.

'You knew there was a young man in the sitting-room?' she said.

'No. Really!' cried the girl. 'What, the young policeman? I'd forgotten all about him. He came in in the storm to warm himself. Hasn't he gone?'

'No, Miss James.'

'How extraordinary of him! What time is it? Quarter to nine! Why didn't he go when he was warm? I must go and see him, I suppose.'

'He says he's lame,' said the housekeeper censoriously and loudly.

'Lame! That's extraordinary. He certainly wasn't last night. But don't shout. I can hear quite well.'

'Is Mr. Marchbanks coming in to breakfast, Miss James?' said the housekeeper, more and more censorious.

'I couldn't say. But I'll come down as soon as mine is ready. I'll be down in a minute, anyhow, to see the policeman. Extraordinary that he is still here.'

She sat down before her window, in the sun, to think a while. She could see the snow outside, the bare, purplish trees. The air all seemed rare and different. Suddenly the world had become quite different: as if some skin or integument had broken, as if the old, mouldering London sky had crackled and rolled back, like an old skin, shrivelled, leaving an absolutely new blue heaven.

'It really is extraordinary!' she said to herself. 'I certainly saw that man's face. What a wonderful face it was! I shall never forget it. Such laughter! He laughs longest who laughs last. He certainly will have the last laugh. I like him for that: he will laugh last. Must be someone really extraordinary! How very nice to be the one to laugh last. He certainly will. What a wonderful being! I suppose I must call him a being. He's not a person exactly.

'But how wonderful of him to come back and alter all the world immediately! *Isn't* that extraordinary. I wonder if he'll have altered

Marchbanks. Of course Marchbanks never *saw* him. But he heard him. Wouldn't that do as well, I wonder! – I *wonder!'*

She went off into a muse about Marchbanks. She and he were *such* friends. They had been friends like that for almost two years. Never lovers. Never that at all. But *friends.*

And after all, she had been in love with him: in her head. This seemed now so funny to her: that she had been, in her head, so much in love with him. After all, life was too absurd.

Because now she saw herself and him as such a funny pair. He so funnily taking life terribly seriously, especially his own life. And she so ridiculously *determined* to save him from himself. Oh, how absurd! *Determined* to save him from himself, and wildly in love with him in the effort. The determination to save him from himself.

Absurd! Absurd! Absurd! Since she had seen the man laughing among the holly bushes – *such* extraordinary, wonderful laughter – she had seen her own ridiculousness. Really, what fantastic silliness, saving a man from himself! Saving anybody. What fantastic silliness! How much more amusing and lively to let a man go to perdition in his own way. Perdition was more amusing than salvation anyhow, and a much better place for most men to go to.

She had never been in love with any man, and only spuriously in love with Marchbanks. She saw it quite plainly now. After all, what nonsense it all was, this being-in-love business. Thank goodness she had never made the humiliating mistake.

No, the man among the holly bushes had made her see it all so plainly: the ridiculousness of being in love, the *infra dig.* business of chasing a man or being chased by a man.

'Is love *really* so absurd and *infra dig.*?' she said aloud to herself.

'Why, of course!' came a deep, laughing voice.

She started round, but nobody was to be seen.

'I expect it's that man again!' she said to herself. 'It really *is* remarkable, you know. I consider it's a remarkable thing that I never really wanted a man, *any* man. And there I am over thirty. It *is* curious. Whether it's something wrong with me, or right with me, I can't say. I don't know till I've proved it. But I believe, if that man kept on laughing something would happen to me.'

She smelt the curious smell of almond blossom in the room, and heard the distant laugh again.

'I do wonder why Marchbanks went with that woman last night – that Jewish-looking woman. Whatever could he want of her? – or she of him? So strange, as if they both had made up their minds to something! How extraordinarily puzzling life is! So messy, it all seems.

'Why does nobody laugh in life like that man? He *did* seem so wonderful. So scornful! And so proud! And so real! With those laughing, scornful, amazing eyes, just laughing and disappearing again. I can't imagine him chasing a Jewish-looking woman. Or chasing any woman, thank goodness. It's all *so* messy. My policeman would be messy if one would let him: like a dog. I do dislike dogs, really I do. And men do seem so doggy! —'

But even while she mused, she began to laugh again to herself with a long, low chuckle. How wonderful of that man to come and laugh like that and make the sky crack and shrivel like an old skin! Wasn't he wonderful! Wouldn't it be wonderful if he just touched her. Even touched her. She felt, if he touched her, she herself would emerge new and tender out of the old, hard skin. She was gazing abstractedly out of the window.

'There he comes, just now,' she said abruptly. But she meant Marchbanks, not the laughing man.

There he came, his hands still shoved down in his overcoat pockets, his head still rather furtively ducked in the bowler hat, and his legs still rather shambling. He came hurrying across the road, not looking up, deep in thought, no doubt. Thinking profoundly, with agonies of agitation, no doubt about his last night's experience. It made her laugh.

She, watching from the window above, burst into a long laugh, and the canaries went off their heads again.

He was in the hall below. His resonant voice was calling, rather imperiously:

'James! Are you coming down?'

'No,' she called. 'You come up.'

He came up two at a time, as if his feet were a bit savage with the stairs for obstructing him.

In the doorway he stood staring at her with a vacant, sardonic look, his grey eyes moving with a queer light. And she looked back at him with a curious, rather haughty carelessness.

'Don't you want your breakfast?' she asked. It was his custom to come and take breakfast with her each morning.

'No,' he answered loudly. 'I went to a tea-shop.'

'Don't shout,' she said. 'I can hear you quite well.'

He looked at her with mockery and a touch of malice.

'I believe you always could,' he said, still loudly.

'Well, anyway, I can now, so you needn't shout,' she replied.

And again his grey eyes, with the queer, greyish phosphorescent gleam in them, lingered malignantly on her face.

'Don't look at me,' she said calmly. 'I know all about everything.'

He burst into a pouf of malicious laughter.

'Who taught you – the policeman?' he cried.

'Oh, by the way, he must be downstairs! No, he was only incidental. So, I suppose, was the woman in the shawl. Did you stay all night?'

'Not entirely. I came away before dawn. What did you do?'

'Don't shout. I came home long before dawn.' And she seemed to hear the long, low laughter.

'Why, what's the matter?' he said curiously. 'What have you been doing?'

'I don't quite know. Why? – are you going to call me to account?'

'Did you hear that laughing?'

'Oh yes. And many more things. And saw things too.'

'Have you seen the paper?'

'No. Don't shout, I can hear.'

'There's been a great storm, blew out the windows and doors of the church outside here, and pretty well wrecked the place.'

'I saw it. A leaf of the church Bible blew right in my face: from the Book of Job —' She gave a low laugh.

'But what else did you see?' he cried loudly.

'I saw *him*.'

'Who?'

'Ah, that I can't say.'

'But what was he like?'

'That I can't tell you. I don't really know.'

'But you must know. Did your policeman see him too?'

'No, I don't suppose he did. My policeman!' And she went off into a long ripple of laughter. 'He is by no means mine. But I *must* go downstairs and see him.'

'It's certainly made you very strange,' Marchbanks said. 'You've got no *soul*, you know.'

'Oh, thank goodness for that!' she cried. 'My policeman has one, I'm sure. *My policeman!*' And she went off again into a long peal of laughter, the canaries pealing shrill accompaniment.

'What's the matter with you?' he said.

'Having no soul. I never had one really. It was always fobbed off on me. Soul was the only thing there was between you and me. Thank goodness it's gone. Haven't you lost yours? The one that seemed to worry you, like a decayed tooth?'

'But what are you *talking* about?' he cried.

'I don't know,' she said. 'It's all so extraordinary. But look here, I *must* go down and see my policeman. He's downstairs in the sitting-room. You'd better come with me.'

They went down together. The policeman in his waistcoat and shirt-sleeves was lying on the sofa, with a very long face.

'Look here!' said Miss James to him. 'Is it true you're lame?'

'It is true. That's why I'm here. I can't walk,' said the fair-haired young man as tears came to his eyes.

'But how did it happen? You weren't lame last night,' she said.

'I don't know how it happened – but when I woke up and tried to stand up, I couldn't do it.' The tears ran down his distressed face.

'How very extraordinary!' she said. 'What can we do about it?'

'Which foot is it?' asked Marchbanks. 'Let us have a look at it.'

'I don't like to,' said the poor devil.

'You'd better,' said Miss James.

He slowly pulled off his stocking, and showed his white left foot curiously clubbed, like the weird paw of some animal. When he looked at it himself, he sobbed.

And as he sobbed, the girl heard again the low, exulting laughter. But she paid no heed to it, gazing curiously at the weeping young police-man.

'Does it hurt?' she asked.

'It does if I try to walk on it,' wept the young man.

'I'll tell you what,' she said. 'We'll telephone for a doctor, and he can take you home in a taxi.'

The young fellow shamefacedly wiped his eyes.

'But have you no idea how it happened?' asked Marchbanks anxi-ously.

'I haven't myself,' said the young fellow.

At that moment the girl heard the low, eternal laugh right in her ear. She started, but could see nothing.

She started round again as Marchbanks gave a strange, yelping cry, like a shot animal. His white face was drawn, distorted in a curious grin, that was chiefly agony but partly wild recognition. He was staring with fixed eyes at something. And in the rolling agony of his eyes was the horrible grin of a man who realises he had made a final, and this time fatal, fool of himself.

'Why,' he yelped in a high voice, 'I knew it was he!' And with a queer shuddering laugh he pitched forward on the carpet and lay writhing for a moment on the floor. Then he lay still, in a weird, distorted position, like a man struck by lightening.

Miss James stared with round, staring brown eyes.

'Is he dead?' she asked quickly.

The young policeman was trembling so that he could hardly speak. She could hear his teeth chattering.

'Seems like it,' he stammered.

There was a faint smell of almond blossom in the air.

IN LOVE

'WELL, my dear!' said Henrietta. 'If I had such a worried look on my face, when I was going down to spend the weekend with the man I was engaged to – and going to be married to in a month – well! I should either try and change my face, or hide my feelings, or something.'

'You shut up!' said Hester curtly. 'Don't look at my face, if it doesn't please you.'

'Now, my dear Hester, don't go into one of your tempers! Just look in the mirror, and you'll see what I mean.'

'Who cares what you mean! You're not responsible for my face,' said Hester desperately, showing no intention of looking in the mirror, or of otherwise following her sister's kind advice.

Henrietta, being the younger sister, and mercifully unengaged, hummed a tune lightly. She was only twenty-one, and had not the faintest intention of jeopardising her peace of mind by accepting any sort of fatal ring. Nevertheless, it *was* nice to see Hester 'getting off', as they say; for Hester was nearly twenty-five, which is serious.

The worst of it was, lately Hester had had her famous 'worried' look on her face, when it was a question of the faithful Joe: dark shadows under the eyes, drawn lines down the cheeks. And when Hester looked like that, Henrietta couldn't help feeling the most horrid jangled echo of worry and apprehension in her own heart, and she hated it. She simply couldn't stand that sudden feeling of fear.

'What I mean to say,' she continued, '*is* – that it's jolly unfair to Joe, if you go down looking like that. Either put a better face on it, or —' But she checked herself. She was going to say 'don't go'. But really, she did hope that Hester would go through with this marriage. Such a weight off her, Henrietta's, mind.

'Oh, hang!' cried Hester. 'Shut up!' And her dark eyes flashed a spark of fury and misgiving at the young Henrietta.

Henrietta sat down on the bed, lifted her chin, and composed her face like a meditating angel. She really was intensely fond of Hester, and the worried look was such a terribly bad sign.

'Look here, Hester!' she said. 'Shall I come down to Markbury with you? *I* don't mind, if you'd like me to.'

'My dear girl,' cried Hester in desperation, 'what earthly use do you think that would be?'

'Well, I thought it might take the edge off the intimacy, if that's what worries you.'

Hester re-echoed with a hollow, mocking laugh.

'Don't be such a *child*, Henrietta, really!' she said.

And Hester set off alone, down to Wiltshire, where her Joe had just started a little farm, to get married on. After being in the artillery, he had got sick and tired of business: besides, Hester would never have gone into a little suburban villa. Every woman sees her home through a wedding ring. Hester had only taken a squint through her engagement ring, so far. But Ye Gods! not Golders Green, not even Harrow!

So Joe had built a little brown wooden bungalow – largely with his own hands: and at the back was a small stream with two willows, old ones. At the sides were brown sheds, and chicken-runs. There were pigs in a hog-proof wire fence, and two cows in a field, and a horse. Joe had thirty-odd acres, with only a youth to help him. But of course, there would be Hester.

It all looked very new and tidy. Joe was a worker. He too looked rather new and tidy, very healthy and pleased with himself. He didn't even see the 'worried look'. Or if he did, he only said:

'You're looking a bit fagged, Hester. Going up to the City takes it out of you, more than you know. You'll be another girl down here.'

'Shan't I just!' cried Hester.

She did like it, too! – the lots of white and yellow hens, and the pigs so full of pep! And the yellow thin blades of willow leaves showering softly down at the back of her house from the leaning old trees. She liked it awfully: especially the yellow leaves on the earth.

She told Joe she thought it was all lovely, topping, fine! And he was awfully pleased. Certainly *he* looked fit enough.

The mother of the helping youth gave them dinner at half-past twelve. The afternoon was all sunshine and little jobs to do, after she had dried the dishes for the mother of the youth.

'Not long now, miss, before you'll be cooking at this range: and a good little range it is.'

'Not long now, no!' echoed Hester, in the hot little wooden kitchen, that was over-heated from the range.

The woman departed. After tea, the youth also departed and Joe and Hester shut up the chickens and the pigs. It was nightfall. Hester went in and made the supper, feeling somehow a bit of a fool, and Joe made a fire in the living-room, he feeling rather important and luscious.

He and Hester would be alone in the bungalow, till the youth appeared next morning. Six months ago, Hester would have enjoyed it. They were so perfectly comfortable together, he and she. They had been friends, and his family and hers had been friends for years, donkey's years. He was a perfectly decent boy, and there would never have been anything messy to fear from him. Nor from herself. Ye Gods, no!

But now, alas, since she had promised to marry him, he had made the wretched mistake of falling 'in love' with her. He had never been that way before. And if she had known he would get this way now, she would have said decidedly: Let us remain friends, Joe, for this sort of thing is a come-down. Once he started cuddling and petting, she couldn't stand him. Yet she felt she ought to. She imagined she even ought to like it. Though where the *ought* came from, she could not see.

'I'm afraid, Hester,' he said sadly, 'you're not in love with me as I am with you.'

'Hang it all!' she cried. 'If I'm not, you ought to be jolly well thankful, that's all I've got to say.'

Which double-barrelled remark he heard, but did not register. He never liked looking anything in the very pin-point middle of the eye. He just left it, and left all her feelings comfortably in the dark. Comfortably for him, that is.

He was extemely competent at motor-cars and farming and all that sort of thing. And surely she, Hester, was as complicated as a motor-car! Surely she had as many subtle little valves and magnetos and accelerators and all the rest of it, to her make-up! If only he would try to handle *her* as carefully as he handled his car! She needed starting, as badly as ever any automobile did. Even if a car had a self-starter, the man had to give it the right twist. Hester felt she would need a lot of cranking up, if ever she was to start off on the matrimonial road with Joe. And he, the fool, just sat in a motionless car and pretended he was making heaven knows how many miles an hour.

This evening she felt really desperate. She had been quite all right doing things with him, during the afternoon, about the place. Then she liked being with him. But now that it was evening and they were alone, the stupid little room, the cosy fire, Joe, Joe's pipe, and Joe's smug sort of hypocritical face, all was just too much for her.

'Come and sit here, dear,' said Joe persuasively, patting the sofa at his side. And she, because she believed a *nice* girl would have been only too delighted to go and sit 'there', went and sat beside him. But she was boiling. What cheek! What cheek of him even to have a sofa! She loathed the vulgarity of sofas.

She endured his arm round her waist, and a certain pressure of his biceps which she presumed was cuddling. He had carefully knocked his pipe out. But she thought how smug and silly his face looked, all its natural frankness and straight-forwardness had gone. How ridiculous of him to stroke the back of her neck! How idiotic he was, trying to be lovey-dovey! She wondered what sort of sweet nothings Lord Byron, for example, had murmured to his various ladies. Surely not so blithering, not so incompetent! And how monstrous of him, to kiss her like that.

'I'd infinitely rather you'd play to me, Joe,' she snapped.

'You don't want me to play to you to-night, do you, dear?' he said.

'Why not to-night? I'd love to hear some Tchaikowsky, something to stir me up a bit.'

He rose obediently and went to the piano. He played quite well. She listened. And Tchaikowsky might have stirred her up all right. The music itself, that is. If she hadn't been so desperately aware that Joe's love-making, if you can call it such, became more absolutely impossible after the sound of the music.

'That was fine!' she said. 'Now do me my favourite nocturne.'

While he concentrated on the fingering, she slipped out of the house.

Oh! she gasped a sigh of relief to be in the cool October air. The darkness was dim. In the west was a half moon freshly shining, and all the air was motionless, dimness lay like a haze on the earth.

Hester shook her hair, and strode away from the bungalow, which was a perfect little drum, re-echoing to her favourite nocturne. She simply rushed to get out of ear-shot.

Ah! the lovely night! She tossed her short hair again, and felt like Mazeppa's horse, about to dash away into the infinite. Though the infinite was only a field belonging to the next farm. But Hester felt herself seething in the soft moonlight. Oh! to rush away over the edge of the beyond! if the beyond, like Joe's bread-knife, did have an edge to it. 'I know I'm an idiot,' she said to herself. But that didn't take away the wild surge of her limbs. Oh! If there were only some other solution, instead of Joe and his spooning. Yes, SPOONING! The word made her lose the last shred of her self-respect, but she said it aloud.

There was, however, a bunch of strange horses in this field, so she made her way cautiously back through Joe's fence. It was just like him, to have such a little place that you couldn't get away from the sound of his piano, without trespassing on somebody else's ground.

As she drew near the bungalow, however, the drumming of Joe's piano suddenly ceased. Oh, Heaven! She looked wildly round. An old willow leaned over the stream. She stretched, crouching, and with the quickness of a long cat, climbed up into the net of cool-bladed foliage.

She had scarcely shuffled and settled into a tolerable position when he came round the corner of the house and into the moonlight, looking for her. How dare he look for her! She kept as still as a bat among the leaves, watching him as he sauntered with erect, tiresomely manly figure and lifted head, staring round in the darkness. He looked for once very ineffectual, insignificant, and at a loss. Where was his supposed male magic? Why was he so slow and unequal to the situation?

There! He was calling softly and self-consciously: 'Hester! Hester! Where have you put yourself?'

He was angry really. Hester kept still in her tree, trying not to fidget. She had not the faintest intention of answering him. He might as well have been on another planet. He sauntered vaguely and unhappily out of sight.

Then she had a qualm. 'Really, my girl, it's a bit thick, the way you treat him! Poor old Joe!'

Immediately something began to hum inside her: 'I hear those tender voices calling Poor Old Joe!'

Nevertheless, she didn't want to go indoors to spend the evening *tête-à-tête* – my word! – with him.

'Of course it's absurd to think I could possibly fall in love like that. I would rather fall into one of his pig-troughs. It's so frightfully common. As a matter of fact, it's just a proof that he doesn't love me.'

This thought went through her like a bullet. 'The very fact of his being in love with me proves that he doesn't love me. No man that loved a woman could be in love with her like that. It's so insulting to her.'

She immediately began to cry, and fumbling in her sleeve for her hanky, she nearly fell out of the tree. Which brought her to her senses.

In the obscure distance she saw him returning to the house, and she felt bitter. 'Why did he start all this mess? I never wanted to marry anybody, and I certainly never bargained for anybody falling in love with me. Now I'm miserable, and I feel abnormal. Because the majority of girls must like this in-love business, or men wouldn't do it. And

607

the majority must be normal. So I'm abnormal, and I'm up a tree. I loathe myself. As for Joe, he's spoilt all there was between us, and he expects me to marry him on the strength of it. It's perfectly sickening! What a mess life is. How I loathe messes!'

She immediately shed a few more tears, in the course of which she heard the door of the bungalow shut with something of a bang. He had gone indoors, and he was going to be righteously offended. A new misgiving came over her.

The willow tree was uncomfortable. The air was cold and damp. If she caught another chill she'd probably snuffle all winter long. She saw the lamplight coming from the window of the bungalow, and she said 'Damn!' which meant, in her case, that she was feeling bad.

She slid down out of the tree, and scratched her arm and probably damaged one of her nicest pair of stockings. 'Oh, hang!' she said with emphasis, preparing to go into the bungalow and have it out with poor old Joe. 'I will *not* call him Poor Old Joe!'

At that moment she heard a motor-car slow down in the lane, and there came a low, cautious toot from a hooter. Headlights shone at a standstill near Joe's new iron gate.

'The cheek of it! The unbearable cheek of it! There's that young Henrietta come down on me!'

She flew along Joe's cinder-drive like a Mænad.

'Hello, Hester!' came Henrietta's young voice, coolly floating from the obscurity of the car. 'How's everything?'

'What cheek!' cried Hester. 'What amazing cheek!' She leaned on Joe's iron gate and panted.

'How's everything?' repeated Henrietta's voice blandly.

'What do you mean by it?' demamded Hester, still panting.

'Now, my girl, don't go off at a tangent! We weren't coming in unless you came out. You needn't think we want to put our noses in your affairs. We're going down to camp on Bonamy. Isn't the weather too divine!'

Bonamy was Joe's pal, also an old artillery man, who had set up a 'farm' about a mile farther along the land. Joe was by no means a Robinson Crusoe in his bungalow.

'Who are you, anyway?' demanded Hester.

'Same old birds,' said Donald, from the driver's seat. Donald was Joe's brother. Henrietta was sitting in front, next to him.

'Same as ever,' said Teddy, poking his head out of the car. Teddy was a second cousin.

'Well,' said Hester, sort of climbing down. 'I suppose you may as well come in, now you *are* here. Have you eaten?'

'Eaten, yes,' said Donald. 'But we aren't coming in this trip, Hester; don't you fret.'

'Why not?' flashed Hester, up in arms.

''Fraid of brother Joe,' said Donald.

'Besides, Hester,' said Henrietta anxiously, 'you know you don't want us.'

'Henrietta, don't be a fool!' flashed Hester.

'*Well*, Hester —!' remonstrated the pained Henrietta.

'Come on in, and no more nonsense!' said Hester.

'Not this trip, Hester,' said Donald.

'No, sir!' said Teddy.

'But what idiots you all are! Why not?' cried Hester.

''Fraid of our elder brother,' said Donald.

'All right,' said Hester. 'Then I'll come along with you.'

She hastily opened the gate.

'Shall I just have a peep? I'm pining to see the house,' said Henrietta, climbing with a long leg over the door of the car.

The night was now dark, the moon had sunk. The two girls crunched in silence along the cinder track to the house.

'You'd say, if you'd rather I didn't come in – or if Joe'd rather,' said Henrietta anxiously. She was very much disturbed in her young mind, and hoped for a clue. Hester walked on without answering. Henrietta laid her hand on her sister's arm. Hester shook it off, saying:

'My dear Henrietta, do be normal!'

And she rushed up the three steps to the door, which she flung open, displaying the lamp-lit living-room, Joe in an arm-chair by the low fire, his back to the door. He did not turn round.

'Here's Henrietta!' cried Hester, in a tone which meant: *'How's that?'*

He got up and faced round, his brown eyes in his stiff face very angry.

'How did *you* get here?' he asked rudely.

'Came in a car,' said young Henrietta, from her Age of Innocence.

'With Donald and Teddy – they're just outside the gate,' said Hester. 'The old gang!'

'Coming in?' asked Joe, with greater anger in his voice.

'I suppose you'll go out and invite them,' said Hester.

Joe said nothing, just stood like a block.

'I expect you'll think it's awful of me to come intruding,' said Henrietta meekly. 'We're just going on to Bonamy's.' She gazed innocently round the room. 'But it's an adorable little place, awfully good taste in a cottagey sort of way. I like it awfully. Can I warm my hands?'

Joe moved from in front of the fire. He was in his slippers. Henrietta dangled her long red hands, red from the night air, before the grate.

'I'll rush right away again,' she said.

'Oh-h,' drawled Hester curiously. 'Don't do that!'

'Yes, I must. Donald and Teddy are waiting.'

The door stood wide open, the headlights of the car could be seen in the lane.

'Oh-h!' Again that curious drawl from Hester. 'I'll tell them you're staying the night with me. I can do with a bit of company.'

Joe looked at her.

'What's the game?' he said.

'No game at all! Only now Tatty's come, she may as well stay.'

'Tatty' was the rather infrequent abbreviation of 'Henrietta'.

'Oh, but Hester!' said Henrietta. 'I'm going on to Bonamy's with Donald and Teddy.'

'Not if I want you to stay here!' said Hester.

Henrietta looked all surprised, resigned helplessness.

'What's the game?' repeated Joe. 'Had you fixed up to come down here to-night?'

'No, Joe, really!' said Henrietta, with earnest innocence. 'I hadn't the faintest idea of such a thing, till Donald suggested it, at four o'clock this afternoon. Only the weather was too perfectly divine, we had to go out somewhere, so we thought we'd descend on Bonamy. I hope *he* won't be frightfully put out as well.'

'And if we had arranged it, it wouldn't have been a crime,' struck in Hester. 'And, anyway, now you're here you might as well all camp here.'

'Oh no, Hester! I know Donald will never come inside the gate. He was angry with me for making him stop, and it was I who tooted. It wasn't him, it was me. The curiosity of Eve, I suppose. Anyhow, I've put my foot in it, as usual. So now I'd better clear out as fast as I can. Good night!'

She gathered her coat round her with one arm and moved vaguely to the door.

'In that case, I'll come along with you,' said Hester.

'But Hester!' cried Henrietta. And she looked inquiringly at Joe.

'I know as little as you do,' he said, 'what's going on.'

His face was wooden and angry, Henrietta could make nothing of him.

'Hester!' cried Henrietta. 'Do be sensible! What's gone wrong! Why don't you at least *explain*, and give everybody a chance! Talk about being normal! – you're always flinging it at *me*!'

There was a dramatic silence.

'What's happened?' Henrietta insisted, her eyes very bright and distressed, her manner showing that she was determined to be sensible.

'Nothing, of course!' mocked Hester.

'Do *you* know, Joe?' said Henrietta, like another Portia, turning very sympathetically to the man.

For a moment Joe thought how much nicer Henrietta was than her sister.

'I only know she asked me to play the piano, and then she dodged out of the house. Since then, her steering-gear's been out of order.'

'Ha-ha-ha!' laughed Hester falsely and melodramatically. 'I like that. I like my dodging out of the house! I went for a breath of fresh fresh air. I should like to know whose steering-gear is out of order, talking about my dodging out of the house!'

'You dodged out of the house,' said Joe.

'Oh, did I? And why should I, pray?'

'I suppose you have your own reasons.'

'I have too. And very good reasons.'

There was a moment of stupefied amazement. . . . Joe and Hester had known each other so well, for such a long time. And now look at them!

'But why did you, Hester?' asked Henrietta, in her most breathless, naïve fashion.

'Why did I what?'

There was a low toot from the motor-car in the lane.

'They're calling me! Good-bye!' cried Henrietta, wrapping her coat round her and turning decisively to the door.

'If you go, my girl, I'm coming with you,' said Hester.

'But why?' cried Henrietta in amazement. The horn tooted again. She opened the door and called into the night:

'Half a minute!' Then she closed the door again, softly, and turned once more in her amazement to Hester.

'But why, Hester?'

Hester's eyes almost squinted with exasperation. She could hardly bear even to glance at the wooden and angry Joe.

611

'Why?'

'Why?' came the soft reiteration of Henrietta's question.

All the attention focused on Hester, but Hester was a sealed book.

'Why?'

'She doesn't know herself,' said Joe, seeing a loop-hole.

Out rang Hester's crazy and melodramatic laugh.

'Oh, doesn't she!' Her face flew into sudden strange fury. 'Well, if you want to know, I absolutely *can't stand* your making love to me, if that's what you call the business.'

Henrietta let go the door-handle and sank weakly into a chair.

The worst had come to the worst. Joe's face became purple, then slowly paled to yellow.

'Then,' said Henrietta in a hollow voice, 'you can't marry him.'

'I couldn't possibly marry him if he kept on being *in love* with me.' She spoke the two words with almost snarling emphasis.

'And you couldn't possibly marry him if he *wasn't*,' said the guardian angel, Henrietta.

'Why not,' cried Hester. 'I could stand him all right till he started being in love with me. Now, he's simply out of the question.'

There was a pause, out of which came Henrietta's:

'After all, Hester, a man's *supposed* to be in love with the woman he wants to marry.'

'Then he'd better keep it to himself, that's all I've got to say.'

There was a pause. Joe, silent as ever, looked more wooden and sheepishly angry.

'But Hester! Hasn't a man *got* to be in love with you —?'

'Not with me! You've not had it to put up with, my girl.'

Henrietta sighed helplessly.

'Then you can't marry him, that's obvious. What an awful pity!'

A pause.

'Nothing can be so perfectly humiliating as a man making love to you,' said Hester. 'I *loathe* it.'

'Perhaps it's because it's the wrong man,' said Henrietta sadly, with a glance at the wooden and sheepish Joe.

'I don't believe I could stand that sort of thing, with *any* man. Henrietta, do you know what it is, being stroked and cuddled? It's too perfectly awful and ridiculous.'

'Yes!' said Henrietta, musing sadly. 'As if one were a perfectly priceless meat-pie, and the dog licked it tenderly before he gobbled it up. It *is* rather sickening, I agree.'

'And what's so awful, a perfectly decent man will go and get that way. Nothing is so awful as a man who has fallen in love,' said Hester.

'I know what you mean, Hester. So doggy!' said Henrietta sadly.

The motor-horn tooted exasperatedly. Henrietta rose like a Portia who has been a failure. She opened the door and suddenly yelled fiercely into the night:

'Go on without me. I'll walk. Don't wait.'

'How long will you be?' came a voice.

'I don't know. If I want to come, I'll walk,' she yelled.

'Come back for you in an hour.'

'Right,' she shrieked, and slammed the door in their distant faces. Then she sat down dejectedly, in the silence. She was going to stand by Hester. That *fool*, Joe, standing there like a mutton-head!

They heard the car start, and retreat down the lane.

'Men are awful!' said Henrietta dejectedly.

'Anyhow, you're mistaken,' said Joe with sudden venom to Hester. 'I'm not in love with you, Miss Clever.'

The two women looked at him as if he were Lazarus risen.

'And I never was in love with you, that way,' he added, his brown eyes burning with a strange fire of self-conscious shame and anger, and naked passion.

'Well, what a liar you must be then. That's all I can say!' replied Hester coldly.

'Do you mean,' said young Henrietta acidly, 'that you put it all on?'

'I thought she expected it of me,' he said, with a nasty little smile that simply paralysed the two young women. If he had turned into a boa-constrictor, they would not have been more amazed. That sneering little smile! Their good-natured Joe!

'I thought it was expected of me,' he repeated, jeering.

Hester was horrified.

'Oh, but how beastly of you to do it!' cried Henrietta to him.

'And what a lie!' cried Hester. 'He liked it.'

'Do you think he did, Hester?' said Henrietta.

'I liked it in a way,' he said impudently. 'But I shouldn't have liked it, if I thought she didn't.'

Hester flung out her arms.

'Henrietta,' she cried, 'why can't we kill him?'

'I wish we could,' said Henrietta.

'What are you to do when you know a girl's rather strict, and you like

613

her for it – and you're not going to be married for a month – and – and you – and you've got to get over the interval somehow – and what else does Rudolf Valentino do for you? – you like *him* —'

'He's dead, poor dear. But I loathed him, *really*,' said Hester.

'You didn't seem to,' said he.

'Well, anyhow, you aren't Rudolf Valentino, and I loathe *you* in the rôle.'

'You won't get a chance again. I loathe *you* altogether.'

'And I'm extremely relieved to hear it, my boy.'

There was a lengthy pause, after which Henrietta said with decision:

'Well, that's that! Will you come along to Bonamy's with me, Hester, or shall I stay here with you?'

'*I* don't care, my girl,' said Hester with bravado.

'Neither do I care what you do,' said he. 'But I call it pretty rotten of you, not to tell me right out, at first.'

'I thought it was real with you then, and I didn't want to hurt you,' said Hester.

'You look as if you didn't want to hurt me,' he said.

'Oh, now,' she said, 'since it was all pretence, it doesn't matter.'

'I should say it doesn't,' he retorted.

There was a silence. The clock, which was intended to be their family clock, ticked rather hastily.

'Anyway,' he said, 'I consider you've let me down.'

'I like that!' she cried, 'considering what you've played off on me!'

He looked her straight in the eye. They knew each other so well.

Why had he tried that silly love-making game on her? It was a betrayal of their simple intimacy. He saw it plainly, and repented.

And she saw the honest, patient love for her in his eyes, and the queer, quiet central desire. It was the first time she had seen it, that quiet, patient, central desire of a young man who has suffered during his youth, and seeks now almost with the slowness of age. A hot flush went over her heart. She felt herself responding to him.

'What have you decided, Hester?' said Henrietta.

'I'll stay with Joe, after all,' said Hester.

'Very well,' said Henrietta. 'And I'll go along to Bonamy's.' She opened the door quietly, and was gone.

Joe and Hester looked at one another from a distance.

'I'm sorry, Hester,' said he.

'You know, Joe,' she said, 'I don't mind what you do, if you love me *really*.'

GLAD GHOSTS

I KNEW Carlotta Fell in the early days before the war. Then she was escaping into art, and was just 'Fell'. That was at our famous but uninspired school of art, the Thwaite, where I myself was diligently murdering my talent. At the Thwaite they always gave Carlotta the Still-life prizes. She accepted them calmly, as one of our conquerors, but the rest of the students felt vicious about it. They called it buttering the laurels, because Carlotta was Hon., and her father a well-known peer.

She was by way of being a beauty too. Her family was not rich, yet she had come into five hundred a year of her own, when she was eighteen; and that, to us, was an enormity. Then she appeared in the fashionable papers, affecting to be wistful, with pearls, slanting her eyes. Then she went and did another of her beastly still-lives, a cactus-in-a-pot.

At the Thwaite, being snobs, we were proud of her too. She showed off a bit, it is true, playing bird of paradise among the pigeons. At the same time, she *was* thrilled to be with us, and out of her own set. Her wistfulness and yearning 'for something else' was absolutely genuine. Yet she was not going to hobnob with us either, at least not indiscriminately.

She was ambitious, in a vague way. She wanted to coruscate, somehow or other. She had a family of clever and 'distinguished' uncles, who had flattered her. What then?

Her cactuses-in-a-pot were admirable. But even she didn't expect them to start a revolution. Perhaps she would rather glow in the wide if dirty skies of life than in the somewhat remote and unsatisfactory ether of Art.

She and I were 'friends' in a bare, stark, but real sense. I was poor, but I didn't really care. She didn't really care either. Whereas I did care about some passionate vision which, I could feel, lay embedded in the half-dead body of this life. The quick body within the dead. I could *feel* it. And I wanted to get at it, if only for myself.

She didn't know what I was after. Yet she could feel that I was It, and, being an aristocrat of the Kingdom of It, as well as the realm of

Great Britain, she was loyal – loyal to me because of It, the quick body which I imagined within the dead.

Still, we never had much to do with one another. I had no money. She never wanted to introduce me to her own people. I didn't want it either. Sometimes we had lunch together, sometimes we went to a theatre, or we drove in the country, in some car that belonged to neither of us. We never flirted or talked love. I don't think she wanted it, any more than I did. She wanted to marry into her own surroundings, and I knew she was of too frail a paste to face my future.

Now I come to think of it, she was always a bit sad when we were together. Perhaps she looked over seas she would never cross. She belonged finally, fatally, to her own class. Yet I think she hated them. When she was in a group of people who talked 'smart', titles and *beau monde* and all that, her rather short nose would turn up, her wide mouth press into discontent, and a languor of bored irritation come even over her broad shoulders. Bored irritation, and a loathing of climbers, a loathing of the ladder altogether. She hated her own class: yet it was also sacrosanct to her. She disliked, even to me, mentioning the titles of her friends. Yet the very hurried resentment with which she said, when I asked her: Who is it —?

'Lady Nithsdale, Lord Staines – old friends of my mother,' proved that the coronet was wedged into her brow, like a ring of iron grown into a tree.

She had another kind of reverence for a true artist: perhaps more genuine, perhaps not; anyhow, more free and easy.

She and I had a curious understanding in common: an inkling, perhaps, of the unborn body of life hidden within the body of this half-death which we call life: and hence a tacit hostility to the commonplace world, its inert laws. We were rather like two soldiers on a secret mission into enemy country. Life, and people, was an enemy country to us both. But she would never declare herself.

She always came to me to find out what I thought, particularly in a moral issue. Profoundly, fretfully discontented with the conventional moral standards, she didn't know how to take a stand of her own. So she came to me. She had to try to get her own feelings straightened out. In that she showed her old British fibre. I told her what, as a young man, I thought: and usually she was resentful. She did so want to be conventional. She would even act quite perversely, in her determination to be conventional. But she always had to come back to me, to ask me again. She depended on me morally. Even when she disagreed with me, it soothed her, and restored her to know my point of view. Yet she disagreed with me.

We had then a curious abstract intimacy, that went very deep, yet showed no obvious contact. Perhaps I was the only person in the world with whom she felt, in her uneasy self, at home, at peace. And to me, she was always of my own *intrinsic* sort, of my own species. Most people are just another species to me. They might as well be turkeys.

But she would always *act* according to the conventions of her class, even perversely. And I knew it.

So, just before the war she married Lord Lathkill. She was twenty-one. I did not see her till war was declared; then she asked me to lunch with her and her husband, in town. He was an officer in a Guards regiment, and happened to be in uniform, looking very handsome and well set-up, as if he expected to find the best of life served up to him for ever. He was very dark, with dark eyes and fine black hair, and a very beautiful, diffident voice, almost womanish in its slow, delicate inflections. He seemed pleased and flattered at having Carlotta for a wife.

To me he was beautifully attentive, almost deferential, because I was poor, and of the other world, those poor devils of outsiders. I laughed at him a little, and laughed at Carlotta, who was a bit irritated by the gentle delicacy with which he treated me.

She was elated too. I remember her saying:

'We need war, don't you think? Don't you think men need the fight, to keep life chivalrous and put martial glamour into it?'

And I remember saying: 'I think we need some sort of fight; but my sort isn't the war sort.' It was August, we could take it lightly.

'What's your sort?' she asked quickly.

'I don't know: single-handed, anyhow,' I said, with a grin. Lord Lathkill made me feel like a lonely sansculotte, he was so completely unostentatious, so very willing to pay all the attention to me, and yet so subtly complacent, so unquestionably sure of his position. Whereas I was not a very sound earthenware pitcher which had already gone many times to the well.

He was not conceited, not half as *conceited* as I was. He was willing to leave me all the front of the stage, even with Carlotta. He felt so sure of some things, like a tortoise in a glittering, polished tortoise-shell that mirrors eternity. Yet he was not quite easy with me.

'You are Derbyshire?' I said to him, looking into his face. 'So am I! I was born in Derbyshire.'

He asked me with a gentle, uneasy sort of politeness, where? But he was a bit taken aback. And his dark eyes, brooding over me, had a sort of fear in them. At the centre they were hollow with a certain misgiving. He was so sure of *circumstances*, and not by any means sure of the man in the middle of the circumstances. Himself! Himself! That was already a ghost.

I felt that he saw in me something crude but real, and saw himself as something in its own way perfect, but quite unreal. Even his love for Carlotta, and his marriage, was a circumstance that was inwardly unreal to him. One could tell by the curious way in which he waited, before he spoke. And by the hollow look, almost a touch of madness, in his dark eyes, and in his soft, melancholy voice.

I could understand that she was fascinated by him. But God help him if ever circumstances went against him!

She had to see me again, a week later, to talk about him. So she asked me to the opera. She had a box, and we were alone, and the notorious Lady Perth was two boxes away. But this was one of Carlotta's conventional perverse little acts, with her husband in France. She only wanted to talk to me about him.

So she sat in the front of her box, leaning a little to the audience and talking sideways to me. Anyone would have known at once there was a *liaison* between us, how *dangereuse* they would never have guessed. For there, in the full view of the world – her world at least, not mine – she was talking sideways to me, saying in a hurried, yet stony voice:

'What do you think of Luke?'

She looked up at me heavily, with her sea-coloured eyes, waiting for my answer.

'He's tremendously charming,' I said, above the theatreful of faces.

'Yes, he's that!' she replied, in the flat, plangent voice she had when she was serious, like metal ringing flat, with a strange far-reaching vibration. 'Do you think he'll be happy?'

'*Be* happy!' I ejaculated. 'When, *be* happy?'

'With me,' she said, giving a sudden little snirt of laughter, like a schoolgirl, and looking up me shyly, mischievously, anxiously.

'If you make him,' I said, still casual.

'How can I make him?'

She said it with flat plangent earnestness. She was always like that, pushing me deeper in than I wanted to go.

'Be happy yourself, I suppose: and quite sure about it. And then *tell* him you're happy, and tell him he is, too, and he'll be it.'

'Must I do all that?' she said rapidly. 'Not otherwise?'

I knew I was frowning at her, and she was watching my frown.

'Probably not,' I said roughly. 'He'll never make up his mind about it himself.'

'How did you know?' she asked, as if it had been a mystery.

'I didn't. It only seems to me like that.'

'Seems to you like that,' she re-echoed, in that sad, clean monotone of finality, always like metal. I appreciate it in her, that she does not murmur or whisper. But I wished she left me alone, in that beastly theatre.

She was wearing emeralds, on her snow-white skin, and leaning forward gazing fixedly down into the auditorium, as a crystal-gazer into a crystal. Heaven knows if she saw all those little facets of faces and plastrons. As for me, I knew that, like a sansculotte, I should never be king till breeches were off.

'I had terrible work to make him marry me,' she said, in her swift, clear, low tones.

'Why?'

'He was frightfully in love with me. *He is!* But he thinks he's unlucky. . . .'

'Unlucky, how? In cards or in love?' I mocked.

'In both,' she said briefly, with sudden cold resentment at my flippancy. There was over her eyes a glaze of fear. 'It's in their family.'

'What did you say to him?' I asked, rather laboured feeling the dead weight.

'I promised to have luck for two,' she said. 'And war was declared a fortnight later.'

'Ah, well!' I said. 'That's the world's luck, not yours.'

'Quite!' she said.

There was a pause.

'Is his family supposed to be unlucky?' I asked.

'The Worths? Terribly! They really are!'

It was interval, and the box door had opened. Carlotta always had her eye, a good half of it at least, on the external happenings. She rose, like a reigning beauty – which she wasn't, and never became – to speak to Lady Perth, and out of spite, did not introduce me.

Carlotta and Lord Lathkill came, perhaps a year later, to visit us when we were in a cottage in Derbyshire, and he was home on leave. She was going to have a child, and was slow, and seemed depressed. He was vague, charming, talking about the country and the history of the lead-mines. But the two of them seemed vague, as if they never got anywhere.

The last time I saw them was when the war was over, and I was leaving England. They were alone at dinner, save for me. He was still haggard, with a wound in the throat. But he said he would soon be well. His slow, beautiful voice was a bit husky now. And his velvety eyes were hardened, haggard, but there was weariness, emptiness in the hardness.

I was poorer than ever, and felt a little weary myself. Carlotta was struggling with his silent emptiness. Since the war, the melancholy fixity of his eyes was more noticeable, the fear at the centre was almost monomania. She was wilting and losing her beauty.

There were twins in the house. After dinner, we went straight up to look at them, to the night nursery. They were two boys, with their father's fine dark hair, both of them.

He had put out his cigar, and leaned over the cots, gazing in silence. The nurse, dark-faced and faithful, drew back. Carlotta glanced at her children; but more helplessly, she gazed at him.

'Bonny children! Bonny boys, aren't they, nurse?' I said softly.

'Yes, sir!' she said quickly. 'They are!'

'Ever think I'd have twins, roistering twins?' said Carlotta, looking at me.

'I never did,' said I.

'Ask Luke whether it's bad luck or bad management,' she said, with that schoolgirl's snirt of laughter, looking up apprehensively at her husband.

'Oh, I!' he said, turning suddenly and speaking loud, in his wounded voice. 'I call it amazing good luck, myself! Don't know what other people think about it.' Yet he had the fine, wincing fear in his body, of an injured dog.

After that, for years I did not see her again. I heard she had a baby girl. Then a catastrophe happened: both the twins were killed in a motor-car accident in America, motoring with their aunt.

I learned the news late, and did not write to Carlotta. What could I say?

A few months later, crowning disaster, the baby girl died of some sudden illness. The Lathkill ill-luck seemed to be working surely.

Poor Carlotta! I had no further news of her, only I heard that she and Lord Lathkill were both living in seclusion, with his mother, at the place in Derbyshire.

When circumstances brought me to England, I debated within myself, whether I should write or not to Carlotta. At last I sent a note to the London address.

I had a reply from the country: 'So glad you are within reach again! When will you come and see us?'

I was not very keen on going to Riddings. After all, it was Lord Lathkill's place, and Lady Lathkill, his mother, was old and of the old school. And I always something of a sansculotte, who will only be king when breeches are off.

'Come to town,' I wrote, 'and let us have lunch together.'

She came. She looked older, and pain had drawn horizontal lines across her face.

'You're not a bit different,' she said to me.

'And you're only a little bit,' I said.

'Am I!' she replied, in a deadened, melancholic voice. 'Perhaps! I suppose while we live we've got to live. What do you think?'

'Yes, I think it. To be the living dead, that's awful.'

'Quite!' she said, with terrible finality.

'How is Lord Lathkill?' I asked.

'Oh,' she said. 'It's finished him, as far as living is concerned. But he's very willing for *me* to live.'

'And you, are you willing?' I said.

She looked up into my eyes, strangely.

'I'm not sure,' she said. 'I need help. What do you think about it?'

'Oh, God, live if you can!'

'Even take help?' she said, with her strange involved simplicity.

'Ah, certainly.'

'Would you recommend it?'

'Why, yes! You are a young thing —' I began.

'Won't you come down to Riddings?' she said quickly.

'And Lord Lathkill – and his mother?' I asked.

'They want you.'

'Do you want me to come?'

'I want you to, yes! Will you?'

'Why, yes, if you want me.'

'When, then?'

'When you wish.'

'Do you mean it?'

'Why, of course.'

'You're not afraid of the Lathkill ill-luck?'

'*I!*' I exclaimed in amazement; such amazement, that she gave her schoolgirl snirt of laughter.

'Very well, then,' she said. 'Monday? Does that suit you?'

We made arrangements, and I saw her off at the station.

I knew Riddings, Lord Lathkill's place, from the outside. It was an old Derbyshire stone house, at the end of the village of Middleton: a house with three sharp gables, set back not very far from the high road, but with a gloomy moor for a park behind.

Monday was a dark day over the Derbyshire hills. The green hills were dark, dark green, the stone fences seemed almost black. Even the little railway station, deep in the green, cleft hollow, was of stone, and dark and cold, and seemed in the underworld.

Lord Lathkill was at the station. He was wearing spectacles, and his brown eyes stared strangely. His black hair fell lank over his forehead.

'I'm so awfully glad you've come,' he said. 'It is cheering Carlotta up immensely.'

Me, as a man myself, he hardly seemed to notice. I was something which had arrived, and was expected. Otherwise he had an odd, unnatural briskness of manner.

'I hope I shan't disturb your mother, Lady Lathkill,' I said as he tucked me up in the car.

'On the contrary,' he sang, in his slow voice, 'she is looking forward to your coming as much as we both are. Oh no, don't look on mother as too old-fashioned, she's not so at all. She's tremendously up to date in art and literature and that kind of thing. She has her leaning towards the uncanny – spiritualism, and that kind of thing – nowadays, but Carlotta and I think that if it gives her an interest, all well and good.'

He tucked me up most carefully in the rugs, and the servant put a foot-warmer at my feet.

'Derbyshire, you know, is a cold county,' continued Lord Lathkill, 'especially among the hills.'

'It's a very dark county,' I said.

'Yes, I suppose it is, to one coming from the tropics. We, of course, don't notice it; we rather like it.'

He seemed curiously smaller, shrunken, and his rather long cheeks were sallow. His manner, however, was much more cheerful, almost communicative. But he talked, as it were, to the faceless air, not really to me. I wasn't really there at all. He was talking to himself. And when once he looked at me, his brown eyes had a hollow look, like gaps with nothing in them except a haggard, hollow fear. He was gazing through the windows of nothingness, to see if I were really there.

It was dark when we got to Riddings. The house had no door in the front, and only two windows upstairs were lit. It did not seem very hospitable. We entered at the side, and a very silent manservant took my things.

We went upstairs in silence, in the dead-seeming house. Carlotta had heard us, and was at the top of the stairs. She was already dressed; her long white arms were bare; she had something glittering on a dull green dress.

'I was so afraid you wouldn't come,' she said, in a dulled voice, as she gave me her hand. She seemed as if she would begin to cry. But of course she wouldn't. The corridor, dark-panelled and with blue carpet on the floor, receded dimly, with a certain dreary gloom. A servant was diminishing in the distance, with my bags, silently. There was a curious, unpleasant sense of the fixity of the materials of the house, the obscene triumph of dead matter. Yet the place was warm, central-heated.

Carlotta pulled herself together and said, dulled:

'Would you care to speak to my mother-in-law before you go to your room? She would like it.'

We entered a small drawing-room abruptly. I saw the water-colours on the walls and a white-haired lady in black bending round to look at the door as she rose cautiously.

'This is Mr. Morier, Mother-in-law,' said Carlotta, in her dull, rather quick way, 'on his way to his room.'

The dowager Lady Lathkill came a few steps forward, leaning from heavy hips, and gave me her hand. Her crest of hair was snow white, and she had curious blue eyes, fixed, with a tiny dot of a pupil, peering from her pink, soft-skinned face of an old and well-preserved woman. She wore a lace fichu. The upper part of her body was moderately slim, leaning forward slightly from her heavy black-silk hips.

She murmured something to me, staring at me fixedly for a long time, but as a bird does, with shrewd, cold far-distant sight. As a hawk, perhaps, looks shrewdly far down, in his search. Then, muttering, she presented to me the other two people in the room: a tall, short-faced, swarthy young woman with the hint of a black moustache; and a plump man in a dinner-jacket, rather bald and ruddy, with a little grey moustache, but yellow under the eyes. He was Colonel Hale.

They all seemed awkward, as if I had interrupted them at a séance. I didn't know what to say: they were utter strangers to me.

'Better come and choose your room, then,' said Carlotta, and I bowed dumbly, following her out of the room. The old Lady Lathkill still stood planted on her heavy hips, looking half round after us with her ferret's blue eyes. She had hardly any eyebrows, but they were arched high up on her pink, soft forehead, under the crest of icily white hair. She had never emerged for a second from the remote place where she unyieldingly kept herself.

Carlotta, Lord Lathkill and I tramped in silence down the corridor and round a bend. We could none of us get a word out. As he suddenly rather violently flung open a door at the end of the wing, he said, turning round to me with a resentful, hang-dog air:

'We did you the honour of offering you our ghost room. It doesn't look much, but it's our equivalent for a royal apartment.'

It was a good-sized room with faded, red-painted panelling showing remains of gilt, and the usual big, old mahogany furniture, and a big pinky-faded carpet with big, whitish, faded roses. A bright fire was burning in the stone fire-place.

'Why?' said I, looking at the stretches of the faded, once handsome carpet.

'Why what?' said Lord Lathkill. 'Why did we offer you this room?'

'Yes! No! Why is it your equivalent for a royal apartment?'

'Oh, because our ghost is as rare as sovereignty in her visits, and twice as welcome. Her gifts are infinitely more worth having.'

'What sort of gifts?'

'The family fortune. She invariably restores the family fortune. That's why we put you here, to tempt her.'

'What temptation should *I* be? – especially to restoring your family fortunes. I didn't think they needed it, anyhow.'

'Well!' he hesitated. 'Not exactly in money: we can manage modestly that way; but in everything else but money —'

There was a pause. I was thinking of Carlotta's 'luck for two'. Poor Carlotta! She looked worn now. Especially her chin looked worn, showing the edge of the jaw. She had sat herself down in a chair by the fire, and put her feet on the stone fender, and was leaning forward, screening her face with her hand, still careful of her complexion. I could see her broad, white shoulders, showing the shoulder-blades, as she leaned forward, beneath her dress. But it was as if some bitterness had soaked all the life out of her, and she was only weary, or inert, drained of her feelings. It grieved me, and the thought passed through my mind that a man should take her in his arms and cherish her body, and start her flame again. If she would let him, which was doubtful.

Her courage was fallen, in her body; only her spirit fought on. She would have to restore the body of her life, and only a living body could do it.

'What *about* your ghost?' I said to him. 'Is she really ghastly?'

'Not at all!' he said. 'She's supposed to be lovely. But I have no experience, and I don't know anybody who has. We hoped you'd come, though, and tempt her. Mother had a message about you, you know.'

'No, I didn't know.'

'Oh yes! When you were still in Africa. The medium said: "There is a man in Africa. I can only see M, a double M. He is thinking of your family. It would be good if he entered your family." Mother was awfully puzzled, but Carlotta said "Mark Morier" at once.'

'That's not why I asked you down,' said Carlotta quickly, looking round, shading her eyes with her hand as she looked at me.

I laughed, saying nothing.

'But, of course,' continued Lord Lathkill, 'you *needn't* have this room. We have another one ready as well. Would you like to see it?'

'How does your ghost manifest herself?' I said, parrying.

'Well, I hardly know. She seems to be a very grateful *presence*, and that's about all I do know. She was apparently quite *persona grata* to everyone she visited. *Gratissima*, apparently!'

'*Benissimo!*' said I.

A servant appeared in the doorway, murmuring something I could not hear. Everybody in the house, except Carlotta and Lord Lathkill, seemed to murmur under their breath.

'What's she say?' I asked.

'If you will stay in this room? I told her you might like a room on the front. And if you'll take a bath?' said Carlotta.

'Yes!' said I. And Carlotta repeated to the maidservant.

'And for heaven's sake speak to me loudly,' said I to that elderly correct female in her starched collar, in the doorway.

'Very good, sir!' she piped up. 'And shall I make the bath hot or medium?'

'Hot!' said I, like a cannon-shot.

'Very good, sir!' she piped up again, and her elderly eyes twinkled as she turned and disappeared.

Carlotta laughed, and I sighed.

We were six at table. The pink Colonel with the yellow creases under his blue eyes sat opposite me, like an old boy with a liver. Next him sat Lady Lathkill, watching from her distance. Her pink, soft old face, naked-seeming, with its pin-point blue eyes, was a real modern witch-face.

Next me, on my left, was the dark young woman, whose slim, swarthy arms had an indiscernible down on them. She had a blackish neck, and her expressionless yellow-brown eyes said nothing, under level black brows. She was inaccessible. I made some remarks, without result. Then I said:

'I didn't hear your name when Lady Lathkill introduced me to you.'

Her yellow-brown eyes stared into mine for some moments before she said:

'Mrs Hale!' Then she glanced across the table. 'Colonel Hale is my husband.'

My face must have signalled my surprise. She stared into my eyes very curiously, with a significance I could not grasp, a long, hard stare. I looked at the bald, pink head of the Colonel bent over his soup, and I returned to my own soup.

'Did you have a good time in London?' said Carlotta.

'No,' said I. 'It was dismal.'

'Not a good word to say for it?'

'Not one.'

'No nice people?'

'Not my sort of nice.'

'What's your sort of nice?' she asked, with a little laugh.

The other people were stone. It was like talking into a chasm.

'Ah! If I knew myself, I'd look for them! But not sentimental, with a lot of soppy emotions on top, and nasty ones underneath.'

'Who are you thinking of?' Carlotta looked up at me as the man brought the fish. She had a crushed sort of roguishness. The other diners were images.

'I? Nobody. Just everybody. No, I think I was thinking of the Obelisk Memorial Service.'

'Did you go to it?'

'No, but I fell into it.'

'Wasn't it moving?'

'Rhubarb, senna, that kind of moving!'

She gave a little laugh, looking up into my face, from the fish.

'What was wrong with it?'

I noticed that the Colonel and Lady Lathkill each had a little dish of rice, no fish, and that they were served second – oh, humility! – and that neither took the white wine. No, they had no wine-glasses. The remoteness gathered about them, like the snows on Everest. The dowager peered across at me occasionally, like a white ermine of the snow, and she had that cold air about her, of being good, and containing a secret of goodness: remotely, ponderously, fixedly knowing better. And I, with my chatter, was one of those fabulous fleas that are said to hop upon glaciers.

'Wrong with it? *It* was wrong, all wrong. In the rain, a soppy crowd, with soppy bare heads, soppy emotions, soppy chrysanthemums and prickly laurustinus! A steam of wet mob-emotions! Ah, no, it shouldn't be allowed.'

Carlotta's face had fallen. She again could feel death in her bowels, the kind of death the war signifies.

'Wouldn't you have us honour the dead?' came Lady Lathkill's secretive voice across at me, as if a white ermine had barked.

'Honour the dead!' My mind opened in amazement. 'Do you think they'd be honoured?'

I put the question in all sincerity.

'They would understand the *intention* was to honour them,' came her reply.

I felt ashamed.

'If I were dead, would I be honoured if a great, steamy wet crowd came after me with soppy chrysanthemums and prickly laurustinus? Ugh! I'd run to the nethermost ends of Hades. Lord, how I'd run from them!'

The manservant gave us roast mutton, and Lady Lathkill and the Colonel chestnuts in sauce. Then he poured the burgundy. It was good wine. The pseudo-conversation was interrupted.

Lady Lathkill ate in silence, like an ermine in the snow, feeding on his prey. Sometimes she looked round the table, her blue eyes peering fixedly, completely uncommunicative. She was very watchful to see that we were all properly attended to; 'The currant jelly for Mr. Morier,' she would murmur, as if it were her table. Lord Lathkill, next her, ate in complete absence. Sometimes she murmured to him, and he murmured back, but I never could hear what they said. The Colonel swallowed the chestnuts in dejection, as if all were weary duty to him now. I put it down to his liver.

It was an awful dinner-party. I never could hear a word anybody said, except Carlotta. They all let their words die in their throats, as if the larynx were the coffin of sound.

Carlotta tried to keep her end up, the cheerful hostess sort of thing. But Lady Lathkill somehow, in silence and apparent humility, had stolen the authority that goes with hostess, and she clung on to it grimly, like a white ermine sucking a rabbit. Carlotta kept glancing miserably at me, to see what I thought. I didn't think anything. I just felt frozen within the tomb. And I drank the good, good warm burgundy.

'Mr. Morier's glass!' murmured Lady Lathkill, and her blue eyes with their black pin-points rested on mine a moment.

'Awfully nice to drink good burgundy!' said I pleasantly.

She bowed her head slightly, and murmured something inaudible.

'I beg your pardon?'

'Very glad you like it!' she repeated, with distaste at having to say it again, out loud.

'Yes, I do. It's good.'

Mrs. Hale, who had sat tall and erect and alert, like a black she-fox, never making a sound, looked round at me to see what sort of specimen I was. She was just a bit intrigued.

'Yes, thanks,' came a musical murmur from Lord Lathkill. 'I think I *will* take some more.'

The man, who had hesitated, filled his glass.

'I'm awfully sorry I can't drink wine,' said Carlotta absently. 'It has the wrong effect on me.'

'I should say it has the wrong effect on everybody,' said the Colonel, with an uneasy attempt to be there. 'But some people like the effect, and some don't.'

I looked at him in wonder. Why was he chipping in? He looked as if he'd liked the effect well enough, in his day.

'Oh no!' retorted Carlotta coldly. 'The effect on different people is quite different.'

She closed with finality, and a further frost fell on the table.

'Quite so,' began the Colonel, trying, since he'd gone off the deep end, to keep afloat.

But Carlotta turned abruptly to me.

'Why is it, do you think, that the effect is so different on different people?'

'And on different occasions,' said I, grinning through my burgundy. 'Do you know what they say? They say that alcohol, if it has an effect on your psyche, takes you back to old states of consciousness, and old reactions. But some people it doesn't stimulate at all, there is only a nervous reaction of repulsion.'

'There's certainly a nervous reaction of repulsion in me,' said Carlotta.

'As there is in all higher natures,' murmured Lady Lathkill.

'Dogs hate whisky,' said I.

'That's quite right,' said the Colonel. 'Scared of it!'

'I've often thought,' said I, 'about those old states of consciousness. It's supposed to be an awful retrogression, reverting back to them. Myself, my desire to go onwards takes me back a little.'

'Where to?' said Carlotta.

'Oh, I don't know! To where you feel it a bit warm, and like smashing the glasses, don't you know?

> *'J'avons bien bu et nous boirons!*
> *Cassons les verres nous les payerons!*
> *Compagnons! Voyez vous bien!*
> *Voyez vous bien!*
> *Voyez! voyez! voyez vous bien*
> *Que les d'moiselles sont belles*
> *Où nous allons!'*

I had the effrontery to sing this verse of an old soldier's song while Lady Lathkill was finishing her celery and nut salad. I sang it quite nicely, in a natty, well-balanced little voice, smiling all over my face meanwhile. The servant, as he went round for Lady Lathkill's plate, furtively fetched a look at me. *Look!* thought I. *You chicken that's come untrussed!*

The partridges had gone, we had swallowed the *flan,* and were at dessert. They had accepted my song in complete silence. Even Carlotta! My *flan* had gone down in one gulp, like an oyster.

'You're quite right!' said Lord Lathkill, amid the squashing of walnuts. 'I mean the state of mind of a Viking, shall we say, or of a Catiline conspirator, might be frightfully good for us, if we could recapture it.'

'A Viking!' said I, stupefied. And Carlotta gave a wild snirt of laughter.

'Why not a Viking?' he asked in all innocence.

'A Viking!' I repeated, and swallowed my port. Then I looked round at my black-browed neighbour.

'Why do you never say anything?' I asked.

'What should I say?' she replied, frightened at the thought.

I was finished. I gazed into my port as if expecting the ultimate revelation.

Lady Lathkill rustled her finger-tips in the finger-bowl, and laid down her napkin decisively. The Colonel, old buck, rose at once to draw back her chair. *Place aux hommes!* I bowed to my neighbour, Mrs. Hale, a most disconcerting bow, and she made a circuit to get by me.

'You won't be awfully long?' said Carlotta, looking at me with her slow, hazel-green eyes, between mischief and wistfulness and utter depression.

Lady Lathkill steered heavily past me as if I didn't exist, perching rather forward, with her crest of white hair, from her big hips. She seemed abstracted, concentrated on something, as she went.

I closed the door, and turned to the men.

> *'Dans la première auberge*
> *J'eus b'en bu!*

sang I in a little voice.

'Quite right,' said Lord Lathkill. 'You're quite right.'

And we sent the port round.

'This house,' I said, 'needs a sort of spring-cleaning.'

'You're quite right,' said Lord Lathkill.

'There's a bit of a dead smell!' said I. 'We need Bacchus, and Eros, to sweeten it up, to freshen it.'

'You think Bacchus and Eros?' said Lord Lathkill, with complete seriousness; as if one might have telephoned for them.

'In the best sense,' said I. As if we were going to get them from Fortnum and Mason's, at least.

'What exactly is the best sense?' asked Lord Lathkill.

'Ah! The flame of life! There's a dead smell here.'

The Colonel fingered his glass with thick, inert fingers uneasily.

'Do you think so?' he said, looking up at me heavily.

'Don't you?'

He gazed at me with blank, glazed blue eyes, that had deathly yellow stains underneath. Something was wrong with him, some sort of breakdown. He should have been a fat, healthy, jolly old boy. Not very old either: probably not quite sixty. But with this collapse on him, he seemed, somehow, to smell.

'You know,' he said, staring at me with a sort of gruesome challenge, then looking down at his wine, 'there's more things than we're aware of happening to us!' He looked up at me again, shutting his full lips under his little grey moustache, and gazing with a glazed defiance.

'Quite!' said I.

He continued to gaze at me with glazed, gruesome defiance.

'Ha!' He made a sudden movement, and seemed to break up, collapse and become brokenly natural. 'There, you've said it. I married my wife when I was a kid of twenty.'

'Mrs. Hale?' I exclaimed.

'Not this one' – he jerked his head towards the door – 'my first wife.' There was a pause; he looked at me with shamed eyes, then turned his wine-glass round and his head dropped. Staring at his twisting glass, he continued: 'I married her when I was twenty, and she was twenty-eight. You might say, she married me. Well, there it was! We had three children – I've got three married daughters – and we got on all right. I suppose she mothered me, in a way. And I never thought a thing. I was content enough, wasn't tied to her apron-strings, and she never asked questions. She was always fond of me, and I took it for granted. I took it for granted. Even when she died – I was away in Salonika – I took it for granted, if you understand me. It was part of the rest of things – war – life – death. I knew I should feel lonely when I got back. Well, then I got buried – shell dropped, and the dug-out caved in – and that queered me. They sent me home. And the minute I saw the Lizard light – it was evening when we got up out of the Bay – I realised that Lucy had been waiting for me. I could feel her there, at my side, more plainly than I feel you now. And do you know, at that moment I woke up to her, and she made an awful impression on me. She seemed, if you get me, tremendously powerful, important; everything else dwindled away. There was the Lizard light blinking a long way off, and that meant home. And all the rest was my wife, Lucy: as if her skirts filled all the darkness. In a way, I was frightened; but that was because I couldn't quite get myself into line. I felt: *Good God! I never knew her!* And she was this tremendous thing! I felt like a child, and as weak as a kitten. And, believe me or not, from that day to this she's never left me. I know quite well she can hear what I'm saying. But she'll let me tell you. I knew that at dinner-time.'

'But what made you marry again?' I said.

'She made me!' He went a trifle yellow on his cheek-bones. 'I could feel her telling me: *"Marry! Marry!"* Lady Lathkill had messages from her too; she was her great friend in life. I didn't think of marrying. But Lady Lathkill had the same message, that I must marry. Then a medium described the girl in detail: my present wife. I knew her at once, friend of my daughters. After that the messages became more insistent, waking me three and four times in the night. Lady Lathkill urged me to propose, and I did it, and was accepted. My present wife was just twenty-eight, the age Lucy had been —'

'How long ago did you marry the present Mrs. Hale?'

'A little over a year ago. Well, I thought I had done what was required of me. But directly after the wedding, such a state of terror came over me – perfectly unreasonable – I became almost unconscious. My present wife asked me if I was ill, and I said I was. We got to Paris. I felt I was was dying. But I said I was going out to see a doctor, and I found myself kneeling in a church. Then I found peace – and Lucy. She had her arms round me, and I was like a child at peace. I must have knelt there for a couple of hours in Lucy's arms. I *never* felt like that when she was alive: why, I couldn't stand that sort of thing! It's all come on after – after — And now, I daren't offend Lucy's spirit. If I do, I suffer tortures till I've made peace again, till she folds me in her arms. Then I can live. But she won't let me go near the present Mrs. Hale. I – I – I daren't go near her.'

He looked up at me with fear, and shame, and shameful secrecy, and a sort of gloating showing in his unmanned blue eyes. He had been talking as if in his sleep.

'Why did your dead wife urge you to marry again?' I said.

'I don't know,' he replied. 'I don't know. She was older than I was, and all the cleverness was on her side. She was a very clever woman, and I was never much in the intellectual line myself. I just took it for granted she liked me. She never showed jealousy, but I think now, perhaps she was jealous all the time, and kept it under. I don't know. I think she never felt quite straight about having married me. It seems like that. As if she had something on her mind. Do you know, while she was alive, I never gave it a thought. And now I'm aware of nothing else but her. It's as if her spirit wanted to live in my body, or at any rate – I don't know —'

His blue eyes were glazed, almost fishy, with fear and gloating shame. He had a short nose, and full, self-indulgent lips, and a once-comedy chin. Eternally a careless boy of thirteen. But now, care had got him in decay.

'And what does your present wife say?' I asked.

He poured himself some more wine.

'Why,' he replied, 'except for her, I shouldn't mind so much. She says nothing. Lady Lathkill has explained everything to her, and she agrees that – that – a spirit from the other side is more important than mere pleasure – you know what I mean. Lady Lathkill says that this is a preparation for my next incarnation, when I am going to serve Woman, and help Her to take Her place.'

He looked up again, trying to be proud in his shame.

'Well, what a damned curious story!' exclaimed Lord Lathkill. 'Mother's idea for herself – she had it in a message too – is that she is coming on earth the next time to save the animals from the cruelty of man. That's why she hates meat at table, or anything that has to be killed.'

'And does Lady Lathkill encourage you in this business with your dead wife?' said I.

'Yes. She helps me. When I get as you might say at cross-purposes with Lucy – with Lucy's spirit, that is – Lady Lathkill helps to put it right between us. Then I'm all right, when I know I'm loved.'

He looked at me stealthily, cunningly.

'Then you're all wrong,' said I, 'surely.'

'And do you mean to say,' put in Lord Lathkill, 'that you don't live with the present Mrs. Hale at all? Do you mean to say you never *have* lived with her?'

'I've got a higher claim on me,' said the unhappy Colonel.

'My God!' said Lord Lathkill.

I looked in amazement: the sort of chap who picks up a woman and has a good time with her for a week, then goes home as nice as pie, and now look at him! It was obvious that he had a terror of his black-browed new wife, as well as of Lucy's spirit. A devil and a deep blue sea with a vengenace!

'A damned curious story!' mused Lord Lathkill. 'I'm not so sure I like it. Something's wrong somewhere. We shall have to go upstairs.'

'Wrong!' said I. 'Why, Colonel, don't you turn round and quarrel with the spirit of your first wife, fatally and finally, and get rid of her?'

The Colonel looked at me, still diminished and afraid, but perking up a bit, as we rose from table.

'How would you go about it?' he said.

'I'd just face her, wherever she seemed to be, and say: *"Lucy, go to blazes!"* '

Lord Lathkill burst into a loud laugh, then was suddenly silent as the door noiselessly opened, and the dowager's white hair and pointed, uncanny eyes peered in, then entered.

'I think I left my papers in here, Luke,' she murmured.

'Yes, mother. There they are. We're just coming up.'

'Take your time.'

He held the door, and ducking forward, she went out again, clutching some papers. The Colonel had blenched yellow on his cheek-bones.

We went upstairs to the small drawing-room.

'You were a long time,' said Carlotta, looking in all our faces. 'Hope the coffee's not cold. We'll have fresh if it is.'

She poured out, and Mrs. Hale carried the cups. The dark young woman thrust out her straight, dusky arm, offering me sugar, and gazing at me with her unchanging, yellow-brown eyes. I looked back at her, and being clairvoyant in this house, was conscious of the curves of her erect body, the sparse black hairs there would be on her strong-skinned dusky thighs. She was a woman of thirty, and she had had a great dread lest she should never marry. Now she was as if mesmerised.

'What do you do usually in the evenings?' I said.

She turned to me as if startled, as she nearly always did when addressed.

'We do nothing,' she replied. 'Talk; and sometimes Lady Lathkill reads.'

'What does she read?'

'About spiritualism.'

'Sounds pretty dull.'

She looked at me again, but she did not answer. It was difficult to get anything out of her. She put up no fight, only remained in the same swarthy, passive, negative resistance. For a moment I wondered that no men made love to her: it was obvious they didn't. But then, modern young men are accustomed to being attracted, flattered, impressed: they expect an effort to please. And Mrs. Hale made none: didn't know how. Which for me was her mystery. She was passive, static, locked up in a resistant passivity that had fire beneath it.

Lord Lathkill came and sat by us. The Colonel's confession had had an effect on him.

'I'm afraid,' he said to Mrs. Hale, 'you have a thin time here.'

'Why?' she asked.

'Oh, there is so little to amuse you. Do you like to dance?'

'Yes,' she said.

'Well, then,' he said, 'let us go downstairs and dance to the Victrola. There are four of us. You'll come, of course?' he said to me.

Then he turned to his mother.

'Mother, we shall go down to the morning-room and dance. Will you come? Will you, Colonel?'

The dowager gazed at her son.

'I will come and look on,' she said.

'And I will play the pianola, if you like,' volunteered the Colonel. We went down and pushed aside the chintz chairs and the rugs. Lady Lathkill sat in a chair, the Colonel worked away at the pianola. I danced with Carlotta, Lord Lathkill with Mrs. Hale.

A quiet soothing came over me, dancing with Carlotta. She was very still and remote, and she hardly looked at me. Yet the touch of her was wonderful, like a flower that yields itself to the morning. Her warm, silken shoulder was soft and grateful under my hand, as if it knew me with that second knowledge which is part of one's childhood, and which so rarely blossoms again in manhood and womanhood. It was as if we had known each other perfectly, as children, and now, as man and woman met in the full, further sympathy. Perhaps, in modern people, only after long suffering and defeat, can the naked intuition break free between woman and man.

She, I knew, let the strain and the tension of all her life depart from her then, leaving her nakedly still, within my arm. And I only wanted to be with her, to have her in my touch.

Yet after the second dance she looked at me, and suggested that she should dance with her husband. So I found myself with the strong, passive shoulder of Mrs. Hale under my hand, and her inert hand in mine, as I looked down at her dusky, dirty-looking neck – she wisely avoided powder. The duskiness of her mesmerised body made me see the faint dark sheen of her thighs, with intermittent black hairs. It was as if they shone through the silk of her mauve dress, like the limbs of a half-wild animal that is locked up in its own helpless dumb winter, a prisoner.

She knew, with the heavy intuition of her sort, that I glimpsed her crude among the bushes, and felt her attraction. But she kept looking away over my shoulder, with her yellow eyes, towards Lord Lathkill.

Myself or him, it was a question of which got there first. But she preferred him. Only for some things she would rather it were me.

Luke had changed curiously. His body seemed to have come alive, in the dark cloth of his evening suit; his eyes had a devil-may-care light in them, his long cheeks a touch of scarlet, and his black hair fell loose over his forehead. He had again some of that Guardsman's sense of well-being and claim to the best in life, which I had noticed the first time I saw him. But now it was a little more florid, defiant, with a touch of madness.

He looked down at Carlotta with uncanny kindness and affection. Yet he was glad to hand her over to me. He, too, was afraid of her: as if with her his bad luck had worked. Whereas, in a throb of crude brutality, he felt it would not work with the dark young woman. So, he handed Carlotta over to me with relief, as if, with me, she would be safe from the doom of his bad luck. And he, with the other woman, would be safe from it too. For the other woman was outside the circle.

I was glad to have Carlotta again: to have that inexpressible delicate and complete quiet of the two of us, resting my heart in a balance now at last physical as well as spiritual. Till now, it had always been a fragmentary thing. Now, for this hour at least, it was whole, a soft, complete, physical flow, and a unison deeper even than childhood.

As she danced she shivered slightly, and I seemed to smell frost in the air. The Colonel, too, was not keeping the rhythm.

'Has it turned colder?' I said.

'I wonder,' she answered, looking up at me with a slow beseeching. Why, and for what was she beseeching me? I pressed my hand a little closer, and her small breasts seemed to speak to me. The Colonel recovered the rhythm again.

But at the end of the dance she shivered again, and it seemed to me I too was chilled.

'Has it suddenly turned colder?' I said, going to the radiator. It was quite hot.

'It seems to me it has,' said Lord Lathkill in a queer voice.

The Colonel was sitting abjectly on the music-stool, as if broken.

'Shall we have another? Shall we try a tango?' said Lord Lathkill. 'As much of it as we can manage?'

'I – I —' the Colonel began, turning round on the seat, his face yellow. 'I'm not sure —'

Carlotta shivered. The frost seemed to touch my vitals. Mrs. Hale stood stiff, like a pillar of brown rock-salt, staring at her husband.

'We had better leave off,' murmured Lady Lathkill, rising.

Then she did an extraordinary thing. She lifted her face, staring to the other side, and said suddenly, in a clear, cruel sort of voice:

'Are you here, Lucy?'

She was speaking across to the spirits. Deep inside me leaped a jump of laughter. I wanted to howl with laughter. Then instantly I went inert again. The chill gloom seemed to deepen suddenly in the room, everybody was overcome. On the piano-seat the Colonel sat yellow and huddled, with a terrible hang-dog look of guilt on his face. There was a silence, in which the cold seemed to creak. Then came again the peculiar bell-like ringing of Lady Lathkill's voice:

'Are you here? What do you wish us to do?'

A dead and ghastly silence, in which we all remained transfixed. Then from somewhere came two slow thuds, and a sound of drapery moving. The Colonel, with mad fear in his eyes, looked round at the uncurtained windows, and crouched on his seat.

'We must leave this room,' said Lady Lathkill.

'I'll tell you what, mother,' said Lord Lathkill curiously; 'you and the Colonel go up, and we'll just turn on the Victrola.'

That was almost uncanny of him. For myself, the cold effluence of these people had paralysed me. Now I began to rally. I felt that Lord Lathkill was sane, it was these other people who were mad.

Again from somewhere indefinite came two slow thuds.

'We must leave this room,' repeated Lady Lathkill in monotony.

'All right, mother. You go. I'll just turn on the Victrola.'

And Lord Lathkill strode across the room. In another moment the monstrous barking howl of the opening of a jazz tune, an event far more extraordinary than thuds, poured from the unmoving bit of furniture called a Victrola.

Lady Lathkill silently departed. The Colonel got to his feet.

'I wouldn't go if I were you, Colonel,' said I. 'Why not dance? I'll look on this time.'

I felt as if I were resisting a rushing, cold, dark current.

Lord Lathkill was already dancing with Mrs. Hale, skating delicately along, with a certain smile of obstinacy, secrecy, and excitement kindled on his face. Carlotta went up quietly to the Colonel, and put her hand on his broad shoulder. He let himself be moved into the dance, but he had no heart in it.

There came a heavy crash, out of the distance. The Colonel stopped as if shot: in another moment he would go down on his knees. And his face was terrible. It was obvious he really felt another presence, other than ours, blotting us out. The room seemed dree and cold. It was heavy work, bearing up.

The Colonel's lips were moving, but no sound came forth. Then, absolutely oblivious of us, he went out of the room.

The Victrola had run down. Lord Lathkill went to wind it up again, saying:

'I suppose mother knocked over a piece of furniture.'

But we were all of us depressed, in abject depression.

'Isn't it awful!' Carlotta said to me, looking up beseechingly.

'Abominable!' said I.

'What do you think there is in it?'

'God knows. The only thing is to stop it, as one does hysteria. It's on a par with hysteria.'

'Quite,' she said.

Lord Lathkill was dancing, and smiling very curiously down into his partner's face. The Victrola was at its loudest.

Carlotta and I looked at one another, with hardly the heart to start again. The house felt hollow and gruesome. One wanted to get out, to get away from the cold, uncanny blight which filled the air.

'Oh, I say, keep the ball rolling,' called Lord Lathkill.

'Come,' I said to Carlotta.

Even then she hung back a little. If she had not suffered, and lost so much, she would have gone upstairs at once to struggle in the silent wrestling of wills with her mother-in-law. Even now, *that* particular fight drew her, almost the strongest. But I took her hand.

'Come,' I said. 'Let us dance it down. We'll roll the ball the opposite way.'

She danced with me, but she was absent, unwilling. The empty gloom of the house, the sense of cold, and of deadening opposition, pressed us down. I was looking back over my life, and thinking how the cold weight of an unliving spirit was slowly crushing all warmth and vitality out of everything. Even Carlotta herself had gone numb again, cold and resistant even to me. The thing seemed to happen wholesale in her.

'One has to choose to live,' I said, dancing on.

But I was powerless. With a woman, when her spirit goes inert in opposition, a man can do nothing. I felt my life-flow sinking in my body.

'This house is awfully depressing,' I said to her, as we mechanically danced. 'Why don't you *do* something? Why don't you get out of this tangle? Why don't you break it?'

'How?' she said.

I looked down at her, wondering why she was suddenly hostile.

'You needn't fight,' I said. 'You needn't fight it. Don't get tangled up in it. Just side-step, on to another ground.'

She made a pause of impatience before she replied:

'I don't see where I am to side-step to, precisely.'

'You do,' said I. 'A little while ago, you were warm and unfolded and good. Now you are shut up and prickly, in the cold. You needn't be. Why not stay warm?'

'It's nothing I do,' she said coldly.

'It is. Stay warm to me. I am here. Why clutch in a tug-of-war with Lady Lathkill?'

'Do I clutch in a tug-of-war with my mother-in-law?'

'You know you do.'

She looked up at me, with a faint little shadow of guilt and beseeching, but with a *moue* of cold obstinacy dominant.

'Let's have done,' said I.

And in cold silence we sat side by side on the lounge.

The other two danced on. They at any rate were in unison. One could see from the swing of their limbs. Mrs. Hale's yellow-brown eyes looked at me every time she came round.

'Why does she look at me?' I said.

'I can't imagine,' said Carlotta, with a cold grimace.

'I'd better go upstairs and see what's happening,' she said, suddenly rising and disappearing in a breath.

Why should she go? Why should she rush off to the battle of wills with her mother-in-law? In such a battle, while one has any life to lose, one can only lose it. There is nothing positively to be done, but to withdraw out of the hateful tension.

The music ran down. Lord Lathkill stopped the Victrola.

'Carlotta gone?' he said.

'Apparently.'

'Why didn't you stop her?'

'Wild horses wouldn't stop her.'

He lifted his hand with a mocking gesture of helplessness.

'The lady loves her will,' he said. 'Would you like to dance?'

I looked at Mrs. Hale.

'No,' I said. 'I won't butt in. I'll play the pianola. The Victrola's a brute.'

I hardly noticed the passage of time. Whether the others danced or

639

not, I played, and was unconscious of almost everything. In the midst of one rattling piece, Lord Lathkill touched my arm.

'Listen to Carlotta. She says closing time,' he said, in his old musical voice, but with the sardonic ring of war in it now.

Carlotta stood with her arms dangling, looking like a penitent schoolgirl.

'The Colonel has gone to bed. He hasn't been able to manage a reconciliation with Lucy,' she said. 'My mother-in-law thinks we ought to let him try to sleep.'

Carlotta's slow eyes rested on mine, questioning, penitent – or so I imagined – and somewhat sphinx-like.

'Why, of course,' said Lord Lathkill. 'I wish him all the sleep in the world.'

Mrs. Hale said never a word.

'Is mother retiring too?' asked Luke.

'I think so.'

'Ah! then supposing we up and look at the supper-tray.'

We found Lady Lathkill mixing herself some nightcap brew over a spirit-lamp: something milky and excessively harmless. She stood at the sideboard stirring her potations, and hardly noticed us. When she had finished she sat down with her steaming cup.

'Colonel Hale all right, mother?' said Luke, looking across at her.

The dowager, under her uplift of white hair, stared back at her son. There was an eye-battle for some moments, during which he maintained his arch, debonair ease, just a bit crazy.

'No,' said Lady Lathkill, 'he is in great trouble.'

'Ah!' replied her son. 'Awful pity we can't do anything for him. But if flesh and blood can't help him, I'm afraid I'm a dud. Suppose he didn't mind our dancing? Frightfully good for *us*! We've been forgetting that we're flesh and blood, mother.'

He took another whisky and soda, and gave me one. And in a paralysing silence Lady Lathkill sipped her hot brew, Luke and I sipped our whiskies, the young woman ate a little sandwich. We all preserved an extraordinary aplomb, and an obstinate silence.

It was Lady Lathkill who broke it. She seemed to be sinking downwards, crouching into herself like a skulking animal.

'I suppose,' she said, 'we shall all go to bed?'

'You go mother. We'll come along in a moment.'

She went, and for some time we four sat silent. The room seemed to become pleasanter, the air was more grateful.

'Look here,' said Lord Lathkill at last. 'What do you think of this ghost business?'

'I?' said I. 'I don't like the atmosphere it produces. There may be ghosts, and spirits, and all that. The dead must be somewhere; there's no such place as nowhere. But they don't affect me particularly. Do they you?'

'Well,' he said, 'no, not directly. Indirectly I suppose it does.'

'I think it makes a horribly depressing atmosphere, spiritualism,' said I. 'I want to kick.'

'Exactly! And ought one?' he asked in his terribly sane-seeming way.

This made me laugh. I knew what he was up to.

'I don't know what you mean by *ought*,' said I. 'If I really want to kick, if I know I can't stand a thing, I kick. Who's going to authorise me, if my own genuine feeling doesn't?'

'Quite,' he said, staring at me like an owl, with a fixed, meditative stare.

'Do you know,' he said, 'I suddenly thought at dinner-time, what corpses we all were, sitting eating our dinners. I thought it when I saw you look at those little Jerusalem artichoke things in a white sauce. Suddenly it struck me, you were alive and twinkling, and we were all bodily dead. Bodily dead, if you understand. Quite alive in other directions, but bodily dead. And whether we ate vegetarian or meat made no difference. We were bodily dead.'

'Ah, with a slap in the face,' said I, 'we come to life! You or I or anybody.'

'I *do* understand poor Lucy,' said Luke. 'Don't you? She forgot to be flesh and blood while she was alive, and now she can't forgive herself, nor the Colonel. That must be pretty rough, you know, not to realise it till you're dead, and you haven't, so to speak, anything left to go on. I mean, it's awfully important to be flesh and blood.'

He looked so solemnly at us, we three broke simultaneously into an uneasy laugh.

'Oh, but I *do* mean it,' he said. 'I've only realised how very extraordinary it is to be a man of flesh and blood, alive. It seems so ordinary, in comparison, to be dead, and merely spirit. That seems so commonplace. But fancy having a living face, and arms, and thighs. Oh, my God, I'm glad I've realised in time!'

He caught Mrs. Hale's hand, and pressed her dusky arm against his body.

'Oh, but if one had died without realising it!' he cried. 'Think how ghastly for Jesus, when He was risen and wasn't touchable! How very awful, to have to say *Noli me tangere!* Ah, touch me, touch me *alive!*'

He pressed Mrs. Hale's hand convulsively against his breast. The tears had already slowly gathered in Carlotta's eyes and were dropping on to her hands in her lap.

'Don't cry, Carlotta,' he said. 'Really, don't. We haven't killed one another. We're too decent, after all. We've almost become two spirits side by side. We've almost become two ghosts to one another, wrestling. Oh, but I want you to get back your body, even if I can't give it to you. I want my flesh and blood, Carlotta, and I want you to have yours. We've suffered so much the other way. And the children, it is as well they are dead. They were born of our will and our disembodiment. Oh, I feel like the Bible. Clothe me with flesh again, and wrap my bones with sinew, and let the fountain of blood cover me. My spirit is like a naked nerve on the air.'

Carlotta had ceased to weep. She sat with her head dropped, as if asleep. The rise and fall of her small, slack breasts was still heavy, but they were lifting on a heaving sea of rest. It was as if a slow, restful dawn were rising in her body, while she slept. So slack, so broken she sat, it occurred to me that in this crucifixion business the crucified does not put himself alone on the cross. The woman is nailed even more inexorably up, and crucified in the body even more cruelly.

It is a monstrous thought. But the deed is even more monstrous. Oh, Jesus, didn't you know that you couldn't be crucified alone? – that the two thieves crucified along with you were the two women, your wife and mother! You called them two thieves. But what would they call you, who had their women's bodies on the cross? The abominable trinity on Calvary!

I felt an infinite tenderness for my dear Carlotta. She could not yet be touched. But my soul streamed to her like warm blood. So she sat slack and drooped, as if broken. But she was not broken. It was only the great release.

Luke sat with the hand of the dark young woman pressed against his breast. His face was warm and fresh, but he too breathed heavily, and stared unseeing. Mrs. Hale sat at his side erect and mute. But she loved him, with erect, black-faced, remote power.

'Morier!' said Luke to me. 'If you can help Carlotta, you will, won't you? I can't do any more for her now. We are in mortal fear of each other.'

642

'As much as she'll let me,' said I, looking at her drooping figure, that was built on such a strong frame.

The fire rustled on the hearth as we sat in complete silence. How long it lasted I cannot say. Yet we were none of us startled when the door opened.

It was the Colonel, in a handsome brocade dressing-gown, looking worried.

Luke still held the dark young woman's hand clasped against his thigh. Mrs. Hale did not move.

'I thought you fellows might help me,' said the Colonel, in a worried voice, as he closed the door.

'What is wrong, Colonel?' said Luke.

The Colonel looked at him, looked at the clasped hands of Luke and the dark young woman, looked at me, looked at Carlotta, without changing his expression of anxiety, fear, and misery. He didn't care about us.

'I can't sleep,' he said. 'It's gone wrong again. My head feels as if there was a cold vacuum in it, and my heart beats, and something screws up inside me. I know it's Lucy. She hates me again. I can't stand it.'

He looked at us with eyes half-glazed, obsessed. His face seemed as if the flesh were breaking under the skin, decomposing.

'Perhaps, poor thing,' said Luke, whose madness seemed really sane this night, 'perhaps you hate *her*.'

Luke's strange concentration instantly made us feel a tension, as of hate, in the Colonel's body.

'I?' The Colonel looked up sharply, like a culprit. 'I! I wouldn't say that, if I were you.'

'Perhaps that's what's the matter,' said Luke, with mad, beautiful calm. 'Why can't you feel kindly towards her, poor thing! She must have been done out of a lot while she lived.'

It was as if he had one foot in life and one in death, and knew both sides. To us it was like madness.

'I – I!' stammered the Colonel; and his face was a study. Expression after expression moved across it: of fear, repudiation, dismay, anger, repulsion, bewilderment, guilt. 'I was good to her.'

'Ah, yes,' said Luke. 'Perhaps *you* were good to her. But was your body good to poor Lucy's body, poor dead thing!'

He seemed to be better acquainted with the ghost than with us.

The Colonel gazed blankly at Luke, and his eyes went up and down, up and down, up and down, up and down.

643

'My body!' he said blankly.

And he looked down amazedly at his little round stomach, under the silk gown, and his stout knee, in its blue-and-white pyjama.

'My body!' he repeated blankly.

'Yes,' said Luke. 'Don't you see, you may have been awfully good to her. But her poor woman's body, were you ever good to that?'

'She had everything she wanted. She had three of my children,' said the Colonel dazedly.

'Ah yes, that may easily be. But your body of a man, was it ever good to her body of a woman? That's the point. If you understand the marriage service: with my body I thee worship. That's the point. No getting away from it.'

The queerest of all accusing angels did Lord Lathkill make, as he sat there with the hand of the other man's wife clasped against his thigh. His face was fresh and naïve, and the dark eyes were bright with a clairvoyant candour, that was like madness, and perhaps was supreme sanity.

The Colonel was thinking back, and over his face a slow understanding was coming.

'It may be,' he said. 'It may be. Perhaps, that way, I despised her. It may be, it may be.'

'I know,' said Luke. 'As if she weren't worth noticing, what you did to her. Haven't I done it myself? And don't I know now, it's a horrible thing to do, to oneself as much as to her? Her poor ghost, that ached, and never had a real body! It's not so easy to worship with the body. Ah, if the Church taught us *that* sacrament: *with my body I thee worship!* that would easily make up for any honouring and obeying the woman might do. But that's why she haunts you. You ignored and disliked her body, and she was only a living ghost. Now she wails in the afterworld, like a still-wincing nerve.'

The Colonel hung his head, slowly pondering. Pondering with all his body. His young wife watched the sunken, bald head in a kind of stupor. His day seemed so far from her day. Carlotta had lifted her face; she was beautiful again, with the tender before-dawn freshness of a new understanding.

She was watching Luke, and it was obvious he was another man to her. The man she knew, the Luke who was her husband was gone, and this other strange, uncanny creature had taken his place. She was filled with wonder. Could one so change, as to become another creature entirely? Ah, if it were so! If she herself could cease to be! If that

644

woman who was married to Luke, married to him in an intimacy of misfortune that was like a horror, could only cease to be, and let a new, delicately-wild Carlotta take her place!

'It may be,' said the Colonel, lifting his head. 'It may be.' There seemed to come a relief over his soul, as he realised. 'I didn't worship her with my body. I think maybe I worshipped other women that way; but maybe I never did. But I thought I was good to her. And I thought she didn't want it.'

'It's no good thinking. We all want it,' asserted Luke. 'And before we die, we know it. I say, before we die. It may be after. But everybody wants it, let them say and do what they will. Don't you agree, Morier?'

I was startled when he spoke to me. I had been thinking of Carlotta: how she was looking like a girl again, as she used to look at the Thwaite, when she painted cactuses-in-a-pot. Only now, a certain rigidity of the will had left her, so that she looked even younger than when I first knew her, having now a virginal, flower-like *stillness* which she had not had then. I had always believed that people could be born again: if they would only let themselves.

'I'm sure they do,' I said to Luke.

But I was thinking, if people were born again, the old circumstances would not fit the new body.

'What about yourself, Luke?' said Carlotta abruptly.

'I!' he exclaimed, and the scarlet showed in his cheek. 'I! I'm not fit to be spoken about. I've been moaning like the ghost of disembodiment myself, ever since I became a man.'

The Colonel said never a word. He hardly listened. He was pondering, pondering. In this way, he, too, was a brave man.

'I have an idea what you mean,' he said. 'There's no denying it, I didn't like her body. And now, I suppose it's too late.'

He looked up bleakly: in a way, willing to be condemned, since he knew vaguely that something was wrong. Anything better than the blind torture.

'Oh, I don't know,' said Luke. 'Why don't you, even now, love her a little with your real heart? Poor disembodied thing! Why don't you take her to your warm heart, even now, and comfort her inside there? Why don't you be kind to her poor ghost, bodily?'

The Colonel did not answer. He was gazing fixedly at Luke. Then he turned, and dropped his head, alone in a deep silence. Then, deliberately, but not lifting his head, he pulled open his dressing-gown at the

645

breast, unbuttoned the top of his pyjama jacket, and sat perfectly still, his breast showing white and very pure, so much younger and purer than his averted face. He breathed with difficulty, his white breast rising irregularly. But in the deep isolation where he was, slowly a gentleness of compassion came over him, moulding his elderly features with strange freshness, and softening his blue eye with a look it had never had before. Something of the tremulous gentleness of a young bridegroom had come upon him, in spite of his baldness, his silvery little moustache, the weary marks of his face.

The passionate, compassionate soul stirred in him and was pure, his youth flowered over his face and eyes.

We sat very still, moved also in the spirit of compassion. There seemed a presence in the air, almost a smell of blossom, as if time had opened and gave off the perfume of spring. The Colonel gazed in silence into space, his smooth white chest, with the few dark hairs, open and rising and sinking with life.

Meanwhile his dark-faced young wife watched as if from afar. The youngness that was on him was not for her.

I knew that Lady Lathkill would come. I could feel her far off in her room, stirring and sending forth her rays. Swiftly I steeled myself to be in readiness. When the door opened I rose and walked across the room.

She entered with characteristic noiselessness, peering in round the door, with her crest of white hair, before she ventured bodily in. The Colonel looked at her swiftly, and swiftly covered his breast, holding his hand at his bosom, clutching the silk of his robe.

'I was afraid,' she murmured, 'that Colonel Hale might be in trouble.'

'No,' said I. 'We are all sitting very peacefully. There is no trouble.' Lord Lathkill also rose.

'No trouble at all, I assure you, mother!' he said.

Lady Lathkill glanced at us both, then turned heavily to the Colonel. 'She is unhappy to-night?' she asked.

The Colonel winced.

'No,' he said hurriedly. 'No, I don't think so.' He looked up at her with shy, wincing eyes.

'Tell me what I can do,' she said in a very low tone, bending towards him.

'Our ghost is walking to-night, mother,' said Lord Lathkill. 'Haven't you felt the air of spring, and smelt the plum-blossom? Don't you feel us all young? Our ghost is walking, to bring Lucy home. The Colonel's breast is quite extraordinary, white as plum-blossom, mother, younger-looking than mine, and he's already taken Lucy into his bosom, in his breast, where he breathes like the wind among trees. The Colonel's breast is white and extraordinarily beautiful, mother. I don't wonder poor Lucy yearned for it, to go home into it at last. It's like going into an orchard of plum-blossom for a ghost.'

His mother looked round at him, then back at the Colonel, who was still clutching his hand over his chest, as if protecting something.

'You see, I didn't understand where I'd been wrong,' he said, looking up at her imploringly. 'I never realised that it was my body which had not been good to her.'

Lady Lathkill curved sideways to watch him. But her power was gone. His face had come smooth with the tender glow of compassionate life, that flowers again. She could not get at him.

'It's no good, mother. You know our ghost is walking She's supposed to be absolutely like a crocus, if you know what I mean: harbinger of spring in the earth. So it says in my great-grandfather's diary: for she rises with silence like a crocus at the feet, and violets in the hollows of the heart come out. For she is of the feet and the hands, the thighs and breast, the face and the all-concealing belly, and her name is silent, but her odour is of spring, and her contact is the all-in-all.' He was quoting from his great-grandfather's diary, which only the sons of the family read. And as he quoted he rose curiously on his toes, and spread his fingers, bringing his hands together till the finger-tips touched. His father had done that before him, when he was deeply moved.

Lady Lathkill sat down heavily in the chair next the Colonel.

'How do you feel?' she asked him, in a secretive mutter.

He looked round at her, with the large blue eyes of candour.

'I never knew what was wrong,' he said, a little nervously. 'She only wanted to be looked after a bit, not to be a homeless, houseless ghost. It's all right! She's all right here.' He pressed his clutched hand on his breast. 'It's all right; it's all right. She'll be all right now.'

He rose, a little fantastic in his brocade gown, but once more manly, candid, and sober.

'With your permission,' he said, 'I will retire.' – He made a little bow. – 'I am glad you helped me. I didn't know – didn't know.'

But the change in him, and his secret wondering were so strong in him, he went out of the room scarcely being aware of us.

Lord Lathkill threw up his arms, and stretched quivering.

'Oh, pardon, pardon,' he said, seeming, as he stretched, quivering, to grow bigger and almost splendid, sending out rays of fire to the dark young woman. 'Oh, mother, thank you for my limbs, and my body! Oh, mother, thank you for my knees and my shoulders at this moment! Oh, mother, thank you that my body is straight and alive! Oh, mother, torrents of spring, torrents of spring, whoever said that?'

'Don't you forget yourself, my boy?' said his mother.

'Oh no, dear no! Oh, mother dear, a man has to be in love in his thighs, the way you ride a horse. Why don't we stay in love that way all our lives? Why do we turn into corpses with consciousness? Oh, mother of my body, thank you for my body, you strange woman with white hair! I don't know much about you, but my body came from you, so thank you, my dear. I shall think of you to-night!'

'Hadn't we better go?' she said, beginning to tremble.

'Why, yes,' he said, turning and looking strangely at the dark woman. 'Yes, let us go; let us go!'

Carlotta gazed at him, then, with strange, heavy, searching look, at me. I smiled to her, and she looked away. The dark young woman looked over her shoulder as she went out. Lady Lathkill hurried past her son, with head ducked. But still he laid his hand on her shoulder, and she stopped dead.

'Good night, mother; mother of my face and my thighs. Thank you for the night to come, dear mother of my body.'

She glanced up at him rapidly, nervously, then hurried away. He stared after her, then switched off the light.

'Funny old mother!' he said. 'I never realised before that she was the mother of my shoulders and my hips, as well as my brain. Mother of my thighs!'

He switched off some of the lights as we went, accompanying me to my room.

'You know,' he said, 'I can understand that the Colonel is happy, now the forlorn ghost of Lucy is comforted in his heart. After all, he married her! And she must be content at last: he has a beautiful chest, don't you think? Together they will sleep well. And then he will begin to live the life of the living again. How friendly the house feels to-night! But, after all, it is my old home. And the smell of plum-blossom – don't you notice it? It is our ghost, in silence like a crocus. There, your fire has died down! But it's a nice room! I hope our ghost will come to you. I think she will. Don't speak to her. It makes her go away.

648

She, too, is a ghost of silence. We talk far too much. But now I am going to be silent too, and a ghost of silence. Good night!'

He closed the door softly and was gone. And softly, in silence, I took off my things. I was thinking of Carlotta, and a little sadly, perhaps, because of the power of circumstance over us. This night I could have worshipped her with my body, and she, perhaps, was stripped in the body to be worshipped. But it was not for me, at this hour, to fight against circumstances.

I had fought too much, even against the most imposing circumstances, to use any more violence for love. Desire is a sacred thing, and should not be violated.

'Hush!' I said to myself. 'I will sleep, and the ghost of my silence can go forth, in the subtle body of desire, to meet that which is coming to meet it. Let my ghost go forth, and let me not interfere. There are many intangible meetings, and unknown fulfilments of desire.'

So I went softly to sleep, as I wished to, without interfering with the warm, crocus-like ghost of my body.

And I must have gone far, far down the intricate galleries of sleep, to the very heart of the world. For I know I passed on beyond the strata of images and words, beyond the iron veins of memory, and even the jewels of rest, to sink in the final dark like a fish, dumb, soundless, and imageless, yet alive and swimming.

And at the very core of the deep night the ghost came to me, at the heart of the ocean of oblivion, which is also the heart of life. Beyond hearing, or even knowledge of contact, I met her and knew her. How I know it I don't know. Yet I know it with eyeless, wingless knowledge.

For man in the body is formed through countless ages, and at the centre is the speck, or spark upon which all his formation has taken place. It is even not himself, deep beyond his many depths. Deep from him calls to deep. And according as deep answers deep, man glistens and surpasses himself.

Beyond all the pearly mufflings of consciousness, of age upon age of consciousness, deep calls yet to deep, and sometimes is answered. It is calling and answering, new-awakened God calling within the deep of man, and new God calling answer from the other deep. And sometimes the other deep is a woman, as it was with me, when my ghost came.

Women were not unknown to me. But never before had woman come, in the depths of night, to answer my deep with her deep. As the ghost came, came as a ghost of silence, still in the depth of sleep.

I know she came. I know she came even as a woman, to my man. But the knowledge is darkly naked as the event. I only know, it was so. In the deep of sleep a call was called from the deeps of me, and answered in the deeps, by a woman among women. Breasts or thighs or face. I remember not a touch, no, nor a movement of my own. It is all complete in the profundity of darkness. Yet I know it was so.

I awoke towards dawn, from far, far away. I was vaguely conscious of drawing nearer and nearer, as the sun must have been drawing towards the horizon, from the complete beyond. Till at last the faint pallor of mental consciousness coloured my waking.

And then I was aware of a pervading scent, as of plum-blossom, and a sense of extraordinary silkiness – though where, and in what contact, I could not say. It was as the first blemish of dawn.

And even with so slight a conscious registering, *it* seemed to disappear. Like a whale that has sounded to the bottomless seas. That knowledge of *it*, which was the mating of the ghost and me, disappeared from me, in its rich weight of certainty, as the scent of the plum-blossom moved down the lanes of my consciousness, and my limbs stirred in a silkiness for which I have no comparison.

As I became aware, I also became uncertain. I wanted to be certain of *it*, to have definite evidence. And as I sought for evidence, *it* disappeared, my perfect knowledge was gone. I no longer knew in full.

Now as the daylight slowly amassed, in the windows from which I had put back the shutters, I sought in myself for evidence, and in the room.

But I shall never know. I shall never know if it was a ghost, some sweet spirit from the innermost of the ever-deepening cosmos; or a woman, a very woman, as the silkiness of my limbs seems to attest; or a dream, a hallucination! I shall never know. Because I went away from Riddings in the morning on account of the sudden illness of Lady Lathkill.

'You will come again,' Luke said to me. 'And in any case, you will never really go away from us.'

'Good-bye,' she said to me. 'At last it was perfect!'

She seemed so beautiful, when I left her, as if it were the ghost again, and I was far down the deeps of consciousness.

The following autumn, when I was overseas once more, I had a letter from Lord Lathkill. He wrote very rarely.

'Carlotta has a son,' he said, 'and I an heir. He has yellow hair, like a little crocus, and one of the young plum trees in the orchard has come out of all season into blossom. To me he is flesh and blood of our ghost itself. Even mother doesn't look over the wall, to the other side, any more. It's all this side for her now.

'So our family refuses to die out, by the grace of our ghost. We are calling him Gabriel.

'Dorothy Hale also is a mother, three days before Carlotta. She has a black lamb of a daughter, called Gabrielle. By the bleat of the little thing, I know its father. Our own is a blue-eyed one, with the dangerous repose of a pugilist. I have no fears of our family misfortune for him, ghost-begotten and ready-fisted.

'The Colonel is very well, quiet, and self-possessed. He is farming in Wiltshire, raising pigs. It is a passion with him, the *crème de la crème* of swine. I admit, he has golden sows as elegant as a young Diane de Poictiers, and young hogs like Perseus in the first red-gold flush of youth. He looks me in the eye, and I look him back, and we understand. He is quiet, and proud now, and very hale and hearty, raising swine *ad maiorem gloriam Dei*. A good sport!

'I am in love with this house and its inmates, including the plum-blossom-scented one, she who visited you, in all the peace. I cannot understand why you wander in uneasy and distant parts of the earth. For me, when I am at home, I am there. I have peace upon my bones, and if the world is going to come to a violent and untimely end, as prophets aver, I feel the house of Lathkill will survive, built upon our ghost. So come back, and you'll find we shall not have gone away....'

NONE OF THAT

I MET Luis Colmenares in Venice, not having seen him for years. He is a Mexican exile living on the scanty remains of what was once wealth, and eking out a poor and lonely existence by being a painter. But his art is only a sedative to him. He wanders about like a lost soul, mostly in Paris or in Italy, where he can live cheaply. He is rather short, rather fat, pale, with black eyes, which are always looking the other way, and a spirit the same, always averted.

'Do you know who is in Venice?' he said to me. 'Cuesta! He is in the Hôtel Romano. I saw him bathing yesterday on the Lido.'

There was a world of gloomy mockery in this last sentence.

'Do you mean Cuesta, the bull-fighter?' I asked.

'Yes. Don't you know, he retired? Do you remember? An American woman left him a lot of money. Did you ever see him?'

'Once,' said I.

'Was it before the revolution? Do you remember, he retired and bought a *hacienda* very cheap from one of Madero's generals, up in Chihuahua? It was after the Carranzista, and I was already in Europe.'

'How does he look now?' I said.

'Enormously fat, like a yellow, round, small whale in the sea. You saw him? You know he was rather short and rather fat always. I think his mother was a Mixtec Indian woman. Did you ever know him?'

'No,' said I. 'Did you?'

'Yes. I knew him in the old days, when I was rich, and thought I should be rich for ever.'

He was silent, and I was afraid he had shut up for good. It was unusual for him to be even as communicative as he had been. But it was evident that having seen Cuesta, the toreador whose fame once rang through Spain and through Latin America, had moved him deeply. He was in a ferment, and could not quite contain himself.

'But he wasn't interesting, was he?' I said. 'Wasn't he just a – a bull-fighter – a brute?'

Colmenares looked at me out of his own blackness. He didn't want to talk. Yet he had to.

'He was a brute, yes,' he admitted grudgingly. 'But not just a brute.

652

Have you seen him when he was at his best? Where did you see him? I never liked him in Spain, he was too vain. But in Mexico he was very good. Have you seen him play with the bull, and play with death? He was marvellous. Do you remember him, what he looked like?'

'Not very well,' said I.

'Short, and broad, and rather fat, with rather a yellow colour, and a pressed-in nose. But his eyes, they were marvellous, also rather small, and yellow, and when he looked at you, so strange and cool, you felt your inside melting. Do you know that feeling? He looked into the last little place of you, where you keep your courage. Do you understand? And you felt yourself melting. Do you know what I mean?'

'More or less, perhaps,' said I.

Colmenares' black eyes were fixed on my face, dilated and gleaming, but not really seeing me at all. He was seeing the past. Yet a curious force streamed out of his face; one understood him by the telepathy of passion, inverted passion.

'And in the bull-ring he was marvellous. He would stand with his back to the bull, and pretend to be adjusting his stockings, while the bull came charging on him. And with a little glance over his shoulder, he would make a small movement, and the bull had passed him without getting him. Then he would smile a little, and walk after it. It is marvellous that he was not killed hundreds of times, but I saw him bathing on the Lido to-day, like a fat, yellow, small whale. It is extra-ordinary! But I did not see his eyes. . . .'

A queer look of abstracted passion was on Colmenares' fat, pale, clean-shaven face. Perhaps the toreador had cast a spell over him, as over so many people in the old and the new world.

'It is strange that I have never seen eyes anywhere else like his. Did I tell you, they were yellow, and not like human eyes at all? They didn't look at you. I don't think they ever looked at anybody. He only looked at the little bit inside your body where you keep your courage. I don't think he could see people, any more than an animal can: I mean see them personally, as I see you and you see me. He was an animal, a marvellous animal. I have often thought, if human beings had not de-veloped minds and speech, they would have become marvellous ani-mals like Cuesta, with those marvellous eyes, much more marvellous than a lion's or a tiger's. Have you noticed a lion or a tiger never sees you personally? It never really looks at you. But also it is afraid to look at the last little bit of you, where your courage lives inside you. But Cuesta was not afraid. He looked straight at it, and it melted.'

'And what was he like, in ordinary life?' said I.

'He did not talk, was very silent. He was not clever at all. He was not even clever enough to be a general. And he could be very brutal and disgusting. But usually he was quiet. But he was always *something*. If you were in a room with him, you always noticed him more than anybody, more than women or men, even very clever people. He was stupid, but he made you physically aware of him; like a cat in the room. I tell you, that little bit of you where you keep your courage was enchanted by him; he put over you an enchantment.'

'Did he do it on purpose?'

'Well! It is hard to say. But he knew he could do it. To some people, perhaps, he could not do it. But he never saw such people. He only saw people who were in his enchantment. And of course, in the bull-ring, he mesmerised everybody. He could draw the natural magnetism of everybody to him – everybody. And then he was marvellous, he played with death as if it were a kitten, so quick, quick as a star, and calm as a flower, and all the time, laughing at death. It is marvellous he was never killed. But he retired very young. And then suddenly it was he who killed the bull, with one hand, one stroke. He was very strong. And the bull sank down at his feet, heavy with death. The people went mad! And he just glanced at them, with his yellow eyes, in a cool, beautiful contempt, as if he were an animal that wrapped the skin of death round him. Ah, he was wonderful! And to-day I saw him bathing on the Lido, in an American bathing-suit, with a woman. His bathing-suit was just a little more yellow than he is. I have held the towel when he was being rubbed down and massaged often. He had the body of an Indian, very smooth, with hardly any hair, and creamy-yellow. I always thought it had something childish about it, so soft. But also, it had the same mystery as his eyes, as if you could never touch it, as if, when you touched it, still it was not he. When he had no clothes on, he was naked. But it seemed he would have many, many more nakednesses before you really came to *him*. Do you understand me at all? Or does it seem to you foolish?'

'It interests me,' I said. 'And women, of course, fell for him by the thousand?'

'By the million! And they were mad because of him. Women went mad, once they felt him. It was not like Rudolf Valentino, sentimental. It was madness, like cats in the night which howl, no longer knowing whether they are on earth or in hell or in paradise. So were the women.

He could have had forty beautiful women every night, and different ones each night, from the beginning of the year to the end.'

'But he didn't, naturally?'

'Oh no! At first, I think, he took many women. But later, when I knew him, he took none of those that besieged him. He had two Mexican women whom he lived with, humble women, Indians. And all the others he spat at, and spoke of them with terrible, obscene language. I think he would have liked to whip them, or kill them, for pursuing him.'

'Only he must enchant them when he was in the bull-ring,' said I.

'Yes. But that was like sharpening his knife on them.'

'And when he retired – he had plenty of money – how did he amuse himself?'

'He was rich, he had a big hacienda, and many people like slaves to work for him. He raised cattle. I think he was very proud to be haciendado and padrón of so many people, with a little army of his own. I think he was proud, living like a king. I had not heard of him for years. Now, suddenly, he is in Venice with a Frenchwoman who talks bad Spanish —'

'How old is he?'

'How old? He is about fifty, or a little less.'

'So young! And will you speak to him?'

'I don't know. I can't make up my mind. If I speak to him, he will think I want money.'

There was a certain note of hatred now in Colmenares' voice.

'Well, why shouldn't he give you money? He is still rich, I suppose?'

'Rich, yes! He must always be rich. He has got American money. An American woman left him half a million dollars. Did you ever hear of it?'

'No. Then why shouldn't he give you money? I suppose you often gave him some, in the past?'

'Oh, that – that is *quite* the past. He will never give me anything – or a hundred francs, something like that! Because he is mean. Did you never hear of the American woman who left him half a million dollars, and committed suicide?'

'No. When was it?'

'It was a long time ago – about 1914 or 1913. I had already lost all my money. Her name was Ethel Cane. Did you never hear of her?'

'I don't think I did,' I said, feeling it remiss not to have heard of the lady.

'Ah! You should have known her. She was extraordinary. I had known her in Paris, even before I came back to Mexico and knew Cuesta well. She was almost as extraordinary as Cuesta: one of those American women, born rich, but what we should call provincial. She didn't come from New York or Boston, but somewhere else. Omaha or something. She was blonde, with thick, straight, blonde hair, and she was one of the very first to wear it short, like a Florentine page-boy. Her skin was white, and her eyes very blue, and she was not thin. At first, there seemed something childish about her – do you know that look, rather round cheeks and clear eyes, so false-innocent? Her eyes especially were warm and naïve and false-innocent, but full of light. Only sometimes they were bloodshot. Oh, she was extraordinary! It was only when I knew her better I noticed how her blonde eyebrows gathered together above her nose, in a diabolic manner. She was much too much a personality to be a lady, and she had all that terrible American energy! Ah, energy! She was a dynamo. In Paris she was married to a dapper little pink-faced American who got yellow at the gills, bilious, running after her when she would not have him. He painted pictures and wanted to be modern. She knew all the people, and had all sorts come to her, as if she kept a human menagerie. And she bought old furniture and brocades; she would go mad if she saw someone get a piece of velvet brocade with the misty bloom of years on it, that she coveted. She coveted such things with lust, and would go into a strange sensual trance, looking at some old worm-eaten chair. And she would go mad if someone else got it, and not she: that nasty old wormy chair of the quattrocento! Things! She was mad about "things". But it was only for a time. She always got tired, especially of her own enthusiasms.

'That was when I knew her in Paris. Then I think she divorced that husband, and, when the revolutions in Mexico became quieter, she came to Mexico. I think she was fascinated by the idea of Carranza. If ever she heard of a man who seemed to have a dramatic sort of power in him, she must know that man. It was like her lust for brocade and old chairs and a perfect æsthetic setting. Now it was to know the most dangerous man, especially if he looked like a prophet or a reformer. She was a socialist also, at this time. She no longer was in love with chairs.

'She found me again in Mexico: she knew thousands of people, and whenever one of them might be useful to her, she remembered him. So she remembered me, and it was nothing to her that I was now poor. I knew she thought of me as "that little Luis Something", but she had a

656

certain use for me, and found, perhaps, a certain little flavour in me. At least she asked me often to dinner, or to drive with her. She was curious, quite reckless and a dare-devil, yet shy and awkward out of her own *milieu*. It was only in intimacy that she was unscrupulous and dauntless as a devil incarnate. In public, and in strange places, she was very uneasy, like one who has a bad conscience towards society, and is afraid of it. And for that reason she could never go out without a man to stand between her and all the others.

'While she was in Mexico, I was that man. She soon discovered that I was satisfactory. I would perform all the duties of a husband without demanding any of the rights. Which was what she wanted. I think she was looking round for a remarkable and epoch-making husband. But, of course, it would have to be a husband who would be a fitting instrument for her remarkable and epoch-making energy and character. She was extraordinary, but she could only work through individuals, through others. By herself she could accomplish nothing. She lay on a sofa and mused and schemed, with the energy boiling inside her. Only when she had a group, or a few real individuals, or just one man, then she could start something, and make them all dance in a tragi-comedy, like marionettes.

'But in Mexico, men do not care for women who will make them dance like puppets. In Mexico, women must run in the dust like the Indian women, with meek little heads. American women are not very popular. Their energy, and their power to make other people do things, are not in request. The men would rather go to the devil in their own way than be sent there by the women, with a little basket in which to bring home the goods.

'So Ethel found not a cold shoulder, but a number of square, fat backs turned to her. They didn't want her. The revolutionaries would not take any notice of her at all. They wanted no women interfering. General Isidor Garabay danced with her, and expected her immediately to become his mistress. But, as she said, she was having *none of that*. She had a terrible way of saying "I'm having none of that!" – like hitting a mirror with a hammer. And as nobody wanted to get into trouble over her, they were having none of her.

'At first, of course, when the generals saw her white shoulders and blonde hair and innocent face, they thought at once: "Here is a *type* for us!" They were not deceived by her innocent look. But they were deceived by what looked like her helplessness. The blood would come swelling into her neck and face, her eyes would go hot, her whole figure would swell with repellent energy, and she would say something very American and very crushing, in French, or in American. None of *that!* Stop *that!*

'She, too, had a lot of power. She could send out of her body a repelling energy, to compel people to submit to her will. Men in Europe or the United States nearly always crumpled up before her. But in Mexico she had come to the wrong shop. The men were a law to themselves. While she was winning and rather lovely, with her blue eyes so full of light and her white skin glistening with energetic health, they expected her to become at once their mistress. And when they saw, very quickly, that she was having *none of that*, they turned on their heels and showed her their fat backs. Because she was clever, and remarkable, and had wonderful energy and a wonderful power for making people dance while she pulled the strings, they didn't care a bit. They, too, wanted *none of that*. They would, perhaps, have carried her off and shared her as a mistress, except for the fear of trouble with the American Government.

'So, soon, she began to be bored, and to think of returning to New York. She said that Mexico was a place without a soul and without a culture, and it had not even brain enough to be mechanically efficient. It was a city and a land of naughty little boys doing obscene little things, and one day it would learn its lesson. I told her that history is the account of a lesson which nobody ever learns, and she told me the world certainly *had* progressed. Only not in Mexico, she supposed. I asked her why she had come, then, to Mexico. And she said she had thought there was something doing, and she would like to be in it. But she found it was only naughty and mostly cowardly little boys letting off guns and doing mediocre obscenities, so she would leave them to it. I told her I supposed it was life. And she replied that since it was not good enough for her, it was not life to her.

'She said all she wanted was to live the life of the imagination and get it acted on. At that time, I thought this ridiculous. I thought she was just trying to find somebody to fall in love with. Later, I saw she was right. She had an imaginary picture of herself as an extraordinary and potent woman who would make a stupendous change in the history of man. Like Catherine of Russia, only cosmopolitan, not merely Russian. And it is true, she *was* an extraordinary woman, with tremendous power of will, and truly amazing energy, even for an American woman. She was like a locomotive-engine stoked up inside and bursting with steam, which it has to let off by rolling a lot of trucks about. But I did not see how this was to cause a change in the tide of mortal affairs. It was only a part of the hubbub of traffic. She sent the trucks bouncing against one another with a clash of buffers, and sometimes she derailed some unfortunate item of the rolling-stock. But I did not see how this was to change the history of mankind. She seemed to have arrived just a little late, as some heroes, and heroines also, to-day, always do.

'I wondered always, why she did not take a lover. She was a woman between thirty and forty, very healthy and full of this extraordinary energy. She saw many men, and was always drawing them out, always on the *qui vive* to start them rolling down some incline. She attracted men, in a certain way. Yet she had no lover.

'I wondered even with regard to myself. We were friends, and a great deal together. Certainly I was under her spell. I came running as soon as I thought she wanted me. I did the things she suggested I should do. Even among my own acquaintances, when I found everybody laughing at me and disliking me for being at the service of an American woman, and I tried to rebel against her, and put her in her place, as the Mexicans say – which means to them, in bed with no clothes on – still, the moment I saw her, with a look and a word she won me round. She was very clever, She flattered me, of course. She made me feel intelligent. She drew me out. There was her cleverness. She made *me* clever. I told her all about Mexico: all my life: all my ideas of history, philosophy. I sounded awfully clever and original, to myself. And she listened with such attention, which I thought was deep interest in what I was saying. But she was waiting for something she could fasten on, so that she could "start something". That was her constant craving, to "start something". But, of course, I thought she was interested in *me*.

'She would lie on a large couch that was covered with old sarapes – she began to buy them as soon as she came to Mexico – herself wrapped in a wonderful black shawl that glittered all over with brilliant birds and flowers in vivid colour, a very fine specimen of the embroidered shawls our Mexican ladies used to wear at a bull-fight or in an open-air *fiesta*: and there, with her white arms glistening through the long fringe of the shawl, the old Italian jewellery rising on her white, dauntless breast, and her short, thick, blonde hair falling like yellow metal, she would draw me out, draw me out. I never talked so much in my life before or since. Always talk! And I believe I talked very well, really, really very clever. But nothing besides talk! Sometimes I stayed till after midnight. And sometimes she would snort with impatience or boredom, rather like a horse, flinging back her head and shaking that

659

heavy blonde hair. And I think some part of her wanted me to make love to her.

'But I didn't. I couldn't. I was there, under her influence, in her power. She could draw me out in talk, marvellously. I'm sure I was very clever indeed. But any other part of me was stiff, petrified. I couldn't even touch her. I couldn't even take her hand in mine. It was a physical impossibility. When I was away from her, I could think of her white, healthy body with a voluptuous shiver. I could even run to her apartment, intending to kiss her, and make her my mistress that very night. But the moment I was in her presence, it left me. I could not touch her. I was averse from touching her. Physically, for some reason, I hated her.

'And I felt within myself, it was because she was repelling me and because she was always hating men, hating all active maleness in a man. She only wanted passive maleness, and then this "talk", this life of the imagination, as she called it. Inside herself she seethed, and she thought it was because she wanted to be made love to, very much made love to. But it wasn't so. She seethed against all men, with repulsion. She was cruel to the body of a man. But she excited his mind, his spirit. She loved to do that. She loved to have a man hanging round, like a servant. She loved to stimulate him, especially his mind. And she, too, when the man was not there, she thought she wanted him to be her lover. But when he was there, and he wanted to gather for himself that mysterious fruit of her body, she revolted against him with a fearful hate. A man must be *absolutely* her servant, and only that. That was what she meant by the life of the imagination.

'And I was her servant. Everybody jeered at me. But I said to myself. I would make her my mistress. I almost set my teeth to do it. That was when I was away from her. When I came to her, I could not even touch her. When I tried to make myself touch her, something inside me began to shudder. It was impossible. And I knew it was because, with her inner body, she was repelling me, always really repelling me.

'Yet she wanted me too. She was lonely: lonesome, she said. She was lonesome, and she would have liked to get me making love to her external self. She would even, I think, have become my mistress, allowed me to take her sometimes for a little, miserable humiliating moment, then quickly have got rid of me again. But I couldn't do it. Her inner body *never* wanted me. And I couldn't just be her prostitute. Because immediately she would have despised me, and insulted me if I had persisted in trying to get some satisfaction of her. I knew it. She had already had two husbands, and she was a woman who always ached to tell *all*, everything. She had told me too much. I had seen one of her American husbands. I did not choose to see myself in a similar light: or plight.

'No, she wanted to live the life of the imagination. She said the imagination could master everything; so long, of course, as one was not shot in the head, or had an eye put out. Talking of the Mexican atrocities, and of the famous case of raped nuns, she said it was all nonsense that a woman was broken because she had been raped. She could rise above it. The imagination could rise above *anything*, that was not real organic damage. If one lived the life of the imagination, one could rise above any experience that ever happened to one. One could even commit murder, and rise above that. By using the imagination, and by using cunning, a woman can justify herself in anything, even the meanest and most bad things. A woman uses her imagination on her own behalf, and she becomes more innocent to herself than an innocent child, no matter what bad things she has done.'

'Men do that, too,' I interrupted. 'It's the modern dodge. That's why everybody to-day is innocent. To the imagination all things are pure, if you did them yourself.'

Colmenares looked at me with quick, black eyes, to see if I were mocking him. He did not care about me and my interruptions. He was utterly absorbed in his recollections of that woman, who had made him so clever, and who had made him her servant, and from whom he had never had any satisfaction.

'And then what?' I asked him. 'Then did she try her hand on Cuesta?'

'Ah!' said Colmenares, rousing, and glancing at me suspiciously again. 'Yes! That was what she did. And I was jealous. Though I couldn't bring myself to touch her, yet I was excruciated with jealousy, because she was interested in someone else. She was interested in someone besides myself, and my vanity suffered tortures of jealousy. Why was I such a fool? Why, even now, could I kill that fat, yellow pig Cuesta? A man is always a fool.'

'How did she meet the bull-fighter?' I asked. 'Did you introduce him to her?'

'She went once to the bull-fight, because everyone was talking about Cuesta. She did not care for such things as the bull-ring; she preferred the modern theatre, Duse and Reinhardt, and "things of the imagination". But now she was going back to New York, and she had never seen a bull-fight, so she must see one. I got seats in the shade – high up, you know – and went with her.

'At first she was very disgusted, and very contemptuous, and a little bit frightened, you know, because a Mexican crowd in a bull-ring is not very charming. She was afraid of people. But she sat stubborn and sulky, like a sulky child, saying: "Can't they do anything more subtle than this, to get a thrill? It's on such a low level!"'

'But when Cuesta at last began to play with a bull, she began to get excited. He was in pink and silver, very gorgeous, and looking very ridiculous, as usual. Till he began to play; and then there really was something marvellous in him, you know, so quick and so light and so playful – do you know? When he was playing with a bull and playing with death in the ring, he was the most playful thing I have ever seen: more playful than kittens or leopard cubs: and you know how they play; do you? Oh, marvellous! More gay and light than if they had lots of wings all over them, all wings of playing! Well, he was like that, playing with death in the ring, as if he had all kinds of gay little wings to spin him with the quickest, tiniest, most beautiful little movements, quite unexpected, like a soft leopard cub. And then at the end, when he killed the bull and the blood squirted past him, ugh! it was as if all his body laughed, and still the same soft, surprised laughter like a young thing, but more cruel than anything you can imagine. He fascinated me, but I always hated him. I would have liked to stick him as he stuck the bulls.

'I could see that Ethel was trying not to be caught by his spell. He had the most curious charm, quick and unexpected like play, you know, like leopard kittens, or slow sometimes, like tiny little bears. And yet the perfect cruelty. It was the joy in cruelty! She hated the blood and messiness and dead animals. Ethel hated all that. It was not the life of the imagination. She was very pale, and very silent. She leaned forward and hardly moved, looking white and obstinate and subdued. And Cuesta had killed three bulls before she made any sign of any sort. I did not speak to her. The fourth bull was a beauty, full of life, curling and prancing like a narcissus-flower in January. He was a very special bull, brought from Spain, and not so stupid as the others. He pawed the ground and blew the breath on the ground, lowering his head. And Cuesta opened his arms to him with a little smile, but endearing, lovingly endearing, as a man might open his arms to a little maiden he really loves, but, really, for her to come to his body, his warm, open body, to come softly. So he held his arms out to the bull, with love. And that was what fascinated the women. They screamed and they fainted, longing to go into the arms of Cuesta, against his soft, round body, that was more yearning than a fico. But the bull, of course, rushed past him, and only got two darts sticking in his shoulder. That was the love.

'Then Ethel shouted, *Bravo! Bravo!* and I saw that she, too, had gone mad. Even Cuesta heard her, and he stopped a moment and looked at her. He saw her leaning forward, with her short, thick hair hanging like yellow metal, and her face dead-white, and her eyes glaring to his, like a challenge. They looked at one another, for a second, and he gave a little bow, then turned away. But he was changed. He didn't play so unconsciously any more: he seemed to be thinking of something, and forgetting himself. I was afraid he would be killed; but so afraid! He seemed absent-minded, and taking risks too great. When the bull came after him over the gangway barrier, he even put his hand on its head as he vaulted back, and one horn caught his sleeve and tore it just a little. Then he seemed to be absent-mindedly looking at the tear, while the bull was almost touching him again. And the bull was mad. Cuesta was a dead man it seemed, for sure: yet he seemed to wake up and *waked* himself just out of reach. It was like an awful dream, and it seemed to last for hours. I think it must have been a long time, before the bull was killed. He killed him at last, as a man takes his mistress at last because he is almost tired of playing with her. But he liked to kill his own bull.

'Ethel was looking like death, with beads of perspiration on her face. And she called to him: "That's enough! That's enough now! *Ya es bastante! Basta!*" He looked at her, and heard what she said. They were both alike there, they heard and saw in a flash. And he lifted his face, with the rather squashed nose and the yellow eyes, and he looked at her, and though he was so far away, he seemed quite near. And he was smiling like a small boy. But I could see he was looking at the little place in her body, where she kept her courage. And she was trying to catch his look on her imagination, not on her naked body inside. And they both found it difficult. When he tried to look at her, she set her imagination in front of him, like a mirror they put in front of a wild dog. And when she tried to catch him in her imagination, he seemed to melt away, and was gone. So neither really had caught the other.

'But he played with two more bulls, and killed them, without ever looking at her. And she went away when the people were applauding him, and did not look at him. Neither did she speak to me of him. Neither did she go to any more bull-fights.

'It was Cuesta who spoke to me of her, when I met him at Clavel's house. He said to me in his very coarse Spanish: "And what about your American skirt?" I told him, there was nothing to say about her. She was leaving for New York. So he told me to ask her if she would like to come and say good-bye to Cuesta, before she went. I said to him: "But why should I mention your name to her, She has never mentioned yours to me." He made an obscene joke to me.

'And it must have been because I was thinking of him that she said that evening: "Do you know Cuesta?" I told her I did, and she asked me what I thought of him. I told her I thought he was a marvellous beast, but he wasn't really a man. "But he is a beast with imagination," she said to me. "Couldn't one get a response out of him?" I told her I didn't know, but I didn't want to try. I would leave Cuesta to the bull-ring. I would never dream of trying my imagination on him. She said, always ready with an answer: "But wasn't there a marvellous *thing* in him, something quite exceptional?" I said, maybe! But so has a rattle-snake a marvellous thing in him: two things, one in his mouth, one in his tail. But I didn't want to try to get response out of a rattlesnake. She wasn't satisfied, though. She was tortured. I said to her: "Anyhow, you are leaving on Thursday." "No, I've put it off," she said. "Till when?" "Indefinite," she said.

'I could tell she was tormented. She had been tormented ever since she had been to the bull-fight, because she couldn't get past Cuesta. She couldn't get past him, as the Americans say. He seemed like a fat, squat, yellow-eyed demon just smiling at her, and dancing ahead of her. "Why don't you bring him here?" she said at last, though she didn't want to say it. – "But why? What is the good of bringing him here? Would you bring a criminal here, or a yellow scorpion?" – "I would if I wanted to find out about it." – "But what is there to find out about Cuesta? He is just a sort of beast. He is less than a man." – "Maybe he's a *schwarze Bestie*," she said, "and I'm a *blonde Bestie*. Anyway, bring him."

'I always did what she wanted me, though I never wanted to myself. So it was now. I went to a place where I knew Cuesta would be, and he asked me: "How is the blonde skirt? Has she gone yet?" I said, "No. Would you like to see her?" He looked at me with his yellow eyes, and that pleasant look which was really hate undreaming. "Did she tell you to ask me?" he said. "No," I said. "We were talking of you, and she said, bring the fabulous animal along and let us see what he really is." – "He is the animal for her meat, this one," he said, in his vulgar way.

664

Then he pretended he wouldn't come. But I knew he would. So I said I would call for him.

'We were going in the evening, after tea, and he was dressed to kill, in a light French suit. We went in his car. But he didn't take flowers or anything. Ethel was nervous and awkward, offering us cocktails and cigarettes, and speaking French, though Cuesta didn't understand any French at all. There was another old American woman there, for chaperon.

'Cuesta just sat on a chair, with his knees apart and his hands between his thighs, like an Indian. Only his hair, which was done up in his little pigtail, and taken back from his forehead, made him look like a woman, or a Chinaman; and his flat nose and little yellow eyes made him look like a Chinese idol, maybe a god or a demon, as you please. He just sat and said nothing, and had that look on his face which wasn't a smile, and wasn't a grimace, it was nothing. But to me it meant rhapsodic hate.

'She asked him in French if he liked his profession, and how long he had been doing it, and if he got a great kick out of it, and was he a pure-blood Indian? – all that kind of thing. I translated to him as short as possible, Ethel flushing with embarrassment. He replied just as short, to me, in his coarse, flat sort of voice, as if he knew it was mere pretence. But he looked at her, straight into her face, with that strange, far-off sort of stare, yet very vivid, taking no notice of her, yet staring right into her: as if all that she was putting forward to him was merely window-dressing, and he was just looking way in, to the marshes and the jungle in her, where she didn't even look herself. It made one feel as if there was a mountain behind her, Popocatepetl, that he was staring at, expecting a mountain-lion to spring down off a tree on the slopes of the mountain, or a snake to lean down from a bough. But the mountain was all she stood for, and the mountain-lion or the snake was her own animal self, that he was watching for, like a hunter.

'We didn't stay long, but when we left she asked him to come in whenever he liked. He wasn't really the person to have calling on one: and he knew it, as she did. But he thanked her, and hoped he would one day be able to receive her at her – meaning his – humble house in the Guadalupe Road, where everything was her own. She said: "Why, sure, I'll come one day. I should love to." Which he understoood, and bowed himself out like some quick but lurking animal: quick as a scorpion, with silence of venom the same.

'After that he would call fairly often, at about five o'clock, but never

665

alone, always with some other man. And he never said anything, always responded to her questions in the same short way, and always looked at her when he was speaking to the other man. He never once *spoke* to her – always spoke to his interpreter, in his flat, coarse Spanish. And he always looked at her when he was speaking to someone else.

'She tried every possible manner in which to touch his imagination: but never with any success. She tried the Indians, the Aztecs, the history of Mexico, politics, Don Porfirio, the bull-ring, love, women, Europe, America – and all in vain. All she got out of him was *Verdad!* He was utterly uninterested. He actually *had* no mental imagination. Talk was just noise to him. The only spark she roused was when she talked of money. Then the queer half-smile deepened on his face, and he asked his interpreter if the Señora was very rich. To which Ethel replied she didn't really know what he meant by rich: he must be rich himself. At which he asked the interpreter friend if she had more than a million American dollars. To which she replied that perhaps she had – but she wasn't sure. And he looked at her so strangely, even more like a yellow scorpion about to sting.

'I asked him later, what made him put such a crude question? Did he think of offering to marry her? "Marry a —?" he replied, using an obscene expression. But I didn't know even then what he really intended. Yet I saw he had her on his mind.

'Ethel was gradually getting into a state of tension. It was as if something tortured her. She seemed like a woman who would go insane. I asked her: "Why, whatever's wrong with you?" "I'll tell you, Luis," she said, "but don't you say anything to anybody, mind. It's Cuesta! I don't know whether I want him or not." – "You don't know whether he wants *you* or not," said I. – "I can handle that," she said, "if I know about myself: if I know my own mind. But I don't. My mind says he's a nada-nada, a dumb-bell, no brain, no imagination, no anything. But my body says he marvellous, and he's got something I haven't got, and he's stronger than I am, and he's more an angel or a devil than a man, and I'm too merely human to get him – and all that, till I feel I shall just go crazy, and take an overdose of drugs. What am I to *do* with my body, I tell you? What am I to *do* with it? I've got to master it. I've got to be *more* than that man. I've got to get all round him, and past him. I've *got* to." – "Then just take the train to New York to-night, and forget him," I said. – "I can't! That's side-tracking. I *won't* side-track my body. I've got to get the best of it. I've got to." – "Well," I said, "you're a point or two beyond me. If it's a question of getting all round Cuesta, and getting past him, why, take the train, and you'll forget him in a fortnight. Don't fool yourself you're in love with the fellow." – "I'm afraid he's stronger than I am," she cried out. – "And what then? He's stronger than I am, but that doesn't prevent me sleeping. A jaguar even is stronger than I am, and an anaconda could swallow me whole. I tell you, it's all in a day's march. There's a kind of animal called Cuesta. Well, what of it?"

'She looked at me, and I could tell I made no impression on her. She despised me. She sort of wanted to go off the deep end about something. I said to her: "God's love, Ethel, cut out the Cuesta caprice! It's not even good acting." But I might just as well have mewed, for all the notice she took of me.

'It was as if some dormant Popocatepetl inside her had begun to erupt. She didn't love the fellow. Yet she was in a blind kill-me-quick sort of state, neither here nor there, nor hot or cold, not desirous nor undesirous, but just simply *insane*. In a certain kind of way, she seemed to want him. And in a very definite kind of way she seemed *not* to want him. She was in a kind of hysterics, lost her feet altogether. I tried might and main to get her away to the United States. She'd have come sane enough, once she was there. But I thought she'd kill me, when she found I'd been trying to interfere. Oh, she was not quite in her mind, that's sure.

' "If my body is stronger than my imagination, I shall kill myself," she said. – "Ethel," I said, "people who talk of killing themselves always call a doctor if they cut their finger. What's the quarrel between your body and your imagination? Aren't they the same thing?" – "No!" she said. "If the imagination has the body under control, you can do anything, it doesn't matter what you do, physically. If my body was under the control of my imagination, I could take Cuesta for my lover, and it would be an imaginative act. But if my body acted without my imagination, I – I'd kill myself." – "But what do you mean by your body acting without your imagination?" I said. "You are not a child. You've been married twice. You know what it means. You even have two children. You must have had at least several lovers. If Cuesta is to be another of your lovers, I think it is deplorable, but I think it only shows you are very much like the other woman who fall in love with him. If you've fallen in love with him, your imagination has nothing to do but accept the fact and put as many roses on the ass's head as you like." She looked at me very solemnly, and seemed to think about it. Then she said: "But my imagination has not fallen in love

667

with him. He wouldn't meet me imaginatively. He's a brute. And once I start, where's it going to end? I'm afraid my body has fallen – not fallen in love with him, but fallen *for* him. It's abject! And if I can't get my body on its feet again, and either forget him or else get him to make it an imaginative act with me – I – I shall kill myself." – "All right," said I. "I don't know what you are talking about, imaginative acts and unimaginative acts. The act is always the same." – "It isn't!" she cried, furious with me. "It is either imaginative or else it's *impossible* – to me." Well, I just spread my hands. What could I say, or do? I simply hated her way of putting it. Imaginative act! Why, I would hate performing an imaginative act with a woman. Damn it, the act is either real, or let it alone. But now I knew why I had never touched her, or even kissed her, not once: because I couldn't stand that imaginative sort of bullying from her. It is death to a man.

'I said to Cuesta: "Why do you go to Ethel? Why don't you stay away, and make her go back to the United States? Are you in love with her?" He was obscene, as usual. "Am I in love with a cuttlefish, that is all arms and eyes, and no legs or tail! That blonde is a cuttlefish. She is an octopus, all arms and eyes and beak, and a lump of jelly." – "Then why don't you leave her alone?" – " "Even cuttlefish is good when it's cooked in sauce," he said. "You had much better leave her alone," I said. – "Leave her alone yourself, my esteemed Señor," he said to me. And I knew I had better go no further.

'She said to him one evening, when only I was there – and she said it in Spanish, direct to him: "Why do you never come alone to see me? Why do you always come with another person? Are you afraid?" He looked at her, and his eyes never changed. But he said, in his usual flat, meaningless voice: "It is because I cannot speak, except Spanish." – "But we could understand one another," she said, giving one of her little violent snorts of impatience and embarrassed rage. "Who knows!" he replied, imperturbably.

'Afterwards, he said to me: "What does she want? She hates a man as she hates a red-hot iron. A white devil, as sacred as the communion wafer!" – "Then why don't you leave her alone?" I said. – "She is so rich," he smiled. "She has all the world in her thousand arms. She is as rich as God. The Archangels are poor beside her, she is so rich and so white-skinned and white-souled." – "Then all the more, why don't you leave her alone?" But he did not answer me.

'He went alone, however, to see her. But always in the early evening.

And he never stayed more than half an hour. His car, well-known everywhere, waited outside: till he came out in his French-grey suit and glistening brown shoes, his hat rather on the back of his head.

'What they said to one another, I don't know. But she became always more distraught and absorbed, as if she were brooding over a single idea. I said to her: "Why take it seriously? Dozens of women have slept with Cuesta, and think no more of it. Why take him seriously?" – "I don't," she said. "I take myself seriously, that's the point." – "Let it be the point. Go on taking yourself seriously, and leave him out of the question altogether."

'But she was tired of my playing the wise uncle, and I was tired of her taking herself seriously. She took herself so seriously, it seemed to me she would deserve what she got, playing the fool with Cuesta. Of course she did not love him at all. She only wanted to see if she could make an impression on him, make him yield to her will. But all the impression she made on him was to make him call her a squid and an octopus and other nice things. And I could see their "love" did not go forward at all.

' "Have you made love to her?" I asked him. – "I have not touched the zopilote," he said. "I hate her bare white neck."

'But still he went to see her: always, for a very brief call, before sundown. She asked him to come to dinner with me. He said he could never come to dinner, nor after dinner, as he was always engaged from eight o'clock in the evening onwards. She looked at him as much as to tell him she knew it was a lie and a subterfuge, but he never turned a hair. He was, she put it, utterly unimaginative: an impervious animal.

' "You, however, come one day to your poor house in the Guadalupe Road," he said – meaning his house. He had said it, suggestively, several times.

' "But you are always engaged in the evening," she said.

' "Come, then, at night – come at eleven, when I am free," he said, with supreme animal impudence, looking into her eyes.

' "Do you receive calls so late?" she said, flushing with anger and embarrassment and obstinacy.

' "At times," he said. "When it is very special."

'A few days later, when I called to see her as usual, I was told she was ill, and could see no one. The next day, she was still not to be seen. She had had a dangerous nervous collapse. The third day, a friend rang me up to say Ethel was dead.

'The thing was hushed up. But it was known she had poisoned herself. She left a note to me, in which she merely said: "It is as I told you. Good-bye. But my testament holds good."

'In her will, she had left half her fortune to Cuesta. The will had been made some ten days before her death – and it was allowed to stand. He took the money —'

Colmenares' voice tailed off into silence.

'Her body had got the better of her imagination, after all,' I said.

'It was worse than that,' he said.

'How?'

He was a long time before he answered. Then he said: 'She actually went to Cuesta's house that night, way down there beyond the Volador market. She went by appointment. And there in his bedroom he handed her over to half a dozen of his bull-ring gang, with orders not to bruise her. Yet at the inquest there were a few deep, strange bruises, and the doctors made reports. Then apparently the visit to Cuesta's house came to light, but no details were ever told. Then there was another revolution, and in the hubbub this affair was dropped. It was too shady, anyhow. Ethel had certainly encouraged Cuesta at her apartment.'

'But how do you know he handed her over like that?'

'One of the men told me himself. He was shot afterwards.'

THE MAN WHO LOVED ISLANDS

I

THERE was a man who loved islands. He was born on one, but it didn't suit him, as there were too many other people on it, besides himself. He wanted an island all of his own: not necessarily to be alone on it, but to make it a world of his own.

An island, if it is big enough, is no better than a continent. It has to be really quite small, before it *feels* like an island; and this story will show how tiny it has to be, before you can presume to fill it with your own personality.

Now circumstances so worked out that this lover of islands, by the time he was thirty-five, actually acquired an island of his own. He didn't own it as freehold property, but he had a ninety-nine years' lease of it, which, as far as a man and an island are concerned, is as good as everlasting. Since, if you are like Abraham, and want your offspring to be numberless as the sands of the sea-shore, you don't choose an island to start breeding on. Too soon there would be over-population, over-crowding, and slum conditions. Which is a horrid thought, for one who loves an island for its insulation. No, an island is a nest which holds one egg, and one only. This egg is the islander himself.

The island acquired by our potential islander was not in the remote oceans. It was quite near at home, no palm trees nor boom of surf on the reef, nor any of that kind of thing; but a good solid dwelling-house, rather gloomy, above the landing-place, and beyond, a small farmhouse with sheds, and a few outlying fields. Down on the little landing-bay were three cottages in a row, like coastguards' cottages, all neat and whitewashed.

What could be more cosy and home-like? It was four miles if you walked all round your island, through the gorse and the blackthorn bushes, above the steep rocks of the sea and down in the little glades where the primroses grew. If you walked straight over the two humps of hills, the length of it, through the rocky fields where the cows lay chewing, and through the rather sparse oats, on into the gorse again, and so to the low cliffs' edge, it took you only twenty minutes. And when you came to the edge, you could see another, bigger island lying beyond. But the sea was between you and it. And as you returned over the turf where the short, downland cowslips nodded, you saw to the east still another island, a tiny one this time, like the calf of a cow. This tiny island also belonged to the islander.

Thus it seems that even islands like to keep each other company.

Our islander loved his island very much. In early spring, the little ways and glades were a snow of blackthorn, a vivid white among the Celtic stillness of close green and grey rock, blackbirds calling out in the whiteness their first long, triumphant calls. After the blackthorn and the nestling primroses came the blue apparition of hyacinths, like elfin lakes and slipping sheets of blue, among the bushes and under the glade of trees. And many birds with nests you could peep into, on the island all your own. Wonderful what a great world it was!

Followed summer, and the cowslips gone, the wild roses faintly fragrant through the haze. There was a field of hay, the foxgloves stood looking down. In a little cove, the sun was on the pale granite where you bathed, and the shadow was in the rocks. Before the mist came stealing, you went home through the ripening oats, the glare of the sea fading from the high air as the fog-horn started to moo on the other island. And then the sea-fog went, it was autumn, the oat-sheaves lying prone, the great moon, another island, rose golden out of the sea, and rising higher, the world of the sea was white.

So autumn ended with rain, and winter came, dark skies and dampness and rain, but rarely frost. The island, your island, cowered dark, holding away from you. You could feel, down in the wet, sombre hollows, the resentful spirit coiled upon itself, like a wet dog coiled in gloom, or a snake that is neither asleep nor awake. Then in the night, when the wind left off blowing in great gusts and volleys, as at sea, you felt that your island was a universe, infinite and old as the darkness; not an island at all, but an infinite dark world where all the souls from all the other bygone nights lived on, and the infinite distance was near.

Strangely, from your little island in space, you were gone forth into the dark, great realms of time, where all the souls that never die veer and swoop on their vast, strange errands. The little earthly island has dwindled, like a jumping-off place, into nothingness, for you have jumped off, you know not how, into the dark wide mystery of time, where the past is vastly alive, and the future is not separated off.

This is the danger of becoming an islander. When, in the city, you wear your white spats and dodge the traffic with the fear of death down your spine, then you are quite safe from the terrors of infinite time. The moment is your little islet in time, it is the spatial universe that careers round you.

But once isolate yourself on a little island in the sea of space, and the moment begins to heave and expand in great circles, the solid earth is gone, and your slippery, naked dark soul finds herself out in the timeless world, where the chariots of the so-called dead dash down the old streets of centuries, and souls crowd on the footways that we, in the moment, call bygone years. The souls of all the dead are alive again, and pulsating actively around you. You are out in the other infinity.

Something of this happened to our islander. Mysterious 'feelings' came upon him that he wasn't used to; strange awarenessess of old, far-gone men, and other influences; men of Gaul, with big moustaches, who had been on his island, and had vanished from the face of it, but not out of the air of night. They were there still, hurtling their big, violent, unseen bodies through the night. And there were priests, with golden knives and mistletoe; then other priests with a crucifix; then pirates with murder on the sea.

Our islander was uneasy. He didn't believe, in the day-time, in any of this nonsense. But at night it just was so. He had reduced himself to a single point in space, and, a point being that which has neither length nor breadth, he had to step off it into somewhere else. Just as you must step into the sea, if the waters wash your foothold away, so he had, at night, to step off into the other worlds of undying time.

He was uncannily aware, as he lay in the dark, that the blackthorn grove that seemed a bit uncanny even in the realm of space and day, at night was crying with old men of an invisible race, around the altar stone. What was a ruin under the hornbeam trees by day, was a moaning of blood-stained priests with crucifixes, on the ineffable night. What was a cave and a hidden beach between coarse rocks, became in the invisible dark the purple-lipped imprecation of pirates.

To escape any more of this sort of awareness, our islander daily concentrated upon his material island. Why should it not be the Happy Isle at last? Why not the last small isle of the Hesperides, the perfect place, all filled with his own gracious, blossom-like spirit? A minute world of pure perfection, made by man himself.

He began, as we begin all our attempts to regain Paradise, by spending money. The old, semi-feudal dwelling-house he restored, let in more light, put clear lovely carpets on the floor, clear, flower petal curtains at the sullen windows, and wines in the cellars of rock. He brought over a buxom housekeeper from the world, and a soft-spoken, much-experienced butler. These two were to be islanders.

In the farmhouse he put a bailiff, with two farm-hands. There were Jersey cows, tinkling a slow bell, among the gorse. There was a call to meals at midday, and the peaceful smoking of chimneys at evening, when rest descended.

A jaunty sailing-boat with a motor accessory rode in the shelter in the bay, just below the row of three white cottages. There was also a little yawl, and two row-boats drawn up on the sand. A fishing-net was drying on its supports, a boat-load of new white planks stood criss-cross, a woman was going to the well with a bucket.

In the end cottage lived the skipper of the yacht, and his wife and son. He was a man from the other, large island, at home on this sea. Every fine day he went out fishing, with his son, every fair day there was fresh fish in the island.

In the middle cottage lived an old man and wife, a very faithful couple. The old man was a carpenter, and man of many jobs. He was always working, always the sound of his plane or his saw; lost in his work, he was another kind of islander.

In the third cottage was a mason, a widower with a son and two daughters. With the help of his boy, this man dug ditches and built fences, raised buttresses and erected a new out-building, and hewed stone from the little quarry. One daughter worked at the big house.

It was a quiet, busy little world. When the islander brought you over as his guest, you met first the dark-bearded, thin, smiling skipper, Arnold, then his boy Charles. At the house, the smooth-lipped butler who had lived all over the world valeted you, and created that curious creamy-smooth, disarming sense of luxury around you which only a perfect and rather untrustworthy servant can create. He disarmed you and had you at his mercy. The buxom housekeeper smiled and treated you with the subtly respectful familiarity that is only dealt out to the true gentry. And the rosy maid threw a glance at you, as if you were very wonderful, coming from the great outer world. Then you met the smiling but watchful bailiff, who came from Cornwall, and the shy farm-hand from Berkshire, with his clean wife and two little children: then the rather sulky farm-hand from Suffolk. The mason, a Kent man, would talk to you by the yard if you let him. Only the old carpenter was gruff and elsewhere absorbed.

Well then, it was a little world to itself, and everybody feeling very safe, and being very nice to you, as if you were really something special.

But it was the islander's world, not yours. He was the Master. The special smile, the special attention was to the Master. They all knew how well off they were. So the islander was no longer Mr. So-and-so. To everyone on the island, even to you yourself, he was 'the Master'.

Well, it was ideal. The Master was no tyrant. Ah, no! He was a delicate, sensitive, handsome Master, who wanted everything perfect and everybody happy. Himself, of course, to be the fount of this happiness and perfection.

But in his way, he was a poet. He treated his guests royally, his servants liberally. Yet he was shrewd, and very wise. He never came the boss over his people. Yet he kept his eye on everything, like a shrewd, blue-eyed young Hermes. And it was amazing what a lot of knowledge he had at hand. Amazing what he knew about Jersey cows, and cheese-making, ditching and fencing, flowers and gardening, ships and the sailing of ships. He was a fount of knowledge about everything, and this knowledge he imparted to his people in an odd, half-ironical, half-portentous fashion, as if he really belonged to the quaint, half-real world of the gods.

They listened to him with their hats in their hands. He loved white clothes; or creamy white; and cloaks, and broad hats. So, in fine weather, the bailiff would see the elegant tall figure in creamy-white serge coming like some bird over the fallow, to look at the weeding of the turnips. Then there would be a doffing of hats, and a few minutes of whimsical, shrewd, wise talk, to which the bailiff answered admiringly, and the farm-hands listened in silent wonder, leaning on their hoes. The bailiff was almost tender, to the Master.

Or, on a windy morning, he would stand with his cloak blowing in the sticky sea-wind, on the edge of the ditch that was being dug to drain a little swamp, talking in the teeth of the wind to the man below, who looked up at him with steady and inscrutable eyes.

Or at evening in the rain he would be seen hurrying across the yard, the broad hat turned against the rain. And the farm-wife would hurriedly exclaim: 'The Master! Get up, John, and clear him a place on the sofa.' And then the door opened, and it was a cry of: 'Why, of all things, if it isn't the Master! Why, have ye turned out then, of a night like this, to come across to the like of we?' And the bailiff took his cloak, and the farm-wife his hat, the two farm-hands drew their chairs to the back, he sat on the sofa and took a child up near him. He was wonderful with children, talked to them simply wonderful, made you think of Our Saviour Himself, said the woman.

He was always greeted with smiles, and the same peculiar deference, as if he were a higher, but also frailer being. They handled him almost tenderly, and almost with adulation. But when he left, or when they spoke of him, they had often a subtle, mocking smile on their faces. There was no need to be afraid of 'the Master'. Just let him have his own way. Only the carpenter was sometimes sincerely rude to him; so he didn't care for the old man.

It is doubtful whether any of them really liked him, man to man, or even woman to man. But then it is doubtful if he really liked any of them, as man to man, or man to woman. He wanted them to be happy, and the little world to be perfect. But anyone who wants the world to be perfect must be careful not to have real likes or dislikes. A general goodwill is all you can afford.

The sad fact is, alas, that general goodwill is always felt as something of an insult, by the mere object of it; and so it breeds a quite special brand of malice, Surely general goodwill is a form of egoism, that it should have such a result!

Our islander, however, had his own resources. He spent long hours in his library, for he was compiling a book of references to all the flowers mentioned in the Greek and Latin authors. He was not a great classical scholar; the usual public-school equipment. But there are such excellent translations nowadays. And it was so lovely, tracing flower after flower as it blossomed in the ancient world.

So the first year on the island passed by. A great deal had been done. Now the bills flooded in, and the Master, conscientious in all things, began to study them. The study left him pale and breathless. He was not a rich man. He knew he had been making a hole in his capital to get the island into running order. When he came to look, however, there was hardly anything left but hole. Thousands and thousands of pounds had the island swallowed into nothingness.

But surely the bulk of the spending was over! Surely the island would now begin to be self-supporting, even if it made no profit! Surely he was safe. He paid a good many of the bills, and took a little heart. But he had had a shock, and the next year, the coming year, there must be economy, frugality. He told his people so in simple and touching lanuage. And they said: 'Why, surely! Surely!'

So, while the wind blew and the rain lashed outside, he would sit in his library with the bailiff over a pipe and pot of beer, discussing farm projects. He lifted his narrow, handsome face, and his blue eyes became dreamy. '*What* a wind!' It blew like cannon-shots. He thought of his island, lashed with foam, and inaccessible, and he exulted.... No, he must not lose it. He turned back to the farm projects with the zest of genius, and his hands flicked white emphasis, while the bailiff intoned 'Yes, sir! Yes, sir! You're right, Master!'

But the man was hardly listening. He was looking at the Master's blue lawn shirt and curious pink tie with the fiery red stone, at the enamel sleeve-links, and at the ring with the peculiar scarab. The brown searching eyes of the man of the soil glanced repeatedly over the fine, immaculate figure of the Master, with a sort of slow, calculating wonder. But if he happened to catch the Master's bright, exalted glance, his own eye lit up with a careful cordiality and deference, as he bowed his head slightly.

Thus between them they decided what crops should be sown, what fertilisers should be used in different places, which breed of pigs should be imported, and which line of turkeys. That is to say, the bailiff, by continually cautiously agreeing with the Master, kept out of it, and let the young man have his own way.

The Master knew what he was talking about. He was brilliant at grasping the gist of a book, and knowing how to apply his knowledge. On the whole, his ideas were sound. The bailiff even knew it. But in the man of the soil there was no answering enthusiasm. The brown eyes smiled their cordial deference, but the thin lips never changed. The Master pursed his own flexible mouth in a boyish versatility, as he cleverly sketched in his ideas to the other man, and the bailiff made eyes of admiration, but in his heart he was not attending, he was only watching the Master as he would have watched a queer, caged animal, quite without sympathy, not implicated.

So, it was settled, and the Master rang for Elvery, the butler, to bring a sandwich. He, the Master, was pleased. The butler saw it, and came back with anchovy and ham sandwiches, and a newly opened bottle of vermouth. There was always a newly opened bottle of something.

It was the same with the mason. The Master and he discussed the drainage of a bit of land, and more pipes were ordered, more special bricks, more this, more that.

Fine weather came at last; there was a little lull in the hard work on the island. The Master went for a short cruise in his yacht. It was not really a yacht, just a little bit of a thing. They sailed along the coast of the mainland, and put in at the ports. At every port some friend turned up, the butler made elegant little meals in the cabin. Then the Master

677

was invited to villas and hotels, his people disembarked him as if he were a prince.

And oh, how expensive it turned out! He had to telegraph to the bank for money. And he went home again to economise.

The marsh-marigolds were blazing in the little swamp where the ditches were being dug for drainage. He almost regretted, now, the work in hand. The yellow beauties would not blaze again.

Harvest came, and a bumper crop. There must be a harvest-home supper. The long barn was now completely restored and added to. The carpenter had made long tables. Lanterns hung from the beams of the high-pitched roof. All the people of the island were assembled. The bailiff presided. It was a gay scene.

Towards the end of the supper the Master, in a velvet jacket, appeared with his guests. Then the bailiff rose and proposed 'The Master! Long life and health to the Master!' All the people drank the health with great enthusiasm and cheering. The Master replied with a little speech: They were on an island in a little world of their own. It depended on them all to make this world a world of true happiness and content. Each must do his part. He hoped he himself did what he could, for his heart was in his island, and with the people of his island.

The butler responded: As long as the island had such a Master, it could not help but be a little heaven for all the people on it. This was seconded with virile warmth by the bailiff and the mason, the skipper was beside himself. Then there was dancing, the old carpenter was fiddler.

But under all this, things were not well. The very next morning came the farm-boy to say that a cow had fallen over the cliff. The Master went to look. He peered over the not very high declivity, and saw her lying dead on a green ledge under a bit of late-flowering broom. A beautiful, expensive creature, already looking swollen. But what a fool, to fall so unnecessarily!

It was a question of getting several men to haul her up the bank, and then of skinning and burying her. No one would eat the meat. How repulsive it all was!

This was symbolic of the island. As sure as the spirits rose in the human breast, with a movement of joy, an invisible hand struck malevolently out of the silence. There must not be any joy, nor even any quiet peace. A man broke a leg, another was crippled with rheumatic fever. The pigs had some strange disease. A storm drove the yacht on a rock. The mason hated the butler, and refused to let his daughter serve at the house.

Out of the very air came a stony, heavy malevolence. The island itself seemed malicious. It would go on being hurtful and evil for weeks at a time. Then suddenly again one morning it would be fair, lovely as a morning in Paradise, everything beautiful and flowing. And everybody would begin to feel a great relief, and a hope for happiness.

Then as soon as the Master was opened out in spirit like an open flower, some ugly blow would fall. Somebody would send him an anonymous note, accusing some other person on the island. Somebody else would come hinting things against one of his servants.

'Some folks think they've got an easy job out here, with all the pickings they make!' the mason's daughter screamed at the suave butler, in the Master's hearing. He pretended not to hear.

'My man says this island is surely one of the lean kine of Egypt, it would swallow a sight of money, and you'd never get anything back out of it,' confided the farm-hand's wife to one of the Master's visitors.

The people were not contented. They were not islanders. 'We feel we're not doing right by the children,' said those who had children. 'We feel we're not doing right by ourselves,' said those who had no children. And the various families fairly came to hate one another.

Yet the island was so lovely. When there was a scent of honeysuckle and the moon brightly flickering down on the sea, then even the grumblers felt a strange nostalgia for it. It set you yearning, with a wild yearning; perhaps for the past, to be far back in the mysterious past of the island, when the blood had a different throb. Strange floods of passion came over you, strange violent lusts and imaginations of cruelty. The blood and the passion and the lust which the island had known. Uncanny dreams, half-dreams, half-evoked yearnings.

The Master himself began to be a little afraid of his island. He felt here strange, violent feelings he had never felt before, and lustful desires that he had been quite free from. He knew quite well now that his people didn't love him at all. He knew that their spirits were secretly against him, malicious, jeering, envious, and lurking to down him. He became just as wary and secretive with regard to them.

But it was too much. At the end of the second year, several departures took place. The housekeeper went. The Master always blamed self-important women most. The mason said he wasn't going to be monkeyed about any more, so he took his departure, with his family. The rheumatic farm-hand left.

And then the year's bills came in, the Master made up his accounts.

In spite of good crops, the assets were ridiculous, against the spending. The island had again lost, not hundreds but thousands of pounds. It was incredible. But you simply couldn't believe it! Where had it all gone?

The Master spent gloomy nights and days going through accounts in the library. He was thorough. It became evident, now the housekeeper had gone, that she had swindled him. Probably everybody was swindling him. But he hated to think it, so he put the thought away.

He emerged, however, pale and hollow-eyed from his balancing of unbalanceable accounts, looking as if something had kicked him in the stomach. It was pitiable. But the money had gone, and there was an end of it. Another great hole in his capital. How could people be so heartless?

It couldn't go on, that was evident. He would soon be bankrupt. He had to give regretful notice to his butler. He was afraid to find out how much his butler had swindled him. Because the man was such a wonderful butler, after all. And the farm bailiff had to go. The Master had no regrets in that quarter. The losses on the farm had almost embittered him.

The third year was spent in rigid cutting down of expenses. The island was still mysterious and fascinating. But it was also treacherous and cruel, secretly, fathomlessly malevolent. In spite of all its fair show of white blossom and bluebells, and the lovely dignity of foxgloves bending their rose-red bells, it was your implacable enemy.

With reduced staff, reduced wages, reduced splendour, the third year went by. But it was fighting against hope. The farm still lost a good deal. And once more there was a hole in that remnant of capital. Another hole in that which was already a mere remnant round the old holes. The island was mysterious in this also: it seemed to pick the very money out of your pocket, as if it were an octopus with invisible arms stealing from you in every direction.

Yet the Master still loved it. But with a touch of rancour now.

He spent, however, the second half of the fourth year intensely working on the mainland, to be rid of it. And it was amazing how difficult he found it, to dispose of an island. He had thought that everybody was pining for such an island as his; but not at all. Nobody would pay any price for it. And he wanted now to get rid of it, as a man who wants a divorce at any cost.

It was not till the middle of the fifth year that he transferred it, at a considerable loss to himself, to an hotel company who were willing to

680

speculate in it. They were to turn it into a handy honeymoon-and-golf island.

There, take that, island which didn't know when it was well off. Now be a honeymoon-and-golf island!

THE SECOND ISLAND

The islander had to move. But he was not going to the mainland. Oh, no! He moved to the smaller island, which still belonged to him. And he took with him the faithful old carpenter and wife, the couple he never really cared for; also a widow and daughter, who had kept house for him the last year; also an orphan lad, to help the old man.

The small island was very small; but being a hump of rock in the sea, it was bigger than it looked. There was a little track among the rocks and bushes, winding and scrambling up and down around the islet, so that it took you twenty minutes to do the circuit. It was more than you would have expected.

Still, it was an island. The islander moved himself, with all his books, into the commonplace six-roomed house up to which you had to scramble from the rocky landing-place. There were also two joined-together cottages. The old carpenter lived in one, with his wife and the lad, the widow and daughter lived in the other.

At last all was in order. The Master's books filled two rooms. It was already autumn, Orion lifting out of the sea. And in the dark nights, the Master could see the lights on his late island, where the hotel company were entertaining guests who would advertise the new resort for honeymoon-golfers.

On his lump of rock, however, the Master was still master. He explored the crannies, the odd hand-breadths of grassy level, the steep little cliffs where the last harebells hung and the seeds of summer were brown above the sea, lonely and untouched. He peered down the old well. He examined the stone pen where the pig had been kept. Himself, he had a goat.

Yes, it was an island. Always, always underneath among the rocks the Celtic sea sucked and washed and smote its feathery greyness. How many different noises of the sea! Deep explosions, rumblings, strange long sighs and whistling noises; then voices, real voices of people clamouring as if they were in a market, under the waters: and again, the far-off ringing of a bell, surely an actual bell! Then a tremendous trilling noise, very long and alarming, and an undertone of hoarse gasping.

On this island there were no human ghosts, no ghosts of any ancient race. The sea, and the spume and the weather, had washed them all out, washed them out so there was only the sound of the sea itself, its own ghost, myriad-voiced, communing and plotting and shouting all winter long. And only the smell of the sea, with a few bristly bushes of gorse and coarse tufts of heather, among the grey, pellucid rocks, in the grey, more-pellucid air. The coldness, the greyness, even the soft, creeping fog of the sea, and the islet of rock humped up in it all, like the last point in space.

Green star Sirius stood over the sea's rim. The island was a shadow. Out at sea a ship showed small lights. Below, in the rocky cove, the row-boat and the motor-boat were safe. A light shone in the carpenter's kitchen. That was all.

Save, of course, that the lamp was lit in the house, where the widow was preparing supper, her daughter helping. The islander went in to his meal. Here he was no longer the Master, he was an islander again and he had peace. The old carpenter, the widow and daughter were all faithfulness itself. The old man worked while ever there was light to see, because he had a passion for work. The widow and her quiet, rather delicate daughter of thirty-three worked for the Master, because they loved looking after him, and they were infinitely grateful for the haven he provided them. But they didn't call him 'the Master'. They gave him his name: 'Mr. Cathcart, sir!' softly and reverently. And he spoke back to them also softly, gently, like people far from the world, afraid to make a noise.

The island was no longer a 'world'. It was a sort of refuge. The islander no longer struggled for anything. He had no need. It was as if he and his few dependants were a small flock of sea-birds alighted on this rock, as they travelled through space, and keeping together without a word. The silent mystery of travelling birds.

He spent most of his day in his study. His book was coming along. The widow's daughter could type out his manuscript for him, she was not uneducated. It was the one strange sound on the island, the type-writer. But soon even its spattering fitted in with the sea's noises, and the wind's.

The months went by. The islander worked away in his study, the people of the island went quietly about their concerns. The goat had a

682

little black kid with yellow eyes. There were mackerel in the sea. The old man went fishing in the row-boat with the lad, when the weather was calm enough; they went off in the motor-boat to the biggest island for the post. And they brought supplies, never a penny wasted. And the days went by, and the nights, without desire, without ennui.

The strange stillness from all desire was a kind of wonder to the islander. He didn't want anything. His soul at last was still in him, his spirit was like a dim-lit cave under water, where strange sea-foliage expands upon the watery atmosphere, and scarcely sways, and a mute fish shadowily slips in and slips away again. All still and soft and uncrying, yet alive as rooted seaweed is alive.

The islander said to himself: 'Is this happiness?' He said to himself: 'I am turned into a dream. I feel nothing, or I don't know what I feel. Yet it seems to me I am happy.'

Only he had to have something upon which his mental activity could work. So he spent long, silent hours in his study, working not very fast, nor very importantly, letting the writing spin softly from him as if it were drowsy gossamer. He no longer fretted whether it were good or not, what he produced. He slowly, softly spun it like gossamer, and if it were to melt away as gossamer in autumn melts, he would not mind. It was only the soft evanescence of gossamy things which now seemed to him permanent. The very mist of eternity was in them. Whereas stone buildings, cathedrals for example, seemed to him to howl with temporary resistance, knowing they must fall at last; the tension of their long endurance seemed to howl forth from them all the time.

Sometimes he went to the mainland and to the city. Then he went elegantly, dressed in the latest style, to his club. He sat in a stall at the theatre, he shopped in Bond Street. He discussed terms for publishing his book. But over his face was that gossamy look of having dropped out of the race of progress, which made the vulgar city people feel they had won it over him, and made him glad to go back to his island.

He didn't mind if he never published his book. The years were blending into a soft mist, from which nothing obtruded. Spring came. There was never a primrose on his island, but he found a winter-aconite. There were two little sprayed bushes of blackthorn, and some windflowers. He began to make a list of the flowers of his islet, and that was absorbing. He noted a wild currant bush and watched for the elder flowers on a stunted little tree, then for the first yellow rags of the broom, and wild roses. Bladder campion, orchids, stitchwort, celandine, he was prouder of them than if they had been people on his island.

When he came across the golden saxifrage, so inconspicuous in a damp corner, he crouched over it in a trance, he knew not for how long, looking at it. Yet it was nothing to look at. As the widow's daughter found, when he showed it her.

He had said to her in real triumph:

'I found the golden saxifrage this morning.'

The name sounded splendid. She looked at him with fascinated brown eyes, in which was a hollow ache that frightened him a little.

'Did you, sir? Is it a nice flower?'

He pursed his lips and tilted his brows.

'Well – not showy exactly. I'll show it you if you like.'

'I should like to see it.'

She was so quiet, so wistful. But he sensed in her a persistency which made him uneasy. She said she was so happy: really happy. She followed him quietly, like a shadow, on the rocky track where there was never room for two people to walk side by side. He went first, and could feel her there, immediately behind him, following so submissively, gloating on him from behind.

It was a kind of pity for her which made him become her lover: though he never realised the extent of the power she had gained over him, and how *she* willed it. But the moment he had fallen, a jangling feeling came upon him, that it was all wrong. He felt a nervous dislike of her. He had not wanted it. And it seemed to him, as far as her physical self went, she had not wanted it either. It was just her will. He went away, and climbed at the risk of his neck down to a ledge near the sea. There he sat for hours, gazing all jangled at the sea, and saying miserably to himself: 'We didn't want it. We didn't really want it.'

It was the automatism of sex that had caught him again. Not that he hated sex. He deemed it, as the Chinese do, one of the great life-mysteries. But it had become mechanical, automatic, and he wanted to escape that. Automatic sex shattered him, and filled him with a sort of death. He thought he had come through to a new stillness of desireless-ness. Perhaps beyond that there was a new fresh delicacy of desire, an unentered frail communion of two people meeting on untrodden ground.

Be that as it might, this was not it. This was nothing new or fresh. It was automatic, and driven from the will. Even she, in her true self, hadn't wanted it. It was automatic in her.

When he came home, very late, and saw her face white with fear and

684

apprehension of his feeling against her, he pitied her, and spoke to her delicately, reassuringly. But he kept himself remote from her.

She gave no sign. She served him with the same silence, the same hidden hunger to serve him, to be near where he was. He felt her love following him with strange, awful persistency. She claimed nothing. Yet now, when he met her bright, brown, curiously vacant eyes, he saw in them the mute question. The question came direct at him, with a force and a power of will he never realised.

So he succumbed, and asked her again.

'Not,' she said, 'if it will make you hate me.'

'Why should it?' he replied, nettled. 'Of course not.'

'You know I would do anything on earth for you.'

It was only afterwards, in his exasperation, he remembered what she said, and was more exasperated. Why should she pretend to do this *for him*? Why not herself? But in his exasperation, he drove himself deeper in. In order to achieve some sort of satisfaction, which he never did achieve, he abandoned himself to her. Everybody on the island knew. But he did not care.

Then even what desire he had left him, and he felt only shattered. He felt that only with her will had she wanted him. Now he was shattered and full of self-contempt. His island was smirched and spoiled. He had lost his place in the rare, desireless levels of Time to which he had at last arrived, and he had fallen right back. If only it had been true, delicate desire between them, and a delicate meeting on the third rare place where a man might meet a woman, when they were both true to the frail, sensitive, crocus-flame of desire in them. But it had been no such thing: automatic, an act of will, not of true desire, it left him feeling humiliated.

He went away from the islet, in spite of her mute reproach. And he wandered about the continent, vainly seeking a place where he could stay. He was out of key, he did not fit in the world any more.

There came a letter from Flora – her name was Flora – to say she was afraid she was going to have a child. He sat down as if he were shot, and he remained sitting. But he replied to her: 'Why be afraid? If it is so, it is so, and we should rather be pleased than afraid.'

At this very moment, it happened there was an auction of islands. He got the maps, and studied them. And at the auction he bought, for very little money, another island. It was just a few acres of rock away in the north, on the outer fringe of the isles. It was low, it rose low out of the great ocean. There was not a building, not even a tree on it. Only northern sea-turf, a pool of rain-water, a bit of sedge, rock, and sea-birds. Nothing else. Under the weeping wet western sky.

He made a trip to visit his new possession. For several days, owing to the seas, he could not approach it. Then, in a light sea-mist, he landed, and saw it hazy, low, stretching apparently a long way. But it was illusion. He walked over the wet, springy turf, and dark-grey sheep tossed away from him, spectral, bleating hoarsely. And he came to the dark pool, with the sedge. Then on in the dampness, to the grey sea sucking angrily among the rocks.

This was indeed an island.

So he went home to Flora. She looked at him with guilty fear, but also with a triumphant brightness in her uncanny eyes. And again he was gentle, he reassured her, even he wanted her again, with that curious desire that was almost like toothache. So he took her to the mainland, and they were married, since she was going to have his child.

They returned to the island. She still brought in his meals, her own along with then. She sat and ate with him. He would have it so. The widowed mother preferred to stay in the kitchen. And Flora slept in the guest-room of his house, mistress of his house.

His desire, whatever it was, died in him with nauseous finality. The child would still be months coming. His island was hateful to him, vulgar, a suburb. He himself had lost all his finer distinction. The weeks passed in a sort of prison, in humiliation. Yet he stuck it out, till the child was born. But he was meditating escape. Flora did not even know.

A nurse appeared, and ate at table with them. The doctor came sometimes, and, if the sea were rough, he too had to stay. He was cheery over his whisky.

They might have been a young couple in Golders Green.

The daughter was born at last. The father looked at the baby, and felt depressed, almost more than he could bear. The millstone was tied round his neck. But he tried not to show what he felt. And Flora did not know. She still smiled with a kind of half-witted triumph in her joy, as she got well again. Then she began again to look at him with those aching, suggestive, somehow impudent eyes. She adored him so.

This he could not stand. He told her that he had to go away for a time. She wept, but she thought she had got him. He told her he had settled the best part of his property on her, and wrote down for her what income it would produce. She hardly listened, only looked at him with those heavy, adoring, impudent eyes. He gave her a cheque-book, with the amount of her credit duly entered. This did arouse her interest. And he told her, if she got tired of the island, she could choose her home wherever she wished.

She followed him with those aching, persistent brown eyes, when he left, and he never even saw her weep.

He went straight north, to prepare his third island.

III

THE THIRD ISLAND

The third island was soon made habitable. With cement and the big pebbles from the shingle beach, two men built him a hut, and roofed it with corrugated iron. A boat brought over a bed and table, and three chairs, with a good cupboard, and a few books. He laid in a supply of coal and paraffin and food – he wanted so little.

The house stood near the flat shingle bay where he landed, and where he pulled up his light boat. On a sunny day in August the men sailed away and left him. The sea was still and pale blue. On the horizon he saw the small mail-steamer slowly passing northwards, as if she were walking. She served the outer isles twice a week. He could row out to her if need be, in calm weather, and he could signal her from a flagstaff behind his cottage.

Half a dozen sheep still remained on the island, as company; and he had a cat to rub against his legs. While the sweet, sunny days of the northern autumn lasted, he would walk among the rocks, and over the springy turf of his small domain, always coming to the ceaseless, restless sea. He looked at every leaf, that might be different from another, and he watched the endless expansion and contraction of the water-tossed sea-weed. He had never a tree, not even a bit of heather to guard. Only the turf, and tiny turf-plants, and the sedge by the pool, the seaweed in the ocean. He was glad. He didn't want trees or bushes. They stood up like people, too assertive. His bare, low-pitched island in the pale blue sea was all he wanted.

He no longer worked at his book. The interest had gone. He liked to sit on the low elevation of his island, and see the sea; nothing but the pale, quiet sea. And to feel his mind turn soft and hazy, like the hazy ocean. Sometimes, like a mirage, he would see the shadow of land rise

687

hovering to northwards. It was a big island beyond. But quite without substance.

He was soon almost startled when he perceived the steamer on the near horizon, and his heart contracted with fear, lest it were going to pause and molest him. Anxiously he watched it go, and not till it was out of sight did he feel truly relieved, himself again. The tension of waiting for human approach was cruel. He did not want to be approached. He did not want to hear voices. He was shocked by the sound of his own voice, if he inadvertantly spoke to his cat. He rebuked himself for having broken the great silence. And he was irritated when his cat would look up at him and mew faintly, plaintively. He frowned at her. And she knew. She was becoming wild, lurking in the rocks, perhaps fishing.

But what he disliked most was when one of the lumps of sheep opened its mouth and baa-ed its hoarse, raucous baa. He watched it, and it looked to him hideous and gross. He came to dislike the sheep very much.

He wanted only to hear the whispering sound of the sea, and the sharp cries of the gulls, cries that came out of another world to him. And best of all, the great silence.

He decided to get rid of the sheep when the boat came. They were accustomed to him now, and stood and stared at him with yellow or colourless eyes, in an insolence that was almost cold ridicule. There was a suggestion of cold indecency about them. He disliked them very much. And when they jumped with staccato jumps off the rocks, and their hoofs made the dry, sharp hit, and the fleece flopped on their square backs, he found them repulsive, degrading.

The fine weather passed, and it rained all day. He lay a great deal on his bed, listening to the water trickling from his roof into the zinc water-butt, looking through the open door at the rain, the dark rocks, the hidden sea. Many gulls were on the island now: many sea-birds of all sorts. It was another world of life. Many of the birds he had never seen before. His old impulse came over him, to send for a book, to know their names. In a flicker of the old passion, to know the name of everything he saw, he even decided to row out to the steamer. The names of these birds! He must know their names, otherwise he had not got them, they were not quite alive to him.

But the desire left him, and he merely watched the birds as they wheeled or walked around him, watched them vaguely, without discrimination. All interest had left him. Only there was one gull, a big, handsome fellow, who would walk back and forth, back and forth in front of the open door of the cabin, as if he had some mission there. He was big, and pearl-grey, and his roundnesses were as smooth and lovely as a pearl. Only the folded wings had shut black pinions, and on the closed black feathers were three very distinct white dots, making a pattern. The islander wondered very much, why this bit of trimming on the bird out of the far, cold seas. And as the gull walked back and forth, back and forth in front of the cabin, strutting on pale-dusky gold feet, holding up his pale yellow beak, that was curved at the tip, with curious alien importance, the man wondered over him. He was portentous, he had a meaning.

Then the bird came no more. The island, which had been full of sea-birds, the flash of wings, the sound and cut of wings and sharp eerie cries in the air, began to be deserted again. No longer they sat like living eggs on the rocks and turf, moving their heads, but scarcely rising into flight round his feet. No longer they ran across the turf among the sheep, and lifted themselves upon low wings. The host had gone. But some remained, always.

The days shortened, and the world grew eerie. One day the boat came: as if suddenly, swooping down. The islander found it a violation. It was torture to talk to those two men, in their homely clumsy clothes. The air of familiarity around them was very repugnant to him. Himself, he was neatly dressed, his cabin was neat and tidy. He resented any intrusion, the clumsy homeliness, the heavy-footedness of the two fishermen was really repulsive to him.

The letters they had brought he left lying unopened in a little box. In one of them was his money. But he could not bear to open even that one. Any kind of contact was repulsive to him. Even to read his name on an envelope. He hid the letters away.

And the hustle and horror of getting the sheep caught and tied and put in the ship made him loathe with profound repulsion the whole of the animal creation. What repulsive god invented animals and evil-smelling men? To his nostrils, the fishermen and the sheep alike smelled foul; an uncleanness on the fresh earth.

He was still nerve-racked and tortured when the ship at last lifted sail and was drawing away, over the still sea. And sometimes, days after, he would start with repulsion, thinking he heard the munching of sheep.

The dark days of winter drew on. Sometimes there was no real day at all. He felt ill, as if he were dissolving, as if dissolution had already set in inside him. Everything was twilight, outside, and in his mind and soul. Once, when he went to the door, he saw black heads of men swimming in his bay. For some moments he swooned unconscious. It was the shock, the horror of unexpected human approach. The horror in the twilight! And not till the shock had undermined him and left him disembodied, did he realise that the black heads were the heads of seals swimming in. A sick relief came over him. But he was barely conscious, after the shock. Later on, he sat and wept with gratitude, because they were not men. But he never realised that he wept. He was too dim. Like some strange, ethereal animal, he no longer realised what he was doing.

Only he still derived his single satisfaction from being alone, absolutely alone, with the space soaking into him. The grey sea alone, and the footing of his sea-washed island. No other contact. Nothing human to bring its horror into contact with him. Only space, damp, twilit, sea-washed space! This was the bread of his soul.

For this reason, he was most glad when there was a storm, or when the sea was high. Then nothing could get at him. Nothing could come through to him from the outer world. True, the terrific violence of the wind made him suffer badly. At the same time, it swept the world utterly out of existence for him. He always liked the sea to be heavily rolling and tearing. Then no boat could get at him. It was like eternal ramparts round his island.

He kept no track of time, and no longer thought of opening a book. The print, the printed letters, so like the depravity of speech, looked obscene. He tore the brass label from his paraffin stove. He obliterated any bit of lettering in his cabin.

His cat had disappeared. He was rather glad. He shivered at her thin, obtrusive call. She had lived in the coal-shed. And each morning he had put her a dish of porridge, the same as he ate. He washed her saucer with repulsion. He did not like her writhing about. But he fed her scrupulously. Then one day she did not come for her porridge; she always mewed for it. She did not come again.

He prowled about his island in the rain, in a big oilskin coat, not knowing what he was looking at, nor what he went out to see. Time had ceased to pass. He stood for long spaces, gazing from a white, sharp face, with those keen, far-off blue eyes of his, gazing fiercely and almost cruelly at the dark sea under the dark sky. And if he saw the labouring sail of a fishing-boat away on the cold waters, a strange malevolent anger passed over his features.

Sometimes he was ill. He knew he was ill, because he staggered as he walked, and easily fell down. Then he paused to think what it was. And he went to his stores and took out dried milk and malt, and ate that. Then he forgot again. He ceased to register his own feelings.

The days were beginning to lengthen. All winter the weather had been comparatively mild, but with much rain, much rain. He had forgotten the sun. Suddenly, however, the air was very cold, and he began to shiver. A fear came over him. The sky was level and grey, and never a star appeared at night. It was very cold. More birds began to arrive. The island was freezing. With trembling hands he made a fire in his grate. The cold frightened him.

And now it continued, day after day, a dull, deathly cold. Occasional crumblings of snow were in the air. The days were greyly longer, but no change in the cold. Frozen grey daylight. The birds passed away, flying away. Some he saw lying frozen. It was as if all life were drawing away, contracting away from the north, contracting southwards. 'Soon,' he said to himself, 'it will all be gone, and in all these regions nothing will be alive.' He felt a cruel satisfaction in the thought.

Then one night there seemed to be a relief; he slept better, did not tremble half-awake, and writhe so much, half-conscious. He had become so used to the quaking and writhing of his body, he hardly noticed it. But when for once it slept deep, he noticed that.

He woke in the morning to a curious whiteness. His window was muffled. It had snowed. He got up and opened his door, and shuddered. Ugh! How cold! All white, with a dark leaden sea, and black rocks curiously speckled with white. The foam was no longer pure. It seemed dirty. And the sea ate at the whiteness of the corpse-like land. Crumbles of snow were silting down the dead air.

On the ground the snow was a foot deep, white and smooth and soft, windless. He took a shovel to clear round his house and shed. The pallor of morning darkened. There was a strange rumbling of far-off thunder in the frozen air, and through the newly-falling snow, a dim flash of lightning. Snow now fell steadily down in the motionless obscurity.

He went out for a few minutes. But it was difficult. He stumbled and fell in the snow, which burned his face. Weak, faint, he toiled home. And when he recovered, took the trouble to make hot milk.

It snowed all the time. In the afternoon again there was a muffled rumbling of thunder, and flashes of lightning blinking reddish through the falling snow. Uneasy, he went to bed and lay staring fixedly at nothingness.

691

Morning seemed never to come. An eternity long he lay and waited for one alleviating pallor on the night. And at last it seemed the air was paler. His house was a cell faintly illuminated with white light. He realised the snow was walled outside his window. He got up, in the dead cold. When he opened his door, the motionless snow stopped him in a wall as high as his breast. Looking over the top of it, he felt the dead wind slowly driving, saw the snow-powder lift and travel like a funeral train. The blackish sea churned and champed, seeming to bite at the snow, impotent. The sky was grey, but luminous.

He began to work in a frenzy, to get at his boat. If he was to be shut in, it must be by his own choice, not by the mechanical power of the elements. He must get to the sea. He must be able to get at his boat.

But he was weak, and at times the snow overcame him. It fell on him, and he lay buried and lifeless. Yet every time he struggled alive before it was too late, and fell upon the snow with the energy of fever. Exhausted, he would not give in. He crept indoors and made coffee and bacon. Long since he had cooked so much. Then he went at the snow once more. He must conquer the snow, this new, white brute force which had accumulated against him.

He worked in the awful, dead wind, pushing the snow aside, pressing it with his shovel. It was cold, freezing hard in the wind, even when the sun came out for a while, and showed him his white, lifeless surroundings, the black sea rolling sullen, flecked with dull spume, away to the horizons. Yet the sun had power on his face. It was March.

He reached the boat. He pushed the snow away, then sat down under the lee of the boat, looking at the sea, which swirled nearly to his feet, in the high tide. Curiously natural the pebbles looked, in a world gone all uncanny. The sun shone no more. Snow was falling in hard crumbs, that vanished as if by a miracle as they touched the hard blackness of the sea. Hoarse waves rang in the shingle, rushing up at the snow. The wet rocks were brutally black. And all the time the myriad swooping crumbs of snow, demonish, touched the dark sea and disappeared.

During the night there was a great storm. It seemed to him he could hear the vast mass of snow striking all the world with a ceaseless thud; and over it all, the wind roared in strange hollow volleys, in between which came a jump of blindfold lightning, then the low roll of thunder heavier than the wind. When at last the dawn faintly discoloured the dark, the storm had more or less subsided, but a steady wind drove on. The snow was up to the top of his door.

Sullenly, he worked to dig himself out. And he managed through sheer persistency to get out. He was in the tail of a great drift, many feet high. When he got through, the frozen snow was not more than two feet deep. But his island was gone. Its shape was all changed, great heaping white hills rose where no hills had been, inaccessible, and they fumed like volcanoes, but with snow powder. He was sickened and overcome.

His boat was in another, smaller drift. But he had not the strength to clear it. He looked at it helplessly. The shovel slipped from his hands, and he sank in the snow, to forget. In the snow itself, the sea resounded.

Something brought him to. He crept to his house. He was almost without feeling. Yet he managed to warm himself, just that part of him which leaned in snow-sleep over the coal fire. Then again he made hot milk. After which, carefully, he built up the fire.

The wind dropped. Was it night again? In the silence, it seemed he could hear the panther-like dropping of infinite snow. Thunder rumbled nearer, crackled quick after the bleared reddened lightning. He lay in bed in a kind of stupor. The elements! The elements! His mind repeated the word dumbly. You can't win against the elements.

How long it went on, he never knew. Once, like a wraith, he got out and climbed to the top of a white hill on his unrecognisable island. The sun was hot. 'It is summer,' he said to himself, 'and the time of leaves.' He looked stupidly over the whiteness of his foreign island, over the waste of the lifeless sea. He pretended to imagine he saw the wink of a sail. Because he knew too well there would never again be a sail on that stark sea.

As he looked, the sky mysteriously darkened and chilled. From far off came the mutter of the unsatisfied thunder, and he knew it was the signal of the snow rolling over the sea. He turned, and felt its breath on him.

THE OVERTONE

His wife was talking to two other women. He lay on the lounge pretending to read. The lamps shed a golden light, and, through the open door, the night was lustrous, and a white moon went like a woman, unashamed and naked across the sky. His wife, her dark hair tinged with grey looped low on her white neck, fingered as she talked the pearl that hung in a heavy, naked drop against the bosom of her dress. She was still a beautiful woman, and one who dressed like the night, for harmony. Her gown was of silk lace, all in flakes, as if the fallen, pressed petals of black and faded-red poppies were netted together with gossamer about her. She was fifty-one, and he was fifty-two. It seemed impossible. He felt his love cling round her like her dress, like a garment of dead leaves. She was talking to a quiet woman about the suffrage. The other girl, tall, rather aloof, sat listening in her chair, with the posture of one who neither accepts nor rejects, but who allows things to go on around her, and will know what she thinks only when she must act. She seemed to be looking away into the night. A scent of honeysuckle came through the open door. Then a large grey moth blundered into the light.

It was very still, almost too silent, inside the room. Mrs. Renshaw's quiet, musical voice continued:

'But think of a case like Mrs. Mann's now. She is a clever woman. If she had slept in my cradle, and I in hers, she would have looked a greater lady than I do at this minute. But she married Mann, and she has seven children by him, and goes out charring. Her children she can never leave. So she must stay with a dirty, drunken brute like Mann. If she had an income of two pounds a week, she could say to him: "Sir, good-bye to you," and she would be well rid. But no, she is tied to him for ever.'

They were discussing the State-endowment of mothers. She and Mrs. Hankin were bitterly keen upon it. Elsa Laskell sat and accepted their talk as she did the scent of the honeysuckle or the blundering adventure of the moth round the silk: it came burdened, not with the meaning of the words, but with the feeling of the woman's heart as she spoke. Perhaps she heard a nightingale in the park outside – perhaps

694

she did. And then this talk inside drifted also to the girl's heart, like a sort of inarticulate music. Then she was vaguely aware of the man sprawled in his homespun suit upon the lounge. He had not changed for dinner: he was called unconventional.

She knew he was old enough to be her father, and yet he looked young enough to be her lover. They all seemed young, the beautiful hostess, too, but with a meaningless youth that cannot ripen, like an unfertilised flower which lasts a long time. He was a man she classed as a Dane – with fair, almost sandy hair, blue eyes, long loose limbs, and a boyish activity. But he was fifty-two – and he lay looking out on the night, with one of his hands swollen from hanging so long inert, silent. The women bored him.

Elsa Laskell sat in a sort of dreamy state, and the feelings of her hostess, and the feeling of her host drifted like iridesence upon the quick of her soul, among the white touch of that moon out there, and the exotic heaviness of the honeysuckle, and the strange flapping of the moth. So still, it was, behind the murmur of talk: a silence of being. Of the third woman, Mrs Hankin, the girl had no sensibility. But the night and the moon, the moth, Will Renshaw and Edith Renshaw and herself were all in full being, a harmony.

To him it was six months after his marriage, and the sky was the same, and the honeysuckle in the air. He was living again his crisis, as we all must, fretting and fretting against our failure, till we have worn away the thread of our life. It was six months after his marriage, and they were down at the little bungalow on the bank of the Soar. They were comparatively poor, though her father was rich, and his was well-to-do. And they were alone in the little two-roomed bungalow that stood on its wild bank over the river, among the honeysuckle bushes. He had cooked the evening meal, they had eaten the omelette and drank the coffee, and all was settling into stillness.

He sat outside, by the remnants of the fire, looking at the country lying level and lustrous grey opposite him. Trees hung like vapour in a perfect calm under the moonlight. And that was the moon so perfectly naked and unfaltering, going her errand simply through the night. And that was the river faintly rustling. And there, down the darkness, he saw a flashing of activity white betwixt black twigs. It was the water mingling and thrilling with the moon. So! It made him quiver, and reminded him of the starlit rush of a hare. There was vividness then in all this lucid night, things flashing and quivering with being, almost as the soul quivers in the darkness of the eye. He could feel it. The night's

695

great circle was the pupil of an eye, full of the mystery, and the un-known fire of life, that does not burn away, but flickers unquenchable.

So he rose, and went to look for his wife. She sat with her dark head bent into the light of a reading lamp, in the little hut. She wore a white dress, and he could see her shoulders' softness and curve through the lawn. Yet she did not look up when he moved. He stood in the doorway, knowing that she felt his presence. Yet she gave no sign.

'Will you come out?' he asked.

She looked up at him as if to find out what he wanted, and she was rather cold to him. But when he had repeated his request, she had risen slowly to acquiesce, and a tiny shiver had passed down her shoulders. So he unhung from its peg her beautiful Paisley shawl, with its temp-ered colours that looked as if they had faltered through the years and now were here in their essence, and put it round her. They sat again outside the little hut, under the moonlight. He held both her hands. They were heavy with rings. But one ring was his wedding ring. He had married her, and there was nothing more to own. He owned her, and the night was the pupil of her eye, in which was everything. He kissed her fingers, but she sat and made no sign. It was as he wished. He kissed her fingers again.

Then a corncrake began to call in the meadow across the river, a strange, dispassionate sound, that made him feel not quite satisfied, not quite sure. It was not all achieved. The moon, in her white and naked candour, was beyond him. He felt a little numbness, as one who has gloves on. He could not feel that clear, clean moon. There was some-thing betwixt him and her, as if he had gloves on. Yet he ached for the clear touch, skin to skin – even of the moonlight. He wanted a further purity, a newer cleanness and nakedness. The corncrake cried too. And he watched the moon, and he watched her light on his hands. It was like a butterfly on his glove, that he could see, but not feel. And he wanted to unglove himself. Quite clear, quite, quite bare to the moon, the touch of everything, he wanted to be. And after all, his wife was everything – moon, vapour of trees, trickling water and drift of perfume – it was all his wife. The moon glistened on her finger-tips as he cher-ished them, and a flash came out of a diamond, among the darkness. So, even here in the quiet harmony, life was at a flash with itself.

'Come with me to the top of the red hill,' he said to his wife quietly.

'But why?' she asked.

'Do come.'

And dumbly she acquiesced, and her shawl hung gleaming above the white flash of her skirt. He wanted to hold her hand, but she was walking apart from him, in her long shawl. So he went to her side, humbly. And he was humble, but he felt it was great. He had looked into the whole of the night, as into the pupil of an eye. And now, he would come perfectly clear out of all his embarrassments of shame and darkness, clean as the moon who walked naked across the night, so that the whole night was as an effluence from her, the whole of it was hers, held in her effluence of moonlight, which was her perfect nakedness, uniting her to everything. Covering was barrier, like cloud across the moon.

The red hill was steep, but there was a tiny path from the bungalow, which he had worn himself. And in the effort of climbing, he felt he was struggling nearer and nearer to himself. Always he looked half round, where, just behind him, she followed, in the lustrous obscurity of her shawl. Her steps came with a little effort up the steep hill, and he loved her feet, he wanted to kiss them as they strove upwards in the gloom. He put aside the twigs and branches. There was a strong scent of honeysuckle like a thick strand of gossamer over his mouth.

He knew a place on the ledge of the hill, on the lip of the cliff, where the trees stood back and left a little dancing-green, high up above the water, there in the midst of miles of moonlit, lonely country. He parted the boughs, sure as a fox that runs to its lair. And they stood together on this little dancing-green presented towards the moon, with the red cliff cumbered with bushes going down to the river below, and the haze of moon-dust on the meadows, and the trees behind them, and only the moon could look straight into the place he had chosen.

She stood always a little way behind him. He saw her face all compounded of shadows and moonlight, and he dared not kiss her yet.

'Will you,' he said, 'will you take off your things and love me here?'

'I can't,' she said.

He looked away to the moon. It was difficult to ask her again, yet it meant so much to him. There was not a sound in the night. He put his hand to his throat and began to unfasten his collar.

'Take off all your things and love me,' he pleaded.

For a moment she was silent.

'I can't,' she said.

Mechanically, he had taken off his flannel collar and pushed it into his pocket. Then he stood on the edge of the land, looking down into all that gleam, as into the living pupil of an eye. He was bareheaded to the moon. Not a breath of air ruffled his bare throat. Still, in the dropping folds of her shawl, she stood, a thing of dusk and moonlight, a little back. He ached with the earnestness of his desire. All he wanted was to give himself, clean and clear, into this night, this time. Of which she was all, she was everything. He could go to her now, under the white candour of the moon, without shame or shadow, but in his completeness loving her completeness, without a stain, without a shadow between them such as even a flower could cast. For this he yearned as never in his life he could yearn more deeply.

'Do take me,' he said, gently parting the shawl on her breast. But she held it close, and her voice went hard.

'No – I can't,' she said.

'Why?'

'I can't – let us go back.'

He looked again over the countryside of dimness, saying in a low tone, his back towards her:

'But I love you – and I want you so much – like that, here and now. I'll never ask you anything again,' he said quickly, passionately, as he turned to her. 'Do this for me,' he said. 'I'll never trouble you for anything again. I promise.'

'I can't,' she said stubbornly, with some hopelessness in her voice.

'Yes,' he said. 'Yes. You trust me, don't you?'

'I don't want it. Not here – not now,' she said.

'Do,' he said. 'Yes.'

'You can have me in the bungalow. Why do you want me here?' she asked.

'But I do. Have me, Edith. Have me now.'

'No,' she said, turning away. 'I want to go down.'

'And you won't?'

'No – I can't.'

There was something like fear in her voice. They went down the hill together. And he did not know how he hated her, as if she had kept him out of the promised land that was justly his. He thought he was too generous to bear her a grudge. So he had always held himself deferential to her. And later that evening he had loved her. But she had hated it, it had been really his hate ravaging her. Why had he lied, calling it love? Ever since, it had seemed the same, more or less. So that he had ceased to come to her, gradually. For one night she had said: 'I think a man's body is ugly – all in parts with mechanical joints.' And now he had scarcely had her for some years. For she thought him an ugliness. And there were no children.

Now that everything was essentially over for both of them, they lived on the surface, and had good times. He drove to all kinds of unexpected places in his motor-car, bathed where he liked, said what he liked, and did what he liked. But nobody minded very much his often aggressive unconventionality. It was only fencing with the foils. There was no danger in his thrusts. He was a castrated bear. So he prided himself on being a bear, on being known as an uncouth bear.

It was not often he lay and let himself drift. But always when he did, he held it against her that on the night when they climbed the red bank, she refused to have him. There were perhaps many things he might have held against her, but this was the only one that remained: his real charge against her on the Judgment Day. Why had she done it? It had been, he might almost say, a holy desire on his part. It had been almost like taking off his shoes before God. Yet she refused him, she who was his religion to him. Perhaps she had been afraid, she who was so good – afraid of the big righteousness of it – as if she could not trust herself so near the Burning Bush, dared not go near for transfiguration, afraid of herself.

It was a thought he could not bear. Rising softly, because she was still talking, he went out into the night.

Elsa Laskell stirred uneasily in her chair. Mrs. Renshaw went on talking like a somnambule, not because she really had anything to say about the State-endowment of mothers, but because she had a weight on her heart that she wanted to talk away. The girl heard, and lifted her hand, and stirred her fingers uneasily in the dark-purple porphyry bowl, where pink rose-leaves and crimson, thrown this morning from the stem, lay gently shrivelling. There came a slight acrid scent of new rose-petals. And still the girl lifted her long white fingers among the red and pink in the dark bowl, as if they stirred in blood.

And she felt the nights behind like a purple bowl into which the woman's heart-beats were shed, like rose-leaves fallen and left to wither and go brown. For Mrs. Renshaw had waited for him. During happy days of stillness and blueness she had moved, while the sunshine glancing through her blood made flowers in her heart, like blossoms underground thrilling with expectancy, lovely fragrant things that would have delight to appear. And all day long she had gone secretly and quietly saying, saying: 'To-night – to-night they will blossom for him. To-night I shall be a bed of blossom for him, all narcissi and fresh fragrant things shaking for joy, when he comes with his deeper sunshine, when he turns the darkness like mould, and brings them forth with his sunshine for spade. Yea, there are two suns; him in the sky and that other, warmer one whose beams are our radiant bodies. He is a sun to me, shining full on my heart when he comes, and everything stirs.' But he had come like a bitter morning. He had never bared the sun of himself to her – a sullen day he had been on her heart, covered with cloud impenetrable. She had waited so heavy anxious, with such a wealth of possibility. And he in his blindness had never known. He could never let the real rays of his love through the cloud of fear and mistrust. For once she had denied him. And all her flowers had been shed inwards so that her heart was like a heap of leaves, brown, withered, almost scentless petals that had never given joy to anyone. And yet again she had come to him pregnant with beauty and love, but he had been afraid. When she lifted her eyes to him, he had looked aside. The kisses she needed like warm raindrops he dared not give, till she was parched and gone hard, and did not want them. Then he gave kisses enough. But he never trusted himself. When she was open and eager to him, he was afraid. When she was shut, it was like playing at pride, to pull her petals apart, a game that gave him pleasure.

So they had been mutually afraid of each other, but he most often. Whenever she had needed him at some mystery of love, he had overturned her censers and her sacraments, and made profane love in her sacred place. Which was why, at last, she had hated his body; but perhaps she had hated it at first, or feared it so much that it was hate.

And he had said to her: 'If *we* don't have children, you might have them by another man —' which was surely one of the cruellest things a woman ever heard from her husband. For so little was she his, that he would give her a caller and not mind. This was all the wife she was to him. He was a free and easy man, and brought home to dinner any man who pleased him, from a beggar upwards. And his wife was to be as public as his board.

Nay, to the very bowl of her heart, any man might put his lips and he would not mind. And so, she sadly set down the bowl from between her two hands of offering, and went always empty, and aloof.

Yet they were married, they were good friends. It was said they were the most friendly married couple in the county. And this was it. And all the while, like a scent, the bitter psalm of the woman filled the room.

'Like a garden in winter, I was full of bulbs and roots, I was full of little flowers, all conceived inside me.

'And they were all shed away unborn, little abortions of flowers.

'Every day I went like a bee gathering honey from the sky and among the stars I rummaged for yellow honey, filling it in my comb.

'Then I broke the comb, and put it to your lips. But you turned your mouth aside and said: "You have made my face unclean, and smeared my mouth."

'And week after week my body was a vineyard, my veins were vines. And as the grapes, the purple drops grew full and sweet, I crushed them in a bowl, I treasured the wine.

'Then when the bowl was full I came with joy to you. But you in fear started away, and the bowl was thrown from my hands, and broke in pieces at my feet.

'Many times, and many times, I said: "The hour is striking," but he answered: "Not yet."

'Many times and many times he has heard the cock crow, and gone out and wept, he knew not why.

'I was a garden and he ran in me as in the grass.

'I was a stream, and he threw his waste in me.

'I held the rainbow balanced on my outspread hands, and he said: "You open your hands and give me nothing."

'What am I now but a bowl of withered leaves, but a kaleidoscope of broken beauties, but an empty bee-hive, yea, a rich garment rusted that no one has worn, a dumb singer, with the voice of a nightingale yet making discord.

'And it was over with me, and my hour is gone. And soon like a barren sea-shell on the strand, I shall be crushed underfoot to dust.

'But meanwhile I sing to those that listen with their ear against me, of the sea that gave me form and being, the everlasting sea, and in my song is nothing but bitterness, for of the fluid life of the sea I have no more, but I am to be dust, that powdery stuff the sea knows not. I am to be dead, who was born of life, silent who was made a mouth, formless who was all of beauty. Yea, I was a seed that held the heavens lapped up in bud, with a whirl of stars and a steady moon.

'And the seed is crushed that never sprouted, there is a heaven lost, and stars and a moon that never came forth.

'I was a bud that never was discovered, and in my shut chalice, skies and lake water and brooks lie crumbling, and stars and the sun are smeared out, and birds are a little powdery dust, and their singing is dry air, and I am a dark chalice.'

And the girl, hearing the hostess talk, still talk, and yet her voice like the sound of a sea-shell whispering hoarsely of despair, rose and went out into the garden, timidly, beginning to cry. For what should she do for herself?

Renshaw, leaning on the wicket that led to the paddock, called:

'Come on, don't be alarmed – Pan is dead.'

And then she bit back her tears. For when he said, 'Pan is dead,' he meant Pan was dead in his own long, loose Dane's body. Yet she was a nymph still, and if Pan were dead, she ought to die. So with tears she went up to him.

'It's all right out here,' he said. 'By Jove, when you see a night like this, how can you say that life's tragedy – or death either, for that matter?'

'What is it then?' she asked.

'Nay, that's one too many – a joke, eh?'

'I think,' she said, 'one has no business to be irreverent.'

'Who?' he asked.

'You,' she said, 'and me, and all of us.'

Then he leaned on the wicket, thinking till he laughed.

'Life's a real good thing,' he said.

'But why protest it?' she answered.

And again he was silent.

'If the moon came nearer and nearer,' she said, 'and were a naked woman, what would you do?'

'Fetch a wrap, probably,' he said.

'Yes – you would do that,' she answered.

'And if he were a man, ditto?' he teased.

'If a star came nearer and were a naked man, I should look at him.'

'That is surely very improper,' he mocked, with still a tinge of yearning.

'If he were a star come near —' she answered.

Again he was silent.

'You are a queer fish of a girl,' he said.

They stood at the gate, facing the silver-grey paddock. Presently their hostess came out, a long shawl hanging from her shoulders.

'So you are here,' she said. 'Were you bored?'

'I was,' he replied amiably. 'But there, you know I always am.'

'And I forgot,' replied the girl.

'What were you talking about?' asked Mrs. Renshaw, simply curious. She was not afraid of her husband's running loose.

'We were just saying "Pan is dead",' said the girl.

'Isn't that rather trite?' asked the hostess.

'Some of us miss him fearfully,' said the girl.

'For what reason?' asked Mrs. Renshaw.

'Those of us who are nymphs – just lost nymphs among farm-lands and suburbs. I wish Pan were alive.'

'Did he die of old age?' mocked the hostess.

'Don't they say, when Christ was born, a voice was heard in the air saying: "Pan is dead." I wish Christ needn't have killed Pan.'

'I wonder how He managed it,' said Renshaw.

'By disapproving of him, I suppose,' replied his wife. And her retort cut herself, and gave her a sort of fakir pleasure.

'The men are all women now,' she said, 'since the fauns died in a frost one night.'

'A frost of disapproval,' said the girl.

'A frost of fear,' said Renshaw.

There was a silence.

'Why was Christ afraid of Pan?' said the girl suddenly.

'Why was Pan so much afraid of Christ that he died?' asked Mrs. Renshaw bitterly.

'And all his fauns in a frost one night,' mocked Renshaw. Then a light dawned on him. 'Christ was woman and Pan was man,' he said. It gave him a real joy to say this bitterly, keenly – a thrust into himself, and into his wife. 'But the fauns and satyrs are there – you have only to remove the surplices that all men wear nowadays.'

'Nay,' said Mrs. Renshaw, 'it is not true – the surplices have grown into their limbs, like Hercules's garment.'

'That his wife put on him,' said Renshaw.

'Because she was afraid of him – not because she loved him,' said the girl.

'She imagined that all her lonely wasted hours wove him a robe of love,' said Mrs. Renshaw. 'It was to her horror she was mistaken. You can't weave love out of waste.'

'When I meet a man,' said the girl, 'I shall look down the pupil of his eye, for a faun. And after a while it will come, skipping —'

'Perhaps a satyr,' said Mrs. Renshaw bitterly.

'No,' said the girl, 'because satyrs are old, and I have seen some fearfully young men.'

'Will is young even now – quite a boy,' said his wife.

'Oh no!' cried the girl. 'He says that neither life nor death is a tragedy. Only somebody very old could say that.'

There was a tension in the night. The man felt something give way inside him.

'Yes, Edith,' he said, with a quiet, bitter joy of cruelty, 'I am old.'

The wife was frightened.

'You are always preposterous,' she said quickly, crying inside herself. She knew she herself had been never young.

'I shall look in the eyes of my man for the faun,' the girl continued in a sing-song, 'and I shall find him. Then I shall pretend to run away from him. And both our surplices, and all the crucifix, will be outside the wood. Inside nymph and faun, Pan and his satyrs – ah, yes: for Christ and the Cross is only for day-time, and bargaining. Christ came to make us deal honourably.

'But love is no deal, nor merchant's bargaining, and Christ neither spoke of it nor forbade it. He was afraid of it. If once His faun, the faun of the young Jesus had run free, seen one white nymph's brief breast, He would not have been content to die on a Cross – and then the men would have gone on cheating the women in life's business, all the time. Christ made one bargain in mankind's business – and He made it for the women's sake – I suppose for His mother's, since He was fatherless. And Christ made a bargain for me, and I shall avail myself of it. I won't be cheated by my man. When between my still hands I weave silk out of the air, like a cocoon, He shall not take it to pelt me with. He shall draw it forth and weave it up. For I want to finger the sunshine I have drawn through my body, stroke it, and have joy of the fabric.

'And when I run wild on the hills, with Dionysus, and shall come home like a bee that has rolled in floury crocuses, he must see the wonder on me, and make bread of it.

'And when I say to him, "It is harvest in my soul", he shall look in my eyes and lower his nets where the shoal moves in a throng in the dark, and lift out the living blue silver for me to see, and know, and taste.

'All this, my faun in commerce, my faun at traffic with me.

'And if he cheat me, he must take his chance.

'But I will not cheat him, in his hour, when he runs like a faun after me. I shall flee, but only to be overtaken. I shall flee, but never out of the wood to the crucifix. For that is to deny I am a nymph; since how can a nymph cling at the crucifix? Nay, the cross is the sign I have on my money, for honesty.

'In the morning, when we come out of the wood, I shall say to him: "Touch the cross, and prove you will deal fairly," and if he will not, I will set the dogs of anger and judgment on him, and they shall chase him. But if, perchance, some night he contrive to crawl back into the wood, beyond the crucifix, he will be faun and I nymph, and I shall have no knowledge what happened outside, in the realm of the crucifix. But in the morning, I shall say: "Touch the cross, and prove you will deal fairly." And being renewed, he will touch the cross.

'Many a dead faun I have seen, like dead rabbits poisoned lying about the paths, and many a dead nymph, like swans that could not fly and the dogs destroyed.

'But I am a nymph and a woman, and Pan is for me, and Christ is for me.

'For Christ I cover myself in my robe, and weep, and vow my vow of honesty.

'For Pan I throw my coverings down and run headlong through the leaves, because of the joy of running.

'And Pan will give me my children and joy, and Christ will give me my pride.

'And Pan will give me my man, and Christ my husband.

'To Pan I am nymph, to Christ I am woman.

'And Pan is in the darkness, and Christ in the pale light.

'And night shall never be day, and day shall never be night.

'But side by side they shall go, day and night, night and day, for ever apart, for ever together.

'Pan and Christ, Christ and Pan.

'Both moving over me, so when in the sunshine I go in my robes among my neighbours, I am a Christian. But when I run robeless through the dark-scented woods alone, I am Pan's nymph.

'Now I must go, for I want to run away. Not run away from myself, but to myself.

'For neither am I a lamp that stands in the way in the sunshine.

'Now am I a sundial foolish at night.

'I am myself, running through light and shadow for ever, a nymph and a Christian; I, not two things, but an apple with a gold side and a red, a freckled deer, a stream that tinkles and a pool where light is drowned; I, no fragment, no half-thing like the day, but a blackbird with a white breast and underwings, a peewit, a wild thing, beyond understanding.'

'I wonder if we shall hear the nightingale to-night,' said Mrs. Renshaw.

'He's a gurgling fowl – I'd rather hear a linnet,' said Renshaw. 'Come a drive with me to-morrow, Miss Laskell.'

And the three went walking back to the house. And Elsa Laskell was glad to get away from them.

THE LOVELY LADY

AT seventy-two, Pauline Attenborough could still sometimes be mistaken, in the half-light, for thirty. She really was a wonderfully preserved woman, of perfect *chic*. Of course, it helps a great deal to have the right frame. She would be an exquisite skeleton, and her skull would be an exquisite skull, like that of some Etruscan woman, with feminine charm still in the swerve of the bone and the pretty naïve teeth.

Mrs. Attenborough's face was of the perfect oval, and slightly flat type that wears best. There is no flesh to sag. Her nose rode serenely, in its finely bridged curve. Only her big grey eyes were a tiny bit prominent on the surface of her face, and they gave her away most. The bluish lids were heavy, as if they ached sometimes with the strain of keeping the eyes beneath them arch and bright; and at the corners of the eyes were fine little wrinkles which would slacken with haggardness, then be pulled up tense again, to that bright, gay look like a Leonardo woman who really could laugh outright.

Her niece Cecilia was perhaps the only person in the world who was aware of the invisible little wire which connected Pauline's eye-wrinkles with Pauline's will-power. Only Cecilia *consciously* watched the eyes go haggard and old and tired, and remain so, for hours; until Robert came home. Then ping! – the mysterious little wire that worked between Pauline's eyes suddenly began to gleam, the eyelids arched, the queer curved eyebrows which floated in such frail arches on Pauline's forehead began to gather a mocking significance, and you had the *real* lovely lady, in all her charm.

She really had the secret of everlasting youth; that is to say, she could don her youth again like an eagle. But she was sparing of it. She was wise enough not to try being young for too many people. Her son Robert, in the evenings, and Sir Wilfred Knipe sometimes in the afternoon to tea: then occasional visitors on Sunday, when Robert was home: for these she was her lovely and changeless self, that age could not wither, nor custom stale: so bright and kindly and yet subtly mocking, like Mona Lisa, who knew a thing or two. But Pauline knew more, so she needn't be smug at all, she could laugh that lovely mocking

Bacchante laugh of hers, which was at the same time never malicious, always good-naturedly tolerant, both of virtues and vices. The former, of course, taking much more tolerating. So she suggested, roguishly.

Only with her niece Cecilia she did not trouble to keep up the glamour. Ciss was not very observant, anyhow: and more than that, she was plain: more still, she was in love with Robert: and most of all, she was thirty, and dependent on her Aunt Pauline. Oh, Cecilia! Why make music for her!

Cecilia, called by her aunt and by her cousin Robert just Ciss, like a cat spitting, was a big dark-complexioned, pug-faced young woman who very rarely spoke, and when she did, couldn't get it out. She was the daughter of a poor Congregational minister who had been, while he lived, brother to Ronald, Aunt Pauline's husband. Ronald and the Congregational minister were both well dead, and Aunt Pauline had had charge of Ciss for the last five years.

They lived all together in a quite exquisite though rather small Queen Anne house some twenty-five miles out of town, secluded in a little dale, and surrounded by small but very quaint and pleasant grounds. It was an ideal place and an ideal life for Aunt Pauline, at the age of seventy-two. When the kingfishers flashed up the little stream in the garden, going under the alders, something still flashed in her heart. She was that kind of woman.

Robert, who was two years older than Ciss, went every day to town, to his chambers in one of the Inns. He was a barrister, and to his secret but very deep mortification, he earned about a hundred pounds a year. He simply *couldn't* get above that figure, though it was rather easy to get below it. Of course, it didn't matter. Pauline had money. But then what was Pauline's was Pauline's, and though she could give almost lavishly, still, one was always aware of having a *lovely* and *undeserved* present made to one: presents are so much nicer when they are undeserved, Aunt Pauline would say.

Robert too was plain, and almost speechless. He was medium-sized, rather broad and stout, though not fat. Only his creamy, clean-shaven face was rather fat, and sometimes suggestive of an Italian priest, in its silence and its secrecy. But he had grey eyes like his mother, but very shy and uneasy, not bold like hers. Perhaps Ciss was the only person who fathomed his awful shyness and *malaise*, his habitual feeling that he was in the wrong place: almost like a soul that has got into the wrong body. But he never did anything about it. He went up to his chambers and read law. It was, however, all the weird old processes that interested him. He had, unknown to everybody but his mother, a quite extraordinary collection of old Mexican legal documents, reports of processes and trials, pleas, accusations, the weird and awful mixture of ecclesiastical law and common law in seventeenth-century Mexico. He had started a study in this direction through coming across a report of a trial of two English sailors, for murder, in Mexico in 1620, and he had gone on, when the next document was an accusation against a Don Miguel Estrada for seducing one of the nuns of the Sacred Heart Convent in Oaxaca in 1680.

Pauline and her son Robert had wonderful evenings with these old papers. The lovely lady knew a little Spanish. She even looked a trifle Spanish herself, with a comb and a marvellous dark brown shawl embroidered in thick silvery silk embroidery. So she would sit at the perfect old table, soft as velvet in its deep brown surface, a high comb in her hair, ear-rings with dropping pendants in her ears, her arms bare and still beautiful, a few strings of pearls round her throat, a puce velvet dress on and this or another beautiful shawl, and by candle-light she looked, yes, a Spanish high-bred beauty of thirty-two or three. She set the candles to give her face just the chiaroscuro she knew suited her; her high chair that rose behind her face was done in old green brocade, against which her face emerged like a Christmas rose.

They were always three at table; and they always drank a bottle of champagne: Pauline two glasses, Ciss two glasses, Robert the rest. The lovely lady sparkled and was radiant. Ciss, her black hair bobbed, her broad shoulders in a very nice and becoming dress that Aunt Pauline had helped her to make, stared from her aunt to her cousin and back again, with rather confused, mute, hazel eyes, and played the part of an audience suitably impressed. She *was* impressed, somewhere, all the time. And even rendered speechless by Pauline's brilliancy, even after five years. But at the bottom of her consciousness were the data of as weird a document as Robert ever studied: all the things she knew about her aunt and cousin.

Robert was always a gentleman, with an old-fashioned punctilious courtesy that covered his shyness quite completely. He was, and Ciss knew it, more confused than shy. He was worse than she was. Cecilia's own confusion dated from only five years back – Robert's must have started before he was born. In the lovely lady's womb he must have felt *very* confused.

He paid all his attention to his mother, drawn to her as a humble flower to the sun. And yet, priest-like, he was all the time aware, with the tail of his consciousness, that Ciss was there, and that she was a bit shut out of it, and that something wasn't right. He was aware of the third consciousness in the room. Whereas to Pauline, her niece Cecilia was an appropriate part of her own setting, rather than a distinct consciousness.

Robert took coffee with his mother and Ciss in the warm drawing-room, where all the furniture was so lovely, all collectors' pieces – Mrs. Attenborough had made her own money, dealing privately in pictures and furniture and rare things from barbaric countries – and the three talked desultorily till about eight or half-past. It was very pleasant, very cosy, very homely even: Pauline made a real home cosiness out of so much elegant material. The chat was simple, and nearly always bright. Pauline was her *real* self, emanating a friendly mockery and an odd, ironic gaiety. Till there came a little pause.

At which Ciss always rose and said good-night and carried out the coffee-tray, to prevent Burnett from intruding any more.

And then! Oh, then, the lovely glowing intimacy of the evening, between mother and son, when they deciphered manuscripts and discussed points, Pauline with that eagerness of a girl, for which she was famous. And it was quite genuine. In some mysterious way she had *saved up* her power for being thrilled, in connection with a man. Robert, solid, rather quiet and subdued, seemed like the elder of the two: almost like a priest with a young girl pupil. And that was rather how he felt.

Ciss had a flat for herself just across the courtyard, over the old coach-house and stables. There were no horses. Robert kept his car in the coach-house. Ciss had three very nice rooms up there, stretching along in a row one after another, and she had got used to the ticking of the stable clock.

But sometimes she did not go up to her rooms. In the summer she would sit on the lawn, and from the open window of the drawing-room upstairs she would hear Pauline's wonderful heart-searching laugh. And in the winter the young woman would put on a thick coat and walk slowly to the little balustraded bridge over the stream, and then look back at the three lighted windows of that drawing-room where mother and son were so happy together.

Ciss loved Robert, and she believed that Pauline intended the two of them to marry: when she was dead. But poor Robert, he was so convulsed with shyness already, with man or woman. What would he be

710

when his mother was dead – in a dozen more years? He would be just a shell, the shell of a man who had never lived.

The strange unspoken sympathy of the young with one another, when they are overshadowed by the old, was one of the bonds between Robert and Ciss. But another bond, which Ciss did not know how to draw tight, was the bond of passion. Poor Robert was by nature a passionate man. His silence and his agonised, though hidden, shyness were both the result of a secret physical passionateness. And how Pauline could play on this! Ah, Ciss was not blind to the eyes which he fixed on his mother, eyes fascinated yet humiliated, full of shame. He was ashamed that he was not a man. And he did not love his mother. He was fascinated by her. Completely fascinated. And for the rest, paralysed in a life-long confusion.

Ciss stayed in the garden till the lights leapt up in Pauline's bedroom – about ten o'clock. The lovely lady had retired. Robert would now stay another hour or so, alone. Then he too would retire. Ciss, in the dark outside, sometimes wished she could creep up to him and say: 'Oh, Robert! It's all wrong!' But Aunt Pauline would hear. And, anyhow, Ciss couldn't do it. She went off to her own rooms once more, and so for ever.

In the morning coffee was brought up on a tray to each of the three relatives. Ciss had to be at Sir Wilfred Knipe's at nine o'clock, to give two hours' lessons to his little granddaughter. It was her sole serious occupation, except that she played the piano for the love of it. Robert set off to town about nine. And, as a rule, Aunt Pauline appeared at lunch, though sometimes not until tea-time. When she appeared, she looked fresh and young. But she was inclined to fade rather quickly, like a flower without water, in the day-time. Her hour was the candle hour.

So she always rested in the afternoon. When the sun shone, if possible she took a sun-bath. This was one of her secrets. Her lunch was very light, she could take her sun-and-air-bath before noon or after, as it pleased her. Often it was in the afternoon, when the sun shone very warmly into a queer little yew-walled square just behind the stables. Here Ciss stretched out the lying-chair and rugs, and put the light parasol in the silent little enclosure of thick dark yew hedges beyond the red walls of the unused stables. And hither came the lovely lady with her book. Ciss then had to be on guard in one of her own rooms, should her aunt, who was very keen-eared, hear a footstep.

One afternoon it occurred to Cecilia that she herself might while away this rather long afternoon by taking a sun-bath. She was growing restive. The thought of the flat roof of the stable buildings, to which she could climb from a loft at the end, started her on a new adventure. She often went on to the roof: she had to, to wind up the stable clock, which was a job she had assumed to herself. Now she took a rug, climbed out under the heavens, looked at the sky and the great elm-tops, looked at the sun, then took off her things and lay down perfectly serenely, in a corner of the roof under the parapet, full in the sun.

It was rather lovely, to bask all one's length like this in warm sun and air. Yes, it was very lovely! It even seemed to melt some of the hard bitterness of her heart, some of that core of unspoken resentment which never dissolved. Luxuriously, she spread herself, so that the sun should touch her limbs fully, fully. If she had no other lover, she should have the sun! She rolled voluptuously. And suddenly her heart stood still in her body, and her hair almost rose on end as a voice said very softly, musingly in her ear:

'No, Henry dear! It was not my fault you died instead of marrying that Claudia. No, darling. I was quite, quite willing for you to marry her, unsuitable though she was.'

Cecilia sank down on her rug powerless and perspiring with dread. That awful voice, so soft, so musing, yet so unnatural. Not a human voice at all. Yet there must, there must be someone on the roof! Oh! how unspeakably awful!

She lifted her weak head and peeped across the sloping leads. Nobody! The chimneys were far too narrow to shelter anybody. There was nobody on the roof. Then it must be someone in the trees, in the elms. Either that, or terror unspeakable, a bodiless voice! She reared her head a little higher.

And as she did so, came the voice again:

'No, darling! I told you you would tire of her in six months. And you see, it was true, dear. It was true, true, true! I wanted to spare you that. So it wasn't I who made you feel weak and disabled, wanting that very silly Claudia; poor thing, she looked so woebegone afterwards! Wanting her and not wanting her, you got *yourself* into that perplexity, my dear. I only warned you. What else could I do? And you lost your spirit and died without ever knowing me again. It was bitter, bitter —'

The voice faded away. Cecilia subsided weakly on to her rug, after the anguished tension of listening. Oh, it was awful. The sun shone, the sky was blue, all seemed so lovely and afternoony and summery. And yet, oh, horror! – she was going to be forced to believe in the supernatural! And she loathed the supernatural, ghosts and voices and rappings and all the rest.

But that awful creepy bodiless voice, with its rusty sort of whisper of an overtone! It had something so fearfully familiar in it too! and yet was so utterly uncanny. Poor Cecilia could only lie there unclothed, and so all the more agonisingly helpless, inert, collapsed in sheer dread.

And then she heard the thing sigh! A deep sigh that seemed weirdly familiar, yet was not human. 'Ah, well; ah, well, the heart must bleed! Better it should bleed than break. It is grief, grief! But it wasn't my fault, dear. And Robert could marry our poor dull Ciss to-morrow, if he wanted her. But he doesn't care about it, so why force him into anything!' The sounds were very uneven, sometimes only a husky sort of whisper. Listen! Listen!

Cecilia was about to give vent to loud and piercing screams of hysteria, when the last two sentences arrested her. All her caution and her cunning sprang alert. It was Aunt Pauline! It must be Aunt Pauline, practising ventriloquism or something like that! What a devil she was!

Where was she? She must be lying down there, right below where Cecilia herself was lying. And it was either some fiend's trick of ventriloquism, or else thought transference that conveyed itself like sound. The sounds were very uneven. Sometimes quite inaudible, sometimes only a brushing sort of noise. Ciss listened intently. No, it could not be ventriloquism. It was worse, some form of thought transference. Some horror of that sort. Cecilia still lay weak and inert, terrified to move, but she was growing calmer with suspicion. It was some diabolic trick of the unnatural woman.

But *what a devil* of a woman! She even knew that she, Cecilia, had mentally accused her of killing her son Henry. Poor Henry was Robert's elder brother, twelve years older than Robert. He had died suddenly when he was twenty-two after an awful struggle with himself, because he was passionately in love with a young and very good-looking actress, and his mother had humorously despised him for the attachment. So he had caught some sudden ordinary disease, but the poison had gone to his brain and killed him before he ever regained consciousness. Ciss knew the few facts from her own father. And lately she had been thinking that Pauline was going to kill Robert as she had killed Henry. It was clear murder: a mother murdering her sensitive sons, who were fascinated by her: the Circe!

'I suppose I may as well get up,' murmured the dim, unbreaking

713

voice. 'Too much sun is as bad as too little. Enough sun, enough love thrill, enough proper food, and not too much of any of them, and a woman might live for ever. I verily believe for ever. If she absorbs as much vitality as she expends! Or perhaps a trifle more!'

It was certainly Aunt Pauline! How, how horrible! She, Ciss, was hearing Aunt Pauline's thoughts. Oh, how ghastly! Aunt Pauline was sending out her thoughts in a sort of radio, and she, Ciss, had to *hear* what her aunt was thinking. How ghastly! How insufferable! One of them would surely have to die.

She twisted and she lay inert and crumpled, staring vacantly in front of her. Vacantly! Vacantly! And her eyes were staring almost into a hole. She was staring into it unseeing, a hole going down in the corner from the lead gutter. It meant nothing to her. Only it frightened her a little more.

When suddenly out of the hole came a sigh and a last whisper. 'Ah, well! Pauline! Get up, it's enough for to-day!' Good God! Out of the hole of the rain-pipe! The rain-pipe was acting as a speaking-tube! Impossible! No, quite possible. She had read of it even in some book. And Aunt Pauline, like the old and guilty woman she was, talked aloud to herself. That was it!

A sullen exultance sprang into Ciss's breast. *That* was why she would never have anybody, not even Robert, in her bedroom. That was why she never dozed in a chair, never sat absent-minded anywhere, but went to her room, and kept to her room, except when she roused herself to be alert. When she slackened off, she talked to herself! She talked in a soft little crazy voice to herself. But she was not crazy. It was only her thoughts murmuring themselves aloud.

So she had qualms about poor Henry! Well she might have! Ciss believed that Aunt Pauline had loved her big, handsome, brilliant first-born much more than she loved Robert, and that his death had been a terrible blow and a chagrin to her. Poor Robert had been only ten years old when Henry died. Since then he had been the substitute.

Ah, how awful!

But Aunt Pauline was a strange woman. She had left her husband when Henry was a small child, some years even before Robert was born. There was no quarrel. Sometimes she saw her husband again, quite amicably, but a little mockingly. And she even gave him money.

For Pauline earned all her own. Her father had been a consul in the East and in Naples: and a devoted collector of beautiful and exotic things. When he died, soon after his grandson Henry was born, he left

714

his collection of treasures to his daughter. And Pauline, who had really a passion and a genius for loveliness, whether in texture or form or colour, had laid the basis of her fortune on her father's collection. She had gone on collecting, buying where she could, and selling to collectors and to museums. She was one of the first to sell old, weird African wooden figures to the museums, and ivory carvings from New Guinea. She bought Renoir as soon as she saw his pictures. But not Rousseau. And all by herself she made a fortune.

After her husband died, she had not married again. She was not even *known* to have had lovers. If she did have lovers, it was not among the men who admired her most and paid her devout and open attendance. To these she was a 'friend'.

Cecilia slipped on her clothes and caught up her rug, hastened carefully down the ladder to the loft. As she descended she heard the ringing musical call: 'All right, Ciss!' which meant that the lovely lady was finished, and returning to the house. Even her voice was marvellously young and sonorous, beautifully balanced and self-possessed. So different from the little voice in which she talked to herself. *That* was much more the voice of an old woman.

Ciss hastened round to the yew enclosure, where lay the comfortable chaise-longue with the various delicate rugs. Everything Pauline had was choice, to the fine straw mat on the floor. The great yew walls were beginning to cast long shadows. Only in the corner, where the rugs tumbled their delicate colours, was there hot, still sunshine.

The rugs folded up, the chair lifted away, Cecilia stooped to look at the mouth of the rain-pipe. There it was, in the corner, under a little hood of masonry and just projecting from the thick leaves of the creeper on the wall. If Pauline, lying there, turned her face towards the wall, she would speak into the very mouth of the hole. Cecilia was reassured. She had heard her aunt's thoughts indeed, but by no uncanny agency.

That evening, as if aware of something, Pauline was a little quicker than usual, though she looked her own serene, rather mysterious self. And after coffee she said to Robert and Ciss: 'I'm so sleepy. The sun has made me so sleepy. I feel full of sunshine like a bee. I shall go to bed, if you don't mind. You two sit and have a talk.'

Cecilia looked quickly at her cousin.

'Perhaps you would rather be alone,' she said to him.

'No, no,' he replied. 'Do keep me company for a while, if it doesn't bore you.'

The windows were open, the scent of the honeysuckle wafted in with

715

the sound of an owl. Robert smoked in silence. There was a sort of despair in the motionless, rather squat body. He looked like a caryatid bearing a weight.

'Do you remember Cousin Henry?' Cecilia asked him suddenly.

He looked up in surprise.

'Yes, very well,' he said.

'What did he look like?' she said, glancing into her cousin's big, secret-troubled eyes, in which there was so much frustration.

'Oh, he was handsome: tall and fresh-coloured, with mother's soft brown hair.' As a matter of fact, Pauline's hair was grey. 'The ladies admired him very much; he was at all the dances.'

'And what kind of character had he?'

'Oh, very good-natured and jolly. He liked to be amused. He was rather quick and clever, like mother, and very good company.'

'And did he love your mother?'

'Very much. She loved him too – better than she does me, as a matter of fact. He was so much more nearly her idea of a man.'

'Why was he more her idea of a man?'

'Tall – handsome – attractive, and very good company – and would, I believe, have been very successful at law. I'm afraid I am merely negative in all those respects.'

Ciss looked at him attentively, with her slow-thinking hazel eyes. Under his impassive mask, she knew he suffered.

'Do you think you are so much more negative than he?' she said.

He did not lift his face. But after a few moments he replied:

'My life, certainly, is a negative affair.'

She hesitated before she dared ask him:

'And do you mind?'

He did not answer her at all. Her heart sank.

'You see, I am afraid my life is as negative as yours is,' she said. 'And I'm beginning to mind bitterly. I'm thirty.'

She saw his creamy, well-bred hand tremble.

'I suppose,' he said, without looking at her, 'one will rebel when it is too late.'

That was queer, from him.

'Robert,' she said, 'do you like me at all?'

She saw his dusky, creamy face, so changeless in its folds, go pale. 'I am very fond of you,' he murmured.

'Won't you kiss me? Nobody ever kisses me,' she said pathetically.

He looked at her, his eyes strange with fear and a certain haughtiness. Then he rose and came softly over to her and kissed her gently on the cheek.

'It's an awful shame, Ciss!' he said softly.

She caught his hand and pressed it to her breast.

'And sit with me some time in the garden,' she said, mumuring with difficulty. 'Won't you?'

He looked at her anxiously and searchingly.

'What about mother?' he said.

Ciss smiled a funny little smile, and looked into his eyes. He suddenly flushed crimson, turning aside his face. It was a painful sight.

'I know,' he said, 'I am no lover of women.'

He spoke with sarcastic stoicism against himself, but even she did not know the shame it was to him.

'You never try to be!' she said.

Again his eyes changed uncannily.

'Does one have to try?' he said.

'Why, yes! One never does anything if one doesn't try.'

He went pale again.

'Perhaps you are right,' he said.

In a few minutes she left him and went to her room. At least, she had tried to take off the everlasting lid from things.

The weather continued sunny, Pauline continued her sun-baths, and Ciss lay on the roof eavesdropping in the literal sense of the word. But Pauline was not to be heard. No sound came up the pipe. She must be lying with her face away into the open. Ciss listened with all her might. She could just detect the faintest, faintest murmur away below, but no audible syllable.

And at night, under the stars, Cecilia sat and waited in silence, on the seat which kept in view the drawing-room windows and the side door into the garden. She saw the light go up in her aunt's room. She saw the lights at last go out in the drawing-room. And she waited. But he did not come. She stayed on in the darkness half the night, while the owl hooted. But she stayed alone.

Two days she heard nothing, her aunt's thoughts were not revealed and at evening nothing happened. Then the second night, as she sat with heavy, helpless persistence in the garden, suddenly she started. He had come out. She rose and went softly over the grass to him.

'Don't speak,' he murmured.

And in silence, in the dark, they walked down the garden and over

717

the little bridge to the paddock, where the hay, cut very late, was in cock. There they stood disconsolate under the stars.

'You see,' he said, 'how can I ask for love, if I don't feel any love in myself. You know I have a real regard for you —'

'How can you feel any love, when you never feel anything?' she said.

'That is true,' he replied.

And she waited for what next.

'And how can I marry?' he said. 'I am a failure even at making money. I can't ask my mother for money.'

She sighed deeply.

'Then don't bother yet about marrying,' she said. 'Only love me a little. Won't you?'

He gave a short laugh.

'It sounds so atrocious, to say it is hard to begin,' he said.

She sighed again. He was so stiff to move.

'Shall we sit down a minute,' she said. And then as they sat on the hay, she added: 'May I touch you? Do you mind?'

'Yes, I mind! But do as you wish,' he replied, with that mixture of shyness and queer candour which made him a little ridiculous, as he knew quite well. But in his heart there was almost murder.

She touched his black, always tidy hair with her fingers.

'I suppose I shall rebel one day,' he said again, suddenly.

They sat some time, till it grew chilly. And he held her hand fast, but he never put his arms round her. At last she rose and went indoors, saying good night.

The next day, as Cecilia lay stunned and angry on the roof, taking her sun-bath, and becoming hot and fierce with sunshine, suddenly she started. A terror seized her in spite of herself. It was the voice.

'*Caro, caro, tu non l'hai visto!*' it was murmuring away, in a language Cecilia did not understand. She lay and writhed her limbs in the sun, listening intently to words she could not follow. Softly, whisperingly, with infinite caressiveness and yet with that subtle, insidious arrogance under its velvet, came the voice, murmuring in Italian: '*Bravo, si molto bravo, poverino, ma uomo come te non lo sara mai, mai, mai!*' Oh, especially in Italian Cecilia heard the poisonous charm of the voice, so caressive, so soft and flexible, yet so utterly egoistic. She hated it with intensity as it sighed and whispered out of nowhere. Why, why should it be so delicate, so subtle and flexible and beautifully controlled, while she herself was so clumsy! Oh, poor Cecilia, she writhed in the afternoon sun, knowing her own clownish clumsiness and lack of suavity, in comparison.

'No, Robert dear, you will never be the man your father was, though you have some of his looks. He was a marvellous lover, soft as a flower, yet piercing as a humming-bird. No, Robert dear, you will never know how to serve a woman as Monsignor Mauro did. *Cara, cara mia bellissima, ti ho aspettato come l'agonizzante aspetta la morte, morte deliziosa, quasi quasi troppo deliziosa per un' anima humana* – Soft as a flower, yet probing like a humming-bird. He gave himself to a woman as he gave himself to God. Mauro! Mauro! How you loved me!'

The voice ceased in reverie, and Cecilia knew what she had guessed before, that Robert was not the son of her Uncle Ronald, but of some Italian.

'I am disappointed in you, Robert. There is no poignancy in you. Your father was a Jesuit, but he was the most perfect and poignant lover in the world. You are a Jesuit like a fish in a tank. And that Ciss of yours is the cat fishing for you. It is less edifying even than poor Henry.'

Cecilia suddenly bent her mouth down to the tube, and said in a deep voice:

'Leave Robert alone! Don't kill him as well.'

There was a dead silence, in the hot July afternoon that was lowering for thunder. Cecilia lay prostrate, her heart beating in great thumps. She was listening as if her whole soul were an ear. At last she caught the whisper:

'Did someone speak?'

She leaned again to the mouth of the tube.

'Don't kill Robert as you killed me,' she said with slow enunciation, and a deep but small voice.

'Ah!' came the sharp little cry. 'Who is that speaking?'

'Henry!' said the deep voice.

There was a dead silence. Poor Cecilia lay with all the use gone out of her. And there was dead silence. Till at last came the whisper:

'I didn't kill Henry. No. NO! Henry, surely you can't blame me! I loved you, dearest. I only wanted to help you.'

'You killed me!' came the deep, artificial accusing voice. 'Now, let Robert live. Let him go! Let him marry!'

There was a pause.

'How very, very awful!' mused the whispering voice. 'Is it possible, Henry, you are a spirit, and you condemn me?'

'Yes! I condemn you!'

Cecilia felt all her pent-up rage going down that drain-pipe. At the same time, she almost laughed. It was awful.

She lay and listened and listened. No sound! As if time had ceased, she lay inert in the weakening sun. The sky was yellowing. Quickly she dressed herself, went down, and out to the corner of the stables.

'Aunt Pauline!' she called discreetly. 'Did you hear thunder?'

'Yes! I am going in. Don't wait,' came a feeble voice.

Cecilia retired, and from the loft watched, spying, as the figure of the lovely lady, wrapped in a lovely wrap of old blue silk, went rather totteringly to the house.

The sky gradually darkened, Cecilia hastened in with the rugs. Then the storm broke. Aunt Pauline did not appear to tea. She found the thunder trying. Robert also did not arrive till after tea, in the pouring rain. Cecilia went down the covered passage to her own house, and dressed carefully for dinner, putting some white columbines at her breast.

The drawing-room was lit with a softly-shaded lamp. Robert dressed, was waiting, listening to the rain. He too seemed strangely cracking and on edge. Cecilia came in with the white flowers nodding at her breast. Robert was watching her curiously, a new look on his face. Cecilia went to the bookshelves near the door, and was peering for something, listening acutely. She heard a rustle, then the door softly opened. And as it opened, Ciss suddenly switched on the strong electric light by the door.

Her aunt, in a dress of black lace over ivory colour, stood in the doorway. Her face was made up, but haggard with a look of unspeakable irritability, as if years of suppressed exasperation and dislike of her fellow-men had suddenly crumpled her into an old witch.

'Oh, aunt!' cried Cecilia.

'Why, mother, you're a little old lady!' came the astounded voice of Robert: like an astonished boy: as if it were a joke.

'Have you only just found it out?' snapped the old woman venomously.

'Yes! Why, I thought —' his voice tailed out in misgiving.

The haggard, old Pauline, in a frenzy of exasperation, said:

'Aren't we going down?'

She had never even noticed the excess of light, a thing she shunned. And she went downstairs almost tottering.

At table she sat with her face like a crumpled mask of unspeakable

720

irritability. She looked old, very old, and like a witch. Robert and Cecilia fetched furtive glances at her. And Ciss, watching Robert, saw that he was so astonished and repelled by his mother's looks, that he was another man.

'What kind of a drive home did you have?' snapped Pauline, with an almost gibbering irritability.

'It rained, of course,' he said.

'How clever of you to have found that out!' said his mother, with the grisly grin of malice that had succeeded her arch smirk.

'I don't understand,' he said with quiet suavity.

'It's apparent,' said his mother, rapidly and sloppily eating her food.

She rushed through the meal like a crazy dog, to the utter consternation of the servant. And the moment it was over, she darted in a queer, crab-like way upstairs. Robert and Cecilia followed her, thunderstruck, like two conspirators.

'You pour the coffee. I loathe it! I'm going! Good-night!' said the old woman, in a succession of sharp shots. And she scrambled out of the room.

There was a dead silence. At last he said:

'I'm afraid mother isn't well. I must persuade her to see a doctor.'

'Yes!' said Cecilia.

The evening passed in silence. Robert and Ciss stayed on in the drawing-room, having lit a fire. Outside was cold rain. Each pretended to read. They did not want to separate. The evening passed with ominous mysteriousness, yet quickly.

At about ten o'clock, the door suddenly opened, and Pauline appeared in a blue wrap. She shut the door behind her, and came to the fire. Then she looked at the two young people in hate, real hate.

'You two had better get married quickly,' she said in an ugly voice. 'It would look more decent; such a passionate pair of lovers!'

Robert looked up at her quietly.

'I thought you believed that cousins should not marry, mother,' he said.

'I do! But you're not cousins. Your father was an Italian priest.' Pauline held her daintily-slippered foot to the fire, in an old coquettish gesture. Her body tried to repeat all the old graceful gestures. But the nerve had snapped, so it was a rather dreadful caricature.

'Is that really true, mother?' he asked.

'True! What do you think? He was a distinguished man, or he

721

wouldn't have been my lover. He was far too distinguished a man to have had you for a son. But that joy fell to me.'

'How unfortunate all round,' he said slowly.

'Unfortunate for you? *You* were lucky. It was *my* misfortune,' she said acidly to him.

She was really a dreadful sight, like a piece of lovely Venetian glass that has been dropped, and gathered up again in horrible, sharp-edged fragments.

Suddenly she left the room again.

For a week it went on. She did not recover. It was as if every nerve in her body had suddenly started screaming in an insanity of discordance. The doctor came, and gave her sedatives, for she never slept. Without drugs, she never slept at all, only paced back and forth in her room, looking hideous and evil, reeking with malevolence. She could not bear to see either her son or her niece. Only when either of them came, she asked in pure malice:

'Well! When's the wedding! Have you celebrated the nuptials yet?'

At first Cecilia was stunned by what she had done. She realised vaguely that her aunt, once a definite thrust of condemnation had penetrated her beautiful armour, had just collapsed squirming inside her shell. It was too terrible. Ciss was almost terrified into repentance. Then she thought: This is what she always was. Now let her live the rest of her days in her true colours.

But Pauline would not live long. She was literally shrivelling away. She kept to her room, and saw no one. She had her mirrors taken away.

Robert and Cecilia sat a good deal together. The jeering of the mad Pauline had not driven them apart, as she had hoped. But Cecilia dared not confess to him what she had done.

'Do you think your mother ever loved anybody?' Ciss asked him tentatively, rather wistfully, one evening.

He looked at her fixedly.

'Herself!' he said at last.

'She didn't even *love* herself,' said Ciss. 'It was something else – what was it?' She lifted a troubled, utterly puzzled face to him.

'Power!' he said curtly.

'But what power?' she asked. 'I don't understand.'

'Power to feed on other lives,' he said bitterly. 'She was beautiful, and she fed on life. She has fed on me as she fed on Henry. She put a sucker into one's soul and sucked up one's essential life.'

722

'And don't you forgive her?'

'No.'

'Poor Aunt Pauline!'

But even Ciss did not mean it. She was only aghast.

'I *know* I've got a heart,' he said, passionately striking his breast. 'But it's almost sucked dry. I *know* people who want power over others.'

Ciss was silent; what was there to say?

And two days later, Pauline was found dead in her bed, having taken too much veronal, for her heart was weakened. From the grave even she hit back at her son and her niece. She left Robert the noble sum of one thousand pounds; and Ciss one hundred. All the rest, with the nucleus of her valuable antiques, went to form the 'Pauline Attenborough Museum'.

RAWDON'S ROOF

RAWDON was the sort of man who said, privately, to his men friends, over a glass of wine after dinner: 'No woman shall sleep again under my roof!'

He said it with pride, rather vaunting, pursing his lips. 'Even my housekeeper goes home to sleep.'

But the housekeeper was a gentle old thing of about sixty, so it seemed a little fantastic. Moreover, the man had a wife, of whom he was secretly rather proud, as a piece of fine property, and with whom he kept up a very witty correspondence, epistolary, and whom he treated with humorous gallantry when they occasionally met for half an hour. Also he had a love affair going on. At least, if it wasn't a love affair, what was it? However!

'No, I've come to the determination that no woman shall ever sleep under my roof again – not even a female cat!'

One looked at the roof, and wondered what it had done amiss. Besides, it wasn't his roof. He only rented the house. What does a man mean, anyhow, when he says 'my roof'? *My* roof! The only roof I am conscious of having, myself, is the top of my head. However, he hardly can have meant that no woman should sleep under the elegant dome of his skull. Though there's no telling. You see the top of a sleek head through a window, and you say: 'By Jove, what a pretty girl's head!' And after all, when the individual comes out, it's in trousers.

The point, however, is that Rawdon said so emphatically – no, not emphatically, succinctly: 'No woman shall ever again sleep under my roof.' It was a case of futurity. No doubt he had had his ceilings white-washed, and their memories put out. Or rather, repainted, for it was a handsome wooden ceiling. Anyhow, if ceilings have eyes, as walls have ears, then Rawdon had given his ceilings a new outlook, with a new coat of paint, and all memory of any woman's having slept under them – for after all, in decent circumstances we sleep under ceilings, not under roofs – was wiped out for ever.

'And will you neither sleep under any woman's roof?'

That pulled him up rather short. He was not prepared to sauce his gander as he had sauced his goose. Even I could see the thought flitting through his mind, that some of his pleasantest holidays depended on the charm of his hostess. Even some of the nicest hotels were run by women.

'Ah! Well! That's not quite the same thing, you know. When one leaves one's own house one gives up the keys of circumstance, so to speak. But, as far as possible, I make it a rule not to sleep under a roof that is openly, and obviously, and obtrusively a woman's roof!'

'Quite!' said I with a shudder. 'So do I!'

Now I understood his mysterious love affair less than ever. He was never known to speak of this love affair: he did not even write about it to his wife. The lady – for she was a lady – lived only five minutes' walk from Rawdon. She had a husband, but he was in diplomatic service or something like that, which kept him occupied in the sufficiently-far distance. Yes, far enough. And, as a husband, he was a complete diplomat. A balance of power. If he was entitled to occupy the wide field of the world, she, the other and contrasting power, might concentrate and consolidate her position at home.

She was a charming woman, too, and even a beautiful woman. She had two charming children, long-legged, stalky, clove-pink-half-opened sort of children. But really charming. And she was a woman with a certain mystery. She never talked. She never said anything about herself. Perhaps she suffered; perhaps she was frightfully happy, and made *that* her cause for silence. Perhaps she was wise enough even to be beautifully silent about her happiness. Certainly she never mentioned her sufferings, or even her trials: and certainly she must have a fair handful of the latter, for Alec Drummond sometimes fled home in the teeth of a gale of debts. He simply got through his own money and through hers, and, third and fatal stride, through other people's as well. Then something had to be done about it. And Janet, dear soul, had to put her hat on and take journeys. But she never said anything of it. At least, she did just hint that Alec didn't *quite* make enough money to meet expenses. But after all, we don't go about with our eyes shut, and Alec Drummond, whatever else he did, didn't hide his prowess under a bushel.

Rawdon and he were quite friendly, but really! None of them ever talked. Drummond didn't talk, he just went off and behaved in his own way. And though Rawdon would chat away till the small hours, *he* never 'talked'. Not to his nearest male friend did he ever mention Janet save as a very pleasant woman and his neighbour: he admitted he adored her children. They often came to see him.

And one felt about Rawdon, he was making a mystery of something. And that was rather irritating. He went every day to see Janet, and of course we saw him going: going or coming. How can one help but see? But he always went in the morning, at about eleven, and did not stay for lunch: or he went in the afternoon, and came home to dinner. Apparently he was never there in the evening. Poor Janet, she lived like a widow.

Very well, if Rawdon wanted to make it so blatantly obvious that it was only platonic, purely platonic, why wasn't he natural? Why didn't he say simply: 'I'm very fond of Janet Drummond, she is my very dear friend?' Why did he sort of curl up at the very mention of her name, and curdle into silence: or else say rather forcedly: 'Yes, she is a charming woman. I see a good deal of her, but chiefly for the children's sake. I'm devoted to the children!' Then he would look at one in such a curious way, as if he were hiding something. And after all, what was there to hide? If he was the woman's friend, why not? It could be a charming friendship. And if he were her lover, why, heaven bless me, he ought to have been proud of it, and showed just a glint, just an honest man's glint.

But no, never a glint of pride or pleasure in the relation either way. Instead of that, this rather theatrical reserve. Janet, it is true, was just as reserved. If she could, she avoided mentioning his name. Yet one knew, sure as houses, she felt something. One suspected her of being more in love with Rawdon than ever she had been with Alec. And one felt that there was a hush put upon it all. She had had a hush put upon her. By whom? By both the men? Or by Rawdon only? Or by Drummond? Was it for her husband's sake? Impossible! For her children's? But why! Her children were devoted to Rawdon.

It had now become the custom for them to go to him three times a week, for music. I don't mean he taught them the piano. Rawdon was a very refined musical amateur. He had them sing, in their delicate girlish voices, delicate little songs, and really he succeeded wonderfully with them; he made them so true, which children rarely are, musically, and so pure and effortless, like little flamelets of sound. It really was rather beautiful, and sweet of him. And he taught them *music*, the delicacy of the feel of it. They had a regular teacher for the practice.

Even the little girls, in their young little ways, were in love with Rawdon! So if their mother were in love too, in her ripened womanhood, why not?

Poor Janet! She was so still, and so elusive: the hush upon her! She

726

was rather like a half-opened rose that somebody had tied a string round, so that it couldn't open any more. But why? Why? In her there was a real touch of mystery. One could never *ask* her, because one knew her heart was too keenly involved: or her pride.

Whereas there was, really, no mystery about Rawdon, refined and handsome and subtle as he was. He *had* no mystery: at least, to a man. What *he* wrapped himself up in was a certain amount of mystification.

Who wouldn't be irritated to hear a fellow saying, when for months and months he has been paying a daily visit to a lonely and very attractive woman – nay, lately even a twice-daily visit, even if always before sundown – to hear him say, pursing his lips after a sip of his own very moderate port: 'I've taken a vow that no woman shall sleep under my roof again!'

I almost snapped out: 'Oh, what the hell! And what about your Janet?' But I remembered in time, it was not *my* affair, and if he wanted to have his mystifications, let him have them.

If he meant he wouldn't have his wife sleep under his roof again, that one could understand. They were really very witty with one another, he and she, but fatally and damnably married.

Yet neither wanted a divorce. And neither put the slightest claim to any control over the other's behaviour. He said: 'Women live on the moon, men on the earth.' And she said: 'I don't mind in the least if he loves Janet Drummond, poor thing. It would be a change for him, from loving himself. And a change for her, if somebody loved her —'

Poor Janet! But he wouldn't have her sleep under his roof, no, not for any money. And apparently he never slept under hers – if she could be said to have one. So what the deuce?

Of course, if they were friends, just friends, all right! But then in that case, why start talking about not having a woman sleep under your roof? Pure mystification!

The cat never came out of the bag. But one evening I distinctly heard it mewing inside its sack, and I even believe I saw a claw through the canvas.

It was in November – everything much as usual – myself pricking my ears to hear if the rain had stopped, and I could go home, because I was just a little bored about 'cornemuse' music. I had been having dinner with Rawdon, and listening to him ever since on his favourite topic: not, of course, women, and why they shouldn't sleep under his roof, but fourteenth-century melody and windbag accompaniment.

It was not late – not yet ten o'clock – but I was restless, and wanted to go home. There was no longer any sound of rain. And Rawdon was perhaps going to make a pause in his monologue.

Suddenly there was a tap at the door, and Rawdon's man, Hawken, edged in. Rawdon, who had been a major in some fantastic capacity during the war, had brought Hawken back with him. This fresh-faced man of about thirty-five appeared in the doorway with an intensely blank and bewildered look on his face. He was really an extraordinarily good actor.

'A lady, sir!' he said, with a look of utter blankness.

'A what?' snapped Rawdon.

'A lady!' – then with a most discreet drop in his voice: 'Mrs. Drummond, sir!' He looked modestly down at his feet.

Rawdon went deathly white, and his lips quivered.

'Mrs. Drummond! Where?'

Hawken lifted his eyes to his master in a fleeting glance.

'I showed her into the dining-room, there being no fire in the drawing-room.'

Rawdon got to his feet and took two or three agitated strides. He could not make up his mind. At last he said, his lips working with agitation:

'Bring her in here.'

Then he turned with a theatrical gesture to me.

'What this is all about, I *don't* know,' he said.

'Let me clear out,' said I, making for the door.

He caught me by the arm.

'No, for God's sake! For God's sake, stop and see me through!'

He gripped my arm till it really hurt, and his eyes were quite wild. I did not know my Olympic Rawdon.

Hastily I backed away to the side of the fire – we were in Rawdon's room, where the books and piano were – and Mrs. Drummond appeared in the doorway. She was much paler than usual, being a rather warm-coloured woman, and she glanced at me with big reproachful eyes, as much as to say: You intruder! You interloper! For my part, I could do nothing but stare. She wore a black wrap, which I knew quite well, over her black dinner-dress.

'Rawdon!' she said, turning to him and blotting out my existence from her consciousness. Hawken softly closed the door, and I could *feel* him standing on the threshold outside, listening keen as a hawk.

'Sit down, Janet,' said Rawdon, with a grimace of a sour smile, which he could not get rid of once he had started it, so that his face looked very odd indeed, like a mask which he was unable either to fit on or take off. He had several conflicting expressions all at once, and they had all stuck.

She let her wrap slip back on her shoulders, and knitted her white fingers against her skirt, pressing down her arms, and gazing at him with a terrible gaze. I began to creep to the door.

Rawdon started after me.

'No, don't go! Don't go! I specially want you not to go,' he said in extreme agitation.

I looked at her. She was looking at him with a heavy, sombre kind of stare. Me she absolutely ignored. Not for a second could she forgive me for existing on the earth. I slunk back to my post behind the leather arm-chair, as if hiding.

'Do sit down, Janet,' he said to her again. 'And have a smoke. What will you drink?'

'No thanks!' she said, as if it were one word slurred out. 'No thanks.'

And she proceeded again to fix him with that heavy, portentous stare.

He offered her a cigarette, his hand trembling as he held out the silver box.

'Nothanks!' she slurred out again, not even looking at the box, but keeping him fixed with that dark and heavy stare.

He turned away, making a great delay lighting a cigarette, with his back to her, to get out of the stream of that stare. He carefully went for an ash-tray, and put it carefully within reach – all the time trying not to be swept away on that stare. And she stood with her fingers locked, her straight, plump, handsome arms pressed downwards against her skirt, and she gazed at him.

He leaned his elbow on the mantelpiece abstractedly for a moment – then he started suddenly, and rang the bell. She turned her eyes from him for a moment, to watch his middle finger pressing the bell-button. Then there was a tension of waiting, an interruption in the previous tension. We waited. Nobody came. Rawdon rang again.

'That's very curious!' he murmured to himself. Hawken was usually so prompt. Hawken, not being a woman, slept under the roof, so there was no excuse for his not answering the bell. The tension in the room had now changed quality, owing to this new suspense. Poor Janet's sombre stare became gradually loosened, so to speak. Attention was divided. Where was Hawken? Rawdon rang the bell a third time, a long peal. And now Janet was no longer the centre of suspense. Where was Hawken? The question loomed large over every other.

'I'll just look in the kitchen,' said I, making for the door.

'No, no. I'll go,' said Rawdon.

But I was in the passage – and Rawdon was on my heels.

The kitchen was very tidy and cheerful, but empty; only a bottle of beer and two glasses stood on the table. To Rawdon the kitchen was as strange a world as to me – he never entered the servants' quarters. But to me it was curious that the bottle of beer was empty, and both the glasses had been used. I knew Rawdon wouldn't notice.

'That's very curious!' said Rawdon: meaning the absence of his man.

At that moment we heard a step on the servants' stairs, and Rawdon opened the door to reveal Hawken descending with an armful of sheets and things.

'What are you doing?'

'Why! —' and a pause. 'I was airing the clean laundry, like – not to waste the fire last thing.'

Hawken descended into the kitchen with a very flushed face and very bright eyes and rather ruffled hair, and proceeded to spread the linen on chairs before the fire.

'I hope I've not done wrong, sir,' he said in his most winning manner. 'Was you ringing?'

'Three times! Leave that linen and bring a bottle of the fizz.'

'I'm sorry, sir. You can't hear the bell from the front, sir.'

It was perfectly true. The house was small, but it had been built for a very nervous author, and the servants' quarters were shut off, padded from the rest of the house.

Rawdon said no more about the sheets and things, but he looked more peaked than ever.

We went back to the music-room. Janet had gone to the hearth, and stood with her hand on the mantel. She looked round at us, baffled.

'We're having a bottle of fizz,' said Rawdon. 'Do let me take your wrap.'

'And where was Hawken?' she asked satirically.

'Oh, busy somewhere upstairs.'

'He's a busy young man, that!' she said sardonically. And she sat uncomfortably on the edge of the chair where I had been sitting.

When Hawken came with the tray, she said:

'I'm not going to drink.'

Rawdon appealed to me, so I took a glass. She looked inquiringly at the flushed and bright-eyed Hawken, as if she understood something.

The manservant left the room. We drank our wine, and the awkwardness returned.

'Rawdon!' she said suddenly, as if she were firing a revolver at him. 'Alec came home to-night in a bigger mess than ever, and wanted to make love to me to get it off his mind. I can't stand it any more. I'm in love with you, and I simply can't stand Alec getting too near to me. He's dangerous when he's crossed – and when he's worked up. So I just came here. I didn't see what else I could do.'

She left off as suddenly as a machine-gun leaves off firing. We were just dazed.

'You are quite right,' Rawdon began, in a vague and neutral tone. . . .

'I am, am I not?' she said eagerly.

'I'll tell you what I'll do,' he said. 'I'll go round to the hotel to-night, and you can stay here.'

'Under the kindly protection of Hawken, you mean!' she said, with quiet sarcasm.

'Why! – I could send Mrs. Betts, I suppose,' he said.

Mrs. Betts was his housekeeper.

'You couldn't stay and protect me yourself?' she said quietly.

'I! I! Why, I've made a vow – haven't I, Joe?' – he turned to me – 'not to have any woman sleep under my roof again.' – He got the mixed sour smile on his face.

She looked up at the ceiling for a moment, then lapsed into silence. Then she said:

'Sort of monastery, so to speak!'

And she rose and reached for her wrap, adding:

'I'd better go, then.'

'Joe will see you home,' he said.

She faced round on me.

'Do you mind *not* seeing me home, Mr. Bradley?' she said, gazing at me.

'Not if you don't want me,' said I.

'Hawken will drive you,' said Rawdon.

'Oh, no, he won't!' she said. 'I'll walk. Good-night.'

'I'll get my hat,' stammered Rawdon, in an agony. 'Wait! Wait! The gate will be locked.'

'It was open when I came,' she said.

He rang for Hawken to unlock the iron doors at the end of the short drive, whilst he himself huddled into a greatcoat and scarf, fumbling for a flashlight.

'You won't go till I come back, will you?' he pleaded to me. 'I'd be awfully glad if you'd stay the night. The sheets *will* be aired.'

I had to promise – and he set off with an umbrella, in the rain, at the same time asking Hawken to take a flashlight and go in front. So that was how they went, in single file along the path over the fields to Mrs. Drummond's house, Hawken in front, with flashlight and umbrella, curving round to light up in front of Mrs. Drummond, who, with umbrella only, walked isolated between two lights, Rawdon shining his flashlight on her from the rear from under his umbrella. I turned indoors.

So that was over! At least, for the moment!

I thought I would go upstairs and see how damp the bed in the guest-chamber was before I actually stayed the night with Rawdon. He never had guests – preferred to go away himself.

The guest-chamber was a good room across a passage and round a corner from Rawdon's room – its door just opposite the padded service-door. This latter service-door stood open, and a light shone through. I went into the spare bedroom, switching on the light.

To my surprise, the bed looked as if it had just been left – the sheets tumbled, the pillows pressed. I put in my hands under the bedclothes, and it was warm. Very curious!

As I stood looking round in mild wonder, I heard a voice call softly: 'Joe!'

'Yes!' said I instinctively, and, though startled, strode at once out of the room and through the servants' door, towards the voice. Light shone from the open doorway of one of the servants' rooms.

There was a muffled little shriek, and I was standing looking into what was probably Hawken's bedroom, and seeing a soft and pretty white leg and a pretty feminine posterior very thinly dimmed in a rather short night-dress, just in the act of climbing into a narrow little bed, and, then arrested, the owner of the pretty posterior burying her face in the bed-clothes, to be invisible, like the ostrich in the sand.

I discreetly withdrew, went downstairs and poured myself a glass of wine. And very shortly Rawdon returned looking like Hamlet in the last act.

He said nothing, neither did I. We sat and merely smoked. Only as he was seeing me upstairs to bed, in the now immaculate bedroom, he said pathetically:

'Why aren't women content to be what a man wants them to be?'

'Why aren't they!' said I wearily.

'I thought I had made everything clear,' he said.

'You start at the wrong end,' said I.

And as I said it, the picture came into my mind of the pretty feminine butt-end in Hawken's bedroom. Yes, Hawken made better starts, wherever he ended.

When he brought me my cup of tea in the morning, he was very soft and cat-like. I asked him what sort of day it was, and he asked me if I'd had a good night, and was I comfortable.

'Very comfortable!' said I. 'But I turned you out, I'm afraid.'

'Me, sir?' He turned on me a face of utter bewilderment.

But I looked him in the eye.

'Is your name Joe?' I asked him.

'You're right, sir.'

'So is mine,' said I. 'However, I didn't see her face, so it's all right. I suppose you *were* a bit tight, in that little bed!'

'Well, sir!' and he flashed me a smile of amazing impudence, and lowered his tone to utter confidence. 'This is the best bed in the house, this is.' And he touched it softly.

'You've not tried them all, surely?'

A look of indignant horror on his face!

'No, sir, indeed I haven't.'

That day, Rawdon left for London, on his way to Tunis, and Hawken was to follow him. The roof of his house looked just the same.

The Drummonds moved too – went away somewhere, and left a lot of unsatisfied tradespeople behind.

THE ROCKING-HORSE WINNER

THERE was a woman who was beautiful, who started with all the advantages, yet she had no luck. She married for love, and the love turned to dust. She had bonny children, yet she felt they had been thrust upon her, and she could not love them. They looked at her coldly, as if they were finding fault with her. And hurriedly she felt she must cover up some fault in herself. Yet what it was that she must cover up she never knew. Nevertheless, when her children were present, she always felt the centre of her heart go hard. This troubled her, and in her manner she was all the more gentle and anxious for her children, as if she loved them very much. Only she herself knew that at the centre of her heart was a hard little place that could not feel love, no, not for anybody. Everybody else said of her: 'She is such a good mother. She adores her children.' Only she herself, and her children themselves, knew it was not so. They read it in each other's eyes.

There were a boy and two little girls. They lived in a pleasant house, with a garden, and they had discreet servants, and felt themselves superior to anyone in the neighbourhood.

Although they lived in style, they felt always an anxiety in the house. There was never enough money. The mother had a small income, and the father had a small income, but not nearly enough, for the social position which they had to keep up. The father went into town to some office. But though he had good prospects, these prospects never materialised. There was always the grinding sense of the shortage of money, though the style was always kept up.

At last the mother said: 'I will see if *I* can't make something.' But she did not know where to begin. She racked her brains, and tried this thing and the other, but could not find anything successful. The failure made deep lines come into her face. Her children were growing up, they would have to go to school. There must be more money, there must be more money. The father, who was always very handsome and expensive in his tastes, seemed as if he never *would* be able to do anything worth doing. And the mother, who had a great belief in herself, did not succeed any better, and her tastes were just as expensive.

And so the house came to be haunted by the unspoken phrase: *There must be more money! There must be more money!* The children could hear it all the time, though nobody said it aloud. They heard it at Christmas, when the expensive and splendid toys filled the nursery. Behind the shining modern rocking-horse, behind the smart doll's house, a voice would start whispering: 'There *must* be more money! There *must* be more money!' And the children would stop playing, to listen for a moment. They would look into each other's eyes, to see if they had all heard. And each one saw in the eyes of the other two that they too had heard. 'There *must* be more money! There *must* be more money!'

It came whispering from the springs of the still-swaying rocking-horse, and even the horse, bending his wooden, champing head, heard it. The big doll, sitting so pink and smirking in her new pram, could hear it quite plainly, and seemed to be smirking all the more self-consciously because of it. The foolish puppy, too, that took the place of the teddy-bear, he was looking so extraordinarily foolish for no other reason but that he heard the secret whisper all over the house: 'There *must* be more money!'

Yet nobody ever said it aloud. The whisper was everywhere, and therefore no one spoke it. Just as no one ever says: 'We are breathing!' in spite of the fact that breath is coming and going all the time.

'Mother,' said the boy Paul one day, 'why don't we keep a car of our own? Why do we always use uncle's, or else a taxi?'

'Because we're the poor members of the family,' said the mother.

'But why *are* we, mother?'

'Well – I suppose,' she said slowly and bitterly, 'it's because your father has no luck.'

The boy was silent for some time.

'Is luck money, mother?' he asked, rather timidly.

'No, Paul. Not quite. It's what causes you to have money.'

'Oh!' said Paul vaguely. 'I thought when Uncle Oscar said *filthy lucker,* it meant money.'

'*Filthy lucre* does mean money,' said the mother. 'But it's lucre, not luck.'

'Oh!' said the boy. 'Then what *is* luck, mother?'

'It's what causes you to have money. If you're lucky you have money. That's why it's better to be born lucky than rich. If you're rich, you may lose your money. But if you're lucky, you will always get more money.'

'Oh! Will you? And is father not lucky?'

'Very unlucky, I should say,' she said bitterly.

The boy watched her with unsure eyes.

'Why?' he asked.

'I don't know. Nobody ever knows why one person is lucky and another unlucky.'

'Don't they? Nobody at all? Does *nobody* know?'

'Perhaps God. But He never tells.'

'He ought to, then. And aren't you lucky either, mother?'

'I can't be, if I married an unlucky husband.'

'But by yourself, aren't you?'

'I used to think I was, before I married. Now I think I am very unlucky indeed.'

'Why?'

'Well – never mind! Perhaps I'm not really,' she said.

The child looked at her to see if she meant it. But he saw, by the lines of her mouth, that she was only trying to hide something from him.

'Well, anyhow,' he said stoutly, 'I'm a lucky person.'

'Why?' said his mother, with a sudden laugh.

He stared at her. He didn't even know why he had said it.

'God told me,' he asserted, brazening it out.

'I hope He did, dear!' she said, again with a laugh, but rather bitter.

'He did, mother!'

'Excellent!' said the mother, using one of her husband's exclamations.

The boy saw she did not believe him; or rather, that she paid no attention to this assertion. This angered him somewhere, and made him want to compel her attention.

He went off by himself, vaguely, in a childish way, seeking for the clue to 'luck'. Absorbed, taking no heed of other people, he went about with a sort of stealth, seeking inwardly for luck. He wanted luck, he wanted it, he wanted it. When the two girls were playing dolls in the nursery, he would sit on his big rocking-horse, charging madly into space, with a frenzy that made the little girls peer at him uneasily. Wildly the horse careered, the waving dark hair of the boy tossed, his eyes had a strange glare in them. The little girls dared not speak to him.

When he had ridden to the end of his mad little journey, he climbed down and stood in front of his rocking-horse, staring fixedly into its lowered face. Its red mouth was slightly open, its big eye was wide and glassy-bright.

736

'Now!' he would silently command the snorting steed. 'Now take me to where there is luck! Now take me!'

And he would slash the horse on the neck with the little whip he had asked Uncle Oscar for. He *knew* the horse would take him to where there was luck, if only he forced it. So he would mount again and start on his furious ride, hoping at last to get there. He knew he could get there.

'You'll break your horse, Paul!' said the nurse.

'He's always riding like that! I wish he'd leave off!' said his elder sister Joan.

But he only glared down on them in silence. Nurse gave him up. She could make nothing of him. Anyhow, he was growing beyond her.

One day his mother and his Uncle Oscar came in when he was on one of his furious rides. He did not speak to them.

'Hallo, you young jockey! Riding a winner?' said his uncle.

'Aren't you growing too big for a rocking-horse? You're not a very little boy any longer, you know,' said his mother.

But Paul only gave a blue glare from his big, rather close-set eyes. He would speak to nobody when he was in full tilt. His mother watched him with an anxious expression on her face.

At last he suddenly stopped forcing his horse into the mechanical gallop and slid down.

'Well, I got there!' he announced fiercely, his blue eyes still flaring, and his sturdy long legs straddling apart.

'Where did you get to?' asked his mother.

'Where I wanted to go,' he flared back at her.

'That's right, son!' said Uncle Oscar. 'Don't you stop till you get there. What's the horse's name?'

'He doesn't have a name,' said the boy.

'Gets on without all right?' asked the uncle.

'Well, he has different names. He was called Sansovino last week.'

'Sansovino, eh? Won at Ascot. How did you know this name?'

'He always talks about horse-races with Bassett,' said Joan.

The uncle was delighted to find that his small nephew was posted with all the racing news. Bassett, the young gardener, who had been wounded in the left foot in the war and had got his present job through Oscar Cresswell, whose batman he had been, was a perfect blade of the 'turf'. He lived in the racing events, and the small boy lived with him.

Oscar Cresswell got it all from Bassett.

'Master Paul comes and asks me, so I can't do more than tell him, sir,' said Bassett, his face terribly serious, as if he were speaking of religious matters.

'And does he ever put anything on a horse he fancies?'

'Well – I don't want to give him away – he's a young sport, a fine sport, sir. Would you mind asking him yourself? He sort of takes a pleasure in it, and perhaps he'd feel I was giving him away, sir, if you don't mind.'

Bassett was serious as a church.

The uncle went back to his nephew and took him off for a ride in the car.

'Say, Paul, old man, do you ever put anything on a horse?' the uncle asked.

The boy watched the handsome man closely.

'Why, do you think I oughtn't to?' he parried.

'Not a bit of it! I thought perhaps you might give me a tip for the Lincoln.'

The car sped on into the country, going down to Uncle Oscar's place in Hampshire.

'Honour bright?' said the nephew.

'Honour bright, son!' said the uncle.

'Well, then, Daffodil.'

'Daffodil! I doubt it, sonny. What about Mirza?'

'I only know the winner,' said the boy. 'That's Daffodil.'

'Daffodil, eh?'

There was a pause. Daffodil was an obscure horse comparatively.

'Uncle!'

'Yes, son?'

'You won't let it go any further, will you? I promised Bassett.'

'Bassett be damned, old man! What's he got to do with it?'

'We're partners. We've been partners from the first. Uncle, he lent me my first five shillings, which I lost. I promised him, honour bright, it was only between me and him; only you gave me that ten-shilling note I started winning with, so I thought you were lucky. You won't let it go any further, will you?'

The boy gazed at his uncle from those big, hot, blue eyes, set rather close together. The uncle stirred and laughed uneasily.

'Right you are, son! I'll keep your tip private. Daffodil, eh? How much are you putting on him?'

'All except twenty pounds,' said the boy. 'I keep that in reserve.'

The uncle thought it a good joke.

'You keep twenty pounds in reserve, do you, you young romancer? What are you betting, then?'

'I'm betting three hundred,' said the boy gravely. 'But it's between you and me, Uncle Oscar! Honour bright?'

The uncle burst into a roar of laughter.

'It's between you and me all right, you young Nat Gould,' he said, laughing. 'But where's your three hundred?'

'Bassett keeps it for me. We're partners.'

'You are, are you! And what is Bassett putting on Daffodil?'

'He won't go quite as high as I do, I expect. Perhaps he'll go a hundred and fifty.'

'What pennies?' laughed the uncle.

'Pounds,' said the child, with a surprised look at his uncle. 'Bassett keeps a bigger reserve than I do.'

Between wonder and amusement Uncle Oscar was silent. He pursued the matter no further, but he determined to take his nephew with him to the Lincoln races.

'Now, son,' he said, 'I'm putting twenty on Mirza, and I'll put five on for you on any horse you fancy. What's your pick?'

'Daffodil, uncle.'

'No, not the fiver on Daffodil!'

'I should if it was my own fiver,' said the child.

'Good! Good! Right you are! A fiver for me and a fiver for you on Daffodil.'

The child had never been to a race-meeting before, and his eyes were blue fire. He pursed his mouth tight and watched. A Frenchman just in front had put his money on Lancelot. Wild with excitement, he flayed his arms up and down, yelling *Lancelot! Lancelot!* in his French accent.

Daffodil came in first, Lancelot second, Mirza third. The child, flushed and with eyes blazing, was curiously serene. His uncle brought him four five-pound notes, four to one.

'What am I to do with these?' he cried, waving them before the boy's eyes.

'I suppose we'll talk to Bassett,' said the boy. 'I expect I have fifteen hundred now, and twenty in reserve; and this twenty.'

His uncle studied him for some moments.

'Look here son!' he said. 'You're not serious about Bassett and that fifteen hundred, are you?'

'Yes, I am. But it's between you and me, uncle. Honour bright?'

'Honour bright all right, son! But I must talk to Bassett.'

'If you'd like to be a partner, uncle, with Bassett and me, we could all be partners. Only, you'd have to promise, honour bright, uncle, not to let it go beyond us three. Bassett and I are lucky, and you must be lucky, because it was your ten shillings I started winning with....'

Uncle Oscar took both Bassett and Paul into Richmond Park for an afternoon, and there they talked.

'It's like this, you see, sir,' Bassett said. 'Master Paul would get me talking about racing events, spinning yarns, you know, sir. And he was always keen on knowing if I'd made or if I'd lost. It's about a year since, now, that I put five shillings on Blush of Dawn for him: and we lost. Then the luck turned, with that ten shillings he had from you: that we put on Singhalese. And since that time, it's been pretty steady, all things considering. What do you say, Master Paul?'

'We're all right when we're sure,' said Paul. 'It's when we're not quite sure that we go down.'

'Oh, but we're careful then,' said Bassett.

'But when are you *sure*?' smiled Uncle Oscar.

'It's Master Paul, sir,' said Bassett in a secret, religious voice. 'It's as if he had it from heaven. Like Daffodil, now, for the Lincoln. That was as sure as eggs.'

'Did you put anything on Daffodil?' asked Oscar Cresswell.

'Yes, sir. I made my bit.'

'And my nephew?'

Bassett was obstinately silent, looking at Paul.

'I made twelve hundred, didn't I, Bassett? I told uncle I was putting three hundred on Daffodil.'

'That's right,' said Bassett, nodding.

'But where's the money?' asked the uncle.

'I keep it safe locked up, sir. Master Paul he can have it any minute he likes to ask for it.'

'What, fifteen hundred pounds?'

'And twenty! And *forty*, that is, with the twenty he made on the course.'

'It's amazing!' said the uncle.

'If Master Paul offers you to be partners, sir, I would if I were you: if you'll excuse me,' said Bassett.

Oscar Cresswell thought about it.

'I'll see the money,' he said.

740

They drove home again, and, sure enough, Bassett came round to the garden-house with fifteen hundred pounds in notes. The twenty pounds reserve was left with Joe Glee, in the Turf Commission deposit.

'You see, it's all right, uncle, when I'm *sure*! Then we go strong, for all we're worth. Don't we, Bassett?'

'We do that, Master Paul.'

'And when are you sure?' said the uncle, laughing.

'Oh, well, sometimes I'm *absolutely* sure, like about Daffodil,' said the boy; 'and sometimes I have an idea; and sometimes I haven't even an idea, have I, Bassett? Then we're careful, because we mostly go down.'

'You do, do you! And when you're sure, like about Daffodil, what makes you sure, sonny?'

'Oh, well, I don't know,' said the boy uneasily. 'I'm sure, you know, uncle; that's all.'

'It's as if he had it from heaven, sir,' Bassett reiterated.

'I should say so!' said the uncle.

But he became a partner. And when the Leger was coming on Paul was 'sure' about Lively Spark, which was a quite inconsiderable horse. The boy insisted on putting a thousand on the horse, Bassett went for five hundred, and Oscar Cresswell two hundred. Lively Spark came in first, and the betting had been ten to one against him. Paul had made ten thousand.

'You see,' he said, 'I was absolutely sure of him.'

Even Oscar Cresswell had cleared two thousand.

'Look here, son,' he said, 'this sort of thing makes me nervous.'

'It needn't, uncle! Perhaps I shan't be sure again for a long time.'

'But what are you going to do with your money?' asked the uncle.

'Of course,' said the boy, 'I started it for mother. She said she had no luck, because father is unlucky, so I thought if *I* was lucky, it might stop whispering.'

'What might stop whispering?'

'Our house. I *hate* our house for whispering.'

'What does it whisper?'

'Why – why' – the boy fidgeted– 'why, I don't know. But it's always short of money, you know, uncle.'

'I know it, son, I know it.'

'You know people send mother writs, don't you, uncle?'

'I'm afraid I do,' said the uncle.

'And then the house whispers, like people laughing at you behind your back. It's awful, that is! I thought if I was lucky —'

741

'You might stop it,' added the uncle.

The boy watched him with big blue eyes, that had an uncanny cold fire in them, and he never said a word.

'Well, then!' said the uncle. 'What are we doing?'

'I shouldn't like mother to know I was lucky,' said the boy.

'Why not, son?'

'She'd stop me.'

'I don't think she would.'

'Oh!' – and the boy writhed in an odd way – 'I *don't* want her to know, uncle.'

'All right, son! We'll manage it without her knowing.'

They managed it very easily. Paul, at the other's suggestion, handed over five thousand pounds to his uncle, who deposited it with the family lawyer, who was then to inform Paul's mother that a relative had put five thousand pounds into his hands, which sum was to be paid out a thousand pounds at a time, on the mother's birthday, for the next five years.

'So she'll have a birthday present of a thousand pounds for five successive years,' said Uncle Oscar. 'I hope it won't make it all the harder for her later.'

Paul's mother had her birthday in November. The house had been 'whispering' worse than ever lately, and, even in spite of his luck, Paul could not bear up against it. He was very anxious to see the effect of the birthday letter, telling his mother about the thousand pounds.

When there were no visitors, Paul now took his meals with his parents, as he was beyond the nursery control. His mother went into town nearly every day. She had discovered that she had an odd knack of sketching furs and dress materials, so she worked secretly in the studio of a friend who was the chief 'artist' for the leading drapers. She drew the figures of ladies in furs and ladies in silk and sequins for the newspaper advertisements. This young woman artist earned several thousand pounds a year, but Paul's mother only made several hundreds, and she was again dissatisfied. She so wanted to be first in something, and she did not succeed, even in making sketches for drapery advertisements.

She was down to breakfast on the morning of her birthday. Paul watched her face as she read her letters. He knew the lawyer's letter. As his mother read it, her face hardened and became more expressionless. Then a cold, determined look came on her mouth. She hid the letter under the pile of others, and said not a word about it.

'Didn't you have anything nice in the post for your birthday, mother?' said Paul.

'Quite moderately nice,' she said, her voice cold and absent.

She went away to town without saying more.

But in the afternoon Uncle Oscar appeared. He said Paul's mother had had a long interview with the lawyer, asking if the whole five thousand could not be advanced at once, as she was in debt.

'What do you think, uncle?' said the boy.

'I leave it to you, son.'

'Oh, let her have it, then! We can get some more with the other,' said the boy.

'A bird in the hand is worth two in the bush, laddie!' said Uncle Oscar.

'But I'm sure to *know* for the Grand National; or the Lincolnshire; or else the Derby. I'm sure to know for *one* of them,' said Paul.

So Uncle Oscar signed the agreement, and Paul's mother touched the whole five thousand. Then something very curious happened. The voices in the house suddenly went mad, like a chorus of frogs on a spring evening. There were certain new furnishings, and Paul had a tutor. He was *really* going to Eton, his father's school, in the following autumn. There were flowers in the winter, and a blossoming of the luxury Paul's mother had been used to. And yet the voices in the house, behind the sprays of mimosa and almond-blossom, and from under the piles of iridescent cushions, simply trilled and screamed in a sort of ecstasy: 'There *must* be more money! Oh-h-h, there *must* be more money. Oh, now, now-w! Now-w-w – there *must* be more money! – more than ever! More than ever!'

It frightened Paul terribly. He studied away at his Latin and Greek with his tutor. But his intense hours were spent with Bassett. The Grand National had gone by: he had not 'known', and had lost a hundred pounds. Summer was at hand. He was in agony for the Lincoln. But even for the Lincoln he didn't 'know', and he lost fifty pounds. He became wild-eyed and strange, as if something was going to explode in him.

'Let it alone, son! Don't you bother about it!' urged Uncle Oscar. But it was as if the boy couldn't really hear what his uncle was saying.

'I've got to know for the Derby! I've got to know for the Derby!' the child reiterated, his big blue eyes blazing with a sort of madness.

His mother noticed how overwrought he was.

'You'd better go to the seaside. Wouldn't you like to go now to the seaside, instead of waiting? I think you'd better,' she said, looking down at him anxiously, her heart curiously heavy because of him.

But the child lifted his uncanny blue eyes.

'I couldn't possibly go before the Derby, mother!' he said. 'I couldn't possibly!'

'Why not?' she said, her voice becoming heavy when she was opposed. 'Why not? You can still go from the seaside to see the Derby with your Uncle Oscar, if that's what you wish. No need for you to wait here. Besides, I think you care too much about these races. It's a bad sign. My family has been a gambling family, and you won't know till you grow up how much damage it has done. But it has done damage. I shall have to send Bassett away, and ask Uncle Oscar not to talk racing to you, unless you promise to be reasonable about it: go away to the seaside and forget it. You're all nerves!'

'I'll do what you like, mother, so long as you don't send me away till after the Derby,' the boy said.

'Send you away from where? Just from this house?'

'Yes,' he said, gazing at her.

'Why, you curious child, what makes you care about this house so much, suddenly? I never knew you loved it.'

He gazed at her without speaking. He had a secret within a secret, something he had not divulged, even to Bassett or to his Uncle Oscar.

But his mother, after standing undecided and a little bit sullen for some moments, said:

'Very well, then! Don't go to the seaside till after the Derby, if you don't wish it. But promise me you won't let your nerves go to pieces. Promise you won't think so much about horse-racing and *events*, as you call them!'

'Oh no,' said the boy casually. 'I won't think much about them, mother. You needn't worry. I wouldn't worry, mother, if I were you.'

'If you were me and I were you,' said his mother, 'I wonder what we *should* do!'

'But you know you needn't worry, mother, don't you?' the boy repeated.

'I should be awfully glad to know it,' she said wearily.

'Oh, well, you *can*, you know. I mean, you *ought* to know you needn't worry,' he insisted.

'Ought I? Then I'll see about it,' she said.

744

Paul's secret of secrets was his wooden horse, that which had no name. Since he was emancipated from a nurse and a nursery-governess, he had had his rocking-horse removed to his own bedroom at the top of the house.

'Surely you're too big for a rocking-horse!' his mother had remonstrated.

'Well, you see, mother, till I can have a *real* horse, I like to have *some* sort of animal about,' had been his quaint answer.

'Do you feel he keeps you company?' she laughed.

'Oh yes! He's very good, he always keeps me company, when I'm there,' said Paul.

So the horse, rather shabby, stood in an arrested prance in the boy's bedroom.

The Derby was drawing near, and the boy grew more and more tense. He hardly heard what was spoken to him, he was very frail, and his eyes were really uncanny. His mother had sudden seizures of uneasiness about him. Sometimes, for half an hour, she would feel a sudden anxiety about him that was almost anguish. She wanted to rush to him at once, and know he was safe.

Two nights before the Derby, she was at a big party in town, when one of her rushes of anxiety about her boy, her first-born, gripped her heart till she could hardly speak. She fought with the feeling, might and main, for she believed in common sense. But it was too strong. She had to leave the dance and go downstairs to telephone to the country. The children's nursery-governess was terribly surprised and startled at being rung up in the night.

'Are the children all right, Miss Wilmot?'

'Oh yes, they are quite all right.'

'Master Paul? Is he all right?'

'He went to bed as right as a trivet. Shall I run up and look at him?'

'No,' said Paul's mother reluctantly. 'No! Don't trouble. It's all right. Don't sit up. We shall be home fairly soon.' She did not want her son's privacy intruded upon.

'Very good,' said the governess.

It was about one o'clock when Paul's mother and father drove up to their house. All was still. Paul's mother went to her room and slipped off her white fur cloak. She had told her maid not to wait up for her. She heard her husband downstairs mixing a whisky and soda.

And then, because of the strange anxiety at her heart, she stole upstairs to her son's room. Noiselessly she went along the upper corridor. Was there a faint noise? What was it?

She stood, with arrested muscles, outside his door, listening. There was a strange, heavy, and yet not loud noise. Her heart stood still. It was a soundless noise, yet rushing and powerful. Something huge, in violent, hushed motion. What was it? What in God's name was it? She ought to know. She felt that she knew the noise. She knew what it was.

Yet she could not place it. She couldn't say what it was. And on and on it went, like a madness.

Softly, frozen with anxiety and fear, she turned the door-handle.

The room was dark. Yet in the space near the window, she heard and saw something plunging to and fro. She gazed in fear and amazement.

Then suddenly she switched on the light, and saw her son, in his green pyjamas, madly surging on the rocking-horse. The blaze of light suddenly lit him up, as he urged the wooden horse, and lit her up, as she stood, blonde, in her dress of pale green and crystal, in the doorway.

'Paul!' she cried. 'Whatever are you doing?'

'It's Malabar!' he screamed in a powerful, strange voice. 'It's Malabar!'

His eyes blazed at her for one strange and senseless second, as he ceased urging his wooden horse. Then he fell with a crash to the ground, and she, all her tormented motherhood flooding upon her, rushed to gather him up.

But he was unconscious, and unconscious he remained, with some brain-fever. He talked and tossed, and his mother sat stonily by his side.

'Malabar! It's Malabar! Bassett, Bassett, I *know*! It's Malabar!'

So the child cried, trying to get up and urge the rocking-horse that gave him his inspiration.

'What does he mean by Malabar?' asked the heart-frozen mother.

'I don't know,' said the father stonily.

'What does he mean by Malabar?' she asked her brother Oscar.

'It's one of the horses running for the Derby,' was the answer.

And, in spite of himself, Oscar Cresswell spoke to Bassett, and himself put a thousand on Malabar: at fourteen to one.

The third day of the illness was critical: they were waiting for a change. The boy, with his rather long, curly hair, was tossing ceaselessly on the pillow. He neither slept nor regained consciousness, and his eyes were like blue stones. His mother sat, feeling her heart had gone, turned actually into a stone.

In the evening, Oscar Cresswell did not come, but Bassett sent a message, saying could he come up for one moment, just one moment? Paul's mother was very angry at the intrusion, but on second thoughts she agreed. The boy was the same. Perhaps Bassett might bring him to consciousness.

The gardener, a shortish fellow with a little brown moustache and sharp little brown eyes, tiptoed into the room, touched his imaginary cap to Paul's mother, and stole to the bedside, staring with glittering, smallish eyes at the tossing, dying child.

'Master Paul!' he whispered. 'Master Paul! Malabar came in first all right, a clean win. I did as you told me. You've made over seventy thousand pounds, you have; you've got over eighty thousand. Malabar came in all right, Master Paul.'

'Malabar! Malabar! Did I say Malabar, mother? Did I say Malabar? Do you think I'm lucky, mother? I knew Malabar, didn't I? Over eighty thousand pounds! I call that lucky, don't you, mother? Over eighty thousand pounds! I knew, didn't I know I knew? Malabar came in all right. If I ride my horse till I'm sure, then I tell you, Bassett, you can go as high as you like. Did you go for all you were worth, Bassett?'

'I went a thousand on it, Master Paul.'

'I never told you, mother, that if I can ride my horse, and *get there*, then I'm absolutely sure – oh, absolutely! Mother, did I ever tell you? I *am* lucky!'

'No, you never did,' said his mother.

But the boy died in the night.

And even as he lay dead, his mother heard her brother's voice saying to her: 'My God, Hester, you're eighty-odd thousand to the good, and a poor devil of a son to the bad. But, poor devil, poor devil, he's best gone out of a life where he rides his rocking-horse to find a winner.'

MOTHER AND DAUGHTER

VIRGINIA BODOIN had a good job: she was head of a department in a certain government office, held a responsible position, and earned, to imitate Balzac and be precise about it, seven hundred and fifty pounds a year. That is already something. Rachel Bodoin, her mother, had an income of about six hundred a year, on which she had lived in the capitals of Europe since the effacement of a never very important husband.

Now after some years of virtual separation and 'freedom', mother and daughter once more thought of settling down. They had become, in course of time, more like a married couple than mother and daughter. They knew one another very well indeed, and each was a little 'nervous' of the other. They had lived together and parted several times. Virginia was now thirty, and she didn't look like marrying. For four years she had been as good as married to Henry Lubbock, a rather spoilt young man who was musical. Then Henry let her down: for two reasons. He couldn't stand her mother. Her mother couldn't stand him. And anybody whom Mrs. Bodoin could not stand she managed to sit on, disastrously. So Henry had writhed horribly, feeling his mother-in-law sitting on him tight, and Virginia after all, in a helpless sort of family loyalty, sitting alongside her mother. Virginia didn't really want to sit on Henry. But when her mother egged her on, she couldn't help it. For ultimately her mother had power over her; a strange *female* power, nothing to do with parental authority. Virginia had long thrown parental authority to the winds. But her mother had another, much subtler form of domination, female and thrilling, so that when Rachael said: 'Let's squash him!' Virginia had to rush wickedly and gleefully to the sport. And Henry knew quite well when he was being squashed. So that was one of his reasons for going back on Vinny. He called her Vinny, to the superlative disgust of Mrs. Bodoin, who always corrected him: 'My daughter *Virginia* —'

The second reason was, again to be Balzacian, that Virginia hadn't a sou of her own. Henry had a sorry two hundred and fifty. Virginia, at the age of twenty-four, was already earning four hundred and fifty. But she was earning them. Whereas Henry managed to earn about twelve pounds per annum, by his precious music. He had realised that he would find it hard to earn more. So that marrying, except with a wife who could keep him, was rather out of the question. Vinny would inherit her mother's money. But then Mrs. Bodoin had the health and muscular equipment of the Sphinx. She would live for ever, seeking whom she might devour, and devouring him. Henry lived with Vinny for two years, in the married sense of the words: and Vinny felt they *were* married, minus a mere ceremony. But Vinny had her mother always in the background; often as far back as Paris or Biarritz, but still, within letter reach. And she never realised the funny little grin that came on her own elvish face when her mother, even in a letter, spread her skirts and calmly sat on Henry. She never realised that in spirit she promptly and mischievously sat on him too: she could no more have helped it than the tide can help turning to the moon. And she did not dream that he felt it, and was utterly mortified in his masculine vanity. Women, very often, hypnotise one another, and then, hypnotised, they proceed gently to wring the neck of the man they think they are loving with all their hearts. Then they call it utter perversity on his part, that he doesn't like having his neck wrung. They think he is repudiating a heart-felt love. For they are hypnotised. Women hypnotise one another, without knowing it.

In the end, Henry backed out. He saw himself being simply reduced to nothingness by two women, an old witch with muscles like the Sphinx, and a young, spell-bound witch, lavish, elvish, and weak, who utterly spoilt him but who ate his marrow.

Rachel would write from Paris: 'My dear Virginia, as I had a windfall in the way of an investment, I am sharing it with you. You will find enclosed my cheque for twenty pounds. No doubt you will be needing it to buy Henry a suit of clothes, since the spring is apparently come, and the sunlight may be tempted to show him up for what he is worth. I don't want my daughter going around with what is presumably a streetcorner musician, but please pay the tailor's bill yourself, or you may have to do it over again later.' Henry got a suit of clothes, but it was as good as a shirt of Nessus, eating him away with subtle poison.

So he backed out. He didn't jump out, or bolt, or carve his way out at the sword's point. He sort of faded out, distributing his departure over a year or more. He was fond of Vinny, and he could hardly do without her, and he was sorry for her. But at length he couldn't see her apart from her mother. She was a young, weak, spendthrift witch, accomplice of her tough-clawed witch of a mother.

Henry made other alliances, got a good hold on elsewhere, and gradually extricated himself. He saved his life, but he had lost, he felt, a good deal of his youth and marrow. He tended now to go fat, a little puffy, somewhat insignificant. And he had been handsome and striking-looking.

The two witches howled when he was lost to them. Poor Virginia was really half-crazy, she didn't know what to do with herself. She had a violent recoil from her mother. Mrs. Bodoin was filled with furious contempt for her daughter: that she should let such a hooked fish slip out of her hands! That she should allow such a person to turn her down! 'I don't quite see my daughter seduced and thrown over by a sponging individual such as Henry Lubbock,' she wrote. 'But if it has happened, I suppose it is somebody's fault —'

There was a mutual recoil, which lasted nearly five years. But the spell was not broken. Mrs. Bodoin's mind never left her daughter, and Virginia was ceaselessly aware of her mother, somewhere in the universe. They wrote, and met at intervals, but they kept apart in recoil.

The spell, however, was between them, and gradually it worked. They felt more friendly. Mrs. Bodoin came to London. She stayed in the same quiet hotel with her daughter: Virginia had had two rooms in an hotel for the past three years. And, at last, they thought of taking an apartment together.

Virginia was now over thirty. She was still thin and odd and elvish, with a very slight and piquant cast in one of her brown eyes, and she still had her odd, twisted smile, and her slow, rather deep-toned voice, that caressed a man like the stroking of subtle fingertips. Her hair was still a natural tangle of curls, a bit dishevelled. She still dressed with a natural elegance which tended to go wrong and a tiny bit sluttish. She still might have a hole in her expensive and perfectly new stockings, and still she might have to take off her shoes in the drawing-room, if she came to tea, and sit there in her stockinged-feet. True, she had elegant feet: she was altogether elegantly shaped. But it wasn't that. It was neither coquetry nor vanity. It was simply that, after having gone to a good shoemaker and paid five guineas for a pair of perfectly simple and natural shoes, made to her feet, the said shoes would hurt her excrutiatingly, when she had walked half a mile in them, and she would simply have to take them off, even if she sat on the kerb to do it. It was a fatality. There was a touch of the *gamin* in her very feet, a certain sluttishness that wouldn't let them stay properly in nice proper shoes. She practically always wore her mother's old shoes. 'Of course, I go through life in mother's old shoes. If she died and left me without a supply, I suppose I should have to go in a bath-chair,' she would say, with her odd twisted little grin. She was so elegant, and yet a slut. It was her charm, really.

Just the opposite of her mother. They could wear each other's shoes and each other's clothes, which seemed remarkable, for Mrs. Bodoin seemed so much the bigger of the two. But Virginia's shoulders were broad; if she was thin, she had a strong frame, even when she looked a frail rag.

Mrs. Bodoin was one of those women of sixty or so, with a terrible inward energy and a violent sort of vitality. But she managed to hide it. She sat with perfect repose, and folded hands. One thought: What a calm woman! Just as one may look at the snowy summit of a quiescent volcano, in the evening light, and think: What peace!

It was strange *muscular* energy which possessed Mrs. Bodoin, as it possesses, curiously enough, many women over fifty, and is usually distasteful in its manifestations. Perhaps it accounts for the lassitude of the young.

But Mrs. Bodoin recognised the bad taste in her energetic coevals, so she cultivated repose. Her very way of pronouncing the word, in two syllables: re-pòse, making the second syllable run on into the twilight, showed how much suppressed energy she had. Faced with the problem of iron-grey hair and black eyebrows, she was too clever to try dyeing herself back into youth. She studied her face, her whole figure, and decided that it was *positive*. There was no denying it. There was no wispiness, no hollowness, no limp frail blossom-on-a-bending-stalk about her. Her figure, though not stout, was full, strange, and *cambré*. Her face had an aristocratic arched nose, aristocratic, who-the-devil-are-you grey eyes, and cheeks rather long but also rather full. Nothing appealing or youthfully skittish here.

Like an independent woman, she used her wits, and decided most emphatically not to be youthful or skittish or appealing. She would keep her dignity, for she was fond of it. She was positive. She liked to be positive. She was used to her positivity. So she would just *be* positive.

She turned to the positive period; to the eighteenth century, to Voltaire, to Ninon de l'Enclos and the Pompadour, to Madame la Duchesse and Monsieur le Marquis. She decided that she was not much in the line of la Pompadour or la Duchesse, but almost exactly in the line of Monsieur le Marquis. And she was right. With hair silvering to white, brushed back clean from her positive brow and temples, cut short, but sticking out a little behind, with her rather full, pink face and thin black eyebrows plucked to two fine, superficial crescents, her arching nose and her rather full insolent eyes she was perfectly eighteenth-century, the early half. That she was Monsieur le Marquis rather than Madame la Marquise made her really modern.

Her appearance was perfect. She wore delicate combinations of grey and pink, maybe with a darkening iron-grey touch, and her jewels were of soft old coloured paste. Her bearing was a sort of alert repose, very calm, but very assured. There was, to use a vulgarism, no getting past her.

She had a couple of thousand pounds she could lay her hands on. Virginia, of course, was always in debt. But, after all, Virginia was not to be sniffed at. She made seven hundred and fifty a year.

Virginia was oddly clever, and not clever. She didn't *really* know anything, because anything and everything was interesting to her for the moment, and she picked it up at once. She picked up languages with extraordinary ease, she was fluent in a fortnight. This helped her enormously with her job. She could prattle away with heads of industry, let them come from where they liked. But she didn't *know* any language, not even her own. She picked things up in her sleep, so to speak, without knowing anything about them.

And this made her popular with men. With all her curious facility, they didn't feel small in front of her, because she was like an instrument. She had to be prompted. Some man had to set her in motion, and then she worked, really cleverly. She could collect the most valuable information. She was very useful. She worked with men, spent most of her time with men, her friends were practically all men. She didn't feel easy with women.

Yet she had no lover, nobody seemed eager to marry her, nobody seemed eager to come close to her at all. Mrs. Bodoin said: 'I'm afraid Virginia is a one-man woman. I am a one-man woman. So was my mother, and so was my grandmother. Virginia's father was the only man in my life, the only one. And I'm afraid Virginia is the same, tenacious. Unfortunately, the man was what he was, and her life is just left there.'

Henry had said, in the past, that Mrs. Bodoin wasn't a one-man woman, she was a no-man woman, and that if she could have had her way, everything male would have been wiped off the face of the earth, and only the female element left.

However, Mrs. Bodoin thought that it was now time to make a move. So she and Virginia took a quite handsome apartment in one of the old Bloomsbury squares, fitted it up and furnished it with extreme care, and with some quite lovely things, got in a very good man, an Austrian, to cook, and they set up married life together, mother and daughter.

At first, it was rather thrilling. The two reception-rooms, looking down on the dirty old trees of the Square gardens, were of splendid proportions, and each with three great windows coming down low, almost to the level of the knees. The chimney-piece was late eighteenth century. Mrs. Bodoin furnished the rooms with a gentle suggestion of Louis-Seize merged with Empire, without keeping to any particular style. But she had, saved from her own home, a really remarkable Aubusson carpet. It looked almost new, as if it had been woven two years ago, and was startling, yet somehow rather splendid, as it spread its rose-red borders and wonderful florid array of silver-grey and gold-grey roses, lilies and gorgeous swans and trumpeting volutes away over the floor. Very æsthetic people found it rather loud, they preferred the worn, dim yellowish Aubusson in the big bedroom. But Mrs. Bodoin loved her drawing-room carpet. It was positive, but it was not vulgar. It had a certain grand air in its floridity. She felt it gave her a proper footing. And it behaved very well with her painted cabinets and grey-and-gold brocade chairs and big Chinese vases, which she liked to fill with big flowers: single Chinese peonies, big roses, great tulips, orange lilies. The dim room of London, with all its atmospheric colour, would stand the big, free, fisticuffing flowers.

Virginia, for the first time in her life, had the pleasure of making a home. She was again entirely under her mother's spell, and swept away, thrilled to her marrow. She had had no idea that her mother had got such treasures as the carpets and painted cabinets and brocade chairs up her sleeve: many of them the débris of the Fitzpatrick home in Ireland, Mrs. Bodoin being a Fitzpatrick. Almost like a child, like a bride, Virginia threw herself into the business of fixing up the rooms. 'Of course, Virginia, I consider this is *your* apartment,' said Mrs. Bodoin. 'I am nothing but your *dame de compagnie*, and shall carry out your wishes entirely, if you will only express them.'

Of course Virginia expressed a few, but not many. She introduced some wild pictures bought from impecunious artists whom she patronised. Mrs. Bodoin thought the pictures positive about the wrong things, but as far as possible, she let them stay: looking on them as the necessary element of modern ugliness. But by that element of modern ugliness, wilfully so, it was easy to see the things that Virginia had introduced into the apartment.

Perhaps nothing goes to the head like setting up house. You can get drunk on it. You feel you are creating something. Nowadays it is no longer the 'home', the domestic nest. It is 'my rooms', or 'my house', the great garment which reveals and clothes 'my personality'. Mrs. Bodoin, deliberately scheming for Virginia, kept moderately cool over it, but even she was thrilled to the marrow, and of an intensity and ferocity with the decorators and furnishers, astonishing. But Virginia was just all the time tipsy with it, as if she had touched some magic button on the grey wall of life, and with an Open Sesame! her lovely and coloured rooms had begun to assemble out of fairyland. It was far more vivid and wonderful to her than if she had inherited a duchy.

The mother and daughter, the mother in a sort of faded russet crimson and the daughter in silver, began to entertain. They had, of course, mostly men. It filled Mrs. Bodoin with a sort of savage impatience to entertain women. Besides, most of Virginia's acquaintances were men. So there were dinners and well-arranged evenings.

It went well, but something was missing. Mrs. Bodoin wanted to be gracious, so she held herself rather back. She stayed a little distant, was calm, reposed, eighteenth-century, and determined to be a foil to the clever and slightly-elvish Virginia. It was a pose, and alas, it stopped something. She was very nice with the men, no matter what her contempt of them. But the men were uneasy with her: afraid.

What they all felt, all the men guests, was that *for them*, nothing really happened. Everything that happened was between mother and daughter. All the flow was between mother and daughter. A subtle, hypnotic spell encompassed the two women, and, try as they might, the men were shut out. More than one young man, a little dazzled, *began* to fall in love with Virginia. But it was impossible. Not only was he shut out, he was, in some way, annihilated. The spontaneity was killed in his bosom. While the two women sat, brilliant and rather wonderful, in magnetic connection at opposite ends of the table, like two witches, a double Circe turning the men not into swine – the men would have liked that well enough – but into lumps.

It was tragic. Because Mrs. Bodoin wanted Virginia to fall in love and marry. She really wanted it, and she attributed Virginia's lack of forthcoming to the delinquent Henry. She never realised the hypnotic spell, which of course encompassed her as well as Virginia, and made men just an impossibility to both women, mother and daughter alike.

At this time, Mrs. Bodoin hid her humour. She had a really marvellous faculty of humorous imitation. She could imitate the Irish servants from her old home, or the American women who called on her, or the modern ladylike young men, the asphodels, as she called them: 'Of course, you know the asphodel is a kind of onion! Oh yes, just an overbred onion': who wanted, with their murmuring voices and peeping under their brows, to make her feel very small and very bourgeois. She could imitate them all with a humour that was really touched with genius. But it was devastating. It demolished the objects of her humour so absolutely, smashed them to bits with a ruthless hammer, pounded them to nothing so terribly, that it frightened people, particularly men. It frightened men off.

So she hid it. She hid it. But there it was, up her sleeve, her merciless, hammer-like humour, which just smashed its object on the head and left him brained. She tried to disown it. She tried to pretend, even to Virginia, that she had the gift no more. But in vain; the hammer hidden up her sleeve hovered over the head of every guest, and every guest felt his scalp creep, and Virginia felt her inside creep with a little, mischievous, slightly idiotic grin, as still another fool male was mystically knocked on the head. It was a sort of uncanny sport.

No, the plan was not going to work: the plan of having Virginia fall in love and marry. Of course the men *were* such lumps, such *œufs farcis*. There was one, at least, that Mrs. Bodoin had real hopes of. He was a healthy and normal and very good-looking boy of good family, with no money, alas, but clerking to the House of Lords and very hopeful, and not very clever, but simply in love with Virginia's cleverness. He was just the one Mrs. Bodoin would have married for herself. True, he was only twenty-six, to Virginia's thirty-one. But he had rowed in the Oxford eight, and adored horses, talked horses adorably, and was simply infatuated by Virginia's cleverness. To him Virginia had the finest mind on earth. She was as wonderful as Plato, but infinitely more attractive, because she was a woman, and winsome with it. Imagine a winsome Plato with untidy curls and the tiniest little brown-eyed squint and just a hint of woman's pathetic need for a protector, and you may imagine Adrian's feeling for Virginia. He adored her on his knees, but he felt he could protect her.

'Of course, he's just a very nice *boy*!' said Mrs. Bodoin. 'He's a boy, and that's all you can say. And he always will be a boy. But that's the very nicest kind of man, the only kind you can live with: the eternal boy. Virginia, aren't you attracted to him?'

'Yes, mother! I think he's an awfully nice *boy*, as you say,' replied Virginia, in her rather low, musical, whimsical voice. But the mocking little curl in the intonation put the lid on Adrian. Virginia was not marrying a nice *boy*! She could be malicious too, against her mother's taste. And Mrs. Bodoin let escape her a faint gesture of impatience.

For she had been planning her own retreat, planning to give Virginia the apartment outright, and half of her own income, if she would marry Adrian. Yes, the mother was already scheming how best she could live with dignity on three hundred a year, once Virginia was happily married to that most attractive if slightly brainless *boy*.

A year later, when Virginia was thirty-two, Adrian, who had married a wealthy American girl and been transferred to a job in the legation at Washington in the meantime, faithfully came to see Virginia as soon as he was in London, faithfully kneeled at her feet, faithfully thought her the most wonderful spiritual being, and faithfully felt that she, Virginia, could have done wonders with him, which wonders would now never be done, for he had married in the meantime.

Virginia was looking haggard and worn. The scheme of a *ménage à deux* with her mother had not succeeded. And now, work was telling on the younger woman. It is true, she was amazingly facile. But facility wouldn't get her all the way. She had to earn her money, and earn it hard. She had to slog, and she had to concentrate. While she could work by quick intuition and without much responsibility, work thrilled her. But as soon as she had to get down to it, as they say, grip and slog and concentrate, in a really responsible position, it wore her out terribly. She had to do it all off her nerves. She hadn't the same sort of fighting power as a man. Where a man can summon his old Adam in him to fight through his work, a woman has to draw on her nerves, and on her nerves alone. For the old Eve in her will have nothing to do with such work. So that mental responsibility, mental concentration, mental slogging wear out a woman terribly, especially if she is head of a department, and not working *for* somebody.

So poor Virginia was worn out. She was thin as a rail. Her nerves were frayed to bits. And she could never forget her beastly work. She would come home at tea-time speechless and done for. Her mother, tortured by the sight of her, longed to say: 'Has anything gone wrong, Virginia? Have you had anything particularly trying at the office to-day?' But she learned to hold her tongue, and say nothing. The question would be the last straw to Virginia's poor overwrought nerves, and there would be a little scene which, despite Mrs. Bodoin's calm and

756

forbearance, offended the elder woman to the quick. She had learned, by bitter experience, to leave her child alone, as one would leave a frail tube of vitriol alone. But, of course, she could not keep her *mind* off Virginia. That was impossible. And poor Virginia, under the strain of work and the strain of her mother's awful ceaseless mind, was at the very end of her strength and resources.

Mrs. Bodoin had always disliked the fact of Virginia's doing a job. But now she hated it. She hated the whole government office with violent and virulent hate. Not only was it undignified for Virginia to be tied up there, but it was turning her, Mrs. Bodoin's daughter, into a thin, nagging, fearsome old maid. Could anything be more utterly English and humiliating to a well-born Irishwoman?

After a long day attending to the apartment, skilfully darning one of the brocade chairs, polishing the Venetian mirrors to her satisfaction, selecting flowers, doing certain shopping and housekeeping, attending perfectly to everything, then receiving callers in the afternoon, with never-ending energy, Mrs. Bodoin would go up from the drawing-room after tea and write a few letters, take her bath, dress with great care – she enjoyed attending to her person – and come down to dinner as fresh as a daisy, but far more energetic than that quiet flower. She was ready now for a full evening.

She was conscious, with gnawing anxiety, of Virginia's presence in the house, but she did not see her daughter till dinner was announced. Virginia slipped in, and away to her room unseen, never going into the drawing-room to tea. If Mrs. Bodoin heard her daughter's key in the latch, she quickly retired into one of the rooms till Virginia was safely through. It was too much for poor Virginia's nerves even to catch sight of anybody in the house, when she came in from the office. Bad enough to hear the murmur of visitors' voices behind the drawing-room door.

And Mrs. Bodoin would wonder: How is she? How is she to-night? I wonder what sort of a day she's had? And this thought would roam prowling through the house, to where Virginia was lying on her back in her room. But the mother would have to consume her anxiety till dinnertime. And then Virginia would appear, with black lines under her eyes, thin, tense, a young woman out of an office, the stigma upon her: badly dressed, a little acid in humour, with an impaired digestion, not interested in anything, blighted by her work. And Mrs. Bodoin, humiliated at the very sight of her, would control herself perfectly, say nothing but the mere smooth nothings of casual speech, and sit in perfect form

757

presiding at a carefully-cooked dinner thought out entirely to please Virginia. Then Virginia hardly noticed what she ate.

Mrs. Bodoin was pining for an evening with life in it. But Virginia would lie on the couch and put on the loud-speaker. Or she would put a humorous record on the gramophone, and be amused, and hear it again, and be amused, and hear it again, six times, and six times be amused by a mildly funny record that Mrs. Bodoin now knew off by heart. 'Why, Virginia, I could repeat that record over to you, if you wished it, without your troubling to wind up that gramophone.' And Virginia, after a pause in which she seemed not to have heard what her mother said, would reply: 'I'm sure you could, mother.' And that simple speech would convey such volumes of contempt for all that Rachel Bodoin was or ever could be or ever had been, contempt for her energy, her vitality, her mind, her body, her very existence, that the elder woman would curl. It seemed as if the ghost of Robert Bodoin spoke out of the mouth of the daughter, in deadly venom. Then Virginia would put on the record for the seventh time.

During the second ghastly year, Mrs. Bodoin realised that the game was up. She was a beaten woman, a woman without object or meaning any more. The hammer of her awful female humour, which had knocked so many people on the head, all the people in fact, that she had come into contact with, had at last flown backwards and hit herself on the head. For her daughter was her other self, her *alter ego*. The secret and the meaning and the power of Mrs. Bodoin's whole life lay in the hammer, that hammer of her living humour which knocked everything on the head. That had been her lust and her passion, knocking every-body and everything humorously on the head. She had felt inspired in it: it was a sort of mission. And she had hoped to hand on the hammer to Virginia, her clever, unsolid but still actual daughter, Virginia. Virginia was the continuation of Rachel's own self. Virginia was Rachel's *alter ego*, her other self.

But, alas, it was a half-truth. Virginia had had a father. This fact, which had been utterly ignored by the mother, was gradually brought home to her by the curious recoil of the hammer. Virginia was her father's daughter. Could anything be more unseemly, horrid, more perverse in the natural scheme of things? For Robert Bodoin had been fully and deservedly knocked on the head by Rachel's hammer. Could anything, then, be more disgusting than that he should resurrect again in the person of Mrs. Bodoin's own daughter, her own *alter ego* Virginia, and start hitting back with a little spiteful hammer that was David's pebble against Goliath's battle-axe!

But the little pebble was mortal. Mrs. Bodoin felt it sink into her brow, her temple, and she was finished. The hammer fell nerveless from her hand.

The two women were now mostly alone. Virginia was too tired to have company in the evening. So there was the gramophone or loud-speaker, or else silence. Both women had come to loathe the apartment. Virginia felt it was the last grand act of bullying on her mother's part, she felt bullied by the assertive Aubusson carpet, by the beastly Venetian mirrors, by the big over-cultured flowers. She even felt bullied by the excellent food, and longed again for a Soho resturant and her two poky, shabby rooms in the hotel. She loathed the apartment: she loathed everything. But she had not the energy to move. She had not the energy to do anything. She crawled to her work, and for the rest, she lay flat, gone.

It was Virginia's worn-out inertia that really finished Mrs. Bodoin. That was the pebble that broke the bone of her temple: 'To have to attend my daughter's funeral, and accept the sympathy of all her fellow-clerks in her office, no, that is a final humiliation which I must spare myself. No! If Virginia must be a lady-clerk, she must be it henceforth on her own responsibility. I will retire from her existence.'

Mrs. Bodoin had tried hard to persuade Virigina to give up her work and come and live with her. She had offered her half her income. In vain. Virginia stuck to her office.

Very well! So be it! The apartment was a fiasco, Mrs. Bodoin was longing, longing to tear it to pieces again. One last and final blow of the hammer! 'Virginia, don't you think we'd better get rid of this apartment, and live around as we used to do? Don't you think we'll do that?' – 'But all the money you've put into it? and the lease for ten years!' cried Virginia, in a kind of inertia. – 'Never mind! We had the pleasure of making it. And we've had as much pleasure out of living in it as we shall ever have. Now we'd better get rid of it – quickly – don't you think?'

Mrs. Bodoin's arms were twitching to snatch the pictures off the walls, roll up the Aubusson carpet, take the china out of the ivory-inlaid cabinet there and then, at that very moment.

'Let us wait till Sunday before we decide,' said Virginia.

'Till Sunday! Four days! As long as that? Haven't we already decided in our own minds?' said Mrs. Bodoin.

759

'We'll wait till Sunday, anyhow,' said Virginia.

The next evening, the Armenian came to dinner. Virginia called him Arnold, with the French pronunciation, Arnault. Mrs. Bodoin, who barely tolerated him, and could never get his name, which seemed to have a lot of bouyoums in it, called him either the Armenian or the Rahat Lakoum, after the name of the sweetmeat, or simply the Turkish Delight.

'Arnault is coming to dinner to-night, mother.'

'Really! The Turkish Delight is coming to dinner? Shall I provide anything special?' Her voice sounded as if she would suggest snails in aspic.

'I don't think so.'

Virginia had seen a good deal of the Armenian at the office when she had to negotiate with him on behalf of the Board of Trade. He was a man of about sixty, a merchant, had been a millionaire, was ruined during the war, but was now coming on again, and represented trade in Bulgaria. He wanted to negotiate with the British Government, and the British Government sensibly negotiated with him: at first through the medium of Virginia. Now things were going satisfactorily between Monsieur Arnault, as Virginia called him, and the Board of Trade, so that a sort of friendship had followed the official relations.

The Turkish Delight was sixty, grey-haired and fat. He had numerous grandchildren growing up in Bulgaria, but he was a widower. He had a grey moustache cut like a brush, and glazed brown eyes over which hung heavy lids with white lashes. His manner was humble, but in his bearing there was a certain dogged conceit. One notices the combination sometimes in Jews. He had been very wealthy and kow-towed to, he had been ruined and humiliated, terribly humiliated, and now, doggedly, he was rising up again, his sons backing him, away in Bulgaria. One felt he was not alone. He had his sons, his family, his tribe behind him, away in the Near East.

He spoke bad English, but fairly fluent guttural French. He did not speak much, but he sat. He sat, with his short, fat thighs, as if for eternity, *there*. There was a strange potency in his fat immobile sitting, as if his posterior were connected with the very centre of the earth. And his brain, spinning away at the one point in question, business, was very agile. Business absorbed him. But not in a nervous, personal way. Somehow the family, the tribe was always felt behind him. It was business for the family, the tribe.

With the English he was humble, for the English like such aliens to be humble, and he had had a long schooling from the Turks. And he was always an outsider. Nobody would ever take any notice of him in society. He would just be an outsider, *sitting*.

'I hope, Virginia, you won't ask that Turkish-carpet gentleman when we have other people. I can bear it,' said Mrs. Bodoin. 'Some people might mind.'

'Isn't it hard when you can't choose your own company in your own house,' mocked Virginia.

'No! *I* don't care. I can meet anything; and I'm sure, in the way of selling Turkish carpets, your acquaintance is very good. But I don't suppose you look on him as a personal friend —?'

'I do. I like him quite a lot.'

'Well —! As you will. But consider your *other* friends.'

Mrs. Bodoin was really mortified this time. She looked on the Armenian as one looks on the fat Levantine in a fez who tries to sell one hideous tapestries at Port Said, or on the seafront at Nice, as being outside the class of human beings, and in the class of insects. That he had been a millionaire, and might be a millionaire again, only added venom to her feeling of disgust at being forced into contact with such scum. She could not even squash him, or annihilate him. In scum there is nothing to squash, for scum is only the unpleasant residue of that which was never anything but squashed.

However, she was not quite just. True, he was fat, and he sat, with short thighs, like a toad, as if seated for a toad's eternity. His colour was of a dirty sort of paste, his brown eyes were glazed under heavy lids. And he never spoke until spoken to, waiting in his toad's silence, like a slave.

But his thick, fine white hair, which stood up on his head like a soft brush, was curiously virile. And his curious small hands, of the same soft dull paste, had a peculiar, fat, soft masculine breeding of their own. And his dull brown eye could glint with the subtlety of serpents, under the white brush of eyelash. He was tired, but he was not defeated. He had fought, and won, and lost, and was fighting again, always at a disadvantage. He belonged to a defeated race which accepts defeat, but which gets its own back by cunning. He was the father of sons, the head of a family, one of the heads of a defeated but indestructible tribe. He was not alone, and so you could not lay your finger on him. His whole consciousness was patriarchal and tribal. And somehow, he was humble, but he was indestructible.

At dinner he sat half-effaced, humble, yet with the conceit of the

761

humble. His manners were perfectly good, rather French. Virginia chattered to him in French, and he replied with that peculiar nonchalance of the boulevards, which was the only manner he could command when speaking French. Mrs. Bodoin understood, but she was what one would call a heavy-footed linguist, so when she said anything, it was intensely in English. And the Turkish Delight replied in his clumsy English, hastily. It was not his fault that French was being spoken. It was Virginia's.

He was very humble, conciliatory, with Mrs. Bodoin. But he cast at her sometimes that rapid glint of a reptilian glance as if to say: 'Yes! I see you! You are a handsome figure. As an *objet de vertu* you are almost perfect.' Thus his connoisseur's, antique-dealer's eye would appraise her. But then his thick white eyebrows would seem to add: 'But what, under holy Heaven, are you as a woman? You are neither wife nor mother nor mistress, you have no perfume of sex, you are more dreadful than a Turkish soldier or an English official. No man on earth could embrace you. You are a ghoul, you are a strange genie from the underworld!' And he would secretly invoke the holy names to shield him.

Yet he was in love with Virginia. He saw, first and foremost, the child in her, as if she were a lost child in the gutter, a waif with a faint, fascinating cast in her brown eyes, waiting till someone would pick her up. A fatherless waif! And he was tribal father, father through all the ages.

Then, on the other hand, he know her peculiar disinterested cleverness in affairs. That, too, fascinated him: that odd, almost second-sight cleverness about business, and entirely impersonal, entirely in the air. It seemed to him very strange. But it would be an immense help to him in his schemes. He did not really understand the English. He was at sea with them. But with her, he would have a clue to everything. For she was, finally, quite a somebody among these English, these English officials.

He was about sixty. His family was established in the East, his grandsons were growing up. It was necessary for him to live in London for some years. This girl would be useful. She had no money, save what she would inherit from her mother. But he would risk that: she would be an invesment in his business. And then the apartment. He liked the apartment extremely. He recognised the *cachet*, and the lilies and swans of the Aubusson carpet really did something to him. Virginia said to him: 'Mother gave me the apartment.' So he looked on that as safe.

And finally, Virginia was almost a virgin, probably quite a virgin, and, as far as the paternal Oriental male like himself was concerned, entirely virgin. He had a very small idea of the silly puppy-sexuality of the English, so different from the prolonged male voluptuousness of his own pleasures. And last of all, he was physically lonely, getting old and tired.

Virginia, of course, did not know why she liked being with Arnault. Her cleverness was amazingly stupid when it came to life, to living. She said he was 'quaint'. She said his nonchalant French of the boulevards was 'amusing'. She found his business cunning 'intriguing', and the glint in his dark glazed eyes, under the white, thick lashes, 'sheiky'. She saw him quite often, had tea with him in his hotel, and motored with him one day down to the sea.

When he took her hand in his own soft still hands, there was something so caressing, so possessive in his touch, so strange and positive in his leaning towards her, that though she trembled with fear, she was helpless. – 'But you are so thin, dear little thin thing, you need repose, repose, for the blossom to open, poor little blossom, to become a little fat!' he said in his French.

She quivered, and was helpless. It certainly was quaint! He was so strange and positive, he seemed to have all the power. The moment he realised that she would succumb into his power, he took full charge of the situation, he lost all his hesitation and humility. He did not want just to make love to her: he wanted to marry her, for all his multifarious reasons. And he must make himself master of her.

He put her hand to his lips, and seemed to draw her life to his in kissing her thin hand. 'The poor child is tired, she needs repose, she needs to be caressed and cared for,' he said in his French. And he drew nearer to her.

She looked up in dread at his glinting, tired dark eyes under the white lashes. But he used all his will, looking back at her heavily and calculating that she must submit. And he brought his body quite near to her, and put his hand softly on her face, and made her lay her face against his breast, as he soothingly stroked her arm with his other hand. 'Dear little thing! Dear little thing! Arnault loves her so dearly! Arnault loves her! Perhaps she will marry her Arnault. Dear little girl, Arnault will put flowers in her life, and make her life perfumed with sweetness and content.'

She leaned against his breast and let him caress her. She gave a fleeting, half poignant, half vindictive thought to her mother. Then she

763

felt in the air the sense of destiny, destiny. Oh, so nice, not to have to struggle. To give way to destiny.

'Will she marry her old Arnault? Eh? Will she marry him?' he asked in a soothing, caressing voice, at the same time compulsive.

She lifted her head and looked at him: the thick white brows, the glinting, tired dark eyes. How queer and comic! How comic to be in his power! And he was looking a little baffled.

'Shall I?' she said, with her mischievous twist of a grin.

'*Mais oui!*' he said, with all the sang-froid of his old eyes. '*Mais oui! Je te contenterai, tu le verras.*'

'*Tu me contenteras!*' she said, with a flickering smile of real amusement at his assurance. 'Will you really content me?'

'But surely! I assure it you. And you will marry me?'

'You must tell mother,' she said, and hid wickedly against his waistcoat again, while the male pride triumphed in him.

Mrs. Bodoin had no idea that Virginia was intimate with the Turkish Delight: she did not inquire into her daughter's movements. During the famous dinner, she was calm and a little aloof, but entirely self-possessed. When, after coffee, Virginia left her alone with the Turkish Delight, she made no effort at conversation, only glanced at the rather short, stout man in correct dinner-jacket, and thought how his sort of fatness called for a fez and the full muslin breeches of a bazaar merchant in *The Thief of Baghdad*.

'Do you really prefer to smoke a hookah?' she asked him, with a slow drawl.

'What is a hookah, please?'

'One of those water-pipes. Don't you all smoke them in the East?'

He only looked mystified and humble, and silence resumed. She little knew what was simmering inside his stillness.

'Madame,' he said, 'I want to ask you something.'

'You do? Then why not ask it?' came her slightly melancholy drawl.

'Yes! It is this. I wish I may have the honour to marry your daughter. She is willing.'

There was a moment's blank pause. Then Mrs. Bodoin leaned towards him from her distance with curious portentousness.

'What was that you said?' she asked. 'Repeat it!'

'I wish I may have the honour to marry your daughter. She is willing to take me.'

His dark, glazed eyes looked at her, then glanced away again. Still leaning forward, she gazed fixedly on him, as if spellbound, turned to stone. She was wearing pink topaz ornaments, but he judged they were paste, moderately good.

'Did I hear you say she is willing to take you?' came the slow, melancholy, remote voice.

'Madame, I think so,' he said, with a bow.

'I think we'll wait till she comes,' she said, leaning back.

There was silence. She stared at the ceiling. He looked closely round the room, at the furniture, at the china in the ivory-inlaid cabinet.

'I can settle five thousand pounds on Mademoiselle Virginia, madame,' came his voice. 'Am I correct to assume that she will bring this apartment and its appointments into the marriage settlement?'

Absolute silence. He might as well have been on the moon. But he was a good sitter. He just sat until Virginia came in.

Mrs. Bodoin was still staring at the ceiling. The iron had entered her soul finally and fully. Virginia glanced at her, but said:

'Have a whisky-and-soda, Arnault?'

He rose and came towards the decanters, and stood beside her: a rather squat, stout man with white head, silent with misgiving. There was the fizz of the syphon: then they came to their chairs.

'Arnault has spoken to you, mother?' said Virginia.

Mrs. Bodoin sat up straight and gazed at Virginia with big, owlish eyes, haggard. Virginia was terrified, yet a little thrilled. Her mother was beaten.

'Is it true, Virginia, that you are *willing* to marry this – Oriental gentleman?' asked Mrs. Bodoin slowly.

'Yes, mother, quite true,' said Virginia, in her teasing soft voice.

Mrs Bodoin looked owlish and dazed.

'May I be excused from having any part in it, or from having anything to do with your future *husband* – I mean having any business to transact with him?' she asked dazedly in her slow, distinct voice.

'Why, of course!' said Virginia, frightened, smiling oddly.

There was a pause. Then Mrs. Bodoin, feeling old and haggard, pulled herself together again.

'Am I to understand that your future husband would like to possess this apartment?' came her voice.

Virginia smiled again quickly and crookedly. Arnault just sat, planted on his posterior, and heard. She reposed on him.

'Well – perhaps!' said Virginia. 'Perhaps he would like to know that I possessed it.' She looked at him.

Arnault nodded gravely.

'And do you *wish* to possess it?' came Mrs. Bodoin's slow voice. 'Is it your intention to *inhabit* it, with your *husband*?' She put eternities into her long, stressed words.

'Yes, I think it is,' said Virginia. 'You know you *said* the apartment was mine, mother.'

'Very well! It shall be so. I shall send my lawyer to this – Oriental gentleman, if you will leave written instructions on my writing-table. May I ask when you think of getting – *married*?'

'When do you think, Arnault?' said Virginia.

'Shall it be in two weeks?' he said, sitting erect with his fists on his knees.

'In about a fortnight, mother,' said Virginia.

'I have heard? In two weeks! Very well! In two weeks everything shall be at your disposal. And now, please excuse me.' She rose, made a slight general bow, and moved calmly and dimly from the room. It was killing her, that she could not shriek aloud and beat that Levantine out of the house. But she couldn't. She had imposed the restraint on herself.

Arnault stood and looked with glistening eyes round the room. It would be his. When his sons came to England, here he would receive them.

He looked at Virginia. She, too, was white and haggard now. And she flung away from him, as if in resentment. She resented the defeat of her mother. She was still capable of dismissing him for ever, and going back to her mother.

'Your mother is a wonderful lady,' he said, going to Virginia and taking her hand. 'But she has no husband to shelter her, she is unfortunate. I am sorry she will be alone. I should be happy if she would like to stay here with us.'

The sly old fox knew what he was about.

'I'm afraid there's no hope of that,' said Virginia, with a return of her old irony.

She sat on the couch, and he caressed her softly and paternally, and the very incongruity of it, there in her mother's drawing-room, amused her. And because he saw that the things in the drawing-room were handsome and valuable, and now they were his, his blood flushed and he caressed the thin girl at his side with passion, because she represented these valuable surroundings, and brought them to his possession. And he said: 'And with me you will be very comfortable, very content, oh, I shall make you content, not like madame your mother. And you will get fatter, and bloom like the rose. I shall make you bloom like the rose. And shall we say next week, hein? Shall it be next week, next Wednesday, that we marry? Wednesday is a good day. Shall it be then?'

'Very well!' said Virginia, caressed again into a luxurious sense of destiny, reposing on fate, having to make no effort, no more effort, all her life.

Mrs. Bodoin moved into an hotel next day, and came into the apartment to pack up and extricate herself and her immediate personal belongings only when Virginia was necessarily absent. She and her daughter communicated by letter, as far as was necessary.

And in five days' time Mrs. Bodoin was clear. All business that could be settled was settled, all her trunks were removed. She had five trunks, and that was all. Denuded and outcast, she would depart to Paris, to live out the rest of her days.

The last day she waited in the drawing-room till Virginia should come home. She sat there in her hat and street things, like a stranger.

'I just waited to say good-bye,' she said. 'I leave in the morning for Paris. This is my address. I think everything is settled; if not, let me know and I'll attend to it. Well, good-bye! – and I hope you'll be *very happy!*'

She dragged out the last words sinisterly; which restored Virginia, who was beginning to lose her head.

'Why, I think I may be,' said Virginia, with the twist of a smile.

'I shouldn't wonder,' said Mrs. Bodoin pointedly and grimly. 'I think the Armenian grandpa knows very well what he's about. You're just the harem type, after all.' The words came slowly, dropping, each with a plop! of deep contempt.

'I suppose I am! Rather fun!' said Virginia. 'But I wonder where I got it? Not from you, mother —' she drawled mischievously.

'I should say *not.*'

'Perhaps daughters go by contraries, like dreams,' mused Virginia wickedly. 'All the harem was left out of you, so perhaps it all had to be put back into me.'

Mrs. Bodoin flashed a look at her.

'You have *all* my *pity!*' she said.

'Thank you, dear. You have just a bit of mine.'

THE BLUE MOCCASINS

THE fashion in women changes nowadays even faster than women's fashions. At twenty, Lina M'Leod was almost painfully modern. At sixty almost obsolete!

She started off in life to be really independent. In that remote day, forty years ago, when a woman said she was going to be independent, it meant she was having no nonsense with men. She was kicking over the masculine traces, and living her own life, manless.

To-day, when a girl says she is going to be independent, it means she is going to devote her attentions almost exclusively to men; though not necessarily to 'a man'.

Miss M'Leod had an income from her mother. Therefore, at the age of twenty, she turned her back on that image of tyranny, her father, and went to Paris to study art. Art having been studied, she turned her attention to the globe of earth. Being terribly independent, she soon made Africa look small; she dallied energetically with vast hinterlands of China; and she knew the Rocky Mountains and the deserts of Arizona as if she had been married to them. All this, to escape mere man.

It was in New Mexico she purchased the blue moccasins, blue bead moccasins, from an Indian who was her guide and her subordinate. In her independence she made use of men, of course, but merely as servants, subordinates.

When the war broke out she came home. She was then forty-five, and already going grey. Her brother, two years older than herself, but a bachelor, went off to the war; she stayed at home in the small family mansion in the country, and did what she could. She was small and erect and brief in her speech, her face was like pale ivory, her skin like a very delicate parchment, and her eyes were very blue. There was no nonsense about her, though she did paint pictures. She never even touched her delicately parchment face with pigment. She was good enough as she was, honest-to-God, and the country town had a tremendous respect for her.

In her various activities she came pretty often into contact with Percy Barlow, the clerk at the bank. He was only twenty-two when she first set eyes on him in 1914, and she immediately liked him. He was a stranger in the town, his father being a poor country vicar in Yorkshire. But he was of the confiding sort. He soon confided in Miss M'Leod, for whom he had a towering respect, how he disliked his step-mother, how he feared his father, was but as wax in the hands of that downright woman, and how, in consequence, he was homeless. Wrath shone in his pleasant features, but somehow it was an amusing wrath; at least to Miss M'Leod.

He was distinctly a good-looking boy, with stiff dark hair and odd, twinkling grey eyes under thick dark brows, and a rather full mouth and a queer, deep voice that had a caressing touch of hoarseness. It was his voice that somehow got behind Miss M'Leod's reserve. Not that he had the faintest intention of so doing. He looked up to her immensely: 'She's miles above me.'

When she watched him playing tennis, letting himself go a bit too much, hitting too hard, running too fast, being too nice to his partner, her heart yearned over him. The orphan in him! Why should he go and be shot? She kept him at home as long as possible, working with her at all kinds of war-work. He was so absolutely willing to do everything she wanted: devoted to her.

But at last the time came when he must go. He was now twenty-four and she was forty-seven. He came to say good-bye, in his awkward fashion. She suddenly turned away, leaned her forehead against the wall, and burst into bitter tears. He was frightened out of his wits. Before he knew what was happening he had his arm in front of his face and was sobbing too.

She came to comfort him. 'Don't cry, dear, don't! It will all be all right.'

At last he wiped his face on his sleeve and looked at her sheepishly. 'It was you crying as did me in,' he said. Her blue eyes were brilliant with tears. She suddenly kissed him.

'You are such a dear!' she said wistfully. Then she added, flushing suddenly vivid pink under her transparent parchment skin: 'It wouldn't be right for you to marry an old thing like me, would it?'

He looked at her dumbfounded.

'No, I'm too old,' she added hastily.

'Don't talk about old! You're not old!' he said hotly.

'At least I'm too old for *that*,' she said sadly.

'Not as far as I'm concerned,' he said. 'You're younger than me, in most ways, I'm hanged if you're not!'

'Are you hanged if I'm not?' she teased wistfully.

'I am,' he said. 'And if I thought you wanted me, I'd be jolly proud if you married me. I would, I assure you.'

'Would you?' she said, still teasing him.

Nevertheless, the next time he was home on leave she married him, very quietly, but very definitely. He was a young lieutenant. They stayed in her family home, Twybit Hall, for the honeymoon. It was her house now, her brother being dead. And they had a strangely happy month. She had made a strange discovery: a man.

He went off to Gallipoli, and became a captain. He came home in 1919, still green with malaria, but otherwise sound. She was in her fiftieth year. And she was almost white-haired; long, thick, white hair, done perfectly, and perfectly creamy, colourless face, with very blue eyes.

He had been true to her, not being very forward with women. But he was a bit startled by her white hair. However, he shut his eyes to it, and loved her. And she, though frightened and somewhat bewildered, was happy. But she was bewildered. It always seemed awkward to her, that he should come wandering into her room in his pyjamas when she was half dressed, and brushing her hair. And he would sit there silent, watching her brush the long swinging river of silver, of her white hair, the bare, ivory-white, slender arm working with a strange mechanical motion, sharp and forcible, brushing down the long silvery stream of hair. He would sit as if mesmerised, just gazing. And she would at last glance round sharply, and he would rise, saying some little casual thing to her and smiling to her oddly with his eyes. Then he would go out, his thin cotton pyjamas hitching up over his hips, for he was a rather big-built fellow. And she would feel dazed, as if she did not quite know her own self any more. And the queer, ducking motion of his silently going out of her door impressed her ominously, his curious cat head, his big hips and limbs.

They were alone in the house, save for the servants. He had no work. They lived modestly, for a good deal of her money had been lost during the war. But she still painted pictures. Marriage had only stimulated her to this. She painted canvases of flowers, beautiful flowers that thrilled her soul. And he would sit, pipe in fist, silent, and watch her. He had nothing to do. He just sat and watched her small, neat figure and her concentrated movements as she painted. Then he knocked out his pipe and filled it again.

She said that at last she was perfectly happy. And he said that he was

770

perfectly happy. They were always together. He hardly went out, save riding in the lanes. And practically nobody came to the house.

But still, they were very silent with one another. The old chatter had died out. And he did not read much. He just sat still, and smoked, and was silent. It got on her nerves sometimes, and she would think as she had thought in the past, that the highest bliss a human being can experience is perhaps the bliss of being quite alone, quite, quite alone.

His bank firm offered to make him manager of the local branch, and, at her advice, he accepted. Now he went out of the house every morning and came home every evening, which was much more agreeable. The rector begged him to sing again in the church choir: and again she advised him to accept. These were the old grooves in which his bachelor life had run. He felt more like himself.

He was popular: a nice, harmless fellow, everyone said of him. Some of the men secretly pitied him. They made rather much of him, took him home to luncheon, and let him loose with their daughters. He was popular among the daughters too: naturally, for if a girl expressed a wish, he would instinctively say: 'What! Would you like it? I'll get it for you.' And if he were not in a position to satisfy the desire, he would say: 'I only wish I could do it for you. I'd do it like a shot.' All of which he meant.

At the same time, though he got on so well with the maidens of the town, there was no coming forward about him. He was, in some way, not wakened up. Good-looking, and big, and serviceable, he was inwardly remote, without self-confidence, almost without a self at all.

The rector's daughter took upon herself to wake him up. She was exactly as old as he was, a smallish, rather sharp-faced young woman who had lost her husband in the war, and it had been a grief to her. But she took the stoic attitude of the young: You've got to live, so you may as well do it! She was a kindly soul, in spite of her sharpness. And she had a very perky little red-brown Pomeranian dog that she had bought in Florence in the street, but which had turned out a handsome little fellow. Miss M'Leod looked down a bit on Alice Howells and her pom, so Mrs. Howells felt no special love for Miss M'Leod – 'Mrs. Barlow, that is!' she would add sharply. 'For it's quite impossible to think of her as anything but Miss M'Leod!'

Percy was really more at ease at the rectory, where the pom yapped and Mrs. Howells changed her dress three or four times a day, and looked it, than in the semi-cloisteral atmosphere of Twybit Hall, where Miss M'Leod wore tweeds and a natural knitted jumper, her skirts rather long, her hair done up pure silver, and painted her wonderful flower pictures in the deepening silence of the daytime. At evening she would go up to change, after he came home. And though it thrilled her to have a man coming into her room as he dressed, snapping his collar-stud, to tell her something trivial as she stood bare-armed in her silk slip, rapidly coiling up the rope of silver hair behind her head, still, it worried her. When he was there, he couldn't keep away from her. And he would watch her, watch her, watch her as if she was the ultimate revelation. Sometimes it made her irritable. She was so absolutely used to her own privacy. What was he looking at? She never watched *him*. Rather she looked the other way. His watching tried her nerves. She was turned fifty. And his great silent body loomed almost dreadful.

He was quite happy playing tennis or croquet with Alice Howells and the rest. Alice was choir-mistress, a bossy little person outwardly, in-wardly rather forlorn and affectionate, and not very sure that life hadn't let her down for good. She was now over thirty – and had no one but the pom and her father and the parish – nothing in her really intimate life. But she was very cheerful, busy, even gay, with her choir and school work, her dancing, and flirting, and dressmaking.

She was intrigued by Percy Barlow. 'How *can* a man be so nice to *everybody*?' she asked him, a little exasperated. 'Well, why not?' he replied, with the odd smile of his eyes. 'It's not why he shouldn't, but how he manages to do it! How can you have so much good-nature? I *have* to be catty to some people, but you're nice to *everybody*.'

'Oh, am I!' he said ominously.

He was like a man in a dream, or in a cloud. He was quite a good bank-manager, in fact very intelligent. Even in appearance, his great charm was his beautifully-shaped head. He had plenty of brains, really. But in his will, in his body, he was asleep. And sometimes this lethargy, or coma, made him look haggard. And sometimes it made his body seem inert and despicable, meaningless.

Alice Howells longed to ask him about his wife. '*Do* you love her? *Can* you really care for her?' But she daren't. She daren't ask him one word about his wife. Another thing she couldn't do, she couldn't per-suade him to dance. Never, not once. But in everything else he was pliable as wax.

Mrs. Barlow – Miss M'Leod – stayed out at Twybit all the time. She did not even come in to church on Sunday. She had shaken off church, among other things. And she watched Percy depart, and felt just a little humiliated. He was going to sing in the choir! Yes, marriage was also a humiliation to her. She had distinctly married beneath her.

The years had gone by: she was now fifty-seven, Percy was thirty-four. He was still, in many ways, a boy. But in his curious silence, he was ageless. She managed him with perfect ease. If she expressed a wish, he acquiesced at once. So now it was agreed he should not come to her room any more. And he never did. But sometimes she went to him in his room, and was winsome in a pathetic, heart-breaking way.

She twisted him round her little finger, as the saying goes. And yet secretly she was afraid of him. In the early years he had displayed a clumsy but violent sort of passion, from which she had shrunk away. She felt it had nothing to do with her. It was just his indiscriminating desire for Woman, and for his own satisfaction. Whereas she was not just unidentified Woman, to give him his general satisfaction. So she had recoiled, and withdrawn herself. She had put him off. She had regained the absolute privacy of her room.

He was perfectly sweet about it. Yet she was uneasy with him now. She was afraid of him; or rather, not of him, but of a mysterious something in him. She was not a bit afraid of *him*, oh no! And when she went to him now, to be nice to him, in her pathetic winsomeness of an unused woman of fifty-seven, she found him sweet-natured as ever, but really indifferent. He saw her pathos and her winsomeness. In some way, the mystery of her, her thick white hair, her vivid blue eyes, her ladylike refinement still fascinated him. But his bodily desire for her had gone, utterly gone. And secretly, she was rather glad. But as he looked at her, looked at her, as he lay there so silent, she was afraid, as if some finger were pointed at her. Yet she knew, the moment she spoke to him, he would twist his eyes to that good-natured and 'kindly' smile of his.

It was in the late, dark months of this year that she missed the blue moccasins. She had hung them on a nail in his room. Not that he ever wore them: they were too small. Nor did she: they were too big. Moccasins are male footwear, among the Indians, not female. But they were of a lovely turquoise-blue colour, made all of little turquoise beads, with little forked flames of dead-white and dark-green. When, at the beginning of their marriage, he had exclaimed over them, she had said: 'Yes! Aren't they a lovely colour! So blue!' And he had replied: 'Not as blue as your eyes, even then.'

So, naturally, she had hung them up on the wall in his room, and there they had stayed. Till, one November day, when there were **no** flowers, and she was pining to paint a still-life with something blue in it – oh, so blue, like delphiniums! – she had gone to his room for the moccasins. And they were not there. And though she hunted, she could not find them. Nor did the maids know anything of them.

So she asked him: 'Percy, do you know where those blue moccasins are, which hung in your room?' There was a moment's dead silence. Then he looked at her with his good-naturedly twinkling eyes, and said: 'No, *I* know nothing of them.' There was another dead pause. She did not believe him. But being a perfect lady, she only said, as she turned away: 'Well then, how curious it is!' And there was another dead pause. Out of which he asked her what she wanted them for, and she told him. Whereon the matter lapsed.

It was November, and Percy was out in the evening fairly often now. He was rehearsing for a 'play' which was to be given in the church schoolroom at Christmas. He had asked her about it. 'Do you think it's a bit *infra dig.*, if I play one of the characters?' She had looked at him mildly, disguising her real feeling. 'If you don't feel *personally* humiliated,' she said, 'then there's nothing else to consider.' And he had answered: 'Oh, it doesn't upset *me* at all.' So she mildly said: 'Then do it, by all means.' Adding at the back of her mind: If it amuses you, child! – but she thought, a change had indeed come over the world, when the master of Twybit Hall, or even, for that matter, the manager of the dignified Stubb's Bank, should perform in public on a schoolroom stage in amateur theatricals. And she kept calmly aloof, preferring not to know any details. She had a world of her own.

When he had said to Alice Howells: 'You don't think other folk'll mind – clients of the bank and so forth – think it beneath my dignity?' she had cried, looking up into his twinkling eyes: 'Oh, you don't have to keep *your* dignity on ice, Percy – any more than I do mine.'

The play was to be performed for the first time on Christmas Eve: and after the play, there was the midnight service in church. Percy therefore told his wife not to expect him home till the small hours, at least. So he drove himself off in the car.

As night fell, and rain, Miss M'Leod felt a little forlorn. She was left out of everything. Life was slipping past her. It was Christmas Eve, and she was more alone than she had ever been. Percy only seemed to intensify her aloneness, leaving her in this fashion.

She decided not to be left out. She would go to the play too. It was past six o'clock, and she had worked herself into a highly nervous state. Outside was darkness and rain: inside was silence, forlornness. She went to the telephone and rang up the garage in Shrewbury. It was with great difficulty she got them to promise to send a car for her: Mr. Slater would have to fetch her himself in the two-seater runabout: everything else was out.

She dressed nervously, in a dark-green dress with a few modest jewels. Looking at herself in the mirror, she still thought herself slim, young-looking and distinguished. She did not see how old-fashioned she was, with her uncompromising erectness, her glistening knob of silver hair sticking out behind, and her long dress.

It was a three-mile drive in the rain, to the small country town. She sat next to old Slater, who was used to driving horses and was nervous and clumsy with a car, without saying a word. He thankfully deposited her at the gate of St. Barnabas' School.

It was almost half-past-seven. The schoolroom was packed and buzzing with excitement. 'I'm afraid we haven't a seat left, Mrs. Barlow!' said Jackson, one of the church sidesmen, who was standing guard in the school porch, where people were still fighting to get in. He faced her in consternation. She faced him in consternation. 'Well, I shall have to stay somewhere, till Mr. Barlow can drive me home,' she said. 'Couldn't you put me a chair somewhere?'

Worried and flustered, he went worrying and flustering the other people in charge. The schoolroom was simply packed solid. But Mr. Simmons, the leading grocer, gave up his chair in the front row to Mrs. Barlow, whilst he sat in a chair right under the stage, where he couldn't see a thing. But he could see Mrs. Barlow seated between his wife and daughter, speaking a word or two to them occasionally, and that was enough.

The lights went down: *The Shoes of Shagput* was about to begin. The amateur curtains were drawn back, disclosing the little amateur stage with a white amateur back-cloth daubed to represent a Moorish courtyard. In stalked Percy, dressed as a Moor, his face darkened. He looked quite handsome, his pale grey eyes queer and startling in his dark face. But he was afraid of the audience – he spoke away from them, stalking around clumsily. After a certain amount of would-be funny dialogue, in tripped the heroine, Alice Howells, of course. She was an Eastern houri, in white gauze Turkish trousers, silver veil, and – the blue moccasins. The whole stage was white, save for her blue moccasins, Percy's dark-green sash, and a negro boy's red fez.

When Mrs. Barlow saw the blue moccasins, a little bomb of rage exploded in her. This, of all places! The blue moccasins that she had

775

bought in the western deserts! The blue moccasins that were not so blue as her own eyes! *Her* blue moccasins! On the feet of that creature, Mrs. Howells.

Alice Howells was not afraid of the audience. She looked full at them, lifting her silver veil. And of course she saw Mrs. Barlow, sitting there like the Ancient of Days in judgment, in the front row. And a bomb of rage exploded in *her* breast too.

In the play, Alice was the wife of the grey-bearded old Caliph, but she captured the love of the young Ali, otherwise Percy, and the whole business was the attempt of these two to evade Caliph and negro-eunuchs and ancient crones, and get into each other's arms. The blue shoes were very important: for while the sweet Lelia wore them, the gallant Ali was to know there was danger. But when she took them off, he might approach her.

It was all quite childish, and everybody loved it, and Miss M'Leod might have been quite complacent about it all, had not Alice Howells got her monkey up, so to speak. Alice with a lot of make-up, looked boldly handsome. And suddenly bold she was, bold as the devil. All these years the poor young widow had been 'good', slaving in the parish, and only even flirting just to cheer things up, never going very far and knowing she could never get anything out of it, but determined never to mope.

Now the sight of Miss M'Leod sitting there so erect, so coolly 'higher plane', and calmly superior, suddenly let loose a devil in Alice Howells. All her limbs went suave and molten, as her young sex, long pent up, flooded even to her finger-tips. Her voice was strange, even to herself, with its long, plaintive notes. She felt all her movements soft and fluid, she felt herself like living liquid. And it was lovely. Underneath it all was the sting of malice against Miss M'Leod, sitting there so erect, with her great knob of white hair.

Alice's business, as the lovely Leila, was to be seductive to the rather heavy Percy. And seductive she was. In two minutes, she had him spellbound. He saw nothing of the audience. A faint, fascinated grin came on to his face, as he acted up to the young woman in the Turkish trousers. His rather full, hoarse voice changed and became clear, with a new, naked clang in it. When the two sang together, in the simple banal duets of the play, it was with a most fascinating intimacy. And when, at the end of Act One, the lovely Leila kicked off the blue moccasins, saying: 'Away, shoes of bondage, shoes of sorrow!' and danced a little dance all alone, barefoot, in her Turkish trousers, in front of her fasci-

776

nated hero, his smile was so spellbound that everybody else was spellbound too.

Miss M'Leod's indignation knew no bounds. When the blue moccasins were kicked across the stage by the brazen Alice, with the words: 'Away, shoes of bondage, shoes of sorrow!' the elder woman grew pink with fury, and it was all she could do not to rise and snatch the moccasins from the stage, and bear them away. She sat in speechless indignation during the brief curtain between Act One and Act Two. Her moccasins! Her blue moccasins! Of the sacred blue colour, the turquoise of heaven.

But there they were, in Act Two, on the feet of the bold Alice. It was becoming too much. And the love-scenes between Percy and the young woman were becoming nakedly shameful. Alice grew worse and worse. She was worked up now, caught in her own spell, and unconscious of everything save of him, and the sting of that other woman, who presumed to own him. Own him? Ha-ha! For he was fascinated. The queer smile on his face, the concentrated gleam of his eyes, the queer way he leaned forward from his loins towards her, the new, reckless, throaty twang in his voice – the audience had before their eyes a man spellbound and lost in passion.

Miss M'Leod sat in shame and torment, as if her chair was red-hot. She too was fast losing her normal consciousness, in the spell of rage. She was outraged. The second Act was working up to its climax. The climax came. The lovely Leila kicked off the blue shoes: 'Away, shoes of bondage, away!' and flew barefoot to the enraptured Ali, flinging herself into his arms. And if ever a man was gone in sheer desire, it was Percy, as he pressed the woman's lithe form against his body, and seemed unconsciously to envelop her, unaware of everything else. While she, blissful in his spell, but still aware of the audience and of the superior Miss M'Leod, let herself be wrapped closer and closer.

Miss M'Leod rose to her feet and looked towards the door. But the way out was packed, with people standing holding their breath as the two on the stage remained wrapped in each other's arms, and the three fiddles and the flute softly woke up. Miss M'Leod could not bear it. She was on her feet, and beside herself. She could not get out. She could not sit down again.

'Percy!' she said, in a low clear voice. 'Will you hand me my moccasins?'

He lifted his face like a man startled in a dream, lifted his face from the shoulder of his Leila. His gold-grey eyes were like softly-startled flames. He looked in sheer horrified wonder at the little white-haired woman standing below.

'Eh?' he said, purely dazed

'Will you please hand me my moccasins!' – and she pointed to where they lay on the stage.

Alice had stepped away from him, and was gazing at the risen viper of the little elderly woman on the tip of the audience. Then she watched him move across the stage, bending forward from the loins in his queer mesmerised way, pick up the blue moccasins, and stoop down to hand them over the edge of the stage to his wife, who reached up for them.

'Thank you!' said Miss M'Leod, seating herself, with the blue moccasins in her lap.

Alice recovered her composure, gave a sign to the little orchestra, and began to sing at once, strong and assured, to sing her part in the duet that closed the Act. She knew she could command public opinion in her favour.

He too recovered at once, the little smile came back on his face, he calmly forgot his wife again as he sang his share in the duet. It was finished. The curtains were pulled to. There was immense cheering. The curtains opened, and Alice and Percy bowed to the audience, smiling both of them their peculiar secret smile, while Miss M'Leod sat with the blue moccasins in her lap.

The curtains were closed, it was the long interval. After a few moments of hesitation, Mrs. Barlow rose with dignity, gathered her wrap over her arm, and with the blue moccasins in her hand, moved towards the door. Way was respectfully made for her.

'I should like to speak to Mr. Barlow,' she said to Jackson, who had anxiously ushered her in, and now would anxiously usher her out.

'Yes, Mrs. Barlow.'

He led her round to the smaller class-room at the back, that acted as dressing-room. The amateur actors were drinking lemonade, and chattering freely. Mrs. Howells came forward, and Jackson whispered the news to her. She turned to Percy.

'Percy, Mrs. Barlow wants to speak to you. Shall I come with you?'

'Speak to me? Aye, come on with me.'

The two followed the anxious Jackson into the other half-lighted class-room, where Mrs. Barlow stood in her wrap, holding the moccasins. She was very pale, and she watched the two butter-muslin Turkish figures enter, as if they could not possibly be real. She ignored Mrs. Howells entirely.

'Percy,' she said, 'I want you to drive me home.'

'Drive you home!' he echoed.

'Yes, please!'

'Why – when?' he said, with vague bluntness.

'Now – if you don't mind —'

'What – in this get-up?' He looked at himself.

'I could wait while you changed.'

There was a pause. He turned and looked at Alice Howells, and Alice Howells looked at him. The two women saw each other out of the corners of their eyes: but it was beneath notice. He turned to his wife, his black face ludicrously blank, his eyebrows cocked.

'Well, you see,' he said, 'it's rather awkward. I can hardly hold up the third Act while I've taken you home and got back here again, can I?'

'So you intend to play in the third Act?' she asked with cold ferocity.

'Why, I must, mustn't I?' he said blankly.

'Do you *wish* to?' she said, in all her intensity.

'I do, naturally. I want to finish the thing up properly,' he replied, in the utter innocence of his head; about his heart he knew nothing.

She turned sharply away.

'Very well!' she said. And she called to Jackson, who was standing dejectedly near the door: 'Mr Jackson, will you please find some car or conveyance to take me home?'

'Aye! I say, Mr. Jackson,' called Percy in his strong, democratic voice, going forward to the man. 'Ask Tom Lomas if he'll do me a good turn and get my car out of the rectory garage, to drive Mrs. Barlow home. Aye, ask Tom Lomas! And if not him, ask Mr. Pilkington – Leonard. The key's there. You don't mind, do you? I'm ever so much obliged —'

The three were left awkwardly alone again.

'I expect you've had enough with two acts,' said Percy soothingly to his wife. 'These things aren't up to your mark. I know it. They're only child's play. But, you see, they please the people. We've got a packed house, haven't we?'

His wife had nothing to answer. He looked so ludicrous, with his dark-brown face and butter-muslin bloomers. And his mind was so ludicrously innocent. His body, however, was not so ridiculously innocent as his mind, as she knew when he turned to the other woman.

'You and I, we're more on the nonsense level, aren't we?' he said, with the new, throaty clang of naked intimacy in his voice. His wife shivered.

779

'Absolutely on the nonsense level,' said Alice, with easy assurance.

She looked into his eyes, then she looked at the blue moccasins in the hand of the other woman. He gave a little start, as if realising something for himself.

At that moment Tom Lomas looked in, saying heartily: 'Right you are, Percy! I'll have my car here in half a tick. I'm more handy with it than yours.'

'Thanks, old man! You're a Christian.'

'Try to be – especially when you turn Turk! Well—' He disappeared.

'I say, Lina,' said Percy in his most amiable democratic way, 'would you mind leaving the moccasins for the next act? We s'll be in a bit of a hole without them.'

Miss M'Leod faced him and stared at him with the full blast of her forget-me-not blue eyes, from her white face.

'Will you pardon me if I don't?' she said.

'What!' he exclaimed. 'Why? Why not? It's nothing but play, to amuse the people. I can't see how it can hurt the *moccasins*. I understand you don't quite like seeing me make a fool of myself. But, anyhow, I'm a bit of a born fool. What?' – and his blackened face laughed with a Turkish laugh. 'Oh, yes, you have to realise I rather enjoy playing the fool,' he resumed. 'And, after all, it doesn't really hurt *you*, now does it? Shan't you leave us those moccasins for the last act?'

She looked at him, then at the moccasins in her hand. No, it was useless to yield to so ludicrous a person. The vulgarity of his wheedling, the commonness of the whole performance! It was useless to yield even the moccasins. It would be treachery to herself.

'I'm sorry,' she said. 'But I'd so much rather they weren't used for this kind of thing. I never intended them to be.' She stood with her face averted from the ridiculous couple.

He changed as if she had slapped his face. He sat down on top of the low pupils' desk and gazed with glazed interest round the class-room. Alice sat beside him, in her white gauze and her bedizened face. They were like two rebuked sparrows on one twig, he with his great, easy, intimate limbs, she so light and alert. And as he sat he sank into an unconscious physical sympathy with her. Miss M'Leod walked towards the door.

'You'll have to think of something as'll do instead,' he muttered to Alice in a low voice, meaning the blue moccasins. And leaning down, he drew off one of the grey shoes she had on, caressing her foot with the slip of his hand over its slim, bare shape. She hastily put the bare foot behind her other, shod foot.

Tom Lomas poked in his head, his overcoat collar turned up to his ears.

'Car's here,' he said.

'Right-o! Tom! I'll chalk it up to thee, lad!' said Percy with heavy breeziness. Then, making a great effort with himself, he rose heavily and went across to the door, to his wife, saying to her, in the same stiff voice of false heartiness:

'You'll be as right as rain with Tom. You won't mind if I don't come out? No! I'd better not show myself to the audience. Well – I'm glad you came, if only for a while. Good-bye then! I'll be home after the service – but I shan't disturb you. Good-bye! Don't get wet now —' And his voice, falsely cheerful, stiff with anger, ended in a clang of indignation.

Alice Howells sat on the infants' bench in silence. She was ignored. And she was unhappy, uneasy, because of the scene.

Percy closed the door after his wife. Then he turned with a looming slowness to Alice, and said in a hoarse whisper: 'Think o' that, now!'

She looked up at him anxiously. His face, in its dark pigment, was transfigured with indignant anger. His yellow-grey eyes blazed, and a great rush of anger seemed to be surging up volcanic in him. For a second his eyes rested on her upturned, troubled, dark-blue eyes, then glanced away, as if he didn't want to look at her in his anger. Even so, she felt a touch of tenderness in his glance.

'And that's all she's ever cared about – her own things and her own way,' he said, in the same hoarse whisper, hoarse with suddenly-released rage. Alice Howells hung her head in silence.

'Not another damned thing, but what's her own, her own – and her own holy way – damned holy-holy-holy, all to herself.' His voice shook with hoarse, whispering rage, burst out at last.

Alice Howells looked up at him in distress.

'Oh, don't say it!' she said. 'I'm sure she's fond of you.'

'*Fond* of me! Fond of *me*!' he blazed, with a grin of transcendent irony. 'It makes her sick to look at me. I am a hairy brute, I own it. Why, she's never once touched me to be fond of me – never once – though she pretends sometimes. But a man knows —' and he made a grimace of contempt. 'He knows when a woman's just stroking him, good doggie! – and when she's really a bit woman-fond of him. That woman's never been real fond of anybody or anything, all her life – she couldn't, for all her show of kindness. She's limited to herself, that woman is; and I've looked up to her as if she was God. More fool me! If God's not good-natured and good-hearted, then what is He —?'

Alice sat with her head dropped, realising once more that men aren't really fooled. She was upset, shaken by his rage, and frightened, as if she too were guilty. He had sat down blankly beside her. She glanced up at him.

'Never mind!' she said soothingly. 'You'll like her again to-morrow.'

He looked down at her with a grin, a grey sort of grin. 'Are you going to stroke me "good doggie!" as well?' he said.

'Why?' she asked, blank.

But he did not answer. Then after a while he resumed: 'Wouldn't even leave the moccasins! And she's hung them up in my room, left them there for years – any man'd consider they were his. And I did want this show to-night to be a success! What are you going to do about it?'

'I've sent over for a pair of pale-blue satin bed-slippers of mine – they'll do just as well,' she replied.

'Aye! For all that, it's done me in.'

'You'll get over it.'

'Happen so! She's curdled my inside, for all that. I don't know how I'm going to be civil to her.'

'Perhaps you'd better stay at the rectory to-night,' she said softly.

He looked into her eyes. And in that look, he transferred his allegiance.

'*You* don't want to be drawn in, do you?' he asked, with troubled tenderness.

But she only gazed with wide, darkened eyes into his eyes, so she was like an open, dark doorway to him. His heart beat thick, and the faint, breathless smile of passion came into his eyes again.

'You'll have to go on, Mrs. Howells. We can't keep them waiting any longer.'

It was Jim Stokes, who was directing the show. They heard the clapping and stamping of the impatient audience.

'Goodness!' cried Alice Howells, darting to the door.

THINGS

THEY were true idealists from New England. But that is some time ago: before the war. Several years before the war, they met and married; he a tall, keen-eyed young man from Connecticut, she a smallish, demure, Puritan-looking young woman from Massachusetts. They both had a little money. Not much, however. Even added together, it didn't make three thousand dollars a year. Still – they were free. Free!

Ah! Freedom! To be free to live one's own life! To be twenty-five and twenty-seven, a pair of true idealists with a mutual love of beauty, and an inclination towards 'Indian thought' – meaning, alas, Mrs. Besant – and an income a little under three thousand dollars a year! But what is money? All one wishes to do is to live a full and beautiful life. In Europe, of course, right at the fountain-head of tradition. It might possibly be done in America: in New England, for example. But at a forfeiture of a certain amount of 'beauty'. True beauty takes a long time to mature. The baroque is only half-beautiful, half-matured. No, the real silver bloom, the real golden-sweet bouquet of beauty had its roots in the Renaissance, not in any later or shallower period.

Therefore the two idealists, who were married in New Haven, sailed at once to Paris: Paris of the old days. They had a studio apartment on the Boulevard Montparnasse, and they became real Parisians, in the old, delightful sense, not in the modern, vulgar. It was the shimmer of the pure impressionists, Monet and his followers, the world seen in terms of pure light, light broken and unbroken. How lovely! How lovely the nights, the river, the mornings in the old streets and by the flower-stalls and the book-stalls, the afternoons up on Montmartre or in the Tuileries, the evenings on the boulevards!

They both painted, but not desperately. Art had not taken them by the throat, and they did not take Art by the throat. They painted: that's all. They knew people – nice people, if possible, though one had to take them mixed. And they were happy.

Yet it seems as if human beings must set their claws in *something*. To be 'free', to be 'living a full and beautiful life', you must, alas, be attached to something. A 'full and beautiful life' means a tight attachment to *something* – at least, it is so for all idealists – or else a certain boredom supervenes; there is a certain waving of loose ends upon the air, like the waving, yearning nostrils of the vine that spread and rotate, seeking something to clutch, something up which to climb towards the necessary sun. Finding nothing, the vine can only trail, half-fulfilled, upon the ground. Such is freedom! – a clutching of the right pole. And human beings are all vines. But especially the idealist. He is a vine, and he needs to clutch and climb. And he despises the man who is a mere *potato*, or turnip, or lump of wood.

Our idealists were frightfully happy, but they were all the time reaching out for something to cotton on to. At first, Paris was enough. They explored Paris *thoroughly*. And they learned French till they almost felt like French people, they could speak it so glibly.

Still, you know, you never talk French with your *soul*. It can't be done. And though it's very thrilling, at first, talking in French to clever Frenchmen – they seem *so* much cleverer than oneself – still, in the long run, it is not satisfying. The endlessly clever *materialism* of the French leaves you cold, in the end, gives a sense of barrenness and incompatibility with true New England depth. So our two idealists felt.

They turned away from France – but ever so gently. France had disappointed them. 'We've loved it, and we've got a great deal out of it. But after a while, after a considerable while, several years, in fact, Paris leaves one feeling disappointed. It hasn't quite got what one wants.'

'But Paris isn't France.'

'No, perhaps not. France is quite different from Paris. And France is lovely – quite lovely. But *to us*, though we love it, it doesn't say a great deal.'

So, when the war came, the idealists moved to Italy. And they loved Italy. They found it beautiful, and more poignant than France. It seemed much nearer to the New England conception of beauty: something pure, and full of sympathy, without the *materialism* and the *cynicism* of the French. The two idealists seemed to breathe their own true air in Italy.

And in Italy, much more than in Paris, they felt they could thrill to the teachings of the Buddha. They entered the swelling stream of modern Buddhistic emotion, and they read the books, and they practised meditation, and they deliberately set themselves to eliminate from their own souls greed, pain, and sorrow. They did not realise – yet – that Buddha's very eagerness to free himself from pain and sorrow is in itself a sort of greed. No, they dreamed of a perfect world, from which all greed, and nearly all pain, and a great deal of sorrow, were eliminated.

But America entered the war, so the two idealists had to help. They did hospital work. And though their experience made them realise more than ever that greed, pain, and sorrow *should* be eliminated from the world, nevertheless the Buddhism, or the theosophy, didn't emerge very triumphant from the long crisis. Somehow, somewhere, in some part of themselves, they felt that greed, pain, and sorrow would never be eliminated, because most people don't care about eliminating them, and never will care. Our idealists were far too Western to think of abandoning all the world to damnation, while they saved their two selves. They were far too unselfish to sit tight under a bho tree and reach Nirvana in a mere couple.

It was more than that, though. They simply hadn't enough *Seitzfleisch* to squat under a bho tree and get to Nirvana by contemplating anything, least of all their own navel. If the whole wide world was not going to be saved, they, personally, were not so very keen on being saved just by themselves. No, it would be so lonesome. They were New Englanders, so it must be all or nothing. Greed, pain, and sorrow must either be eliminated from *all the world*, or else, what was the use of eliminating them from oneself? No use at all! One was just a victim.

And so, although they still *loved* 'Indian thought', and felt very tender about it: well, to go back to our metaphor, the pole up which the green and anxious vines had clambered so far now proved dry-rotten. It snapped, and the vines came slowly subsiding to earth again. There was no crack and crash. The vines held themselves up by their own foliage, for a while. But they subsided. The beanstalk of 'Indian thought' had given way before Jack and Jill had climbed off the tip of it to a further world.

They subsided with a slow rustle back to earth again. But they made no outcry. They were again 'disappointed'. But they never admitted it. 'Indian thought' had let them down. But they never complained. Even to one another, they never said a word. They were both disappointed, faintly but deeply disillusioned, and they both knew it. But the knowledge was tacit.

And they still had so much in their lives. They still had Italy – dear Italy. And they still had freedom, the priceless treasure. And they still had so much 'beauty'. About the fullness of their lives they were not quite so sure. They had one little boy, whom they loved as parents should love their children, but whom they wisely refrained from fastening upon, to build their lives on him. No, no, they must live their own lives! They still had strength of mind to know that.

But they were now no longer very young. Twenty-five and twenty-seven had become thirty-five and thirty-seven. And though they had had a very wonderful time in Europe, and though they still loved Italy – dear Italy! – yet: they were disappointed. They had got a lot out of it: oh, a very great deal indeed! Still, it hadn't given them quite, not *quite*, what they had expected. Europe was lovely, but it was dead. Living in Europe, you were living on the past. And Europeans, with all their superficial charm were not *really* charming. They were materialistic, they had no *real* soul. They just did not understand the inner urge of the spirit, because the inner urge was dead in them, they were all survivals. There, that was the truth about Europeans: they were survivals, with no more getting ahead in them.

It was another bean-pole, another vine-support crumbled under the green life of the vine. And very bitter it was, this time. For up the old tree-trunk of Europe the green vine had been clambering silently for more than ten years, ten hugely important years, the years of real living. The two idealists had *lived* in Europe, lived on Europe and on European life and European things as vines in an everlasting vineyard.

They had made their home here: a home such as you could never make in America. Their watchword had been 'beauty'. They had rented, the last four years, the second floor of an old palazzo on the Arno, and here they had all their 'things'. And they derived a profound, profound satisfaction from their apartment: the lofty, silent, ancient rooms with windows on the river, with glistening, dark-red floors, and the beautiful furniture that the idealists had 'picked up'.

Yes, unknown to themselves, the lives of the idealists had been running with a fierce swiftness horizontally, all the time. They had become tense, fierce, hunters of 'things' for their home. While their souls were climbing up to the sun of old European culture or old Indian thought, their passions were running horizontally, clutching at 'things'. Of course they did not buy the things for the things' sakes, but for the sake of 'beauty'. They looked upon their home as a place entirely furnished by loveliness, not by 'things' at all. Valerie had some very lovely curtains at the windows of the long *salotto*, looking on the river: curtains of queer ancient material that looked like finely-knitted silk, most beautifully faded down from vermilion and orange, and gold, and black, down to a sheer soft glow. Valerie hardly ever came into the *salotto* without mentally falling on her knees before the curtains. 'Char-

786

tres!' she said. 'To me they are Chartres!' And Melville never turned and looked at his sixteenth-century Venetian bookcase, with its two or three dozen of choice books, without feeling his marrow stir in his bones. The holy of holies!

The child silently, almost sinisterly, avoided any rude contact with these ancient monuments of furniture, as if they had been nests of sleeping cobras, or that 'thing' most perilous to the touch, the Ark of the Covenant. His childish awe was silent and cold, but final.

Still, a couple of New England idealists cannot live merely on the bygone glory of their furniture. At least, one couple could not. They got used to the marvellous Bologna cupboard, they got used to the wonderful Venetian bookcase, and the books, and the Siena curtains and bronzes, and the lovely sofas and side-tables and chairs they had 'picked up' in Paris. Oh, they had been picking things up since the first day they had landed in Europe. And they were still at it. It is the last interest Europe can offer to an outsider: or to an insider either.

When people came, and were thrilled by the Melville interior, then Valerie and Erasmus felt they had not lived in vain: that they still were living. But in the long mornings, when Erasmus was desultorily working at Renaissance Florentine literature, and Valerie was attending to the apartment: and in the long hours after lunch; and in the long, usually very cold and oppressive evenings in the ancient palazzo: then the halo died from around the furniture, and the things became things, lumps of matter that just stood there or hung there, *ad infinitum*, and said nothing; and Valerie and Erasmus almost hated them. The glow of beauty, like every other glow, dies down unless it is fed. The idealists still dearly loved their things. But they had got them. And the sad fact is, things that glow vividly while you're getting them, go almost quite cold after a year or two. Unless, of course, people envy them very much, and the museums are pining for them. And the Melvilles' 'things', though very good, were not quite so good as that.

So, the glow gradually went out of everything, out of Europe, out of Italy – 'the Italians are *dears*' – even out of that marvellous apartment on the Arno. 'Why, if I had this apartment, I'd never, never even want to go out of doors! It's too lovely and perfect.' That was something, of course – to hear that.

And yet Valerie and Erasmus went out of doors: they even went to get away from its ancient, cold-floored, stone-heavy silence and dead dignity. 'We're living on the past, you know, Dick,' said Valerie to her husband. She called him Dick.

They were grimly hanging on. They did not like to give in. They did not like to own up that they were through. For twelve years, now, they had been 'free' people living a 'full and beautiful life'. And America for twelve years had been their anathema, the Sodom and Gomorrah of industrial materialism.

It wasn't easy to own that you were 'through'. They hated to admit that they wanted to go back. But at last, reluctantly, they decided to go, 'for the boy's sake'. – 'We can't *bear* to leave Europe. But Peter is an American, so he had better look at America while he's young.' The Melvilles had an entirely English accent and manner; almost; a little Italian and French here and there.

They left Europe behind, but they took as much of it along with them as possible. Several van-loads, as a matter of fact. All those adorable and irreplaceable 'things'. And all arrived in New York, idealists, child, and the huge bulk of Europe they had lugged along.

Valerie had dreamed of a pleasant apartment, perhaps on Riverside Drive, where it was not so expensive as east of Fifth Avenue, and where all their wonderful things would look marvellous. She and Erasmus house-hunted. But alas! their income was quite under three thousand dollars a year. They found – well, everybody knows what they found. Two small rooms and a kitchenette, and don't let us unpack a *thing*!

The chunk of Europe which they had bitten off went into a warehouse, at fifty dollars a month. And they sat in two small rooms and a kitchenette, and wondered why they'd done it.

Erasmus, of course, ought to get a job. This was what was written on the wall, and what they both pretended not to see. But it had been the strange, vague threat that the Statue of Liberty had always held over them: 'Thou shalt get a job!' Erasmus had the tickets, as they say. A scholastic career was still possible for him. He had taken his exams brilliantly at Yale, and had kept up his 'researches' all the time he had been in Europe.

But both he and Valerie shuddered. A scholastic career! The scholastic world! The *American* scholastic world! Shudder upon shudder! Give up their freedom, their full and beautiful life? Never! Never! Erasmus would be forty next birthday.

The 'things' remained in warehouse. Valerie went to look at them. It cost her a dollar an hour, and horrid pangs. The 'things', poor things, looked a bit shabby and wretched, in that warehouse.

However, New York was not all America. There was the great clean West. So the Melvilles went West, with Peter, but without the things.

They tried living the simple life, in the mountains. But doing their own chores became almost a nightmare. 'Things' are all very well to look at, but it's awful handling them, even when they're beautiful. To be the slave of hideous things, to keep a stove going, cook meals, wash dishes, carry water and clean floors: pure horror of sordid anti-life!

In the cabin on the mountains, Valerie dreamed of Florence, the lost apartment; and her Bologna cupboard and Louis-Quinze chairs, above all, her 'Chartres' curtains, stood in New York and costing fifty dollars a month.

A millionaire friend came to the rescue, offering them a cottage on the Californian coast – California! Where the new soul is to be born in man. With joy the idealists moved a little farther west, catching at new vine-props of hope.

And finding them straws! The millionaire cottage was perfectly equipped. It was perhaps as labour-savingly perfect as is possible: electric heating, and cooking, a white-and-pearl-enamelled kitchen, nothing to make dirt except the human being himself. In an hour or so the idealists had got through their chores. They were 'free' – free to hear the great Pacific pounding the coast, and to feel a new soul filling their bodies.

Alas! the Pacific pounded the coast with hideous brutality, brute force itself! And the new soul, instead of sweetly stealing into their bodies, seemed only meanly to gnaw the old soul out of their bodies. To feel you are under the fist of the most blind and crunching brute force: to feel that your cherished idealist's soul is being gnawed out of you, and only irritation left in place of it: well, it isn't good enough.

After about nine months, the idealists departed from the Californian West. It had been a great experience, they were glad to have had it. But, in the long run, the West was not the place for them, and they knew it. No, the people who wanted new souls had better get them. They, Valerie and Erasmus Melville, would like to develop the old soul a little further. Anyway, they had not felt any influx of new soul on the Californian coast. On the contrary.

So, with a slight hole in their material capital, they returned to Massachusetts and paid a visit to Valerie's parents, taking the boy along. The grandparents welcomed the child – poor expatriated boy – and were rather cold to Valerie, but really cold to Erasmus. Valerie's mother definitely said to Valerie, one day, that Erasmus ought to take a job, so that Valerie could live decently. Valerie haughtily reminded her mother of the beautiful apartment on the Arno, and the 'wonderful' things in store in New York, and of the 'marvellous and satisfying life' she and Erasmus had led. Valerie's mother said that she didn't think her daughter's life looked so very marvellous at present: homeless, with a husband idle at the age of forty, a child to educate, and a dwindling capital: looked the reverse of marvellous to *her*. Let Erasmus take some post in one of the universities.

'What post? What university?' interrupted Valerie.

'That could be found, considering your father's connections and Erasmus's qualifications,' replied Valerie's mother. 'And you could get all your valuable things out of store, and have a really lovely home, which everybody in America would be proud to visit. As it is, your furniture is eating up your income, and you are living like rats in a hole, with nowhere to go to.'

This was very true. Valerie was beginning to pine for a home, with her 'things'. Of course, she could have sold her furniture for a substantial sum. But nothing would have induced her to. Whatever else passed away, religions, cultures, continents, and hopes, Valerie would *never* part from the 'things' which she and Erasmus had collected with such passion. To these she was nailed.

But she and Erasmus still would not give up that freedom, that full and beautiful life they had so believed in. Erasmus cursed America. He did not *want* to earn a living. He panted for Europe.

Leaving the boy in charge of Valerie's parents, the two idealists once more set off for Europe. In New York they paid two dollars and looked for a brief, bitter hour at their 'things'. They sailed 'student class' – that is, third. Their income now was less than two thousand dollars instead of three. And they made straight for Paris – cheap Paris.

They found Europe, this time, a complete failure. 'We have returned like dogs to our vomit,' said Erasmus; 'but the vomit has staled in the meantime.' He found he couldn't stand Europe. It irritated every nerve in his body. He hated America too. But America at least was a darn sight better than this miserable, dirt-eating continent; which was by no means cheap any more, either.

Valerie, with her heart on her things – she had really burned to get them out of that warehouse, where they had stood now for three years, eating up two thousand dollars – wrote to her mother she thought Erasmus would come back if he could get some suitable work in America. Erasmus, in a state of frustration bordering on rage and insanity, just went round Italy in a poverty-stricken fashion, his coat-cuffs frayed hating everything with intensity. And when a post was found for him in

Cleveland University, to teach French, Italian, and Spanish literature, his eyes grew more beady, and his long, queer face grew sharper and more rat-like with utter baffled fury. He was forty, and the job was upon him.

'I think you'd better accept dear. You don't care for Europe any longer. As you say, it's dead and finished. They offer us a house on the college lot, and mother says there's room in it for all our things. I think we'd better cable "Accept".'

He glowered at her like a cornered rat. One almost expected to see rat's whiskers twitching at the sides of the sharp nose.

'Shall I send the cablegram?' she asked.

'Send it!' he blurted.

And she went out and sent it.

He was a changed man, quieter, much less irritable. A load was off him. He was inside the cage.

But when he looked at the furnaces of Cleveland, vast and like the greatest of black forests, with red and white-hot cascades of gushing metal, and tiny gnomes of men, and terrific noises, gigantic, he said to Valerie:

'Say what you like, Valerie, this is the biggest thing the modern world has to show.'

And when they were in their up-to-date little house on the college lot of Cleveland University, and that woebegone débris of Europe: Bologna cupboard, Venice book-shelves, Ravenna bishop's chair, Louis-Quinze side-tables, 'Chartres' curtains, Siena bronze lamps, all were arrayed, and all looked perfectly out of keeping, and therefore very impressive; and when the idealists had had a bunch of gaping people in, and Erasmus had showed off in his best European manner, but still quite cordial and American; and Valerie had been most ladylike, but for all that, 'we prefer America'; then Erasmus said, looking at her with queer, sharp eyes of a rat:

'Europe's the mayonnaise all right, but America supplies the good old lobster – what?'

'Every time!' she said, with satisfaction.

And he peered at her. He was in the cage: but it was safe inside. And she, evidently, was her real self at last. She had got the goods. Yet round his nose was a queer, evil scholastic look of pure scepticism. But he liked lobster.